THE FOUNDING:
A "lost ship" of Terran origin, in the pre-empire colonizing days, lands on a planet with a dim red star, later to be called Darkover.

DARKOVER LANDFALL

THE AGES OF CHAOS:
One thousand years after the original landfall settlement, society has returned to the feudal level. The Darkovans, their Terran technology renounced or forgotten, have turned instead to freewheeling, out-of-control matrix technology, psi powers, and terrible psi weapons. The populace lives under the domination of the Towers and a tyrannical breeding program to staff the Towers with unnaturally powerful, inbred gifts of *laran*.

STORMQUEEN!
HAWKMISTRESS!

THE HUNDRED KINGDOMS:
An age of war and strife retaining many of the decimating and disastrous effects of the Ages of Chaos. The lands which are later to become the Seven Domains are divided by continuous border conflicts into a multitude of small, belligerent kingdoms, named for convenience "The Hundred Kingdoms." The close of this era is heralded by the adoption of the Compact, instituted by Varzil the Good. A landmark and turning point in the history of Darkover, the Compact bans all distance weapons, making it a matter of honor that one who seeks to kill must himself face equal risk of death.

TWO TO CONQUER
THE HEIRS OF THE HAMMERFELL
THE FALL OF NESKAYA
ZANDRU'S FORGE

THE RENUNCIATES:

During the Ages of Chaos and the time of the Hundred Kingdoms, there were two orders of women who set themselves apart from the patriarchal nature of Darkovan feudal society: the priestesses of Avarra and the warriors of the Sisterhood of the Sword. Eventually these two independent groups merged to form the powerful and legally chartered Order of Renunciates or Free Amazons, a guild of women bound only by oath as a sisterhood of mutual responsibility. Their primary allegiance is to each other rather than to family, clan, caste, or any man save a temporary employer. Alone among Darkovan women, they are exempt from the usual legal restrictions and protections. Their reason for existence is to provide the women of Darkover an alternative to their socially restrictive lives.

AGAINST THE TERRANS
—THE FIRST AGE (Recontact):

After the Hastur Wars, the Hundred Kingdoms are consolidated into the Seven Domains, and ruled by a hereditary aristocracy of seven families, called the Comyn, allegedly descended from the legendary Hastur, Lord of Light. It is during this era that the Terran Empire, really a form of confederacy, rediscovers Darkover, which they know as the fourth planet of the Cottman star system. The fact that Darkover is a lost colony of the Empire is not easily or readily acknowledged by Darkovans and their Comyn overlords.

AGAINST THE TERRANS
—THE SECOND AGE (After the Comyn):

With the initial shock of recontact beginning to wear off, and the Terran spaceport a permanent establishment on the outskirts of the city of Thendara, the younger and less traditional elements of Darkovan society begin the first real exchange of knowledge with the Terrans—learning Terran science and technology and teaching Darkovan matrix technology in turn. Eventually Regis Hastur, the young Comyn lord most active in these exchanges, becomes Regent in a provisional government allied to the Terrans. Darkover is once again reunited with its founding Empire.

THE BLOODY SUN
THE HERITAGE OF HASTUR
THE PLANET SAVERS
SHARRA'S EXILE
THE WORLD WRECKERS
EXILE'S SONG
THE SHADOW MATRIX
TRAITOR'S SUN

THE DARKOVER ANTHOLOGIES:

These volumes of stories edited by Marion Zimmer Bradley, strive to "fill in the blanks" of Darkovan history, and elaborate on the eras, tales, and characters which have captured readers' imaginations.

THE KEEPER'S PRICE
SWORD OF CHAOS
FREE AMAZONS OF DARKOVER
THE OTHER SIDE OF THE MIRROR
RED SUN OF DARKOVER
FOUR MOONS OF DARKOVER
DOMAINS OF DARKOVER
RENUNICATES OF DARKOVER
LERONI OF DARKOVER
TOWERS OF DARKOVER
MARION ZIMMER BRADLEY'S DARKOVER
SNOWS OF DARKOVER

DARKOVER: FIRST CONTACT

DARKOVER LANDFALL
TWO TO CONQUER

Marion Zimmer Bradley

DAW BOOKS, INC.

DONALD A. WOLLHEIM, FOUNDER

375 Hudson Street, New York, NY 10014

ELIZABETH R. WOLLHEIM
SHEILA E. GILBERT
PUBLISHERS

http://www.dawbooks.com

First Paperback Printing, September 2004
4   5   6   7   8   9

DAW TRADEMARK REGISTERED
U.S. PAT. OFF. AND FOREIGN COUNTRIES
—MARCA REGISTRADA.
HECHO EN U.S.A.

PRINTED IN THE U.S.A.

CONTENTS

Two to Conquer
For Tanith Lee, to commemorate an old argument
which neither of us won, or lost, or ever will

ACKNOWLEDGMENTS

Darkover Landfall:

The songs quoted in the text from the New Hebrides Commune are all from the *Songs of the Hebrides*, collected by Marjorie Kennedy-Fraser and published 1909, 1922 by Boosey and Hawkes. *The Seagull of the Land-Under-Waves*, English worlds by Mrs. Kennedy-Fraser, from the Gaelic of Kenneth MacLeod. *Caristiona*, words traditional, English by Kenneth MacLeod. *The Fairy's Love Song*, English words by James Hogg (adapted). *The Mull-Fisher's Song*, English words by Marjorie Kennedy-Fraser. The *Coolins of Rum*, English words by Elfrida Rivers, by special permission.

Two to Conquer

To "Cinhil MacAran" of the SCA for the first verse of "Four and Twenty *Leroni*"—to the tune of "The Ball of Kirriemuir"—and to Patricia Mathews for creating the Sisterhood of the Sword and dressing them in red.

DARKOVER LANDFALL

CHAPTER ONE

The landing gear was almost the least of their worries; but it made a serious problem in getting in and out. The great starship lay tilted at a forty-five degree angle with the exit ladders and chutes coming nowhere near the ground, and the doors going nowhere. All the damage hadn't been assessed yet—not nearly—but they estimated that roughly half the crew's quarters and three-fourths of the passenger sections were uninhabitable.

Already half a dozen small rough shelters, as well as the tentlike field hospital, had been hastily thrown up in the great clearing. They'd been made, mostly out of plastic sheeting and logs from the resinous local trees, which had been cut with buzz-saws and timbering equipment from the supply materials for the colonists. All this had taken place over Captain Leicester's serious protests; he had yielded only to a technicality. His orders were absolute when the ship was in space; on a planet the Colony Expedition Force was in charge.

The fact that it wasn't the *right* planet was a technicality that no one had felt able to tackle . . . yet.

It was, reflected Rafael MacAran as he stood on the low peak above the crashed spaceship, a beautiful planet. That is, what they could see of it, which wasn't all that much. The gravity was a little less than Earth's, and the oxygen content a little higher, which itself meant a certain feeling of well-being and euphoria for anyone born and brought up on Earth. No one reared on Earth in the twenty-first century, like Rafael MacAran, had ever smelled such sweet and resinous air, or seen faraway hills through such a clean bright morning.

The hills and the distant mountains rose around them in an apparently endless panorama, fold beyond fold, gradually losing color with distance, turning first dim green, then dimmer blue, and finally to dimmest violet and purple. The great sun was deep red, the color of spilt blood; and that morning they had seen the four moons, like great multicolored jewels, hanging off the horns of the distant mountains.

MacAran set his pack down, pulled out the transit and began to set up its tripod legs. He bent to adjust the instrument, wiping sweat from his forehead. God, how hot it seemed after the brutal ice-cold of last night and the sudden snow that had swept from the mountain-range so swiftly they had barely had time to take shelter! And now the snow lay in melting runnels as he pulled off his nylon parka and mopped his brow.

He straightened up, looking around for convenient horizons. He already knew, thanks to the new-model altimeter which could compensate for different gravity strengths, that they were about a thousand feet above sea level—or what would be sea level if there were any seas on this planet which they couldn't yet be sure of. In the stress and dangers of the crash-landing no one except the Third Officer had gotten a clear look at the planet from space, and she had died twenty minutes after impact while they were still digging bodies out of the wreckage of the bridge.

They knew that there were three planets in this system: one an oversized, frozen-methane giant, the other a small barren rock, more moon than planet except for its solitary orbit, and this one. They knew that this one was what Earth Expeditionary Forces called a Class M planet—roughly Earth-type and probably habitable. And now they knew they were on it. That was just about all they knew about it, except what they had discovered in the last seventy-two hours. The red sun, the four moons, the extremes of temperature, the mountains all had been discovered in the frantic intervals of digging out and identifying the dead, setting up a hasty field hospital and drafting every able-bodied person to care for the injured, bury the dead, and set up hasty shelters while the ship was still inhabitable.

Rafael MacAran started pulling his surveying instruments from his pack but he didn't attend to them. He had needed this brief interval alone more than he had realized; a little time to recover from the repeated and terrible shocks of the last few hours—the crash, and a concussion which would have put him into a hospital on crowded, medically-hypersensitive Earth. Here the medical officer, harried from worse injuries, tested his reflexes briefly, handed him some headache pills and went on to the seriously hurt and the dying. His head still felt like an oversized toothache although the visual blurring had cleared up after the first night's sleep. The next day he had been drafted, with all the other able-bodied men not on the medical staff or the engineering crews in the ship, to dig mass graves for the dead. And then there had been the mind-shaking shock of finding Jenny among them.

Jenny. He had envisioned her safe and well, too busy at her own job to hunt him up and reassure him. Then among the mangled dead, the unmistakable silver-bright hair of his only sister. There hadn't even been time for tears. There were too many dead. He did the only thing he could do. He reported to Camilla Del Rey, deputizing for Captain Leicester on the identity detail, that the name of Jenny MacAran should be transferred from the lists of unlocated survivors to the list of definitely identified dead.

Camilla's only comment had been a terse, quiet "Thank you, MacAran." There was no time for sympathy, no time for mourning or even humane expressions of kindness. And yet Jenny had been Camilla's close friend, she'd really loved that damned Del Rey girl like a sister—just why, Rafael had never known, but Jenny had, and there must have been some reason. He realized somewhere below the surface, that he had hoped Camilla would shed for Jenny the tears he could not manage to weep. Someone ought to cry for Jenny, and he couldn't. Not yet.

He turned his eyes on his instruments again. If they had known their definite latitude on the planet it would have been easier, but the height of the sun above the horizon would give them some rough idea.

Below him in a great bowl of land at least five miles across filled with low brushwood and scrubby trees, the crashed spaceship lay. Rafael, looking at it from this distance, felt a strange sinking feeling. Captain Leicester was supposed to be working with the crew to assess the damage and estimate the time needed to make repairs. Rafael knew nothing about the workings of starships—his own field was geology. But it didn't look to him as if that ship was ever going anywhere again.

Then he turned off the thought. That was for the engineering crews to say. They knew, and he didn't. He'd seen some near-miracles done by engineering these days. At worst this would be an uncomfortable interval of a few days or a couple of weeks, then they'd be on their way again, and a new habitable planet would be charted on the Expeditionary Forces starmaps for colonization. This one, despite the brutal cold at night, looked extremely habitable. Maybe they'd even get to share some of the finder's fees, which would go to improve the Coronis Colony where they'd be by then.

And they'd all have something to talk about when they were Old Settlers in the Coronis Colony, fifty or sixty years from now.

But if the ship never did get off the ground again. . . .

Impossible. This wasn't a charted planet, okayed for colonizing, and already opened up. The Coronis Colony—Phi Coronis Delta—was already the site of a flourishing mining settlement. There was a functioning spaceport and a crew of engineers and technicians had been working there for ten years preparing the planet for settlement and studying its ecology. You couldn't set down, raw and unhelped by technology, on a completely unknown world. It couldn't be done.

Anyway, that was somebody else's job and he'd better do his own now. He made all the observations he could, noted them in his pocket notebook, and packed up the tripod starting down the hill again. He moved easily across the rock-strewn slope through the tough underbrush and trees carrying his pack effortlessly in the light gravity. It was cleaner and easier than a hike on Earth, and he cast a longing eye at the distant mountains. Maybe if their stay stretched out more than a few days, he could be spared to take a brief climb into them. Rock samples and some geological notations should be worth something to Earth Expeditionary and it would be a lot better than a climbing trip on Earth, where every National Park from Yellowstone to Himalaya was choked with jet-brought tourists three hundred days of the year.

He supposed it was only fair to give everyone a chance at the mountains, and certainly the slidewalks and lifts installed to the top of Mount Rainier and Everest and Mount Whitney had made it easier for old women and children to get up there and have a chance to see the scenery. But still, MacAran thought longingly, to climb an actual wild mountain—one with no slidewalks and not even a single chairlift! He'd climbed on Earth, but you felt silly struggling up a rock cliff when teenagers were soaring past you in chairlifts on their effortless way to the top and giggling at the anachronist who wanted to do it the hard way!

Some of the nearer slopes were blackened with the scars of old forest fires, and he estimated that the clearing where the ship lay was second-growth from some such fire a few years before. Lucky the ship's fire-prevention systems had prevented any fire on impact—otherwise if anyone had escaped alive, it might have been quite literally from a frying pan into a raging forest fire. They'd have to be careful in the woods. Earth people had lost their old woodcraft habits and might not be aware anymore of what forest fires could do. He made a mental note of it for his report.

As he re-entered the area of the crash, his brief euphoria vanished. Inside the field hospital, through the semi-transparent plastic of the shelter material, he could see rows and rows of unconscious or semiconscious bodies. A group of men were trimming branches from tree trunks and another small group was raising a dymaxion dome—the kind, based on triangular bracings, which could be built in half a day. He began to wonder what the report of the Engineering crew had been. He could see a crew of machinists crawling around on the crumpled bracings of the starship, but it didn't look as if much had been accomplished. In fact, it didn't look hopeful for getting away very soon.

As he passed the hospital, a young man in a stained and crumpled Medic uniform came out and called.

"Rafe! The Mate said report to the First Dome as soon as you get back—there's a meeting there and they want you. I'm going over there myself for a Medic report—I'm the most senior man they can spare." He moved slowly beside MacAran. He was slight and small, with light-brown hair and a small curly brown beard, and he looked weary, as if he had had no sleep. MacAran asked hesitatingly, "How are things going in the hospital?"

"Well, no more deaths since midnight, and we've taken four more people off critical. There evidently wasn't a leak in the atomics after all—that girl from Comm checked out with no radiation burns; the vomiting was evidently just a bad blow in the solar plexus. Thank God for small favors—if the atomics had sprung a leak, we'd probably all be dead, and another planet contaminated."

"Yeah, the M-AM drives have saved a lot of lives," MacAran said. "You look awfully tired, Ewen—have you had any sleep at all?"

Ewen Ross shook his head. "No, but the Old Man's been generous with wakers, and I'm still racing my motors. About midafternoon I'm probably going to crash and I won't wake up for three days, but until then I'm holding on." He hesitated, looked shyly at his friend and said, "I heard about Jenny, Rafe. Tough luck. So many of the girls back in that area made it out, I was sure she was okay."

"So was I." MacAran drew a deep breath and felt the clean air like a great weight on his chest. "I haven't seen Heather— is she—"

"Heather's okay; they drafted her for nursing duty. Not a scratch on her. I understand after this meeting they're going to post completed lists of the dead, the wounded and the survivors. What were you doing, anyway? Del Rey told me you'd been sent out, but I didn't know what for."

"Preliminary surveying," MacAran said. "We have no idea of our latitude, no idea of the planet's size or mass, no idea about climate or seasons or what have you. But I've established that we can't be too far off the equator, and—well, I'll be making the report inside. Do we go right in?"

"Yeah, in the First Dome." Half unconsciously, Ewen had spoken the words with capital letters, and MacAran thought how human a trait it was to establish location and orientation at once. Three days they had been here and already this first shelter was the First Dome, and the field shelter for the wounded was the Hospital.

There were no seats inside the plastic dome, but some canvas groundsheets and empty supply boxes had been set around and someone had brought a folding chair down for Captain Leicester. Next to him, Camilla Del Rey sat on a box with a lapboard and notebook on her knees; a tall, slender, dark-haired girl with a long, jagged cut across her cheek, mended with plastic clips. She was wrapped in the warm fatigue uniform of a crewmember, but she had shucked the heavy parka-like top and wore only a thin, clinging cotton shirt beneath it.

MacAran shifted his eyes from her, quickly—*damn it, what was she up to, sitting around in what amounted to her underwear in front of half the crew! At a time like this it wasn't decent* . . . then, looking at the girl's drawn and wounded face, he absolved her. She was hot—it *was* hot in here now—and she was, after all, on duty, and had a right to be comfortable.

If anyone's out of line it's me, eyeing a girl like this at a time like this. . . .

Stress. That's all it is. There are too damn many things it's not safe to remember or think about. . . .

Captain Leicester raised his grey head. *He looks like death,* MacAran thought, *probably he hasn't slept since the crash either.* He asked the Del Ray girl, "Is that everyone?"

"I think so."

The Captain said, "Ladies, gentlemen. We won't waste time on formalities, and for the duration of this emergency the protocols of etiquette are suspended. Since my recording officer is in the hospital, Officer Del Rey has kindly agreed to act as communications recorder for this meeting. First of all; I have called you together, a representative from every group, so that each of you can speak to your crews with authority about what is happening and we can minimize the growth of rumors and uninformed gossip about our position. And anywhere that more than twenty-five people are gathered, as I remember from my Pensacola days, rumors and gossip start up. So let's get your information here, and not rely on what somebody told someone else's best friend a few hours ago and what somebody else heard in the mess room—all right? Engineering: let's begin with you. What's the situation with the drives?"

The Chief Engineer—his name was Patrick, but MacAran didn't know him personally—stood up. He was a lanky gaunt man who resembled the folk hero Lincoln. "Bad," he said laconically. "I'm not saying they can't be fixed, but the whole drive room is a shambles. Give us a week to sort it out, and we can estimate how long it will take to fix the drives. Once the mess is cleared away, I'd say—three weeks to a month. But I'd hate to have my year's salary depend on how close I came inside that estimate."

Leicester said, "But it *can* be fixed? It's not hopelessly wrecked?"

"I wouldn't think so," Patrick said. "Hell, it better *not* be! We may need to prospect for fuels, but with the big converter that's no problem, any kind of hydrocarbon will do—even cellulose. That's for energy-conversion in the life-support system, of course; the drive itself works on anti-matter implosions." He became more technical, but before MacAran got too hopelessly lost, Leicester stopped him.

"Save it, Chief. The important thing is, you're saying *it can be fixed*, preliminary estimated time three to six weeks. Officer Del Rey, what's the status on the bridge?"

"Mechanics are in there now, Captain, they're using cutting torches to get out the crumpled metal. The computer console is a mess, but the main banks are all right, and so is the library system."

"What's the worst damage there?"

"We'll need new seats and straps all through the bridge cabin—the mechanics can handle that. And of course we'll have to re-program our destination from the new location, but once we find out exactly where we are, that should be simple enough from the Navigation systems."

"Then there's nothing hopeless there either?"

"It's honestly too early to say, Captain, but I shouldn't think so. Maybe it's wishful thinking, but I haven't given up yet."

Captain Leicester said, "Well, just now things look about as bad as they can; I suspect we're all tending to look on the grim side. Maybe that's good; anything better than the worst will be a pleasant surprise. Where's Dr. Di Asturien? Medic?"

Ewen Ross stood up. "The Chief didn't feel he could leave, sir; he's got a crew working to salvage all remaining medical supplies. He sent me. There have been no more deaths and all the dead are buried. So far there is no sign of any unusual illness of unknown origin, but we are still checking air and soil samples, and will continue to do so, for the purpose of classifying known and unknown bacteria. Also—"

"Go on."

"The Chief wants orders issued about using only the assigned latrine areas, Captain. He pointed out that we're carrying all sorts of bacteria in our own bodies which might damage the local flora and fauna, and we can manage to disinfect the latrine areas fairly thoroughly—but we should take precautions against infecting outside areas."

"A good point," Leicester said. "Ask someone to have the orders posted, Del Rey. And put a security man to make sure everybody knows where the latrines are, and uses them. No taking a leak in the woods just because you're there and there aren't any anti-littering laws."

Camilla Del Rey said, "Suggestion, Captain. Ask the cooks to do the same with the garbage, for a while, anyhow."

"Disinfect it? Good point. Lovat, what's the status on the food synthesizer?"

"Accessible and working, sir, at least temporarily. It might not be a bad idea, though, to check indigenous food supplies and make sure we *can* eat the local fruits and roots if we have to. If it goes on the blink—and it was never intended to run for long periods in planetary gravities—it will be too late to start testing the local vegetation *then*." Judith Lovat, a small, sturdily built woman in her late thirties with the green emblem of Life-support systems on her smock, glanced toward the door of the dome. "The planet seems to be widely forested; there should be something we can eat, with the oxygen-nitrogen system of this air. Chlorophyll and photosynthesis seem to be pretty much the same on all M-type planets and the end product is usually some form of carbohydrate with amino acids."

"I'm going to put a botanist right on it," Captain Leicester said, "which brings me to you, MacAran. Did you get any useful information from the hilltop?"

MacAran stood up. He said, "I would have gotten more if we'd landed in the plains—assuming there are any on this planet—but I did get a few things. First, we're about a thousand feet above sea level here, and definitely in the Northern hemisphere, but not too many degrees of latitude off the equator, considering that the Sun runs high in the sky. We seem to be in the foothills of an enormous mountain range, and the mountains are old enough to be forested—that is, no active apparent volcanoes in sight, and no mountains which look like the result of volcanic activity within the last few millennia. It's not a young planet."

"Signs of life?" Leicester asked.

"Birds in plenty. Small animals, perhaps mammals but I'm not sure. More kinds of trees than I knew how to identify. A good many of them were a kind of conifer, but there seemed to be hardwoods too, of a kind, and some bushes with various seeds and things. A botanist could tell you a lot more. No signs of any kind of artifact, however, no signs that anything has ever been cultivated or touched. As far as I can tell, the planet's untouched by human—or any other—hands. But of course we may be in the middle of the equivalent of the Siberian steppes or the Gobi desert—way, way off the beaten track."

He paused, then said, "About twenty miles due east of here, there's a prominent mountain peak—you can't miss it—from which we could take sightings, and get some rough estimate of the planet's mass, even without elaborate instruments. We might also sight for rivers, plains, water supply, or any signs of civilization."

Camilla Del Roy said, "From space there was no sign of life."

Moray, the heavy swarthy man who was the official representative of Earth Expeditionary, and in charge of the Colonists, said quietly, "Don't you mean no signs of a technological civilization, Officer? Remember, until a scant four centuries ago, a starship approaching Earth could not have seen any signs of intelligent life there, either?"

Captain Leicester said curtly, "Even if there is some form of pre-technological civilization, that is equivalent to no civilization at all, and whatever form of life there may be here, sapient or not, is not of any consequences to our purpose. They could give us no help in repairing our ship, and provided we are careful not to contaminate their ecosystems, there is no reason to approach them and create culture shock."

"I agree with your last statement," Moray said slowly, "but I would like to raise one question you have not yet mentioned, Captain. Permission?"

Leicester grunted, "First thing I said was that we're suspending protocol for the duration—go ahead."

"What's being done to check this planet out for habitability, in the event the drives *can't* be repaired, and we're stuck here?"

MacAran felt a moment of shock which stopped him cold, then a small surge of relief. Someone had said it. Someone else was thinking about it. He hadn't had to be the one to bring it up.

But on Captain Leicester's face the shock had not gone away; it had frozen into a stiff cold anger. "There's very little chance of that."

Moray got heavily to his feet. "Yes. I heard what your crew was saying, but I'm not entirely convinced. I think that we should start, at once, to take inventory of what we have, and what is here, in the event that we are marooned here permanently."

"Impossible," Captain Leicester said harshly. "Are you trying to say you know more than my crew about the condition of our ship, Mr. Moray?"

"No. I don't know a damn thing about starships, don't know as I particularly want to. But I know *wreckage* when I see it. I know a good third of your crew is dead, including some important technicians. I heard officer Del Rey say that she thought—she only *thought*—that the navigational computer could be fixed, and I do know that nobody can navigate a M-AM drive in interstellar space without a computer. We've got to take it into account that this ship may not be going *anywhere*. And in that case, we won't be going anywhere either. Unless we've got some boy genius who can build an interstellar communications satellite in the next five years with the local raw materials and the handful of people we have here, and send a message back to Earth, or to the Alpha Centauri or Coronis colonies to come and fetch their little lost sheep."

Camilla Del Rey said in a low voice, "Just what are you trying to do, Mr. Moray? Demoralize us further? Frighten us?"

"No. I'm trying to be realistic."

Leicester said, making a noble effort to control the fury that congested his face, "I think you're out of order, Mr. Moray. Our first order of business is to repair the ship, and for that purpose it may be necessary to draft every man, *including* the passengers from your Colonists group. We cannot spare large groups of men for remote contingencies," he added emphatically, "so if that was a request, consider it denied. Is there any other business?"

Moray did not sit down. "What happens then if six weeks from now we discover that you *can't* fix your ship? Or six months?"

Leicester drew a deep breath. MacAran could see the desperate weariness in his face and his effort not to betray it. "I suggest we cross that bridge if, and when, we see it in the distance, Mr. Moray. There is a very old proverb that says, sufficient unto the day is the evil thereof. I don't believe that a delay of six weeks will make all that difference in resigning ourselves to hopelessness and death. As for me, I intend to live, and to take this ship home again, and anyone who starts defeatist talk will have to reckon with me. Do I make myself clear?"

Moray was evidently not satisfied; but something, perhaps only the Captain's will, kept him quiet. He lowered himself into his seat, still scowling.

Leicester pulled Camilla's lapboard toward him. "Is there anything else? Very well. I believe that will be all, ladies and gentlemen. Lists of survivors and wounded, and their condition, will be posted tonight. Yes, Father Valentine?"

"Sir, I have been requested to say a Requiem Mass for the dead, at the site of the mass graves. Since the Protestant chaplain was killed in the crash, I would like to offer my services to anyone, of any faith, who can use them for anything whatsoever."

Captain Leicester's face softened as he looked at the young priest, his arm in a sling and one side of his face heavily bandaged. He said, "Hold your service by all means, Father. I suggest dawn tomorrow. Find someone who can work on erecting a suitable memorial here; some day, maybe a few hundred years from now, this planet may be colonized, and they should know. We'll have time for that, I imagine."

"Thank you, Captain. Will you excuse me? I must go back to the hospital."

"Yes, Father, go ahead. Anyone who wants to get back now is excused—unless there are any questions? Very well." Leicester leaned back in his seat and closed his eyes briefly. "MacAran and Dr. Lovat, will you stay a minute, please?"

MacAran came forward slowly, surprised beyond words; he had never spoken to the Captain before, and had not realized that Leicester knew him even by sight. What could he want? The others were leaving the dome, one by one; Ewen touched his shoulder briefly and whispered, "Heather and I will be at the Requiem Mass, Rafe. I've got to go. Come around to the hospital and let me check that concussion. Peace, Rafe; see you later," before he slipped away.

Captain Leicester had slumped in his chair, and he looked exhausted and old, but he straightened slightly as Judith Lovat and MacAran approached him. He said, "MacAran, your profile said you've had some mountain experience. What's your professional specialty?"

"Geology. Its true, I've spent a good deal of time in the mountains."

"Then I'm putting you in charge of a brief survey expedition. Go climb that mountain, if you can get up it, and take your sights from the peak, estimate the planet's mass, and so forth. Is there a meteorologist or weather specialist in the colonist group?"

"I suppose so, sir. Mr. Moray would know for sure."

"He probably would, and it might be a good idea for me to make a point of asking him," Leicester said. He was so weary he was almost mumbling. "If we can estimate what the weather in the next few weeks is likely to do, we can decide how best to provide shelter and so forth for the people. Also, any information about period of rotation, and so forth, might be worth something to Earth Expeditionary. And—Dr. Lovat—locate a zoologist and a botanist, preferably from the colonists, and send them along with MacAran. Just in case the food synthesizers break down. They can make tests and take samples."

Judith said. "May I suggest a bacteriologist too, if there's one available?"

"Good idea. Don't let repair crews go short, but take what you need, MacAran. Anyone else you want to take along?"

"A medical technician, or at least a medical nurse," MacAran requested, "in case somebody falls down a crevasse or gets chewed up by the local equivalent of *Tyrannosaurus Rex*."

"Or picks up some ghastly local bug," Judith said. "I ought to have thought of that."

"Okay, then, if the Medic chief can spare anybody," Leicester agreed. "One more thing. First Officer Del Rey is going with you."

"May I ask what for?" MacAran said, slightly startled. "Not that she isn't welcome, though it might be a rough trek for a lady. This isn't Earth and those mountains haven't any chairlifts!"

Camilla's voice was low and slightly husky. He wondered if it was grief and shock, or whether that was her natural tone. She said, "Captain, MacAran evidently doesn't know the worst of it. How much do you know about the crash and its cause, then?"

He shrugged. "Rumors and the usual gossip. All I know is that the alarm bells began to ring, I got to a safety area—so-called," he added, bitterly, remembering Jenny's mangled body, "and the next thing I knew I was being dragged out of the cabin and hauled down a ladder. Period."

"Well, then, here it is. We don't know where we are. We don't know what sun this is. We don't know even approximately what star cluster we're in. We were thrown off course by a gravitational storm—that's the layman's term, I won't bother explaining what causes it. We lost our orientation equipment with the first shock, and we had to locate the nearest star-system with a potentially habitable planet, and get down in a hurry. So I've got to take some astronomical sightings, if I can, and locate some known stars—I can do that with spectroscopic readings. From there I may be able to triangulate our position in the Galactic Arm, and do at least part of the computer re-programming from the planet's surface. It is easier to take astronomical observations at an altitude where the air is thinner. Even if I don't get to the mountain's peak, every additional thousand feet of altitude will give me a better chance for accurate readings." The girl looked serious and grave, and he sensed that she was holding fear at bay with her deliberately didactic and professional manner. "So if you can have me along on your expedition, I'm strong and fit, and I'm not afraid of a long hard march. I'd send my assistant, but he has burns over thirty percent of his body surface and even if he recovers—and it's not certain he will—he won't be going anywhere for a long, long time. There's no one else who knows as much about navigation and Galactic Geography as I do, I'm afraid, so I'd trust my own readings more than anyone else's."

MacAran shrugged. He was no male chauvinist, and if the girl thought she could handle the expedition's long marches, she could probably do it. "Okay," he said, "it's up to you. We'll need rations for four days minimum, and if your equipment is heavy, you'd better arrange to have someone else carry it; everybody else will have his own scientific paraphernalia." He looked at the thin shirt clinging damply to her upper body and added, a little harshly, "Dress warmly enough, damn it; you'll get pneumonia."

She looked startled, confused, then suddenly angry; her eyes snapped at him, but MacAran had already forgotten her. He said to the Captain, "When do you want us to start? Tomorrow?"

"No, too many of us haven't had enough sleep," said Leicester, dragging himself up again from what looked like a painful doze. "Look who's talking—and half my crew are in the same shape. I'm going to order everybody but half a dozen watchmen to sleep tonight. Tomorrow, except for basic work crews, we'll dismiss everyone for the memorial services for the dead; and there's a lot of inventorying to do, and salvage work. Start—oh, two, three days from now. Any preference about a medical officer?"

"May I have Ewen Ross if the chief can spare him?"

"It's okay by me," Leicester said, and sagged again, evidently for a split second asleep where he sat. MacAran said a soft, "Thank you, sir," and turned away. Camilla Del Rey laid a hand, a feather's touch, on his arm.

"Don't you dare judge him," she said in a low, furious voice, "he's been on his feet since two days before the crash on a steady diet of wakers, and he's too old for that! I'm going to see he gets twenty-four hours straight sleep if I have to shut down the whole camp!"

Leicester pulled himself up again. "—wasn't asleep," he said firmly. "Anything else, MacAran, Lovat?"

MacAran said a respectful, "No, sir," and slipped quietly away, leaving the Captain to his rest, his First Officer standing over him like—the image touched his mind in shock—a fiercely maternal tiger over her cub. *Or over the old lion?* And why did he care anyhow?

CHAPTER TWO

Too much of the passenger section was either flooded with fire-prevention foam, or oil-slick and dangerous; for that reason, Captain Leicester had given orders that all members of the expedition to the mountain were to be issued surface uniforms, the warm, weatherproof garments meant for spaceship personnel to wear on visiting the surface of an alien planet. They had been told to be ready just after sunrise, and they were ready, shouldering their rucksacks of rations, scientific equipment, makeshift campout gear. MacAran stood waiting for Camilla Del Rey, who was giving final instructions to a crewman from the bridge.

"These times for sunrise and sunset are as exact as we can get them, and you have exact azimuth readings for the direction of sunrise. We may have to estimate noon. But every night, at sunset, shine the strongest light in the ship in this direction, and leave it on for exactly ten minutes. That way we can run a line of direction to where we're going, and establish due east and west. You already know about the noon angle readings."

She turned and saw MacAran standing behind her. She said, with composure, "Am I keeping you waiting? I'm sorry, but you must understand the necessity for accurate readings."

"I couldn't agree more," MacAran said, "and why ask me? You outrank everybody in this party, don't you, ma'am?"

She lifted her delicate eyebrows at him. "Oh, is *that* what's worrying you? As a matter of fact, no. Only on the bridge. Captain Leicester put *you* in charge of this party, and believe me, I'm quite content with that. I probably know as much about mountaineering as you do about celestial navigation—if as much. I grew up in the Alpha colony, and you know what the deserts are like there."

MacAran felt considerably relieved—and perversely annoyed. This woman was just too damned perceptive! Oh, yes, it would minimize tensions if he didn't have to ask her as a superior officer to pass along any orders—or suggestions—about the trip. But the fact remained that somehow she'd managed to mike him feel officious, blundering and like a damn fool.

"Well," he said, "any time you're ready. We've got a good long way to go, over some fairly rough ground. So let's get this show on the road."

He moved away toward where the rest of the group stood gathered, mentally taking stock. Ewen Ross was carrying a good part of Camilla Del Roy's astronomical equipment, since, as he admitted, his medical kit was only a light weight. Heather Stuart, wrapped like the others in surface uniform, was talking to him in low tones, and MacAran thought wryly that it must be love, when your girl got up at this unholy hour to see you off. Dr. Judith Lovat, short and sturdy, had an assortment of small sample cases buckled together over her shoulder. He did not know the other two who were waiting in uniform, and before they moved off, he walked around to face them.

"We've seen each other in the recreation rooms, but I don't think I know you. You are—"

The first man, a tall, hawk-nosed, swarthy man in his middle thirties, said, "Marco Zabal. Xenobotanist. I'm coming at Dr. Lovat's request. I'm used to mountains. I grew up in the Basque country, and I've been on expeditions to the Himalayas."

"Glad to have you." MacAran shook his hand. It would help to have someone else along who knew mountains. "And you?"

"Lewis MacLeod. Zoologist, veterinary specialist."

"Crew member or colonist?"

"Colonist." MacLeod grinned briefly. He was small, fat and fair-skinned. "And before you ask, no, no formal mountaineering experience—but I grew up in the Scottish Highlands, and even in this day and age, you still have to walk a good ways to get anywhere, and there's more vertical country around than horizontal."

MacAran said, "Well, that's a help. And now that we're all together—Ewen, kiss your girl goodbye and let's get moving."

Heather laughed softly, turning and putting back the hood of the uniform—she was a small girl, slight and delicately made, and she looked even smaller in some larger woman's uniform—"Come off it, Rafe. I'm going with you. I'm a graduate microbiologist, and I'm here to collect samples for the Medic Chief."

"But—" MacAran frowned in confusion. He could understand why Camilla had to come—she was better qualified for the job than any man. And Dr. Lovat, perhaps, understandably felt concerned. He said, "I asked for men on this trip. It's some mighty rough ground." He looked at Ewen for support, but the younger man only laughed.

"Do I have to read you the Terran Bill of Rights? *No law shall be made or formulated abridging the rights of any human being to equal work regardless of racial origin, religion or sex—*"

"Oh, damn it, don't you spout Article Four at me," MacAran muttered. "If Heather wants to wear out her shoe leather and you want to let her, who am I to argue the point?" He still suspected Ewen of arranging it. Hell of a way to start a trip! And here he'd been, despite the serious purpose of this mission, excited about actually having a chance to climb an unexplored mountain—only to discover that he had to drag along, not only a female crew member—who at least looked hardy and in good training—but Dr. Lovat, who might not be old but certainly wasn't as young and vigorous as he could have wished, and the delicate-looking Heather. He said, "Well, let's get going," and hoped he didn't sound as glum as he felt.

He lined them up, leading the way, placing Dr. Lovat and Heather immediately behind him with Ewen so that he would know if the pace he set was too hard for them, Camilla next with MacLeod, and the mountain-trained Zabal to bring up the rear. As they moved away from the ship and through the small clutter of roughly-made buildings and shelters, the great red sun began to lift above the line of faraway hills, like an enormous, inflamed, bloodshot eye. Fog lay thick in the bowl of land where the ship lay, but as they began to climb up out of the valley it thinned and shredded, and in spite of himself, MacAran's spirits began to lift. It was, after all, no small thing to be leading a party of exploration, perhaps the only party of exploration for hundreds of years, on a wholly new planet.

They walked in silence; there was plenty to see. As they reached the lip of the valley, MacAran paused and waited for them to come up with him.

"I have very little experience with alien planets," he said. "But don't blunder into any strange underbrush, look where you step, and I hope I don't have to warn you not to drink the water or eat anything until Dr. Lovat has given it her personal okay. You two are the specialists—" he indicated Zabal and MacLeod, "anything to add to that?"

"Just general caution," MacLeod said. "For all we know this planet could be alive with poisonous snakes and reptiles, but our surface uniforms will protect us against most dangers we can't see. I have a handgun for use in extreme emergencies—if a dinosaur or huge carnivore comes along and rushes us—but in general it would be better to run away than shoot. Remember this is preliminary observation, and don't get carried away in classifying and sampling—the next team that comes here can do that."

"If there is a next team," Camilla murmured. She had spoken under her breath, but Rafael heard her and gave her a sharp look. All he said was, "Everybody, take a compass reading for the peak, and be sure to mark every time we move off that reading because of rough ground. We can see the peak from here; once we get further into the foothills we may not be able to see anything but the next hilltop, or the trees."

At first it was easy, pleasant walking, up gentle slopes between tall, deeply rooted coniferous trunks, surprisingly small in diameter for their height, with long blue-green needles on their narrow branches. Except for the dimness of the red sun, they might have been in a forest preserve on Earth. Now and again Marco Zabal fell out of line briefly to inspect some tree or leaf or root pattern; and once a small animal scooted away in the woods. Lewis MacLeod watched it regretfully and said to Dr. Lovat, "One thing—there are furred mammals here. Probably marsupials, but I'm not sure."

The woman said, "I thought you were going to take specimens."

"I will, on the way back. I've no way to keep live specimens on the way, how would I know what to feed them? But if you're worried about food supply, I should say that so far every mammal on any planet, without exception, has proved to be edible and wholesome. Some aren't very tasty, but milk-secreting animals are all evidently alike in body chemistry."

Judith Lovat noted that the fat little zoologist was puffing with effort, but she said nothing. She could understand perfectly well the fascination of being the first to see and classify the wildlife of a completely strange planet, a job usually left to highly specialized First Landing teams, and she supposed MacAran wouldn't have accepted him for the trip unless he was physically capable of it.

The same thought was on Ewen Ross' mind as he walked beside Heather, neither of them wasting their breath in talk. He thought, Rafe isn't setting a very hard pace, but just the same I'm not too sure how the women will take it. When MacAran called a halt, a little more than an hour after they had set out, he left the girl and moved over to MacAran's side.

"Tell me, Rafe, how high is this peak?"

"No way of telling, as far off as I saw it, but I'd estimate eighteen-twenty thousand feet."

Ewen asked, "Think the women can handle it?"

"Camilla will have to; she's got to take astronomical observations. Zabal and I can help her if we have to, and the rest of you can stay further down on the slopes if you can't make it."

"I can make it," Ewen said. "Remember, the oxygen content of this air is higher than Earth's; anoxia won't set in quite so low." He looked around the group of men and women, seated and resting, except for Heather Stuart, who was digging out a soil sample and putting it into one of her tubes. And Lewis MacLeod had flung himself down full length and was breathing hard, eyes closed. Ewen looked at him with some disquiet, his trained eyes spotting what even Judith Lovat had not seen, but he did not speak. He couldn't order the man sent back at this distance—not alone, in any case.

It seemed to the young doctor that MacAran was following his thoughts when the other man said abruptly, "Doesn't this seem almost too easy, too good? There has to be a catch to this planet *somewhere*. It's too much like a picnic in a forest preserve."

Ewen thought, *some picnic, with fifty-odd dead and over a hundred hurt in the crash,* but he didn't say it, remembering Rafe had lost his sister. "Why not, Rafe? Is there some law that says an unexplored planet *has* to be dangerous? Maybe we're just so conditioned to a life on Earth without risks that we're afraid to step one inch outside our nice, safe technology." He smiled. "Haven't I heard you bitching because on Earth you said that all the mountains, and even the ski slopes, were so smoothed out there wasn't any sense of personal conquest? Not that I'd know—I never went in for danger sports."

"You may have something there," MacAran said, but he still looked somber. "If that's so, though, why do they make such a fuss about First Landing teams when they send them to a new planet?"

"Search me. But maybe on a planet where man never developed, his natural enemies didn't develop either?"

It should have comforted MacAran, but instead he felt a cold chill. If man didn't *belong* here, could he *survive* here? But he didn't say it. "Better get moving again. We've got a long way to go, and I'd like to get on the slopes before dark."

He stopped by McLeod as the older man struggled to his feet. "You all right, Dr. MacLeod?"

"Mac," the older man said with a faint smile, "we're not under ship discipline now. Yes, I'm fine."

"You're the animal specialist. Any theories why we haven't seen anything larger than a squirrel?"

"Two," MacLeod said with a round grin, "the first, of course, being that there aren't any. The second, the one I'm committed to, is that with six, no, seven of us crashing along through the underbrush this way, anything with a brain bigger than a squirrel's keeps a good long way off!"

MacAran chuckled, even while he revised his opinion of the fat little man upward by a good many notches. "Should we try to be quieter?"

"Don't see how we can manage it. Tonight will be a better test. Larger carnivores—if there's any analogy to Earth—will come out then, hoping to catch their natural prey sleeping."

MacAran said, "Then we'd better make it our business that we don't get crunched up by mistake," but as he watched the others sling their packs and get into formation, he thought silently that this was one thing he had forgotten. It was true; the overwhelming attention to safety on Earth had virtually eliminated all but man-made dangers. Even jungle safaris were undertaken in glass-sided trucks, and it wouldn't have occurred to him that night would be dangerous in that way.

They had walked another forty minutes, through thickening

trees and somewhat heavier underbrush, where they had to push branches aside, when Judith stopped, rubbing her eyes painfully. At about the same time, Heather lifted her hands and stared at them in horror; Ewen, at her side, was instantly alert.

"What's wrong?"

"My hands—" Heather held them up, her face white. Ewen called, "Rafe, hold up a minute," and the straggling line came to a halt. He took Heather's slim fingers gingerly between his own, carefully examining the erupting greenish dots; behind him Camilla cried out:

"Judy! Oh, God, look at her face!"

Ewen swung around to Dr. Lovat. Her cheeks and eyelids were covered with the greenish dots, which seemed to spread and enlarge and swell as he looked at them. She squeezed her eyes shut. Camilla caught her hands gently as she raised them to her face.

"Don't touch your face, Judy—Dr. Ross, what is it?"

"How the hell do I know?" Ewen looked around as the others gathered around them.

"Anybody else turning green?" He added, "All right, then. This is what I'm here for, and everybody else keep your distance until we know just what we've got. Heather!" He shook her shoulder sharply. "Stop that! You're not going to drop dead, as far as I can tell your vital signs are all just fine."

With an effort, the girl controlled herself. "Sorry."

"Now. Exactly what do you feel? Do those spots hurt?"

"No, dammit, they *itch!*" She was flushed, her face red, her copper hair falling loose around her shoulders; she raised a hand to brush it back, and Ewen caught her wrist, careful to touch only her uniform sleeve. "No, don't touch your face," he said, "that's what Dr. Lovat did. Dr. Lovat, how do you feel?"

"Not so good," she said with some effort, "My face burns, and my eyes—well, you can see."

"Indeed I can." Ewen realized that the lids were swelling and turning greenish; she looked grotesque.

Secretly Ewen wondered if he looked as frightened as he felt. Like everyone there, he had been brought up on stories of exotic plagues to be found on strange worlds. But he was a doctor and this was his job. He said, making his voice as firm as he could, "All right, everyone else stand back; but don't panic, if it was an airborne plague we'd all have caught it, and probably the night we landed here. Dr. Lovat, any other symptoms?"

Judy said, trying to smile, "None—except I'm scared."

Ewen said, "We won't count that—yet." Pulling rubber gloves from a steri-pace in his kit, he quickly took her pulse. "No tachycardia, no depressed breathing. You, Heather?"

"I'm fine, except for the damned itching."

Ewen examined the small rash minutely. It was pinpoint at first, but each papule quickly swelled to a vesicle. He said, "Well, let's start eliminating. What did you and Dr. Lovat do that nobody else did?"

"I took soil samples," she said, "looking for soil bacteria and diatoms."

"I was studying some leaves," Judy said, "trying to see if they had a suitable chlorophyll content."

Marco Zabal turned back his uniform cuffs. "I'll play Sherlock Holmes," he said. "There's your answer." He extended his wrists, showing one or two tiny green dots. "Miss Stuart, did you have to move away any leaves to dig up your samples?"

"Why, yes, some flat reddish ones," she said, and he nodded. "There's your answer. Like any good xenobotanist, I handle any plant with gloves until I'm sure what's in it or on it, and I noticed the volatile oil at the time, but took it for granted. Probably some distant relative of urushiol—*rhus toxicodendron*—poison ivy to you. And it's my guess that if it comes out this quickly, it's simple contact dermatitis and there aren't any serious side effects." He grinned, his long narrow face amused. "Try an antihistamine ointment, if you have any, or give Dr. Lovat a shot, since her eyes are swollen so much it's going to be hard for her to see where she's going. And from now on don't go admiring any pretty leaves until I pass on them, all right?"

Ewen followed his instructions, with a relief so great it was almost pain. He felt totally unable to cope with any alien plagues. A massive hypo of antihistamines quickly shrunk Judith Lovat's swollen eyes to normal, although the green color remained. The tall Basque showed them all his specimen leaf, encased in a transparent plastic sample case. "The red menace that turns you green," he said dryly. "Learn to stay away from alien plants, if you can."

MacAran said, "If everyone's all right, let's move along," but as they gathered up their equipment, he felt half sick with relief, and renewed fear. What other dangers could be lurking in an innocent-looking tree or flower? He said half-aloud to Ewen, "I knew this place was too good to be true."

Zabal heard him and chuckled. "My brother was on the First Landing team that went to the Coronis colony. That's one reason I was heading out there. That's the only reason I happen to know all this. The Expedition Force doesn't care to publicize how tricky planets can be, because no one on our nice, safe Earth would dare go out to them. And of course by the time the major colonizing groups get there, like us, the technological crews have removed the obvious dangers and, shall we say, smoothed things down a bit."

"Let's go," MacAran ordered, without answering. This was a wild planet, but what could he do about it? He'd said he wanted to take risks, now he was having his chance.

But they went on without incident, halting near midday to eat lunch from their packs and allow Camilla Del Rey to check her chronometer and come closer to the exact moment of noon. He drew closer to her as she was watching a small pole she had set up in the ground:

"What's the story?"

"The moment when the shadow is shortest is exact noon. So I note the length every two minutes and when it begins to get longer again, noon—the sun exactly on meridian—is in that two-minute period. This is close enough to true local noon for our measurements." She turned to him and asked in a low voice, "Are Heather and Judy really all right?"

"Oh, yes. Ewen's been checking them at every stop. We don't know how long it will take for the color to fade, but they're fine."

"I nearly panicked," she murmured, "Judy Lovat makes me ashamed of myself. She was so calm."

He noticed that imperceptibly the "Lieutenant Del Rey," "Dr. Lovat," "Dr. MacLeod" of the ship—where, after all, you saw only your few intimates except formally—were melting into Camilla, Judy, Mac. He approved. They might be here a long time. He said something like that, then abruptly asked, "Do you have any idea how long we will be here for repairs?"

"None," she said, "but Captain Leicester says—six weeks if we can repair it."

"If?"

"Of course we can repair it," she said suddenly and sharply, and turned away. "We'll have to. We can't stay here."

He wondered if this were fact or optimism, but did not ask. When he spoke next it was to make some banal remark about the quality of the rations they carried and to hope Judy would find some fresh food sources here.

As the sun angled slowly down over the distant ranges, it grew cold again, and a sharp wind sprang up. Camilla looked apprehensively at the gathering clouds.

"So much for astronomical observations," she murmured. "Does it rain *every* night on this damnable planet?"

"Seems like it," MacAran said briefly. "Maybe it's a seasonal thing. But every night, so far, at this season at least—hot at noon, cooling down fast, clouds in the afternoon, rain at evening, snow toward midnight. And fog in the morning."

She said, knitting her brows, "From what I've guessed from the time changes—not that five days can tell us much—it's spring; anyhow the days are getting longer, about three minutes each day. The planet seems to have somewhat more tilt than Earth, which would make for violent weather changes. But maybe after the snow clears and before the fog rises, the sky will clear a little. . . ." and fell silent, thinking. MacAran did not disturb her, but as a thin fine drizzle began to fall, began to search for a camping site. They had better get under canvas before it turned into a downpour.

They were on a downslope; below them lay a broad and almost treeless valley, not in their direct path, but pleasant and green, stretching for two or three miles to the south. MacAran looked down at it, calculating the mile or two lost as against the problems of camping under the trees. Evidently these foothills were interspersed with such little valleys, and through this one ran something like a narrow stream of water—a river? A brook? Could it be used to replenish their water supplies? He raised the question, and MacLeod said, "Test the water, sure. But we'll be safer camping here in the middle of the forest."

"Why?"

For answer MacLeod pointed and MacAran made out something that looked like some herd animal. Details were hard to make out, but they were about the size of small ponies. "That's why," MacLeod said. "For all we know they may be peaceful—or even domesticated. And if they're grazing they're not carnivores. But I'd hate to be in their way if they took a notion to stampede in the night. In the trees we can hear things coming."

Judy came and stood beside them. "They might be good to eat. They might even be domesticable, if anyone ever colonizes this planet some day—save the trouble of importing food animals and beasts of burden from Earth."

Watching the slow, flowing movement of the herd over the gray-green turf, MacAran thought it was a tragedy that man could only see animals in terms of his own needs. *But hell, I like a good steak as well as anyone, who am I to preach?* And maybe within a few weeks they would be gone, and the herd animals, whatever they were, could remain unmolested forever.

They set up a camp on the slope in the midst of the drizzle, and Zabal set about making a fire. Camilla said, "I've got to get to the hilltop at sunset and try to find a line of sight to the ship. They're showing lights to establish sightings."

"You couldn't see anything in this rain," MacAran said sharply. "Visibility's about half a mile now. Even a strong light wouldn't show. Get inside the dome, you're drenched!"

She whirled on him. "*Mister* MacAran, need I remind you that I do not take my orders from you? You are in charge of the exploration party—but I'm here on ship's business and I have duties to perform!" She turned away from the small plastic dome-shaped tent and started up the slope. MacAran, cursing all stubborn female officers, started after her.

"Go back," she said sharply, "I've got my instruments, I can manage."

"You just said I'm in charge of this party. All right, damn it, one of *my* orders is that no one goes off alone! *No* one—and that includes the ship's first officer!"

She turned away without speaking again, forging up the slope, hugging her parka hood around her face against the cold, driving rain. It grew heavier as they climbed, and he heard her slip and stumble in the underbrush, even with the strong handlight she carried. Catching up with her, he put a strong hand under her elbow. She moved to shake it off, but he said harshly, "Don't be a fool, Lieutenant! If you break an ankle we'll all have to carry you—or turn back! Two can find a footing, maybe, where one can't. Come on—take my arm." She remained rigid and he snarled, "Damn it, if you were a man I wouldn't *ask* you politely to let me help—I'd *order* it!"

She laughed shortly. "All right," she said, and gripped his elbow, their two handlights playing on the ground for a path.

He heard her teeth chattering, but she did not speak a word of complaint. The slope grew steeper, and on the last few yards MacAran had to scramble up ahead of the girl and reach downward to pull her up. She looked round, searching for the direction; pointed where a very faint glimmer of light showed through the blinding rain.

"Could that be it?" she said uncertainly, "The compass direction seems about right"

"If they're using a laser, yes, I suppose it might show this far, even through the rain." The light blotted out, gleamed briefly, was wiped out again, and MacAran swore. "This rain's turning to sleet—come on, let's get down before we have to *slide* down—on ice underfoot!"

It was steep and slippery, and once Camilla lost her footing on the icy leafmold and slid, rolled and floundered to a stop against a great tree trunk; she lay there half-stunned until MacAran, flashing his light around and calling, caught her in his beam. She was gasping and sobbing with the cold, but when he reached a hand to help her up she shook her head and struggled to her feet. "I can manage. But thank you," she added, grudgingly.

She felt exhausted, utterly humiliated. She had been trained that it was her duty to work with men as an equal, and in the usual world she knew, a world of buttons to push and machines to run, physical strength was not a factor she had ever had to take into account. She never stopped to reflect that in all her life she had never known any physical effort greater than gymnastics in the exercise room of the ship, or a space station; she felt that she had somehow failed to carry her own weight, she had somehow betrayed her high position. A ship's officer was supposed to be more competent than *any* civilian! She trudged wearily along down the steep slope, setting her feet down with dogged care, and felt the tears of exhaustion and weariness freezing on her cold cheeks.

MacAran, following slowly, was unaware of her inward struggle, but he felt her weariness through her sagging shoulders. After a moment he put his arm around her waist, and said gently, "Like I said before, if you fall again and get hurt badly we'll have to carry you. Don't do that to us, Camilla." He added, hesitatingly, "You'd have let Jenny help you, wouldn't you?"

She did not answer, but she let herself lean on him. He guided her stumbling steps toward the small glow of light through the tent. Somewhere above them, in the thick trees, the harsh call of a night-bird broke through the noise of the beating sleet, but there was no other sound. Even their steps sounded odd and alien here.

Inside the tent MacAran sagged, gratefully taking the plastic cup of boiling tea MacLeod handed him, stepping carefully to where his sleeping bag had been spread beside Ewen's. He sipped at the boiling liquid, brushing ice from his eyelids, hearing Heather and Judy making cooing sounds over Camilla's icy face, bustling around in the cramped quarters and bringing her hot tea, a dry blanket, helping her out of her iced-over parka. Ewen asked, "What's it doing out there—rain? Hail? Sleet?"

"Mixture of all three, I'd guess. We seem to have lucked right into some kind of equinoctial storm, I'd imagine. It *can't* be like this all year round."

"Did you get your readings?" At MacAran's affirmative nod, he said, "One of us should have gone, the Lieutenant's not really up to that kind of climb in this weather. Wonder what made her try?"

MacAran looked across at Camilla, huddled under a blanket, with Judy drying her wet, tangled hair as she sipped the boiling tea. He said, surprising himself, *"Noblesse oblige."*

Ewen nodded. "I know what you mean. Let me get you some soup. Judy did some great things with the ration. Good to have a food expert along."

They were all exhausted and talked little of what they had seen; the howling of the wind and sleet outside made speech difficult in any case. Within half an hour they had downed their food and crawled into their sleeping bags. Heather snuggled close to Ewen, her head on his shoulder, and MacAran, just beyond them, looked at their joined bodies with a slow, undefined envy. There seemed a closeness there which had little to do with sexuality. It spoke in the way they shifted their weight, almost unconsciously, each to ease and comfort the other. Against his will he thought of the moment when Camilla had let herself rest against him, and smiled wryly in the dark. Of all the women in the ship she was the least likely to be interested in him, and probably the one he disliked most. But damn it, he had to admire her!

He lay awake for a time, listening to the noise of wind in the heavy trees, to the sound of a tree cracking and crashing down somewhere in the storm—*God! If one fell on the tent, we'd all be killed*—to strange sounds which might be animals crashing through the underbrush. After a while, fitfully, he slept, but with one ear open, hearing MacLeod gasping in his sleep and moaning, once hearing Camilla cry out, a nightmarish cry, then fall again into exhausted sleep. Toward morning the storm quieted and the rain ceased and he slept like the dead, hearing only through his sleep the sounds of strange beasts and birds moving in the nighted forest and on the unknown hills.

CHAPTER THREE

Some time before dawn he roused, hearing Camilla stirring, and saw across the dark tent that she was struggling into her uniform. He slid quietly from his sleeping bag, and asked softly, "What is it?"

"The rain's stopped and the sky's clear; I want some sky-sightings and spectrograph readings before the fog comes in."

"Right. Need any help?"

"No, Marco can help carry the instruments."

He started to protest, then shrugged and crawled back into his sleeping bag. It wasn't entirely up to him. She knew her business and didn't need his careful watchfulness. She'd made that amply clear.

Some undefined apprehension, however, kept him from sleeping again; he lay in an uneasy doze, hearing around him the noises of the waking forest. Birds called from tree to tree, some harsh and raucous, some soft and chirping. There were small croakings and stirrings in the underbrush, and somewhere a distant sound not unlike the barking of a dog.

And then the silence was shattered by a horrible yell—a shriek of unquestionably human agony, a harsh scream of anguish, repeated twice and breaking off in a ghastly babbling moan, and silence.

MacAran was out of his sleeping bag and out of the tent, half dressed, Ewen less than half a step behind him, and all the others crowding after, sleepy, bewildered, frightened. He ran up the slope toward the sound, hearing Camilla cry out for help.

She had set her equipment in a clearing near the summit,

but now it was knocked over; nearby Marco Zabal lay on the ground, writhing and moaning incoherently. He was swollen and his face had a hideous congested look; Camilla was brushing frantically with her gloved hands. Ewen dropped by the writhing man, with a quick demand to Camilla:

"Quick—what happened!"

"Things—like insects," she said, shaking as she held out her hands. On the gloved palm lay a small crushed thing, less than two inches long, with a curved tail like a scorpion and a wicked fang at the front; it was bright orange and green in color. "He stepped on that mound there, and I heard him scream, and then he fell down—"

Ewen had his medical kit out, and was quickly moving his hands over Zabal's heart. He gave quick directions to Heather, who had dropped beside him, to cut away the man's clothes; the wounded man's face was congested and blackening, and his arm swollen immensely. Zabal was unconscious now, moaning deliriously.

A powerful nerve poison, Ewen thought; his heart is slowing down and his breathing depressed. All he could do now was to give the man a powerful stimulant and stand by in case he needed artificial respiration. He didn't even dare give him anything to ease the agony—almost all narcotics were respiratory depressants. He waited, hardly breathing himself, his stethoscope on Zabal's chest, while the man's faltering heart began to beat a little more regularly; he raised his head to look briefly at the mound, to ask Camilla if she had been bitten— she hadn't, although two of the hideous insects had begun to crawl up her arm—and to demand that everybody stay a good long distance from the mound, or anthill, or whatever it was. *Just dumb luck we didn't camp on top of it in the dark! MacAran and Camilla might have stumbled right into it—or maybe they're dormant in snow!*

Time dragged. Zabal began to breathe again more regularly and to moan a little but he did not recover consciousness. The great red sun, dripping fog, slowly lifted itself up over the foothills surrounding them.

Ewen sent Heather back to the tent for the rest of his medical equipment; Judy and MacLeod began to fix some breakfast. Camilla stoically calculated the few astronomical readings she had been able to take before the attack of the scorpionants—MacLeod, after examining the dead one, had temporarily christened them that. MacAran came and stood beside the unconscious man and the young doctor who knelt beside him.

"Will he live?"

"I don't know. Probably. I never saw anything like it since I treated my one and only case of rattlesnake bite. But one thing's certain—he won't be going anywhere today, probably not tomorrow either."

MacAran asked, "Shouldn't we carry him down to the tent? Could there be more of those things crawling around?"

"I'd rather not move him now. Maybe in a couple of hours."

MacAran stood, looking down in dismay, at the unconscious man. They shouldn't delay—and yet, their party had been rigidly calculated for size and there was no one to spare to send back to the ship for help. Finally he said, "We've got to go on. Suppose we move Marco back to the tent, when it's safe, and you stay to look after him. The others can do their exploration work here as well as anywhere, check out soil, plant, animal samples. But I have to survey what I can from the peak, and Lieutenant Del Rey has to take her astronomical sightings from as high up as possible. We'll go on ahead, as far as we can. If the peak turns out to be unclimbable we won't try, just take what readings we can and come back."

"Wouldn't it be better to wait and see whether we can go on with you? We don't know what kind of dangers there are in the forests here."

"It's a matter of time," Camilla said tautly. "The sooner we know where we are, the sooner we have a chance—" she didn't finish.

MacAran said, "We don't know. The dangers might even be less for a very small party, even for a single person. It's even odds, either way. I think we're going to have to do it that way."

They arranged it like that, and since in two hours Zabal had shown no signs of recovering consciousness, MacAran and the other two men carried him, on an improvised stretcher, down to the tent. There was some protest about the splitting of the party, but no one seriously disputed it, and MacAran realized that he had already become their leader whose word was law. By the time the red sun stood straight overhead they had divided the packs and were ready to go, with only the small emergency shelter-tent, food for a few days, and Camilla's instruments.

They stood in the shelter tent, looking down at the semiconscious Zabal. He had begun to stir and moan but showed no other signs of returning consciousness. MacAran felt desperately uneasy about him, but all he could do was leave him in Ewen's hands. After all, the important business here was the preliminary estimate of this planet—and Camilla's observations as to where in the Galaxy they were!

Something was nagging at his mind. Had he forgotten anything? Suddenly Heather Stuart pulled off her uniform coat and drew off the fut-knit jacket she was wearing under it. "Camilla, it's warmer than yours," she said in a low voice, "please wear it. It snows so here. And you're going to be out with only the small shelter!"

Camilla laughed, shaking her head. "It's going to be cold here too."

"But—" Heather's face was taut and drawn. She bit her lip and pleaded, "*Please,* Camilla. Call me a silly fool, if you like. Say I'm having a premonition, but *please* take it!"

"You too?" MacLeod asked dryly. "Better take it, Lieutenant. I thought I was the only one having freaked-out second sight. I've never taken ESP very seriously, but who knows, on a strange planet it just might turn out to be a survival quality. Anyhow, what can you lose to take a few extra warm clothes?"

MacAran realized that the nagging at his mind *had* been somehow concerned with weather. He said, "Take it, Camilla, if it's extra warm. I'll take Zabal's mountain parka, too, it's heavier than mine, and leave mine for him. And some extra sweaters if you have them. Don't deprive yourselves, but it's true that if it snows you will have more shelter than we do, and it sometimes gets pretty cold on the heights." He was looking at Heather and MacLeod curiously; as a general rule he had no faith in what he had heard about ESP, but if two people in the party both felt it, and he too had some inkling of it—well, maybe it was just a matter of unconscious sensory clues, something they couldn't add up consciously. Anyway, you didn't need ESP to predict bad weather on the mountain heights of a strange planet with a freakishly bad climate! "Take all the clothes anyone can spare, and an extra blanket—we have extras," he ordered, "and then let's get going."

While Heather and Judy were packing, he made time for a word alone with Ewen. "Wait here for at least eight days for us," he said, "and we'll signal every night at sunset if we can.

If there's no word or signal by that time, get back to the ship. If we make it back, no sense disturbing everyone else with this—but if something happens to us, you're in charge."

Ewen felt reluctant to see him go. "What shall I do if Zabal dies?"

"Bury him," MacAran said harshly, "what else?" He turned away and motioned to Camilla. "Let's go, Lieutenant."

They strode away from the clearing without looking back, MacAran setting a steady pace, not too fast, not too slow.

As they climbed higher the land changed, the ground under foot becoming less overgrown, with more bare rocks and sparser trees. The slope of the foothills was not acute, but as they neared the crest of the slope where they had camped, MacAran called a halt to rest and swallow a mouthful of rations. From where they stood they could see the small orange square of the shelter-tent, only a flyspeck at this height, through the heavy trees.

"How far have we come, MacAran?" the woman asked, putting back the fur-lined hood of her jacket.

"I've no way of knowing. Five, six miles perhaps; about two thousand feet of altitude. Headache?"

"Only a little," the girl lied.

"That's the change in air pressure; you'll get used to it presently," he said. "Good thing we have a fairly gradual rise in land."

"It's hard to realize that's really where we slept last night— so far down," she said a little shakily.

"Over this ridge it will be out of sight. If you want to chicken out, this is your last chance. You could make it down in an hour, maybe two."

She shrugged. "Don't tempt me."

"Are you frightened?"

"Of course. I'm not a fool. But I won't panic, if that's what you mean."

MacAran rose to his feet, swallowing the last of his ration. "Let's go, then. Watch your step—there are rocks above us."

But to his surprise she was sure-footed on the piled rocks near the peak, and he did not need to help her, or hunt for an easier pass. From the top of the hill they could see a long panorama beneath them, behind them; the valley where they had camped, with its long plain, the further valley where the starship lay— although even with his strong binoculars MacAran could only make out a tiny dark streak that *might* be the ship. Easier to see was the ragged clearing where they had cut trees for shelters. Passing the glasses to Camilla, he said, "Man's first mark on a new world."

"And last, I hope," she said. He wanted to ask her, put it up to her straight, *could* the ship be repaired? But that wasn't the time for thinking about that. He said, "There are streams among the rocks, and Judy tested the water days ago. We can probably find all the water we need to refill our canteens, so don't ration yourself too much."

"My throat feels terribly dry. Is it just the altitude?"

"Probably. On Earth we couldn't come much higher than this without oxygen, but this planet has a higher oxygen content." MacAran took one last look at the orange tent below them; stowed the glasses and slung them over his shoulder. "Well, the next peak will be higher. Let's get on, then." She was looking at some small orange flowers that grew in the crannies of the rock. "Better not touch them. Who knows what might bite, here?"

She turned around, a small orange flower in her fingers. "Too late now," she said with wry grin. "If I'm going to drop dead when I pick a flower, better find it out now than later. I'm not so sure I *want* to go on living if it's a planet where I can't *touch* anything." She added, more seriously, "We've got to take some risks, Rafe—and even then, something we never thought of might kill us. Seems to me that all we can do is take the obvious precautions—and then take our chances."

It was the first time since the crash that she had called him by his first name, and unwillingly he softened. He said, "You're right of course; short of going around in space suits we haven't any real protection, so there's no point in being paranoid. If we were a First Landing Team we'd know what risks not to take, but as it is I guess all we can do is take our chances." It was growing hot, and he stripped off his outer layer of clothing. "I wonder how much stock to put in Heather's premonitions of bad weather?"

They started down the other side of the ridge. Halfway down the slope, after two or three hours of searching for a path, they discovered a small crystal spring gushing from a split rock, and refilled their canteens; the water tasted sweet and pure, and at MacAran's suggestion they followed the stream down; it would certainly take the shortest way.

At dusk heavy clouds began to scud across the lowering sun. They were in a valley, with no chance to signal the ship or the other camp of their party. While they were setting up the tiny shelter-tent, and MacAran was making fire to heat their rations, a thin fine rain began falling; swearing, he moved the small fire under the flap of the tent, trying to shield it a little from the rain. He managed to get water heated, but not hot, before the gusting sleet put it out again, and he gave up and dumped the dried rations into the barely warm water. "Here. Not tasty but edible—and nourishing, I hope."

Camilla made a face when she tasted it, but to his relief said nothing. The sleet whipped around them and they crawled inside and drew the flap tight. Inside there was barely room enough for one of them to lie at full length while the other sat up—the emergency tents were really only meant for one. MacAran started to make some flippant remark about nice cozy quarters, looked at her drawn face and didn't. He only said, as he wriggled out of his storm parka and pack, and started unrolling his sleeping bag, "I hope you don't suffer from claustrophobia."

"I've been a spaceship officer since I was seventeen. How could I get along with claustrophobia?" In the dark he imagined her smile. "On the contrary."

Neither of them had much to say after that. Once she asked into the darkness, "I wonder how Marco is?" but MacAran had no answer for her, and there was no point in thinking how much better this trip would have been with Marco Zabal's knowledge of the high Himalaya. He did ask, once, just before he dropped off to sleep, "Do you want to get up and try for some star-sights before dawn?"

"No. I'll wait for the peak, I guess, if we get that far." Her breathing quieted into soft exhausted sighs and he knew she slept. He lay awake a little, wondering what lay ahead. Outside, the sleet lashed the branches of the trees and there was a rushing sound which might have been wind or some animal making a rush through the undergrowth. He slept lightly, alert for unexpected sounds. Once or twice Camilla cried out in her sleep and he woke, alert and listening. Had she a touch of altitude sickness? Oxygen content or no oxygen content, the peaks were pretty high and each successive one left their general altitude a little higher. Well, she'd get acclimated, or else she wouldn't. Briefly, on the edge of sleep, MacAran reflected that it was the stuff of entertainment-media, a man alone with a beautiful woman on a strange planet full of dangers. He was conscious of wanting her—hell, he was human and male—but in their present circumstances nothing was further from his mind than sex. *Maybe I'm just too civilized.* In the very thought, exhausted by the day's climbing, he fell asleep.

The next three days were replays of that day, except that on the third night they reached a high pass at dusk and the night's rain had not yet begun. Camilla set up her telescope and made a few observations. He could not forbear, as he set up the shelter-tent in the dark, to ask, "Any luck? Where are we, do you know?"

"Not sure. I knew already that this sun is none of the charted ones, and the only constellations I can spot, from central co-ordinates, are all skewed to the left. I suspect we're right out of the Spiral Arm of the Galaxy—note how few stars there are, compared even to Earth, let alone any centrally located colony planet! Oh, we're a good long way from where we were supposed to be going!" Her voice sounded taut and drawn, and as he moved closer he saw in the darkness that there were tears on her cheeks.

He felt a painful urge to comfort her. "Well, at least when we're on our way again, we'll have discovered a new habitable planet. Maybe you'll even get part of the finder's fee."

"But it's so far—" she broke off. "Can we signal the ship?"

"We can try. We're at least eight thousand feet higher than they are; maybe we're in a line-of-sight. Here, take the glasses, see if you can find any sign of a flash. But of course they could be behind some fold of the hills."

He put his arm around her, steadying the glasses. She did not draw away. She said, "Do you have the bearing for the ship?"

He gave it to her; she moved the glasses slightly, compass in hand. "I see a light—no, I think it's lightning. Oh, what difference does it make?" Impatiently she put the glasses aside. He could feel her trembling. "You *like* these wide open spaces, don't you?"

"Why, yes," he said, slowly, "I've always loved the mountains. Don't you?"

In the darkness she shook her head. Above them the pale violet light of one of the four small moons gave a faint tremulous quality to the dimness. She said, faintly, "No. I'm afraid of them."

"Afraid?"

"I've been either on a satellite or training ship since I was picked for space at fifteen. You—" her voice wavered, "you get kind of—agoraphobic."

"And you volunteered to come on this trip!" MacAran said, but she mistook his surprise and admiration for criticism. "Who else was there?" she said harshly, turned away and went into the tiny tent.

Once again, after they had swallowed their food—hot tonight, since there was no rain to put out their fire—MacAran lay awake long after the girl slept. Usually at night there was only the sound of blowing rain and creaking, lashing branches; tonight the forest seemed alive with strange sounds and noises, as if, on the rare snowless night, all its unknown life came alive. Once there was a faraway howling that sounded like a tape he had heard, once, on Earth, of the extinct timber wolf; once an almost feline snarl, low and hoarse, and the terrified cry of some small animal, and then silence. And then, toward midnight, there was a high, eerie scream, a long wailing cry that seemed to freeze the very marrow of his bones. It sounded so uncannily like the scream Marco had given when attacked by the scorpion-ants that for a dreaming moment MacAran, shocked awake, started to leap to his feet; then as Camilla, roused by his movement, sat up in fright, it came again, and he realized nothing human could possibly have made it. It was a shrill, ululating cry that went on, higher and higher, into what seemed like ultra-sonics; he seemed to hear it long after it had died away.

"What is it?" Camilla whispered, shaking.

"God knows. Some kind of bird or animal, I suppose."

They listened in silence to the ear-shattering scream again. She moved a little closer to him, and murmured, "It sounds as if it were in agony."

"Don't be imaginative. That may be its normal voice, for all we know."

"*Nothing* has a normal voice like that," she said firmly.

"How can we possibly know that?"

"How can you be so matter of fact? Oooh—" she flinched

as the long shrilling sound came again. "It seems to freeze the marrow of my bones!"

"Maybe it uses that sound to paralyze its prey," MacAran said. "It scares me too, damn it! If I were on Earth—well, my people were Irish, and I'd imagine the old Arran banshee had come to carry me off!"

"We'll have to name it *banshee,* when we find out what it is," Camilla said, and she wasn't laughing. The hideous sound came again, and she clapped her hands over her ears, screaming, "Stop it! *Stop it!*"

MacAran slapped her, not very hard. "Stop it yourself, damn you! For all we know it might be prowling around outside and big enough to eat up both of us and the tent too! Let's keep quiet and just lie low until it goes away!"

"That's easier said than done," Camilla murmured, and flinched as the eerie banshee cry came again. She crept closer to him in the crowded quarters of the tent and said, in a very small voice, "Would you—hold my hand?"

He searched for her fingers in the dark. They felt cold and stiff, and he began to chafe them softly between his own. She leaned against him, and he bent down and kissed her softly on the temple. "Don't be afraid. The tent's plastic and I doubt if we smell edible. Let's just hope whatever-it-is, the banshee if you like, catches itself a nice dinner soon and shuts up."

The howling scream sounded again, further away this time and without the ghastly bone-chilling quality. He felt the girl sag against his shoulder and eased her down again, letting her head rest against him. "You'd better get some sleep," he said gently.

Her whisper was almost inaudible. "Thanks, Rafe."

After he knew, by the sound of her steady breathing, that she slept again, he leaned over and kissed her softly. This was one hell of a time to start something like that, he told himself, angry at his own reactions, they had a job to do and there was nothing personal about it. Or shouldn't be. But still it was a long time until he slept.

They came out of the tent in the morning to a world transformed. The sky was clear and unstained by cloud or fog, and underfoot the hardy colorless grass had been suddenly carpeted by quick-opening, quick-spreading colored flowers. No biologist, MacAran had seen something like this in deserts and other barren areas and he knew that places with violent climates often developed forms of life which could take advantage of tiny favorable changes in temperature or humidity, however brief. Camilla was enchanted with the multicolored low-growing flowers and with the beelike creatures who buzzed among them, although she was careful not to disturb them.

MacAran stood surveying the land ahead. Across one more narrow valley, crossed by a small running stream, lay the last slopes of the high peak which was their destination.

"With any luck we should be near the peak tonight, and tomorrow, just at noon, we can take our survey readings. You know the theory—triangulate the distance between here and the ship, calculate the angle of the shadow, we can estimate the size of the planet. Archimedes or somebody like that did it for Earth, thousands of years before anyone ever invented higher mathematics. And if it doesn't rain tonight you may be able to get some clearer sightings from the heights."

She was smiling. "Isn't it wonderful what just a little change in the weather can do? Will it be much of a climb?"

"I don't think so. It looks from here as if we could walk straight up the slope—evidently the timberline on this planet is higher than most worlds. There's bare rock and no trees near the peak, but only a couple of thousand feet below there's vegetation. We haven't reached the snowline yet."

On the higher slopes, in spite of everything. MacAran recovered his old enthusiasm. A strange world perhaps, but still, a mountain beneath him, the challenge of a climb. An easy climb it was true, without rocks or icefalls, but that simply freed him to enjoy the mountain panorama, the high clear air. It was only Camilla's presence, the knowledge that she feared the open heights, that kept him in touch with reality at all. He had expected to resent this, the need to help an amateur over easy stretches which he could have climbed with one leg in a cast, the waiting for her to find footing on the stretches of steep rocky scree, but instead he found himself curiously in rapport with her fear, her slow conquest of each new height. A few feet below the high peak he stopped.

"Here. We can run a perfectly good line of sight from here, and there's a flat spot to set up your equipment. We'll wait here for noon."

He had expected her to show relief; instead she looked at

him, with a certain shyness, and said, "I thought you'd like to climb the peak, Rafe. Go ahead, if you want to, I don't mind."

He started to snap at her that it would be no fun at all with a frightened amateur, then realized this was no longer true. He pulled his pack off his shoulder and smiled at her, laying a hand on her arm. "That can wait," he said gently, "this isn't a pleasure trip, Camilla. This is the best spot for what we want to do. Did you adjust your chronometer so that we can catch noon?"

They rested side by side on the slope, looking down across the panorama of forests and hills spread out below them. *Beautiful,* he thought, *a world to love, a world to live in.*

He asked idly, "Do you suppose the Coronis colony is this beautiful?"

"How would I know? I've never been there. Anyway, I don't know all that much about planets. But this one is beautiful. I've never seen a sun quite this color, and the shadows—" she fell silent, staring down at the pattern of greens and dark-violet shade in the valleys.

"It would be easy to get used to a sky this color," MacAran said, and was silent again.

It was not long until the shortening shadows marked the approach of the meridian. After all the preparation, it seemed a curious anticlimax; to unfold the hundred-foot-high aluminum rod, to measure the shadows exactly, to the millimeter. When it was finished and he was refolding the rod, he said as much, wryly:

"Forty miles and an eighteen-thousand-foot climb for a hundred and twenty seconds of measurements."

Camilla shrugged. "And God-knows-how-many light-years to come here. Science is all like that, Rafe."

"Nothing to do now but wait for the night, so you can take your observations." Rafe folded the rod and sat down on the rocks, enjoying the rare warmth of the sunlight. Camilla went on moving around their campsite for a little, then came back and joined him. He asked, "Do you really think you can chart this planet's position, Camilla?"

"I hope so. I'm going to try and observe known Cepheid variables, take observations over a period of time, and if I can find as many as three that I can absolutely identify, I can compute where we are in relation to the central drift of the Galaxy."

"Let's pray for a few more clear nights, then," Rafe said, and was silent.

After some time, watching him study the rocks less than a hundred feet above them, she said, "Go on, Rafe. You know you want to climb it. Go ahead, I don't mind."

"You don't? You won't mind waiting here?"

"Who said I'd wait here? I think I can make it. And—" she smiled a little, "I suppose I'm as curious as you are—to get one glimpse of what's beyond it!"

He rose with alacrity. "We can leave everything but the canteens here," he said. "It *is* an easy enough climb—not a climb at all, really; just a steep sort of scramble." He felt light-hearted, joyous at her sudden sharing of his mood. He went ahead, searching out the easiest route, showing her where to set her feet. Common sense told him that this climb, based only on curiosity to see what lay beyond and not on their mission's needs, was a little foolhardy—who could risk a broken ankle?—but he could not contain himself. Finally they struggled up the last few feet and stood looking out over the peak. Camilla cried out in surprise and a little dismay. The shoulder of the mountain on which they stood had obscured the real range which lay beyond; an enormous mountain range which lay, seemingly endless and to the very edge of their sight, wrapped in eternal snow, enormous and jagged and covered with glaciated ridges and peaks below which pale clouds drifted, lazily and slow.

Rafe whistled. "Good God, it makes the Himalayas look like foothills," he muttered.

"It seems to go on forever! I suppose we didn't see it before because the air wasn't so clear, with clouds and fog and rain, but—" Camilla shook her head in wonder. "It's like a wall around the world!"

"This explains something else," Rafe said slowly. "The freak weather. Flowing over a series of glaciers like that, no wonder there's almost perpetual rain, fog, snow—you name it! And if they are really as high as they look—I can't tell how far away they are, but they could easily be a hundred miles on a clear day like this—it would also explain the tilt of this world on its axis. They call the Himalayas, on Earth, a third pole. This is a *real* third pole! A third icecap, anyway."

"I'd rather look the other way," Camilla said, and faced back toward the folds and folds of green-violet valleys and forests. "I prefer my planets with trees and flowers—and sunlight, even if the sunlight is the color of blood."

"Let's hope it shows us some stars tonight—and some moons."

CHAPTER FOUR

"I simply can't believe this weather," Heather Stuart said, and Ewen, stepping to the door of the tent, jeered gently, "What price your blizzard warnings now?"

"I'm glad to be wrong," Heather said firmly, "Rafe and Camilla need it, on the mountain." An expression of disquiet passed over her face. "I'm not so sure I *was* wrong, though, there's something about this weather that scares me a little. It seems all wrong for this planet somehow."

Ewen chuckled. "Still defending the honor of your old Highland granny and her second sight?"

Heather did not smile. "I never believed in second sight. Not even in the Highlands. But now I'm not so sure. How is Marco?"

"Not much change, although Judy did manage to get him to swallow a little broth. He seems a little better, although his pulse is still awfully uneven. Where is Judy, by the way?"

"She went into the woods with MacLeod. I made her promise not to go out of sight of the clearing, though." A sound inside of the tent drew them both back; for the first time in three days, something other than inarticulate moans from Zabal. Inside he was moving, struggling to sit up. He muttered, in a hoarse astonished voice, *"Que pasó? O Dio, mi duele—duele tanto—"*

Ewen bent over him, saying gently, "It's all right, Marco, you're here, we're with you. Are you in pain?"

He muttered something in Spanish. Ewen looked blankly up at Heather, who shook her head. "I don't speak it; Camilla does, but I only know a few words." But before she could muster any of them, Zabal muttered, "Pain? You'd better believe! What *were* those things? How long—where's Rafe?"

Ewen checked the man's heart-rate before he spoke. He said, "Don't try to sit up; I'll put a pillow behind your head. You've been very ill; we thought you weren't going to make it." *And I'm still not so sure,* he thought grimly, even while he wadded his spare coat to put behind the injured man's head and Heather encouraged him to swallow some soup. *No, please, there have been too many deaths.* But he knew this would make no difference. On Earth only the old died, as a rule. Here—well, it was different. Damn different.

"Don't waste your breath talking. Save your strength and we'll tell you everything," he said.

The night fell, still miraculously clear and free of fog or rain. Even on the heights, no fog closed in, and Rafe, setting up Camilla's telescope and other instruments on the flat place of their camp, saw for the first time the stars rise over the peaks, clear and brilliant but very far away. He did not know a Cepheid variable from a constellation, so much of what she was trying to do was incomprehensible to him; but with a carefully shielded light—not to spoil the dark-adaptation of her eyes—he wrote down careful strings of figures and co-ordinates as she gave them. After what seemed hours of this, she sighed and stretched cramped muscles.

"That's all I can do for now; I can take more readings just before dawn. Still no sign of rain?"

"None, thank goodness."

Around them the scent from the flowers on the lower slopes was sweet and intoxicating, as quick-blooming shrubs, vivified by two days of heat and dryness, burst and opened all around. The unfamiliar scents were a little dizzying. Over the mountain floated a great gleaming moon, with a pale iridescent glow; then, following it by only a few moments, another, this one with pale violet lustre.

"Look at the moon," she whispered.

"Which moon?" Rafe smiled in the darkness. "Earthmen get used to saying, *the* moon; I suppose some day someone will give them names. . . ."

They sat on the soft dry grass, watching the moons swing free of the mountains and rise. Rafe quoted softly, "If the stars shone only one night in a thousand years, how men would look and wonder and adore."

She nodded. "Even after ten days, I find I miss them."

Rationally Rafe knew that it was madness to sit here in the dark. If nothing else, birds or beasts of prey—perhaps the banshee-screamer from the heights they had heard last night— might be abroad in the dark. He said so, finally, and Camilla, like the breaking of a spell, started and said, "You're right. I must wake well before dawn."

Rafe was somehow reluctant to go into the stuffy darkness of the shelter-tent. He said, "In the old days it used to be believed it was dangerous to sleep in the moonlight—that's where the word lunatic came from. Would it be four times as dangerous to sleep under four moons, I wonder?"

"No, but it would be—lunatic," Camilla said, laughing gently. He stopped, took her shoulders in a gentle grip and for a moment the girl, biting back a tart remark, thought in a mixture of fear and anticipation that he would bend down and kiss her; but then he turned away and said, "Who wants to be sane? Good night, Camilla. See you an hour before sunrise," and strode away, leaving her to go before him into the shelter.

A clear night, over the planet of the four moons. Banshees prowled on the heights, freezing their warm-blooded prey with their screams, blundering toward them by the heat of their blood, but never coming below the snowline; on a snowless night, anything on rock or grass was safe. Above the valleys, great birds of prey swung, beasts still unknown to the Earthmen prowled in the depths of the deep forest, living and dying, and trees unheard crashed to the ground. Under the moonlight, in the unaccustomed heat and dryness of a warm wind blowing away from the glaciated ridges, flowers bloomed and opened, and shed their perfume and pollen. Night-blooming and strange, with a deep and intoxicating scent. . . .

The red sun rose clear and cloudless, a brilliant sunrise with the sun like a giant ruby in a clear garnet sky. Rafe and Camilla, who had been at the telescope for two hours, sat and watched it with the pleasant fatigue of a light task safely over for some time.

"Shall we start down? This weather is too good to last,"

Camilla said, "and although I've gotten used to the mountain in the sun, I don't think I'd care to navigate it on ice."

"Right. Pack up the instruments—you know how they go—and I'll fix a bite of rations and strike the tent. We'll start down while the weather holds—not that it doesn't look like a gorgeous day. If it's still fine tonight we can stop on one of the hilltops and camp out, and you can take some more sightings," he said.

Within forty minutes they were going down. Rafe cast a wistful look back at the huge unknown range before turning his back on it. His own undiscovered range, and probably he would never see it again.

Don't be too sure, a voice remarked precisely in his mind, but he shrugged it off. He didn't believe in precognition.

He sniffed the light flower-scents, half enjoying them, half disturbed by their faintly acrid sweetness. The most noticeable were the tiny orange flowers Camilla had plucked the day before, but there was also a lovely white flower, star-shaped with a golden corolla, and a deep blue bell-like blossom with inner stalks covered with a shimmering gold-colored dust. Camilla bent over, inhaling the spicy fragrance. Rafe thought to warn her, after a moment;

"Remember Heather and Judy turning green? Serve you right if you do!"

She looked up, laughing. Her face looked faintly gold from the flower-dust. "If it was going to hurt me it would have already—the air's full of the scent, or haven't you noticed? Oh, it's so beautiful, so beautiful, I feel like a flower myself, I feel as if I could get drunk on flowers—"

She stood rapt, gazing at the beautiful bell-shaped blossom and seeming to shimmer with the golden dust. *Drunk,* Rafe thought, *drunk on flowers.* He let his pack slip from his shoulder and roll away.

"You *are* a flower," he said hoarsely. He seized her and kissed her; she raised her lips to his, shyly at first, then with growing passion. They clung together in the field of waving flowers; she broke free first, and ran toward the stream which flowed down the slope, laughing, bending to toss her hands in the water.

Rafe thought in astonishment, *what has happened to us,* but the thought slid lightly over his mind and vanished. Camilla's slight body seemed to flicker, to go in and out of focus. She stripped off her climbing boots and thick socks, dabbling her feet in the water.

Rafe bent over her and pulled her down into the long grass.

In the camp on the lower heights, Heather Stuart woke slowly, feeling the hot sun through the orange silk of the tent. Marco Zabal still drowsed in his corner, his blanket drawn over his head; but as she looked at him he began to stir, and smiled at her.

"So you sleep too, still?"

"I suppose the others are out in the clearing," Heather said, stirring. "Judy said she wanted to test some of the nuts on the trees for edible carbohydrates—I notice her test kits aren't here. How are you feeling, Marco?"

"Better," he said, stretching. "I think maybe I get up for a minute today. Something in this air and sun, it does me good."

"It's lovely," she agreed. She too was conscious of some extra sense of well-being and euphoria in the scented air. *It must be the higher oxygen content.*

She stepped into the bright air, stretching like a cat in the sunshine.

A clear picture came into her mind, bright and intrusive and strangely exciting; Rafe, drawing Camilla into his arms. . . . "That's lovely," she said aloud, and breathed deeply, smelling the curious, somehow golden scent which seemed to fill the light warm wind.

"What's lovely? *You* are," said Ewen, coming around the tent and laughing. "Come on, let's walk in the forest—"

"Marco—"

"Marco's better. Do you realize that with all these people I've hardly spoken to you alone since before the crash?"

Hand in hand, they ran toward the trees; MacLeod, coming from the edge of the forest, his hands filled with ripe round clear-greenish fruits, held out a handful. His lips were dripping with their juice. "Here. They're marvelous—"

Laughing, Heather bit into the round smooth globe. It was bursting with sweet, fragrant juice; she ate it all, greedily, and reached for another. Ewen tried to pull it away.

"Heather, you're mad, they haven't even been tested yet—"

"I tested them," MacLeod laughed, "I ate half a dozen for breakfast and I feel wonderful! Say I'm psychic, if you like.

They won't hurt you and they're chock full of every vitamin we know on Earth and a couple we don't! I *know,* I tell you!"

He caught Ewen's eye, and the young doctor, a curious awareness growing in him, said slowly, "Yes. Yes, you do know, of course they're good. Just as those mushrooms—" he pointed to a grayish fungus growing on the tree, "are wholesome and full of protein, but those—" he pointed to an exquisitely-colored golden nut, "are deadly, two bites will give you a hell of a bellyache and half a cup will kill you—how the hell do I know all this?" He rubbed his forehead, feeling the odd itch through it all, and took a fruit from Heather.

"Here, we'll all be crazy together then. Marvelous! Better than rations any day . . . where's Judy?"

"She's all right," MacLeod said, laughing. "I'm going off and look for some more fruits!"

Marco Zabal lay alone in the shelter-tent, eyes closed, half-dreaming through closed lids of the sun on the Basque hills of his childhood. Far away in the forest it seemed that he heard singing, singing which seemed to go on, and on, high and clear and sweet. He got to his feet, not stopping to draw any garment about him, disregarding the warning pounding of his heart. An incredible glow of well-being and beauty seemed to surge through him. The sunlight was brilliant on the sloping clearing, the trees seemed to hang darkly and protectively like a beckoning roof, the flowers seemed to sparkle and glitter with a brilliance that was like gold, orange, blue; colors he had never seen before danced and sparkled before his eyes.

Deep in the forest came the sound of singing, high, shrill, unbelievably sweet; the pipes of Pan, the lyre of Orpheus, the call of the sirens. He felt his weakness fade; his youth restored.

Across the clearing he saw three of his companions, lying on the grass laughing, the girl kicking flowers into the air with her bare toes. He stood enraptured, watching her, entangled for a moment in the webs of her fantasy . . . *I am a woman made of flowers* . . . but the far-off singing lured him on; they beckoned him to join them, but he smiled, blew the girl a kiss, and bounded like a young man into the forest.

Far ahead he saw the gleam of white—a bird? A naked body?—he never knew how far he ran, hardly feeling the rapid pounding of his heart, wrapped in the glorious euphoria of freedom from pain, following the white gleam of the distant figure—or bird?—calling out in mingled rapture and anguish, "Wait, wait—"

The song shrilled and seemed to fill his whole head and heart. Gently, without pain, he fell into the long sweet-scented grass. The singing went on, and on, and he saw bending over him a fair face, long colorless hair waving around her eyes, a voice too sweet, too heart-wrenchingly sweet to be human, and hair turned to silver by the sun slanting through the trees, and he went happily, joyously down into darkness with the woman's face, sweet and mad, imprinted on his dying eyes.

Rafe ran through the forest, his heart pounding, slipping and falling on the steep path. He shouted, as he ran, "Camilla! Camilla!"

What had happened? One moment she was at peace in his arms—then pure terror had surged across her face and she had screamed and begun babbling something about faces on the heights, faces in the clouds, wide-open spaces waiting to fall on her and crush her, and the next moment she had wrenched away from him and dashed away between the trees, screaming wildly.

The trees seemed to waver and dip before his eyes, to form long black witch-claws to entangle him, tripping him up, throwing him full length into briars that raked along his arm and stung like fire. Lightning flashed with the color of the pain in his arm; he felt a wild and sudden terror as some unknown animal crashed a path in the forest, a stampede, hoofs, beating, beating, crushing him . . . he flung his arms around the bole of a tree and clung to it, the pounding of his heart driving out all other thought. The tree's bark was soft and smooth, like the fur of some animal; he laid his hot face against it. Faces were watching him from the trees, faces, faces. . . .

"Camilla," he murmured, dazed, slipped to the ground and lay insensible.

On the heights, clouds gathered; fog began to rise. The wind died, and a thin fine rain began to fall, slowly turning to sleet; first on the heights, then in the valley. The flowers closed their bells; the bees and insects sought their holes in the tree-trunks and underbrush; and the pollen dropped, its work done, to the ground. . . .

Camilla woke, dazed, into dim darkness. She remembered nothing after she had run, screaming, panicked at the wideness as of interstellar space, nothing between her and the spreading stars . . . no. That had been delirium. Had it *all* been delirium? She explored slowly in the darkness, was rewarded by a gleam of light—a cave-mouth. She crept to the door of the cave and shivered with sudden icy cold. She was wearing only a thin cotton shirt and slacks, torn and disordered—no. Thank God, her parka was tied around her neck by its sleeves. Rafe had done it while they lay together by the bank of the stream.

Rafe. Where was he? Come to think of it, where was *she*? How much of the wild and disordered dreams were real and how much insane fantasy? Evidently she had caught some fever, some illness which lay in wait here. This horrible planet! This horrible place! How long had elapsed? Why was she alone here? Where were her scientific instruments, where her pack? Where—this was the burning question—where was Rafe?

She struggled into her parka and zipped it up, and felt the worst of the shivering subside, but she felt cold and hungry and nauseous, and her body ached and throbbed with a hundred scratches and bruises. Had Rafe left her here in the shelter of the cave while he went to fetch help? Had she been lying in fever and delirium for long? No, he would have left some message in case she recovered consciousness.

She looked through the falling snow, trying to figure out where she could possibly be. Above her, a dark slope rose. She must have dived into the cave in mad terror of the open spaces around her, seeking any darkness and shelter against the fear that lay on her. Perhaps MacAran was out in this wild weather looking for her, and they could wander for hours in the dark, missing one another by a few feet in the driving snow.

Logic bade her sit down and take stock of her situation. She was warmly clad now, and could shelter in the cave till daybreak. But suppose MacAran, too, was lost on the hillside? *Had it attacked them both, that sudden fear, that panic? And where had it come from, that joy, the abandon . . . No, that was for later, she couldn't think now about that.*

Where would MacAran seek her? The best thing was to climb up, toward the peak. Yes. They had left their packs there;

and it was the one place from which they could orient themselves when the sun rose and the snow subsided. She would climb, and chance that logic would prompt MacAran to do the same. If not, and she found herself alone when dawn broke, she could make her way back to the camp where the others could help—or to the ship.

She climbed in the dark, driving snow, seeking each step for the way straight upward. After a time she began to guess that she was on the path they had made in their upward climb. *Yes. This is right.* It was a sureness inside her, so that she began to move quickly in the dark, and after a time she saw, without surprise, a small bobbing light, making orange sparks against the snowflakes; and MacAran came straight toward her, and clasped her hands.

"How did you know where to look for me?" she asked.

"Hunch—or something," he said. In the small light of the handlamp she could just see the snow clinging to his eyebrows and lashes. "I just knew. Camilla—let's not waste breath on trying to figure it all out now. It's a long climb still to where we left our packs and equipment."

She said, twisting her lips in bitterness against the memory of how she had flung her pack from her, "Do you suppose they'll still be where we left them?"

MacAran's hand closed over hers. "Don't worry about it. Come," he added gently, "you need rest. We can talk about it some other time."

She relaxed, letting him guide her steps in the darkness. MacAran moved along at her side, exploring this new sureness and wondering from where it had come. Never for a moment had he doubted that he was moving directly toward Camilla in the darkness, he could *feel* her in front of him, but there was no way to say that without sounding quite mad.

They found the small shelter-tent set up in the lee of the rocks. Camilla crept inside gratefully, glad MacAran had spared her the struggle in the dark. MacAran felt confused; when had they set the tent up? Surely they had taken it down and stowed it in their packs before descending this morning? Had it been before or after they lay together by the stream-bank? The worry nagged at him but he dismissed it—we were both pretty freaked-out, we might have done *anything,* and hardly been conscious of it. He felt considerable relief at realizing that their packs were neatly piled inside—*God, we were lucky, might have lost all our calculations* . . .

"Shall I fix us something to eat before you sleep?"

She shook her head. "I couldn't eat. I feel as if I'd been dream-dusting! What *happened* to us, Rafe?"

"Search me." He felt unaccountably shy with her. "Did you eat anything in the forest—fruit, anything?"

"No. I remember wanting to, it looked so good, but at the last minute—I drank the water, though."

"Forget it. Water's water and Judy tested it, so that's out."

"Well, it must have been *something*," she argued.

"I can't quarrel with that. But not tonight, please. We could hash it ever for hours and not be any closer to an answer." He extinguished the light. "Try to sleep. We've already lost a day."

Into the darkness Camilla said, "Let's hope Heather was wrong about the blizzard, then."

MacAran didn't answer. He thought, did she say *blizzard*, or was it just *weather?* Could the freak weather have had anything to do with what happened? He had the uncanny sense, again, that he was near an answer and could not quite grasp it, but he was desperately tired, and it eluded him, and still groping, he slept.

CHAPTER FIVE

They found Marco Zabal after a vain hour of searching and calling in the woods, laid out smooth and straight and already rigid beneath the grayish trunk of an unknown tree. The light snow had shrouded him in a pall a quarter of an inch thick, and at his side Judith Lovat knelt, so white and still beneath the drifting flakes that at first they thought in dismay that she had died too.

Then she stirred and looked up at them with dazed eyes and Heather knelt beside her, wrapping a blanket around her shoulders and trying to get her attention with soft words. She did not speak during all the time that MacLeod and Ewen were carrying Marco back to the tent, and Heather had to guide her steps as if she were drugged or in a trance.

As the small dismal procession wound through the falling snow Heather felt, or fantasied, that she could still feel their thoughts spinning in her own brain, Ewen's black despair . . . *what kind of doctor am I, lie fooling around on the grass while my patient runs out berserk and dies* . . . MacLeod's curious confusion entangled in her own fantasy, an old tale of the fairy folk she had heard in childhood, *the hero should never have woman or wife either of flesh and blood nor of the faery folk, and so they fashioned for him a woman made of flowers . . . I was the woman of flowers . . .*

Inside the tent Ewen sank down, staring straight ahead, and did not move. But Heather, desperately anxious at Judy's continued daze, went and shook him.

"Ewen! Marco's dead, there's nothing you can do for him, but Judy's alive; come and see if you can rouse her!"

Dragging, weary, *his thoughts look like a black cloud around him,* Heather thought, and shook herself. Ewen bent over Judith Lovat, checking her pulse, her heartbeat. He flashed a small light in her eyes, then said quietly, "Judy, did you lay out Marco's body the way we found it?"

"No," she whispered, "not I. It was the beautiful one, the beautiful one. I thought at first it was a woman, like a bird singing, and his eyes . . . his eyes . . ."

Ewen turned away in despair. "She's still delirious," he said shortly. "Fix her something to eat, Heather, and try to get it down her. We all need food—plenty of it; low blood sugar is half what's wrong with us now, I suspect."

MacLeod smiled a wry smile. "I got a contraband dose of Alpha happy-juice once," he said, "felt just about like that. What happened to us, anyhow, Ewen? You're the doctor, you tell us."

"As God is my witness, I don't know," Ewen said. "I thought at first it was the fruits, but we only began eating them *afterward.* And we all drank the water three days ago and no harm done. Anyway neither Judy nor Marco touched the fruit."

Heather put a bowl of hot soup into his hand, went and knelt by Judith, alternately spooning soup between her lips and trying to eat her own. MacLeod said, "I've no idea what happened first. It seemed like—I'm not sure; suddenly it was like a cold wind blowing through my bones, shaking me—shaking me *open* somehow. That was when I knew the fruits were good to eat and I ate one. . . ."

"Foolhardy," said Ewen, but MacLeod, still with that *openness,* knew that the young doctor was only cursing his own neglect. He said, "Why? The fruits *were* good, or we'd be sick now."

Heather said, hesitantly, "I can't help feeling it was something to do with the weather. Some difference."

"A psychedelic wind," jeered Ewen, "a ghostly wind that drove us all temporarily insane!"

"Stranger things have happened," Heather said, and artfully maneuvered another spoonful of soup into Judy's slack mouth. The older woman blinked dazedly and said, "Heather? How did I get here?"

"We brought you, love. You're all right now."

"Marco—I saw Marco—"

"He's dead," Ewen said gently. "he ran into the woods

when we all went mad; I never saw him. He must have strained his heart—I'd warned him not even to sit up."

"It *was* his heart, then? You're sure?"

"As sure as I can be without autopsy, yes," Ewen said. He swallowed the last of his soup. His head was clearing, but the guilt still lay on him; he knew he would never be wholly free of it. "Look, we've got to compare notes, while it's still fresh in our minds. There must be some one common factor, something we all did. Ate, or drank—"

"Or breathed," Heather said. "It had to be something in the air, Ewen. Only the three of us ate the fruits. You didn't eat anything, did you, Judy?"

"Yes, some grayish stuff on the edge of a tree—"

"But we didn't touch that," Ewen said, "only MacLeod. We three ate the fruits, but neither Marco nor Judy did. MacLeod ate some of the gray fungus but none of us did. Judy was smelling the flowers and MacLeod was handling them, but neither Heather nor I did, until afterward. The three of us were lying in the grass—" he saw Heather's face turn pink, but went on steadily, "and both of us were making love to her, and all three of us were hallucinating. If Marco got up and ran into the woods I can only assume that he must have been hallucinating too. How did it begin with you, Judy?"

She only shook her head. "I don't know," she said. "I only know—the flowers were brighter, the sky seemed—seemed to break up like rainbows. Rainbows and prisms. Then I heard singing, it must have been birds, but I'm not sure. I went where the shadows were, and they were all purple, lilac-purple and blue. Then *he* came. . . ."

"Marco?"

She shook her head. "No. He was very tall, and had silver hair. . . ."

Ewen said pityingly, "Judy, you were hallucinating. I thought Heather was made out of flowers."

"The four moons—I could see them even though the sky was bright," Judy said. "He didn't say anything but I could hear him *thinking.*"

MacLeod said, "We all seem to have had *that* delusion. If it's a delusion."

"It's sure to be," Ewen said. "We've found no trace of any other form of intelligent life here. Forget it, Judy," he added gently, "sleep. When we all get back to the ship—well, there will have to be some form of inquiry."

Dereliction, neglect of duty is the least it will be. Can I plead temporary insanity?

He watched Heather settle Judy down into her sleeping bag. When the older woman finally slept he said wearily, "We ought to bury Marco. I hate to do it without an autopsy, but the only alternative is to carry him back to the ship."

MacLeod said, "We're going to look awfully damned foolish going back and claiming we all went mad at once." He did not took at Heather and Ewen as he added, rather sheepishly, "I feel like a ghastly fool—group sex never has been my kick—"

Heather said firmly, "We'll all have to forgive each other, and forget about it. It just happened, that's all. And for all we know it happened to them too—" she stopped, struck with a horrifying thought. "Imagine that sort of thing happening to *two hundred people . . .*"

"It doesn't bear thinking about," MacLeod said with a shudder.

Ewen said that mass insanity was nothing new. "Whole villages. The dancing madness in the middle ages. And attacks of ergotism—from spoiled rye made into bread."

Heather said, "I don't think whatever it was got far enough down the mountain."

"Another of your hunches, I suppose," Ewen said, but not unkindly. "At this point I suspect we're all too close to it. Let's stop theorizing without facts and wait until we *have* some facts."

"Does this qualify as a fact?" Judy said, sitting up suddenly. They had all thought her asleep; she fumbled in the torn neck of her blouse and drew out something wrapped in leaves. "This—or these." She handed Ewen a small blue stone, like a star sapphire.

"Beautiful," he said slowly, "but you found it in the woods—"

"Right," she said. "I found this, too."

She stretched it out to him, and for a moment the others, crowding close, literally could not believe their eyes.

It was less than six inches long. The handle was made of something like shaped bone, delicate but quite without ornamentation. As for the rest, there was no question what it was.

It was a small flint knife.

CHAPTER SIX

In the ten days the exploring party had been absent from the ship in the clearing, the clearing seemed to have grown. Two or three more small buildings had grown up around the ship; and at one edge of the clearing a fenced-off area had been plowed and a small sign proclaimed AGRICULTURAL TESTING AREA.

"That ought to do something for our food," MacLeod said, but Judith made no answer, and Ewen looked at her sharply. She had been curiously apathetic since That Day—that was how they all thought of it—and he was desperately worried about her. He wasn't a psychologist, but he knew that there was something gravely wrong. *Damn it, I did everything wrong. I let Marco die, I haven't been able to bring Judy back to reality.*

They came into the camp almost unnoticed, and for a moment MacAran felt a sharp stab of apprehension. Where was everybody? Had they all run amuck that day, had the madness overtaken all of them down here too? When he and Camilla had come down to the lower camp, to find Heather and Ewen and MacLeod still talking themselves hoarse in the attempt to find some explanation, it had been a bad moment. If madness lay on this planet, ready to claim them all, how could they survive? What worse things lay here waiting for them? Now, looking around the empty clearing, MacAran felt again the sharp stab of fear; then he saw a little group of people in Medic uniform coming out of the hospital tent, and further on, a crew going up into the ship. He relaxed; everything *looked* normal.

But then, so do we. . . .

"What's the first thing to do?" he asked. "Do we report straight to the Captain?"

"I should, at least," Camilla said. She looked thinner, almost haggard. MacAran wanted to take her hand and comfort her, although he was not sure for what. Since they had lain in each other's arms on the mountainside, he had felt a deep gnawing hunger for her, an almost fierce protectiveness; yet she turned away from him at every point, withdrawing into her old sharp self-sufficiency. MacAran felt hurt and resentful, and somehow lost. He dared not touch her, and it made him irritable.

"I expect he'll want to see all of us," he said. "We have to report Marco's death, and where we buried him. And we have a lot of information for him. Not to mention the flint knife."

"Yes. If the planet's inhabited that creates another problem," MacLeod said, but he did not elaborate.

Captain Leicester was with a crew inside the ship but an officer outside told the party that he had given orders that he was to be called the moment they returned, and sent for him. They waited in the small dome, none of them knowing what they were going to say.

Captain Leicester came into the dome. He looked somehow older, his face drawn with new lines. Camilla rose as he came in, but he motioned her to a seat again.

"Forget the protocol, Lieutenant," he said kindly, "you all look tired; was it a hard trip? I see Dr. Zabal is not with you."

"He's dead, sir," Ewen said quietly, "he died from the bites of poisonous insects. I'll make a complete report later."

"Make it to the Medic Chief," the Captain said, "I'm not qualified to understand anyway. You others can bring up your reports at the next meeting—tonight, I suppose. Mr. MacAran, did you manage to get the calculations you were hoping for?"

MacAran nodded. "Yes; as near as we can figure, the planet is somewhat larger than Earth, which means, with the lighter gravity, that its mass must be somewhat less. Sir, I can discuss all that later; just now I must ask you one question. Did anything unusual happen here while we were gone?"

The Captain's lined face ridged, displeased. "How do you mean, unusual? This whole planet is unusual, and nothing that happens here can be called routine."

Ewen said, "I mean anything like illness or mass insanity, sir."

Leicester frowned. "I can't imagine what you could be

talking about," he said. "No, no reports from Medic of any illness."

"What Dr. Ross means is that we all had an attack of something like delirium," MacAran told him. "It was the day after the second night without rain. It was widespread enough to hit Camilla—Lieutenant Del Rey—and myself, on the peaks, and to hit the other group almost six thousand feet lower down. We all behaved—well, irresponsibly, sir."

"Irresponsibly?" He scowled, his eyes fierce on them. "Irresponsibly," Ewen met the Captain's eyes, his fists clenched. "Dr. Zabal was recovering; we ran off into the woods and left him alone so that he got up in delirium, ran off on his own and strained his heart—which is why he died. Judgment was impaired; we ate untested fruits and fungus. There were—various delusional processes."

Judith Lovat said firmly, "They were not all delusional."

Ewen looked at her and shook his head. "I don't think Dr. Lovat is in any state to judge, sir. We seem all to have had delusions about reading one another's thoughts, anyway."

The Captain drew a long, harried breath. "This will have to go to the Medics. No, we had nothing like that here. I suggest you all go and make your reports to the appropriate chiefs, or write them up to present at the meeting tonight. Lieutenant Del Rey, I want your report myself. I'll see the rest of you later."

"One more thing, sir," MacAran said. "This planet is inhabited." He drew out the flint knife from his pack, handed it over. But the Captain barely looked at it. He said, "Take it to Major Frazer; he's the staff anthropologist. Tell him I'll want a report tonight. Now if the rest of you will excuse us, please—"

MacAran felt the curious flatness of anticlimax as they left the Captain and Camilla together. While he hunted through the camp for anthropologist Frazer, he slowly identified his own feeling as jealousy. How could he compete with Captain Leicester? Oh, this was rubbish, the captain was old enough to be Camilla's father. Did he honestly believe Camilla was in love with the Captain?

No. But she's emotionally all tied up with him and that's worse.

If he had been disappointed by the Captain's lack of response to the flint knife, Major Frazer's response left nothing to be desired.

"I've been saying since we landed that this world was habitable," he said, turning the knife over in his hands, "and here's proof that it's inhabited—by something intelligent, at least."

"Humanoid?" MacAran asked, and Frazer shrugged. "How could we know that? There have been intelligent life-forms reported from three or four other planets; so far they have reported one simian, one feline, and three unclassifiable—xenobiology isn't my speciality. One artifact doesn't tell us anything—how many shapes are there that a knife could be designed in? But it fits a human hand well enough, although it's a little small."

Meals for crew and passengers were served in one large area, and when MacAran went for his noon meal he hoped to see Camilla; but she came in late and went directly to a group of other crew members. MacAran could not catch her eye and had the distinct feeling that she was avoiding him. While he was morosely eating his plateful of rations, Ewen came up to him.

"Rafe, they want us all at a Medical meeting if you have nothing else to do. They're trying to analyze what happened to us."

"Do you honestly think it will do any good, Ewen? We've all been talking it over—"

Ewen shrugged. "Mine is not to reason why," he said. "You're not under the authority of the Medic staff, of course, but still—"

MacAran asked, "Were they very rough on you about Zabal's death?"

"Not really. Both Heather and Judy testified that we were all out of contact. But they want your report, and everything you can tell them about Camilla."

MacAran shrugged and went along with him.

The Medic meeting was held at one end of the hospital tent, half empty now—the more seriously injured had died, the less so had been restored to duty. There were four qualified doctors, half a dozen nurses, and a few assorted scientific personnel to listen to the reports they made.

After listening to all of them in turn, the Chief Medical Officer, a dignified white-haired man named Di Asturien, said slowly, "It sounds like some form of airborne infection. Possibly a virus."

"But nothing like that turned up in our air samples," MacLeod argued, "and the effect was more like that of a drug."

"An airborne drug? It seems unlikely," Di Asturien said, "although the aphrodisiac effect seems to have been considerable also. Do I correctly assume that there was some sexual stimulation effect on all of you?"

Ewen said, "I already mentioned that, sir. It seemed to affect all three of us—Miss Stuart, Dr. MacLeod and myself. It had no such effect on Dr. Zabal to my knowledge, but he was in a moribund condition."

"Mr. MacAran?"

He felt for some strange reason embarrassed, but before Di Asturien's cool clinical eyes he said, "Yes, sir. You can check this with Lieutenant Del Rey if you like."

"Hm. I understand, Dr. Ross, that you and Miss Stuart are currently paired in any case, so perhaps we can discount that. But Mr. MacAran, you and the Lieutenant—"

"I'm interested in her," he said steadily, "but as far as I know she's completely indifferent to me. Even hostile. Except under the influence of—of whatever happened to us." He faced it, then. Camilla had not turned to him as a woman to a man she cared for. She had simply been affected by the virus, or drug, or whatever strange thing had sent them all mad. What to him had been love, to her had been madness—and now she resented it.

To his immense relief the Medic Chief did not pursue the subject. "Doctor Lovat?"

Judy did not look up. She said quietly, "I can't say. I can't remember. What I think I remember may very well be entirely delusion."

Di Asturien said, "I wish you would co-operate with us, Dr. Lovat."

"I'd rather not." Judy went on fingering something in her lap, and no persuasion could force her to say any more.

Di Asturien said, "In about a week, then, we'll have to test all three of you for possible pregnancy."

"How can that be necessary?" Heather asked. "I, at least, am taking regular anti shots. I'm not sure about Camilla, but I suspect crew regulations require it for anyone between twenty and forty-five."

Di Asturien looked disturbed. "That's true," he said, "but

there is something very peculiar which we discovered in a Medic meeting yesterday. Tell them, Nurse Raimondi."

Margaret Raimondi said, "I'm in charge of keeping records and issuing contraceptive and sanitary supplies for all women of menstrual age, both crew and passengers. You all know the drill; every two weeks, at the time of menstruation and halfway between, every woman reports for either a single shot of hormone or, in some cases, a patch strip to send small doses of hormones into the blood, which suppress ovulation. There are a total of one hundred and nineteen women surviving in the right age bracket, which means, with an average arbitrary cycle of thirty days, approximately four women would be reporting every day, either for menstrual supplies or for the appropriate shot or patch which is given four days after onset of menstruation. It's been ten days since the crash, which means about one-third of the women should have reported to me for one reason or the other. Say forty."

"And they haven't been," Dr. Di Asturien said. "How many women have reported since the crash?"

"Nine," said Nurse Raimondi grimly. "*Nine*. This means that two-thirds of the women involved have had their biological cycles disrupted on this planet—either by the change in gravity, or by some hormone disruption. And since the standard contraceptive we use is entirely keyed to the internal cycle, we have no way of telling whether it's effective or not."

MacAran didn't need to be told how serious this was. A wave of pregnancies could indeed be emotionally disruptive. Infants—or even young children—could not endure interstellar FTL drive; and since the universal acceptance of reliable contraceptives, and the population laws on overcrowded Earth, a wave of feeling had made abortion completely unthinkable. Unwanted children were simply never conceived. But would there be any alternative here?

Dr. Di Asturien said, "Of course, on new planets women are often sterile for a few months, largely because of the changes in air and gravity. But we can't count on it."

MacAran was thinking, *if Camllla is pregnant, will she hate me?* The thought that a child of theirs might have to be destroyed was frightening. Ewen asked soberly, "What are we going to do, Doctor? We can't demand that two hundred adult men and women take a vow of chastity!"

"Obviously not. That would be worse for mental health

than the other dangers," Di Asturien said, "but we must warn everyone that we're no longer sure about the effectiveness of our contraceptive program."

"I can see that. And as soon as possible."

Di Asturien said, "The Captain has called a mass meeting tonight—crew *and* colonists. Maybe I can announce it there." He made a wry face. "I'm not looking forward to it. It's going to be an awfully damned unpopular announcement. As if we didn't have enough troubles already!"

The mass meeting was held in the hospital tent, the only place big enough to hold the crew and passengers all at once. It had begun to cloud over by midafternoon and when the meeting was called, a thin fine cold rain was falling and distant lightning could be seen over the peaks of the hills. The members of the exploring party sat together at the front, in case they were called on for a report, but Camilla was not among them. She came in with Captain Leicester and the rest of the crew officers, and MacAran noticed that they had all put on formal uniform. Somehow that struck him as a bad sign. Why should they try to emphasize their solidarity and authority that way?

The electricians on the crew had put up a rostrum and rigged an elementary public address system, so that the Captain's voice, low and rather hoarse, could be heard throughout the big room.

"I have asked you all to come here tonight," he said, "instead of reporting only to your leaders, because in spite of every precaution, in a group this size rumors can get started, and can also get out of hand. First, I will give you what good news there is to give. To the best of our knowledge and belief, the air and water on this planet will support life indefinitely without damage to health, and the soil will probably grow Earth crops to supplement our food supply during the period of time while we are forced to remain here. Now I must give you the news which is not so good. The damage to the ship's drive units and computers is far more extensive than originally believed, and there is no possibility of immediate or rapid repairs. Although eventually it may be possible to become spaceborne, with our current personnel and materials, we cannot make repairs at all."

He paused, and a stir of voices, appalled, apprehensive, rose in the room. Captain Leicester raised his hand.

"I am not saying that we should lose hope," he said. "But in our current state we cannot make repairs. To get this ship off the surface of the planet is going to demand extensive changes in our present setup and will be a very long-range project demanding the total co-operation of every man and woman in this room."

Silence, and MacAran wondered what he meant by that. What exactly was the Captain saying? *Could* repairs be made or *couldn't* they?

"This may sound like a contradictory statement," the Captain went on. "We have not the material to make repairs. However, we *do* have, among all of us, the *knowledge* to make repairs; and we have an unexplored planet at our disposal, where we can certainly find the raw materials and *build* the material to make repairs."

MacAran frowned, wondering exactly how that was meant. Captain Leicester proceeded to explain.

"Many of you people bound for the colonies have skills which will be useful there but which are of no use to us here," he said. "Within a day or two we will set up a personnel department to inventory all known skills. Some of you who have registered as farmers or artisans will be placed under the direction of our scientists or engineers to be trained. I demand a total push."

At the back of the room, Moray rose. He said, "May I ask a question, Captain?"

"You may."

"Are you saying that the two hundred of us in this room can, within five or ten years, develop a technological culture capable of building—or rebuilding—a starship? That we can discover the metals, mine them, refine them, machine them, and build the necessary machinery?"

The Captain said quietly, "With the full co-operation of every person here, this can be done. I estimate that it will take between three and five years."

Moray said flatly, "You're insane. You're asking us to evolve a whole technology!"

"What man has done, man can do again," Captain Leicester said imperturbably. "After all, Mr. Moray, I remind you that we have no alternative."

"The hell we don't!"

"You are out of order," the Captain said sternly. "Please take your seat."

"No, damn it! If you really believe all this can be done," Moray said, "I can only assume that you're stark raving mad. Or that the mind of an engineer or spaceman works so differently from any sane man's that there's no way to communicate. You say this will take three to five years. May I respectfully remind you that we have about a year to eighteen months' supply of food and medical supplies? May I also remind you that even now—moving toward summer—the climate is harsh and rigorous and our shelters are insufficient? The winter on this world, with its exaggerated tilt on the axis, is likely to be more brutal than anything any Earthman has ever experienced."

"Doesn't that prove the necessity of getting off this world as soon as possible?"

"No, it proves the need of finding reliable sources of food and shelter," Moray said. "*That's* where we need our total push! Forget your ship, Captain. It isn't going anywhere. Come to your senses. We're colonists, not scientists. We have everything we need to survive here—to settle down here. But we can't do it if half our energies are devoted to some senseless plan of diverting all our resources to repair a hopelessly crashed ship!"

There was a small uproar in the hall, a flood of cries, questions, outrage. The Captain repeatedly called for order, and finally the cries died down to dull mutterings. Moray demanded, "I call for a vote," and the uproar rose again.

The Captain said, "I refuse to consider your proposal, Mr. Moray. The matter will not come to a vote. May I remind you that I am currently in supreme command of this ship? Must I order your arrest?"

"Arrest, hell," Moray said scornfully. "You're not in space now, Captain. You're not on the bridge of your ship. You have no authority over any of us, Captain—except maybe your own crew, if they want to obey you."

Leicester stood on the rostrum, as white as his shirt, his eyes gleaming with fury. He said, "I remind all of you that MacAran's party, sent out to explore, has discovered traces of intelligent life on this planet. Earth Expeditionary has a standard policy of not placing colonies on inhabited planets. If we settle here we are likely to bring cultural shock to the stone age culture."

Another uproar. Moray shouted angrily, "Do you think your attempts to evolve a technology here for your repairs wouldn't do that? In God's name, sir, we have everything we need to establish a colony here. If we divert all our resources to your insane effort to repair the ship, it's doubtful if we can even survive!"

Captain Leicester made a distinct effort to master himself, but his fury was obvious. He said harshly, "You are suggesting that we abandon the effort—and relapse into barbarism?"

Moray was suddenly very grave. He came forward to the rostrum and stood beside the Captain. His voice was level and calm.

"I hope not, Captain. It is man's mind that makes him a barbarian, not his technology. We may have to do without top-level technology, at least for a few generations, but that doesn't mean we can't establish a good world here for ourselves and our children, a civilized world. There have been civilizations which have existed for centuries almost without technology. The illusion that man's culture is only the history of his technostructures is propaganda from the engineers, sir. It has no basis in sociology—or in philosophy."

The Captain said harshly, "I'm not interested in your social theories, Mr. Moray."

Doctor Di Asturien rose. He said, "Captain, one thing must be taken into account. We made a most disquieting discovery today—"

At that moment a violent clap of thunder rocked the hospital tent. The hastily rigged lights went out. And from the door one of the security men shouted:

"Captain! Captain! The woods are on fire!"

CHAPTER SEVEN

Everyone kept their heads; Captain Leicester bellowed from the platform, "Get some lights in here; security, get some lights!" One of the young men on the Medic staff found a handlamp for the Captain and one of the bridge officers shouted, "Everyone! Stay in place and wait for orders, there is no danger here! Get those lights rigged as fast as you can!"

MacAran was near enough to the door to see the distant rising glare against the darkness. In a few minutes lamps were being distributed, and Moray, from the platform, said urgently, "Captain, we have tree-felling and earth-moving equipment. Let me order a detail to work on firebreaks around the encampment."

"Right, Mr. Moray. Get with it," Leicester said harshly. "All bridge officers, gather here; get to the ship and secure any flammable or explosive material." He hurried away toward the back of the tent. Moray ordered all able-bodied men to the clearing, and requisitioned all available handlamps not in use on the bridge. "Form up in the same squads you did for gravedigging detail," he ordered. MacAran found himself in a crew with Father Valentine and eight strangers, felling trees in a ten-foot swath around the clearing. The fire was still a distant roar on a slope miles away, a red glare against the sky, but the air smelled of smoke, with a strange acrid undertone.

Someone said at MacAran's elbow, "How can the woods catch fire after all this rain?"

He brought back memory of something Marco Zabal had said that first night. "The trees are heavily resined—practically tinder. Some few of them may even burn when they're wet—

we built a campfire of green wood. I suppose lightning can set off a fire at almost any time." We were lucky, he thought, we camped out in the center of the woods and never thought of fire, or of firebreaks. "I suspect we'll need a permanent firebreak around any encampment or work area."

Father Valentine said, "You sound as if you thought we were going to be here a long time."

MacAran bent to his saw. He said, not looking up, "No matter whose side you're on—the Captain's or Moray's—it looks as if we'll be here for years." He was too weary, and too unsure of anything at this moment, to decide for himself if he had any real preference and in any case he was sure no one would consult him about his choice, but down deep he knew that if they ever left this world again he would regret it.

Father Valentine touched his shoulder. "I think the Lieutenant is looking for you."

He straightened to see Camilla Del Rey walking toward him. She looked worn and haggard, her hair uncombed and her uniform dirty. He wanted to take her in his arms but instead he stood and watched her attempt not to meet his eyes as she said, "Rafe, the Captain wants to talk with you. You know the terrain better than anyone else. Do you think it could be fought or contained?"

"Not in the dark—and not without heavy equipment," MacAran said, but he accompanied her back toward the Captain's field quarters. He had to admire the efficiency with which the firebreak operation had been set up, the small amount of ship's firefighting equipment moved to the hospital. *The Captain had sense enough to use Moray here. They're really two of a kind—if they could only work together for the same objectives. But just now they're the irresistible force and the immovable object.*

The fine rain was changing to heavy sleet as they came into the dome. The small dark crowded dome was dimly lit by a single handlamp, and the battery seemed to be already failing.

Moray was saying: "—our power sources are already giving way. Before we can do anything else, sir, in your plan *or* mine, some sources of light and heat have to be found. We have wind-power and solar-power equipment in the colonizing materials, although I somehow doubt if this sun has enough light and radiation for much solar power. MacAran—" he turned, "I take it there are mountain streams? Any big enough for damming?"

"Not that we saw in the few days we were in the mountains," MacAran said, "but there's plenty of wind."

"That will do for a temporary makeshift," Captain Leicester said. "MacAran, do you know exactly where the fire is located?"

"Far enough to be no immediate danger to us," MacAran said, "although we're going to need firebreaks from now on, anywhere we go. But this fire's no danger, I think. The rain's turning to snow and I think that will smother it out."

"If it can burn in the rain—"

"Snow's wetter and heavier," MacAran said, and was interrupted by what sounded like a volley of gunfire. "What's that?"

Moray said, "Game stampede—probably getting away from the fire. Your officers are shooting food. Captain, once again, I suggest conservation of ammunition for absolute emergencies. Even on Earth, game has been hunted recreationally with bow and arrow. There are prototypes in the recreation department, and we'll need them for enlarging the food supply."

"Full of ideas, aren't you," Leicester grunted, and Moray said, tight-mouthed, "Captain, running a spaceship is your business. Setting up a viable society with the most economical use of resources is *mine.*"

For a moment the two men stared at one another in the failing light, the others in the dome forgotten. Camilla had edged around behind the Captain and it seemed to MacAran that she was supporting him mentally as well as backing him up physically. Outside there were all the noises of the camp, and behind it all the small hiss of snow striking the dome. Then a gust of high wind struck it and a blast of cold air came in through the flapping doorway; Camilla ran to shut it, struggling against the wild blast, and was flung back. The door swung wildly, came loose from the makeshift hinges and knocked the girl off her feet; MacAran ran to help her up. Captain Leicester swore softly and began to shout for one of his aides.

Moray raised a hand. He said quietly, "We need stronger and more permanent shelters, Captain. These were built to last six weeks. May I order them built to last for a few years, then?"

Captain Leicester was silent, and with that new and exaggerated sensitivity it almost seemed to MacAran that he could hear what the Captain was thinking. Was this an entering wedge? Could he use Moray's undoubted talents without giving him too much power over the colonists, and diminishing his own? When he spoke his voice was bitter; but he gave way gracefully.

"You know survival, Mr. Moray. I'm a scientist—and a spaceman. I'll put you in charge of the camp, on a temporary basis. Get your priorities in order and requisition what you need." He strode to the door and stood there looking out at the whirling snow. "No fire can live in that. Call in the men and feed them before they go back to making firebreaks. You're in charge, Moray—for the time being." His back was straight and indomitable, but he sounded tired. Moray bowed slightly. There was no hint of subservience in it.

"Don't think I'm giving way," Leicester warned. "That ship is going to be repaired."

Moray shrugged a little. "Maybe so. But it can't be repaired unless we survive long enough to do it. For now, that's all I'm concerned about."

He turned to Camilla and MacAran, ignoring the Captain.

"MacAran, your party knows at least some of the terrain. I want a local survey made of all resources, including food—Dr. Lovat can handle that. Lieutenant Del Rey, you're a navigator; you have access to instruments. Can you arrange to make some sort of climate survey which we might manage to use for weather prediction?" He broke off. "The middle of the night isn't the time for this. We'll get moving tomorrow." He moved to the door and, finding his way blocked by Captain Leicester standing and staring into the whirling snowflakes, tried to move past him a time or two, finally touched him on the shoulder. The Captain started and moved aside. Moray said, "The first thing to do is to get those poor devils in out of the storm. Will you give orders, Captain, or shall I?"

Captain Leicester met his eyes levelly and with taut hostility. "It doesn't matter," he said quietly, "I'm not concerned with which of us gives the orders, and God help you, if *you're* just looking for the power to give them. Camilla, go and tell Major Layton to secure from firelighting operations and make sure that everyone who was on the firebreak line gets hot food before he turns in." The girl pulled her hood over her head and hurried off through the snow.

"You may have your talents, Moray," he said, "and as far as I'm concerned you're welcome to use mine. But there's an old saying in the Space Service. Anyone who intrigues for power, deserves to get it!"

He strode out of the dome, leaving the wind to blow through it, and MacAran, watching Moray, felt that somehow, obscurely, the Captain had come off best.

CHAPTER EIGHT

The days were lengthening, but even so there seemed never to be enough light or enough time for the work which had to be done in the settlement. Three days after the fire, extensive firebreaks thirty feet wide had been constructed around the encampment, and firefighting squads had been organized for emergency outbreaks. It was about that time that MacAran went off, with a party of the colonists, to make Moray's survey. The only members of the previous party to accompany him were Judith Lovat and MacLeod. Judy was still quiet and contained, almost unspeaking; MacAran was worried about her, but she did her work efficiently and seemed to have an almost psychic awareness of where to find the sort of thing they were looking for.

For the most part, this woodland exploration trip was uneventful. They laid out trails for possible roadways toward the valley where they had first seen herds of game, assessed the amount of fire damage—which was not really very great—mapped the local streams and rivers, and MacAran collected rock samples from the local heights to assess their potential ore contents.

Only one major event broke the rather pleasant monotony of the trip. One evening toward sunset they were blazing trail through an unusually thick level of forest when MacLeod, slightly ahead of the main party, stopped short, turned back, laying a finger on his lips to enjoin silence, and beckoned to MacAran.

MacAran came forward, Judy tiptoeing at his side. She looked oddly excited.

MacLeod pointed upward through the thick trees. Two huge trunks rose dizzyingly high, without auxiliary branches for at least sixty feet; and spanning them, swung a bridge. There was nothing else to call it; a bridge of what looked like woven wickerwood, elaborately constructed with handrails.

MacLeod said in a whisper, "There are the proofs of your aborigines. Can they be arboreal? Is that why we haven't seen them?"

Judy said sharply, "Hush!" In the distance there was a small, shrill, chattering sound; then, above them on the bridge, a creature appeared.

They all got a good look at it in that moment; about five feet tall, either pale-skinned or covered with pale fur, gripping the bridge rail with undoubted hands—none of them had presence of mind to count the fingers—a flat but oddly humanoid face, with a flat nose and red eyes. For nearly ten seconds it clung to the bridge and looked down at them, seeming nearly as startled as they were themselves; then, with a shrill birdlike cry it rushed across the bridge, swung up into the trees and vanished.

MacAran let out a long sigh. So this world was inhabited, not free and open for mankind. MacLeod asked quietly, "Judy, were these the people you saw that day? The one you called *the beautiful one?*"

Judy's face took on the strange stubbornness which any mention of that day could bring on. "No," she said, quietly but very positively. "These are the little brothers, the small ones who are not wise."

And nothing could move her from that, and very quickly they gave over questioning her. But MacLeod and Major Fraser were in seventh heaven.

"Arboreal humanoids. Nocturnal, to judge by their eyes, probably simian, although more like tarsiers than apes. Obviously sapient—they're tool-users and makers of artifacts. *Homo arborens.* Men living in trees," MacLeod said.

MacAran said hesitatingly, "If we have to stay here—how can two sapient species survive on one planet? Doesn't that invariably mean a fatal war for dominance?"

Fraser said, "God willing, no. After all, there were four sapient species on Earth for a long time. Mankind—and dolphins, whales, and probably elephants too. We just happened to be the only *technological* species. They're tree-dwelling;

we're ground-dwelling. No conflict, as far as I can see—anyway no *necessary* conflict."

MacAran wasn't so sure, but kept his qualms to himself.

Peaceful as their trip was, there were unexpected dangers. In the valley with the game, which they named for convenience the Plains of Zabal, the game was stalked by great cat-like predators and only nighttime fires kept them away. And on the heights MacAran caught his first sight of the birds with the banshee voices; great wingless birds with vicious claws, moving at such speeds that only a last desperate recourse to the laser beam they carried for emergencies kept Dr. Fraser from being disemboweled by a terrible stroke; MacLeod, dissecting the dead bird, discovered that it was completely blind. "Does it get at its prey by hearing? Or something else?"

"I suspect it senses body warmth," MacAran said, "they seem only to live in the snows." They christened the dreadful birds *banshees,* and avoided the passes except in broad daylight after that. They also found mounds of the scorpion-like ants whose bites had killed Dr. Zabal, and debated poisoning them; MacLeod was against it, on the grounds that these ants might form some important part of an ecological chain which could not be disturbed. They finally agreed to exterminate only the mounds within three square miles of the ship, and warn everyone about the dangers of their bite. It was an interim measure, but then everything they did on this planet was an interim measure.

"If we leave the damn place," Dr. Fraser said harshly, "we'll have to leave it pretty much the way we found it."

When they returned to the encampment, after a three week survey, they found that two permanent buildings of wood and stone had already been erected; a common recreation hall and refectory, and a building for use as a laboratory. It was the last time MacAran measured anything by weeks; they still did not know the length of the planet's year, but they had for the sake of convenience and the assignment of duties and work shifts set up an arbitrary ten-day cycle, with one day in every ten a general holiday. Large gardens had been laid out and seeds were already sprouting, and a careful harvesting was being made of a few tested fruits from the woods.

A small wind generator had been rigged, but power was strictly rationed and candles made from resin from the trees were being issued for night use. The temporary domes still housed most of the personnel except those who were located in the hospital; MacAran shared his with a dozen other single men.

The day after his return Ewen Ross summoned both him and Judy to the hospital. "You missed Dr. Di Asturien's announcement," he said. "In brief, our hormone contraceptives are worthless—no pregnancies so far except one very doubtful early miscarriage, but we've been relying on hormones so long that no one knows much about the prehistoric kind any more. We don't have pregnancy-testing equipment, either, since nobody needs it on a spaceship. Which means if we *do* get any pregnancies they may be too far advanced for safe abortions before they're even diagnosed!"

MacAran smiled wryly. "You can save your breath where I'm concerned," he said, "the only girl I'm currently interested in doesn't know I'm alive—or at least wishes I weren't." He had not even seen Camilla since his return.

Ewen said, "Judy, what about you? I looked up your Medic record; you're at the age where contraception is voluntary instead of mandatory—"

She smiled faintly. "Because at my age I'm not likely to be taken unawares by emotion. I've not been sexually active on this voyage—there's no one I've been interested in, so I've not bothered with the shots."

"Well, check with Margaret Raimondi anyhow—she's giving out emergency information just in case. Sex is voluntary, Judy, but information is mandatory. You can choose to abstain—but you ought to be free to choose not to, so run along to Margaret and pick up the information."

She began to laugh and it struck MacAran that he had not seen Judith Lovat laugh since the day of the strange madness that had attacked them all. But the laughing seemed to have a hysterical note which made him uneasy, and he was relieved when she said at last, "Oh, very well. What harm can it do?" and went. Ewen looked after her with disquiet, too.

"I'm not happy about her. She seems to have been the only one permanently affected by whatever it was that hit us, but we haven't psychiatrists to spare and anyhow she is able to do her work—which is a legal definition of sanity in any terms. Still, I hope she snaps out of it. Was she all right on the trip?"

MacAran nodded. He said thoughtfully, "Perhaps she had some experience she hasn't told us about. She certainly seems at home here. Something like what you told me about MacLeod knowing the fruits were good to eat. Could an emotional shock develop latent psi powers?"

Ewen shook his head. "God only knows, and we're too busy to check it out. Anyhow, how would you check out anything like that? As long as she's normal enough to do her assigned work I can't interfere with her."

After leaving the hospital, MacAran walked through the encampment. Everything looked peaceful, from the small shop where farm tools were being constructed, to the ship area where machinery was being removed and stored. He found Camilla in the dome which had been wind-damaged the night of the fire; it had been repaired and reinforced, and the computer controls set up inside. She looked at him with what seemed open hostility.

"What do you want? Has Moray sent you here to order me to transform this into a weather station or some such thing?"

"No, but it sounds like a good idea," MacAran said. "Another blizzard like the one that hit us the night of the fire, could wreck us if we weren't warned."

She came and looked up at him. Her arms were straight down at her sides, clenched into fists, and her face taut with anger. She said, "I think you must all be quite insane. I don't expect anything more of the colonists—they're just civilians and all they care about is getting their precious colony set up. But you, Rafe! You've had a scientist's training, you ought to see what it *means!* All we *have* is the hope of repairing the ship—if we waste our resources on anything else, the chances get smaller and smaller!" She sounded frantic. "And we'll be here forever!"

MacAran said slowly, "Remember, Camilla, I was one of the colonists, too. I left Earth to join the Coronis colony—"

"But that's a regular colony, with everything set up to make it—to make it part of civilization," Camilla said. "I can understand *that*. Your skills, your education, they'd be *worth* something!"

MacAran reached out and took her shoulders in his hands. "Camilla—" he said, and put all his yearning into the sound of her name. She didn't actually respond, but she was quiet between his hands, looking up at him. Her face was drawn and miserable.

"Camilla, will you listen to me a minute? I'm with the Captain all the way, as far as acts go. I'm willing to do anything needful to make sure the ship gets off the ground. But I'm keeping in mind that it may not, after all, be possible, and I want to make sure we can survive if it isn't."

"Survive for what?" Camilla said, almost frantic. "To revert to savagery, survive as farmers, barbarians, with nothing that makes life worth living? We'd do better to die in a last effort!"

"I don't know why you say that, my love. After all, the first humans started with less than we have. Their world, maybe, had a little better climate, but then we have ten or twelve thousand years of human know-how. A group of people that Captain Leicester thinks capable of repairing a starship, ought to have enough know-how to build a pretty good life for themselves and their children—and all the generations after that." He tried to draw her into his arms, but she wrenched away, white and furious.

"I'd rather *die*," she said harshly, "any civilized human being would! You're worse than the New Hebrides group out there—Moray's people—that damnfool back-to-nature crew, playing right into his hands—"

"I don't know anything about them—Camilla, my darling, please don't be angry with me. I'm only trying to look at both sides—"

"But there *is* only one side," she flung at him, angry and implacable, "and if you don't see it that way then you aren't even worth talking with! I'm ashamed—I'm ashamed of myself that I ever let myself think you might be different!" Tears were running down her face, and she angrily flung off his hands. "Get out and stay out! Get out, damn you!"

MacAran had the temper usually associated with his hair. He dropped his hands as if he had been burned, and spun on his heel. "It will be a positive pleasure," he said between his teeth, and strode out of the dome, slamming the reinforced door until it rattled on its hinges. Behind him Camilla collapsed on a bench, her face in her hands, and cried herself sick, weeping frantically until a wave of violent nausea racked her, forcing her to stagger away toward the women's latrine area. At last she crept away, her head pounding, her face flushed and sore, aching in every nerve.

As she returned to the computer dome, a memory struck her. This had happened three times now—in a surge of violent fear and rejection, her hands went up to her mouth, and she bit at her knuckles.

"Oh, *no*," she whispered, "Oh, no, no . . ." and her voice trailed off in whispered pleas and imprecations. Her gray eyes were wild with terror.

MacAran had gone into the combined recreation area-refectory, which had quickly become a center for the huge and disorganized community, when he noticed on an improvised bulletin board a notice about a meeting of the New Hebrides Commune. He had seen this before—the colonists accepted by Earth Expeditionary had consisted not only of individuals like himself and Jenny, but of small groups or communes, extended families, even two or three business companies wishing to extend their trade or open branch offices. They were all carefully screened to determine how they would fit into the balanced development of the colony, but apart from that they were a most heterogeneous crew. He suspected that the New Hebrides Commune was one of the many small neo-rural communes who had drawn away from the mainstream society on latter-day Earth, resenting its industrialization and regimentation. Many such communities had gone out to the star colonies; everyone agreed that while misfits on Earth, they made excellent colonists. He had never paid the slightest attention to them before; but after Camilla's words he was curious. He wondered if their meeting was open to outsiders?

He vaguely remembered that this group had occasionally reserved one of the ship's recreation areas for their own meetings, they seemed to have a strongly knit community life. Well, at worst they could ask him to leave.

He found them in the empty, between-meal refectory area. Most of them were sitting in a circle and playing musical instruments; one of them, a tall youth with long braided hair, raised his head and said, "Members only, friend," but another, a girl with red hair hanging loose to her waist, said, "No, Alastair. It's MacAran, and he was on the exploring team, he knows a lot of the answers we need. Come in, man, make yourself welcome."

Alastair laughed. "Right you are, Fiona, and with a name like MacAran he should be an honorary member anyway."

MacAran came in. To his faint surprise he saw, somewhere

in the circle, the round, pudgy, ginger-haired little figure of Lewis MacLeod. He said, "I didn't meet any of you on the ship, I'm afraid I don't know what you people are supposed to stand for."

Alastair said quietly, "We're neo-ruralists, of course; world-builders. Some members of the Establishment call us anti-technocrats, but we're not the destroyers. We're simply looking for an honorable alternative for the society of Earth, and we're usually just as welcome in the colonies as they are glad to have us away from Earth. So—tell us, MacAran. What's the story here? How soon can we get out to make our own settlement?"

MacAran said, "You know as much as I do. The climate is pretty brutal, you know; if it's like this in summer, it's going to be a lot rougher in winter."

Fiona laughed. She said, "Most of us grew up in the Hebrides or even the Orkneys. They have about the worst climate on Earth. Cold doesn't scare us, MacAran. But we want to be established in community life, so we can set up our own ways and customs, before the winter sets in."

MacAran said slowly, "I'm not sure Captain Leicester will let anyone leave the encampment. The priority is still on repairing the ship, and I think he regards all of us as a single community. If we begin to break up—"

"Come *off* it," Alastair said, "none of us are scientists. We can't spend five years working on a starship; it's against our entire philosophy!"

"Survival—"

"—survival." MacAran understood only a little of the Gaelic of his forefathers, but he realized Alastair was being indecent. "Survival, to us, means setting up a colony here as fast as possible. We signed on to go to Coronis. Captain Leicester made a mistake and set us down here, but it's all the same to us. For our purposes, this is even better."

MacAran raised his eyebrows at MacLeod. He said, "I didn't know you belonged to this group."

"I didn't," MacLeod said, "I'm a fringe member, but I agree with them—and I want to stay here."

"I thought they didn't approve of scientists."

The girl Fiona said, "Only in their place. When they use their knowledge to serve and help mankind—not to manipulate it, or to destroy its spiritual strength. We're happy to have Dr.

MacLeod—Lewis, we don't use titles—as one of us, with his knowledge of zoology."

MacAran said, in amazement, "Are you intending to mutiny against Captain Leicester?"

"Mutiny? We're not his crew or his subjects, man," said a strange boy, "we just intend to live the way we would have made for ourselves on the new world. We can't wait three years until he gives up this wild idea of rebuilding his ship. By that time we could have a functional community."

"And if he does repair the ship, and goes on to Coronis? Will you stay here?"

"This is our world," the girl Fiona said, coming to Alastair's side. Her eyes were gentle but implacable. "Our children will be born here."

MacAran said, in shock, "Are you trying to tell me—"

Alastair said, "We don't know, but some of our women may already be pregnant. It is our sign of commitment to this world, our sign of rejection of Earth and the world Captain Leicester wants to force on us. And you can tell him so."

As MacAran left them, the musical instruments began again, and the mournful sound of a girl's voice, in the eternal melancholy of an old song of the Isles; a lament for the dead, out of a past more torn and shattered with wars and exiles than any other people of Earth:

> Snow-white seagull, say,
> Tell me, pray,
> Where our fair young lads are resting.
> Wave on wave they lie,
> Breath nor sigh,
> From their cold lips coming;
> Sea-wrack their shroud,
> Harp and dirge the sea's sad crooning.

The song tightened MacAran's throat, and against his will tears came to his eyes. *They lament,* he thought, *but they know life goes on. The Scots have been exiles for centuries, for millennia. This is just another exile, a little further than most, but they will sing the old songs under the new stars and find new mountains and new seas. . . .*

Going out of the hall he drew up his hood—by now it would be beginning to rain. But it wasn't.

CHAPTER NINE

MacAran had already seen what a couple of rainless and snowless nights could do on this planet. The garden areas blossomed with vegetation, and flowers, mostly the small orange ones, covered the ground everywhere. The four moons came out in their glory from before sunset until well after sunrise, turning the sky into a flood of lilac brilliance.

The woods were dry, and they began to worry about keeping a firewatch. Within a few miles of the encampment, Moray got the idea of rigging lightning-rods to each of the hilltops, each anchored to an enormously tall tree. It might not prevent fire in the event of a serious storm, but might lessen the dangers somewhat.

And above them on the heights, the great bell-shaped golden flowers opened wide, their sweet-scented pollen drifting in the upper slopes. It had not reached the valleys.

Not yet. . . .

After a week of snowless evenings, moonlit nights and warm days—warm by the standards of this planet, which would have made Norway seem like a summer resort—MacAran went to ask Moray's assent to another trip into the foothills. He felt he should take advantage of the rare seasonable weather to collect further geological specimens, and perhaps to locate caves which might serve as emergency shelter during later exploration. Moray had taken a small room at the corner of the Recreation building for an office, and while MacAran waited outside, Heather Stuart came into the building.

"What do you think of this weather?" he asked her, the old habit from Earth asserting itself. *When in doubt talk about the weather. Well, there's plenty of weather on this planet to talk about, and it's all so bad.*

"I don't like it," Heather said seriously, "I haven't forgotten what happened on the mountain when we had a few clear days."

You too? MacAran thought, but he demurred. "How could the weather be responsible, Heather?"

"Airborne virus. Airborne pollen. Dust-borne chemicals. I'm a microbiologist, Rafe, you'd be surprised what can be in a few cubic inches of air or water or soil. In the debriefing session Camilla said the last thing she remembered before freaking out was smelling the flowers, and I remember that the air was full of their scent." She smiled weakly. "Of course what I remember may not be any kind of evidence and I hope to God that I don't find out by trial and error again. I've just found out for certain that I'm not pregnant, and I never want to go through *that* again. When I think of the way women must have had to live before the really safe contraceptives were invented, from month to month never *knowing.* . . ." She shuddered. "Rafe, is Camilla sure yet? She won't talk to me about it any more."

"I don't know," MacAran said sombrely, "she won't talk to me at all."

Heather's fair mobile face registered dismay. "Oh, I'm so sorry, Rafe! I was so happy about you two, Ewen and I both hoped—oh, here, I think maybe Moray's ready to see you." The door had opened and the big redhead Alastair bumped into them as he came barging out; he turned and half shouted, "The answer is still *no,* Moray! We're pulling out—all of us, our whole Community! Now, tonight!"

Moray followed him to the door. He said, "Selfish crew, aren't you? You talk about community, and it turns out that you mean only your own little group—not the larger community of mankind on this planet. Did it ever occur to you that all of us, the whole two-hundred-odd of us, are perforce a commune? We *are* humanity, we *are* society. Where's that big sense of responsibility toward your fellow man, laddie?"

Alastair bent his head. He muttered, "The rest of you don't stand for what we stand for."

"We all stand for common good and survival," Moray said

quietly. "The Captain will come around. Give me a chance to talk to the others, at least."

"I was appointed to speak for them—"

"Alastair," said Moray gravely, "you're violating your own standards, you know. If you're a true philosophical anarchist, you have to give them an opportunity to hear what I have to say."

"You're just trying to manipulate us all—"

"Are you afraid of what I'll say to them? Are you afraid they won't stick to what *you* want?"

Alastair, maneuvered into a corner, burst out, "Oh, talk to them and be damned to you, then! Much good may it do you!"

Moray followed them out, saying to MacAran as he passed, "Whatever it is, it'll have to keep, lad. I have to talk these young lunatics into trying to see us all as one big family—not just their little family!"

Out in the open space, the thirty members or so of the New Hebrides community were gathered. MacAran noticed that they had put aside the ship-issued surface uniform and were wearing civilian clothing and carrying backpacks. Moray went forward and began to harangue them. From where he stood at the door of the Recreation Hall MacAran could not hear his words, but there was a lot of shouting and argument. MacAran stood watching the small swirls and eddies of dust blow up across the plowed ground, the backlog of wind in the trees at the edge of the clearing like a sea-noise that never quieted. It seemed to him that there was a song in the wind. He looked down at Heather beside him, and her face seemed to gleam and glow in the dark sunlight, almost a visible song.

She said hoarsely, "Music—music on the wind. . . ."

MacAran muttered, "In God's name what are they doing out there? Holding a *dance?*"

He moved away from Heather, as a group of the uniformed Security guards came across from the ship. One of them faced Alastair and Moray and started to speak; MacAran, moving into range, heard "—put down your packs. I have the Captain's orders to take you all into custody, for desertion in the face of an emergency."

"Your Captain hasn't any power over us, emergency or otherwise, fuzz-face," the big redhead yelled, and one of the girls scooped up a handful of dirt and flung it, evoking screams of riotous laughter from the others.

Moray said urgently to the Security men, "No! There is no need for this! Let me handle them!"

The officer hit by the thrown dirt unslung his gun. MacAran, gripped by a surge of all too familiar fear, muttered, "That's torn it," and ran forward just as the young men and women of the communes threw down their rucksacks and charged, howling and screaming like demons.

One Security officer threw down his rifle and burst into wild manic laughter. He flung himself on the ground and rolled there, screaming. MacAran, in split-second awareness, ran forward. He grabbed up the thrown-down gun; wrested another away from the second man, and ran toward the ship as the third Security man, who had only a handgun, fired. In MacAran's rocking brain the shot sounded like an infinite gallery of echoes, and with a wild high scream, one of the girls fell on the ground, rolling where she lay in agony.

MacAran, dragging the rifles, burst into the Captain's presence in the computer dome; Leicester raised his beetling brows, demanding explanation, and MacAran watched the eyebrows crawl up like caterpillars, take wing and flutter loose in the dome . . . *no.* NO! Fighting the spinning attack of unreality, he gasped, "Captain, it's happening again! What happened to us all on the slopes! For the love of God, lock up the guns and ammo before someone gets killed! One girl's already been shot—"

"What?" Leicester stared at him in frank disbelief. "Surely you're exaggerating . . ."

"Captain, I went through it," MacAran said, fighting desperately against the urge to fling himself down and roll on the floor, to grab the Captain by the throat and shake him to death. . . . "It's real. It's—you know Ewen Ross. You know he's had careful, complete Medic training—and he lay in the woods fooling around with Heather and MacLeod while a dying patient ran right past him and collapsed with a burst aorta. Camilla—Lieutenant Del Rey—threw away her telescope and ran off to chase butterflies."

"And you think this—this epidemic is going to strike here?"

"Captain, I *know* it," MacAran pleaded, "I'm—I'm fighting it off now—"

Leicester had not become Captain of a starship by being unimaginative or by refusing to meet emergencies. As the sound of a second shot erupted in the space before the clearing, he ran for the door, hitting an alarm button as he ran. When no one answered he shouted, running across the clearing.

MacAran, at his heels, sized up the situation in the flicker of an eye. The girl shot by the officer was still lying on the ground, writhing in pain; as they burst into the area Security men and the young people of the Commune were grappling hand to hand, shouting wild obscenities. A third shot rang out; one of the Security officers howled in pain and fell, clutching his kneecap.

"Danforth!" the Captain bellowed.

Danforth swung round, gun levelled, and for a split second MacAran thought he would pull the trigger again, but the years-long habit of obedience to the Captain made the berserk officer hesitate. Only a minute, but by that time MacAran's flying body struck him in a rough tackle; the man came crashing to the ground and the gun rolled away. Leicester dived for it, broke it, thrust the cartridges in his pocket.

Danforth struggled like a mad thing, clawing at MacAran, grappling for his throat; MacAran felt the surge of wild rage rising in him too, with spinning red colors before his eyes. He wanted to claw, to bite, to gouge out the man's eyes . . . with savage effort, remembering what had happened before, he brought himself back to reality and let the man rise to his feet. Danforth stared at the Captain and began to blubber, wiping his streaming eyes with doubled fists and muttering incoherently.

Captain Leicester snarled, "I'll break you for this, Danforth! Get to quarters!"

Danforth gave a final gulp. He relaxed and smiled lazily at his superior officer. "Captain," he murmured tenderly, "did anybody ever tell you that you got beautiful big blue eyes? Listen, why don't we—" straight-faced, smiling, in perfect seriousness, he made an obscene suggestion that made Leicester gasp, turn purple with rage, and draw breath to bellow at him again. MacAran grabbed the Captain's arm urgently.

"Captain, don't do anything you'll be sorry for. Can't you see he doesn't know what he's doing or saying?"

Danforth had already lost interest and ambled off, idly kicking at pebbles. Around them the nucleus of the fight had lost momentum; half the combatants were sitting on the ground crooning; the others had separated into little clumps of two and three. Some were simply stroking one another with total animal absorption and a complete lack of inhibitions, lying on the rough grass; others had already proceeded, totally without discrimination—man and woman, woman and woman, man and man—to more direct and active satisfactions. Captain Leicester stared at the daylight orgy in consternation and began to weep.

A surge of disgust flared up in MacAran, blotting out his early concern and compassion for the man. Simultaneously he was torn between reeling, struggling emotions; a rising surge of lust, so that he wanted to fall to the ground with the crowded, entwined bodies, a last scrap of compunction for the Captain—*he doesn't know what he's doing, not even as much as I do* . . . and a wave of rising sickness. Abruptly he bolted, sick panic blotting out everything else, stumbled and ran from the scene.

Behind him a long-haired girl, little more than a child, came up to the Captain, urged him down with his head on her lap, and rocked him like a baby, crooning softly in Gaelic. . . .

Ewen Ross saw and felt the first wave of rising unreason . . . it hit him as panic . . . and simultaneously, inside the hospital building, a patient still shrouded in bandages and comatose for days rose, ripped off his bandages and, while Ewen and a nurse stared in horrified consternation, tore his wounds open and laughing, bled to death. The nurse hurled a huge carboy of green soap at the dying man; then Ewen, fighting wildly for control of the waves of madness that threatened to overcome him (*the ground was rocking in earthquake, wild vertigo rippled his guts and head with nausea, insane colors spun before his eyes* . . .) leaped for the nurse and after a moment's struggle, took away the scalpel with which she was ripping at her wrists. He resisted her entwining arms (*throw her down on the bed now, tear her dress off* . . .) and ran for Dr. Di Asturien, to gasp out a terrified plea to lock up all poisons, narcotics and surgical instruments. Hastily drafting Heather (she had, after all, some memory of her own first attack) they managed to get more of them locked away and the key safely hidden before the whole hospital went berserk. . . .

Deep in the forest, the unaccustomed sunlight glazed the forest lawns and clearings with flowers and filled the air with pollen sweeping down from the heights on the wind.

Insects hurried from flower to flower, from leaf to leaf; birds mated, built nests of warm feathers with their eggs encased in insulating mud-and-straw walls, to hatch enclosed and feed on stored nectars and resins until the next warm spell. Grasses and grains scattered their seed, which the next snows would fertilize and moisten to sprout.

On the plains, the staglike beasts ran riot, stampeding, fighting, coupling in broad daylight, as the pollen-laden winds sent their curious scents deep into the brain. And in the trees of the lower slopes, the small furred humanoids ran wild, venturing to the ground—some of them for the only time in their lives—feasting on the abruptly-ripening fruits, bursting through the clearings in maddened disregard of the prowling beasts. Generations and millennia of memory, in their genes and brains, had taught them that at this time, even their natural enemies were unable to sustain the long effort of chase.

Night settled over the world of the four moons; the dark sun sank in a strange clear twilight and the rare stars appeared. One after another, the moons climbed the sky; the great violet-gleaming moon, the paler green and blue gemlike discs, the small one like a white pearl. In the clearing where the great starship, alien to this world, lay huge and strange and menacing, the men from Earth breathed the strange wind and the strange pollen borne on its breath, and curious impulses struggled and erupted in their forebrains.

Father Valentine and half a dozen strange crewmen sprawled in a thicket, exhausted and satiated.

In the hospital, fevered patients moaned untended, or ran wildly into the clearing and into the forest, in search of they knew not what. A man with a broken leg ran a mile through the trees before his leg gave way beneath him and he lay laughing in the moonlight while a tigerlike beast licked his face and fawned on him.

Judith Lovat lay quietly in her quarters, swinging the great blue jewel on the chain around her throat; she had kept it, all this time, concealed beneath her clothing. Now she drew it out, as if the strange starlike patterns within it exerted some hypnotic influence on her. Memories swirled in her mind, of the strange smiling madness that had been on her before. After a time, following some invisible call, she rose, dressed warmly, calmly appropriating her room-mate's warmest clothing (her room-mate, a girl named Eloise, who had been a communications officer on shipboard, was sitting under a longleafed tree, listening to the strange sounds of the wind in its leaves and singing wordlessly). Judy went calmly through the clearing, and struck into the forest. She was not sure where she was going, but she knew she would be guided when the time came, so she followed the upward trail, never deviating, listening to the music in the wind.

Phrases heard on another planet echoed dimly in her mind, *by woman wailing far her demon lover. . . .*

No, not a demon, she thought, *but too bright, too strange and beautiful to be human . . .* she heard herself sob as she walked, remembering the music, the shimmering winds and flowers, and the strange, glowing eyes of the half-remembered being, the clutch of fear that had quickly turned to enchantment and then to a happiness, a sense of closeness more intense than anything she had ever known.

Had it been something like this, then, those old Earth-legends of a wanderer lured away by the fairy-folk, the poet who had cried out in his enchantment:

> I met a Lady in the wood,
> A fairy's child
> Her hair was long, her foot was light
> And her eyes were wild. . . .

Was it like that? Or was it—*And the Son of God looked on the daughters of men, and beheld they were fair. . . .*

Judy was enough of a disciplined scientist to be aware that in the curious actions of this time there was something of madness. She was certain that some of her memories were colored and changed by the strange state of consciousness she had been in then. Yet experience and reality testing counted for something, too. If there was a touch of madness in it, behind the madness lay something real, and it was as real as the tangible touch on her mind now, that said, *"Come. You will be led, and you will not be harmed."*

She heard the curious rustle in the leaves over her head, and stopped, looking up, her breath catching in anticipation. So deep was her hope and longing to see the strange unforgotten face that she could have wept when it was only one of the little ones, the small red-eyed aliens, who peered at her shy and wild through the leaves, then slid down the trunk and stood before her, trembling and yet confident, holding out his hands.

She could not entirely reach his mind. She knew the little ones were far less developed than she, and the language barrier was great. Yet, somehow, they communicated. The small tree-man knew that she was the one he sought, and why; Judy knew that he had been sent for her, and that he bore a message she desperately hungered to hear. In the trees she saw other strange and shy faces, and in another moment, once they were aware of her good will, they slipped down and were all around her. One of them slid a small cool hand into her fingers: another garlanded her with bright leaves and flowers. Their manner was almost reverent as they bore her along, and she went with them without protest, knowing that this was only a prologue to the real meeting she longed for.

High in the wrecked ship an explosion thundered. The ground shook, and the echoes rolled through the forest, frightening the birds from the trees. They flew up in a cloud that darkened the sun for a moment, but no one in the clearing of the Earthmen heard. . . .

Moray lay outstretched on the soft ploughed soil of the garden unit, listening with a deep inner knowledge to the soft ways of growth of the plants embedded in the soil. It seemed to him, in those expanding moments, that he could hear the grass and leaves growing, that some of the alien Earth-plants were complaining, weeping, dying, while others, in this strange ground, throve and changed, their inner cells altering and changing as they must to adapt and survive. He could not have put any of this into words, and, a practical and materialistic man, he would never rationally believe in ESP. Yet, with the unused centers of his brain stimulated by the strange madness of this time, he did not try to rationalize or believe. He simply knew, and accepted the knowledge, and knew it would never leave him.

Father Valentine was awakened by the rising sun over the clearing. At first, dazed, and still flooded with the strange awarenesses, he sat staring in wonder at the sun and the four moons which, by some trick of the light or his curiously heightened senses, he could see quite clearly in the deep-violet sunrise; green, violet, alabaster-pearl, peacock-blue. Then memory came flooding in, and horror, as he saw the crewmen scattered around him, still deep in sleep, exhausted. The full hideous horror of what he had done, in those last hours of darkness and animal hungers, bore in on a mind too confused and hyperstimulated even to be aware of its own madness.

One of the crewmen had a knife in his belt. The little priest, his face streaming with tears, snatched it out and began very seriously expunging all the witnesses to his sin, muttering to himself the phrases of the last rites as he watched the streaming blood. . . .

It was the wind, MacAran thought. Heather had been right; it was something in the wind. Some substance, airborne, dust or pollen, which caused this madness to run riot. He had known it before, and this time he had had some idea what was happening; enough to work all through the early stages, swept only by recurrent attacks of sudden panic or euphoria, at locking up weapons, ammunition, poisons from the hospital or the chemistry lab. He knew that Heather and Ewen were doing the same thing, to some limited extent, in the hospital. But even so he was numbed with horror at the events of the last day and night, and when night fell, knowing rationally that one semi-sane man could do little against two hundred completely crazed men and women, he had simply hidden in the woods, desperately clinging to sanity against the recurrent waves of madness that clutched at him. This damned planet! This damned world, with the winds of madness that crept like ghosts from the towering hills, ravening madness that touched men and beasts alike. An encompassing, devouring, ghost wind of madness and terror!

The Captain is right. We've got to get off this world. No one can survive here, nothing human, we're too vulnerable . . .

He was gripped with desperate anxiety for Camilla. In this mad night of rape, murder, panic, terror out of control, savage battle and destruction, where had she gone? His earlier search for her had been fruitless, even though, aware of his heightened senses, he had tried to "listen" in that strange way which, on the mountain, had allowed him to find her unerringly through the blizzard. But his own fear acted like static blurring a sensitive receptor; he could feel her, but where? Had she hidden, like himself after he knew the hopelessness of his search, simply trying to escape the madness of the others? Had she been gripped by the lust and wild sensual euphoria of some of the others, and was she simply caught up in one of the groups madly pleasuring and indifferent to all else? The thought was agony to MacAran, but it was the safest alternative. It was the only bearable alternative—otherwise the thought that she might have met some murder-crazed crewman before the weapons were safely locked away, the fear that she might have run into the woods in a recurrence of panic and there been clawed or savaged by some animal, would have driven him quite witless with fear.

His head was buzzing, and he staggered as he walked across the clearing. In a thicket near the stream he saw motionless bodies—dead or wounded or sated, he could not tell; a quick glance told him Camilla was not there and he went on. The ground seemed to rock under his feet and it took all his concentration not to dash madly off into the trees, looking for . . . looking for . . . he wrenched himself back to awareness of his search and grimly went on.

Not in the recreation hall, where members of the New Hebrides Commune were sprawled in exhausted sleep or vacantly strumming musical instruments. Not in the hospital, although on the floor a snowstorm of paper showed him where someone had gone berserk with the medical records . . . *stoop down, scoop up a handful of paper scraps, sift them through your fingers like falling snow, let them whirl away on the wind . . .* MacAran never knew how long he stood there listening to the wind and watching the playing clouds before the wave of surging madness receded again, like a tidal wave dragging and sucking back from the shore. But the racing clouds had covered the sun, and the wind was blowing ice-cold by the time he recovered himself and began, in a wave of panic, hunting madly in every corner and clearing for Camilla.

He entered the computer dome last, finding it darkened (*what had happened to the lights! Had that explosion knocked them all out, all the power controls from the ship?*) and at first MacAran thought it was deserted. Then, as his eyes grew accustomed to the dim light, he made out shadowy figures back in the corner of the building; Captain Leicester, and—yes—Camilla, kneeling at his side and holding his hand.

By now he took it for granted that he was actually hearing the Captain's thoughts, *why have I never really seen you before, Camilla?* MacAran was amazed and in a small sane part of his mind, ashamed at the wave of primitive emotion that surged over him, a roaring rage that snarled in him and said, *this woman is mine!*

He came toward them, rising on the balls of his feet, feeling his throat swelling and his teeth drawn back and bared, his voice a wordless snarl. Captain Leicester sprang up and faced him, defiantly, and again with that odd, heightened sensitivity, MacAran was aware of the mistake the Captain was making . . .

Another madman, I must protect Camilla against him, that much duty I can still do for my crew . . . and coherent thought blurred out in a surge of rage and desire. It maddened MacAran; Leicester crouched and sprang at him, and the two men went down, gripping one another, roaring deep in their throats in primitive battle. MacAran came uppermost and in a flick of a moment he saw Camilla lying back tranquilly against the wall; but her eyes were dilated and eager and he knew that she was excited by the sight of the struggling men, that she would accept—passively, not caring—whichever of them now triumphed in the fight—

Then a wash of sanity came over MacAran. He tore himself free of the Captain, struggling to his feet. He said, in a low, urgent voice, "Sir, this is idiotic. If you fight it, you can get out of this. Try to fight it, try to stay sane—"

But Leicester, rolling free, came up to his feet, snarling with rage, his lips flecked with foam and his eyes unfocused and quite mad. Lowering his head, he charged full steam at MacAran; Rafe, quite cool-headed now, stepped back. He said regretfully, "I'm sorry, Captain," and a well-aimed single blow to the point of the chin connected and knocked the crazed man senseless to the floor.

He stood looking down at him, feeling rage drain out of him like running water. Then he went to Camilla and knelt beside her. She looked up at him and smiled, and suddenly, in the way he could no longer doubt, they were in contact again. He said gently, "Why didn't you tell me you were pregnant, Camilla? I would have worried, but it would have made me very happy, too."

I don't know. At first, I was afraid, I couldn't accept it; it would have changed my life too much.

But you don't mind now?

She said aloud, "Not just at this minute, I don't mind, but things are so different now. I might change again."

"Then it isn't an illusion," MacAran said, half aloud, "we *are* reading each other's minds."

"Of course," she said, still with that tranquil smile, "didn't you know?"

Of course, then, MacAran thought; this is why the winds bring madness.

Primitive man on Earth must have had ESP, the whole gamut of psi powers, as a reserve survival power. Not only would it account for the tenacious belief in them against only the sketchiest proof, but it would account for survival where mere sapience would not. A fragile being, primitive man could not have survived without the ability to *know* (with his eyesight dimmer than the birds', his hearing less than a tenth of that of any dog or carnivore) where he could find food, water, shelter; how to avoid natural enemies. But as he evolved civilization and technology, these unused powers were lost. The man who walks little, loses the ability to run and climb; yet the muscles are there and can be developed, as every athlete and circus performer learns. The man who relies on notebooks loses the ability of the old bards, to memorize day-long epics and genealogies. But for all these millennia the old ESP powers lay dormant in his genes and chromosomes, in his brain—and some chemical in the strange wind (pollen? dust? virus?) had restimulated it.

Madness, then. Man, accustomed to using only five of his senses, bombarded by new data from the unused others, and his primitive brain also stimulated to its height, could not face it, and reacted—some by total, terrifying loss of inhibition; some with ecstasy; some with blank, blind refusal to face the truth.

If we are to survive on this world, then, we must learn to listen to it; to face it; to use it, not to fight it.

Camilla took his hand. She said aloud, in a soft voice, "Listen, Rafe. The wind is dying; it will rain, soon, and this will be over. We may change—I may change again with the wind, Rafe. Let us enjoy being together now—while I can." Her voice sounded so sad that the man, too, could have wept. Instead, he took her hand and they walked quietly out of the dome; at the door Camilla paused, slipped her hand gently free of Rafe's and went back. She bent over the Captain, slid her rolled-up windbreaker gently under his head; knelt at his side for a moment and kissed his cheek. Then she rose and came back to Rafe, clinging to him, shaking softly with unshed tears, and he led her out of the dome.

High on the slopes, mists gathered and a soft fine foggy rain began to fall. The small red-eyed furred creatures, as if waking from a long dream, stared wildly about themselves and scurried for the safety of their tree-roads and shelters of woven wood and wicker. The cavorting beasts in the valleys bellowed softly in confusion and hunger, abandoned their cavorting and stampeding and began quietly to graze along the streams again. And, as if waking from a hundred long confused nightmares, the alien men from Earth, feeling the rain on their faces, the effects of the wind receding in their minds, woke and found that in many cases, the nightmare, acted out, was dreadfully real.

Captain Leicester came up slowly to consciousness in the deserted computer dome, hearing the sounds of rain beating in the clearing outside. His jaw ached; he struggled up to his feet, feeling his face ruefully, fighting for memory out of the strange confused thoughts of the past thirty-six hours or so. His face was furred with stubble, unshaven; his uniform filthy and mussed. Memory? He shook his head, confused; it hurt, and he put his hands to his throbbing temples.

Fragments spun in his mind, half real like a long dream. Gunfire, and a fight of some sort; the sweet face of a red-headed girl, and a sharp unmistakable memory of her body, naked and welcoming—had that been real or a wild fantasy? An explosion that had rocked the clearing—the ship? His mind was still too fuzzed with dream and nightmare to know what he had done or where he had gone after that, but he remembered coming back here to find Camilla alone, *of course she would protect the computer, like a mother hen her one chick,* and a vague memory of a long time with Camilla, holding her hand while some curious, deep-rooted communion went on, intense and complete, achingly close, yet somehow not sexual, although there had been that too—*or was that illusion, confused memory of the redheaded girl whose name he did not know*—the strange songs she had sung—and another surge of fear and protectiveness, an explosion in his mind, and then black darkness and sleep.

Sanity returned, a slow rise, a receding of the nightmare. What had been happening to the ship, to the crew, to the others, in this time of madness? He didn't know. He'd better find out. He vaguely remembered that someone had been shot, before he freaked out—or was that, too, part of the long madness? He pressed the button by which he summoned the ship's Security men, but there was no response and then he realized that the lights were not working, either. So someone had gotten to the power sources, in madness. What other damage? He'd better go and find out. Meanwhile, where was Camilla?

(At this moment she slipped reluctantly away from Rafe, saying gently, "I must go and see what damage has been done in the ship, *querido*. The Captain, too; remember I am still part of the crew. Our time is over—at least for now. There's going to be plenty for all of us to do. I must go to him—yes, I know, but I love him too, not as I do you, but I'm learning a lot about love, my darling, and he may have been hurt.")

She walked across the clearing, through the blowing rain which was beginning to be mixed with heavy wet snow. *I hope someone finds some kind of fur-bearing animals,* she thought, *the clothes made for Earth won't face a winter here.* It was a quiet routine thought at the back of her mind as she went into the darkened dome.

"Where have you been, Lieutenant?" the Captain said thickly. "I have a queer feeling I owe you some kind of apology, but I can't remember much."

She looked around the dome, quickly assessing damage. "It's foolish to call me Lieutenant here, you've called me Camilla before this—before we ever landed here."

"Where is everybody, Camilla? I suppose it's the same thing that hit you in the mountains?"

"I suppose so. I imagine before long we'll be up to our ears in the aftermath," she said with a sharp shudder. "I'm frightened, Captain—" she broke off with an odd little smile. "I don't even know your name."

"It's Harry," Captain Leicester said absent-mindedly, but his eyes were fixed on the computer and with a sudden, sharp exclamation Camilla went toward it. She found one of the resin-candles issued for lights and lit it, holding it up to examine the console.

The main banks of storage information were protected by plates from dust, damage, accidental erasure or tampering. She caught up a tool and began to unfasten the plates, working with feverish haste. The Captain came, caught up by her air of urgency, and said, "I'll hold the light." Once he had taken it, she moved faster, saying between her teeth, "Someone's been at the plates, Captain, I don't like this—"

The protective plate came away in her hands, and she stared, her face slowly whitening, her hands dropping to her sides in horror and dismay.

"You know what's happened," she said, her voice sticking in her throat. "It's the computer. At least half the programs—maybe more—have been erased. Wiped. And without the computer—"

"Without the computer," Captain Leicester said slowly, "the ship is nothing but a few thousand tons of scrap metal and junk. We're finished, Camilla. Stranded."

CHAPTER TEN

High above the forest, in a close-woven shelter of wicker-work and leaves, the rain beating softly outside, Judy rested on a sort of dais covered with soft woven fabric and took in, not with words entirely, what the beautiful alien with the silver eyes was trying to tell her.

"Madness comes upon us too, and I am deeply sorrowful to have intruded into your people's lives this way. There was a time—not now, but lost in our history—when our folk travelled, as yours do, between the stars. It may even be that all men are of one blood, back in the beginning of time, and that your people too are our little brothers, as with the furred people of the trees. Indeed it would seem so, since you and I came together under the madness in the winds and now you bear this child. It is not that I regret, entirely—"

A feather's-touch upon her hand, no more, but Judy felt she had never known anything as tender as the sad eyes of the alien. *"Now, with no madness in my blood, I feel only deep grief for you, little one. No one of our own would be allowed to bear a child in loneliness, and yet you must return to your own people, we could not care for you. You could not even bear the cold of our dwelling-places in high summer, in winter you would surely die, my child."*

All of Judy's being was one great cry of anguish, *will I never see you again?*

I can reach you so clearly only at these times, the answer flowed, *although your mind is more open to me than before, the minds of your people are like half-shut doors at other times. It would be wisest for me to let you go now, for you never to look back to the time of madness, and yet*—long silence, and a great sigh. *I cannot, I cannot, how can I let you go from me and never know* . . .

The strange alien reached out, touching the jewel which hung about her neck on a fine chain, and drew it forth. *We use these—sometimes—for the training of our children. Mature, we do not need them. It was a love-gift to you; an act of madness, perhaps, perhaps unwise, my elders would certainly say so. Yet perhaps, if your mind is opened enough to master the jewel, perhaps I can reach you at times, and know that all is well with you and the child.*

She looked at the jewel, which was blue, like a star-sapphire, with small inner flecks of fire, only a moment; then raised her eyes to look again with grief on the alien being. Taller than mortal, with great pale-gray eyes, almost silver, fair-skinned and delicate of feature, with long slender fingers and bare feet even in the bitter chill, and with long almost colorless hair floating like weightless silk about the shoulders; strange and bizarre and yet beautiful, with a beauty that struck at the woman like pain. With infinite tenderness and sadness, the alien reached for her and folded her very briefly against the delicate body, and she sensed that this was a rare thing, a strange thing, a concession to her despair and loneliness. *Of course. A telepathic race would have little use for demonstrative displays.*

And now you must go, my poor little one. I will take you to the edge of the forest, the Little Folk will guide you from there. (I fear your people, they are so violent and savage and your minds . . . your minds are closed . . .)

Judy stood looking up at the stranger, her own grief at parting blurring in the perception of the other's fear and anguish. "I understand," she whispered aloud, and the other's drawn face relaxed a little.

Shall I see you again?

There are so many chances, both for good and evil, child. Only time knows, I dare not promise you. With a gentle touch, he folded her in the fur-lined cloak in which, earlier, he had wrapped her. She nodded, trying to hold back her tears; only when he had disappeared into the forest did she break down and follow, weeping, the small furred alien who came to lead her down the strange paths.

* * *

"You are the logical suspect," Captain Leicester said harshly. "You have never made any secret of the fact that you don't want to leave this planet, and the sabotage of the computer means that you will get your way, and that we will never be able to leave here."

"No, Captain, you're quite wrong," Moray looked him in the face without flinching. "I have known all along that we would never leave this planet. It did occur to me, during the— what the hell shall we call it? During the mass freakout? Yes; it occurred to me during the mass freakout that maybe it would be a good thing if the computer was nonfunctional, it would force you to stop pretending we could fix the ship—"

"I was not *pretending*," said the Captain icily.

Moray shrugged. "Words don't matter that much. Okay, force you to stop kidding yourself about it, and get down to the serious business of survival. But I didn't do it. To be honest, I might have if it had ever occurred to me, but I don't know one end of a computer from the other—I wouldn't know how to go about putting it out of action. I suppose I *could* have blown it up—I know I heard the explosion—but as it happens, when I heard the explosion I was lying in the garden having—" suddenly he laughed, embarrassed, "having the time of my life talking to a cabbage sprout, or something like that."

Leicester frowned at him. He said, "Nobody blew the computer up, or even put it out of action. The programs have simply been erased. Any literate person could do that."

"Any literate person familiar with a starship, maybe," Moray said. "Captain, I don't know how to convince you, but I'm an ecologist, not a technician. I can't even make up a computer program. But if it's not out of commission, what's all the fuss about? Can't you re-program it, or whatever the word is? Are the tapes, or whatever they are, so irreplaceable?"

Leicester was abruptly convinced. Moray didn't *know*. He said dryly, "For your information, the computer contained about half of the sum total of human knowledge about physics and astronomy. Even if my crew contained four dozen Fellows of the Royal College of Astronomy of Edinburgh, it would take them thirty years to re-program just the navigational data. That's not even counting the medical programs—we haven't checked those yet—or any of the material from the ship's Library. All things considered, the sabotage of the computer is a worse piece of human vandalism than the burning of the Library at Alexandria."

"Well, I can only repeat that I didn't do it and I don't know who did," Moray said. "Look for someone on your crew with the technical know-how." He gave a dry, unamused laugh. "And someone who could keep their head long enough. Have the Medics figured out what hit us?"

Leicester shrugged. "The best guess I've heard so far is an airborne dust containing some violent hallucinogen. Still unidentified, and probably will be until things settle down at the hospital."

Moray shook his head. He knew the Captain believed him now, and to tell the truth he was not entirely happy about the destruction of the computer. As long as Leicester's whole efforts were taken up in attempting to manage the ship repairs he was unlikely to interfere with what Moray was doing to assure the Colony's survival. Now, a Captain without a ship, he was likely to get seriously in the way of their assault on a strange world. For the first time Moray understood the old joke about the Space fleet:

"You can't retire a starship Captain. You have to shoot him."

The thought stirred dangerous fears in him. Moray was not a violent man, but during the thirty-six hours of the strange wind, he had discovered painful and unsuspected depths in himself. *Maybe someone else will think of that, next time— what makes me so sure there will be a next time? Or maybe I will, can I ever be sure now?*

Turning away from the unwelcome thought, he said, "Have you a report on damages yet?"

"Nineteen dead—no medical reports, but at least four hospital patients died of neglect," Leicester said shortly. "Two suicides. One girl cut herself and bled to death on broken glass, but probably accident rather than suicide. And—I suppose you heard about Father Valentine."

Moray shut his eyes. "I heard about the murders. I don't know all the details."

Leicester said, "I doubt if anyone alive does. He doesn't himself, and probably won't unless Chief Di Asturien wants to give him narcosynthesis or something. All I know is somehow he got mixed up with a gang of the crewmen who were doing some messing around—sexual messing around—down by the edge of the river. Things got fairly wild. When the first wave subsided a little he realized what he'd been doing, and I gather he couldn't face it, and started cutting throats."

"I take it, then, that he was one of the suicides?"

Leicester shook his head. "No. I gather he came out of it just in time to realize that suicide, too, was a mortal sin. Funny. I guess I'm just getting hardened to horrors on this wonderful paradise planet of yours—all I can think about now is how much trouble he'd have saved if he'd gone ahead with it. Now I've got to try him for murder, and then decide, or make the people decide, whether or not we have capital punishment here."

Moray smiled bleakly. "Why bother?" he said. "What verdict could you possibly get except *temporary insanity?*"

"My God, you're right!" Leicester passed his hand over his forehead.

"In all seriousness, Captain. We may have to cope with this again, and again, and again. At least until we know the cause. I suggest that you immediately disarm your Security crew; the first sign happened when a Security man shot first a girl, then a fellow officer. I suggest that if we ever again have a rainless night, that all lethal weapons, kitchen knives, surgical instruments, and the like, be locked up. It probably won't prevent all the trouble, we can't lock up every rock and hunk of stovewood on the planet, and to look at you, somebody evidently forgot who you were and took a swing at you."

Leicester rubbed his chin. "Would you believe a fight over a girl, at my age?"

For the first time the two men grinned at one another with the beginnings of a brief mutual human liking, then it receded. Leicester said, "I'll think about it. It won't be easy."

Moray said grimly, "Nothing here's going to be easy, Captain. But I have a feeling that unless we start up a serious campaign for an ethic of nonviolence—one that will hold even under stress like the mass freakout—none of us will live through the summer."

CHAPTER ELEVEN

The days of the Wind had spared the garden, MacAran thought. Perhaps some deep survival-instinct had told the maddened colonists that this was their lifeline. Repairs to the hospital were underway, and work crews drafted for manual labor were doing salvage work on the ship—Moray had made it bitterly clear that for many years this would be their only stock of metal for tools and implements. Bit by bit, the interior fabric of the great starship was being cannibalized; furniture from the living quarters and recreation areas was being brought out and converted for use in the dormitory and community buildings, tools from the repair shops, kitchen areas and even the bridge decks were being inventoried by groups of clerical workers. MacAran knew that Camilla was busy checking the computer, trying to discover what programs had been salvaged. Down to the smallest implement, ballpoint pens and women's cosmetics in the canteen supplies, everything was being inventoried and rationed. When the supplies of a technologically oriented Earth culture ran out, there would be no more, and Moray made it clear that replacements were already being devised for an orderly transition.

The clearing presented a curious blend, he thought; the small domes constructed with plastic and fiber, damaged in the blizzard and repaired with tougher local woods; the mixed piles of complex machinery, tended and guarded by uniformed crewmen with Chief Engineer Patrick in charge; the people from the New Hebrides Commune working—by their own choice, MacAran understood—in the garden and woods.

He held in his hand two slips of paper—the old habit of

posting memoranda still held; he imagined that eventually dwindling paper supplies would phase it out. What would they substitute? Systems of bells coded to each person, as was done in some large department stores to attract the attention of a particular person? Word of mouth messages? Or would they manage to discover some way to make paper of local products and continue their centuries-long reliance on written memoranda? One of the slips he held told him to check in at the hospital for what was called routine examination; the other asked him to report to Moray's office for work analysis and assignment.

By and large, the announcement that the computer was useless and the ship perforce abandoned had been greeted without much outcry. One or two crewmen had been heard to mutter that whoever did it should be lynched, but there was at the moment no way of discovering either who had wiped the Navigation tapes from the computer, nor of finding out who had dynamited one of the inner drive chambers with an improvised bomb. Suspicion for the latter fell by default on a crewmember who had recently asked admission into the New Hebrides Commune and whose mangled body had been found inside the ship near the explosion site; and everyone was content to let it stay there.

MacAran suspected that the quiet was temporary, the result of shock, and that sooner or later there would be fresh storms, but for the moment everyone had simply accepted the urgent necessity to join together to repair damages and assure survival against the unguessed harshness of the unknown winter. MacAran himself was not sure how he felt about it, but he had in any case been ready for a colony, and secretly it seemed to him that it might be more interesting to colonize a "wild" planet than one extensively terraformed and worked over by Earth Expeditionary. But he hadn't been prepared to be cut off from the mainstream of Earth—no starships, no contact or communication with the rest of the Galaxy, perhaps for generations, perhaps forever. *That* hurt. He hadn't accepted it yet; he knew he might never accept it.

He went into the building where Moray's office was located, read the sign on the door (DON'T KNOCK, COME IN) and went in to find Moray talking to an unknown girl who must be, from her dress, one of the New Hebrides people.

"Yes, yes, dear, I know you want a work assignment to the garden, but your history shows you worked in art and ceramics and we're going to need you there. Do you realize that the first craft developed in almost every civilization is pottery? In any case, didn't I see a report that you were pregnant?"

"Yes, the Annunciation Ceremony for me was yesterday. But our kind of people always work right up to delivery."

Moray smiled faintly. "I'm glad you feel well enough to go on working. But women in colonies are never permitted to do manual work."

"Article four—"

"Article four," said Moray, and his face was grim, "was developed for Earth, Earth conditions. Get wise to the facts of life on planets with alien gravity, light and oxygen content, Alanna. This planet is one of the lucky ones; oxygen on the high side, light gravity, no anoxic or crush-syndrome babies. But even on the best planets, just the *change* does it, and it's a grim statistic for a population as low as ours. Half the women are sterile for five to ten years, half the fertile women miscarry for five to ten years. And half the live births die before they're a month old for five to ten years. Colony women have to be *pampered,* Alanna. Co-operate, or you'll be sedated and hospitalized. If you want to be one of the lucky ones with a live baby instead of a messed-up dead one, *co-operate,* and start doing it *now.*"

When she had gone away with a slip for the hospital, looking dazed and shocked, MacAran took her place before the cluttered desk, and Moray grimaced up at him, "I take it you heard that. How'd you like *my* job—scaring the hell out of young pregnant girls?"

"Not much." MacAran was thinking of Camilla, also carrying a child. So she was not sterile. But one chance in two that she would miscarry—and then a fifty-fifty chance that her child would die. Grim statistics, and they sent a clutch of horror through him. Had she been advised of this? Did she know? Was she co-operating? He didn't know; she had been locked up with the Captain, hovering over the computer, for half the last tenday.

Moray said, frowning slightly, "Come out of the clouds. You're one of the lucky ones, MacAran—you're not technologically unemployed."

"Huh?"

"You're a geologist and we need you doing what you were trained for. You heard me tell Alanna that one of the first industries we need, in a hurry, at that, is *pottery*. For pottery, you need china clay, or a good substitute for it. We also need reliable building stone—we need concrete or cement of some sort—we need limestone, or something with the same properties; and we need silicates for glass, various ores . . . in fact, what we need is a geological assay of this part of the planet, and we need it before the winter sets in. You aren't priority one, Mac—but you're in category two or three. Can you draw up a plan for an assay and exploration in the next day or two, and tell me roughly how many men you'll need for sampling and testing?"

"Yes, I can do that easy enough. But I thought you said we couldn't go in for a technological civilization. . . ."

"We can't," Moray told him, "not as Engineer Patrick uses the word. No heavy industry. No mechanized transport. But there's no such thing as a non-technological civilization. Even the cave men had technology—they manufactured flints, or didn't you ever see one of their factory sites? Man is a tool-user—a technician. I never had any notion of starting us out as savages. The question is, *which* technologies can we manage, especially during the first three or four generations?"

"You plan that far ahead?"

"I have to."

"You said my job wasn't priority one. What's priority one?"

"Food," Moray said realistically. "Again, we're lucky. The soil's arable here—although I suspect marginally, so we're going to have to use fertilizers and composts—and agriculture *is* possible. I've known planets where the food-securing priority would have taken up so much time that even minimal *crafts* might have to be postponed for two or three generations. Earth doesn't colonize them, but we could have been marooned on one. There may even be domesticable animals here; MacLeod's on that now. Priority two is shelter—and by the way, when you make that survey, check some lower slopes for *caves*. They may be warmer than anything we can build, at least during the winter. After food and shelter come simple crafts—the amenities of life; weaving, pottery, fuel and lights, clothing, music, garden tools, furniture. You get the idea. Go draw up your survey, MacAran, and I'll assign you enough men to carry it out." He gave another of those grim smiles. "Like I say; you're one of the lucky ones. This morning I've got to tell a deep-space communications expert with absolutely no other skills, that his job is completely obsolete for at least ten generations, and offer him a choice of agriculture, carpentry or blacksmithing!"

As MacAran left the office, his thoughts flew again, compulsively, to Camilla. Was this what lay in store for her? No, certainly not, any civilized group of people must have some use for a computer library of information! But would Moray, with his grim priorities, see it that way?

He walked through the midday sunlight, pale violet shadows, the sun hanging high and red like an inflamed and bloodshot eye, toward the hospital. In the distance a solitary figure was toiling over rocks, building a low fence, and MacAran looked at Father Valentine, doing his solitary penance. MacAran accepted, in principle, the theory that the colony could spare no single pair of hands; that Father Valentine could atone for his crimes by useful work more easily than by hanging by the neck until dead; and MacAran, with the memory of his own madness lying heavy on him (*how easily he could have killed the Captain, in his rage of jealousy!*) could not even find it in his heart to shun the priest or feel horror at him. Captain Leicester's judgment would have done justice to King Solomon; Father Valentine had been commanded to bury the dead, those he had killed, and the others, to create a graveyard, and enclose it with a fence against wild beasts or desecration, and to build a suitable memorial to the mass grave of those who had died in the crash. MacAran was not certain what useful purpose a graveyard would serve, except perhaps to remind the Earthmen of how near death lay to life, and how near madness lay to sanity. But this work would keep the Father away from the other crewmen and colonists, who might not have the same awareness of how near they might have come to repeating his crime, until the memory had mercifully died down a little; and would provide enough hard work and penance to satisfy even the despairing man's need for punishment.

Somehow the sight of the lonely, bent figure put him out of the mood to keep his other appointment in the hospital. He walked away toward the woods, passing the garden area where New Hebrideans were tending long rows of green sprouting plants. Alastair, on his knees, was transplanting small green shoots from a flat screened pan; he returned MacAran's wave with a smile. *They were happy at the outcome of this, this life would suit them perfectly.* Alastair spoke a word to the boy holding the box of plants, got up and loped toward MacAran.

"The *padrón*—Moray—told me you were going to do geological work. What's the chances of finding materials for glassmaking?"

"Can't say. Why?"

"Climate like this, we need greenhouses," Alastair said, "concentrated sunlight. Something to protect young plants against blizzards. I'm doing what I can with plastic sheets, foil reflectors and ultraviolet, but that's a temporary makeshift. Check natural fertilizers and nitrates, too. The soil here isn't too rich."

"I'll make a note of it," MacAran promised. "Were you a farmer by trade on Earth?"

"Lord, no. Auto mechanic—transit specialist," Alastair grimaced. "The Captain was talking about converting me to a machinist. I'm going to be sittin' up nights praying for whoever it was blew up the damn ship."

"Well, I'll try to find your silicates," MacAran promised, wondering how high, on Moray's austere priorities, the art of glassmaking would come. And what about musical instruments? Fairly high, he'd imagine. Even savages had music and he couldn't imagine life without them, nor, he'd guess, could these members of a singing folk.

If the winter's as bad as it probably will be, music just might keep us all sane, and I'll bet that Moray—cagey bastard that he is—has that already figured out.

As if in answer to his thought, one of the girls working in the field raised her voice in low, mournful song. Her voice, deep and husky, had a superficial resemblance to Camilla's, and the words of the song rang out, in question and sadness, an old sad melody of the Hebrides:

> My Caristiona,
> Wilt answer my cry?
> No answering tonight?
> My grief, ah me . . .
> My Caristiona . . .

Camilla, why do you not come to me, why do you not answer me? Wilt answer my cry . . . my grief, ah me . . .

> Deep my heart is grieving, grieving,
> And my eyes are streaming, streaming . . .
> My Caristiona . . . wilt answer my cry?

I know you are unhappy, Camilla, but why, why do you not come to me . . . ?

Camilla came into the hospital slowly and rebelliously, clutching the examination slip. It was a comforting hangover from ship routine, but when, instead of the familiar face of Medic Chief Di Asturien (*at least he speaks Spanish!*) she was confronted with young Ewen Ross, she frowned with irritation.

"Where's the Chief? You haven't the authority to do examinations for Ship personnel!"

"The Chief's operating on that man who was shot in the kneecap during the Ghost Wind; anyway I'm in charge of routine examinations, Camilla. What's the matter?" His round young face was ingratiating, "won't I do? I assure you my credentials are wonderful. Anyhow, I thought we were friends— fellow victims from the first of the Winds! Don't damage my self-esteem!"

Against her will she laughed. "Ewen, you rascal, you're impossible. Yes, I guess this is routine. The Chief announced the contraceptive failure a couple of months ago, and I seem to have been one of the victims. It's just a case of putting in for an abortion."

Ewen whistled softly. "Sorry, Camilla," he said gently; "can't be done."

"But I'm *pregnant!*"

"So congratulations or something," he said, "maybe you'll have the first child born here, or something, unless one of the Commune girls gets ahead of you."

She heard him, frowning, not quite understanding. She said stiffly, "I guess I'll have to take it up with the Chief after all; you evidently don't understand the rules of the Space Service."

His eyes held a deep pity; he understood all too well. "Di Asturien would give you the same answer," he said gently. "Surely you know that in the Colonies abortions are performed only to save a life, or prevent the birth of a grossly defective child, and I'm not even sure we have facilities for *that* here. A high birth rate is absolutely imperative for at least the first three generations—you surely know that women volunteers aren't even accepted for Earth Expeditionary unless they're childbearing age and sign an agreement to have children?"

"I would be exempt, even so," Camilla flashed, "although I

didn't volunteer for the colony at all; I was crew. But you know as well as I do that women with advanced scientific degrees are exempt—otherwise no woman with a career she valued would ever go out to the colonies! I'm going to fight this, Ewen! Damn you, I'm not going to accept forced childbearing! No woman is *forced* to have a child!"

Ewen smiled ruefully at the angry woman. He said, "Sit down, Camilla; be sensible. In the first place, love, the very fact that you have an advanced degree makes you valuable to us. We need your genes a lot more than we need your engineering skills. We won't be needing skills like that for half a dozen generations—if then. But genes for high intelligence and mathematical ability have to be preserved in the gene pool, we can't risk letting them die out."

"Are you trying to tell me I'll be *forced* to have children? Like some savage woman, some walking womb from the prehistoric planets?" Her face was white with rage. "This is completely unendurable! Every woman on the crew will go out on strike when they hear that!"

Ewen shrugged. "I doubt it," he said. "In the first place, you've got the law wrong. Women are not allowed to volunteer for colonies unless they have intact genes, are of childbearing age and sign an agreement to have children—but women *over* childbearing age are *occasionally* accepted if they have medical or scientific degrees. Otherwise the end of your fertile years means the end of your chance to be accepted for a Colony—and do you know how long the waiting lists are for the Colonies? I waited four years; Heather's parents put her name down when she was ten, and she's twenty-three. The Over-population laws on Earth mean that some women have been on waiting lists for twelve years to have a *second* child."

"I can't imagine why they'd bother," Camilla said in disgust. "One child ought to be enough for any woman, if she has anything above the neck, unless she's a real neurotic with no independent sense of self-esteem."

"Camilla," Ewen said very gently, "this is biological. Even back in the twentieth century, they did experiments on rats and ghetto populations and things, and found that one of the first results of crucial social overcrowding was the failure of maternal behavior. It's a pathology. Man is a rationalizing animal, so sociologists called it 'Women's Liberation' and things like that, but what it amounted to was a pathological reaction to

overpopulation and overcrowding. Women who couldn't be allowed to have children, had to be given some other work, for
the sake of their mental health. But it wears off. Women sign
an agreement, when they go to the colonies, to have a minimum of two children; but most of them, once they're out of the
crowding of Earth, recover their mental and emotional health,
and the average Colony family is four children—which is
about right, psychologically speaking. By the time the baby
comes, you'll probably have normal hormones too, and make
a good mother. If not, well, it will at least have your genes, and
we'll give it to some sterile woman to bring up for you. Trust
me, Camilla."

"Are you trying to tell me that I've *got* to have this baby?"

"I sure as hell am," Ewen said, and suddenly his voice went
hard, "and others too, provided you can carry them to term.
There's a one in two chance that you'll have a miscarriage."
Steadily, unflinching, he rehearsed the statistics which MacAran
had heard from Moray earlier that same day. "If we're lucky,
Camilla, we have fifty-nine fertile women now. Even if they
all became pregnant this year, we'll be lucky to have twelve
living children . . . and the viable level for this colony to survive means we've got to bring our numbers up to about four
hundred before the oldest women start losing their fertility. It's
going to be touch and go, and I have a feeling that any woman
who refuses to have as many children as she can physically
manage, is going to be awfully damned unpopular. Public
Enemy Number One isn't in it."

Ewen's voice was hard, but with the heightened sensitivity
he had known ever since the first Wind blasted him wide open
to the emotions of others, he realized the hideous pictures that
were spinning in Camilla's mind:

*not a person, just a thing, a walking womb, a thing used for
breeding, my mind gone, my skills useless . . . just a brood
mare . . .*

"It won't be that bad," he said in deep sympathy. "There
will be plenty for you to do. But that's the way it's got to be,
Camilla. I'm sure it's worse for you than it is for some others,
but it's the same for everyone. Our survival depends on it." He
looked away from her; he could not face the blast of her agony.

She said, her lips tightening to a hard line, "Maybe it would
be better *not* to survive, under conditions like that."

"I won't discuss that with you until you're feeling better,"

Ewen said quietly, "it's not worth the breath. I'll set up a pre-natal examination for you with Margaret—"

"—I *won't!*"

Ewen got quickly to his feet. He signalled to a nurse behind her back and gripped her wrist in a hard grip, immobilizing her. A needle went into her arm; she looked at him with angry suspicion, her eyes already glazing slightly.

"What—"

"A harmless sedative. Supplies are short, but we can spare enough to keep you calmed down," Ewen said calmly. "Who's the father, Camilla? MacAran?"

"None of your affair!" she spat at him.

"Agreed, but I ought to know, for genetic records. Captain Leicester?"

"MacAran," she said with a surge of dull anger, and suddenly, with a deep gnawing pain, she remembered . . . *how happy they had been during the Winds* . . .

Ewen looked down at her senseless form with deep regret. "Get hold of Rafael MacAran," he said, "have him with her when she comes out of it. Maybe he can talk some sense into her."

"How can she be so selfish?" the nurse said in horror.

"She was brought up on a space satellite," Ewen said, "and in the Alpha colony. She joined the space service at fifteen and all her life she's been brainwashed into thinking childbearing was something she shouldn't be interested in. She'll learn. It's only a matter of time."

But secretly he wondered how many women of the crew felt the same—sterility could be psychologically determined too—and how long it would take to overcome this conditioned fear and aversion.

Could it even be done, in time to bring them up to a viable number, on this harsh, brutal and inhospitable world?

CHAPTER TWELVE

MacAran sat beside the sleeping Camilla, thinking back over the hospital interview just past with Ewen Ross. After explaining about Camilla, Ewen had asked him only one further question:

"Do you remember having sex with anyone else during the Wind? I'm not just being idly curious, believe me. Some women, and some men, simply can't remember, or named at least half a dozen. By putting together everything that anyone *does* remember, we can eliminate certain people; that is, for genetic records later on. For instance, if some woman names three men as *possibly* responsible for her pregnancy, we only need to blood-test three men to establish—within rough limits, that is—the actual father."

"Only Camilla," MacAran said, and Ewen had grinned. "At least you're consistent. I hope you can talk that girl into some sense."

"I can't somehow see Camilla as much of a mother," MacAran said slowly, feeling disloyal, and Ewen shrugged. "Does it matter? We're going to have plenty of women either wanting children and unable to have them, miscarrying during pregnancy or losing them at birth. If she doesn't want the child when it's born, one thing we're *not* going to be short of is foster mothers!"

Now that thought stirred Rafael MacAran to a slow resentment as he sat watching the drugged girl. The love between them, even at best, had arisen out of hostility, been an up-and-down thing of resentment and desire, and now the anger got out of control. *Spoiled brat,* he thought, *she's had everything her own way all her life, and now at the first hint she might have to give way to some consideration other than her own convenience, she starts making a fuss! Damn her!*

As if the violence of his angry thoughts had penetrated the thinning veils of the drug, Camilla's gray eyes, fringed by heavy dark lashes, flicked open, and she looked around, in momentary bewilderment, at the translucent walls of the hospital dome, and MacAran by the side of her cot.

"Rafe?" A look of pain flicked over her face, and MacAran thought, *at least she's not calling me MacAran any more.* He spoke as gently as he could. "I'm sorry you're not feeling well, love. They asked me to come and sit with you a while."

Her face hardened as memory came back; he could feel her anger and misery and it was like pain inside him, and it turned off his own resentment like a switch being turned.

"I really am sorry, Camilla. I know you didn't want this. Hate me, if you've got to hate someone. It's my fault; I wasn't acting very responsibly, I know."

His gentleness, his willingness to take all the blame, disarmed her. "No, Rafe," she said painfully, "that's not fair to you. At the time it happened I wanted it as much as you did, so there's no point in blaming you. The trouble is, we've all gotten out of the *habit* of connecting pregnancy and sex, we all have a civilized attitude about it now. And of course none of us could have been *expected* to know that the regular contraceptives weren't working."

Rafe reached out to touch her hand, "Well, we'll share the blame, then. But can't you try to remember how you felt about it during the Wind? We were so happy then."

"I was *insane* then. So were you." The deep bitterness in her voice made him flinch with pain, not only for himself but for her. She tried to pull her hand free, but he held on to the slim fingers.

"I'm sane now—at least I think I am—and I still love you, Camilla. I haven't words to tell you how much."

"I should think you'd hate me."

"I couldn't hate you. I'm not happy that you don't want this child," he added, "and if we were on Earth I'd probably admit that you had a right to choose—not to bear it, if you didn't want to. But I wouldn't be happy about that either, and you can't expect me to be sorry that it's going to have a chance to live."

"So you're glad I'm going to be trapped into bearing it?" she flung at him, furious.

"How can I be glad about anything that makes you so miserable?" MacAran demanded in despair. "Do you think I get any satisfaction out of seeing you unhappy? It tears me up, it's killing me! But you're pregnant, and you're sick, and if it makes you feel any better to say these things—I love you, and what can I do about it, except listen and wish I could say something helpful? I only wish you felt happier about it, and I wasn't so completely helpless."

Camilla could feel his confusion and distress as if they were her own, and this persistence of an effect she had associated only with the time of the winds shocked her out of her anger and self-pity. Slowly, she sat up in bed and reached for his hand.

"It's not your fault, Rafe," she said softly, "and if it makes you so unhappy for me to act like this, I'll try to make the best of it. I can't pretend I *want* a child, but if I have to have one—and it seems I do—I'd rather it was yours than someone else's." She smiled faintly, and added, "I suppose—the way things were going then—it could have been anyone, but I'm glad it was you."

Rafe MacAran found himself unable to speak—and then realized he didn't have to. He bent down and kissed her hand. "I'll do everything I can to make it easier," he promised, "and I only wish it were more."

Moray had finished work assignments for most of the colonists and crew by the time Chief Engineer Laurence Patrick found himself, with Captain Leicester, consulting the Colony Representative.

Patrick said, "You know, Moray, long before I became a M-AM drive expert I was a specialist in small all-terrain craft. There's enough metal in the ship, salvaged, to create several such craft, and they could be powered with small converted drive units. It would be a tremendous help to you in locating and structuring the resources of the planet, and I'm willing to handle the building. How soon can I get to it?"

Moray said, "Sorry, Patrick, not in your lifetime or mine."

"I don't understand. Wouldn't it help a great deal in exploring, and in maximizing use of resources? Are you *trying* to create as savage and barbarian an environment as you can possibly manage?" Patrick demanded angrily. "Lord help us, has the Earth Expeditionary become nothing but a nest of anti-technocrats and neo-ruralists?"

Moray shook his head, unruffled. "Not at all," he said. "My first colony assignment was on a planet where I designed a highly technical civilization based on maximal use of electric power and I'm extremely proud of it—in fact, I'm intending, or in view of our mutual catastrophe I should say I *had* been intending, to go back there at the end of my days and retire. My assignment to the Coronis colony meant I was designing technological cultures. But as things turned out—"

"It's still possible," said Captain Leicester. "We can pass down our technological heritage to our children and grandchildren, Moray, and some day, even if we're marooned here for life, our grandchildren will go back. Don't you know your history, Moray? From the invention of the steamboat to man's landing on the Moon was less than two hundred years. From there to the M-AM drives which landed us on Alpha Centauri, less than a hundred. We may all die on this Godforsaken lump of rock, we probably *will*. But if we can preserve our technology intact, enough to take our grandchildren back into the mainstream of human civilization, we won't be dying for nothing."

Moray looked at him with a deep pity. "Is it possible that you still don't understand? Let me spell it out for you, Captain, and you, Patrick. This planet will not support *any* advanced technology. Instead of a nickel-iron core, the major metals are low-density non-conductors, which explains why the gravity is so low. The rock, as far as we can tell without sophisticated equipment we don't have and can't build, is high in silicates but low in metallic ores. Metals are always going to be rare here—terrifyingly rare. The planet I spoke about, with enormous use of electric power, had huge fossil-fuel deposits *and* huge amounts of mountain streams to convert energy . . . *and* a very tough ecological system. This planet appears to be only marginally agricultural land, at least here. The forest cover is all that keeps it from massive erosion, so we must harvest timber with the greatest care, and preserve the forests as a lifeline. Added to that, we simply can't spare enough manual labor to build the vehicles you want, to service and maintain them, or to build such small roadways as they would need. I can give you exact facts and figures if you like, but in brief, if you insist on a mechanized technology you're handing down a death sentence—if not for all of us, at least for our grandchildren; we might make it through three generations, because with such small numbers we could move on to a new part of the planet when we'd burned out one area. But no more."

Patrick said with deep bitterness, "Is it worth while surviving, or even *having* grandchildren, if they're going to live this way?"

Moray shrugged. "I can't make you have grandchildren," he said. "But I have a responsibility to the ones already on the way, and there are colonies without advanced technology which have just as long a waiting list as the one planned around massive use of electricity. Our lifeline isn't you people, I'm sorry to say; you are—to put it bluntly, Chief—just so much dead weight. The people we need on this world are the ones in the New Hebrides Commune—and I suspect if we survive at all, it's going to be their doing."

"Well," Captain Leicester said, "I guess that tells us where we stand." He thought it over a minute. "What's ahead for us, then, Moray?"

Moray looked at the records, and said, "I note on your personnel printout that your hobby at the academy was building musical instruments. That isn't very high priority, but this winter we can use plenty of people who know something about it. Meanwhile, do you know anything about glass blowing, practical nursing, dietetics, or elementary teaching?"

"I joined the service as a Medical Corpsman," Patrick said surprisingly, "before I went into Officer's Training."

"Go talk to Di Asturien in the hospital, then. For the time being I'll mark you down as assistant orderly, subject to drafts of all able-bodied men in the building program. An engineer should be able to handle architectural work and designing. As for you, Captain—"

Leicester said irritably, "It's idiotic to call me *Captain*. Captain of *what*, for God's sake, man!"

"Harry, then," Moray said, with a small wry grin. "I suspect titles and things will just quietly disappear within three or four years, but I'm not going to deprive anyone of one, if he wants to keep it."

"Well, consider I've phased mine out," Leicester said. "Going to draft me to hoe in the garden? Once I'm out as a spaceship captain, it's all I'm good for."

"No," Moray said bluntly. "I'm going to need whatever it was in you that made you a Captain—leadership, maybe."

"Any law against salvaging what technological know-how we have? Programming it into the computer, maybe, for those hypothetical grandchildren of ours?"

"Not so hypothetical in your case," Moray said, "Fiona MacMorair—she's over in the hospital as 'possible early pregnancy'—gave us your name as the probable father."

"Who the *hell,* pardoning the expression, who on this hellfired world is Fiona Macwhatsis?" Leicester scowled. "I never heard of the damn girl."

Moray chuckled. "Does that matter? I happened to spend most of this wind making love to cabbage sprouts and baby bean plants, or at least listening to them telling me their troubles, but most of us spent it a little less—seriously, shall we say. Dr. Di Asturien's going to ask you the names of any possible female contacts."

Leicester said, "The only one I remember, I had to fight for, and I lost." He rubbed the fading bruise on his chin. "Oh, wait—is this a redheaded girl, one of the Commune group?"

Moray said, "I don't know the girl by sight. But about three-fourths of the New Hebrides people are red-haired—they're mostly Scots, and a few Irish. I'd say the chances were better than average that unless the girl miscarries, you'll have a redheaded son or daughter come nine-ten months from now. So you see, Leicester, you have a stake in this world."

Leicester flushed, a slow angry blush. He said, "I don't want my descendants to live in caves and scratch the ground for a living. I want them to know what kind of world we came from."

Moray did not answer for a moment. Finally he said, "I ask you seriously—don't answer. I'm not the keeper of your conscience, but think it over—might it not be best to let our descendants evolve a technology indigenous to this world? Rather than tantalizing them with the knowledge of one that could destroy this planet?"

"I'm counting on my descendants having good sense," Leicester said.

"Go ahead and program the stuff into the computer, then, if you want to," Moray said with the same small shrug, "maybe they'll have too much good sense to use it."

Leicester turned to go. "Can I have my assistant back? Or has Camilla Del Rey been assigned to something *important,* like cooking or making curtains for the hospital?"

Moray shook his head. "You can have her back when she's out of the hospital," he said, "although I've got her listed as pregnant, for assignment to light work only, and I thought we'd ask her to write some elementary mathematics texts. But the computer isn't very strenuous; if she wants to go back to it, I've no objection."

He looked pointedly at the work charts cluttering his desk, and Harry Leicester, ex-captain of the starship, realized that he had been, for all practical purposes, dismissed.

CHAPTER THIRTEEN

Ewen Ross hesitated over the genetic charts and looked up at Judith Lovat. "Believe me, Judy. I'm not trying to make trouble for you, but it's going to make our records a lot simpler. Who was the father?"

"You didn't believe me when I told you before," Judy said flatly, "so if you know the answer better than I do, say whatever you like."

"I hardly know how to answer you," Ewen said. "I don't remember being with you, but if you say I was—"

She shook her head stubbornly, and he sighed. "The same story of an alien. Can't you see how fantastic that is? How completely unbelievable? Are you trying to postulate that the aborigines of this world are human enough to crossbreed with our women?" He hesitated. "You aren't by any chance being funny, Judy?"

"I'm not postulating anything, Ewen. I'm not a geneticist, I'm simply an expert in dietetics. I'm simply telling you what happened."

"During a time when you were insane. Two times."

Heather touched his arm gently. "Ewen," she said, "Judy's not lying. She's telling the truth—or what she believes to be the truth. Take it easy."

"But damn it, her beliefs aren't evidence." Ewen sighed and shrugged. "All right, Judy, have it your way. But it must have been MacLeod—or Zabal. Or me. Whatever you think you remember, it must have been."

"If you say so, of course it must have been," Judy said, quietly stood up and walked away, knowing without needing to look that what Ewen had written down was *father unknown; possible: MacLeod, Lewis; Zabal, Marco; Ross, Ewen.*

Heather said quietly behind the closing door, "Darling, you were a little rough on her."

"I happen not to think we have room for fantasy on a world as rough as this. Damn it, Heather, I was trained to save life at all costs—*all* costs. And I've already had to see people die . . . I've *let* them die—when we're sane, we've got to be *supersane* to compensate!" the young doctor said wildly.

Heather thought about that for a minute and finally said, "Ewen, how do you judge? Maybe what seems sanity on Earth might be foolishness here. For instance, you know the Chief is training groups of the women for prenatal care and mid-wifery—in case, he says, we lose too many people this winter for the Medical staff to cope. He also said that he himself hadn't delivered a baby since he was an intern—you don't in the Space Service of course. Well, one of the first things he told us was; if a woman's going to miscarry, don't take any extraordinary measures to prevent it. If having the mother rest and keep warm won't save the child, nothing else; no hormones, no fetal-support drugs, nothing."

"That's fantastic," Ewen said, "it's almost criminal!"

"That's what Dr. Di Asturien said," Heather told him. "On Earth, it *would* be criminal. But here, he said, first of all, a threatened miscarriage may be one way of nature discarding an embryo which can't adapt to the environment here—gravity, and so forth. Better to let the woman miscarry early and start over, instead of wasting six months carrying a child who will die, or grow up defective. Also, on Earth, we could afford to save defective children—lethal genes, mental retardates, congenital deformities, fetal insults and so forth. We had elaborate machinery and medical structure for such things as exchange transfusions, growth-hormone transplants, rehabilitation and training if the child grew up defective. But here, unless some day we want to take the harsh step of exposing defective infants or killing them, we'd better keep them down to an absolute minimum—and about half the defective children born on Earth—maybe ninety percent, nobody knows, it's such routine now on Earth to prevent a miscarriage at any cost—are the result of preventing children who really should have died, nature's mistakes, from being selected out. On a world like this, it's absolute survival for our race; we can't let lethal genes and defects get into our gene pool. See what I mean? Insanity on Earth—harsh facts for survival here. Natural selection has to take its course—and this means no heroic methods to prevent miscarriages, no extreme methods to save moribund or birth-damaged babies."

"And what's all this got to do with Judy's wild story about an alien being fathering her child?" Ewen demanded.

"Only this," Heather said, "we've got to learn to think in new ways—and not to reject things out of hand because they sound fantastic."

"You *believe* some nonhuman alien—oh, come, Heather! For God's sake!"

"What God?" Heather asked. "All the Gods I ever heard of belong to Earth. I don't *know* who fathered Judy's baby. I wasn't there. But she was, and in the absence of proof about it, I'd take *her* word. She's not a fanciful woman, and if she says that some alien came along and made love to her, and that she found herself pregnant, damn it, I'll believe it until it's proved otherwise. At least until I see the baby. If it's the living image of you, or Zabal, or MacLeod, maybe I'll believe Judy had a brainstorm. But during this second Wind, you behaved rationally, up to a point. MacAran behaved rationally, up to a point. Evidently after the first exposure, a *little* control remains on subsequent exposures to the drug, or pollen. She gave a rational account of what she did this time, and it was consistent with what happened the first time. So why not give her the benefit of the doubt?"

Slowly, Ewen crossed out the names, leaving only *"Father; unknown."*

"That's all we can say for sure," he said at last, "I'll leave it at that."

In the large building which still served as refectory, kitchen and recreation hall—although a separate group-kitchen was going up, built of the heavy pale translucent native stone—a group of women from the New Hebrides Commune, in their tartan skirts and the warm uniform coats they wore with them now, were preparing dinner. One of them, a girl with long red hair, was singing in a light soprano voice:

> When the day wears away,
> Sad I wander by the water,
> Where a man, born of sun,

Wooed the fairy's daughter,
Why should I sit and sigh,
Pulling bracken, pulling bracken
All alone and weary?

She broke off as Judy came in:

"Dr. Lovat, everything's ready, I told them you were over at the hospital. So we went ahead without you."

"Thank you, Fiona. Tell me, what was that you were singing?"

"Oh, one of our island songs," Fiona said. "You don't speak Gaelic? I thought not—well, it's called the "Fairy's Love Song"—about a fairy who fell in love with a mortal man, and wanders the hills of Skye forever, still looking for him, wondering why he never came back to her. It's prettier in Gaelic."

"Sing it in Gaelic, then," Judy said, "it would be fearfully dull if only one language survived here! Fiona, tell me, the Father doesn't come to meals in the common room, does he?"

"No, someone takes it out to him."

"Can I take it out today? I'd like to talk to him," Judy said, and Fiona checked a rough work-schedule posted on the wall. "I wonder if we'll ever get permanent work-assignments until we know who's pregnant and who isn't? All right, I'll tell Elsie you've got it. It's one of those sacks over there."

She found Father Valentine toiling away in the graveyard, surrounded by the great stones he was heaving into place in the monument. He took the food from her and unwrapped it, laying it out on a flat stone. She sat down beside him and said quietly, "Father, I need your help. I don't suppose you'd hear my confession?"

He shook his head slowly. "I'm not a priest any more, Dr. Lovat. How in the name of anything holy can I have the insolence to pass judgment in the name of God on someone else's sins?" He smiled faintly. He was a small slight man, no older than thirty, but now he looked haggard and old. "In any case, I've had a lot of time to think, heaving rocks out here. How can I honestly preach or teach the Gospel of Christ on a world where He never set foot? If God wants this world saved he'll have to send someone to save it . . . whatever that means." He put a spoon into the bowl of meat and grain. "You brought your own lunch? Good. In theory I accept isolation. In practice

I find I crave the company of my fellow man much more than I ever thought I would."

His words dismissed the question of religion, but Judy, in her inner turmoil, could not let it drop so easily. "Then you're just leaving us without pastoral help of any sort, Father?"

"I don't think I ever did much in that line," Father Valentine said. "I wonder if any priest ever did? It goes without saying that anything I can do for anyone as a friend, I'll do—it's the least I can do; if I spent my life at it, it wouldn't begin to balance out what I did, but it's better than sitting around in sackcloth and ashes mouthing penitential prayers."

The woman said, "I can understand that, I suppose. But do you really mean there's no room for faith, or religion, Father?"

He made a dismissing gesture. "I wish you wouldn't call me 'father.' Brother, if you want to. We've all got to be brothers and sisters in misfortune here. No, I didn't say that, Doctor Lovat—I don't know your Christian name—Judith? I didn't say that, Judith. Every human being needs belief in the goodness of some power that created him, no matter what he calls it, and some religious or ethical structure. But I don't think we need sacraments or priesthoods from a world that's only a memory, and won't even be that to our children and our children's children. Ethics, yes. Art, yes. Music, crafts, knowledge, humanity—yes. But not rituals which will quickly dwindle down into superstitions. And certainly not a social code or a set of purely arbitrary behavioral attitudes which have nothing to do with the society we're in now."

"Yet you would have worked in the Church structure at the Coronis colony?"

"I suppose so. I hadn't really thought about it. I belong to the Order of Saint Christopher of Centaurus, which was organized to carry the Reformed Catholic Church to the stars, and I simply accepted it as a worthy cause. I never really thought about it—not serious, hard, deep thought. But out here on my rock pile I've had a lot of time to think." He smiled faintly. "No wonder they used to put criminals to breaking rocks, back on Earth. It keeps your hands busy and gives you all your time for thought."

Judy said slowly, "So you don't think behavioral ethics are absolute, then? There's nothing definite or divinely ordained about them here?"

"How can there be? Judith, you know what I did. If I hadn't

been brought up with the idea that certain things were in themselves, and of their very nature, enough to send me straight to hell, then when I woke up after the Wind, I could have lived with it. I might have been ashamed, or upset, or even sick at my stomach, but I wouldn't have had the conviction, deep down in my mind, that none of us deserved to *live* after it. In the seminary there were no shades of right and wrong, just virtue and sin, and nothing in between. The murders didn't trouble me, in my madness, because I was taught in seminary that lewdness was a mortal sin for which I could go to hell, so how could murder be any worse? You can go to hell only once, and I was already damned. A rational ethic would have told me that whatever those poor crewmen, God rest them, and I, had done during that night of madness, it had harmed only our dignity and our sense of decency, if that mattered. It was miles away, galaxies away, from murder."

Judy said, "I'm no theologian, Fa—er—Valentine, but can anyone truly commit a mortal sin in a state of complete insanity?"

"Believe me, I've been through that one and out the other side. It doesn't help to know that if I'd been able to run to my own confessor and get his forgiveness for all the things I did in my madness—ugly things by some standards, but essentially harmless—I might have been able to keep from killing those poor men. There has to be something wrong with a system that means you can take guilt on and off like an overcoat. As for madness—nothing can come out in madness that wasn't there already. What I really couldn't face, I begin to realize, wasn't just the knowledge that in madness I'd done some forbidden things with other men, it was the knowledge that I'd done them gladly and willingly, that I no longer believed they were very wrong, and that forever after, any time I saw those men, I'd remember the time when our minds were completely open to one another and we knew each other's minds and bodies and hearts in the most total love and sharing any human beings could know. I knew I could never hide it again, and so I took out my little pocket knife and started trying to hide from *myself*." He smiled wryly, a terrible death's head grin. "Judith, Judith, forgive me, you came to ask me for help, you asked me to hear your confession, and you've ended up listening to mine."

She said very gently, "If you're right, we'll all have to be priests to each other, at least as far as listening to each other and giving what help we can." One phrase he had spoken seized on her, and she repeated it aloud. *"Our minds were open to one another . . . the most total love and sharing any human beings could know.* That seems to be what this world has done to us. In different degrees, yes—but to all of us in some way or other. That's what he said"—and slowly, searching for words, she told him about the alien, their first meeting in the wood, how he had sent for her during the Wind, and the strange things he had told her, without speech.

"He told me—our people's minds were like half-shut doors," she said. "Yet we understood each other, perhaps more so because there had been that—that total sharing. But no one believes me!" she finished with a cry of despair. "They believe I'm mad, or lying!"

"Does it matter so much what they believe?" the priest asked slowly. "By their disbelief you might even be shielding him. You told me he was afraid of us—of your people—and if his kind are gentle people, I'm not surprised. A telepathic race tuned in to us during the Ghost Wind would probably have decided we were a horrifyingly violent, frightening people, and they wouldn't have been entirely wrong, although there's another side to us. But if they once begin believing in your— what is Fiona's phrase?—your fairy lover, they might seek out his people, and the results might not be very good." He smiled faintly. "Our race has a bad reputation when we meet other cultures we consider inferior. If you care about your child's father, Judy, I'd let them go on disbelieving in him."

"Forever?"

"As long as necessary. This planet is already changing us," Valentine said, "maybe some day our children and his will find some way of coming together without catastrophe, but we'll have to wait and see."

Judy pulled at the chain around her neck and he said, "Didn't you used to wear a cross on that?"

"Yes, I took it off, forgive me."

"Why? It doesn't mean anything here. But what is this?"

It was a blue jewel, blazing, with small silvery patterns moving within. "He said—they used these things for the training of their children; that if I could master the jewel I could reach him—let him know it was well with me and the child."

"Let me see it," Valentine said, and reached for it, but she flinched and drew away.

"What—?"

"I can't explain it. I don't understand it. But when anyone else touches it, now, it—it *hurts,* as if it was part of *me*," she said fumblingly. "Do you think I'm mad?"

The man shook his head. "What's madness?" he asked. "A jewel to enhance telepathy—perhaps it has some peculiar properties which resonate to the electrical signals sent off by the brain—telepathy can't just exist, it must have some natural phenomenal basis. Perhaps the jewel is attuned to whatever it is in your mind that makes you *you.* In any case, it exists, and—have you reached him with it?"

"It seems so sometimes," said Judy, fumbling for words. "It's like hearing someone's voice and knowing whose it is by the sound—no, it's not quite like that either, but it does happen. I feel—very briefly, but it's quite real—as if he were standing beside me, touching me, and then it fades again. A moment of reassurance, a moment of—of love, and then it's gone. And I have the strange feeling that it's only a beginning, that a day will come when I'll know other things about it—"

He watched while she tucked the jewel away inside her dress again. At last he said, "If I were you, I'd keep it a secret for a while. You said this planet's changing us all, but perhaps it isn't changing us *fast* enough. There are some of the scientists who would want to test this thing, to work at it, perhaps even to take it from you, experiment, destroy it to see how it works. Perhaps even interrogate and test you again and again, to see if you are lying or hallucinating. Keep it secret, Judith. Use it as he told you. A day may come when it will be important to know how it works—the way it is supposed to work, not the way the scientists might want to make it work."

He rose, shaking the crumbs of his meal off his lap.

"It's back to the rock pile for me."

She stood on the tips of her toes and kissed his cheek. "Thank you," she said softly, "you've helped me a lot."

The man touched her face. "I'm glad," he said. "It's—a beginning. A long road back, but it's a beginning. Bless you, Judith."

He watched her walk away, and a curious near-blasphemous thought touched his mind, *how do I know God isn't sending a Child . . . a strange child, not quite man . . . here on this strange world?* He dismissed the thought, Thinking *I'm mad,* but another thought made him cringe with mingled memory and dismay, *how do we know the Child I worshipped all these years was not some such strange alliance?*

"Ridiculous," he said aloud, and bent over his self-imposed penance again.

CHAPTER FOURTEEN

"I never thought I'd find myself praying for bad weather," Camilla said. She closed the door of the small repaired dome where the computer was housed, joining Harry Leicester inside. "I've been thinking. With what data we have about the length of the days, the inclination of the sun, and so forth, couldn't we find out the exact length of this planet's year?"

"That's elementary enough," Leicester said. "Write up your program and feed it through. Might tell us how long a summer to expect and how long a winter."

She moved to the console. Her pregnancy was beginning to show now, although she was still light and graceful. He said, "I managed to salvage almost all of the information about the matter-anti-matter drives. Some day—Moray told me the other day that from the steam engine to the stars is less than three hundred years. Some day our descendants will be able to return to Earth, Camilla."

She said, "That's assuming they'll want to," and sat down at her desk. He looked at her in mild question. "Do you doubt it?"

"I'm not doubting anything, I'm just not presuming to know what my great-great-great-great—oh, hell, what my ninth-generation grandsons will want to be doing. After all, Earthmen lived for generations without even wanting to invent things which could easily have been invented any time after the first smelting of iron was managed. Do you honestly think Earth would have gone into space without population pressure and pollution? There are so many social factors too."

"And if Moray has his way our descendants will all be barbarians," Leicester said, "but as long as we have the computer and it's preserved, the knowledge will be *there*. There for them to use, whenever they feel the need."

"*If* it's preserved," she said with a shrug. "After the last few months I'm not sure anything we brought here is going to outlive this generation."

Consciously, with an effort, Leicester reminded himself, *she's pregnant and that's why they thought for years that women weren't fit to be scientists—pregnant women get notions.* He watched her making swift notations in the elaborate shorthand of the computer. "Why do you want to know the length of the year?"

What a stupid question, the girl thought, then remembered he was brought up on a space station, weather is nothing to him. She doubted if he even realized the relationship of weather and climate to crops and survival. She said, explaining gently, "First, we want to estimate the growing season and find out when our harvests can come in. Its simpler than trial and error, and if we'd colonized in the ordinary way, someone would have observed this planet through several year cycles. Also, Fiona and Judy and—and the rest of us would like to know when our children will be born and what the climate's likely to be like. I'm not making my own baby clothes, but someone's got to make them—and know how much chill to allow for!"

"You're planning already?" he asked, curiously. "The odds are only one in two that you'll carry it to term and the same that it won't die."

"I don't know. Somehow I never doubted that mine would be one of the ones to live. Premonition, maybe; ESP" she said, thinking slowly as she spoke. "I had a feeling Ruth Fontana would miscarry, and she did."

He shuddered. "Not a pleasant gift to have."

"No, but I seem to be stuck with it," she said matter-of-factly, "and it seems to be helping Moray and the others with the crops. Not to mention the well Heather helped them dig. Evidently it's simply a revival of latent human potential and there's nothing weird about it. Anyhow, it seems we'll have to learn to live with it."

"When I was a student," Leicester said, "all the facts known positively about ESP were fed into a computer and the answer was that the probability was a thousand to one that there was no such thing . . . that the very few cases not totally and conclusively disproven were due to investigator error, not human ESP."

Camilla grinned and said, "That just goes to show you that a computer isn't God."

Captain Leicester watched the young woman stretch back and ease her cramped body. "Damn these bridge seats, they were never meant for use in full gravity conditions. I hope comfortable furniture gets put on a fair priority; Junior here doesn't approve of my sitting on hard seats these days."

Lord, how I love that girl, who'd have believed it at my age! To remind himself more forcefully of the gap, Leicester said sharply, "Are you planning to marry MacAran, Camilla?"

"I don't think so," she said with the ghost of a smile. "We haven't been thinking in those terms. I love him—we came so close during the first Wind, we've shared so much, we'll always be part of each other. I'm living with him, when he's here—which isn't very often—if that's what you really want to know. Mostly because he wants me so much, and when you've been that close to anyone, when you can—" she fumbled for words, "when you can feel how much he wants you, you can't turn your back on him, you can't leave him—hungry and unhappy. But whether or not we can make any kind of home together, whether we want to live together for the rest of our lives—I honestly don't know; I don't think so. We're too different." She gave him a straightforward smile that made the man's heart turn over and said, "I'd really be happier with you, on a long-term basis. We're so much more alike. Rafe's so gentle, so sweet, but you understand me better."

"You're carrying his child, and you can say this to me, Camilla?"

"Does it shock you?" she asked, grieved. "I'm sorry, I wouldn't upset you for the world. Yes, it's Rafe's baby, and I'm glad, in a funny way. *He* wants it, and one parent *ought* to want a child; for me—I can't help it, I was brainwashed—it's still an accident of biology. If it was yours, for instance—and it could have been, the same kind of accident, just as Fiona's having *your* child and you hardly know her by sight—you'd have hated it, you'd have wanted me to fight against having it."

"I'm not so sure. Maybe not. Not now, anyhow," Harry Leicester said in a low voice. "Saying these things still upsets me, though. Shocks me. I'm too old, maybe."

She shook her head. "We've got to learn not to hide from

each other. In a society where our children will grow up knowing that what they feel is an open book, what good is it going to be to keep sets of masks to wear from each other?"

"Frightening."

"A little. But they'll probably take it for granted." She leaned a little against him, easing her back against his chest. She reached back and took his fingers in hers. She said slowly, "Don't be shocked at this. But—if I live—if we both live—I'd like my next child to be yours."

He bent and kissed her on the forehead. He was almost too much moved to speak. She tightened her hand on his, then drew it away.

"I told MacAran this," she said matter-of-factly. "For genetic reasons, it's going to be a good thing for women to have children by different fathers. But—as I said—my reasons aren't quite as cold and unemotional as all that."

Her face took on a distant look—for a moment it seemed to Leicester that she was looking at something invisible through a veil—and for a moment contracted in pain; but to his quick, concerned question, she summoned a smile.

"No, I'm all right. Lets see what we can do about this year-length thing. Who knows, it might turn out to be our first National Holiday!"

The windmills were visible several miles from the Base Camp now, huge wooden-sailed constructs which supplied power for grinding flour and grain (nuts, harvested in the forest, made a fine slightly-sweet flour which would serve until the first crops of rye and oats were harvested) and also brought small trickles of electric power into the camp. But such power would always be in short supply on this world, and it was carefully rationed; for lights in the hospital, to operate essential machinery in the small metal shops and the new glass-house. Beyond the camp, with its own firebreak, was what they had begun to call New Camp, although the Hebrides Commune people who worked there called it New Skye; an experimental farm where Lewis MacLeod, and a group of assistants, were checking possibly domesticable animals.

Rafe MacAran, with his own small crew of assistants, paused to look back from the peak of the nearest hill before setting off into the forest. The two camps could both clearly be seen, from here, and around them both was swarming activity, but there was some indefinable difference from any camp he had seen on Earth, and for a moment he could not put his finger on it. Then he knew what it was; it was the quiet. Or was it? There was really plenty of sound. The great windmills creaked and heaved in the strong wind. There were crisp distant sounds of hammerings and sawings where the building crews were constructing winter buildings. The farm had its noises, including the noisy sounds of animals, the bellowings of the antlered mammals, the curious grunts, chirps, squeaks of unfamiliar life forms. And finally Rate put his finger on it. There were no sounds which were not of natural origin. No traffic. No machinery, except the softly whirring potter's wheels and the clinkings of tools. Each one of these sounds had some immediate human deliberation behind it. There were almost no impersonal sounds. Every sound seemed to have a purpose, and it seemed strange and lonesome to Rafe. All his life he had lived in the great cities of Earth, where even in the mountains, the sounds of all-terrain vehicles, motorized transit, high-tension power lines, and jet planes overhead, provided a comforting background. Here it was quiet, frighteningly quiet because whenever a sound broke the stillness of wind, there was some immediate *meaning* to the sound. You couldn't tune it out. Whenever there was a sound, you *had* to listen to it. There were no sounds which could be carelessly disregarded because, like jets passing overhead or the drive of the starship, you knew they had nothing to do with you. Every sound in the landscape had some immediate application to the listener, and Rafe felt tense most of the time, listening.

Oh well. He supposed he'd get used to it.

He started instructing his group. "We'll work along the lower rock-ridges today, and especially in the stream-beds. We want samples of every new-looking kind of earth—oh hell— *soil*. Every time the color of the clay or loam changes, take a sample of it, and locate it on the map—you're doing the mapping, Janice?" he asked the girl, and she nodded. "I'm working on grid paper. We'll get a location for every change of terrain."

The morning's work was relatively uneventful, except for one discovery near a stream-bed, which Rafe mentioned when they gathered to kindle a fire and make their noon-day meal— nut-flour rolls to be toasted and "tea" of a local leaf which had a pleasant, sweet taste like sassafras. The fire was kindled in a quickly-piled rock fireplace—the colony's strongest law was never to build a fire on the ground without firebreaks or rock enclosures—and as the quick resinous wood began to burn down to coals, a second small party came down the slope toward them: three men, two women.

"Hello, can we join you for dinner? It'll save building another fire," Judy Lovat greeted them.

"Glad to have you," MacAran agreed, "but what are you doing in the woods, Judy? I thought you were exempt from manual work now."

The woman gestured. "As a matter of fact, I'm being treated like surplus luggage," she said. "I'm not allowed to lift a finger, or do any real climbing, but it minimizes bringing samples back to camp if I can do preliminary field-testing on various plants. That's how we discovered the ropeweed. Ewen says the exercise will do me good, if I'm careful not to get overtired or chilled." She brought her tea and sat down beside him. "Any luck today?"

He nodded. "About time. For the last three weeks, every day, everything I brought in was just one more version of quartzite or calcite," he said. "Our last strike was graphite."

"Graphite? What good is that?"

"Well, among other things, it's the lead in a pencil," MacAran said, "and we have plenty of wood for pencils, which will help when supplies run low of other writing instruments. It can also be used to lubricate machinery, which will conserve supplies of animal and vegetable fats for food purposes."

"It's funny, you never think of things like that," Judy said. "The *millions* of little things you need that you always took for granted."

"Yes," said one of MacAran's crew. "I always thought of cosmetics as something extra—something people could do without in an emergency. Marcia Cameron told me the other day that she was working on a high-priority program for face cream, and when I asked why, she reminded me that in a planet with all this much snow and ice, it was an urgent necessity to keep the skin soft and prevent chapping and infections."

Judy laughed. "Yes, and right now we're going mad trying to find a substitute for cornstarch to make baby powder with. Adults can use talc, and there's plenty of that around, but if babies breathe the stuff they can get lung troubles. All the local grains and nuts won't grind fine enough; the flour is fine to eat but not absorbent enough for delicate little baby bottoms."

MacAran asked, "Just how urgent is that now, Judy?"

Judy shrugged. "On Earth, I'd have about two-and-a-half months to go. Camilla and I, and Alastair's girl Alanna, are running about neck-and-neck; the next batch is due about a month after that. Here—well, it's anybody's guess." She added, quietly, "We expect the winter will set in before that. But you were going to tell me about what you found today."

"Fuller's earth," MacAran said, "or something so like it I can't tell the difference." At her blank look he elucidated, "It's used in making cloth. We get small supplies of animal fiber, something like wool, from the rabbit-horns, and they're plentiful and can be raised in quantity on the farm, but fuller's earth will make the cloth easier to handle and shrink."

Janice said, "You never think of asking a geologist for something to make *cloth*, for goodness' sake."

Judy said, "When you come down to it, every science is interrelated, although on Earth everything was so specialized we lost sight of it." She drank the last of her tea. "Are you heading bank to Base Camp, Rafe?"

He shook his head. "No, it's into the woods for us, probably back in the hills where we went that first time. There may be streams which rise in the far hills and we're going to check them out. That's why Dr. Frazer is with us—he wants to find further traces of the people we sighted last trip, get some more accurate idea of their cultural level. We know they build bridges from tree to tree—we haven't tried to climb in them, they're evidently a lot lighter than we are and we don't want to break their artifacts or frighten them."

Judy nodded. "I wish I were going," she said, rather wistfully, "but I'm under orders never to be more than a few hours from Base Camp until after the baby is born." MacAran caught a look of deep longing in her eyes and, with that new ability to pick up emotions, reached out for her and said gently, "Don't worry, Judy. We won't trouble anyone we find, whether the little people who build the bridges, or—anyone else. If any of the beings here were hostile to us, we'd have found it out by now. We've no intention of bothering them. One of our reasons for going is to make sure we won't inadvertently infringe on their living space, or disturb anything they need for *their* survival. Once we know where *they're* settled, we'll know where we ought *not* to settle."

She smiled. "Thank you, Rafe," she said, softly. "That's

good to know. If we're thinking along those lines, I guess I needn't worry."

Shortly after the two groups separated, the food-testing crew working back toward Base Camp, while MacAran's crew moved further into the deep hills.

Twice in the next ten-day period they saw minor traces of the small furred aliens with the big eyes; once, over a mountain watercourse, a bridge constructed of long linked and woven loops of reed, carefully twined together and fastened with rope ladders leading up toward it from the lower levels of the trees. Without touching it, Dr. Frazer examined the vines of which it was constructed, saying that the need for fiber, rope and heavy twines were likely to be greater than the small supplies of what they called ropeweed could provide. Almost a hundred miles further into the hills, they found what looked like a ring of trees planted in a perfect circle, with more of the rope ladders leading up into the trees; but the place looked deserted and the platform which seemed to have been built between the trees, of something like wickerwork, was dilapidated and the sky could be seen through wormholes in the bottom.

Frazer looked covetously upward. "I'd give five years off my life to get a look up there. Do they use furniture? Is it a house, a temple, who knows what? But I can't climb those trees and the rope ladders probably wouldn't even hold Janice's weight, let alone mine. As I remember, none of them was much bigger than a ten-year-old child."

"There's plenty of time," MacAran said. "The place is deserted, we can come back some day with ladders and explore to your heart's content. Personally I think it's a farm."

"A *farm?*"

MacAran pointed. On the regularly spaced tree trunks were extraordinarily straight lines; the delicious gray fungus which MacLeod had discovered before the first of the Winds was growing there in rows as neatly spaced as if they had been drawn on with a ruler. "They could hardly grow as neatly as this," MacAran said, "they must have been planted here. Maybe they come back every few months to harvest their crop, and the platform up there could be anything—a resthouse, a storage granary, an overnight camp. Or of course this could be a farm they abandoned years ago."

"It's nice to know the stuff can be cultivated," Frazer said, and began carefully making notes in his notebook about the exact kind of tree on which it was growing, the spacing and height of the rows. "Look at this! It looks for all the world like a simple irrigation system, to divert water *away* from where the fungus is growing and directly to the roots of the tree!"

As they went on into the hills, the location of the alien "farm" firmly fixed on Janice's map, MacAran found himself thinking about the aliens. Primitive, yes, but what other type of society was seriously possible on this world? Their intelligence level must be comparable to that of many men, judging by the sophistication of their devices.

The Captain talks about a return to savagery. But I suspect we couldn't return if we tried. In the first place we're a selected group, half of us educated at the upper levels, the rest having been through the screening process for the Colonies. We come with knowledge acquired over millions of years of evolution and a few hundred years of forced technology pressured by an overpopulated, polluted world. We may not be able to transplant our culture whole, this planet wouldn't survive it, and it would probably be suicide to try. But he doesn't have to worry about dropping back to a primitive level. Whatever we finally do with this world, the end result, I suspect, won't at least be below what we had on Earth, in terms of the human mind making the best use of what it finds. It will be different . . . probably in a few generations even I couldn't relate it to Earth culture. But humans can't be less than human, and intelligence doesn't function below its own level.

These small aliens had developed according to the needs of this world; a forest people, wearing fur (MacAran, shivering in the icy rain of a summer night, wished he had it) and living in symbiosis with the forests. But as nearly as he could judge their constructs were indicative of a high level of elegance and adaptiveness.

What had Judy called them? *The little brothers who are not wise.* And what about the *other* aliens? This planet had evidently brought forth *two* wholly sapient races, and they must co-exist to some degree. It was a good sign for humanity and the others. But Judy's alien—it was the only name he had and even now he found himself doubting the very existence of the others—must be near enough to human to father a child on an Earthwoman, and the thought was strangely disturbing.

On the fourteenth day of their journey they reached the lower slopes of the great glacier which Camilla had christened

The Wall Around the World. It soared above them cutting off half the sky, and MacAran knew that even at this oxygen level it was unclimbable. There was nothing beyond these slopes except bare ice and rock, buffeted by the eternal icy winds, and nothing was to be gained by going on. But even as MacAran's party turned their back on the enormous mountain mass, his mind rejected that *unclimbable*. He thought, *no, nothing is impossible.* We can't climb it now. Perhaps not in my lifetime; certainly not for ten, twenty years. But, it's not in human nature to accept limits like this. Some day either I'll come back and climb it, or my children will. Or *their* children.

"So that's as far as we go in one direction," Dr. Frazer said. "Next expedition had better go in the other direction. This way it's all forest, and more forest."

"Well, we can make use of the forests," MacAran said. "Maybe the other direction there's a desert. Or an ocean. Or for all we know, fertile valleys and even cities. Only time will tell."

He checked the maps they had been making, looking with satisfaction on the filled-in parts, but realizing that there was a lifetime to go. They camped that night at the very foot of the glacier, and MacAran woke up before dawn, perhaps wakened by the cessation of the soft thick nightly snow. He went out and looked at the dark sky and the unfamiliar stars, three of the four moons hanging like jewelled pendants below the high ridge of the mountain above, then his eyes and thoughts went back to the valley. His people were there, and Camilla, carrying his child. Far to the east was a dim glow where the great red sun would rise. MacAran was suddenly overcome with a great and unspeakable content.

He had never been happy on Earth. The Colony would have been better, but even there, he would have fitted into a world designed by other men, and not all his kind of men. Here he could have a share in the original design of things, carve out and create what he wanted for himself and his children to come and their children's children. Tragedy and catastrophe had brought them here, madness and death had ravaged them, and yet MacAran knew that he was one of the lucky ones. He had found his own place, and it was good.

It took them much of that day and the next to retrace their steps from the foot of the glacier, through sullen grey weather and heavy gathering cloud, and MacAran, who had begun to mistrust fine weather on this planet, nevertheless felt the now-familiar prickle of disquiet. Toward evening of the second day the snow began, heavy and harder than anything he had yet seen on this world. Even in their warm clothes the Earthmen were freezing, and their sense of direction was quickly lost in the world which had turned to a white whirling insanity without color, form or place. They dared not stop and yet it soon became obvious that they could not go on much longer through the deepening layers of soft powdery snow, through which they floundered, clinging to one another. They could only keep going *down*. Other directions no longer had meaning. Under the trees it was a little better, but the howling wind from the heights above them, the creaking and heaving of branch after branch like wind in the gigantic rigging of some sailing ship immense beyond imagining, filled the twilight with uncanny voices. Once, trying to shelter beneath a tree, they attempted to set up their tent, but the gale made it flap wildly and twice it was lost and they had to chase the blowing fabric through the snow until it became entangled around a tree and they could, after a fashion, reclaim it. But it was useless to them as shelter, and they grew colder and colder, their coats keeping them dry indeed, but doing almost nothing against the piercing cold.

Frazer muttered with chattering teeth, as they held on to one another in the lee of a larger tree than usual, "If it's like this in the summer, what the hell kind of storms are we going to have in the winter?"

MacAran said grimly, "I suspect, in the winter, none of us had better set foot outside the Base Camp." He thought of the storm after the first of the Winds, when he had searched for Camilla through the light snow. It had seemed like a blizzard to him then. How little he had known this world! He was overcome with poignant fear and a sense of regret. *Camilla. She's safe in the settlement, but will we ever get back there, will any of us?* He thought with a painful twinge of self-pity that he would never see his child's face, then angrily dismissed the thought. They needn't give up and lie down to die yet, but there had to be some shelter somewhere. Otherwise they wouldn't outlast the night. The tent was no more good to them than a piece of paper, but there had to be a way.

Think. You were boasting to yourself about what a selected, intelligent group we were. Use it, or you might as well be an Australian bushman.

You might better. Survival is something they're damn good at. But you've been pampered all your life.

Survive, damn you.

He gripped Janice by one arm, Dr. Frazer by the other; reached past him to young Domenick, the boy from the Commune who had been studying geology for work in the Colony. He drew them all close together, and spoke over the howling of the storm.

"Can anyone see where the trees are thickest? Since there's not likely to be a cave here, or any shelter, we've got to do the best we can with underbrush, or anything to break the wind and keep dry."

Janice said, her small voice almost inaudible, "It's hard to see, but I had the impression there's something dark over there. If it isn't solid, the trees must be so thick I can't see through them. Is that what you mean?"

MacAran had had the same impression himself; now, with it confirmed, he decided to trust it. *He'd been led straight to Camilla, that other time.*

Psychic? Maybe so. What did he have to lose?

"Everyone hold hands," he directed, more in gesture than words, "If we lose each other we'll never find each other again." Gripping one another tightly, they began to struggle toward the place that was only a darker darkness against the trees.

Dr. Frazer's grip tightened hard on his arm. He put his face close to MacAran's and shouted, "Maybe I'm losing my mind, but I saw a *light.*"

MacAran had thought it was afterimages spinning behind his wind-buffeted eyes. What he thought he saw beyond it was even more unlikely; the figure of a man? Tall and palely shining and naked even in the storm—no, it was gone, it had been only a vision, but he thought the creature had beckoned from the dark loom . . . they struggled toward it. Janice muttered, "Did you see it?"

"Thought I did."

Afterward, when they were in the shelter of the thickly laced trees, they compared notes. No two of them had seen the same thing. Dr. Frazer had seen only the light. MacAran had seen a naked man, beckoning. Janice had seen only a face with a curious light around it, as if the face—she said—were really inside her own head, vanishing like the Cheshire cat when she narrowed her eyes to see it better; and to Domenick it had been a figure, tall and shining—"Like an angel," he said, "or a woman—a woman with long shining hair." But, stumbling after it, they had come against trees so thickly grown that they could hardly force their way between them; MacAran dropped to the ground and wriggled through, dragging them after.

Inside the clump of thickly growing trees the snow was only a light spray, and the howling wind could not reach them. They huddled together, wrapped in blankets from their packs and sharing body warmth, nibbling at rations cold from their dinner. Later, MacAran struck a light, and saw, against the bole of the tree, carefully fastened flat pieces of wood. A ladder, against the side of the tree, leading upwards. . . .

Even before they began climbing he guessed that this was not one of the houses of the small furred folk. The rungs were far enough apart to give even MacAran some trouble, and Janice, who was small, had to be pulled up them. Dr. Frazer demurred, but MacAran never hesitated.

"If we all saw something different," he said, "we were *led* here. *Something* spoke directly to our minds. You might say we were *invited.* If the creature was naked—and two of us saw him, or it, that way—evidently the weather doesn't bother them, whatever they are, but it knows that we're in danger from it. I suggest we accept the invitation, with a proper respect."

They had to wriggle through a loosely tied door up through on to a platform, but then they found themselves inside a tightly-built wooden house. MacAran started to strike his light carefully again, and discovered that it was not necessary, for there was indeed a dim light inside, coming from some kind of softly glowing, phosphorescent stuff against the walls. Outside the wind wailed and the boughs of the great trees creaked and swayed, so that the soft floor of the dwelling had a slight motion, not unpleasant but a little disquieting. There was a single large room; the floor was covered with something soft and spongy, as if moss or some soft winter grass grew there of itself. The exhausted, chilled travellers stretched out gratefully, relaxing in the comparative warmth, dryness, shelter, and slept.

Before MacAran slept it seemed to him that in the distance he heard a high sweet sound, like singing, through the storm. Singing? Nothing could live out there, in this blizzard! Yet the impression persisted, and at the very edge of sleep, words and pictures persisted in his mind.

Far below in the hills, astray and maddened after his first exposure to the Ghost Wind, coming back to sanity to discover the tent carefully set up and their packs and scientific equipment neatly piled inside. Camilla thought he had done it. He had thought *she* had done it.

Someone's been watching us. Guarding us.

Judy was telling the truth.

For an instant a calm beautiful face, neither male nor female, swam in his mind. "Yes. We know you are here. We mean you no harm, but our ways lie apart. Nevertheless we will help you as we can, even though we can only reach you a little, through the closed doors of your minds. It is better if we do not come too close; but sleep tonight in safety and depart in peace. . . ."

In his mind there was a light around the beautiful features, the silver eyes, and neither then nor ever did MacAran ever know whether he had seen the eyes of the alien or the lighted features, or whether his mind had received them and formed a picture made up of childhood dreams of angels, of fairy-folk, of haloed saints. But to the sound of the faraway singing, and the lulling noise of the wind, he slept.

CHAPTER FIFTEEN

". . . and that was really all there was to it. We stayed inside for about thirty-six hours, until the snow ended and the wind quieted, then we went away again. We never had a glimpse of whoever lived there; I suspect he carefully kept away until we were gone. It wasn't there that he took you, Judy?"

"Oh, no. Not so far. Not nearly. And it wasn't to any home of his own people. It was, I think, one of the cities of the little people, the men of the tree-roads, he called them, but I couldn't find the place again, I wouldn't want to," she said.

"But they have good will toward us, I'm sure of that," MacAran said, "I suppose—it wasn't the same one you knew?"

"How can I possibly know? But they're evidently a telepathic race; I suspect anything known to one of them is known to others—at least to his intimates, his family—if they have families."

MacAran said. "Perhaps, some day, they'll know we mean them no harm."

Judy smiled faintly and said, "I'm sure they know that you—and I—mean them no harm; but there are some of us they don't know, and I suspect that perhaps time doesn't matter to them as much as it does to us. That's not even so alien, except to us Western Europeans—Orientals even on Earth often made plans and thought in terms of generations instead of months or even years. Possibly he thinks there's time to get to know us any century now."

MacAran chuckled. "Well, we're not going anyplace. I guess there's time enough. Dr. Frazer is in seventh heaven, he's got anthropological notes enough to provide him with a spare-time job for three years. He must have written down everything he saw in the house—I hope they're not offended by his looking at everything. And of course he made notes of everything used as food—if we're anywhere near the same species, anything they can eat we can evidently eat," MacAran added. "We didn't touch his supplies, of course, but Frazer made notes of everything he had. I say he for convenience, Domenick was sure it was a woman who had led us there. Also the one piece of furniture—major furniture—was what looked like a loom, with a web strung on it. There were pods of some sort of vegetable fiber—it looked something like milkweed on Earth—soaking, evidently to prepare them for spinning into thread; we found some pods like it on the way back and turned them over to MacLeod on the farm, they seem to make a very fine cloth."

Judy said, as he rose to go, "You realize there are still plenty of people in the camp who don't even believe there are any alien peoples on this planet."

MacAran met her lost eyes and said very gently, "Does it matter, Judy? We know. Maybe we'll just have to wait, and start thinking in terms of generations, too. Maybe our children will all know."

On the world of the red sun, the summer moved on. The sun climbed daily a little higher in the sky, a solstice was passed, and it began to angle a little lower; Camilla, who had set herself a task of keeping calendar charts, noted that the daily changes in sun and sky indicated that the days, lengthening for their first four months on this world, were shortening again toward the unimaginable winter. The computer, given all the information they had, had predicted days of darkness, mean temperatures in the level of zero centigrade, and virtually constant glacial storms. But she reminded herself that this was only a mathematical projection of probabilities. It had nothing to do with actualities.

There were times, during that second third of her pregnancy, when she wondered at herself. Never before this had it occurred to her to doubt that the severe discipline of mathematics and science, her world since childhood, had any lacunae; or that she would ever come up against any problem, except for strictly personal ones, which these disciplines could not solve. As far as she could tell, the old disciplines still held good for her crewmates. Even the growing evidence of her own increasing ability to read the minds of others, and to look uncannily into the future and make unsettlingly accurate guesses based only on quick flashes of what she had to call "hunch"— even this was laughed at, shrugged aside. Yet she knew that some of the others experienced much the same thing.

It was Harry Leicester—she still secretly thought of him as Captain Leicester—who put it most clearly for her, and when she was with him she could see it almost as he did.

"Hold on to what you *know,* Camilla. That's all you can do; it's known as intellectual integrity. If a thing is impossible, it's *impossible.*"

"And if the impossible happens? Like ESP?"

"Then," he said hardily, "you have somehow misinterpreted your facts, or are making guesses based on subliminal cues. Don't go overboard on this because of your will to believe. Wait for *facts.*"

She asked him quietly, "Just what would you consider evidence?"

He shook his head. "Quite frankly, there is nothing I would consider evidence. If it happened to me, I should simply certify myself as insane and the experience of my senses therefore worthless."

She thought then, *what about the will to disbelieve? And how can you have intellectual integrity when you throw out one whole set of facts as impossible before you even test them?* But she loved the Captain and the old habits held. Some day, perhaps, there would be a showdown, but she hoped, with a quiet desperation, that it would not come soon.

The nightly rain continued, and there were no more of the frightening winds of madness, but the tragic statistics which Ewen Ross had foreseen went on, with a fearful inevitability. Of one hundred and fourteen women, some eighty or ninety should, within five months, have become pregnant; forty-eight actually did so, and of these, twenty-two miscarried within two months. Camilla knew she was going to be one of the lucky ones, and she was; her pregnancy went on so uneventfully that there were times when she completely forgot about it. Judy, too, had an uneventful pregnancy; but the girl from the Hebrides Commune, Alanna, went into labor in the sixth month and gave birth to premature twins who died within seconds of delivery. Camilla had little contact with the girls of the Commune—most of them were working at New Skye, except for the pregnant ones in the hospital—but when she heard that, something went through her that was like pain, and she sought out MacAran that night and stayed with him a long time, clinging to him in a wordless agony she could neither explain nor understand. At last she said, "Rafe, do you know a girl named Fiona?"

"Yes, fairly well; a beautiful redhead in New Skye. But you needn't be jealous, darling, as a matter of fact, I think she's living with Lewis MacLeod just now. Why?"

"You know a lot of people in New Skye. Don't you?"

"Yes, I've been there a lot lately, why? I thought you had them down for disgusting savages," Rafe said, a little defensively, "but they're nice people and I like their way of life. I'm not asking you to join them. I know you wouldn't, and they won't let me in without a woman of my own—they try to keep the sexes balanced, though they don't marry—but they treat me like one of them."

She said with unusual gentleness, "I'm very glad, and I'm certainly not jealous. But I'd like to see Fiona, and I can't explain why. Could you take me to one of their meetings?"

"You don't have to explain," he said, "They're having a concert—oh, informal, but that's what it is—tonight, and anyone who wants to come is welcome. You could even join in, if you felt like singing, I do sometimes. You know some old Spanish songs, don't you? There's a sort of informal project to preserve as much music as we can remember."

"Some other time, I'll be glad to; I'm too short of breath to do much singing now," she said. "Maybe after the baby's born." She clasped his hand, and MacAran felt a wild pang of jealousy. *She knows Fiona's carrying the Captain's child, and she wants to see her. And that's why she isn't jealous, she couldn't care less. . . .*

I'm jealous. But would I want her to lie to me? She does love me, she's having my child, what more do I want?

They heard the music beginning before they reached the new Community Hall at the New Skye farm, and Camilla looked at MacAran in startled dismay. "Good Lord, what's that unholy racket!"

"I forgot you weren't a Scot, darling, don't you like the bagpipes? Moray and Domenick and a couple of others play them, but you don't have to go in until they're finished unless you like," he laughed.

"It sounds worse than a banshee on the loose," Camilla said firmly. "The music isn't all like that, I hope?"

"No, there are harps, guitars, lutes, you name it, they've got it. And building new ones." He squeezed her fingers as the pipes died, and they walked toward the hall. "It's a tradition, That's all. The pipes. And the Highland regalia—the kilts and swords."

Camilla felt, surprisingly, a brief pang almost of envy as they came into the hall, brightly lit with candles and torches; the girls in their brilliant tartan skirts and plaids, the men resplendent in kilts, swords, buckled plaids swaggering over their shoulders. So many of them were bright-haired redheads. *A colorful tradition. They pass it on, and our traditions—die. Oh, come, damn it, what traditions? The annual parade of the Space Academy? Theirs fit, at least, into this strange world.*

Two men. Moray and the tall, redheaded Alastair, were doing a sword dance, leaping nimbly across the gleaming blades to the sound of the piper. For an instant Camilla had a strange vision of gleaming swords, not used in games, but deadly serious, then it flickered out again and she joined in the applause for the dancers.

There were other dances and songs, mostly unfamiliar to Camilla, with a strange, melancholy lilt and a rhythm that made her think of the sea. And the sea, too, ran through many of the words. It was dark in the hall, even by the torchlight, and she did not anywhere see the coppery-haired girl she sought, and after a time she forgot the urgency that had brought her there, listening to the mournful songs of a vanished world of islands and seas;

> O Mhari Oh, Mhari my girl
> Thy sea-blue eyes with witchery
> Draw me to thee, off Mull's wild shore
> My heart is sore, for love of thee. . . .

MacAran's arm tightened around her and she let herself lean against him.

She whispered, "How strange, that on a world without seas, so many sea-songs should be kept alive. . . ."

He murmured, "Give us time. We'll find some seas to sing about—" and broke off, for the song had died, and someone called, "Fiona! Fiona, you sing for us!" Others took up the cry, and after a time the slight red-haired girl, wearing a full green-and-blue skirt which accentuated, almost flaunting, her pregnancy, came through the crowd. She said, in her light sweet voice, "I can't do much singing, I'm short of breath these days. What would you like to hear?"

Someone called out in Gaelic; she smiled and shook her head, then took from another girl a small harp and sat on a wooden bench. Her fingers moved in soft arpeggios for a moment, and then she sang:

> The wind from the island brings songs of our sorrow
> The cry of the gulls and the sighing of streams;
> In all of my dreaming, I'm hearing the waters
> That flow from the hills in the land of our dreams.

Her voice was low and soft, and as she sang Camilla caught the picture of green, low hills, familiar outlines of childhood, memories of an Earth few of them could remember, kept alive only in songs such as this; memories of a time when the hills of Earth were green beneath a golden-yellow sun, and sea-blue skies. . . .

> Blow westward, O sea-wind, and bring us some murmur
> Adrift from our homeland of honor and truth;
> In waking and sleeping, I'm hearing the waters
> That flow from the hills in the land of our youth.

Camilla's throat tightened with half a sob. The lost land, the forgotten . . . for the first time, she made a clear effort to open the eyes of her mind to the special awareness she had known since the first wind. She fixed her eyes and her mind, almost fiercely, with a surge almost of passionate love, on the singing girl; and then she saw, and relaxed.

She won't die. Her child will live.

I couldn't have borne it, for him to be wiped out as if he'd never been . . .

What's wrong with me? He's only a few years older than Moray, there's no reason he shouldn't outlive most of us . . .

but the anguish was there, and the intense relief, as Fiona's song swelled into a close;

> We sing in this far land the songs of our exile,
> The pipes and the harps are as fair as before;
> But never shall music run sweet as the waters
> That flow in that land we shall never see more.

Camilla discovered that she was weeping; but she was not alone. All around her, in the darkened room, the exiles were mourning their lost world; unable to bear it, Camilla rose and blindly made her way toward the door, groping through the crowds. When they saw that she was pregnant they courteously cleared a way for her. MacAran followed, but she took no notice of him; only when they were outside, she turned to him and stood, clinging to him, weeping wildly. But when at last she began to hear his concerned questions, she turned them aside. She did not know how to answer.

Rafe tried to comfort her, but somehow he picked up her disquiet, and for some time he did not know why, until abruptly it came to him.

Overhead the night was clear, with no cloud or sign of rain. Two great moons, lime-green, peacock blue, hung low in the darkening violet sky. And the winds were rising.

Inside the Hall of the New Hebrides Commune, music passed imperceptibly into an almost ecstatic group dance, the growing sense of togetherness, of love and communion binding them together into bonds of closeness which were never to be forgotten or broken. Once, late in the night when the torches were flaring and guttering low, two of the men sprang up, facing one another in a flare-up of violent wrath, swords flickering from their flamboyant Highland regalia, crossing in a clash of steel. Moray, Alastair and Lewis MacLeod, acting like the fingers of a single hand, dived at the two angry men and brought them sprawling down, knocking the swords out of their hands, and sat on them—literally—until the gleam of wolfish anger died in the two. Then, gently freeing them they poured whisky down their throats (*Scots will somehow manage to make whisky at the far ends of the Universe,* Moray thought, *no matter what else they go without*) until the two fighting men embraced one another drunkenly and pledged eternal friendship and the love-feast went on, until the red sun rose, clear and cloudless in the sky.

Judy woke, feeling the stir of the wind like a breath of cold through her very bones, the waking strangeness in her brain and bones. She felt quickly, as if seeking to reassure herself, where her child stirred with a strange strong life. *Yes. It is well with her, but she too feels the winds of madness.*

It was dark in the room where she lay, and she listened to the sounds of distant song. *It is beginning, but this time . . . this time do they know what it is, can they meet it without fear or strangeness?* She herself felt perfect calm, a silence at her center of being. She knew, without surprise, exactly what had brought the madness at first; and knew that for her, at least, madness would not return. There would always, in the season of the winds, be strangeness, and a greater openness and awareness; the latent powers, so long dormant, would always be stronger under the influence of the powerful psychedelic borne on the wind. But she knew, now, how to cope with them, and there would be only the small madness which eases the mind and rests the unquiet brain from stress, leaving it free to cope with further stress another time. She let herself drift on it now, reaching out with her thoughts for a half-felt touch that was like a memory. She felt as if she were spinning, floating on the winds that tossed her thoughts, and briefly her thoughts clasped and linked with the alien (even now she had no name for him, she needed none, they knew each other as a mother knows the face of her child or as twin recognizes twin, they would be together always even if her living eyes never again beheld his face) in a brief, half-ecstatic joining. Brief as the touch was, she needed, desired no more.

She drew out the jewel, his love-gift. It seemed to her to glow in the darkness with its own inner fire, as it had glowed in his hand when he laid it in hers in the forest, echoing the strange silver blue glow of his eyes. *Try to master the jewel.* She focused her eyes and thoughts on it, struggling to know, with that curious inner sight, what was meant.

It was dark in her room, for as the night moved on the moons sank behind the shuttered window and the starlight was dim. The jewel still clasped in her hand, Judy reached for a resin-candle; sleep was far from her. She felt about in the darkness for a light, missed it and heard the small chemical-tipped

splinter fall to the floor. She whispered a small irritable impre-
cation, now she would have to get out of bed and find it. She
stared fiercely at the resin-candle, somehow looking *through*
the jewel in her hand.

Light, damn you.

The resin-candle on its carven stick suddenly flared into
brilliant flame, untouched. Judy, gasping and feeling her heart
pound, quickly snuffed the flame, took her hand away; again
centered all her thoughts on the jewel and the flame and saw
the light flare out again between her fingers.

So this is what they were. . . .

*This could be dangerous. I will hide it until the proper
time comes.* In that moment she knew she had made a discovery which might, one day, step into the gap between the
transplanted knowledge of Earth and the old knowledge of
this strange world, but she also knew that she would not
speak of it for a long time, if ever. *When the time comes and
their minds are strong and ready, then—then perhaps they
can be trusted with it. If I show them now, half of them will
not believe—and the rest will begin to scheme how to use it.*
Not now.

Since the destruction of the starship and his acceptance that
they were marooned on this world (*A lifetime? Forever? Forever for me, at least*) Captain Leicester had had only one hope,
a lifework, something to give reason to his existence and some
glimmer of optimism to his despair.

Moray could structure a society which would tie them to
the soil of this world, rooting like hogs for their daily food.
That was Moray's business; maybe it was necessary for the
time being, to evolve a stable society which could insure survival. But survival didn't matter if it was *only* survival, and
he now realized it could be more. It would some day take
their children back to the stars. He had the computer; and he
had a technically trained crew, and he had a lifetime of
knowledge. For the last three months he had systematically,
piece by piece, stripped the ship of every bit of equipment,
every bit of his own training for a lifetime, and programmed,
with the help of Camilla and three other technicians, everything he knew into it. He had read every surviving textbook
from the library into it, from astronomy to zoology, from
medicine to electronic engineering; he had brought in every

surviving crew member, one by one, and helped them to transfer all their knowledge to the computer. Nothing was too small to program into the computer, from how to build and repair a food synthesizer, to the making and repair of zippers on uniforms.

He thought, in triumph; there's a whole technology here, a whole heritage, preserved entire for our descendants. It won't be in my lifetime, or Moray's, or perhaps in my children's lifetime. But when we grow past the small struggles of day-to-day survival, the knowledge will be there, the heritage. It will be here for now, whether the knowledge for the hospital of how to cure a brain tumor or glaze a cooking-pot for the kitchen; and when Moray runs up against problems in his structured society, as he inevitably will, the answers will be here. The whole history of the world we came from; we can pass by all the blind alleys of society, and go straight to a technology which will take us back to the stars one day—to rejoin the greater community of civilized man, not crawling around on one planet, but spreading like a great branching tree from star to star, universe upon universe.

We can all die, but the thing which made us human will survive—entire—and some day we will go back. Some day we will reclaim it.

He lay and listened to the distant sound of singing from the New Skye hall, in the dome which had become his whole life. Vaguely it occurred to him that he should get up; dress; go over to them, join them. *They had something to preserve too.* He thought of the lovely copper-haired girl he had known so briefly; who, amazingly, bore his child.

She would be glad to see him, and surely he had some responsibility, even though he had fathered the child half-knowing, maddened like a beast in rut—he flinched at the thought. Still she had been gentle and understanding, and he owed her something, some kindness for having used and forgotten her. What was her strange and lovely name? *Fiona?* Gaelic, surely. He rose from his bed, searching quickly for some garments, then hesitated, standing at the door of the dome and looking out at the clear bright sky. The moons had set and the pale false dawn was beginning to glow far to the east, a rainbow light like an aurora, which he supposed was reflected from the faraway glacier he had never seen; would never see; never cared to see.

He sniffed the wind and as he drew it into his lungs a strange, angry suspicion came over him. Last time they had destroyed the ship; this time they would destroy him, and his work. He slammed the dome and locked it; double-locked it with the padlock he had demanded from Moray. This time no one would approach the computer, not even those he trusted most. Not even Patrick. Not even Camilla.

"Lie still, beloved. Look, the moons have set, it will be morning soon," Rafe murmured. "How warm it is, under the stars in the wind. Why are you crying, Camilla?"

She smiled in the darkness. "I'm not crying," she said softly, "I'm thinking that some day we'll find an ocean—and islands—for the songs we heard tonight, and that some day our children will sing them there."

"Have you come to love this world as I do, Camilla?"

"Love? I don't know," she said tranquilly, "it's *our* world. We don't have to love it. We only have to learn to live with it, somehow. Not on our terms but on its own."

All across Base Camp, the minds of the Earthmen flickered into madness, unexplained joy or fear; women wept without knowing why, or laughed in sudden joy they could not explain. Father Valentine, asleep in his isolated shelter, woke and came quietly down the mountain, and unnoticed, came into the Hall in New Skye, mingling with them in love and complete acceptance. When the winds died he would return to solitude, but he knew he would never be wholly alone again.

Heather and Ewen, sharing the night duty in the hospital, watched the red sun rise in the cloudless sky. Arms enlaced, they were shaken out of their silent ecstatic watching of the sky (a thousand ruby sparkles, the brilliant rush of light driving back the darknesses) by a cry behind them; a shrill, moaning wail of pain and terror.

A girl rushed toward them from her bed, panicked at the sudden pain, the gushing blood; Ewen lifted her and laid her down, mustering his strength and calm, trying to focus sanity (*you can get on top of it! Fight! Try!*) but stopped in the very act, arrested by what he saw in her frightened eyes. Heather touched him compassionately.

"No," she said, "no need to try."

"Oh, God, Heather, I can't, not like that, I can't bear it—"

The girl's eyes were wide and terrified. "Can't you help me?" she begged. "Oh, help me, help me—"

Heather knelt and gathered the girl in her arms. "No, darling," she said gently. "No, we can't help you, you're going to die. Don't be afraid, Laura darling, it will be very quick, and we'll be with you. Don't cry, darling, don't cry, there's nothing to be afraid of." She held the girl close in her arms, murmuring to her, comforting her, sensing every bit of fear and trying with the strength of their rapport to soothe her, until the girl lay quiet and peaceful on her shoulder. They held her like that, crying with her, until she stopped breathing; then they laid her gently on the bed, covered her with a sheet, and sorrowfully, hand in hand, walked out into the sunrise and wept for her.

Captain Harry Leicester saw the sun rise, rubbing weary eyes. He had not taken his eyes from the console of the computer, watching over the only hope to save this world from barbarism. Once, shortly before dawn, he had thought he heard Camilla's voice calling to him from the doorway, but it was surely delusion. (*Once she had shared his dream. What had happened?*)

Now, in a strange, uneasy half-doze, half-trance, he watched a procession through his mind of strange creatures, not quite men, lifting strange starships into the red sky of this world, and, centuries later, returning. (*What had they been seeking, in the world beyond the stars? Why had they not found it?*) Could the quest after all be endless or even come full circle and end in its beginning?

But we have something to build on, the history of a world. *Another world. Not this one.*

Are the answers of another world fit for this one?

He told himself furiously that knowledge was knowledge, that knowledge was power, and could save them—

—or *destroy*. After the long struggle to survive, will they not seek old answers, ready-made from the past, and try to re-create the desperate history of Earth, here on a world with a more fragile chain of life? Suppose, one day, they come to believe, as I seemed to believe for a time, that the computer really does have all the answers?

Well, doesn't it?

He rose and went to the doorway of the dome. The shuttered window, made small against the bitter cold, and high, swung wide at his touch and he looked out at the sunrise and the strange sun. *Not mine. But theirs.* Someday they will unlock its secrets.

With my help. My single-handed struggle to keep for them a heritage of true knowledge, a whole technology to take them back to the stars.

He breathed deep, and began to listen silently to the sounds of this world. The winds in the trees and the forests, the running of the streams, the beasts and birds that lived their own strange secret lives deep in the woods, the unknown aliens whom his descendants would one day know.

And they would not be barbarian. They would *know.* If they were tempted to explore some blind alley of knowledge, the answer would be there, ready for their asking, ready with its reply.

(Why did Camilla's voice echo in his mind? *"That only proves that a computer isn't God."*)

Isn't the truth a form of God? he demanded wildly of himself and of the universe. *Ye shall know the truth and the truth shall make you free.*

(Or enslave you? Can one truth hide another?)

Suddenly a horrid vision came into his mind, as his thoughts burst free from time and slid into the future, which lay quivering before him. A race taught to go for all its answers here, to the shrine which had all the *right* answers. A world where no question could ever be left open, for it had *all* the answers, and what lay outside it was not possible to explore.

A barbarian world with the computer worshipped as a God.

A God. A God. A God.

And he was creating that God.

God! Am I insane?

And the answer came, clear and cold. No. I have been insane since the ship crashed, but now I am sane. Moray was right all along. The answers of another world are not the answers we can use here. *The* technology, *the* science, are only a technology and a science for Earth, and if we try to transfer them here, whole, we will destroy this planet. Some day, not as soon as I would wish, but in their own good time, they will evolve a technology rooted in the soil, the stones, the sun, the resources of this world. Perhaps it will take them to the stars, if they want to go. Perhaps it will take them into time or the inner spaces of their own hearts. But it will be theirs, not mine. I am not a God. I cannot make a world in my own image.

He had brought all the supplies of the ship from the bridge to this dome. Now, quietly, he turned and began to fashion what he sought, old words from another world ringing in his mind;

> Endless the world's turn, endless the sun's spinning
> Endless the quest;
> I turn again, back to my own beginning,
> And here, find rest.

With steady hands he lighted a resin-candle and, deliberately, set a light to the long fuse.

Camilla and MacAran heard the explosion and ran toward the dome, just in time to see it erupt skyward in a shower of debris, and rising flame.

Fumbling with the padlock, Harry Leicester began to realize that he wasn't going to get out. This time he wasn't going to make it. Staggering from the blow and concussion, but coldly, gladly sane, he looked at the wreckage. *I've given you a clean start,* he thought confusedly, maybe I am God after all, the one who drove Adam and Eve out of Eden and stopped telling them all the answers, letting them find their own way, and grow . . . no lifelines, no cushions, let them find their own way, live or die. . . .

He hardly knew it when they forced the door open and took him up gently, but he felt Camilla's gentle touch on his dying mind and opened his eyes into the gray compassionate stare.

He whispered in confusion, *"I am a very foolish fond old man. . . ."*

Her tears fell on his face. "Don't try to talk. I know why you did it. We began to do it together, last time, and then . . . oh, Captain, Captain. . . ."

He closed his eyes. "Captain of *what?"* he whispered. And

then, at his last breath, "You can't retire a Captain. You have to shoot him . . . and I shot him. . . ."

And then the red sun went out, forever, and blazed into luminous galaxies of light.

EPILOGUE

Even the struts of the starship were gone, carried away to the hoarded stores of metal; mining would always be slow on this world, and metals scarce for many, many generations. Camilla, from habit, gave the place a glance, but no more, as she went across the valley. She walked lightly, a tall woman, her hair lightly touched with frost, as she followed a half-heard awareness. Beyond the range of vision she saw the tall stone memorial to the crash victims, the graveyard where all the dead of the first terrible winter were buried beside the dead from the first summer and the winds of madness. She drew her fur cloak around her, looking with a regret so long past that it was no longer even sadness, at one of the green mounds.

MacAran, coming down the valley from the mountain road, saw her, wrapped in her furs and her tartan skirt, and raised his hand in greeting. His heart still quickened at the sight of her, after so many years; and when he reached her, he took both her hands for a moment and held them before he spoke.

She said, "The children are well—I visited Mhari this morning. And you, I can tell without asking that you had a good trip." Letting her hand rest in his, they turned back together through the streets of New Skye. Their household was at the very end of the street, where they could see the tall East Peak, beyond which the red sun rose every morning in cloud; at one end, the small building which was the weather station; Camilla's special responsibility.

As they came into the main room of the house they shared with half a dozen other families, MacAran threw off his fur jacket and went to the fire. Like most men in the colony who did not wear kilts, he wore leather breeches and a tunic of woven tartan cloth. "Is everyone else out?"

"Ewen is at the hospital; Judy is at the school; Mac went off with the herding drive," she said, "and if you're dying for a look at the children I think they're all in the schoolyard but Alastair. He's with Heather this morning."

MacAran walked to the window, looking at the pitched roof of the school. How quickly they grew tall, he thought, and how lightly fourteen years of childbearing lay on their mother's shoulders. The seven who had survived the terrible famine winter five years ago were growing up. Somehow they had weathered, together, the early storms of this world; and although she had had children by Ewen, by Lewis MacLeod, by another whose name he had never known and he suspected Camilla herself did not know, her two oldest children and her two youngest were his. The last, Mhari, did not live with them; Heather had lost a child three days before Mhari's birth and Camilla, who had never cared to nurse her own children if there was a wet-nurse available, had given her to Heather to nurse; when Heather was unwilling to give her up after she was weaned, Camilla had agreed to let Heather keep her, although she visited her almost every day. Heather was one of the unlucky ones; she had borne seven children but only one had lived more than a month after birth. Ties of fosterage in the community were stronger than blood; a child's mother was only the one who cared for it, its father the one who taught it. MacAran had children by three other women, and cared for them all equally, but he loved best Judy's strange young Lori, taller than Judy at fourteen and yet childlike and peculiar, called a changeling by half the community, her unknown father still a secret to all but a few.

Camilla said, "Now you're back, when are you off again?"

He slid an arm around her. "I'll have a few days at home first, and then—we're off to find the sea. There must be one, somewhere on this world. But first—I have something for you. We explored a cave, a few days ago—and found these, in the rock. We don't have much use for jewels, I know, it's really a waste of time to dig them out, but Alastair and I liked the looks of these, so we brought some home to you and the girls. I had a sort of feeling about them."

From his pocket he took a handful of blue stones, pouring them into her hands, looking at the surprise and pleasure in her eyes. Then the children came running in, and MacAran found himself swamped in childish kisses, hugs, questions, demands.

"Da, can I go to the mountains with you next time? Harry goes and he's only fourteen!"

"Da, Alanna took my cakes, make her give them back!"

"Dada, Dada, look here, look here! See me climb!"

Camilla, as always, ignored the hullabaloo, calmly gesturing them to quiet. "One question at a time—what is it, Lori?"

The silver-haired child with grey eyes picked up one of the blue stones, looking at the starlike patterns coiled within. She said gravely, "My mother has one like this. May I have one, too? I think perhaps I can work it as she does."

MacAran said, "You may have one," and over her head looked at Camilla. Some day, in Lori's own time, they would know exactly what she meant, for their strange fosterling never did anything without reason.

"You know," Camilla said, "I think some day these are going to be very, very important to all of us."

MacAran nodded. Her intuition had been proven right so many times that now he expected it; but he could wait. He walked to the window and looked up at the high, familiar skyline of the mountains, daydreaming beyond them to the plains, the hills, and the unknown seas. A pale blue moon, like the stone into which Lori still stared, entranced, floated up quietly over the rim of the clouds around the mountain; and very gently, rain began to fall.

"Some day," he said, offhand, "I suppose someone will give those moons—and this world—a name."

"Some day," Camilla said, "but we'll never know."

A century later they named the planet DARKOVER. But Earth knew nothing of them for two thousand years.

TWO TO CONQUER

PROLOGUE: *THE ALIEN*

Paul Harrell woke, blurred and semi-conscious, with a sense of having survived nightmares for a long time. Every muscle in his body ached like a separate toothache, and his head felt as if he had a truly monumental hangover. Blurred memories, vague, a man with his face, his own voice asking, *Who the hell are you, you're not the devil, by any chance?* Not that he believed in the devil, or hell, or any of those things invented to try to force men to do what other people thought they should do instead of what they wanted to do.

He moved his head, and the pain in it made him wince. *Whew! I really must have tied one on last night!*

He stretched, trying to turn over, and found that he was lying, his legs flung out at ease, comfortably stretched out. That brought him wide awake, in shock.

He could move, stretch; *he wasn't in the stasis box!*

Had it all been a nightmare, then? The flight from the Alpha police, the rebellion he had led in the colony, the final confrontation, with his men shot down around him, the capture and the trial, and finally the horror of the stasis box closing around him forever.

Forever. That had been his last thought. Forever.

Painless, of course. Even pleasant, like going to sleep when you were completely exhausted. But he had struggled and fought for that last instant of consciousness, knowing that it *would* be the last; he would never waken.

Humane governments had abolished the death penalty long ago. Too often, new evidence, a few years after the prisoner was executed, had proved him innocent. Death made the mistake irrevocable, and embarrassed the whole judicial system. The stasis box kept the prisoner safely removed from society . . . but he could always be reprieved and recalled to life. And no prisons, no traumatic memories of association with hardened criminals, no prison riots, no need for counseling, recreation, rehabilitation. Just stick them away in a stasis box and let them age there, naturally, and finally die, unconscious, lifeless . . . unless they were proved innocent. Then you could take them out.

But, Paul Harrell thought, they couldn't prove him innocent. He was guilty as hell, and furthermore, he'd admitted it, and tried as hard as he could to be shot down before capture. What was more, he made sure he took about ten of the damn cops with him, so they couldn't legally grant him the option of Rehab.

The rest of his men, the ones they didn't shoot down, went meekly down to Rehabilitation like so many sheep, to be made over into the conformist nothings which are all they want in this stupid world. Pussycats. Gutless wonders. And right up to the end, he could see that the judge and all his legal advisers were hoping he'd break down and beg for executive clemency— a chance for Rehab, so they could tinker with his brain, with drugs and re-education and brainwashing, so they could make him over into a nobody, to march along in lockstep just like everybody else through what they call life. *But not me, thanks. I wouldn't play their damned game. When I finished my run, I was ready to go, and I went.*

And it had been a good life while it lasted, he thought. He'd made hash of their stupid laws because for years they couldn't even imagine that anyone would break laws except through accident or ignorance! He'd had all the women he wanted, and all the high living.

Especially women. He didn't play the stupid games women tried to make men play. He was a man, and if they wanted a man instead of a sheep, they learned right away that Paul Harrell didn't play by their conformist, ball-less rules.

That damned woman who led the police down on me.

Her mother had probably taught her that you had to make noises about rape, unless the man got down on his knees and pretended to be a capon, a gutless wonder who'd let a woman lead him around by the nose and never touch her unless she *said* she wanted it! Hell, he knew better than that. That was what women wanted and they loved it, when you gave it to them and didn't take no for an answer! Well, she found out; he didn't play their games, even with the stasis box hanging over him! She probably thought he'd go and whine for a chance at Rehab, and they'd make him over into a pussycat she could lead around by the balls!

Well, the hell with her, she'll wake up nights all the rest of her life, remembering that for once she had a real man. . . .

And when he had gotten this far in his memories Paul Harrell sat up and stared. He wasn't in the stasis box, but he wasn't anywhere else he could remember being, either. Had it all been a nightmare, then, the girl, the rebellion, the shoot-out with the police, the judge, trial, the stasis box. . . .

Had he ever been there at all, had any of it ever happened?

And if so, what had gotten him out?

He was lying on a soft mattress, covered with clean coarse linens, and over them, thick wool blankets and quilts and a fur cover. All around him was a very faint, dim, reddish light. He reached out and found that the light was coming through heavy bed-curtains; that he was in a high curtained bed such as he'd seen somewhere once in a museum, and that curtains around the bed were closing out the light. Red curtains.

He thrust them aside. He was in a room he had never seen before. Not only had he never seen the room before, he had never seen anything remotely like it before.

One thing was for damn sure. He wasn't in the stasis box, unless part of the punishment was a series of bizarre dreams. Nor was he anywhere in the Rehab center. In fact, he thought, glancing out the high arched window at a huge red sun beyond, he wasn't on Alpha at all, nor on Terra, nor on any of the planets of the Confederated Worlds that he had ever visited before.

Maybe this was Valhalla, or something. There were old legends about a perfect place for warriors who met a hero's end. And he had certainly gone down fighting; at his trial, they said he had killed eight policemen and crippled another for life. He'd gone out like a man, not a brainwashed conformist; he hadn't cringed and whimpered and begged for a chance to crawl around on his knees a while longer in a world with no respect for anyone who'd rather die on his feet!

Anyway, he was out of the box, that was a good place to start. But he was naked, just the way he'd gone into the box. His hair was still clipped short, as when he'd gone into the box . . . no. They'd shaved it then, so he'd been in there a month or two, anyhow, because he could feel the thick soft nap of it. He looked at the room around him. The room had a stone floor with a few thick fur and skin rugs. There was no furniture except the bed and a heavy chest carved richly of some dark wood.

And now, through the pain that still pounded in his head, he remembered something else; flaring pain, blue lightnings around him, a circle of faces, falling as if from a great height—pain, and then a man. A man with his own face, and his own voice asking, *Who are you? You're not the devil, by any chance?* Old legends. If you met a man with your own face, your double, your *doppelganger,* your fetch, it was either the devil or a warning of death. But he had died, for all practical purposes, when they put him into the stasis box, so what more could anyone do to him? Anyway, that had been a dream. Hadn't it? Or, when he went into the box, had they cloned him and brainwashed the clone into being the good respectable, conformist citizen they'd always wanted *him* to be?

Somehow, something had brought him here. But who, and when, and how? And above all, why?

And then the door opened, and the man with his face came in.

Not a close resemblance, as of brothers or twins. *Himself.*

Like himself, the man had blond hair; only on the strange man, it was thick and long and twisted into a tight braid, wrapped with a red cord. Paul had never known a man who wore his hair that way.

He had never seen a man dressed as the man with his face was dressed, either, in garments of heavy wool and leather; a laced leather jerkin, a thick tunic under it of unbleached wool, leather breeches, high boots. Now that Paul was part way out from under the covers, he realized it was cold enough in the room for that kind of clothing to make sense; and now, through the windows, he saw that snow lay thickly on the ground. Well, he already knew he wasn't on Alpha; if he'd had any doubts, the faint purple shadows on the snow, and the great red sun, would have told him.

But beyond all that, the man with his face. Not just a close resemblance. Not a likeness which would fade at close range. Not even the image he would have seen in a mirror, reversed, but the face he had seen, watching taped video of himself, at his trial.

A clone, if anyone except rich eccentrics could have afforded such a thing. An absolute, identical replica of himself, down to the cleft chin and the small brown birthmark on his left thumb. *What the hell was going on here?*

He demanded, "Who the hell are you?"

The man in the leather jerkin said, "I was coming here to ask the same question of you."

Paul heard the strangeness of the syllables. They sounded a little like Old Spanish—a language of which Paul knew only a few words. But he could clearly understand the stranger's meaning, and that frightened him worse than anything else that had happened yet. They were reading each other's thoughts.

"Hell," he blurted out. "You're *me!*"

"Not quite," said the other man, "but near enough. And that is why we brought you here."

"Here," Paul said, fastening on that. "Where is *here?* What world is this? What sun is that? And how did I get here? And who are you?"

The man shook his head, and again Paul had the eerie sense that he was watching himself.

"The sun is the sun," he said, "and we are in what they call the Hundred Kingdoms; this is the Kingdom of Asturias. As for what world this is, it is called Darkover, and it is the only world I know. When I was a boy they told me some fable about the other stars being suns like our own, with a million million other worlds circling them like ours, and perhaps men like ours on them, but I always thought that was a story to frighten babes and girl children! But I have seen stranger things, and heard stranger things than that, in the last night. My father's sorcery brought you here, and if you wish to know why, you must ask him. But we mean you no harm."

Paul hardly heard the explanation. He was staring at the man with his face, his body, his own hands, and trying to understand what he felt about the man.

His brother. Himself. He'd understand me. Those thoughts flickered through his mind. And at the same time, crowding them, a sudden raging anger: *How does he dare to go around wearing my face?* And then, in total confusion, *if he's me, who in hell am I?*

And the other man spoke his question aloud. "If you are me," he said, and his fists clenched, "then who am I?"

Paul said, with a harsh half-laugh, "Maybe you're the devil after all. What's your name?"

"Bard," said the man, "but they call me *Wolf*. Bard di Asturien, the Kilghard Wolf. And you?"

"My name is Paul Harrell," he said, and swayed. Was this all a bizarre dream of the stasis box? Had he died and wound up in Valhalla?

None of it made sense to him. None at all.

Seven Years Earlier . . .

BOOK ONE

The Foster Brothers

CHAPTER ONE

Light blazed from every window and embrasure of Castle Asturias; on this night King Ardrin of Asturias held high festival, for he was handfasting his daughter Carlina to his foster son and nephew, Bard di Asturien, son of his brother, Dom Rafael of High Fens. Most of the nobles of Asturias, and a few from the neighboring kingdoms, had come to do honor to the handfasting and to the king's daughter, and the courtyard was ablaze with brilliance; strange horses and riding beasts to be stabled, nobles richly dressed, commoners crowding in to spy what they could from outside the gates and accept the dole of food and wine and sweets given out from the kitchens to all comers, servants running here or there on real or invented errands.

High in the secluded chambers of the women, Carlina di Asturien looked with distaste on the embroidered veils and the blue velvet over-gown, set with pearls from Temora, that she would wear for the handfasting ceremony. She was fourteen years old; a slender, pale, young woman, with long dark braids looped below her ears, and wide gray eyes which were the only good feature in a face too thin and thoughtful for beauty. Her face was reddened around the eyelids; she had been crying for a long time.

"Come, now, come, now," her nurse, Ysabet, urged. "You mustn't cry like this, *chiya*. Look at the pretty gown, you will never have one so fine again. And Bard is so handsome and brave; just think, your father made him banner bearer on the field for bravery in the battle of Snow Glen. And, after all, dear child, it is not as if you would be marrying a stranger; Bard is your foster brother, reared here in the king's house since he was ten years old. Why, when you were children, you were always playing together, I thought you loved him well!"

"And so I do—as a brother," Carlina said in a whisper. "But to marry Bard—no, Nurse, I don't want to. I don't want to marry at all—"

"Now that is folly," said the older woman, clucking, and she held up the pearl-broidered overdress to help her nursling into it. Carlina submitted like a doll being dressed, knowing that resistance would do her no good.

"Why don't you want to marry Bard, then? He is handsome, and brave—how many young men have distinguished themselves before reaching their sixteenth year?" Ysabet demanded. "One day, I have no doubt, he will be general of all your father's armies! You are not holding it against him that he is *nedestro,* are you? The poor lad did not choose to be born to one of his father's fancy-women instead of to his lawful wife!"

Carlina smiled faintly at the thought of anyone calling Bard "poor lad."

Her nurse pinched her cheek. She said, "Now, that is the right way to go to your handfasting, with a smile! Let me do up these laces properly." She tugged at the lacings, then tucked in the ribbons. "Sit here, my pretty, while I do up your sandals. Look how dainty, your mother had them made to match the gown, blue leather with pearls! How pretty you are, Carlie, like a blue flower! Let me fasten the ribbons here in your hair. I do not think there is a prettier bride anywhere in nine kingdoms this night! And Bard handsome enough, surely, to be worthy of you, so fair where you are so dark. . . ."

"What a pity," Carlina said dryly, "that he cannot marry you, Nurse, since you like him so much."

"Oh, come now, he wouldn't want me, old and withered as I am," said Ysabet, bridling. "A handsome young warrior like Bard must have a young and beautiful bride, and so your father has ordained it . . . I cannot imagine why the wedding is not on this night as well, and the bedding too!"

"Because," Carlina said, "I begged my mother, and she spoke for me to my father and my lord; and he consented that I should not be married until I had completed my fifteenth year. The wedding will be a year from tonight, at Midsummer Festival."

"How can you bear to wait so long? Evanda bless you, child, if I had a handsome young lover like Bard, I could not wait so long. . . ." She saw Carlina flinch and spoke more gently. "Are you afraid of the marriage bed, child? No woman ever died of it, and I have no doubt you will find it pleasurable; but it will be less frightening to you at first, since your husband is playfellow and foster brother as well."

Carlina shook her head. "No, it is not *that,* Nurse, though, as I told you, I have no mind to marriage; I would rather spend my life in chastity and good works among the priestesses of Avarra."

"Heavens protect us!" The woman made a shocked gesture. "Your father would never allow it!"

"I know that, Nurse. The Goddess knows, I besought him to spare me this marriage and let me go, but he reminded me that I was a princess and that it was my duty to marry, to bring strong powerful alliances to his throne. As my sister Amalie has already been sent to wed with King Lorill of Scathfell. Beyond the Kadarin, poor girl, alone in those northern mountains, and my sister Marilla married south to Dalereuth. . . ."

"Are you angry that they were wedded to princes and kings, and you, only, to your father's brother's bastard son?"

Carlina shook her head. "No, no," she said impatiently. "I know what is in father's mind; he wishes to bind Bard to him with a strong tic, so that one day Bard will be his strongest champion and protector. There was no thought for me, or for Bard; it is only one of my father's maneuvers to protect the throne and the kingdom!"

"Well," said the nurse, "most marriages are made for reasons less worthy than that."

"But it is not necessary," Carlina said, impatiently. "Bard would be content with any woman, and my father could have found some woman of noble rank who would satisfy Bard's ambition! Why should I be forced to spend my life with a man who does not care whether it is me, Carlina, or another, provided she is high-born enough to satisfy his ambition, and has a pretty face and a willing body! Avarra have mercy, do you think I do not know that every servant girl in the castle has shared his bed? They brag of it after!"

"As for that," said Ysabet, "he is no better and no worse than any of your brothers or foster brothers. You cannot blame a young man for wenching, and at least you know from their bragging that he is neither maimed nor a lover of men! When he is wedded to you, you must simply give him enough to do in your bed to keep him out of others!"

Carlina gestured displeasure at the vulgarity. "They are welcome to Bard and to his bed," she said, "and I will not dispute their place there. But I have heard worse, that he will not hear a refusal; that if a girl answers him *no,* or if he has reason to think she might give him a *no,* his pride is so great that he will put a compulsion on her, a glamour, so that she cannot refuse, but will go to his bed will-less, without the power to help herself—"

"I have heard of men who have that *laran,*" Ysabet grinned. "It is a useful thing, even if a young man is handsome and hearty; but I never put much stock in such tales of spellbinding. What young woman needs to be spelled to go to a young man's bed? No doubt they use that old tale to excuse themselves if they are found big-bellied out of season—"

"No, Nurse," Carlina said. "At least once, I know, it is true, for my own maid Lisarda, she is a good girl, and she told me that she could not help herself—"

Ysabet said with a coarse laugh, "Any slut says afterward that she could not help herself!"

"But no," Carlina interrupted angrily, "Lisarda is scarce twelve years old; she is motherless and hardly knew what he wanted of her, only that she could not choose but to do as he would. Poor child, she was hardly come into womanhood, and she cried, after, in my arms, and I was hard put to it to explain why a man could want a woman *that* way—"

Ysabet frowned. She said, "I wondered what had happened to Lisarda—"

"I find it hard to forgive Bard, that he could do that to a young girl who had never harmed him!" Carlina said, still angry.

"Well, well," said the nurse, sighing, "men do such things now and again, and women are expected to accept them."

"I don't see why!"

"It is the way of the world," Ysabet said, then started, and looked at the timepiece on the wall. "Come, Carlina, my pet, you must not be late to your own handfasting!"

Carlina rose, sighing with resignation, as her mother, Queen Ariel, came into her chamber,

"Are you ready, my daughter?" The queen surveyed the young woman from head to foot, from the braids looped under her ears to the delicate blue slippers embroidered with pearls. "There will be no prettier bride, at least, in the Hundred Kingdoms. You have done well, Ysabet."

The old woman bent in a curtsy, acknowledging the compliment.

"You need just a touch of powder on your face, Carlie, your eyes are red," said the lady. "Bring the puff, Ysabet. Carlina, have you been crying?"

Carlina lowered her head and did not answer.

Her mother said firmly, "It is unseemly for a bride to shed tears, and this is only your handfasting." With her own hands she dabbed with the powder puff at her daughter's eyelids. "There. Now a touch of the crayon there, at the brow—" she said, pointing for Ysabet to repair the makeup. "Lovely. Come, my dear, my women are waiting. . . ."

There was a small chorus of cooing noises and admiration as Carlina in her bridal finery joined the women. Ariel, Queen of Asturias, attended by her ladies, held out her hand to Carlina.

"Tonight you will sit among my ladies, and when your father calls for you, you will go forward and join Bard before the throne," she began.

Carlina looked at her mother's serene face and contemplated a final appeal. She knew that her mother did not like Bard—although for the wrong reasons; she simply objected to his bastard status. She had never liked it, that he should be foster brother to Carlina and Beltran. However, it was not her mother who had made this marriage, but her father. And she knew that King Ardrin was not accustomed to listening overmuch to what his womenfolk wanted. Her mother had won this one concession, that she should not be married until she was full fifteen years old.

When they call me forth to be handfasted I will scream and refuse to speak, I will cry out No when they ask me to consent, I will run out of the room. . . . But in her heart Carlina knew that she would not do any of these disgraceful things, but would go through the ceremony with the decorum befitting a princess of Asturias.

Bard is a soldier, she thought despairing, perhaps he will die in battle before the wedding; and then she felt guilty, for there had been a time when she had loved her playmate and foster brother. Quickly she amended her thoughts: perhaps he will find some other woman he wishes to wed, perhaps my father will change his mind. . . .

Avarra, merciful Goddess, Great Mother, pity me, spare me this marriage somehow. . . .

Angry, despairing, she blinked back the tears that threatened to flood her eyes again. Her mother would be angry if she disgraced them all this way.

In a lower room in the castle, Bard di Asturien, foster son to the king, and his banner bearer, was being dressed for his handfasting by his two comrades and foster brothers: Beltran, the king's son, and Geremy Hastur, who, like Bard, had been reared in the king's house, but was a younger son of the Lord of Carcosa.

The three youths were very different. Bard was tall and heavily built, already a man's height, with thick blond hair twisted into the warrior's braid at the back of his head, and the strong arms and heavy thews of a swordsman and rider; he towered like a young giant over the others. Prince Beltran was tall, too, although not quite as tall as Bard; but he was still thin and coltish, bony with a boy's roundness, and his cheeks still fuzzed with a boy's first traces of beard. His hair was cropped short and tightly curled, but as blond as Bard's own.

Geremy Hastur was smaller than either, red-haired and thin-faced, with sharp gray eyes and the quickness of a hawk or ferret. He wore dark, plain clothing, the dress of a scholar rather than a warrior, and his manner was quiet and unassuming.

Now he looked up at Bard, laughing, and said, "You will have to sit down, foster brother; neither Beltran nor I can reach your head to tie the red cord about your braid! And you cannot go to a ceremonial occasion without it!"

"No indeed," Beltran said, hauling Bard down into a seat. "Here, Geremy, you tie it, your hands are defter than mine, or Bard's. I remember last autumn when you stitched that guardsman's wound—"

Bard chuckled as he bent his head for his young friends to tie on the red cord which signified a warrior tried in battle and commended for bravery. He said, "I always thought you were cowardly, Geremy, that you did not fight in the field, and your hands as soft as Carlina's; yet when I saw that, I decided you had more courage than I, for I wouldn't have done it. I think it a pity there is no red cord for you!"

Geremy said, in his muted voice, "Why, then, we should have to give a red cord to every woman in childbirth, or every messenger who slips unseen through the enemy's lines. Courage takes many forms. I can do without warrior's braid or red cord, I think."

"Perhaps, one day," Beltran said, "when the day comes when I rule over this land—may my father's reign be long!—perhaps we may reward courage in some other form than that we see on the battlefield. What about it, Bard? You will be my champion then, if we all live so long." He frowned suddenly at Geremy and said, "What ails you, man?"

Geremy Hastur shook his red head. He said, "I do not know—a sudden chill; perhaps, as they say in the hills, some wild animal pissed on the ground which will be my grave." He finished twisting the red cord around Bard's warrior braid, handed him sword and dagger and helped him to bind them on.

Bard said, "I am a soldier; I know very little of other kinds of courage." He shrugged his ceremonially embroidered cape into place, bright red to match the red cord twisted into the braid all along its length. "I tell you, it demands more courage to face this nonsense tonight; I prefer to face my enemies sword in hand!"

"What's this talk of enemies, foster brother?" Beltran asked, surveying his friend. "You surely have no enemies in my father's hall! Why, how many young men your age have been given a warrior's cord, and made the king's banner bearer on the field of war, before they were full sixteen years old? And when you killed Dom Ruyven of Serrais and his paxman, twice saving the king's life at Snow Glen—"

Bard shook his head. "The Lady Ariel does not love me. She would stop this marriage to Carlina if she could. And she is angry because it was I, and not you, who won renown on the battlefield, Beltran."

Beltran shook his head. "Perhaps it is simply the way of a mother," he hazarded. "It is not enough for her that I am prince, and heir to my father's throne, I must have renown as a warrior too. Or perhaps—" he tried to make a joke of it, but Bard could tell that there was bitterness, too—"she fears that your courage and renown will cause my father to think better of you than he does of his son."

Bard said, "Well, Beltran, you had the same teaching as I; you too could have won a warrior's decorations. It is the fortune of war, I suppose, or the luck of the battlefield."

"No," Beltran said. "I am not a warrior born, and I have not your gift for it. It is all I can do to acquit myself honorably and keep my skin in one piece by killing anyone who wants to have a swing at it."

Bard laughed and said, "Well, believe me, Beltran, that is all I do."

But Beltran shook his bead gloomily. "Some men are warriors born, and others are warriors made; I am neither."

Geremy broke in, trying to lighten the tone, "But you need not be a great warrior, Beltran; you must prepare yourself to rule Asturias one day, and then you can have as many warriors as you like, and if they serve you well, it will not matter whether or not you know which end of a sword to take hold by! You will be the one who rules all your warriors, and all your sorcerers, too. . . . Will you have me, on that day, to serve you as *laranzu?*" He used the old word for *sorcerer, wizard,* and Beltran grinned and clapped him on the shoulder.

"So I will have a wizard and a warrior for foster brothers, and we three will rule Asturias together against all its enemies, battle and sorcery both! But may that day, be the gods merciful to us, be long in coming. Geremy, send your page to the courtyard again to see if Bard's father has come to see the handfasting of his son."

Geremy started to signal to the youngster who waited to run their errands, but Bard shook his head.

"Save the child trouble." His jaw tightened. "He will not come, and there is no need to pretend that he will, Geremy."

"Not even to see you married to his king's own daughter?"

"Perhaps he will come for the wedding, if the king makes it clear that he will be offended if he does not," Bard said, "but not for a mere handfasting."

"But the handfasting is the true binding," Be!tran said. "From the moment of the handfasting, you are Carlina's lawful husband and she cannot take another while you live! It is only that my mother thinks her too young for bedding, so that part of the ceremony is delayed for another year. But Carlina is your wife; and you, Bard, are my brother."

He said it with a shy smile, and Bard, for all his calm façade, was touched. He said, "That's probably the best part of it."

Geremy said, "But I am astonished that Dom Rafael should not come to see your handfasting! Surely he has been sent word that you were decorated on the field for bravery, made the king's banner bearer, killed Dom Ruyven and his paxman at a single blow—if my father heard such things of me, he would be beside himself with pride and pleasure!"

"Oh, I have no doubt Father is proud of me," Bard said, and his face twisted into a bitterness strange in one so young. "But he listens in all things to the Lady Jerana, his lawful wife; and she has never forgotten that he forsook her bed when she was childless for twelve years of their marriage; nor did she ever forgive my mother for giving him a son. And she was angry because my father brought me up in his own house, and had me schooled in arms and the ways of a court instead of having me nursed and fostered to follow the plow or scratch the fields farming mushrooms!"

Beltran said, "She should have been glad that someone had given her husband a son when she could not."

Bard shrugged. "That is not the Lady Jerana's way! Instead she surrounded herself with *leroni* and sorceresses— half her ladies-in-waiting have red hair and are trained witches—until sooner or later one of them could give her a spell to cure her barrenness. Then she bore my baby brother, Alaric. And then, when my father could deny her nothing because she had given him a legitimate son and heir, she set herself to get rid of me. Oh, Jerana could not show enough kindness to me, until she had her own son; she pretended she was a true mother to me, but I could see the blow held back behind every false kiss she gave me! I think, she feared I would stand in her own son's light, because Alaric was little and sickly and I was strong and well, and she hated me worse than ever because Alaric loved me."

"I would have thought," Beltran said again, "that she would welcome a strong brother and guardian for her son, one who could care for him. . . ."

"I love my brother," Bard said. "There are times when I think there is no one else in the world to whom it would matter whether I lived or died; but since Alaric was old enough to know one face from another, he smiled at me, and held up his little arms for me to carry him piggyback and begged for rides on my horse. But for Lady Jerana it was not seemly that a bastard half-brother should be *her* little princelet's chosen paxman and playmate; *she* would have princes' and noble-men's sons for her child's companions! And so a time came when I saw him only by guile; and once I angered her when he was sick, because I sneaked without permission into his precious nursery. A child of four, and she was angry because his brother could sing him to sleep and he would not sleep for *her* coaxing." His face was hard, bitter, closed away into memory.

"And after that, she gave my father no peace until he sent me away. And instead of bidding her be silent, and ruling his own house, as a man should do, he chose to have peace in his bed and at his fireside by sending me away from home and brother!"

Beltran and Geremy were, momentarily, silenced by his bit-terness. Then Geremy patted his arm and said, with a half-embarrassed tenderness, "Well, you have two brothers to stand at your side tonight, Bard, and soon you will have kin here."

Bard's smile was bleak, unforgiving. "Queen Ariel loves me no more than my stepmother. I am sure she will find some way to turn Carlina against me, and perhaps both of you. I do not blame my father, except for listening to a woman's words; Zandru twist my feet if I ever listen to what a woman says!"

Beltran laughed and said, "One would not think you a woman-hater, Bard. From what the maids say, quite the re-verse—on the day you are bedded with Carlina, there will be weeping all over the kingdom of Asturias!"

"Oh, as for *that*," Bard said, making a deliberate effort to match the mood of merriment, "I listen to women only in one place, and you may guess what that place is. . . ."

"And yet," said Beltran, "when we were young lads and girls all together, I remember that you always listened to Car-lina; you would climb a tree no one else would hazard to fetch down her kitten, and when she and I quarreled, I soon learned I must give way or you would pummel me, taking her part!"

"Oh—Carlina," Bard said, and his bitter face relaxed into a smile. "Carlina is not like other women; I would not speak of her in the same breath as most of the bitches and sluts in this place! When I am wedded to her, believe me, I shall have no leisure for the rest! I assure you, she will have no need to surround herself with spells as Lady Jerana did, to keep me faithful to her. Since first I came here, she has been kind to me—"

"We would all have been kind to you," Beltran protested, "but you would not speak to anyone and threatened to fight us—"

"Still, Carlina made me feel that perhaps, for once, someone cared whether I lived or died," Bard said, "and I would not fight *her*. Now your father has chosen to give her to me—which I never thought I could win, being bastard born. Lady Jerana may have driven me from my home, and from my father, and from my brother, but now, perhaps, I have a home here."

"Even if you must take Carlina with it?" Beltran mocked. "She is not what I would choose for a wife; skinny, dark, plain—I'd as soon bed the stick-poppet they mount in the fields to scare away the crows!"

Bard said genially, "I wouldn't expect her brother to be aware of her beauty, and it's not for her beauty I want her."

Geremy Hastur, who had the red hair and the *laran* gift of the Hastur kin of Carcosa, the gift to read thoughts even without the starstones which the *leroni* or sorceresses used, could sense Bard's thoughts as they went up toward the great hall for the handfasting ceremony.

There are plenty of women in this world for the bedding, Bard thought. But Carlina is different. She is the king's daughter; wedding her, I am no longer bastard and nobody, but the king's banner bearer and champion; I shall have home, family, brothers, children someday . . . for a woman who can bring me all this, I shall be grateful to her all my life; I swear she shall never have cause to reproach her father that he gave her to his brother's bastard. . . .

Surely, Geremy thought, this was enough reason for a marriage. Perhaps he does not want Carlina for herself, but as a symbol of all that she can bring him. Yet marriages are made in the kingdoms every day, with less reason than this. And if he is good to Carlina, surely she will be content.

But he felt disquiet, for he knew that Carlina was afraid of Bard. He had been present when King Ardrin mentioned the marriage to his daughter, and had heard Carlina's shocked cry and seen her weeping.

Well, there was no help for it, the king would have his way, and surely it was right that he should reward his banner bearer, who was also his nephew, though a bastard, with honors and a rich marriage into his household; this would cement Bard to King Ardrin's throne as champion. Perhaps it was a pity for Carlina, but all girls were given in marriage, soon or late, and she might have been married to some elderly lecher, or some grizzled old warrior, or even to some bandit barbarian from one of the little kingdoms across the Kadarin, if her father found it expedient to seal an alliance with another kingdom. Instead he was giving her to a close relative, one who had been her own playmate and foster brother and had championed her in childhood. Carlina would resign herself to it soon enough.

But his sharp eyes spotted the reddened eyelids, even behind the careful touch of powder and paint. He raised his eyes and looked compassionately at Carlina, wishing she knew Bard as well as he did. Perhaps, if she understood her hand-fasted husband, she could lessen his bitterness, make him feel less withdrawn, less outcaste among others. Geremy sighed, thinking of his own exile.

For Geremy Hastur had not come willingly to King Ardrin's court, either. He was the youngest son of King Istvan of Carcosa; and he had been sent, half hostage, half diplomat, to be fostered in King Ardrin's household as a token of friendly relations between the royal house of Asturias and the house of the Hasturs of Carcosa. He would have wished to be his father's counselor, a sorcerer, a *laranzu*—he had known all his life that he had not the makings of a soldier—but his father had found him one son too many and had sent him away as a hostage, as he might have sent a daughter away to marry. At least, Geremy thought, Carlina would not be sent away from her home for this marriage!

The court rose for King Ardrin's entrance. Bard, standing beside Beltran, listening to the crying of the heralds, still found that he was glancing about the crowd to see if, perhaps, his father had come at the last moment, wishing to surprise him; desisted and angrily faced forward. Why should he care? King Ardrin thought more of him than his own father did, the king had decorated him in battle, given him lands and a rich estate, and a warrior's red cord, and the hand of his youngest daughter in marriage. With all this, why should he worry about his father, sitting home and listening to the poison that filthy hag Jerana poured into his ears?

But I wish my brother were here. I wish Alaric could know I am the king's champion and his son-in-law . . . he would be seven, now. . . .

At the appointed time he stepped forward, prompted by Beltran and Geremy. Carlina was standing at the right hand of her father's seat. Bard's ears were ringing, and he hardly heard the king's words.

"Bard mac Fianna, called di Asturien, whom I have made my banner bearer," Ardrin of Asturias said, "we have called you here tonight to handfast you to my youngest daughter, the lady Carlina. Say, Bard, is it your will to enter my household?"

Bard's voice sounded perfectly steady; he wondered at that, because inside he was shaking. He supposed it was like riding into battle, there was something that steadied you when you had to be steady. "My king and my lord, it is my will."

"Then," said Ardrin, taking Bard's hand in one of his, and Carlina's in the other, "I bid you join hands before all this company and exchange your pledge."

Bard felt Carlina's hand in his; very soft, the fingers so slender that they felt boneless. She was icy cold, and did not look at him.

"Carlina," said Ardrin, "do you consent to have this man for your husband?"

She whispered something Bard could not hear. He supposed it was a formal phrase of consent. At least she had not refused.

He bent forward, as ritual demanded, and kissed her trembling lips. She was shaking. Hellfire! Was the girl afraid of him? He smelled the flowery scent of her hair, of some cosmetic that had been dabbed on her face. As he drew back, a corner of her stiff embroidered collar scratched his cheek a little. Well, he thought, he had had enough women; soon enough she would lose her fear in his arms, they always did; even if now she was a dressed-up doll. The thought of Carlina in his bed made him feel dizzy, almost faint. Carlina. His, forever, his princess, his wife. And then no one could ever again call him bastard or outcast. Carlina, his home, his beloved . . . his own. He felt his throat thicken as he whispered the ritual words.

"Before our kin assembled I pledge to wed you, Carlina, and to cherish you forever."

He heard her voice, only a whisper.

"Before . . . kin assembled . . . pledge to wed . . ." but try as he might he could not hear her speak his name.

Damn Queen Ariel and her idiotic plans to rid herself of him! They should have had the wedding and the bedding tonight, so that Carlina could quickly lose her fear of him! He was trembling, thinking of that. He had never wanted any woman this much. He tightened his hand on her fingers trying to reassure her, but felt only her involuntary flinching of pain.

King Ardrin said, "May you be forever one," and he loosed Carlina's hand, reluctantly. Together, they drank from a wine cup held to their lips. It was done; Carlina was his bride. Now it was too late for King Ardrin to change his mind. Bard realized that until this moment he had felt that something would come between him and his good fortune even as they stood together for the handfasting, that his stepmother's malice, or Queen Ariel's, would come between him and Carlina, who meant to him a home, a place, honor . . . *damn all women! All women except Carlina, that is!*

Beltran drew him into a kinsman's embrace and said, "Now you are truly my brother!" and Bard sensed that somehow Beltran had always been jealous of his friendship with Geremy, too; now the tie with Beltran was so strong that Geremy had nothing to equal it. Beltran and Geremy had sworn brotherhood, exchanging daggers, before they were out of childhood. No one, Bard thought with a brief surge of resentment, had ever asked *him* to swear the oath of *bredin*; not him, bastard and outcast. . . . well, that was over, over for his life-time. Now he was the king's son-in-law, Carlina's pledged husband. Brother-in-law, even if not sworn brother, to Prince Beltran. Somehow it seemed to him that he walked taller; catching a glimpse of himself in one of the long mirrors adorning the Great Hall, it seemed that he looked handsome for once, that he was a bigger and somehow a better man than had ever looked into that mirror before.

Later, when the minstrels struck up for dancing, he led Carlina out. The dance broke couples up and recombined them in elaborate twisting measures, brought them together again; as they passed and re-passed in the dance, joining and loosing hands, it seemed to him that Carlina was less reluctant to take his hand. Geremy was dancing with one of the queen's youngest ladies, a red-haired maiden named Ginevra—Bard did not know her other name; she had played with Carlina when they were little girls, then become a waiting-woman. Bard wondered briefly if Ginevra shared Geremy's bed. Probably; what man would spend so much time and trouble on a woman if she would not? Or perhaps Geremy was still trying to persuade her. Well, if so, Geremy was a fool. Bard himself never bothered about high-born maidens, they tended to want too much in the way of flattery and promises of devotion. Nor did he care for the prettier ones; they promised more, he had found, and yielded less. Ginevra was almost plain enough to be properly grateful for masculine attention. But what was he doing, thinking of such things when he had Carlina?

Or rather, he thought sullenly, as he led her toward the buffet for a glass of wine after the hearty dancing, he *didn't* have Carlina, not yet! A year to wait! Damn it, why had her mother done this?

Carlina shook her head as he would have refilled her glass. "No, thank you, I don't really like it, Bard—and I think you have had enough," she said soberly.

He blurted out, "I would rather have a kiss from you than any drink ever brewed!"

Carlina looked up at him in astonishment; then her red mouth crinkled in a small smile. "Why, Bard, I have never heard you make a pretty speech before! Can it be that you have been taking lessons in gallantry from our cousin Geremy?"

Bard said, abashed, "I don't know any pretty speeches. I'm sorry, Carlina, do you want me to learn the art of flattering you? I've never had time for such things." And the unspoken part of that, with resentment, *Geremy has nothing else to do but sit home and learn to say pretty things to women,* was perfectly audible to Carlina.

Suddenly she thought of Bard as he had been when first he came to be fostered there, three years ago, and he had seemed to her a great countrified sullen lout, refusing to use the manners he had, sulking, refusing to join in their games and play. Even then, he had been taller than any of them, taller than most men, and more broadly built. He had little interest in anything but the arms-play of their lessons, and had spent his playtime listening to the guardsmen tell tales of campaigns and war. None of them had liked him much, but Geremy said he was lonely, and had gone to some trouble to try to coax him into joining their games.

She felt, suddenly, almost sorry for the boy to whom she had been pledged. She did not want to marry him; but he had not been consulted either, and no man could be expected to refuse marriage to a king's daughter. He had spent so much of his life in war and preparation for war; it was not his fault that he was not gallant and a courtier like Geremy. She would rather have married Geremy—although, as she had told her nurse, she would rather not marry at all. Not because she had any great fondness for Geremy; simply that he was a gentler boy and she felt she understood him better. But Bard looked so unhappy.

She said, drinking the last unwanted drops in her glass, "Shall we sit and talk a while? Or would you like to dance again?"

"I'd rather talk," he said. "I'm not very good at dancing, or any of those courtly arts!"

Again she smiled at him, showing her dimples. She said, "If you are light enough on your feet to be a swordsman—and Beltran tells me you are unequalled—then you should be a fine dancer too. And remember, we used to dance together at lessons when we were children; would you have me believe you have forgotten how to dance since you were twelve years old?"

"To tell you the truth, Carlina," Bard said hesitantly, "I got my man's growth so young, when the rest of you were all so little. And, big as my body was, I felt always that my feet were bigger still, and that I was a great hulking brute! When I came to ride to war, and to fight, then my size and weight gave me the advantage . . . but I find it hard to think of myself as a courtier."

Something in this confession touched her beyond endurance. She suspected he had never said anything like this to anyone before, or even thought it. She said, "You're not clumsy, Bard, I find you a fine dancer. But if it makes you uncomfortable, you need not dance again, at least not with me. We will sit here and talk awhile." She turned, smiling. "You will have to learn to offer me your arm, when we cross a room together. With the help of the Goddess, I may indeed civilize you one day!"

"You have a considerable task on your hands, *damisela*," Bard said, and let the tips of her fingers rest lightly on his arm.

They found a seat together at the edge of the room, out of the way of the dancers, near where some elderly folk were playing at cards and dice. One of the men of the king's household came toward them, evidently intending to claim a dance with Carlina, but Bard glowered at him and he discovered some urgent business elsewhere.

Bard reached out with the hand he thought was clumsy and touched the corner of her temple. "I thought, when we stood before your father, that you had been crying. Carlie, has someone ill-used you?"

She shook her head and said, "No." But Bard was just enough of a telepath—although when the household *leronis* had tested him, at twelve, he had been told he had not much *laran*—to sense that she would not speak the true reason for her tears aloud; and he managed to guess it.

"You are not happy about this marriage," he said, with his formidable scowl, and felt her flinch again as she had done when he squeezed her hand.

She lowered her head. She said at last, "I have no wish to marry; and I wept because no one asks a girl if she wishes to be given in marriage."

Bard frowned, hardly believing what he heard. "What would a woman do, in the name of Avarra, if she was *not* married? Surely you do not wish to stay at home all your days till you are old?"

"I would like to have the choice to do that, if I wished," Carlina said. "Or perhaps to choose for myself whom I would marry. But I would rather not marry at all. I would like to go to a Tower as a *leronis*, perhaps to keep my virginity for the Sight, as some of mother's maidens have done, or perhaps to live among the priestesses of Avarra, on the holy isle, belonging only to the Goddess. Does that seem so strange to you?"

"Yes," Bard said. "I have always heard that every woman's greatest desire is to marry as soon as possible."

"And so it is, for many women, but why should women be any more alike than you and Geremy? You choose to be a soldier, and he to be a *laranzu;* would you say that everyone should choose to be a soldier?"

"It's different with men," Bard said. "Women don't understand these things, Carlie. You need a home and children and someone to love you." He picked up her hand and carried the small soft fingers to his lips.

Carlina felt sudden anger, mingled with a flood almost of pity.

She felt like giving him an angry reply, but he was looking at her so gently, with so much hopefulness, that she forbore to speak what she thought.

He could not be blamed; if there was blame, it was her father's, who had given her to Bard as if she were the red cord he wore about the warrior's braid, a reward for his bravery in battle. Why should she blame him for the customs of the land which made of a woman only a chattel, a pawn for her father's political ambitions?

He followed some of this, his brow knitted as he sat holding her hand. "Do you not want to wed with me at all, Carlie?"

"Oh, Bard—" she said, and he could hear the pain in her voice—"it is not *you.* Truly, truly, my foster brother and my promised husband, since I must marry, there is no other man I would rather have. Perhaps one day—when I am older, when we are both older—then, if the gods are kind to us, we may come to love one another as is seemly for married people." She clasped his big hand in her two small ones, and said, "The gods grant it may be so."

And then someone came up to claim Carlina for a dance; and though Bard glowered again, she said, "Bard, I must; one of the duties of a bride is to dance with all who ask her, as you very well know, and every maiden here who wishes to marry this year thinks it lucky to dance with the groom. Later we can speak together, my dear."

Bard yielded her, reluctantly, and, recalled to his duty, moved about the room, dancing with three or four of Queen Ariel's women, as was suitable for a man attached to the king's household, his banner bearer. But again and again, his eyes sought out Carlina, where her blue robe, pearl-embroidered, and her dark hair, drew his awareness back again.

Carlina. Carlina was *his,* and he realized that he hated, with a violent surge of loathing, every man who touched her. How dare they? What was she about, flirting, raising her eyes to any man who came to dance with her, as if she were some shameless camp follower? Why did she encourage them? Why couldn't she be shy and modest, refusing dances except with her promised husband? He knew this was unreasonable, but it seemed to him that she was trying to win the approval and the flirtatious smile of every man who touched her. He restrained his wrath when she danced with Beltran, and her father, and the grizzled veteran of sixty whose granddaughter had been her foster sister, but every time she danced with some young soldier or guardsman of the king's household, he fancied that Queen Ariel was looking at him triumphantly.

Of course what she had said about not wanting to marry at all—that was girlish nonsense, he didn't believe a word of it. No doubt she was cherishing some girl's passion for some man, someone not really worthy of her, to whom her parents would not give her; and now that she was handfasted, and old enough to dance with men who were not her kinsmen, she could seek him out. Bard knew that if he found Carlina with another man, he would tear the man limb from limb, and Carlina herself he would—would he hurt her? No. He would simply demand of her what she had given the other man, make her so much his that she would never think of any other man alive. He scanned the ranks of guardsmen jealously, but Carlina seemed to pay no more attention to any one than another, dancing courteously with all comers but never accepting a second dance with any.

But no, she was dancing again with Geremy Hastur, a little closer to him than she had been to any other, she was laughing with him, his head was bent over her dark one. Was she sharing confidences, had she told *him* that she did not want to marry Bard? Was it Geremy, perhaps, she wished to marry? After all, Geremy was of the Hastur kin, descended from the legendary sons and daughters of Cassilda, Robardin's daughter . . . kin to the very gods, or so they said. Damn all the Hastura, the di Asturiens were an ancient and noble lineage too, why should she prefer Geremy? Rage and jealousy surging in him, he crossed the floor toward them; he still had enough awareness of good manners to refrain from interrupting their dance, but as the music halted and they stepped apart, laughing, he moved toward them so purposefully that he shoved another couple, without apology.

"It is time again to dance with your promised husband, my lady," he said.

Geremy chuckled. "How impatient you are, Bard, considering that you will have the rest of your lives together," he said, resting an affectionate hand on Bard's elbow. "Well, Carlie, at least you know your promised husband is eager!"

Bard felt the twist of malice in the taunt and said angrily, "My *promised wife*—" he put heavy emphasis on the words, "is *Lady Carlina* to you, not *Carlie!*"

Geremy stared up at him, still not believing he was not making a joke. "It is for my foster sister to tell me when I am no longer welcome to call her by the name I called her when her hair was too short to braid," he said genially. "What has come over you, Bard?"

"The Lady Carlina is pledged as my wife," Bard said stiffly. "You will conduct yourself toward her as is seemly for a married woman."

Carlina opened her mouth in amazement, and shut it again. "Bard," she said with careful patience. "perhaps when we are truly man and wife and not merely a handfasted couple I shall allow you to tell me how I am to conduct myself toward my foster brothers; and perhaps not. At the moment, I shall continue to do exactly as I please in that respect! Apologize to Geremy, or don't presume to show your face again to me tonight!"

Bard stared at her in dismay and anger. Did she intend to make him crawl before this sandal wearer, this *laranzu* wizard? Was she willing to insult her promised husband in public over Geremy Hastur? Was it really Geremy she cared for then?

Geremy stared, too, hardly believing what he was hearing, but King Ardrin was looking in their direction, and there was enough trouble in this household tonight—he sensed it—so that a quarrel would not be wise. Besides, he didn't want to quarrel with his friend and foster brother. Bard was alone here, with no father to stand beside him, and no doubt he was feeling touchy because his closest kin could not be troubled to make half a day's ride to see him honored as the king's champion, and married to the king's daughter, so he tried to ease it over.

"I don't need any apologies from Bard, foster sister," he said. "If I offended him, I'll willingly beg his pardon instead. And there is Ginevra waiting for me. Bard, my good friend, be the first to wish us well; I have asked her for leave to write my father to make arrangements for a handfasting in *that* quarter, and she has not refused me, only said that she must ask leave of *her* father to accept my offer. So if all the old folk are agree-able, I may stand, a year or so from now, where you stand tonight! Or even, if the gods are kind, in the hills of my own country—"

Carlina touched Geremy's arm. "Are you homesick, Geremy?" she asked gently.

"Homesick? Not really, I suppose. I was sent from Carcosa before it could truly be my home," he said. "But sometimes—at sunset—my heart sickens for the lake, and for the towers of Carcosa, rising against the setting sun, and for the frogs that cry there after the sun goes down, the sound that was my first lullaby."

Carlina said gently, "I have never been far from home; but it must be sadness beyond all other sadness. I am a woman and I was brought up to know that whatever happened, I must leave my home someday. . . ."

"And now," said Geremy touching her hand, "the gods have been kind, for your father has given you to a member of his household and you need never leave your home."

She smiled up at him, forgetting Bard, and said, "If one thing could reconcile me to this marriage, I think it would be that."

The words were like salt in a raw wound to Bard, where he stood listening. He broke in sharply, "Go, then, and join Ginevra," and put his hand, not gently, on Carlina's, drawing her away. When they were out of earshot he spun her around roughly to face him.

"So—did you tell Geremy, then, that you did not want to marry me? Have you been babbling this tale to every man you dance with, making a game of me behind my back?"

"Why, no," she said, looking up at him in surprise. "Why should I? I spoke my heart to Geremy because he is my foster brother and Beltran's sworn brother, and I think of him as I would of my own blood kin, born of my father and my mother!"

"And are you sure it is so innocent with him? He comes from the mountain country," Bard said, "where a brother may lie with his sister; and the way he touched you—"

"Bard, that is too ridiculous for words," Carlina said, impa-tiently. "Even if we were wedded and bedded, such jealousy would be unseemly! Are you going to call challenge, when we are wedded, on every man to whom I speak civilly? Must I be afraid to say a pleasant word to my own foster brothers? Will you be jealous next of Beltran, or of Dom Cormel?" He was the veteran of fifty years service with her father and grandfather.

Before her wrathful gaze he lowered his eyes. "I can't help it, Carlina. I am frantic with fear that I would lose you," he said. "It was cruel of your father not to give you to me now, since he had decided on the wedding. I cannot help but think he is making game of me, and that later, before we are bedded, he will give you to someone else he likes better, or who will pay a bigger bride-price, or whose station would make him a more powerful alliance! Why should he give you to his brother's bastard son?"

Before the dismay in his eyes Carlina was flooded with pity. Behind the arrogance of his words, was he so insecure? She reached out to take his hand. "No, Bard, you must not think that. My father loves you well, my promised husband, he has promoted you over the head of my own brother Beltran, he has made you his banner bearer and given you the red cord; how can you think he would play you false that way? But he would have cause to be angry if you made a silly quarrel with Geremy Hastur at our festival! Now promise me you will not be so silly and jealous again, Bard, or I will quarrel with you too!"

"If we were truly wedded and bedded," he said, "I should have no cause for jealousy, for I would know you were mine beyond recall. Carlina," he begged, suddenly, taking up both her hands and covering them with kisses, "the law recognizes that we are man and wife; the law allows us to consummate our marriage whenever we will. Let me have you tonight and I will *know* that you are mine, and be certain of you!"

She couldn't help herself; she shrank away in mortal terror. She had won a respite, and now he made this demand of her, as the price of ending his jealous scenes. She knew that her shrinking was hurting him, but she lowered her eyes and said, "No, Bard. I do not seek to—to pluck fruit from the blossoming tree, nor should you. All things come in their proper time." She felt stupid, prim, as she mouthed the old proverb. "It is unseemly to ask me this at our handfasting!"

"You said you hoped you might come to love me—"

"At the proper time," she said, and knew her voice was shrill.

He retorted, "This *is* the proper time, and you know it! Unless you know something I do not, that your father plans to play me false and give to another, meanwhile binding me to him!"

Carlina swallowed, knowing that he really believed this, and really sorry for him.

He saw her hesitation, sensing her pity, and put his arm around her, but she drew back with such distress that he let her go. He said bitterly, "It's true, then. You do not love me."

"Bard," she begged, "give me time. I promise you, when the time has come, I will not shrink from you then. But I was not . . . not told of this, I was told I should have a year . . . perhaps when I am older—"

"Will it take a year to resign yourself to the horrible fate of sharing my bed?" he asked, with such bitterness that she wished she did not feel this dreadful reluctance.

"Perhaps," she said, faltering, "when I am older, I will not feel this way—my mother says I am too young for wedding or for bedding, so perhaps when I am old enough—"

"That is folly," he said scornfully. "Younger maidens than you are wedded every day, and bedded too. That is a ruse to reconcile me to waiting and then to losing you altogether; but if we have lain down together, my sweetheart, then no living person can separate us, not your father nor your mother. . . . I give you my word you are not too young, Carlina! Let me prove that to you!" He took her in his arms, kissing her, crushing her mouth under his; she struggled silently, in such dismay that he let her go.

She said bitterly, "And if I refuse you, will you put compulsion on me, as you did on Lisarda, who was also too young for such things? Will you put enchantment on me, so that I cannot refuse you whatever you want from me, so that I must do your will whether it is my own desire or no?"

Bard bent his head, his lips pressed bitterly together, a thin angry line. "So that is it," he said. "So that little whore went wailing to you and filled your mind with evil lies against me?"

"She did not lie, Bard, for I read her thoughts."

"Whatever she says to you, she was not unwilling," Bard said, and Carlina said in real anger now, "No; that is what is worse; that you forced her will so that she did not *want* to resist you!"

"You would find as much pleasure in it as she did," Bard said hotly, and she replied with equal anger, "And you could

accept that—that I would not be Carlina, but only some wish
of yours forced on my real self? No doubt I would do your
will, and even do it willingly, if you put that compulsion on
me—just as Lisarda did! And just as she does, I should hate
you for every moment of the rest of my life!"

"I think not," Bard said. "I think, perhaps, when you were
rid of your silly fears, you would come to love me and know
that I had done what was best for us both!"

"No," she said, shaking. "No, Bard . . . I beg you . . . Bard,
I am your wife." A guileful thought touched her; she was
ashamed of herself for trying to manipulate him this way, but
she was frightened and desperate. "Would you use me as if I
were no better than one of my maids?"

He let her go, shocked. He said, "All gods forbid that I
should show you dishonor, Carlie!"

"Then," she said, pressing her advantage swiftly, "you will
wait until the appointed time." She drew quickly out of reach.
"I promise you," she said, "I will be faithful to you. There is
no need for you to fear you will lose me; but all things come
in their proper time." She touched his hand lightly and went
away.

Bard, watching her as she went out of sight, thought to himself that she had made a fool of him. No, she was right; it was
a matter of honor, that she, his wife, should come to him of her
own free will and without compulsion. Yet he was excited,
anger contributing to the uproar in his mind and body.

No woman had ever complained of his advances! How did
that damned wench Lisarda have the presumption to complain
of him? She hadn't minded, the little slut, he had only given
her a chance to do what she wanted to do anyway! He remembered her; yes, she had been frightened at first, but before he was done he had made her moan with pleasure, what
right had she to change her mind afterward and go and bewail
her precious virginity to Carlina, as if it had any particular
value? *She* wasn't an heiress who must keep it for honor and
dowry!

And now Carlina had roused him, and left him in a state of
need! Anger and resentment mingled in him; did the girl think
he was going to await her convenience as patiently as a
maiden?

Suddenly he knew what he should do to have proper revenge on them both, both damned women who had made a

fool of him! Women were all alike, starting with the unknown mother who had been willing to give him up to his father's wealth and position. And Lady Jerana who had poisoned his father's mind and had him sent from his home. And that wretched little slut Lisarda with her whimpering and her tales to Carlina. And even Carlina herself was not free of the general damnableness of women!

In a rage he went out toward the galleries where the upper servants were watching the festivities. He saw Lisarda among them, a slender childish-looking girl with soft brown hair, her slight body just barely rounding into womanhood; Bard's own body tightened with excitement, remembering.

She had been untouched, even ignorant, and frightened, but she had soon enough lost her reluctance. And yet she had the presumption to go complaining to Carlina, as if she had minded! Damned girl, he would show her better this time!

He waited until she was looking in his direction, then caught her eye. He saw her shiver and try to look away, but he reached out, as he had learned how to do, into her mind, touching something deep down in her, below the conscious will, the response of body to body. What did it matter what she *thought* she wanted? This was there and it was real too, and all her arrogant notions about her pridefully held innocence meant nothing in the face of this reality. He held her until he felt her senses stirring, watched with a detached, malicious amusement as she made her way toward him. Staying out of sight, he drew her behind a pillar, kissed her expertly, felt her response flooding them both.

Far away, in a detached corner of her mind, he could sense, could see in her eyes, the panic of the conscious mind, now in abeyance, her dread and horror that this thing was happening to her again in spite of what she wanted, that her body was responding to him when her will did not. Bard laughed soundlessly and whispered to her; watched her go, like a sleepwalker, up the stairs to his room, where, he knew, she would be waiting for him, naked and eager, whenever he chose to come.

He'd keep her waiting awhile. That would prove to her what she really wanted, make her wait for him; her tears and cries would remind her that she had really wanted it all along. *That* would teach her to go complaining to Carlina as if he had mishandled her, or taken her unwilling!

And if Carlina did somehow come to hear of it, well, that was her fault too. She was his wife, in law and in fact, and if she did not recognize that as a responsibility, she had no right to complain if he went elsewhere.

CHAPTER TWO

The year was well advanced, and early hay harvest had begun, when Bard di Asturien sought out King Ardrin in his presence-chamber.

"Uncle," he said, for he had this privilege, the king being his foster father, "will we ride to war before apple harvest?"

King Ardrin raised his eyebrows. He was a tall, imposing man, fair-haired like most of the di Asturiens, and had once been powerful, but he had taken a wound in the arm some years ago and it had left the arm paralyzed. He bore other scars too, the marks of a man who has had to keep his realm by force of arms for most of his life. He said, "Why, I had hoped not, foster son. But you know more than I of what is doing on the borders, since you have been there with the guardsmen these past forty days; what news?"

"No news of the border," Bard said, "for all is quiet; after Snow Glens there is no question of rebellion in *that* area again. But this gossip I heard as I rode homeward; did you know that Dom Eiric Ridenow, the younger, has married his sister to the Duke of Hammerfell?"

King Ardrin looked thoughtful, but all he said was, "Go on."

"One of my guardsmen has a brother-in-law who is a mercenary soldier to the duke," Bard said. "He slew a man by misadventure, and went into exile for three years, so he took service in Hammerfell, and he has been released from his service oath. My guardsman said that when his brother-in-law took service at Hammerfell he made it a condition that he should not ride against Asturias; and I find it interesting that he should be released from his oath now, instead of at midwinter, which is customary."

"Then you think—"

"I think the Duke of Hammerfell is cementing his new kin tie to Ridenow of Serrais," Bard said, "by gathering his army against Asturias. We might have expected that in the spring. If he strikes at us before the winter snow, he will hope to find us unprepared. Also, Beltran has a *laranzu* with his men, whose gift is for rapport with sentry bird; he said that although there were no armies on the road, men were gathering in the market town of Tarquil, which lies not all that far from Hammerfell. True, it is hiring fair there; but the *laranzu* said there were too few men with pitchforks and milking pails, and too many on horseback. It would seem that mercenaries are gathering there. And there was a train of pack beasts riding from Dalereuth Tower, and you know as well as I do what is made in Dalereuth. What does the Duke of Hammerfell want with clingfire, if not to ride against us with the Ridenow of Serrais?"

King Ardrin nodded, slowly. He said, "I am sure you are right. Well, Bard, you who have seen this campaign coming against us, what would you do if the command was yours?"

It was not the first time Bard had been asked this question. It had never meant anything, except that his foster father wished to see if he had a strong sense of military tactics; he would have asked Beltran and Geremy the same question, had they been present, and then would have gone to his ordinary advisers. Nevertheless, Bard gave his best thought to the problem.

"I would ride against them now, before they can gather their mercenaries, before ever they leave Hammerfell," he said. "I would lay siege to Hammerfell, long before he expects us to know what is happening. He does not expect the war to come to his country, he is merely gathering mercenaries to send to the aid of Dom Eiric, so when the Ridenow come against us this summer, as they are sure to do, we will find his forces unpleasantly swollen. But if we strike at Hammerfell *now*, and lay siege to the duke until he is willing to take oath and send hostages not to move against you, you will confound Dom Eiric and confuse his advisers. Also, if I were in command, I would send a few of the troops south to capture and destroy the clingfire before it can be used against us; perhaps to add to our own stockpiles. And since it will certainly be guarded by sorcerers, I would send a *laranzu* or two in that party."

"How soon could we be ready to move against Hammerfell?" King Ardrin asked.

"Within a tenday, sir. Roundup of the horse levies will be finished by then, and the men will be free to answer the war call," Bard said. "But I would send it out in secret, rather than summoning men with the beacon fires; they may have wizards spying to see the beacons from afar. Then we can strike Hammerfell within a tenday of the time he knows we have crossed the border—if we can move swiftly, with a few picked men, we can cut off the bridges over the Valeron, and hold anyone who rides against us, sending one detachment inside to lay siege to the castle."

King Ardrin's stern face broke into a smile. He said, "I could not have made a better plan myself; in fact, Bard, I doubt I could have made one so good. Now I have another question for you: if I lead the troops north to Hammerfell, can you go south to capture the clingfire? I can give you some *leroni*, and three dozen picked horsemen—you may choose them yourself—but no more; will it be enough?"

Bard did not answer for a moment. He said, "Can you not spare four dozen, sir?"

"No; I shall need those extra dozen horsemen to ride to Hammerfell," King Ardrin said.

"Then I shall have to make do with three dozen, sir. At least they can move swiftly when the need arises." His heart was pounding. He had never been given an independent command before.

"Prince Beltran will lead you—officially," King Ardrin said, "but the men will follow you. You understand me, Bard? I must give this command to Beltran. But I shall make it clear to him that you are the military adviser."

Bard nodded. That was simply the reality of the matter; a member of the royal house must be in nominal command. King Ardrin was a seasoned war leader; but he, Bard, was being given a tricky fast mission with a picked striking force. "I will go and choose my men, sir."

"A moment." King Ardrin gestured him back. "A time will come when you, as my son-in-law, will be empowered to command. Your bravery is welcome to me, Bard; but I forbid you to run into too much danger. I need your skill at strategy more than I need your strong arm or your courage. Don't get yourself killed, Bard. I have my eye on you; I am too old to be my own general for more than a few more years. You know what I am trying to say."

Bard bowed deeply and said, "I am at your command, my king and my lord."

"And a day will come when I will be at yours, kinsman. Go now and choose your men."

"May I bid farewell to the Lady Carlina, my lord?"

Ardrin smiled. "You may, certainly."

Bard thought, exultantly, about his good fortune. Now it seemed that his career was assured, and it might be that if he brought this mission successfully to an end, King Ardrin would grant him a further favor, that he might have Carlina at Midwinter festival. Or he might prevail upon her, at least, to consummate their marriage on that night of traditional license! Surely, when he was the king's commander and champion, she would not continue to refuse him!

He admitted it to himself; he was tired of casual wenching. It was Carlina he wanted. At first he had cared for her only as a sign that the king regarded him highly, as a gateway to position and power in the realm, a power which a *nedestro* could not otherwise have within the realm of Asturias. But when she had spoken to him so gently at midsummer, he knew that she was the only woman he really wanted.

He was tired of casual wenching. He was tired of Lisarda, tired even of the game he played with her, making her unwilling body respond even while she wept and insisted she hated him. Wretched little spoilsport, when he had done his best to pleasure her! But now he no longer cared. He wanted no one but Carlina.

He found her in the sewing rooms, supervising the women who were making linen cushions, and beckoned her away from them. Again it struck him with wonder, why should he want this plain girl when there were so many pretty ones around her? Was it only that she was the king's daughter, that she had been his playmate when they were children? Her hair had been hastily braided and shoved back out of the way, but even so, lint was clinging to it, and her blue tartan dress was one he had seen her wear, it seemed, every day since she was ten years old; or did she simply have another one made for her when she had outgrown or outworn the old one?

He said, "There are feathers in your hair, Carlina."

She dabbed at it, preoccupied, laughed. "No doubt; some of

the women are stuffing comforters for the winter to come, and making cushions and pillows; I rule over the feathers, while my mother's women are salting and pickling the bird's flesh for the winter." She looked at the bits of feather fluff clinging to her fingers. "Do you remember, foster brother, the year that you and I and Beltran got into the feather vats and feathers flew all over the sewing rooms? I felt so guilty, for you and Beltran were beaten, and I was only sent to my room without dinner!"

Bard laughed. "Then we had the best of it, for I would rather be beaten any day than go fasting, and I have no doubt Beltran feels much the same! And for all these years I have felt you had the worst of it!"

"But the prank was mine; you and Beltran, and Geremy too, were always being beaten for mischief that I thought up," she said. "We had merry times, did we not, foster brother?"

"We did indeed," Bard said, and took her hands in his. "But I would not call you foster sister now, Carlina *mea*. And I came to bear you great news!"

She smiled up at him. "What is it, my promised husband?" she asked, using the words shyly.

"The king your father has given me command of troops," he burst out exultantly. "I am to go with three dozen picked men and capture a caravan of clingfire. . . . Beltran is nominally in command, but you know, and I too, that the command is truly mine . . . and I am to pick my own men, and to have *leroni* with us. . . ."

"Oh, Bard, how wonderful," she said, warming against her will as he poured out his good news. "I am so glad for you! Surely this means, as you have hoped, I know, that from banner bearer you will rise to one of his captains, and perhaps one day to lead all his armies!"

Bard said, trying not to show too much pride, "Surely that day will be many years from now. But it does show that your father continues to think well of me; and I have thought, Carlina *mea*, that if this mission comes off well, then perhaps he will put forward our wedding by half a year and we can be married at midsummer—"

Carlina tried to control her involuntary flinching. She and Bard must be married; it was her father's will, which was law in the land of Asturias. She genuinely wished Bard well; there was no reason they should be unfriends. There was not, after all, so much difference between midwinter and midsummer. Yet, however she tried to tell herself this, she was still, helplessly, reluctant.

But Bard's delight in the thought was so great that she could not bear to quench it. She temporized. "That must be as my father and my lord wills it, Bard."

Bard saw only a proper maidenly shyness in the words. He tightened his fingers on her hands and said, "Will you kiss me in farewell, my promised wife?"

How could she deny him so much? She let him draw her close, felt his lips, hard and insistent, over hers, stifling her breath. He had never kissed her before except for the brotherly and respectful kiss they had exchanged, before witnesses, at their handfasting. This was different, and somehow frightening, as she felt him trying to open her lips with his mouth; she did not struggle, submitting, scared and passive, to the touch, and somehow this was more exciting to Bard than the most violent passion could have been.

As they moved apart he said in a low voice, half afraid of his own emotion, "I love you, Carlina."

At the shaking of his voice she was moved, again, with reluctant tenderness. She touched his cheek with her fingertips and said gently, "I know, my promised husband."

When he had left her again, she stood staring after the closed door, her emotions in turmoil. Her whole heart yearned after the silence and peace of the Isle of Silence; yet it seemed that it was never to be, that she must go, will she nill she, to be the wife of her cousin, her foster brother, her promised husband, Bard di Asturien. Perhaps, she told herself, perhaps it will not be so bad, when we were little children we loved one another well.

"Ah, Carlina," called one of the women, "what am I to do with this bolt of material; the threads are all drawn at the edge and there is a big piece spoilt here—"

Carlina came and bent over the material. She said, "You will have to straighten it as best you can; and if it is not wide enough after for a sheet, then you must save this end for cushion covers, which can be worked over in wool, with colored designs embroidered here to hide the crooked weave. . . ."

"Why, lady," mocked one of the girls, "how can you give thought to such things, when you have had a visit here from your lover. . . ."

She had used the inflection that changed the word subtly from *promised husband* to *paramour,* and Carlina flushed, feeling the heat flooding into her cheeks. But all she said, schooling her voice to calm and uninvolvement, "Why, Catriona, I thought you had been sent here to learn weaving and embroidery and all manner of womanly arts among the queen's women, but I see you need schooling in *casta* too, to say *promised husband* with the proper courtesy; if you say it like that among the queen's other women, they will mock at you for being countrified."

CHAPTER THREE

Bard rode forth before dawn the next morning. The hour was so early that the easternmost sky had not yet begun to flush with the red dawn; all four of the moons were in the sky, though only one near the full; three small crescents, and the pale disk of Mormallor, floating over the distant hills behind them. Bard's mind was filled with the memory of Carlina's shy kiss; perhaps a day would come when she would kiss him of her own free will, when she would be glad and proud of being married to the king's banner bearer, the king's champion, perhaps the general of all his armies. . . . His thoughts were pleasant enough as he rode at the head of his first command, small though it was.

On the other hand, Beltran, somberly dressed and wrapped in a great cape, was sullen and morose; Bard sensed that he was angered and wondered why.

Beltran growled, "You seem content enough, and perhaps for *you* this command is welcome, but I would rather ride north to Hammerfell at my father's side, where he could see whether I do well or ill; and here I am sent to capture a caravan, sent off like the leader of a bandit gang!"

Bard tried to tell his foster brother how important it might be, to make sure that the clingfire from Dalereuth never reached Serrais, to be used against the fields and villages and forests of Asturias; but Beltran could only see that he had not been given the privilege of riding at his father's right hand, in sight of his armies. "My only comfort is that you will not take my rightful place there," he grumbled. "*That* post he gave to Geremy . . . damn him, damn all the Hasturs!"

Here Bard shared Beltran's displeasure and thought it politic to let him know it.

"Right; he promised me I should have Geremy at the head of the sorcerers riding with us, and at the last moment he tells me he cannot spare Geremy to me, and has given me three strangers," he added his grumbling to Beltran's. He looked ahead to where they rode, a little apart from the picked combat men he had chosen; a tall *laranzu*, graying, his red moustaches hiding half his lower face, and two women, one overplump for riding, ambling on a donkey, and one thin, childish girl, so deeply shrouded in her gray sorcerer's cloak that Bard could not make out whether she was fair or plain. He knew nothing of these three, nothing of their competence, and he wondered nervously if they would be willing to accept him as leader of this expedition. The *laranzu* in particular; although, like all of his kind, he rode unarmed except for a dagger at his side, a small knife such as a woman might wear, he looked as if he had been riding on campaigns such as this since long before Bard was born.

He wondered if this was Beltran's apprehension, too, but he soon found that the prince's displeasure was from quite another cause.

"Geremy and I pledged one another we would ride together to battle this year, and now he has chosen to remain at the king's side—"

"Foster brother," Bard said seriously, "a soldier hears only the voice of his commander, and his own wishes must be subordinate to that."

Prince Beltran's voice was petulant. "I am sure, if he had told my father of this, Father would have honored our promise and given Geremy to this expedition. After all, it is only a stupid matter of chasing down caravans, not much more important than riding out to capture bandit raiders on the border," he added; and Bard, frowning, knew suddenly why the king had said firmly to him that he, and not Prince Beltran, was really in command of this expedition; quite obviously, the prince had no notion of the strategic importance of the clingfire caravans!

If Prince Beltran has no military sense, no wonder my lord the king is eager to train me for command at last; so that if he cannot leave his armies in the hands of his son, he may leave them to his son-in-law. . . . If he has no son fit for a general of

*all his armies, he will marry his daughter to his own general
instead of to a rival outside his borders. . . .*

He tried to make Prince Beltran see something of the importance of his mission, but Beltran was sulking, and at last
said, "I can see that you want it to be important, Bard, because
it makes *you* feel more important." And Bard shrugged and let
it go.

By midafternoon they were near to the southern border of
Asturias; and during the midafternoon rest to breathe the
horses, Bard rode toward the sorcerers, who had stopped a little apart from the rest. This was customary; most fighting men
(and Bard was no exception) were wary of *leroni*.

He thought King Ardrin must have regarded this mission as
important, else he would hardly have sent a man long seasoned
in campaign, but would have given them the young and inexperienced Geremy, if only to please his son and his foster son.
Still, Bard found himself echoing the wish of the prince, that
Geremy, whom he knew so well, had been with them, rather
than this stranger. He did not know how to talk to a *laranzu*.
Geremy, from the time they were all twelve years old, had had
lessons apart, not in swordplay and unarmed combat and dagger fighting like the rest of the king's fosterlings, but in the oc-
cult mastery of the starstones, the blue wizard's crystals which
gave the *leroni* their powers. Geremy had shared their lessons
in military tactics and strategy, in riding and hunting, and had
gone with them on fire watch and ridden with them against
bandits, but it was clear even then that he was not intended for
a soldier, and when he had given up wearing a sword, exchanging it for the dagger of a sorcerer, and saying he needed
no weapon but the starstone about his neck, a great gulf had
opened between them.

And now, as he faced the *laranzu* the king had sent with
them, he felt something of the same gulf. Yet the man looked
hardened to campaigns, rode like a soldier, and even had a sol-
dierly way of handling his home. He had thin, hawklike features and keen, colorless eyes, the gray hardness of tempered
steel.

"I am Bard di Asturien," he said. "I do not know your name,
sir."

"Gareth MacAran, a ves ordras, vai dom . . ." said the
man, saluting briefly.

"What have you been told about this expedition, Master Gareth?"

"Only that I was at *your* orders, sir." Bard had just enough *laran* to catch the very faint, almost undetectable emphasis put on *your*. Inwardly he felt a definite satisfaction. So he was not the only one to believe Beltran was completely hopeless in military matters.

He said, "Have you a sentry bird?"

Master Gareth pointed. He said, gently, but in definite reproof, "I was riding on campaign before you were begotten, sir. If you will tell me what information is needed. . . ."

Bard felt the sting of the reproof. He said stiffly, "I am young, sir, but not untried in campaign. I have spent most of my time with the sword, and am not accustomed to the proper courtesy in dealing with wizardry. I need to know where the clingfire caravan rides to the south, so that we can take them by surprise, and before they have a chance to destroy what they have."

Master Gareth set his mouth. He said, "Clingfire, is it? I'd be glad to see all that stuff dumped into the sea. At least it will not be used to set siege to Asturias this year, then. Melora!" he called, and the older *leronis* came toward him. He had thought her, from her thick body, to be an older woman; now he saw that she was young, but heavy-bodied, her face round and moon-shaped, with pale, vague eyes. Her hair, brilliantly fire red, was twisted into an untidy bun.

"Bring the bird to me. . . ."

Bard watched with amazement—an amazement not new to him, but one that never failed—as the woman deftly unhooded the great bird riding on a block on her saddle. He had had occasion to handle sentry birds; by comparison, even the fiercest of hunting hawks were gentle as a child's cage-bird. The long snakelike neck writhed around and the bird screamed at Bard, a high snarling cry, but when Melora stroked its feathers it quieted, giving a chirp which seemed almost plaintive, eager for caresses. Gareth took the bird, while Bard cringed inwardly at the proximity of those fierce, unclipped talons near his eyes; but Master Gareth handled it as Carlina would have held one of her tiny singing birds.

"There, my beauty . . ." he said, stroking the bird lovingly. "Go and see what they are doing. . . ."

He flung the bird into the air; it winged away on long,

strong pinions, wheeling overhead and disappearing into the clouds. Melora slumped in her saddle, her vague eyes closed, and Gareth said in an undertone, "There is no need for you to stay here, sir. I'll stay in rapport with her and see all she sees through the eyes of the bird. I'll come and make my report to you when we ride on again."

"How long will it take?"

"How should I know, sir?"

Again, Bard felt the sense of a reproof from the old campaigner. Was this, he wondered, why King Ardrin had given him this command, to show him all the little things he should know, in addition to fighting . . . including the courtesy one should show to a skilled *laranzu*. Well, he would learn.

Master Gareth said, "When the bird has seen all it needs to see, and is on its way back to us, then we can ride on. It will find us wherever we are; but Melora cannot ride and stay in rapport with her bird. She would fall from her donkey, and she is no skilled rider at the best of times."

Bard frowned, wondering why they had sent a woman with the troops who could scarcely sit a donkey, let alone a horse!

Master Gareth said, "Because, sir, she is the most skilled at rapport with sentry bird of any *leronis* in Asturias; that is a woman's art, and I am not myself so skilled. I can share rapport with the birds enough to handle them without being pecked to death, but Melora can fly with them and see all they see, and interpret it to me. And now, sir, if you will forgive me, I must not talk any more, I must follow Melora." His face shut down, his eyes rolled up into his head, and Bard, looking at the whites of his eyes, felt a shudder of dismay. The man was not *there;* some essential part of himself was off with Melora and the sentry bird. . . .

Suddenly he was glad that Geremy had not come with them. It was bad enough to see this stranger go away into some eerie realm where he could not follow; if it had been his friend and foster brother, he would have found it unendurable.

The third of the *leroni* had removed her gray riding cloak, throwing back the hood; he could see now that it was a slender young girl, with a pretty, remote face, her flaming hair curling around her cheeks, beautiful and serious. As she saw Bard's eyes on her, she colored and turned away, and something in the shy gesture reminded him of Carlina, frail, almost wraithlike.

She was leading her horse toward the spring, with only the

faintest glance at her two colleagues, entranced on their mounts. Bard dismounted and went to take her horse's bridle.

"*Damisela,* may I assist you?"

"Thank you." She surrendered the reins to him. She did not meet his eyes; he tried to catch her glance, but only saw the color rising in her face. How pretty she was! He led the horse to the water hole, standing with one hand on the reins.

He said, "When Master Gareth and Dame Melora come back to themselves, I will send two of my men to care for their horses."

"Thank you, sir; they will be grateful, for they are always weary after long rapport with the birds. I cannot do it at all," the girl said. She had a small, whispery voice.

"But you are a skilled *leronis?*"

"No, *vai dom,* only a beginner, an apprentice. Perhaps I shall be one day," she said. "My gift at the moment is to see where they cannot send a bird." Again she lowered her eyes and colored.

"And what is your name, *damisela?*"

"Mirella Lindir, sir."

The horse had finished drinking. Bard said, "Have you a food bag for your horse?"

"By your leave, not now, sir. The horse of a *leronis* is trained to stand quietly for a long time without moving—" She gestured to the two motionless figures, Master Gareth and Melora. "But if I feed mine, it will disturb the others."

"I see. Well, as you will," Bard said, recalling that he should go among his men and see what they were doing. Prince Beltran should see to them, of course, but already he had begun to mistrust Beltran's skill, or even his interest in this campaign. Well, so much the better; if this went well, it would be all the more to Bard's credit.

Mirella said shyly, "Don't let me keep you from your duties, sir."

He bowed to her, and went; her eyes, he thought, were beautiful, and she had a shyness not unlike Carlina's. He wondered if she was still a virgin. She had looked at him with interest, certainly. He had promised himself that he would give up his wenching, remain faithful to Carlina, but on campaign a soldier should take what was offered. He was whistling when he rejoined his men.

He was pleased when, some time later, the pretty Mirella,

shrouded in her gray cloak again, modestly, before the eyes of the soldiers, rode toward him and said timidly, "By your leave, sir, Master Gareth has reported that the bird is on its way back and we can ride on."

"I thank you, *damisela,*" Bard said, and meticulously turned to Prince Beltran for orders.

"Give the order to ride," Beltran said indifferently, getting into his own saddle. When the men were all on the road again, Bard, who had watched them all ride past, his eyes alert for anything amiss in any one of them, a piece of equipment rusty, a horse that might be showing the first signs of having picked up a stone or throwing a shoe, rode on to join the three *leroni*.

"What word from your sentry bird, Master Gareth?"

The old *laranzu*'s lined face looked taut and weary. He was chewing on a strip of dried meat as he rode. Melora, next to him, looked almost equally exhausted, her eyes reddened as if with crying, and she too was eating, cramming mouthfuls of dried fruit with honey between her smeared lips.

"The caravan lies about two days' ride yonder," Master Gareth said, pointing, "as the bird flies. There are four wagons; I counted two dozen men beside the wagon drovers, and I saw from their gear and horses, and the fashion of their swords, that they are Dry-town mercenaries."

Bard pursed his lips, for the Dry-town mercenaries were the fiercest fighters known, and he wondered how many of his men had ever fought against their curious curved swords and the daggers they used in lieu of shields to their other side.

"I will warn my men," he said. Among the picked men were several veterans of the wars against Ardcarran. It had been, he thought, a good instinct prompting him to choose men who had fought against the Dry towns. Perhaps they could give the others some advice on how to cope with that style of attack and defense.

And another thing. He glanced at Master Gareth and said with a faint frown, "You are an old campaigner, sir. I do not expect the women to know this, but I was taught it was unsoldierly to eat in the saddle except in the gravest emergencies."

He sensed the smile behind the old man's copper-colored moustaches. "It is clear you know little of *laran,* my lord; how it drains the body of strength. Ask your quartermasters; they will tell you they have been issued triple rations for us, and with good reason. I eat in my saddle so that I will have the strength not to fall out of it, sir, which would be far more disruptive than eating as I ride."

Much as Bard hated to be reproved, he tucked the lesson away, as he did all military matters, for when he would have need of it. But he scowled at Master Gareth and rode away with the briefest of courtesies.

Riding among the men, he dropped the word to each of them that they would be fighting, when it came time to capture the caravan, against Dry-town mercenaries; and he listened for some time to the reminiscences of an elderly campaign veteran who had ridden to war with his own father, Dom Rafael, years before Bard was born.

"There's a trick to fighting Dry-towners; you have to watch both hands, because they're as good with those damned little daggers they wear as any of us is with an honest sword, and when you have your sword engaged, they'll come at you with the other hand, and bury the dagger in your ribs; They're trained to fight with both hands."

"Be sure to warn the men against that, Larion," he said, and rode on, deep in thought. What an honor it would be to him, if he could capture the clingfire intact and take it back to King Ardrin! Like most soldiers, he hated clingfire, thinking it a coward's weapon, although he knew the strategic importance it could have in burning an enemy's objective. At least he could make sure it would not be hurled against the towers of Asturias! Or used to burn their woodlands!

They made camp that night over the borders of Asturias, in a small village which lay on the outskirts of the Plains of Valeron, a no-man's-land which owed allegiance to no king, and the villagers gathered sullenly around Bard's men as if they would have denied them leave to camp there. Then, looking at the three *leroni* in their gray robes, they scowled and withdrew.

"These lands," Bard said to Beltran, as they dismounted, "should be under allegiance to some lord; it is dangerous having them here, ready to shelter outlaws and bandits and perhaps open to some malcontent who could set himself up as king or baron here."

Beltran looked scornfully around, at the lean fields of scanty grain, the orchards of sparse trees of poor-quality nuts, some so scanty of leaves that the farmers had been reduced to growing mushrooms on them. "Who would bother? They can pay no tribute. It would be a poor lord indeed who would stoop to conquer such folk! What honor could an eagle have in battling an army of rabbithorns?"

"That's not the point," Bard said. "The point is, that some enemy to Asturias could come here and put them against us, so that we would have enemies on our very borders. I shall speak to my lord the king about it, and perhaps next spring he will send me here, to make certain that if they pay no tribute to Asturias, at least they will pay none to Ridenow or Serrais! Will you speak with the men and make sure all is in good order, or shall I?"

"Oh, I'll do it," Beltran said with a yawn. "I suppose they must know that their prince cares for their welfare. I don't know much of soldiering, but there are enough veterans here who can tell me if there is anything amiss."

Bard smiled wryly as Beltran went off. Beltran knew little of military tactics, perhaps; but he knew enough of statecraft so that he wanted to win the men's liking and allegiance. A king ruled by the loyalty of his soldiers. Beltran was intelligent enough to know that Bard had the military command of this campaign; it could hardly be otherwise. But he was taking no chances that the men would think their prince indifferent to their personal welfare! Bard watched Prince Beltran go from man to man, making inquiries about their horses, their blankets and gear, their rations. The mess cooks were building fires and something was stewing in a cookpot. It smelled extremely good, after a long day of riding, with no more noon meal than a hunk of hard journey-bread and a handful of nuts!

Left for a moment without occupation, he found himself drifting in the direction of the place, somewhat apart, where the *leroni* had their camp. The memory of the eyes of the pretty Mirella was like a magnet; she could not have been much more than fifteen.

He found her making a fire. A tent had been pitched, and through the fabric he could see the hefty form of the *leronis* Melora moving around inside. He knelt beside her and said, "May I offer you fire, *damisela?*" He held out the oil-fed flint-striker which was simpler to use than an ordinary tinder-box.

She did not turn her eyes toward him. He could see the blush he found so adorable, flooding over her pale neck.

She said, "I thank you, my lord. But I do not need it." And indeed, as she gazed at the piled tinder, her hand laid on the silken bag at her throat where, he guessed, she kept the star-stone, the tinder burst suddenly into flame.

He laid a light hand on her wrist and whispered, "If you would only look into my eyes, *damisela,* I too would burst into flame."

She turned a little toward him, and although she did not raise her eyes, be saw the curve of a faint smile at the corners of her mouth.

Suddenly a shadow fell across them.

"Mirella," said Master Gareth sternly, "get inside the tent and help Melora with your bedding."

Coloring, she rose quickly and hurried inside the tent. Bard rose too, angrily, facing the elderly sorcerer.

"With all respect, I warn you, *vai dom,*" Master Gareth said, "do your wenching elsewhere. That one is not for you."

"What is it to you, old man? Is she your daughter? Or perhaps your light-o-love, or handfasted bride?" Bard demanded in a rage. "Or have you won her loyalty with your spells?"

Master Gareth shook his head, smiling. "None of those," he said, "but on campaign I am responsible for the women who ride with me, and they are not to be touched."

"Except, perhaps, by you?"

Again the silent headshake and the smile. "You know nothing of the world in which the *leroni* live, sir. Melora is my daughter; I will not have her touched by casual amours except at her own wish. As for Mirella, she is to be kept virgin for the Sight, and there is a curse on any who should take her, unless she resigns it of her free will. I warn you, avoid her."

Stung, red-faced, feeling like a scolded schoolboy before the level eyes of the old sorcerer, Bard bent his head and muttered, "I did not know."

"No, and that is why I am telling you," said the old man genially. "For Mirella was too shy to do so herself. She is not accustomed to men who cannot read her thoughts."

Bard cast a resentful look toward the tent. He thought it should have been the fat and ugly Melora, the old man's daughter, kept virgin for the Sight, for what man would want her unless he could first hide her face with a horse bag? Why the pretty Mirella? Master Gareth was still smiling amiably, but Bard had the uncanny sudden sense that the old man was actually reading his mind.

"Come, come, sir," said Master Gareth with a good-natured

grin, "you are handfasted to the princess Carlina. It's not worthy of you to look to a simple *leronis*. Lie alone tonight, and perhaps you will dream of the high-born woman who waits at home for you. After all, you can't have every woman on whom you cast your roving eyes. Don't show such ugly temper!"

Bard ripped out a curse and turned away. He knew enough not to anger a *laranzu,* on whom the fate of the campaign might rest, but the old man's voice, as if he spoke to the greenest of boys, infuriated him. What business was it of Master Gareth's?

The servant who rode to attend on the officers had made a small third camp for them, apart from the others. Bard went to taste the food cooked for the men—he had learned never to eat his own meal until horses and men were safely settled for the night—and to inspect the picket lines of the horses, then came back to find Beltran awaiting him.

"You look ill-tempered, Bard. What ails you?"

"Damned old bird of prey," Bard growled. "Afraid I should touch his precious maiden *leroni,* when I did no more than offer the young one a bit of tinder!"

Beltran chuckled. "Well, it's a compliment, Bard. He knows you have a way with the women! Your reputation, after all, has simply preceded you, that is all, and he is afraid no maiden could resist you, nor retain her maidenhood in your presence!"

Put like that, Bard began to recover a little of his self-esteem, to feel less like a reprimanded schoolboy.

"As for me," Beltran said, "I feel it's wrong to bring women on campaign—good women, that is. I suppose any army should have camp followers, though I've no taste for them myself. If I must have women about, I prefer the kind who look as if they washed more often than when they got caught out of doors during the fall rains! But good women with a campaign are a temptation to the unchaste, and an annoyance to the chaste whose mind is on their business of fighting!"

Bard nodded, admitting the justice of what Beltran said.

"And what's more, if they're available, the men will fight over 'em; and if they're not, they'll moon about over them," he said.

Beltran said, "Should the day come when I command my father's armies, I will forbid any *leronis* to ride with the army; there are *laranzu'in* enough, and myself I think men better at that kind of skill; women are too squeamish and have no place with an army, no more than Carlina or one of our baby brothers! How old is your little brother now?"

"He must be eight now," Bard said. "Nine at midwinter. I wonder if he has forgotten me? I have not been home since my father sent me here for fostering."

Beltran patted his shoulder in sympathy. He said, "Well, well, no doubt you can have leave to go home before midwinter."

"If the fighting in Hammerfell is over before the snow closes the roads," Bard said, "I will do so. My foster mother does not love me, but she cannot keep me from home. It would be good to see if Alaric still holds me in affection." To himself he thought that perhaps he would ask his father to come to his wedding. It was not every one of the king's fosterlings who would be joined in *catenas* marriage by King Ardrin himself!

They sat late talking, and when at last they slept, Bard was well content. He thought briefly and with regret, of the pretty Mirella, but after all, what Master Gareth had said was true: he had Carlina, and soon enough they would be married. Beltran was right, after all. Virtuous women had no place with the king's armies.

The next morning, after a brief conference with Master Gareth and Beltran, they turned their steps toward the ford of Moray's Mills. No one now alive knew who Moray might have been, though stories in the countryside made him everything from a giant to a dragon keeper: but there was still a ruined mill near the ford, and a little upstream from it another mill still in operation. A toll gate closed the road, and as Bard's men came toward it, the toll-keeper, a fat and graying man, came out to say, "By order of the Lord of Dalereuth, this road is closed, my lords. I have sworn not to open for anyone who does not pay him tribute, or have his safe-conduct within his borders."

"Now, by all of Zandru's hells—" Bard began, but Prince Beltran rode forward, looming over the little man in his miller's apron.

"I am very willing to pay a head tax to the Lord of Dalereuth." he said. "I am sure he would appreciate the head of an insolent fellow like you. Rannvil—" he gestured, and one of the horsemen drew his sword. "Open the gates, man; don't be a fool."

The toll-keeper, his teeth chattering, went to the mechanism that trundled the great toll gate aside. Beltran contemptuously flung the man a few coins. "Here's your tribute. But if this gate is barred against us when we come back, take my word for it, I'll have my men tear it out of the ground and set your head on top of it to scare away crows!"

As they passed through, Bard heard the man grumbling and leaned down from his horse to grab him by the shoulder.

"Whatever you said, say it aloud to our faces, you!"

The man looked up, his jaw set and wrathful. He said, "I have no part in the quarrels of my betters, *vai dom.* Why should I suffer because you noblemen can't keep your borders? All I care about is running my mill. But you won't come back this way, or at all. I have nothing to do with what waits for you at the ford yonder. Now, if you wish, win honor by killing an unarmed man!"

Bard let him go and straightened up. He said, "Kill you? Why? Thanks for your warning; you've been well paid." He watched the man go off toward his mill, and although he had been a soldier since his fourteenth year, he frowned and suddenly wondered why it should be this way. Why should every nobleman who chose demand that he be sovereign over his own land? That only made more work for mercenaries.

Perhaps, he thought, *all this land should be under one rule, with peace at the borders, from the Hellers to the sea . . . and little men like this could grow their crops and turn their mills in peace . . . and I could live on the estates the king has given me, with Carlina. . . .*

But there was no leisure to think of that now. He called urgently to Master Gareth, raising his hand to halt the men.

"I have had a warning," he said, "that something waits for us at that ford; but I see nothing. Does your bird give you warning, or has either of your women seen anything by their spells?"

Master Gareth beckoned to Mirella, shrouded in her cloak, and spoke to her, softly. She took her starstone from about her throat and gazed into it.

After a moment she said, in a low, neutral voice, "There is neither man nor beast at the ford to wait for us; but there is darkness there, and a barrier we may not be able to pass. We must go with great care, kinsman."

Master Gareth raised his eyes and met Bard's. He said,

"She has the Sight; if there is a darkness that she cannot penetrate, we must indeed go with the greatest of care, sir."

But the ford lay calm and peaceful in the sunlight, shallow ripples swirling with glints of crimson. Bard frowned, trying to assess what lay before them. He could see nothing, no signs of ambush, no twig or branch stirring on the far side of the ford, where a path led up between overgrown trees. That would, indeed, be a good place for ambush.

"If you cannot see beyond the ford by sorcery or the Sight," he said, "can the sentry bird pass and see if there is any ambush hidden beyond?"

Master Gareth nodded. "To be sure; the bird is only a beast and has nothing to do with sorcery or the magic of the trained mind. The only magic about the bird is the skill Melora and I have to remain in rapport with the creature. Melora," he called, "child, let the sentry bird go."

Bard watched as the fierce bird rose high over the ford, circling. After a time, Master Gareth shook himself, waked, beckoned to Melora, who reached out her hand and took the bird as it came circling back, stroking its feathers and feeding it tidbits before slipping the hood over its head. Master Gareth said, "There is no one, man or beast, hidden beyond the ford; no living creature for many leagues except a girl herding a flock of rabbithorns. Whatever waits here at the ford, *vai dom,* it is not an ambush of armed men."

Bard and Beltran exchanged glances. Finally Beltran said, "We cannot wait here all day for a terror no one can see. I think we must ride to the ford; but Master Gareth, stay back, for we must keep you in reserve if you are needed. I have known sorcerers to set a forest or a field ablaze in the path of armies on the march; and I suppose there could be something like that beyond the ford. We must be wary of that. Bard, will you order the men to ride?"

Bard's skin prickled. He had had this reaction once or twice before in the presence of *laran;* he had little enough of it himself, but somehow he could scent it. There was, he knew, a talent which could sniff out the use of *laran;* perhaps, if he had been trained in its use, he would have had that. It might have been useful after all. He had always thought that Geremy, training as a *laranzu,* was somehow less a man, less a soldier, than Beltran and himself. Now, watching Master Gareth, he began to realize that this work might have its own dangers and terrors, even though a *laranzu* rode unarmed into battle. *That, in itself, might be frightening enough,* Bard thought, laying his hand for reassurance on his sword.

He turned to the men and commanded, "Count off by fours!" He could not order any man to be first to ride into some unknown terror. When they had done so, he said, "Group two, ride forward," and took lead of them.

His skin prickled again as he rode forward, and his horse tossed her head in protest as she set a fastidious foot within the ford; but the water was quiet, and he gave the order.

"Ride, slowly, keep together!"

Above them, at the very edge of his vision, he saw a flicker of motion. He thought Master Gareth had recalled the sentry bird. . . . A quick glance showed him that Melora's bird sat, hooded and quiet, on the woman's saddle. *So, they were being watched from afar. Was there any defense against that?*

They were in the center of the ford now, the water at its deepest swirling around the hocks of the horses; thigh-deep on a tall man. One of his soldiers said, "There's nothing here, sir. We can call the others to come."

Bard shook his head. Inwardly he felt that prickling that warned of danger, growing, so that he clamped his teeth, wondering if he would spew up his breakfast like a breeding woman. . . .

He heard Master Gareth shouting, wheeled his horse in midstream. "Back," he yelled. "Get back—"

The water swirled upward, rising around his horses' withers, and suddenly the peaceful ford was a raging, foaming torrent, a racing undertow sucking, pulling. He felt his horse stumble under him as if he had ridden into a mountain stream swollen by spring thaw into furious rapids. *Witch-waters!* He tugged at the reins, trying to soothe his neighing, plunging horse, hold her steady, against the threat of being swept away downstream. Around him every one of the group was struggling with horses maddened with fear at the peaceful water suddenly gone wild. Cursing, fighting his terrified horse, Bard managed to get her under control, urge her back toward the water's edge. He saw one of his men slip from his saddle, go down into the torrent. Another horse stumbled, and Bard reached over and grabbed the rein, trying to hold his own horse with one hand.

"Hold them! In the name of all the gods, hold them! Back to the bank!" he shouted. "Keep together!"

The surprise was the worst; his horse was used to mountain streams and fords. Warned in advance, he could perhaps have held her against this. Gripping with his knees, urging her carefully against the water that now raced up to her neck, he managed to get her back to dry land, stood grabbing the bridles of the others as they came up. One horse was down and had broken a leg; it lay kicking, screaming like a woman in the torrent, until it drowned. Bard swore, his throat tight. The poor creature had never harmed any living thing, and it had died a terrible death. Of the rider there was no sign. Another horse had gone down, and its rider, leaping off into the water, had managed to get it up, limping, and drag it back to the shore; he went down himself and floundered, half-drowned, until one of the men, leaping down the bank, grabbed him and hauled him out.

Bard saw the last man out of the water; then cried out in awe and dismay. For once again the water lay calm and shallow before them, the peaceful, normal ford of Moray's Mill.

So that was what the little man had meant. . . .

Grimly, they took stock of their losses. The horse that had broken a leg lay motionless now, lifeless; and of his rider there was no sign whatever. Either he lay dead beneath the waters of the ford or had been swept away on the torrent and his body would surface far downstream. Another man had gotten free but his horse was lamed and useless; still a third horse had thrown his rider and gotten to shore, but the man lay senseless, his body washing up and down at the edge of the water. Bard motioned to one of his fellows to go and drag him to dry land, ran his fingers briefly across the gaping wound in the skull. It was likely he would never waken.

Bard blessed whatever precognitive warning had prompted him to send only a quarter of the men into the stream. At that rate they would have lost half a dozen men, instead of two men and horses, and perhaps had more horses lamed or damaged. But he beckoned to Master Gareth and his voice was grim.

"So this is what lay in the darkness your girl could not read!"

The man shook his head, sighing. "I am sorry, *vai dom. . . .* We are psychics, not sorcerers, and our powers are not infinite. May I venture to say in our defense that without us your men would have ridden completely unwarned into the ford?"

"True," Bard admitted, "but now what do we do? If the ford is spelled against us—have we sprung the trap, or will it rise again the moment we set foot within it?"

"I cannot say, my lord. But perhaps Mirella's Sight will tell us," he said, beckoning her forward. He spoke in a low voice, and again the girl gazed into her starstone, finally saying in her wandering, neutral, drugged spell-voice, "I can see nothing . . . there is a darkness on the water. . . ."

Bard swore, morosely. The spell was still there against them, then. He said to Beltran, "Do you think we can take the ford now we are warned?"

Beltran said, "Perhaps; if the men know what they must face, they are picked men and good riders, all of them. But Master Gareth, and the *leroni,* probably cannot pass, and certainly the one who rides on a donkey cannot. . . ."

Master Gareth said, "We are trained *leroni,* sir; we take what risks the army takes, and my daughter and my foster daughter go where I go. They are not afraid."

"It is not their courage I am doubting," Bard said impatiently. "It is their skill as horsewomen. Besides, that little donkey would be drowned at the first wave. I don't want to see any woman killed out of hand, but we will need you when battle is joined, too. And before we do anything, can you keep us from being spied on?" He gestured up impatiently at the sentry bird wheeling above them.

"I would do what I can, sir, but I think our spells will be needed more against the witch-waters of the ford," Master Gareth said.

Bard nodded, thinking about that. As a commander made the best use of his fighting men, so, he was beginning to know, he must hoard the strength of his army's *leroni* and use them to best advantage.

Did King Ardrin give me this command so that I might have a chance to command not fighting men alone, but sorcerers? Even in the press of decisions, he thought with excitement that this meant well for his future. *If . . .* he thought, quickly sobering, *he could carry off this apparently simple commission without losing all his men at the witched ford!*

"Master Gareth, this is the province of your special knowledge. What do you recommend to me?"

"We can try to set a counter-spell on the waters, sir. I cannot guarantee—I do not know who we are facing or what their

powers may be—but we will do our best to quiet the waters.
We have this in our favor; to meddle this way with nature takes
tremendous power, and they cannot keep it up for very long.
Nature takes always the way toward the normal again; the
water seeks its proper flow, and so we have the force of natural water working for us, while they must fight *against* that
natural force. So our counter-spell should not be too difficult."

"All the gods grant you are right," Bard said, "but still, I
will warn the men to be prepared for rapids." He rode among
them, speaking to first one and then the other, telling the man
whose horse had been lamed to take the one whose rider had
been killed. Then he moved close to Beltran, saying. "Ride by
me, foster brother; I don't want to face my lord and king if I
let you be killed in the rapids! If you die in battle, I suppose he
could face it; but I will not be responsible otherwise!"

Beltran laughed. "Do you think you ride so much better
than I do, Bard? I don't! I think you overstep your authority—
I, not you, command this expedition!" But he said it laughing,
and Bard shrugged.

"As you will, Beltran; but in God's name, mind what you
are about. My horse is bigger and heavier than yours, because
it takes a big horse to carry weight like mine, and I had all I
could do to keep my seat!"

He wheeled and rode forward to Master Gareth. "There is
no way mistress Melora can cross the ford on that little donkey; certainly not if your spells fail. Can she sit a horse?"

Master Gareth said, "I am her father, not her mentor or the
master of her destiny; why not ask the lady herself?"

Bard set his jaw. "I am not given to asking women questions when there is a man to command them. But if you insist—well, *damisela,* can you ride? If you can, your father will
take mistress Mirella before him on his horse, since she rides
lighter than you, and you shall ride her horse, which looks
steady enough."

"I would rather trust to my father's spells and my own,"
Melora said firmly. "Do you think I will abandon my poor little donkey to drown?"

"Oh, hell and damnation, woman," Bard burst out. "If you
can manage to sit on a horse, one of my men will lead your
donkey. I suppose the beast can swim!"

"You must do your best to ride, Melora," Master Gareth
said. "And Whitefur must make shift to swim for himself. I am

sure he can fend for himself in the ford better than you can. Mirella, my child, let Melora have your horse and climb up behind me on my saddle."

She scrambled up nimbly enough, although the watching men had a glimpse of long shapely legs in striped red and blue stockings, as she clambered up behind the elderly *laranzu* and settled herself, smoothing down her skirts, and clinging to his waist. Bard went himself to help lift the plump and ungainly Melora into the saddle of the other girl's horse. She sat a horse, he told himself uncharitably, like a sack of meal dumped into a saddle.

"Sit a bit straighter, I implore you, *vai leronis,* and hold more carefully to the reins," he said, then sighed. "I think perhaps I had better ride at your side and lead your horse."

"That would be good of you," Master Gareth said, "for we will need to concentrate on setting the counter-spell; and I would take it as a kindness, too, if one of your men can lead Melora's donkey, for she will be afraid for him."

One of the veterans burst out, laughing, "Mistress Melora, if you can set a spell to quiet these waters, I will myself carry your little donkey across my saddle like a baby!"

She giggled. Fat and ungainly as she was, she had a sweet voice and a lovely laugh. "I am afraid that would frighten him worse than the rapids, sir. I think, if you will lead him, he can manage somehow to swim, after your horse's tail."

The veteran brought a tie-rope and secured the bridle of the donkey to his own bridle. Bard took Melora's rein, thinking what a pity it was that it was not the pretty Mirella; and heard again Melora's sweet giggle. He wondered, uneasily, if she could read his mind, and cut off the thought. This was no time for thinking about women, not with a spelled ford to cross and a battle coming up!

"For the love of all the gods, Master Gareth, set your counter-spell."

Melora's heavy figure was motionless on her horse. The look of strangeness, of concentration, settled down over Master Gareth's face. Mirella's hood slid down over her face so that nothing was visible but her small chin. Bard watched the three *leroni,* feeling the prickling in his spine that meant *laran* was powerful somewhere near. . . . How could he tell, what was it?

Silently, feeling a curious reluctance to shatter the scary silence by a word or a shout, Bard beckoned the men forward. Still weighted by that sense of prickling intensity in the air, he twitched at his horse's rein and urged the animal forward. The mare tossed her head and whickered uneasily, remembering what had happened when she had set foot in the ford before.

"Easy. Easy, girl," he urged in a low voice, thinking, *I don't blame her at all, I feel the same way*. . . . But he was a reasoning human, not a brute beast, and he would not give way to blind, unreasoning fear. Urged on by voice and hands, the mare set foot into the ford, and Bard beckoned to the men behind him.

Nothing happened . . . but then, nothing had happened, before, until they were in midstream. Bard urged the horse on, holding to Melora's rein, half-turned in his saddle. Behind him Master Gareth rode, Mirella clinging to his waist, and behind him, the men of the party, Prince Beltran bringing up the rear.

They were all in the water now, and Bard felt his skin tighten on his face. If the spell was working, it would strike them now, sweep down on them like a torrent. He braced himself in his saddle, feeling the prickle, prickle, prickle that was his personal awareness of *laran* at work, growing in strength as if he could almost see the flare and interplay between the spell set on the ford and the counter-spell; his horse seemed to step through a tangle of thick weed although there was nothing tangible there . . .

Then, suddenly, it was gone; just gone, vanished, the ford running silent and innocent, just water again. Bard let out his breath and dug his heels into his mare's side. The first riders were partway up the far bank by now, and he held his mount there in midstream, watching them ride past and up the other side of the stream.

For now, at least, their *leroni* had out-spelled the wizards set against them.

So far, on this campaign, the weather had held fine. But now, as the day waned, the sky grew dark with thickening clouds and toward evening snow began to fall, softly, but with persistence; first a few thick, clumped, wet flakes at a time, then thick and fine and hard, coming down and down and down with idiot persistence. Melora, back on her donkey, swaddled herself in her gray cloak and wrapped a blanket over her head. The soldiers, one by one, got out scarves and mufflers and thick hoods, and rode, sullen and glowering. Bard

knew what they were thinking. By tradition, war was a summer business, and in winter, all but the mad, or the desperate,
kept to their own firesides. There was a certain amount of danger in a winter campaign. The men might say, and with some
justice, that while they owed service to King Ardrin, this went
beyond what was customary and right, and riding like this into
a snowstorm which might easily turn into a blizzard in intensity was not customary and therefore the king had no right to
ask it of them. How could he command their loyalty? For the
first time he wished he were not in command here, but that he
was riding north to Hammerfell at King Ardrin's right hand,
his sovereign's banner bearer. The king could command loyalty from his troops, use his personal influence and power to
demand loyalty beyond custom. He could make the men promises, and make those promises good. Bard was painfully aware
that he was only seventeen years old; that he was only the
king's bastard nephew and fosterling; that he had been promoted over the heads of many seasoned officers. There were
probably men in the ranks, even among these picked men he
had chosen for this campaign, who might be waiting to see him
come to grief; to make some dreadful mistake that he could
never recoup. Had the king given him this command only that
he might overstep his powers, see himself as the green and un-
seasoned warrior that he was?

Despite his triumph and promotion on the field of Snow
Glen, he was only a boy. Could he carry through this mission
at all? Was the king hoping he would fail, so that he could deny
him Carlina? What would lie ahead for him if he failed? Would
he be demoted, sent home in disgrace?

He rode ahead to join Master Gareth, who had wrapped his
lower face in a thick, red, knitted muffler under the gray sorcerer's cape. He said with asperity, "Can't you do anything
about this weather? Is this a blizzard coming up, or only a
snow flurry?"

"You ask too much of my powers, sir," said the older man.
"I am a *laranzu,* not a god; the weather is not mine to command." A touch of humor wrinkled up one corner of his face in
a wry smile. "Believe me, Master Bard, if I had command over
the weather, I would use it to my own advantage. I am as cold
as you, and as blinded by snow, and my bones are older and
feel the cold more."

Bard said, hating to confess his own inadequacy, "The men are

grumbling, and I am a little afraid of mutiny. A winter campaign—
while the weather held fine, they did not care. But now—"

Master Gareth nodded. "I can see that. Well, I will try to see
how far this storm extends, and if we will ride out of it soon;
although weather magic is not my special gift. Only one of his
majesty's *laranzu'in* has that, and Master Robyl rode north to
Hammerfell with the king; he felt he would be needed more on
the northern border of the Hellers where the snows are fiercer.
But I will do my best."

And as Bard turned away, he added, "Cheer up, sir. The
snow may make it hard for us to ride, but not nearly as hard as
for the caravan with the clingfire; they have all those carts and
wagons to push along through the snow, and if it gets too deep
they won't be able to move at all."

Bard realized that he should have thought of that. Snow
would immobilize the carts and wagons of the caravan, while
the light horsemen of the picked group were still well able to
ride and to fight. Furthermore, if it was true that Dry-town
mercenaries had been hired to escort the caravan, they were
accustomed to warmer weather, and the snow would confuse
them. He rode among the men, listening to their grumblings
and protests, and reminded them of this. Even though the snow
continued to fall, and even grew heavier, that thought seemed
to cheer them a little.

However, the clouds and falling snow grew ever thicker, and
after a word with Beltran, they called a halt early. Nothing was
to be gained by forcing grumbling men to press on through the
same snow that would immobilize their prey. Riding through
the snow, the men were weary and disheartened, and some of
them would have eaten a few bites of cold food and rolled into
their blankets at once, but Bard insisted that fires must be
lighted and hot food cooked, knowing this would do more for
the men's morale than anything else. With fires lighted on stone
slabs and blazing away, fed by the fallen tree branches of an
abandoned orchard—hit by the nut blight of a few seasons
ago—the camp looked cheerful, and one of the men brought out
a small drone-pipe and began to play, mournful old laments
older than the world. The young women slept in their shared
tent, but Master Gareth joined the men around the fire, and after
a time, though he protested that he was neither minstrel nor
bard, consented to tell them the tale of the last dragon. Bard sat
beside Beltran in the shadows of the fire, chewing on dried fruit

and listening to the story of how the last dragon had been slain by one of the Hastur kin, and how, sensing with the *laran* of beasts that this last of his folk was dead, every beast and bird within the Hundred Kingdoms had set up a wail, a keen, even the banshees joining in the lament for the last of the wise serpents . . . and the son of Hastur himself, standing beside the corpse of the last dragon on Darkover, had vowed never again to hunt for any living thing for sport. When Master Gareth finished his tale, the men applauded and begged for more, but he shook his head, saying that he was an old man and had been riding all day, and that he was away to his blankets.

Soon the camp was dark and silent; only the small red eye of the fire, covered with green branches against the morning's need for hot porridge, sizzled and watched from its cover. All around the fire dark triangles marked where the men lay in their blankets, beneath the waterproof sheets, stretched up at an angle, to protect them from the still falling snow; miniature open halftents pitched on a forked stick apiece, each with two or three or four men beneath, huddled together and sharing blankets and body warmth. Beltran lay at Bard's side, looking curiously small and boyish, but Bard lay awake, staring at the fire and the white-silver streaks of snow that made pale arrows across the light. Somewhere, not far from them, the enemy lay immobilized, heavy carts mired in snow, pack beasts floundering.

At his side Beltran said softly, "I wish Geremy were with us, foster brother."

Bard laughed almost noiselessly. "So did I, at first. Now I'm not so sure. Perhaps two green boys in command are enough, and we are well off to have Master Gareth's experience and wisdom; while Geremy as an untried *laranzu* rides with your father who is well skilled in command. . . . Perhaps he thought if we three went together it would seem too much like one of the hunting trips we used to ride on, the three of us, when we were only lads. . . ."

"I remember," Beltran said, "when we three were younger and we rode out like this. Lying together and looking into the fire and talking of the days when we would be men, and on campaign together, in command, in real war and not our mock battles against *chervine* herds. . . . Do you remember, Bard?"

Bard smiled in the dark. "I remember. What mighty campaigns and wars we planned, how we would subdue all this countryside from the Hellers to the shores of Carthon, and beyond the seas. . . . Well, this much has come true of what we planned, that we are all on campaign, and at war, just as we said when we were boys who hardly knew which end of a sword to take hold by. . . ."

"And now Geremy is a *laranzu* riding with the king, and he thinks only of Ginevra, and you are the king's banner bearer, promoted in battle, and handfasted to Carlina, and I—" Prince Beltran sighed in the darkness. "Well, no doubt, one day I will know what it is that I want from my life, or if I do not, my father and king will tell me what it is that I will have."

"Oh, you," Bard said, laughing, "some day the throne of Asturias will be yours."

"That is no laughing matter," Beltran said, and he sounded somber. "To know that I will come to power only over my father's grave and by his death. I love my father, Bard, and yet at times I think I shall go mad if I must stand at his footstool and wait for something real to do. . . . I cannot even go forth out of the kingdom and seek adventure, as any other subject is free to do." Bard felt the younger lad shiver. "I am so cold, foster brother."

For a moment Beltran seemed, to Bard, no older than the little brother who had clung to his neck and wept when he went away to the king's house. Awkwardly, he patted Beltran's shoulder in the dark. "Here, have some more of the blanket, I don't feel the cold as badly as you do, I never did. Try to sleep. Tomorrow, perhaps, we'll have a fight on our hands, a real fight, not one of the mock battles we used to take so much pleasure in, and we must be ready for it."

"I'm afraid, Bard. I'm always afraid. Why are you and Geremy never afraid?"

Bard snorted brief laughter. "What makes you think we're not afraid? I don't know about Geremy, but I was afraid enough to wet my breeches like a babe, and no doubt I'll be so again. Only I haven't time to talk about it when it's happening, and no wish to do so when it isn't. Don't worry, foster brother. You did well enough at Snow Glens, I remember."

"Then why did my father promote you on the field, and not me?"

Bard half sat up in the darkness and stared at him. He said, "Is that flea still biting you? Beltran, my friend, your father knows you have all you need already. You are his son and his legitimate heir, you ride at his side, you are already acknowledged just one breath away from the throne. He promoted me because I was his fosterling, and a bastard. Before he could set me over his men, to command them, he had to make me somebody he could legitimately promote, which he could not do without acknowledging me specially. Promoting me was only sharpening a tool he wished to use, no more, not a mark of his love or special regard! By the cold whirlwind of Zandru's third hell, I know it if you don't! Are you fool enough to be jealous of me, Beltran?"

"No," Beltran said slowly in the dark. "No, I suppose not, foster brother." And after a time, hearing Beltran's silent breathing in the dark, Bard slept.

CHAPTER FOUR

In the morning it was still snowing, and the sky was so dark that Bard's heart sank as he watched the men going glumly about the business of caring for their horses, cooking up a great pot of porridge, making ready and saddling up to ride. He heard muttering among the men to the effect that King Ardrin had no right to send them out in winter, that this campaign was the work of his fosterling, who didn't know what was proper and right; who ever heard of a campaign like this with winter coming on?

"Come on, lads," Bard urged. "If the Dry-towners can ride in weather like this, are we going to stand back and let them bring clingfire to hurl against our villages and our families?"

"Dry-towners are likely to do anything," one of the men grumbled. "Next thing, they'll be holding harvest in spring-time! War is a business for the summertime!"

"And because they believe we will stay snug at home, they think it safe to strike at us," Bard argued. "Do you want to stay home and let them attack?"

"Yes, why not stay home and let them come to us? Defending our homes against attack's one thing," a burly veteran growled, "but going out looking for trouble, that's something else!"

But, though there was grumbling and muttering, there was no open mutiny or rebellious behavior. Beltran was pale and silent, and Bard, remembering their talk last night, realized that the youngster was terrified. It was easy to think of Beltran as younger than himself, although in solid fact there was less than half a year between them; Bard had always been so much the larger of the foster brothers, the strongest, always best at swordplay and wrestling and hunting, their unquestioned leader.

So he made occasion to speak to Beltran about his fears that the men would mutiny, and asked Beltran to go among them and try to sound out their mood as they rode.

"You are their prince, and you represent the will of their king. A time might come when they would not obey me, but they would not be willing, I think, to defy their king's own son," he suggested guilefully, and Beltran, looking at Bard with a sullen scowl—after all, should he take orders from Bard?— finally nodded and drew back to ride alongside first one, then another of the men, asking questions, talking to one after the other. Bard watched, thinking that perhaps in this task Beltran had put aside his fears—and perhaps that touch of personal concern from their prince had quieted the men's rebelliousness.

And still the snow continued to fall. It was up, now, to the fetlocks of the horses, and Bard began seriously to worry about whether the horses could get through. He asked Master Gareth to send out the sentry birds, but received the halfway expected answer that they would not fly in such weather.

"Sensible birds," Bard grumbled. "I wish I needn't! Well, is there any way to find out how far from us the caravan is traveling, and whether we will come up with them today?"

Master Gareth said, "I will ask Mirella; this is why she is with us, so that she can use the Sight."

Bard watched as Mirella, seated on her horse amid the falling snow, her hair showing bright copper through the thickly salted flakes on her braids, sat staring into her crystal. The light reflected, faintly blue, on her face; the only light, it seemed, anywhere in that dismal day, was the blue light and the flame of her coppery hair. She was muffled in cloak and shawls, but they could not hide the slender grace of her body, and Bard found himself, once again, letting his mind linger on her beauty. She was, doubtless, the most beautiful young girl he had even seen; next to her Carlina was a pale stick. Yet Mirella was completely beyond his reach, sacrosanct, a *leronis,* vowed virgin for the Sight, and there were uncanny warning tales about what could befall the manhood of any man who would assail the virginity of a *leronis* against her will. He told himself that he could, with his gift; assure himself that it would *not* be against her will, that he could force her to come to his bed willingly. . . .

But that would make an enemy of Master Gareth. Damn, there were enough willing women in this world, and he was handfasted to a princess, and anyway this was no time to be thinking of women at all!

Mirella sighed and opened her eyes, the blue light dimming from her face, and her glance rested on him, shy, serious, so direct that Bard wondered, a little abashed, if she could read what he had been thinking.

Instead she only said, in her still neutral voice, "They are not far from us, *vai dom.* Three hours' ride over that ridge yonder—" She pointed, but the ridge she spoke of was invisible in the falling snow. "They have encamped because the snow has fallen deeper there, and thicker, and their carts cannot move. They are up to the hubs of the wheels, and the draft animals cannot move. One broke a leg in the harness and the others tried to stampede and nearly kicked themselves to death. If we ride on as we are going now, we will come upon them soon after midday."

Bard rode to relay this news to his men, and found them grim, not at all pleased by the news.

"That means we have to fight in deep snow, and what do we do with the caravan when we have captured it, if their pack beasts are not working?" one old veteran inquired sourly. "I suggest we make camp here and wait for a thaw, when we can take it easier. If they're unable to move, they'll wait there for us!"

"We'd run out of food and fodder for the horses," Bard said, "and there's an advantage to doing battle when *we* choose. Come on, let's get there as soon as we can!"

They rode on, the snow continuing to fall. Bard watched the gray-cloaked *leroni,* frowning. Finally he rode forward and asked Master Gareth, "How shall we protect the women in battle, sir? We cannot spare a man to guard them."

"I said it before," Master Gareth said. "These women are skilled *leroni;* they are capable of looking after themselves. Melora has been in battle before this, and although Mirella has not, I have no fear for her."

"But these men we shall fight are accompanied by Dry-town mercenaries," Bard said. "And if your daughter and foster daughter are taken prisoner—*leroni* or no—they will be dragged in chains to be sold in a Daillon brothel."

Melora, riding near them on her ambling donkey, said quietly, "Have no fear for us, *vai dom.*" She put her hand on the small dagger she wore at her waist, under the cloak. "My sister and I will not fall into Dry-town hands alive."

The calm, matter-of-fact way she spoke made a cold shudder run up Bard's spine. Curiously, the note was one of kinship. He, too, had known that he faced death or worse in battle, and had come early to that knowledge, and the note in Melora's voice made him think of his own early battles. He found himself grinning at her, a tight, spontaneous grin. He said, "The Goddess forbid that it should come to that, *damisela*. But I did not know there were women capable of such decisions, or courage in war."

"It is not courage," Melora said, in her sweet voice. "It is only that I fear the chains and brothels of the Dry towns more than I fear death. Death, I have been taught, is a gateway to another and better life; and life would have no sweetness for me as a chained whore in Daillon. And my dagger is very sharp, so I could end my life very swiftly and without much pain—I am, I think, rather afraid of pain, but not of death."

"Why," he said, reining in his horse so that he rode beside her donkey, "I should use you to hearten my men, mistress Melora. I did not know women were capable of such courage." He found himself wondering if Carlina would be able to talk this way when she rode into battle. He did not know. He had never thought to ask her.

It occurred to Bard that he had known many women intimately, since his fifteenth year. And yet it seemed to him, suddenly, that he really knew very little about what women were like. He had known their bodies, yes, but nothing of the rest of them; it had not occurred to him that any woman could be interesting to him, except for coupling with them.

And yet, he remembered, when they were all children, he had talked with Carlina as freely as he had talked with his foster brothers, had spent time with her; he had known her favorite foods, the colors of frocks and ribbons she liked best to wear, knew her fear of owls and of nightflyers, her dislike of nut porridge and seed cake, her dislike of pink frocks and shoes with over-high heels, how bored she became at sitting for long hours over her sewing; he had comforted her for the callouses on her fingers as she learned to play the *rryl* and the tall harp, and helped her with her lessons.

And yet, when he had become a man, and begun thinking of women in terms of lust, he had grown away from Carlina;

he did not know what kind of woman the child had become. What now seemed worse to him, he had not really cared; he had thought of her mostly as his promised wife. He had, lately, thought a great deal of bedding her; but somehow it had never occurred to him to talk with her, just talk with her as he was doing with this odd, soft-spoken, unbeautiful *leronis.*

It was disquieting; he had no particular interest in bedding this woman. In fact, the thought rather repelled him, she was so fat and so ungainly and so plain; she was one of the few women he had met who did not stir his manhood even slightly. Yet he wanted to go on talking with her; he felt closer to her, in a strange way, than he had felt in many years to anyone else except his foster brothers. He looked ahead of them, to where Mirella rode, silent and distant, and bewitchingly pretty, and as before, he felt the sudden stir of desire, and then he looked back at the solidly built, ungainly Melora, slumped on her donkey like, again the uncharitable comparison, a sack of grain. Why, he wondered, could not the beautiful Mirella also be soft-voiced and warm and friendly like this, why could she not ride at his side and look into his eyes with such sympathetic interest? Melora's hair was almost the same flame color as Mirella's; and behind her moon-faced chubby cheeks there was some faint hint of the same delicate bone structure. He said, "Mistress Mirella—you and she are very similar; is Mirella your sister or half-sister?"

"No," she said, "but we are kinswomen; her mother is my eldest sister. But I have another sister who is a *leronis* as well—all of us are gifted with *laran.* Are you not the son of Dom Rafael di Asturien? Why, then, my youngest sister Melisendra is one of your foster mother's women; she went to serve Domna Jerana three seasons ago. Have you never seen her there?"

"I have not been home for many years," Bard said shortly.

"Ah, that is sad," she said with warm sympathy, but Bard did not want to pursue that topic.

He said, "Have you been in battle before this, that you are so calm and not afraid?"

"Why, yes, I was beside my father at the battle of Snow Glen, with the sentry birds. I saw you given the king's banner."

"I did not know there were women there," he said, "not even among the *leroni.*"

"But I saw you," she said. "Nor was I the only woman

there. There was a detachment of Renunciates, the sworn Sister-hood of the Sword, and they, too, fought valiantly; had they been men, they would have won honor and the king's praise, even as you did. When the men broke through with axes on the southern flank, they held their shield-line against them until horsemen under Captain Syrtis could come to their aid. Two of them were killed, and one lost a hand; but they held that flank where they were stationed."

Bard grimaced. "I have heard of the Renunciates; I did not know King Ardrin would stoop to use them in battle! It is bad enough that they share fire-watch with men. I do not think a woman's place is on the field of war!"

"Nor do I," Melora said. "But then, I do not think a man's place is on the field of war either; nor does my father. He would rather abide at home, playing the lute and the *rryl,* and using our starstones to heal sickness and bring metals from under the earth. But while there is war, we must even fight as our lord and king wills it, Master Bard."

Bard smiled genially and said, "Women don't understand these things. War is a man's business, and men are never happier than when they are fighting, I think; but women should be able to stay at home and make songs and heal our wounds."

"Do you truly think a man's business is fighting?" Melora asked. "Well, I do not, and I hope that a day may come when men are as free from war as you would like to have all women."

"I am a soldier, *damisela,*" Bard said. "In a world of womanly peace I would have no place and no occupation. But if you love peace so well, why do you not leave war to men, who enjoy it?"

"Because," she said with spirit, "I do not know many men who truly enjoy it!"

"I do, *damisela.*"

"Do you truly? Or is it only that you have never had much opportunity for anything else?" Melora asked. "There was a day when all these lands were at peace, under the Hastur kings; but now we have a hundred petty kingdoms, all fighting year in and year out because they cannot agree! Do you really think that is the way the world should go?"

Bard smiled and said, "The world will go as it will, Mistress Melora, and not as you or I would have it."

"But," Melora said, "the world goes as men make it go; and men are free to make it go otherwise, if they have the courage!"

He smiled at her. She actually looked pretty to him now, her eyes animated, her round moon-face crinkled like fresh cream. It struck him that in her own way, she had a warm and sensuous presence, that her heavy body might be warm, welcoming; certainly she would not whimper like that stupid doll Lisarda, but would speak up to him spiritedly. He said, "It might be a better world if you had the making of it, Mistress Melora. Perhaps it is a pity that women have no part in the decisions which make our world."

Beltran came riding up to him. With a word of apology, Bard excused himself and rode forward with the prince.

"Master Gareth says they are encamped just beyond that wood," he said. "We should draw up here, and let the men rest their horses and eat well. Then, since one of the wenches has the Sight, we can be certain how best to attack them."

"Right," Bard said, and gave the orders which brought the men into a close circle, alert for possible attack—it was not impossible that the Dry-towners, knowing they were fixed in one spot for an attack, would ride out to take the initiative.

"Possible," Beltran said, "but not likely. If possible they like the snow less than we do. And they have the caravan to defend." He dismounted and rummaged in his saddlebags for a nosebag of feed for his horse. "I see you were sweetening one of our *leroni*. You must indeed be an incorrigible wencher, if you can find it in your heart to say a word to that fat cow! How stupid she looks!"

Bard shook his head. "Oh, she is attractive enough, in her own way and her voice is sweet," he said. "And whatever one may say of her, she is far from stupid."

Beltran said, with a sardonic laugh, "Watching you, I begin to think the old proverb is true, that all women are alike when the lamp is out, for certainly you will play at gallantry with anything that wears a skirt! Are you so desperate for female companionship, then, that you will hanker after a fat, ugly *leronis?*"

Bard said, exasperated, "I give you my word I don't *hanker after her.* I have nothing on my mind now but the battle we have to face over that hill, and whether we will have to face clingfire or sorcery! I show her courtesy because she is Master Gareth's daughter, no more than that! In heaven's name, foster brother, give your attention to our mission, not to my short-comings as a wencher!"

His helmet hung at the horn of his saddle. He pulled it free, fastening it over his head with the leather strap, meticulously tucking the warrior's braid out of his way. Beltran slowly followed his example. His face was white, and Bard felt a moment's sympathy, remembering their talk last night; but he had no time for that now.

He rode back along the line, checking each man's equipment, saying a word to each of them. His stomach was tight, and he felt braced, as always, by danger.

"We will come as near the top of the hill as we can, without being sighted," he said, "and wait there until Master Gareth signals. Then we will charge down at them as fast as we can and try to take them by surprise."

One of the men grumbled, "If their *larazu'in* are all sleeping!"

Bard said, "If they have sentry birds or sorcery watching us, perhaps we cannot take them entirely by surprise. But they cannot know in advance quite how many we are, or how fiercely we will fight! Remember, men, they're Dry-town mercenaries, this war is nothing to them, and the snow is our best ally, for they're not used to it."

"We're not, either," one man muttered in the ranks. "Sane men don't fight in snow!"

"Would you rather let this clingfire go through? If they can move clingfire in winter, we can capture it," Bard said sharply. "All right, men, no more talking now, they may hear us, and I want to surprise them as much as we can."

He rode ahead to Master Gareth, saying, "Try to see how many men are guarding the wagons."

Master Gareth gestured at Mirella. "I have done so already, sir. I cannot count up more than fifty; that is not counting the drovers, who may be armed, but who may have their hands full with the beasts."

Bard nodded. He beckoned to two experienced men, the best riders in the group, and said, "You two, just before we charge, take your shields for cover and ride down toward the head of the train; cut the animals loose and try to stampede them back toward the train. That will create more confusion. Ride warily; they may pick you off with arrows."

They nodded. Skilled men, veterans of many campaigns, each wore the red cord twisted around his warrior braid. One settled his helmet on his head and grinned, loosening the dagger he wore belted at his waist. "This is better for such work than a sword."

"Master Gareth," Bard said, "your part is done, and well done. You may stay here with the women. In any case you need not ride down into the charge with us. If they throw spells against us, you will be needed for counter-spells against their sorcery, but you are worse than useless in battle."

"Sir," said the *laranzu,* "I know my part in battle. And so do my daughter and my foster daughter. With respect, sir, mind you your fighting men, and leave my part to me."

Bard shrugged. "On your own head, then, sir. We shall have no time for you once the fighting begins." He met Melora's eyes and was suddenly troubled at the thought that she would ride, unarmed except for a dagger, on her little donkey, into the thick of the battle. But what could be do? She had made it amply clear that she needed none of his protection.

Still, he looked at her, troubled, feeling the fear grow. It pulsed through him like a living thing, stark, unreasoning terror. He saw the flesh sliced living from her bones, saw her dragged away in chains, Dry-town bandits squabbling for her maimed body, saw his foster brother Beltran stricken down. . . . He heard himself moan with terror. One of the men in the ranks cried out, a high, shrill sound of sheer panic.

"Ah, no—look where it flies, the demon. . . ."

Bard jerked his head up, seeing the darkness hovering over them, clawed and terrible, swooping down, down; heard Mirella scream aloud . . . flame spouted over them and he shrank away, feeling the withering breath of fire. . . .

Suddenly reality struck; nothing smelled burned or charred.

"Hold your line, men," he shouted. "It's illusion, a show to frighten babies . . . no worse than fireworks at midsummer day! Come on, men, is this the best they can do? They'd set a real forest blazing if they could, but this thing can't burn anybody; nothing will burn in the snow—come on!" he shouted, knowing that action was the best thing to shake off illusion. "Charge! Down the hill, you men there!" He kicked at his horse's ribs, felt her break into a gallop, crested the hill and looked down, at last, on the wagons. There were four of them, and he saw his men racing, swooping swiftly down to slash across the reins of the pack beasts, lash at them with their long whips. Bellowing, the animals broke into a lumbering gallop, and one of the carts swayed and overturned with a crash. Bard yelled, and rode on. A Dry-towner, a tall, pale man with blond hair flying loose, rose up with a long spear, aiming at his horse. Bard leaned down and cut him down. Out of the corner of his eye he saw Beltran riding down one of the Dry-towners, who stumbled, rolled, screamed under his horse's hoofs. Then he lost sight of his foster brother as three of the Dry-town mercenaries came at him at once.

He never remembered anything, afterward, of that battle; only noise, blood spattered on the snow, choking cold, and that through it all the snow continued to fall. Somewhere his horse stumbled and he fell and found himself fighting on foot. He had no idea how many he fought, or whether he killed them or just beat them off. At one point he saw Beltran down, facing two huge mercenaries, and ran through the snow, feeling his boots soaking wet, drawing his dagger and striking down one of the men; then the battle swept them apart again. Then he was standing on the first of the wagons, shouting to his men to rally there, to hold the wagons. All around them were the noises of battle, clashing sword and dagger, the screams of wounded men and dying horses.

And then all was quiet and Bard saw his men clambering toward the wagons, through the snow, rallying around them. He saw with relief that Beltran, though his face was bleeding under the helmet, was still on his feet. He sent one of the men to count their dead and wounded, and went with Master Gareth to inspect the wagons. He was thinking what a damned fool he would feel if these barrels contained dried fruits for the army quartermasters, instead of the clingfire they had been promised.

He set his foot into the wagons, cautiously unstoppered one barrel. He sniffed the bitter-acrid smell, nodding grimly. Yes, it was clingfire, the vicious stuff which, once set alight, went on burning whatever it touched, burning through clothing and flesh and bone. . . . It did not occur normally in nature; it was made by sorcery. He and his men were fortunate that, in the snow, probably the Dry-towners had felt that it would not ignite. Or perhaps they had not been told what they guarded; sometimes arrows tipped with clingfire were used to strike horses out from under men in the field, a cruel and unsoldierly trick, for the horses, maddened by the burning, went wild and ran amok, doing more damage than the fires.

He told off half a dozen unwounded or slightly wounded men to guard the wagons, placing them under Master Gareth. He saw with relief that Melora was unhurt, though her face was smeared with blood.

She said quietly, "A man came at me, and I stabbed him. It's his blood, not mine."

He ordered another three men to round up the missing horses. Of the Dry-towners who had not fled, the worst wounded were given a swift death. Those who could ride, or even run, had gone.

He was turning to take final inventory of how many pack beasts could be found—for they could not move the wagons without them—when there was a sudden yell behind him and he found himself facing a tall Dry-towner, rushing at him with sword and dagger. The man had evidently been hidden behind the wagons. He was bleeding from a great wound in the leg, but he parried Bard's sword stroke, thrusting under his guard with a dagger. Bard managed to get him away, strike down the sword, snatch his own dagger from his belt. Then they were in a deadly clinch, struggling, swaying, daggers raised, scissoring to Bard's throat. With his free hand Bard knocked up the two daggers, grabbed his own as it fell free and drove it, hard, into the man's ribs. He yelled, still struggling, and died.

Shaking, still sick with the shock of the surprise attack, Bard picked up his sword and sheathed it; bent to wrench his dagger free. But it was stuck in one of the vertebrae and resisted all attempts to pull it out; and finally he laughed mirthlessly, said, "Bury it with him. Let him take it with him into Zandru's hells. I'll have his in exchange, then." He picked up the Dry-towner's dagger, a beautifully ornamented one with a blade of dark metal and a hilt set with worked copper and green gems. He looked at it appreciatively. "He was a brave man," he said, and slid the dagger into his own sheath.

It took the rest of the day to round up the wagons and pack beasts, to bury the three men they had lost. Seven more were hurt more or less badly; one of those, Bard knew, and grieved, would never survive the long trek in winter back to Asturias. Master Gareth had taken a thigh wound but said that he would probably be able to ride the next day.

And through it all, with merciless silence and justice, the snow continued to fall. The short autumn day darkened early into night. Bard's men raided the wagons for the best of their supplies and cooked a feast. One of the pack beasts had broken a leg, and one man who had experience as a butcher slaughtered it properly, and set its carcass for pit roasting. The Dry-towners had plenty of wine with them, too, the sweet heavy treacherous stuff from Ardcarran, and Bard gave his men license to drink whatever they would, since the sentry bird, and Mirella's Sight, confirmed that there were no enemy near them. They sat and sang rowdy songs and bragged of what they had done in the battle, and Bard sat and watched them.

Melora said, standing behind him in her gray cloak, "I wonder how they can sit so, and laugh and sing, after such a day of blood and slaughter, and so many of their friends, and even their enemies, lying dead."

Bard said, "Why, *damisela,* you are not afraid of the ghosts of the dead, are you? Do you think the dead come around, jealous because the living are enjoying themselves?"

She shook her head silently. Then she said, "No. But for me this would be a time of mourning."

"You are not a soldier, lady. For a soldier, each battle he survives is an occasion to rejoice that he continues to live. And so they feast, and sing, and drink, and if we were on the march with a regular army, not a foray alone like this, they would take their pleasure with the camp followers, too, or be off to the nearest town for women."

She shuddered and said, "At least there are no towns near for them to pillage and rape—"

"Why, *damisela,* if men go into danger of death, it is the fortunes of war; why should women be immune from that fortune? Most women accept it peacefully enough," he said, laughing, and noticed that she did not look away or simper or giggle as most of the women he knew would have done, shocked or pretending to be so.

She only said, quietly, "I suppose it is so; the excitement, the relief of being alive, instead of dead, the general shock of battle. . . . I had not thought. I would not have accepted it peacefully if the Dry-towners had won, though. I am very glad they did not; glad I am still alive." She was standing close enough to him so that he could smell some faint perfume from her hair and her cloak. "I was frightened, for fear, if the battle went against us, I should not have courage to kill myself, but would accept—ravage, bondage, rape—rather than death—death seemed very horrible to me as I stood and watched men die—"

He turned and took her hand in his; she did not protest. He said in a low voice, "I am glad you are still alive, Melora."

She said, just as low, "So am I."

He drew her against him and kissed her, feeling with amazement how very soft her heavy body and full breasts felt against him, how warm her lips were under his. He could feel her yielding herself wholly to the kiss; but she drew back afterward, a little, and said softly, "No, I beg you, Bard. Not here, not like this, not with all your men around us. . . . I would not refuse you, you have my word of that," she said, "but not like this; I have been told . . . it is not right. . . ."

Reluctantly, Bard let her go. *I could love her so easily,* he thought. *She is not beautiful, but she is so warm, so sweet . . .* and all the pent-up excitement of the day surged in him. And yet he knew that she was right, too. Where there were no accessible women for the other men, it went against all decency and custom for the commander to have his own; Bard was a soldier and he knew better than to take any privilege his men could not share. Her willingness made it all the worse. He had never before felt so close to any woman.

Yet—he drew a deep breath of resignation. He said, "The fortunes of war, Melora. Perhaps—one day—"

"Perhaps," she said gently, giving him her hand and looking into his eyes. It seemed to him that he had never wanted any woman so much. Next to her all the women he had known were like children, Lisarda no more than a child playing with her dolls, even Carlina childish and unripe. And yet, to his surprise, he had no desire to press the matter. He knew perfectly well that he could put a compulsion on her, so that she would come, unseen by any of his men, to his bed after the whole camp slept; and yet the very thought filled him with loathing. He wanted her just as she was, her whole self, of her free will, desiring him. He knew that if he had only her body, all that made her *Melora* would be gone. Her body, after all, was only that of a fat, ungainly woman, young but already sagging and slovenly. It was something more that made her so infinitely desirable to him, and for a moment he wondered, and raised his eyes, blurting out the question.

"Have you put a spell on me, Melora?"

She raised her hands, laying them on either side of his face, the fat fingers closing around his cheeks with great tenderness, and looked straight into his eyes. Beyond the fire the men were singing a rowdy song:

> Four-and-twenty *leroni* went to Ardcarran,
> When they came back again, they couldn't use their
>   *laran*—

"Ah, no, Bard," Melora said very gently. "It is only that we have touched, you and I; we have been honest with each other, and that is a rare thing between a man and a woman. I love you well; I wish things were different, that we were somewhere else than in this place tonight." She leaned forward and touched his lips, very gently, with her own, not with desire but with a tenderness which warmed him more than the wildest passion. "Good night, my dear friend."

He pressed her fingers and let her go, watching her walk away, with regret and a sadness that was new to him.

> All the trailmen came, the place
>   was bursting at the seams;
> We watched them a-doing it, a-swinging
>   from the beams.
> Four-and-twenty farmers, bringing sacks of
>   nuts;
> Couldn't get the strings untied. . . .

Beltran said behind him, "They seem to be enjoying themselves. They've got some new verses I hadn't heard." He chuckled. "I remember when our tutors beat us for copying the dirtier verses of that one in Carlina's copybook."

Bard said, glad to have something else to think about, "I remember you telling him that it proved girls shouldn't learn to read."

"But I would as soon leave reading to women who have nothing more important to do," Beltran said, "though I suppose I will have to sign state papers and such matters." He leaned over Bard; his breath was sweet and winy, and Bard realized the boy had been drinking, perhaps a bit more than he could handle. "It's a good night to get drunk."

"How is your wound?"

Beltran chuckled and said, "Wound, hell! My horse ran

away with me down the hill and I slipped in my saddle and bashed my face into the saddle horn, and gave myself a nose-bleed; so I fought all the battle with blood pouring down my face! I think I must have looked very fearsome!" He edged under Bard's tarpaulin, pitched with the open end toward the fire, and sat down there. The tarpaulin over them kept the snow off. "It seems to be clearing, at last."

"We'll have to find out if any of the men have any skill at driving wagons and handling pack beasts."

Beltran yawned hugely. "Now that it's over, I feel I could sleep for a tenday. Look, it's early still, but most of the men are drunk as monks at midwinter."

"What else do you expect them to do, with no women around?"

Beltran shrugged. "I don't grudge them their skinful. Between you and me, Bard, I'm as well pleased. . . . I remember after the battle of Snow Glens, a group of the younger men dragged me with them to a whorehouse in the town—" He made a fastidious grimace. "I've no taste for such games."

"I prefer willing companions, not paid ladies, myself," Bard agreed, "though, after a battle like this, I doubt I'd know the difference." Yet inwardly he knew he was not telling the truth. Tonight he wanted Melora, and even if he had had the pick of all the courtesans of Thendara or Carcosa, he would still have chosen her. Would he have chosen her over Carlina? He found he did not want to think about that. Carlina was his handfasted wife, and that was different.

"You haven't had enough to drink, foster brother," Beltran said, and handed him a bottle. Bard put it to his lips and drank, long and deep, glad to feel the strong wine blurring away the pain of knowing that Melora had wanted him, as much as he wanted her, and that he had, surprising himself, agreed to let her go. Had she scorned him, regarded him as easy, a soft touch, a green boy who was afraid to impose his will on a woman? Was she playing games with him? No, he would have staked his manhood on her honesty. . . .

One of the men was playing a *rryl*. They shouted for Master Gareth to come and sing for them, but Melora came quietly from their tent.

"My father begs that you will excuse him," she said. "He is in great pain from his wound and cannot sing."

"Will you come and share our wine, lady?" But their tone

was very respectful, and Melora shook her head. "I will take my father a glass, if I may. It will help him to sleep, perhaps; but my kinswoman and I must care for him, and so we will not drink. But I thank you." Her eyes sought out Bard where he sat in the darkness across the fire, and he thought there was a new sadness in them.

"I thought he was not much wounded," Bard said.

"Why, so did I," Beltran said, "though I have heard that sometimes the Dry-towners put poisons of one sort or another on their blades. Never heard of anyone who died from it, though." Again he yawned, hugely.

The men around the fire sang ballad after ballad. At last the fire sank down and was covered, and the men, in groups of two or three or four against the cold, settled down into their blankets. Bard went quietly to the tent shared by the women and now by the wounded *laranzu.*

"How does Master Gareth?" he asked, stooping close to the entrance.

"The wound is greatly inflamed, but he is sleeping," Mirella whispered, kneeling at the doorway. "I thank you for inquiring."

"Is Melora within?"

Mirella looked up at him, her eyes wide and serious, and suddenly he knew that Melora had confided in her—or had the younger girl read Melora's mind and her thoughts?

"She is sleeping, sir." Mirella hesitated, then said in a rush, "She cried herself to sleep, Bard." Their eyes met, with sympathy and warmth. She touched his hand, lightly. He found that he spoke through a lump in his throat.

"Good night, Mirella."

"Good night, my friend," she said softly, and he knew that she did not lightly use the word. Filled with a strange mixture of bitterness and warmth, he strode away, back to the dying campfire and the darkened half-tent he shared with Beltran. In silence, he drew off boots, sword belt, unstrapped the dagger at his waist.

"You are *bredin* to a Dry-town bandit, Bard." Beltran laughed in the darkness. "For you have exchanged daggers, one for the other. . . ."

Bard hefted the dagger in his hand. "I doubt I shall ever fight with it, for it is too light for my hand," be said, "but it is marvelously ornamental, worked with copper and gems, and it is a legitimate prize of war; so I will wear it upon great occasions, and excite the envy of all." He slid the weapon under the flap of the tarpaulin. "Poor devil, he lies colder than we do tonight."

They stretched out, side by side. Bard's thoughts were with the woman who cried herself to sleep, across the camp. He had drunk enough to blur the worst of the pain, but not all.

Beltran said into the darkness, "I was not as much afraid as I thought I would be. Now it is over, it does not seem so frightening. . . ."

"It never does," Bard said. "Afterward it is simple—even exhilarating—and all you want is a drink, or a woman, or both. . . ."

"Not I," Beltran said. "I think a woman would sicken me at this point; I would rather drink with my comrades. What have women to do with war?"

"Ah, well, you're still young," Bard said affectionately, and his hand closed over his foster brother's. Not knowing whether it was his own thought or Beltran's, a vagrant thought floated across his mind, *I wish Geremy were with us.* . . . He remembered, at the edge of sleep, nights when all three of them had slept together like this, on hunting trips, fire-watch; fumbled, childish experimentation in the dark; memories pleasant, kindly, soothing the raw edges of his pain over Melora; he had loyal friends and comrades, foster brothers who loved him well.

At the edge of sleep, half dreaming, he felt Beltran's body pressed tight against his, and the boy whispered, "I would— would pledge to you, too, foster brother; shall we exchange knives, too?"

Bard, shocked awake, stared and burst out laughing.

"By the Goddess!" he said coarsely, "you are younger than I thought, Beltran! Do you still think I am boy enough to take my pleasure with boys? Or do you think because you are Carlina's brother I will take you for her?" He could not stop laughing. "Well, well, who would have thought it—that Geremy Hastur is still young enough to take field-license with his playmates!" The word he used was a coarser one, army gutter slang, and he heard Beltran's choked cry of shame and shock in the darkness. "Well, whatever Geremy may choose to do, Beltran, I am not fond of such childish games. Can't you behave like a man?"

Even in the dark he could see that Beltran's face was

flooded with angry color. The boy choked, half crying, and sat up. He said, through a sob of rage, "Damn you, you whoreson bastard! I swear, I will kill you for that, Bard—"

"What, from love to hatred so quickly?" mocked Bard. "You are still drunk, *bredillu*. Come, little brother, it's only a game, you'll outgrow it someday. Lie down and go back to sleep now, and don't be silly." He spoke kindly, now that his first shock was past. "It's all right."

But Beltran was sitting bolt upright in the darkness, his whole body stiff with rage. He said between his teeth, "You taunt me, you—! Bard mac Fianna, I swear to you, roses will grow us Zandru's ninth hell before you take Carlina to bed!" He got up and strode away, snatching up his boots and thrusting his feet into them; and Bard, shocked, sat staring after him.

He knew, sobered as if by a dash of the still-falling snow, that he had made a grave mistake. He should have remembered how young Beltran really was, and refused him more gently. What the boy wanted, no doubt, was only affection and closeness; as Bard himself had wanted. He need not have taunted the youngster's manhood. He felt a sudden impulse to scramble up and run after his foster brother, apologize for mocking him, make up the quarrel.

But the memory of the insult Beltran had flung held him motionless. He called me *whoreson, Bard mac Fianna, not di Asturien as is my right now.* Although down deep he knew that Beltran had simply spoken the first insult that came into his head, the truth of it hurt beyond enduring. Angrily, gritting his teeth, he lay down again. Let Prince Beltran sleep in the wagons, or among the horses, for all he cared!

CHAPTER FIVE

At midwinter-night, Ardrin of Asturias celebrated his victory over the Duke of Hammerfell.

The winter was unusually mild, and folk came from far and wide. The son of the duke was there; Lord Hammerfell had sent him to be fostered at the court of Asturias—so it was said. They all knew, as the boy himself knew, that he was a hostage for peace between Hammerfell and Asturias. Nevertheless, King Ardrin, who was a kindly man, introduced the boy as his fosterling, and it was obvious that he was being well treated and given the best of everything, from tutors and governesses to lessons in swordplay and languages, the proper education for a prince. The same education, Bard thought, looking at the child in his elaborate festival clothing, that he himself had had, at the side of Geremy Hastur and Prince Beltran.

"Still," Carlina said, "I feel sorry for the child, sent so young away from his home. You were older, Bard. You were turned twelve, and already as tall as a man. How old is young Garris—eight, or is it nine?"

"Eight, I think," Bard said, thinking that his own father could have come, or could, if he wished, have sent his young legitimate son Alaric. He could not count bad weather an excuse, and Alaric was old enough to be sent for fostering.

"Would you like to dance again, Carlina?"

"Not yet, I think," she said, fanning herself. She wore a green gown, just a little less elaborate than the one she had worn at midsummer to their handfasting; he felt that the color did not suit her, making her look pale and sallow.

Geremy came toward them and said, "Carlie, you have not

yet danced with me. Come now, Bard, you've had your share, and Ginevra is not here. She has gone to stay with her mother for the holiday, and I am not sure she will come back. Her mother has quarreled with Queen Ariel—"

"For shame on you for gossiping, Geremy!" Carlina struck him playfully with her fan. "I am sure that my mother and the Lady Marguerida will soon make it up, and then we shall have Ginevra back with us. Bard, go and dance with one of my mother's ladies. You cannot stand here all night beside me! There are many ladies eager to dance with the king's own banner bearer!"

Bard said sullenly, "Most of them don't want to dance with me. I am too clumsy!"

"Still, we cannot spend all evening here! Go and dance with Lady Dara. She is so clumsy herself that you will be graceful as a *chieri* beside her, and she will never notice if you step on her feet, for she is so fat she has not been on speaking terms with her own feet twenty years. . . ."

"And you reprove *me* for talking gossip, Carlie?" Geremy chuckled and took his foster sister's arm. "Come and dance, *breda*. So already you are giving Bard orders as if he were your husband?"

"Why, he is all but so," Carlina said, laughing. "I think we have the right to give orders to one another already!" She smiled gaily at Bard and moved away on Geremy's arm.

Left alone, Bard did not take her advice, or go and offer himself to the ungainly Lady Dara as a partner. He went toward the buffet and poured himself a glass of wine. King Ardrin and a group of his councillors were standing there, and amiably made room for Bard to join them.

"A good festival to you, foster son."

"And to you, kinsman," Bard said—he called the king foster father only in private.

"I have been telling Lord Edelweiss what you told me about the folk who live near Moray's Mill," the King said. "It is chaos and anarchy for so many folk to live with no proper overlord. Come spring thaw, I think we must ride out and set things in order there. If every little village claims to be independent and to make its own laws, there will be borders everywhere, and a man will not be able to ride half a day without needing to cope with some new set of laws."

"The lad has a head on his shoulders," said Lord Edelweiss, a gray-haired man dressed like an elaborate fop, and behind Bard's back, he heard the old man say, "Pity your own older son shows no such talent for strategy and war skills. Let's hope he has some skill at statesmanship, or that boy there will have the kingdom in his hands before he's twenty-five years old!"

King Ardrin said stiffly, "Bard is Beltran's devoted foster brother; they are *bredin.* I need fear nothing for Beltran in Bard's hands."

Bard bit his lip, troubled. He and Beltran had been hardly on speaking terms since that battle and its aftermath; Beltran, tonight, had given him no midwinter gift, though he had meticulously sent the prince an egg from his best hunting hawk, to be hatched under a palace hen; a thoughtful gift and one that would normally have brought delighted thanks from his foster brother. In fact, it seemed that Beltran was avoiding him.

Again Bard cursed himself for his own folly in quarreling with Beltran. Raw-edged over his own frustration, the enforced separation from Melora—for he knew that she had wanted him then, as much as he wanted her—he had lashed out at Beltran because the boy was the most convenient object on which to vent his own fury. He should, instead, have taken that chance to cement his own bond with the young prince. Damn it, he missed their old closeness! Well, at least Beltran had not yet poisoned Geremy's mind against him . . . he hoped. It was hard to tell what went on behind Geremy's somber face, and although it might only have been that Geremy was missing his Ginevra, Bard found that hard to believe. They were not handfasted, and Ginevra was not really of sufficiently noble birth to be a proper match for the heir to Hastur of Carcosa.

Perhaps tonight he should seek out Beltran, make his apologies and explain to his foster brother why he had been so sharp with him. . . . His outraged pride cringed at that thought. But a serious and unmended quarrel with the prince could damage his own career, and if some of the king's councillors were already wondering if Bard stood dangerously close to the throne—he was, after all, the eldest son of the king's own brother—then he had better make sure that Beltran did not perceive him as a threat!

But before he could put his resolve into action, a voice at

his shoulder said genially, "A good festival to you, dom Bard."

Bard turned to face the elderly *laranzu*. "And to you, Master Gareth. Ladies," he acknowledged, bowing to Mirella, lovely in her pale-blue gauze draperies, and to Melora, who wore a low-necked gown of green with a high collar; the dress cut as loose as a pregnant woman's, and indeed, her heavy body made her look very much as if she were pregnant, but the color showed the high color of her clear skin, made her red hair glow.

"You are not dancing, Master Gareth?"

The old man shook his head with a rueful smile. He said, "I cannot," and Bard saw that he leaned on a stout walking stick. "A memory, sir, of that fight with the Dry-towners."

"Why, such a wound should be long healed," Bard said, with concern, and he shrugged.

"I think perhaps there was poison on the dagger; had it not been diluted by many other fights, I should have lost the leg," Master Gareth said. "It has never healed completely, and now I begin to think it never will. Even *laran* has not sufficed. But it does not keep me from the festival," he said, courteously dismissing the subject.

The young son of Hammerfell's duke came up and said shyly, "Will the Lady Mirella dance with me?"

She glanced at her guardian for permission—Mirella was too young to dance at public balls except with kinsmen—but evidently Master Gareth considered the youngster far too young to represent any threat; they were obviously children together. He gestured approval and they moved away together. The boy was not nearly as tall as Mirella, so they made a somewhat incongruous partnership.

Bard said to Melora, "Will you honor me, Melora?"

Master Gareth raised his eyebrows slightly at the informal use of her name, but she said, "Certainly," and held out her hand. She was, Bard reflected, probably several years older than he was himself, and he was surprised that she was not yet married or pledged.

After a moment, as they danced, he put the question, and she said, "I am promised to Neskaya Tower. I dwelt at Dalereuth for a time; but they set us to making clingfire, and I feel it very strongly—that *leroni* should be neutral in wars. So

I am bound to Neskaya, where the Keeper has pledged to neutrality in all wars among the Domains."

"That seems to me an ill choice," said Bard. "If we must fight, why should *leroni* be exempt from battle? Already they do not carry weapons, even in battle. Are they to live at peace when the rest of us must fight for our lives?"

"Someone must begin the fight for peace," Melora said. "I have spoken with Varzil and I think him a great man."

Bard shrugged. "A deluded idealist, no more," he said. "They will burn the Tower of Neskaya about your heads, and go on making war as always. I only hope, Lady, that you may not share in their fall."

"I hope so, too," she said, and they were silent, dancing. She was singularly light on her feet, moving like a breath of air.

He said, "Dancing, you are very beautiful, Melora. How strange, when first I saw you, I did not think you beautiful at all."

"And now that I look at you, I see you are a handsome man," she said. "I do not know how much you have heard about *leroni*—I am a telepath and I do not look much at people, what their outward aspect may be. I had no idea even whether you were fair or dark, when I talked with you on campaign. And now, you are the king's banner bearer and a handsome man and all the ladies envy me because you do not dance often with them."

From any other woman, Bard thought, this would have sounded unendurably coy and flirtatious. Melora stated it simply, like any other fact.

They danced, silently, the old sympathy beginning to build up again between them. In an isolated corner of the room, he drew her to him and kissed her. She sighed and allowed the kiss, but then, regretfully, drew away.

"No, my dear," she said, very gently. "Let's not allow this to go so far that we cannot part as friends, and no more."

"But why not, Melora? I know that you feel as I do, and now we are not hindered as we were after the battle—"

She looked straight at him. She said, "What we might have done, had occasion offered, in hot blood and after the excitement and danger of battle, is a thing apart; now, in cold blood, you know and I know that it would not be suitable. You are here with your promised wife; and the Princess Carlina has been most gracious to me. I would not step on the hem of her robe before her very eyes. Bard, you know I am right."

He did, but in his outraged pride, he would not acknowledge it. He flung at her, wrathfully, "What man except some sandal-wearer wishes to be only friend to a woman?"

"Oh, Bard," she said, shaking her head, "I think you are two men! One of you is heartless and cruel, especially with women, and cares nothing how you hurt! The other is the man I have seen, the man I dearly love—even though I will not share your bed this night, nor any other," she added firmly. "But I hope with all my heart, for Carlina's sake that it is always this other man I know that you show to her. For *that* one, I shall cherish all my life." She pressed his hand gently, turned away from him, and quickly lost herself in the crowd of dancers.

Bard, left alone, his cheeks burning with outrage, tried to follow her green-clad form through the crowds; but she had hidden herself from him as completely as if she had vanished right out of the hall. He had the faint prickling sense of *laran* in use and wondered if she had thrown a mantle of invisibility over herself, as he knew some *leroni* could do. His rage and wounded pride knew no bounds.

Fat, stupid woman, probably she had cast a glamour over him so that he wanted her, because no man before had ever done so. . . . Well, Varzil of Neskaya was welcome to her, damn him, and he hoped the Tower was burned over their heads! He went back to the buffet and wrathfully drank another glass of wine, and another, knowing that he was getting drunk, knowing King Ardrin, himself an abstemious man, would not approve.

Nor did Carlina; when she met with him again, there was gentle reproof in her voice.

"Bard, you have been drinking more than is seemly."

"Are you going to make me a henpecked husband even before the wedding?" he snarled at her.

"Oh, my dear, don't talk that way," she said, flushing to the neck of her green gown. "But my father will be angry too. You know that he hates it when any of his young officers drink so much that they cannot behave in a seemly manner."

"Have I done anything unseemly?" he demanded of her.

"No," she admitted, smiling a little, "but promise me not to drink any more, Bard."

"*A ves ordras, domna*," be conceded, "but only if you will dance with me."

It was a couple-dance again, and, with the license allowed to a handfasted pair, he could hold her tightly, not at the decorous distance required of most couples. Geremy, he noticed, had been given the privilege of dancing with Queen Ariel, at a most respectful distance indeed. Beltran had (probably at Carlina's request) chosen to dance with the ungainly Lady Dara. She too was graceful on her feet, as much as Melora, was it so common for ladies who were over-plump to dance so gracefully? Damn it, he would not think of Melora now! She might dance with the fiends from Zandru's hells, for all he cared! He drew Carlina vengefully close to him, aware of her thin, bony slenderness in his arms. A man could be bruised on those bones!

"Not so tightly, Bard, you are hurting me . . ." she protested. "And it is not suitable. . . ."

He let her go, stung with compunction. He said, "I wouldn't hurt you for the world, Carlie. Anyone or everyone else, but never you."

The dance ended. The king and queen, with the more elderly and dignified ladies and lords of the court, were withdrawing, so that their presence might not inhibit the younger people at their revels. He saw that the young son of Hammerfell was being taken away by his governess, and that the pretty Mirella was being folded into her cloak by Master Gareth. King Ardrin made a little speech, wishing the youngsters a merry festival and bidding them dance till dawn if they wished.

Carlina stood beside Bard, smiling as her parents departed. She said, "Last year I, too, was taken away at mid-night when the elders and children were sent to bed. This year, I suppose, they think that as a handfasted bride I am in no danger, with my promised husband to guard me." Her smile was merry.

And, in truth, Bard knew that midwinter revels sometimes grew a little rowdy. They were certainly noisier, after the old people and children departed; there was more drinking, many boisterous kissing games, and the dances grew wilder and less decorous. As the night moved on toward dawn, more and more couples slipped away into the gallery and side passages of the castle, and once Bard and Carlina, dancing past a long passage, saw a couple closely embraced, so intimately so that Carlina quickly turned away her eyes. But Bard steered her into the galleries.

He murmured, "Carlina, you are promised to me already. I think already most of the couples here who are pledged or handfasted have gone apart—" He drew her into his arms, straining her close to him. "You know what I want of you, my promised wife. It is midwinter, we are handfasted, why not make it complete now, since the laws permit?" His mouth fastened over hers; when she twisted away to breathe he murmured thickly, "Even your father could not protest!"

She said softly, "Bard, no, no." He could sense the rising panic in her, but she spoke in an undertone, trying desperately for calm.

"I have resigned myself to this marriage, Bard. I'll honor my father's wish, I promise you. But not—not now." He sensed, and it struck pain deep into him, that she was fighting hard not to show her dismay and revulsion. "Give me time. Not—not now, not tonight."

It seemed that he could hear again the threatening words Beltran had hurled at him: *roses will grow in Zandru's ninth hell before you take Carlina to bed!*

He snarled at her, "Has Beltran made good his threat, then?"

Melora had refused him, too, though a scant forty days before she wanted him. Melora was a telepath; she must have been aware of the quarrel with Beltran, knew Beltran could poison the king's mind against him; a liaison with an out-of-favor courtier could do Melora no good. . . . Beltran had turned Melora against him, too, and now Carlina. . . .

Carlina said, her voice shaking, "I don't know what you are talking about, Bard. Have you quarreled with my brother?"

"And if I had, would that change your mind about me?" he demanded, bitterly. "So, you too are like all women, you will tease me as if I had no manhood! You are my promised wife, why do you draw away from me as if I meant rape?"

"You just now said," she replied, staring up at him with bitterness as great as his own, "that you would never want to hurt me. Does that hold only when I agree to everything you want of me? Do you think it would not be rape because I am your promised wife? I love you as foster brother and friend, and if the Goddess is merciful to us both, a day will come when I will love you as the husband my father has given to me. But that time is not yet; I have been promised that I shall have till midsummer. Bard, I beg you, let me go!"

"So that your father may have enough time to change his mind about me? So that Beltran may poison his mind against me, have you given to his own minion?"

"How dare you say that of Geremy," she demanded furiously, and somehow the name ignited the last reserves of Bard's wrath.

"So, you are so careful of *his* honor, that *ombredin*, that half-man—"

"Don't speak that way of my foster brother," she said in a rage.

"I'll speak as I choose, and no woman shall prevent me," he flung at her.

"Bard, you are still drunk; the wine cup speaks, not you," she said, and his own fury blazed up, the last vestiges of his self-control flaring. He had let Melora go out of respect for Carlina! How dare she refuse him now, as if he were nothing to her? He would not be un-manned twice on midwinter night by some damned woman's whims! He dragged her into the gallery, gripping her so hard that she cried out, and forced his lips down on hers, ignoring her struggles. Mingled wrath and desire flamed high in him; for the second time, a woman he wanted and felt he had a right to have had denied him, and this time he would not submit to her meekly, but he would impose his will on her! Damn it, she was his wife, and tonight he would have her, willingly if she chose, but in any case he would have her! She struggled in his arms, in growing panic, exciting him unendurably.

"Bard, no, no," she pleaded, sobbing. "Not like this, not like this . . . oh, please, please. . . ."

He held her, fiercely, knowing that he was hurting her with the violence of his grasp. "Come to my room, then! Don't make me force you, Carlina!" How could she possibly be indifferent to this raging torrent of desire in him? Somehow, he must *make* her feel it! What he wanted was for her to want him as fiercely as he wanted her, to match his own desire and need with her own, and here she was fighting and struggling against him as if she were an unkissed child who did not even know what he wanted of her!

A hand alighted on his shoulder; tore them apart.

"Bard, you are drunk, or completely out of your mind?" Geremy asked, staring at them in dismay. Carlina covered her face with her hands, weeping with relief and shame.

"Damn you, how dare you interfere, you half-man—"

"Carlina is my foster sister," Geremy said. "I won't have her raped at a party, even by her promised husband! Bard, in the name of all the gods, go and slosh your face with cold water and apologize to Carlina, and we'll say no more of this; and next time, stop drinking while you can still master yourself!"

"Damn you—" Bard advanced on Geremy with fury, his fists clenched; Beltran seized him from behind. He said, "No, you don't, Bard. Carlina, you didn't want this, did you?"

She sobbed, "No, I didn't," and Bard said angrily, "She is my promised wife! She had no right to refuse herself to me this way—you did not hear her crying out, certainly! By what right do you assume she wishes to be released from me? She liked it well enough, until you came along to interfere—"

"Now there you lie," Beltran said in a rage. "For everyone in this hall with a scrap of *laran* must have heard her cry out against you! I'll see that my father hears of this! Damnable bastard, trying to take by force what he could never have had willing—"

Bard whipped his dagger out of its sheath. The green gems glittered in the light. He said low, between his teeth, "You meddling catamite, don't presume to interfere in what you don't know the first thing about! Get out of my way—"

"No!" Geremy grabbed his wrist. "Bard, you are raving mad! To draw steel at midwinter, before your prince? Beltran, he's drunk, don't listen to what he says! Bard, go and sober up, and I'll give you my word of honor, the king will hear no more of this—"

"So you're in this against me too, you filthy boy-lover, you and your minion," Bard yelled, and sprang at him. Geremy stepped aside, trying to avoid the thrust of the dagger, but Bard, beside himself with rage, hurled himself at Geremy and they slammed to the floor, struggling. Geremy twisted his body, grabbing his own dagger. He was still begging, "Bard, no—foster brother, don't—" but Bard did not even hear, and Geremy knew that he must fight in real earnest now, or Bard would kill him. They had fought before this, as boys, but never, before this, with real weapons in their hands. Bard was stronger than he was. He thrust up, trying to knock the dagger aside, to shove his knee between himself and Bard's descending blade. He felt his knife go into Bard's arm, slit the leather and scrape flesh; and in the next moment Bard's dagger went deep into his thigh, high up near the groin. He cried out, harshly, in agony, feeling the leg go numb.

Then a dozen of the king's men were dragging them apart, and Bard, abruptly sobered by the flood of adrenalin, like a cold wash over him, stared at Geremy, rolling about in convulsive agony on the floor.

"Zandru's hells! *Bredu*—" he begged, dropping to his knees beside his foster brother; but he knew Geremy did not hear him. Carlina was sobbing in Beltran's arms.

Beltran said to one of the soldiers, "Escort my sister to her apartments, and find her maids; then go and awaken my father. I will be responsible."

He dropped to his knees beside Geremy, shoving Bard viciously aside.

"Don't touch him, you—! You've done enough! Geremy, *bredu*, my beloved brother—speak to me, I beg you, speak to me—" He sobbed, and Bard heard the anguish in his voice. But Geremy was beyond hearing.

One of the soldiers grabbed Bard, not gently, and took the dagger, "Poisoned," he said. "A Dry-town dagger." And Bard, in horror, recalled, for the first time that evening, that it was the dagger he had taken in the fight. The slightest wound from a Dry-town dagger, poisoned like this, had meant that Master Gareth had been lamed, probably for life. And he had struck Geremy, in his rage, deep into the hamstrings. Shocked, too horrified to speak, he let the soldiers take him away and place him under arrest.

He spent forty days under house arrest, and no one came near him. He had plenty of time to regret his rashness, his drunken rage; but there were times, too, when he blamed Carlina for it all. Food was brought to his rooms by soldiers, who told him that for a week Geremy had raved in delirium and hung between life and death; but they had sent for a *laranzu* from Neskaya who had saved his life and even his leg. But the leg, they had heard, envenomed by the poison, had withered and shrunk, and he would probably never walk again without support.

In a cold wash of terror, Bard wondered what they would do with him. To draw steel at midwinter festival was a crime enough; to wound a foster brother even in play was a serious offense. Beltran had broken Bard's nose once, at one of their games, and he had been severely beaten, prince or no, by their tutors, had been forced to apologize at dinner time before everyone in the king's household, and had been required by the king to give Bard, in fine, his best hawk, and his finest cloak. He still had the cloak.

He tried to bribe the soldier who guarded him to smuggle out a message to Carlina. If she would intercede for him—she was his only hope. The least he could expect would be a year's exile, and forfeiture of the king's favor. They could not void his marriage to Carlina, but they could put some trouble in his way. If Geremy had died, he would have faced three years exile, at least, and blood-money to Geremy's family; but Geremy was not dead. But the soldier curtly refused, saying the king had forbidden any messages to be carried.

Wholly alone, thrown on his own resources, Bard's bitterness washed away his remorse. It was Melora's doing; if she had not refused him, he would not have had to take out his rage and frustration on Carlina, he could have given Carlina the extra half-year she wanted, until their appointed time. Melora had led him on, then refused him, damned tease!

And then Carlina! She said that she would love him as a husband, yet she put him off this way! And how dared Geremy and Beltran, damned *ombredin-y*, to come interfering? Beltran was jealous, damn him, because Bard had refused him, and he had called his minion to fight him. . . . It was their fault! He had done nothing wrong!

Rage hardened his remorse, until the day, with soft spring rain flooding the castle roofs and the spring thaw at hand, when two soldiers came into his room and said, "Best dress yourself, Dom Bard; the king has called you to audience."

Bard dressed carefully in his best, shaving himself closely and braiding his hair into the warrior's braid, twisting the red cord around it. When the king saw it, perhaps he would remember how well Bard had served him, and for how long. If he had killed or maimed the king's son, he knew, nothing could have saved him; he would count himself lucky to be allowed a quick death and not be torn on hooks. But Geremy was a hostage, son of the king's enemies—

Geremy was the king's foster son and his own foster brother. It would not save him.

He came into the king's presence-chamber with a defiant stride, standing tall, staring down everyone in the room. Carlina was there, among the queen's women, pale and drawn, her hair dragged back from her face into a thin knot, her eyes huge and frightened. Beltran looked angry, defiant and would not meet Bard's eyes. Bard looked for Geremy. He was there, leaning on crutches, and Bard noticed that the wounded leg still bore a slipper rather than a boot and that Geremy did not set it to the ground.

He felt his throat tighten. He would not have harmed Geremy. Damn it, why hadn't Geremy kept out of it, why had they insisted on interfering in what was between Bard and his promised wife?

King Ardrin said, "Well, Bard mac Fianna, what have you to say for yourself?" The name of a bastard—the name of his unknown mother, not the *di Asturien* he was called in courtesy, boded ill.

Bard bent the knee before his foster father. He said, "Only this, kinsman; the fight was not of my seeking, but they forced it upon me. And that I have served you for five years, and I think I have served you well. With your own hand you commended me at Snow Glens and gave me a red cord, and I captured clingfire for your armies. I love my foster brother well and I would never have harmed him willingly; I did not know the dagger was poisoned, I swear it."

"He lies," Beltran said passionlessly, "for we made jokes about his having become *bredin* to a Dry-towner, and he had heard mistress Melora, the *leronis,* say that her father's wound was poisoned."

"I had forgotten it was not my own dagger," Bard protested angrily. "I admit it, kinsman, I should not have drawn my steel at Festival. I am so far guilty; but Geremy forced the fight upon me! Did Prince Beltran tell you that he was only jealous?"

King Ardrin said, "Was it Geremy who drew his dagger first?"

"No, kinsman," Bard said, dropping his head, "but I swear I did not know the dagger was poisoned; I had forgotten. And I was drunk; if they are just, they will tell you that, too, and that they forced the quarrel by laying rough hands on me. I drew my dagger in self-defense. I did not want to be beaten by them like a lackey, and there were two of them!"

"Geremy," asked the king, "did you and Beltran lay hands on Bard first? I will have the truth of this matter, all the truth."

"We did, Uncle," Geremy said, "but he had laid hands on Carlina in a way she did not like, and Beltran and I would not have her mauled, or even raped."

"Is this true, Bard?" The king looked at him with surprise and displeasure. He said, "They had spared to tell me this! Did you so far forget yourself as to mishandle Carlina when you were drunk?"

"As to that," Bard said, feeling caution desert him with the remembered rage, "Carlina is my pledged wife and they had no right to interfere! Beltran has made a great thing of this because he is jealous, he wants to give Carlina to his *bredu* there, to bind them closer still! He is jealous because I have showed myself his better at swordplay and in war, and with women too—not that he would know what to do with a woman when he is alone with her! Where was Beltran when I defended you at Snow Glens, Uncle?"

He knew that he had struck inside the king's guard there; for Ardrin of Asturias flinched, and looked angrily at his son, then from one to the other of his foster sons.

"Father," Beltran said, "is it not clear to you that he has plotted to seize the kingdom from your hands, to take Carlina whether she will or no, to win your armies' allegiance behind your back? If he were still your loyal and obedient subject, would he have drawn steel at midwinter festival?"

King Ardrin said, "Whether or no, it is clear that I have reared a wolf cub to bite my hand. Was it not enough to you, Bard, that Carlina was pledged to you and should have been yours at the proper time?"

"By all the laws of this kingdom, Carlina is mine," Bard protested, but the king stopped him with an upraised hand.

"Enough. You presume too much. A handfasting is not a marriage, and not even the king's foster son can lay a hand undesired upon the king's daughter. You have broken too many of the laws of this court, Bard; you are a troublemaker. I will have no lawbreaker and kin-maimer within this household. Get you gone from here. I give you horse and sword and hunting bow and armor, and purse of four hundred silver royals; and thus do I reward your past services to me. But I name you outlaw within Asturias. I give you three days to leave this realm; and after that, if you are seen within the borders of Asturias for seven years from midwinter, no law shall protect you. Any man may slay you like an animal, without blood-guilt, or blood-feud begun, or blood-money paid to your kinsmen for wounding or death."

Bard stood blinking in outrage at the severity of the punishment. He had expected to lose his place at court—the king could have done no less. He could have accepted, with equanimity, the usual sentence of a year's outlawry; had even steeled himself, if the king was in a mood to be severe, to the knowledge that he might have to go into exile for three years. He had also been sure that when next King Ardrin had gone to war and had need of him, he would have been forgiven and recalled to court. But *seven years' exile!*

"This is hard, *vai dom*," he protested, kneeling before the king. "I have served you faithfully and well, and I am not yet even full grown. How do I deserve such hard treatment?"

King Ardrin's face was like stone. "If you are old enough to behave like a man, and a vicious one," he said, "you are old enough to suffer the penalty I would lay on such a man. Some of my councillors have thought me over-lenient that I do not order you killed. I have taken a pet dog to my heart and I find a wolf biting my heels! I name you wolf and outlaw, and I bid you begone from this court before sunset and from this realm within three days, before I take second thought and decide I want no such man living within my kingdom. I love your father well, and I would prefer not to have the blood of his son on my hands; but don't presume on this, Bard, because if I see your face within the borders of Asturias within seven years, I shall certainly strike you down like the wolf you are!"

"Not in seven years, not in seven times seven, tyrant," Bard cried, leaping to his feet, and flung down at the king's feet the red cord the king had given him in battle. "All the gods grant that we meet in battle when you are guarded only by your son there and his trustworthy catamite! You speak of lawbreaking? What law is stronger than that which binds a man to his wife, and you, sir, are flouting that!" He turned away from the king and strode toward where Carlina stood among the women.

"What do you say, my wife? Will you, at least, show justice within the law, and follow me into exile as a wife should do?"

She raised her eyes to him, cold and tearless.

"No, Bard, I will not. An outlaw has no claim, and no protection in law. I would have done my father's will and married you; but I begged him once to spare me this marriage, and now I rejoice that he has changed his mind; and you know why."

"There was a time when you said you could love—"

"No," she interrupted him. "I call Avarra to witness; I thought, perhaps, when I had grown older and you, perhaps, wiser, if the Goddess was merciful to us, we might one day come to love each other as it was suitable for married people. It would have been even more truthful to say that I hoped for it, not that I believed it would come to pass. There was a time when I loved you well as foster brother and friend. But you have forfeited that."

His face twisted in a gesture of contempt. "So you are like all the other women, bitch! And I thought you something different and above them!"

Carlina said, "No, Bard, I—" but King Ardrin gestured her to silence.

"No more, girl. You need hold no more parley with him. Henceforth he is nothing to you. Bard mac Fianna," he said, "I give you three days to quit my realm. After that time I lay on you the doom of an outlaw; no man, woman or child in this realm may give you roof or shelter, food or drink, fire or fuel, aid or counsel. And for the space of seven years, if you are found within the borders of this realm, you shall be slain like a wolf at any man's hand, and your body given to wild beasts without public mourning or burial. Now go."

Custom demanded that the outlaw should bend the knee to his king in token that he accepted his doom. Perhaps, if King Ardrin had given him the customary sentence, Bard would have done so; but he was young and proud, and raging with frustration.

"I will go, since you leave me no remedy," he snarled. "You have named me wolf; wolf I shall be from this day forth! I leave you to the mercy of those two you have chosen over me; and I shall return when you cannot forbid me. And as for you, Carlina—" his eyes sought her out, and the girl cringed. "I swear that I will have you, one day, whether you will or no; and that I vow to you, I, Bard mac Fianna, I, the wolf!"

He spun on his heel and went forth from the great hall, and the doors swung shut behind him.

CHAPTER SIX

"But where will you go?" Dom Rafael of Asturias asked his son. "What are your plans, Bard? You are over-young to set forth outside the realms of your own kingdom, alone and outlawed!" Bard's father all but wrung his hands. "Lord of Light, what folly and what misfortune!"

Bard shook his head impatiently. "What's done is done, Father," he said, "and bewailing will not better it. 1 was ill-done-by; the king your brother showed me small justice and no mercy, for a quarrel I never wanted. All I can do is to set my back to the court of Asturias and seek better fortune elsewhere."

They were standing in the room that had been Bard's own since his father had brought him to his own house, to rear with his own legitimate son; out of kindness or sentiment, Dom Rafael had kept the room ready for Bard, though he had not set foot in it since he was twelve years old. It was a boy's room, not a man's, and there was not much in it that Bard cared to take with him into exile.

"Come, Father," be said, almost affectionately, laying his hand on the older man's shoulder, "it's not worth grieving. Even if the king had showed me leniency, and had only sent me from court for that damnable midwinter folly, I could hardly have stayed here; Lady Jerana loves me as little as ever. And now she can hardly conceal her rejoicing that I am well out of her way, for good and all." His grin was fierce. "I wonder if she thinks I would try to seize Alaric's heritage, as the king came to think I coveted Beltran's? After all, in days past, the elder son was often shown preference over the legitimate son. Come, Father, has it never crossed your mind, that perhaps I would not be content to see Alaric preferred before me, and try to take what is lawfully his?"

Dom Rafael di Asturien looked up at his tall son seriously. He was a man a little past the prime of age, broad-shouldered, with the look of a muscular and active man who has let himself go soft in retirement. He said, "Would you so, Bard?"

Bard said, "No," and turned over in his fingers a hawk hood he had made when he was eight years old. "No, Father, do you think me wholly without honor, because of this quarrel I have had with my foster brothers? That was folly, drunken folly and something akin to madness, and if I could mend it—but not even the Lord of Light can turn back time, or undo what has been done. And as for Alaric and his heritage—Father, there are many bastard sons who grow up as outcasts, with no name but the name of a dishonored mother, and no man's hand to guide them, and no more fortune than they can wrest from the world by the toil of their hands, or by banditry. But you reared me in your own house, and from childhood I had good companions, and was well taught, and was fostered in the king's house when it was time for me to learn the skills of manhood." With a shyness surprising in the arrogant young warrior, he reached out and embraced his father. "You could have had peace in your bed and at your fireside, had you been willing to send me away to be prentice to a smith or a farmer or some tradesman. Instead I had horses and hawks and was raised as a nobleman's son, and you endured strife with your lawfully wedded lady for this. Do you think I can forget that, or try to have more than this generous portion, from the brother who has always called me brother, and never *bastard?* Alaric is my brother, and I love him; I would be worse than ingrate, I would be wholly without honor, if I laid a hand on what is rightfully his. And if I have any regret for my quarrel with that damnable sandal-wearer Beltran, it is that I might somehow have harmed you or Alaric."

"You have not harmed me, my son," Dom Rafael said, "though I shall find it hard to forgive Ardrin for what he has done to you. When he cast a slight upon your loyalty, he cast a slight upon mine, causing me to question what I have never questioned before, that he was rightfully king of this land. And as for harming Alaric—" he broke off, laughed and said, "you may ask him that for yourself. I think he is glad enough to see you home that he would welcome whatever sent you here."

As he spoke the door opened, and a very small boy, about eight years old, came into the room. Bard turned away from the saddlebags he was packing. "Well, Alaric, you were only a little boy when I went away to the king's court, and now you are nearly old enough for your own spurs and honor!" He hugged the child and swung him up in his arms.

"Let me go with you into exile, my brother," the child said fiercely. "Father wants me to go and be fostered in the house of that old king! I don't want to serve a king who would exile my brother!" He saw Bard laugh and shake his head, and he insisted, "I can ride; I can serve as your page, even your squire, take care of your horse and carry your arms—"

"No, now, my lad," Bard said, setting the boy on his feet, "I shall have no need for page or squire on the roads I must ride now; you must stay and be a good son to our father while I am in outlawry, and that means learning to be a good man. As for the king, if you are quiet and reasonable and speak low, he will like that better than being brave and speaking your mind; he is a fool, but he is the king and he must be obeyed, were he as stupid as Durraman's donkey."

"But where will you go, Bard?" the child insisted. "I heard the men crying the doom of outlawry on you at the crossroads, and they said that no one could give you food or fire or help—"

Bard laughed. "I shall carry food for three days," he said, "and before that time is over I shall be well out of Asturias, into lands where no one gives heed to King Ardrin's dooms and justices. I have money with me and a good horse."

"Will you go and be a bandit, Bard?" the boy asked, his eyes wide in wonder, and Bard shook his head.

"No; only a soldier. There are many overlords who can use a skilled man."

"But *where?* Will we know?" the boy asked, and Bard chuckled, answering only with a snatch of an old ballad:

> I shall fare forth to the setting sun
> Where it sinks beyond the sea;
> An outlaw's doom shall be my fate
> And all men flee from me.

"I wish I were going with you," the boy said, but Bard shook his head.

"Each man rides with his own fate, brother, and your road is to the king's house. His own son is grown, but he has a new fosterling, Garris of Hammerfell, who is your own age, and no doubt you'll be foster brothers and *bredin;* which, no doubt, is why he sent for you."

"That," Dom Rafael said with a sardonic curl of his lip, "and to make it certain I understood that his quarrel was with you, and not with me. Well, if he wishes to think me so quickly forgetful, be it so. And as for you, Bard, you could ride to the border and take service with The MacAran. He holds El Haleine against strife on all sides, and there are bandits, and cat-things coming down out of the Venza hills; he will be glad enough of a good sword."

"I had thought of that," Bard said, "though it is over near Thendara and there are Hasturs there. Some of Geremy's kin might declare blood-feud on me, and I would need to guard my back night and day. I would rather be out of Hastur country for a few years." He bit his lip and stared at the floor. A picture of Geremy was before his eyes, white and wasted from illness, halting on the lame leg. Damn Beltran who had drawn Geremy into their quarrel! If he must have maimed a foster brother, why could it not have been the one with whom he truly had a quarrel? A foolish quarrel, but still a quarrel; he and Geremy had seldom exchanged a cross word; and by his hand Geremy had been lamed for life. He set his teeth and mentally turned his back on the memory. What was done was done. It was all too late for regrets. But he felt he would give the best ten years of his life to see Geremy whole again, and feel his foster brother's hand in his. He swallowed fiercely and clenched his jaw.

"I had thought of riding to the east and taking service with Edric of Serrais. It would feed my soul to make war on King Ardrin! It would teach him, perhaps, that I am better as friend than foe!"

Dom Rafael said, "I cannot advise you, my son. Far less can I lay a command on you. You are of age, and soon you will be far beyond the reach of my word; and you have your own way to make in the world for seven years. But I beg of you; spend the years of your exile far from Asturias, and make no war upon our kinsmen."

"I had not thought of that," Bard said. "If I join the ranks of King Ardrin's enemies, he will consider you his enemy as well; in a sense, Alaric is hostage for my good behavior. I cannot face him in battle while he is foster father to the brother I love."

"Not only that," Dom Rafael said. "Seven years, at your age, will but bring you well into manhood. When you return— and after seven years have come and gone you will be free to return—you can make your peace with Ardrin, and make for yourself an honorable career in the land of your birth."

Bard snorted amusement. "Ardrin of Asturias will make his peace with me when the she-wolf of Alar leaves off gnawing at her victim's heart, and when the *kyorebni* in winter bring food to the starving rabbithorns! Father, while Beltran and Geremy live, I will never find peace here, even if Ardrin no longer lives."

"You cannot be sure of that," Dom Rafael said. "One day Geremy will return to his own country; and Prince Beltran may die in battle. And Ardrin has no other son. Should Beltran die sonless, Alaric is the king's next heir, and I think he knows it; and that is why Alaric is being fostered in his house, for the proper education of a possible prince."

"Queen Ariel is not yet past childbearing," Bard said. "She might yet give the king another son."

"Still, if it came to that, the new king could have no quarrel with you, and might well be glad of a kinsman, even *nedestro*, with your skill at war."

Bard shrugged. "Be it so," he said. "For your sake, and my brother's, and for the sake of that claim to the throne, I will make no war on King Ardrin; though it would do my heart good to ride against him in war, or to storm Asturias and take Carlina by force of arms."

Alaric asked, wide-eyed, "Is the Princess Carlina so beautiful?"

"Why, as to that," Bard said, "I suppose all women are much the same when the lamp is out. But Carlina was the king's daughter, and she was reared as my foster sister, and I loved her well; and she was promised to me, and by all the laws she is my handfasted wife. It goes against all the laws and against all justice that some other man shall take my promised wife to bed!" And again the bitterness surged in him, rage against Carlina who had refused to follow him into exile as a promised wife should do, rage against Beltran and Geremy who had come between them, rage against Melora who had driven him to Carlina in such frustration that he had lost his self-control and drunk too much and laid rough hands on her. . . .

"Perhaps," said little Alaric, "you will do some foreign king a great service, and he will give you his daughter—"

Bard laughed. "And half his kingdom, as the old tales have it? Stranger things have happened, I suppose, little brother."

"Have you everything you need?" his father asked.

"King Ardrin, damn him, paid me off well," Bard said. "I rode away in a fury, too angry to claim what he had given me, and here comes a flunkey after me, hot-foot, with all the things the king had promised me, a golden gelding from the plains of Valeron, and a sword and dagger which might well have been heirlooms among the Hastur kin, and the suit of leather armor I wore on the fields of Snow Glen, and a purse of four hundred silver royals, and when I came to count it I found he had added fifty copper *reis* too. So I cannot say I was ill-paid for my years of service to him; he could hardly have been more generous to one of his captains of twenty years going home to retirement! He bought me off, Zandru lash him with scorpion whips! I would like to send it all back to him, saying that since he had defrauded me of my lawful wife, I would be no better than a pimp to take money and goods for her; yet—" he shrugged, "I must be practical. Such a gesture would not get me Carlina, and I shall need horse and sword and armor when I ride out of Asturias—"

He broke off as the door opened and a young woman, full-bodied, her hair falling in two long copper braids over her shoulders, came into the room. In an instant of shock he thought he looked on Melora; but no, this woman was slenderer, and much younger. She had the same round face, the same big, vague gray eyes. She said shyly, "My lord, the Lady Jerana has sent to ask if she shall make anything ready before your son leaves us. She said that if Bard mac Fianna has any needs he should make them known at once, to me or to her, so that we may fetch them from the storerooms and have them ready."

Bard said, "I shall need three days' journey food; and I would be grateful for a bottle or two of wine. I will not trouble the lady further." His eyes lingered on the familiar, yet subtly strange, features and body. The red-haired girl was prettier than Melora, more slender, younger, but she roused in Bard the same subtle combination of resentment and desire he had felt for Melora.

"You see," Dom Rafael said, "my wife bears you no ill will, Bard; she is eager to make certain you do not suffer from want in your exile. Have you a good store of blankets, and would you like a cooking pot or two?"

Bard laughed. "Would you persuade me of Lady Jerana's love, Father? By no means! Like the king, she is eager to pay me off and hurry me on my way! But I shall take advantage of her generosity; a blanket or two would not be amiss, and perhaps a waterproof cover for my packs. Are you going to supply them, *damisela?* You are new among my lady mother's waiting-women?"

"Melisendra is not a waiting-woman, but a fosterling of my wife," said Dom Rafael, "and your kinswoman, too; she is a MacAran, and your mother was of that kindred."

"Is it so? Why, *damisela*, I know your kinsman," Bard said, "for Master Gareth was *laranzu* when I rode to battle for King Ardrin, and so, too, was your sister Melora, and your kinswoman Mirella—"

Her face lighted with a quick smile. "Is it so? Melora is far more skilled than I as a *leronis;* she sent me word she was to go to Neskaya," she said. "How does my father, sir?"

"When I saw him last, at midwinter, he was well," Bard said, "although, I suppose, you know that he was lamed at the battle near Moray's mill, with a stroke from a Dry-towner's poisoned dagger; and he was still walking with the aid of a stick."

"He sent me a letter," she said. "Melora wrote it; and she spoke well of your bravery—" and suddenly she dropped her eyes and blushed.

He said with calm courtesy, "I am glad Melora thinks well of me," but inwardly he was raging with conflict. Melora, who had refused him, despite all of her fine words of friendship!

He said, "If your kinsmen think well of me, *damisela,* I am glad; for it had entered my mind to ride to El Haleine and take service with The MacAran."

She said, "But The MacAran has no need of mercenary soldiers, sir; he has signed a truce with the Hasturs and with Neskaya, and they have pledged to keep peace only within their borders and wage no war outside them. You can save yourself the trouble of traveling there, sir, for they will hire no mercenaries from outside their borders."

Bard raised his eyebrows. So the Hasturs of Thendara and Hali were extending their influence, then, to El Haleine? "I thank you for the warning, *damisela,*" he said. "Peace may be welcome to the farmers, but it is always unwelcome news to a soldier."

"But," said Melisendra, with her ingenuous smile, "if there is peace long enough, a day may come when men may do more with their lives than soldiering, and men such as my father may do more with their talents than risk their lives, unweaponed, in battle!"

Dom Rafael broke in, and somehow he looked a little displeased. "Go to your lady, my girl, and make my son's wants known to her; and tell her he will be riding out at sunset."

"Why, Father, are you so eager to be rid of me?" Bard asked. "I intend to lie this night in my father's house; I shall not see it again, nor you, for seven long years!"

"Eager to be rid of you? God forbid," said Dom Rafael, "but you have only three days to leave Asturias."

"It will take me only a day's ride to reach the border, if I ride north to the Kadarin," Bard said, "for if El Haleine is in Hastur hands, that is closed to me; I shall away into the Hellers, then, and see if the Lord Ardais has need for a hired sword who is also a leader of men. Or do you think your worthy kinsmen will send assassins to waylay me on my way out of the kingdom, sir?"

Dom Rafael stopped and considered it. He said, "I sincerely hope not. Still, if you have a blood-quarrel with Geremy, and with the prince—one of them might seek to assure that you do not seek to return and make peace with Ardrin after your seven years. I would go with great care, my son, and I would not delay until the last moment."

"I shall be careful, Father," Bard said, "but I shall not sneak forth into exile like a whipped dog, tail between my legs, either! And I shall lie this last night in my father's house." His eyes met Melisendra's in a long glance. The girl colored and tried to turn her glance away but Bard held her eyes, holding her in that close compulsion. Master Gareth had warned him away from Mirella as if he were an unruly schoolboy, and Melora had teased him, tormented him, finally refused him. He held Melisendra's eyes until she squirmed, her face flooding crimson, and finally managed to break eye contact and hurry out of the room, her head bent.

Then Bard laughed and bent to Alaric. He said, "Come, you shall take choice of all my bows and arrows and all my playthings. I am a man and will not need them, and who should have them, when I am gone, if not my own brother? Stay and look through these things and I will tell you what you will do in the king's house as his fosterling."

Later, when the child had gone away, his hands full of balls and shuttlecocks and hunting bows and such gear, Bard stood by the window, smiling in pleasant anticipation. The girl Melisendra would come. She would not be able to resist the compulsion he had put on her. Damn all women, who thought they could tease him and refuse him and make him less than a man with their whims! And so he smiled, not with surprise, but with a kind of fulfilled greed, when he heard the light step on the stairs.

She came slowly, with lagging step, into the room.

"Why, mistress Melisendra," he said, with a grin that showed his white teeth, "what are you doing here?"

She looked up at him, the big gray eyes wide and vague and somehow frightened. "Why—I don't know," she said shakily, "I thought—it seemed to me that I had to come—"

He reached for her, with a lazy smile, dragged her close and kissed her, pressing her roughly. Under his hand he felt her heart beating, and knew that she was terrified and confused.

He should have tried this with Carlina, then there would have been no trouble; he wouldn't have hurt her, she wouldn't have protested. He had been a fool. Somehow he had believed Carlina must somehow share the torment that raged in him, would want him as he wanted her. He still wanted her, like a ravenous itch in his blood, a thirst no other woman could slake; she was *his,* his wife, the king's daughter, sign and symbol of all he had done, of his honor, his achievement, and King Ardrin had dared to come between them!

His hands went to the laces of her undertunic, thrusting inside, and she let him do what he would, in terrified silence, like a rabbithorn in the grip of a banshee. She whimpered, a little, as his hand closed over her nipple. Her breasts were full, not like Carlina's meager bosom; this was a sow, a fat pig like Melora, like Melora who had teased him and played with his emotions! Well, this one would not do so! He dragged her toward the bed, keeping the relentless pressure on her mind and body. She did not struggle, even when he thrust her down on the bed, hauling at her skirts. She kept up the mindless whimpering, but he did not listen, flinging himself down on top of her. Once, she screamed. Then she lay silent, shaking, not even crying. Well, she knew better than that. Her very terror excited him, as Carlina's had done. *This* woman would not resist him, *this* one knew better!

He rolled away from her and lay spent, exhausted and triumphant. What was she sniveling about? She had wanted it as much as he did; and he had given her what all women wanted, once you got through the silly nonsense of pretty speeches and flattery. He supposed he would have owed some of that to a wedded wife. He remembered, with a sudden throb of pain, how he and Melora had sat beside the campfire, talking. He had not wanted to put compulsion on her; and so she had made a fool of him. Well, this woman would have no such opportunity to do that! Women were all whores anyway; he had had enough of them. They didn't make any fuss; why should a high-born girl be any different? They all had the same thing under their skirts, didn't they? It was only that their price was different, the whores demanding money, the noblewomen demanding pretty talk and flattery and a sacrifice of his very manhood!

And then, suddenly, he was deathly sick and exhausted. Going into exile, leaving his home for years, and he was forced to waste time and thought on women, damn them all! Melisendra still lay with her back to him, shaking with sobs again. Damn her! It wouldn't have been like this with Carlina. She loved him, she would have learned to love him, they had been friends since childhood, all he should have done was to show her that he wouldn't hurt her. . . . It *should* have been Carlina. What was he doing with this damnable little whore in his bed? Had it been some confused notion of revenge on Melora? The red hair, limp on the pillow, somehow filled him with dismay. Master Gareth would have been angry, Master Gareth would know that Bard mac Fianna was no boy to be warned away from a woman he wanted. But her soft sobbing filled him with disquiet.

He put out a hesitant hand to her. "Melora," he said, don't cry.

She turned over and faced him. Her eyes, lashes damp and

tangled, looked enormous in her white face. "I am not Melora." She said, "If you had served Melora so, she would have killed you with her *laran*."

No, he thought. Melora had wanted him, but for her own quixotic reasons had chosen to frustrate them both. This one— what was her name again—Mirella—Melisendra, that was it. She had been a virgin. He had not foreseen that; he knew that most *leroni* took the privilege of choosing lovers as they would. He wished it had been Melora. Melora would have responded to his own hunger. Melisendra had been only a limp, unwilling body in his arms. And yet—and yet, that was exciting too, knowing that he forced his will upon her and she could not make a fool of him as Melora had done.

"Never mind," he said. "It's done. Damn it, stop crying!"

She struggled to control her sobs. "Why are you angry with me, now that you have had your will?"

Why did she talk as if she had been so unwilling? He had seen her looking at him; he had simply given her the chance to do what she wanted to do, without need of silly scruples like those that had kept Melora from his arms!

"My lady will be angry," she said. "And what will I do, cousin, if you have gotten me with child?"

He thrust her clothing at her. "It's nothing to do with me," he said. "I am going into exile; unless you have grown so maddened with love for me that you wish to ride with me in male disguise, like a maiden in some old ballad, following her lover as a page, in men's dress—no? Well, then *damisela*, you will be neither the first nor the last to bear a bastard to di Asturien; do you think yourself better than my own mother? If it should be so, I am sure that my father would not let you or the babe starve in the fields."

She stared at him, her eyes wide, wiping away the tears that still flooded down her face.

"Why," she whispered, "you are not a man, but a fiend!"

"No," he said, with a bitter laugh. "Have you not heard? I am an outlaw, and wolf. The king has said so. Do you truly expect me to behave like a man?"

She caught up her clothes and fled, and he heard her sobbing fade away as her light footfall died out on the stairs.

He flung himself down on his bed. The sheets smelled of the scent of her hair. *Damn it*, he thought miserably, *it should have been Carlina. . . .*

Without Carlina I am an outlaw, a bastard . . . a wolf . . .
and his rage and pride and longing overcame him.

It would have been so different with you . . . Carlina, Carlina!

He rode away at midmorning, taking leave of his father and
Alaric with embraces and regrets; but he was young, and he
knew that he was bound outward into the world to seek adventure. He could not remain cast down for long. They could
call it exile, but for a young man with experience in war, there
was adventure and the hope of gain, and he could return in
seven years.

As he rode the mists cleared and the weather became fine.
Perhaps he would ride into the Dry towns, and see if the Lord
of Ardcarran had need of a hired sword, a bodyguard who
spoke the languages of Asturias and the western country, to in-
struct his guardsmen in swordplay and defend him against his
enemies. He must certainly have many. Somehow that made
him think of his soldiers' rowdy song:

> Four-and-twenty *leroni* went to Ardcarran,
> When they came back, they couldn't use their *laran*

They must, he thought, have been like Mirella, *leroni* kept
virgin for the Sight. Why, he wondered, should it be so, that
only a maiden could exercise that particular form of *laran?* He
knew so little about *laran,* except to fear it, and yet it could
have been different, he could have been chosen, like Geremy,
to become a *laranzu,* to carry a starstone rather than a sword in
battle. . . . He whistled a few more verses of the improper ballad, but his voice died away alone in the vast spaces. He
wished that he had some friend or kinsman, even a serving
man, riding with him. Or a woman; Melora, riding at his side,
on her little ambling donkey, to talk with him about war and
ethics and ambitions as he had never talked with any living
woman, or even a man . . . no. He wouldn't think of Melora.
When he thought of Melora he thought of her shining red hair,
and that made him think of Melisendra, limp, struggling in his
arms. . . .

Carlina. If Carlina had agreed, as a wife should, to follow
him into exile. She would have ridden at his side, laughing and
talking as they had when they were children. And when they
dismounted to make camp at night, he would hold her gently
in his arms and fold his blankets around her, so tenderly . . . it

made him faint to think of it. And then it made him dizzy with rage, to think that King Ardrin would lose no time in giving her to some other man, perhaps to Geremy Hastur. Savagely he wished Carlina joy of Geremy, crippled, with his withered leg . . . but the thought tormented him. Carlina, giving herself to Geremy as she would not to him! Damn them all, what did he want with women, anyway?

He stopped at midday to breathe his horse, tethering him to a featherpod tree, taking hard-baked journey-bread and meat paste from his saddlebags, and munching while the horse cropped the new spring grass. He had food for several days— Domna Jerana had been generous with her stores—and he would not risk trying to buy food, or grain for his horse, until he was across the borders of Asturias. And he would fill his water bottles from springs, rather than at the wells in the towns; he was under a writ of outlawry, and they would have every right to refuse it to him. He was not really afraid he would be killed; King Ardrin had put no price on his head, and as long as he kept out of reach of Geremy's kindred, who might well declare blood-feud, he had little to fear.

But he felt very much alone, and he was not used to it. He would have enjoyed the company of someone, even a serving man. He remembered that once he and Beltran had ridden out this way, on a hunting trip. They had been thirteen or so, not yet declared men, and some trouble at home had made them talk of running away, of riding into the Dry towns together to seek employment as hired mercenaries. Even while they knew it was half a game, it had been very real to them. They had been good friends then. A sudden snowstorm had made them seek shelter in one of the ruined barns, and they had shared blankets and talked very late, and before they slept they had turned to each other and given one another the pledge of *bredin,* as young boys do . . . why, in the name of all the gods, had he quarreled with Beltran about something like that? It had been that damned girl Melora, he had been raw-edged about her refusal, and it had caused him to fall out with his foster brother. Why should any woman come between the bonds between men? None of them was worth it! And because Melora had refused him, he had quarreled with Beltran, and spoken the unforgivable, and that had led to this . . . even if he had outgrown such boyish games, he should have remembered the long years of friendship with Beltran, his brother and his prince. Bard put his hands over his face, and for the first and the last time since his childhood, he wept, remembering the years of closeness among them, and that Beltran had become his enemy and that Geremy was lamed for life. The fire burned down, but he lay exhausted, his head in his arms, sick with grief, despairing. What had come over him, to fling away ambition, friendship, the life he had made for himself, for the sake of a woman? And now he had lost Carlina too. The sun set, but he could not make himself rise, wash his face, get on his horse again. He wished he had died at the battle at Moray's mill, that Geremy's dagger had found him instead.

I am alone. I will always be alone. I am the wolf my foster father named me. Every man's hand is against me and my hand is against every man. Never before had he been fully aware of the meaning of the word *outlaw*, even when he stood before the king and heard his doom declared.

At last, exhausted, he slept.

When he woke, coming up out of sleep all at once like a wild animal, feeling his face stiff with the salt of the tears that had dried on his face, the tears of his last childhood, he knew suddenly that he had slept too long; someone was near him. He caught up his sword before his eyes were even fully open, and leaped to his feet.

It was gray with dawn; and Beltran, wrapped in a blue cape and hood, his hand on a naked sword, stood before him.

"So," Bard said, "you are not content with having me exiled; you felt that even seven years would not make you safe, Beltran?" He was sick with hate and weakness; had he wept himself to sleep last night over the quarrel with his foster brother who would have killed him in his sleep?

"How brave you are, my Prince," he said, "to kill a sleeping man! Did you feel that even seven years could not make you safe from me?"

"I won't chop words with you, Wolf," Beltran said. "You chose to idle your way out of this kingdom instead of making all speed; now the doom is on you that any man may slay you unpunished. My father chose to show you mercy; but I do not want you in my kingdom. Your life is mine."

Bard snarled, "Come and take it," and ran at Beltran with his sword.

They were evenly matched. They had had lessons together,

from the best arms masters in the kingdom, and they had always practiced together; they knew one another's weaknesses too well. Bard was taller, and his reach longer; yet never, before this, had they fought with real weapons, but only with blunted practice swords. And always before his eyes was the memory of that accursed midwinter night when he had fought Geremy, and maimed him for life. . . . He did not want to kill Beltran; he found it impossible that Beltran, despite their quarrel, would try to kill him. *Why, in Zandru's name, why?*

Only that he might give Carlina lawfully to Geremy, that Carlina would be widow before she was ever a wife? The thought enraged him; he beat down Beltran's defense, and, fighting like a berserker, managed to knock the sword from his hand. It fell some distance away.

He said, "I don't want to kill you, foster brother. Let me go peacefully out of this kingdom. If after seven years you are still ready to kill me, I will call challenge and fight you fair at that time."

"Dare to cut me down unarmed," Beltran said, "and your life will be worth nothing anywhere in the Hundred Kingdoms!"

Bard snarled, "Go, then, and pick up your sword, and I'll show you again that you are no match for me! Do you think, little boy, that you'll make yourself my equal by killing me?"

Beltran went slowly to pick up the sword. As he stooped to pick it up, there was a noise of racing hooves, and a horse dashed toward them at full gallop. As it jerked to a halt between them, Bard saw, stepping back in amazement, that the rider was Geremy Hastur, white as death. He flung himself from his saddle and stood, clinging to the saddle straps, unable to stand alone without support.

"I beg you—Bard, Beltran—" he said, breathlessly. "Will nothing amend this quarrel between you but death? Don't do this, *bredin-y.* I will never walk again; Bard must go outlaw into exile for half a lifetime. I beg you, Beltran—if you love me—let this be enough!"

"Don't interfere, Geremy," Beltran said, his lips drawn back in a snarl.

But Bard said, "This time, Geremy, I swear by my father's honor and my love for Carlina, the quarrel was none of my making; Beltran would have killed me as I slept, and when I disarmed him, I forbore to kill. If you can talk some sense into the damned little fool, in God's name, do it, and let me go in peace."

Geremy smiled at him. He said, "I don't hate you, foster brother. You were drunk, beside yourself, and I believe it, if the king does not, that you had forgotten you were not carrying that same old blunted dagger you had cut your meat with since we were boys. Beltran, you idiot, put away that sword. I came to say farewell, Bard, and make peace with you. Come and embrace me, kinsman."

He held out his arms, and Bard, his sight blurring with a mist of tears, went to embrace his foster brother, kissing him on either cheek. He felt that he would weep again. And then the world blurred in rage and hate as over his shoulder he saw Beltran rushing at him with a drawn sword.

"Traitor! Damned traitor," he shouted, tore himself from Geremy's arms, and whirled, his sword flashing out. Two strokes beat down Beltran's sword, and even as he heard Geremy cry out in horror and dismay, he ran Beltran through the heart, felt the other man crumple on his sword and fall.

Geremy had fallen, striking his lame leg hard, and lay moaning on the ground. Bard stood looking down at him, bitterly.

"The *cristoforos* tell a tale of their Bearer of Burdens," he said, "that he too was betrayed by his foster brother while he stood in kinsman's embrace. I did not know you were a *cristoforo*, Geremy, or that you would play such a treacherous game on me. I believed you." He felt his mouth twist in a weeping grimace, but he bit his tongue hard and betrayed nothing.

Geremy set his teeth and struggled to rise. He said, "I did not betray you, Bard. I swear it. Help me up, foster brother."

Bard shook his head. "Not twice," he said bitterly. "Did you plot with Beltran to have your revenge?"

"No," said Geremy. Clutching at the stirrup, he managed to struggle to his feet. "Believe it or not, Bard, I came to try to make peace." He was crying. "Is Beltran dead?"

Bard said, "I don't know," and bent to feel his heart. There was no sign of life; and he looked at Beltran in despair, and at Geremy. "I had no choice."

"I know," said Geremy, and his voice broke. "He would have killed you. Merciful Avarra, how did we come to this?"

Bard set his teeth, nerving himself to wrench the sword out of Beltran's body. He wiped the blade on a handful of grass, and sheathed it. Geremy stood weeping, no longer making any attempt to conceal his tears. At last he said, "I know not what I shall say to King Ardrin. He was in my care. He was always so much the youngest of us—" He couldn't go on.

Bard said, "I know. Long after we were men, he was still a boy. I should have known—" and fell silent.

Geremy said at last, "Each man must ride the road of his own fate. Bard, I hate to ask this of you; but I cannot walk alone. Will you set Beltran's body on his horse, that I may lead it back to the castle? If I had paxman or serving man with me—"

"But," said Bard. "you wanted no witness to treachery."

"Do you still believe that?" Geremy shook his head. "No, to weakness, for I was ready to plead with Beltran to make his peace with you. I am not your enemy, Bard. There has been enough death. Do you want my life too?"

Bard knew he could have it easily enough. Geremy, as befitted a *laranzu,* was unarmed. He shook his head, and went to catch Beltran's horse and lead it to where be could lift the prince's lifeless form and tie it across the saddle.

"Do you need help to mount, Geremy?"

Geremy bent his head, unwilling to meet Bard's eyes. He accepted, reluctantly, Bard's hand to help him into his saddle, and sat there, swaying, shaking from head to foot. Their eyes met, and they both knew there was nothing more that they could say. Even a formal farewell would be too much. Geremy pulled at the reins, taking the reins of the horse which bore Beltran's lifeless body, and slowly turned on the trail and rode away toward Asturias. Bard watched him go, his face set and drawn, until he was out of sight; then he sighed, saddled his own horse, and rode away without looking back, out of the kingdom of Asturias and into exile.

BOOK TWO

The Kilghard Wolf

CHAPTER ONE

Half a year before the seven years of his outlawry had passed, Bard mac Fianna, called the Wolf, had news of the death of King Ardrin, and knew that he was free to return to Asturias.

He was far away in the Hellers then, in the little kingdom of Scaravel, helping to hold Sain Scarp against the assault of bandits from beyond Alardyn; a little time after the siege was lifted, Dom Rafael sent word to his son with news of the kingdom.

Three years after the death of Prince Beltran, Queen Ariel had borne the king another son. When Ardrin died, and the infant Prince Valentine succeeded to his father's throne, the queen had prudently fled to her kinsmen on the Plains of Valeron, leaving Asturias to whatever hands could take and hold it. The principal claim was being made by Geremy Hastur, whose mother was a cousin of King Ardrin, and who claimed that in times past all these lands had lain under the dominion of the old Hasturs and should still be under their wardship.

Dom Rafael had written: *I will never again bow the knee to the Hastur kindred, and my claim is better than Geremy's; Alaric is my rightful heir, and the heir to Ardrin, after Valentine. Come, my son, and help me take Alaric from Geremy's warding, and hold this kingdom for your brother.*

Bard pondered the message, standing half armored in the guard room of Scaravel, where it had reached him. In seven years he had served as mercenary, and later as captain of mercenaries, in as many little kingdoms; and he had no doubt at all that the fame of the Kilghard Wolf had spread beyond the Hellers and into the lowlands, even to Valeron. In those years he had seen plenty of fighting, and he read into the message the subtler news that there would be more fighting ahead; but at the end of *that* fighting there would be peace and honor, and a place near the throne of Asturias. He looked, frowning, at the messenger.

"And my father gave you no more message than this, no private intelligence for my ears alone?"

"No, *vai dom*."

No news, Bard wondered, of my wife? Has Geremy had the effrontery to marry Carlina? What else could give him the effrontery to claim Ardrin's throne, if not that he is wedded to Ardrin's daughter? All that talk of old Hastur kin is so much stable sweepings, and Geremy must know it as well as I do!

"But I bear you a message from the Lady Jerana," the messenger offered. "She bade me say to you that Domna Melisendra sends you greetings, and the greetings of your son Erlend."

Bard scowled, and the messenger flinched at the angry gesture.

He had all but forgotten Melisendra. There had been women enough in the time between, and it was likely that he had a son or two, scattered about the kingdoms. In fact, he gave one camp follower money, when he had it, because her son was so much like he had been as a child, and because she washed his clothes and trimmed his hair when it wanted cutting, and her cooking was better than he got in the guard room. He thought now with distaste of Melisendra. Whimpering, whining baggage! That encounter had left a bad taste in his mouth. It was the last time he had used his gift to lay compulsion on any woman to come to his bed. Well, she had been a maiden, right enough, and it was likely that the foolish girl had known no better than to tell her mistress all that had happened. Lady Jerana's knife had been sharp for him ever since he was a boy, and his brother Alaric had preferred him to any other companion. Now Jerana would have one more evil deed, or so she would certainly say, to hold over his head.

Melisendra's presence would be a good reason to avoid Asturias. And yet, it was not entirely unpleasant, to think he might have a son by a girl of good family, a son gently reared as a nobleman's *nedestro* son. The boy would be six or so. Old enough for some training in the manly arts; and no doubt Melisendra would try her best to make him into a milksop out of her grudge against his father. He wanted no son of *his* reared by that whimpering whey-faced wench, nor by her sour mistress. So if Lady Jerana thought she was warning him off, with the news that his mishandling of Melisendra was common knowledge, well, she had better think again.

"Say to my father," he said to the messenger, "that I will ride for Asturias within three days' time. My work here is done."

Before he left, he went down among the camp followers to find the woman Lilla, and gave her most of the money he had earned at Scaravel.

"You should, perhaps, buy yourself a little farm somewhere in these hills," he said, "and perhaps a husband to help you to care for it, and to rear your son."

"By that," Lilla said, "I take it that you will not be coming back when your business in your homeland is done?"

Bard shook his head. "I don't think so," he said.

He saw her swallow hard, and flinched in anticipation of a scene; but Lilla was too sensible a woman for that. She stood on tiptoe and gave him a hearty kiss and hug.

"Then Godspeed you, Wolf, and may you fare well in the Kilghards."

He returned the kiss, grinning at her. "That's a soldier's woman! I'd like to say good-bye to the boy," he said, and she called the chubby boy, who came and stared up at Bard in his shining helmet, ready for the road southward. Bard picked him up and chucked him under the chin.

"I can't acknowledge him, Lilla," he said. "I don't know if I'll have a home to take him to; and in any case there were enough men before me and after me."

"I don't expect it, Wolf. Any husband I marry can rear my son as his own, or find some other woman."

"Just the same," Bard went on, smiling at the boy's bright eyes, "if he should show any talent for arms, in twelve years or so, and you have other children, so that you don't need his work on the farm to support you in your old age, send him to me at Asturias, and I'll put him in the way to earn his bread with the sword, or do better than that for him if I can."

"That's generous," Lilla said, and he laughed.

"It's easy to be generous with what may never come to pass; all this is supposing I'm still alive in twelve years or so, and that's the one thing no soldier can ever tell. If you hear that I'm dead—well, then, girl, your son must make his way in the world as his father did, with his wits and his strong arm, and may all the devils be kinder to him than they've been to me."

Lilla said, "That's a strange blessing you give to your son, Wolf."

"A wolf's blessing?" Bard laughed again and said, "It may be that he is not my son at all; and a kinsman's blessing would do him no good, just as my curse would do him no harm. I hold no faith in such things, Lilla. Curses and blessings are all one. I wish him well, and you too." He gave the boy a rough smack on the cheek and set him down, and gave Lilla another kiss. Then he got on his horse and rode away, and if Lilla wept, she had sense enough not to do it until Bard was well out of sight.

Bard, however, was elated as he rode southward. He had freed himself of the one tie he had made in all those years, and he had done it at no more cost than by lightening himself of money he did not need. Probably the boy was not his son, for all small fair-haired children looked very much alike anyhow, without need of kin ties, and would grow up with his feet firmly rooted in the dung of his mother's dairy, and he would never need to take any thought for either of them again.

He rode south alone, toward the Kadarin. He made his way through a countryside ravaged by small wars, for the Aldarans who had, in his father's time, kept peace through all this country had fallen out, and now there were four small kingdoms, and the forests lay waste where the four brothers, all greedy and land hungry, had fought through them with clingfire and sorcery. Bard had taken service one year with one of them; and when they fell out—Dom Anndra of Scathfell had taken for himself a girl Bard wanted, a wisp of a thing fourteen years old, with long dark hair and eyes that reminded Bard of Carlina—he had left and taken service with the man's brother and led Dom Lerrys right into the stronghold by a secret way he had learned when he served Scathfell. But then the two brothers had made up their quarrel, and banded together, swearing many oaths, against a third brother, and the girl had warned Bard that one price of their compact was Bard's head, for they both felt he would betray either or both of them; and so she let him out by the same secret door, and he fled to Scaravel, vowing he would never become involved again in kin strife!

And now he was riding homeward, to do just that. But at least these were his own kin!

He crossed the Kadarin and rode through the Kilghard

Hills, seeing in the countryside the signs of war. When he crossed the borders of Asturias, he noted the tokens of fighting in the countryside, and wondered if he should hasten to the king's household? But no; Geremy claimed the throne, and sat in King Ardrin's stronghold, and if Dom Rafael had already laid seige to that place, his message would have sent for Bard to join him there; and so he rode toward his old family home.

He had not realized how much the countryside would change in seven years; nor, paradoxically, how much it would remain the same. It was early spring; a heavy snow had fallen during the night, and the featherpod trees had put on their snow pods. When he and Carlina were children they bad played under a featherpod tree in the courtyard. He was already well beyond children's games, but he had climbed the tree to bring down pods for Carlina, so that she could make beds for her dolls with the feathery pods and the wool inside them. Once they found a really huge pod, and Carlina had put a kitten to bed inside the pod, cuddled in the feathery stuff, and sung it lullabyes; but the kitten had tired of the game and torn its way out of the pod. He remembered Carlina, her hair hanging in untidy ripples to her waist, standing with the torn pod in her hands, sucking on a finger where the kitten had scratched her, her eyes filling with tears. He had caught the kitten and threatened to wring its neck, but Carlina had grabbed it and sheltered it against her breast, warding him away with her small fingers.

Carlina. He was coming back to Carlina, who was his wife under the old law, and he would demand that his father enforce it. If they had given Carlina to another man, first he would kill the other man, and then he would marry Carlina. And if the other man was Geremy, he would cut off Geremy's *cuyones* and roast them before his face!

By the time he saw from afar the towers of Dom Rafael's Great Hall, he had worked himself into a fine frenzy against Geremy, and against Carlina; if she had stayed with him, even Ardrin could not have parted them lawfully!

The sun had set, but it was a clear night, and three moons were in the sky. He thought of that as a lucky omen, but when he rode up to the gates of the Great Hall the gates were barred against him, and when he dismounted and beat on them, the voice of his father's old *coridom*, Gwynn, came gruffly though: "Be off with you? Who rides here when honest folk be abed? If you ha' business with Dom Rafael, come back by daylight when the rogues run back to their dens!"

"Open this gate, Gwynn," Bard shouted, laughing, "for it is the Kilghard Wolf, and if you do not I shall leap the wall, and make you pay blood money if the rogues get my home! What, would you bar me from my father's hearthside?"

"Young Master Bard! Is it really you? Brynat, Haldran, come here and unbar these gates! We heard you were on your way, young sir, but who'd think that you'd come at this hour?" The gate swung wide. Bard dismounted and led his horse in, and old Gwynn came and fumbled one-handed to embrace him. He was ancient, gray and stooped; he walked lamely, and one arm had been taken off at the elbow when he had held the towers of the Great Hall single-handed before Bard was born, and hidden the lady, Dom Rafael's first wife, in the lofts. For that service, Dom Rafael had sworn that none but old Gwynn should ever be *coridom* while he lived, and while the old man was long past his office, he jealously held on to it, refusing to let any younger man take over for him. He had shown Bard his first moves at swordplay when Bard was not seven years old. Now he hugged and kissed him, saying, "Foster father, why are the gates barred in this peaceful countryside?"

"There's no peace anywhere these days, Master Bard," the old man said soberly. "Not with the Hasturs swearing all this land round here is theirs from away back, land that's been held all these years by the di Asturiens—why, the very name *Asturias* means *land of di Asturiens;* how come all these damned Hasturs try to claim it? And now folk at Hali swearing to make all this one land under their tyrants, and trying to take weapons away from honest folk so we'll all be at the mercy of cutthroats and bandits! Oh, Master Bard, it's evil days in this land since you went away!"

"I heard King Ardrin was dead," Bard said.

"True, sir, and young Prince Beltran murdered by assassins, about that same time you left us, sir, though between you and me I've never been sure that Hastur who's trying to claim the throne now didn't have some hand in it. He and the young prince rode out together, so they said, and only one of them came back, and of course it was the Hastur, and him a dirty *laranzu* and sandal-wearer. So with Beltran dead, and Queen Ariel fled out of the country—Dom Rafael said it, when the old king died, *'That land fares ill where the king's but a babe,'* and sure enough, they're fighting all up and down the land, and honest folk can't get their crops in for the bandits in the fields, if it's not the soldiers! And now, I hear, if the Hasturs win this war they'll take away all our weapons, even bows for hunting, leave us with no more than daggers and pitchforks, and if they have their way, I dare say a shepherd won't be allowed to carry a club to keep off the wolves!"

He added, taking the reins of Bard's horse with his good arm, "But come away in, sir, Dom Rafael's going to be glad to hear you've come!" He shouted for a couple of grooms to come and unsaddle him, to carry his packs inside the Great Hall, and to bring lights and servants; in a little while, there were people running everywhere in the courtyard, dogs barking, noise and confusion.

Bard said, "I wonder, has my father gone to bed?"

"No, sir," said the childish voice almost under his feet, "for I told him you would come tonight; I saw it in my starstone. And so grandsire waited for you in the Hall."

Old Gwynn started back in dismay.

"Young Master Erlend!" he said crossly. "Ye've been forbidden the stables, ye uncanny wee man, you might have been trampled under all the horses! Yeur mammy will be angry with me!"

"The horses know me, and my voice," said the child, coming out into the light. "They won't step on me." He looked to be about six years old, small for his age, and with a great mop of curly red hair, like freshly minted copper in the torchlight. Bard knew who he must be, even before the boy bent his knee in an odd, old-fashioned bow, and said, "Welcome home to you, sir my father, I wanted to be the first to see you. Gwynn, you must not be afraid, I shall tell Grandsire not to be angry with you."

Bard scowled down at the boy. He said, "So you are Erlend." Strange that he had not thought of that; Melisendra had had the red hair of the old kindreds, bred into them generations ago, the blood of the Hastur kin, of Hastur and Cassilda; but he had not thought that the boy might be *laran* gifted. "And you know who I am, then?" How, he wondered, had Melisendra spoken of him?

"Yes," he said, "I have seen you in my mother's mind and memory, though more when I was smaller than now; now she is too busy, she says, bringing up a great boy like me, to have time for remembering the past days. And I have seen you in my

starstone, and Grandsire has told me that you are a great warrior, and that you are called Wolf. I think perhaps I would like
to be a great warrior too, though my lady mother said that
more likely I will be a *laranzu,* a wielder of magic like *her* father. May I look at your sword, Father?"

"Yes, certainly." Bard smiled at the small, serious boy, and
knelt beside him, drawing his sword from the sheath. Erlend
laid a small, respectful hand on the hilt. Bard started to warn
him not to touch the blade, then realized that the boy already
knew better. He sheathed the blade and swung the boy to his
shoulder.

"So my son is the first to welcome me home after all these
years of exile, and that is very fitting," he said. "Come with me
when I greet my father."

The Great Hall seemed smaller than when he had last seen
it, and shabbier. A long, low room, stone-floored, with the
shields and banners of generations of di Asturien men hanging
on the walls, and weapons too old for use displayed there too:
pikes, and the old spears which were too clumsy for the close
in fighting of the day, and tapestries woven hundreds of years
ago, showing old gods and goddesses, the harvest goddess
driving a banshee from the fields, Hastur sleeping on the
shores of Hali, Cassilda at her loom. The stone floor was uneven under foot, and a fire was burning at each end of the long
hall. At the far end, women were clustered together, and Bard
heard the sound of a *rryl;* at the near fireside, Dom Rafael di
Asturien rose from his armchair as Bard came near with his
son in his arms.

He was wearing a long indoor gown of woven dark-green
wool with embroideries at neck and sleeves. The di Asturien
men were blond, all of them, and Dom Rafael's hair was so
light it was impossible to see whether it was graying, or not;
but his beard was white. He looked very much as he had
looked when Bard had last seen him, only thinner, his eyes
somewhat sunken as if with worry.

He held out his arms, but Bard set Erlend down on his feet,
and knelt to his father. He had never done this to any of the
overlords he had served in his seven years of exile.

"I have come back, my father," he said, sensing somewhere
in his mind the surprise of his son, that his father, the renowned
warrior and the outlaw, should kneel to his grandfather just as
the vassals did. He felt his father's hand touch his hair.

"Take my blessing, son. And whatever gods there are, if any, be praised that they have brought you safely back to me. But then, I never doubted that. Get up, dear son, and embrace me," Dom Rafael said, and Bard, obeying, saw the lines in his father's face and felt the sharp thinness of his bones. He thought, with shock and dismay, *Why, he is already old. The giant of my youth is already an old man!* It troubled him, that he was taller than his father, and so much broader that he could have lifted him in his arms as he had done with Erlend!

So swiftly had the years passed, while he fought in strange wars in foreign lands! *Time has left its hand heavy on me too,* he thought, and sighed.

"I see that Erlend came to greet you," Dom Rafael said, as Bard joined him on the seat before the fire. "But now you must away to your bed, grandson; what was your nurse thinking of, to let you out into the night so late?"

"I suppose she was thinking I was already in bed, for that is where she left me," Erlend said, "but I felt it most seemly to go and greet my father. Good night, Grandsire, good night, sir," he added, with his funny, precocious little bow, and Dom Rafael laughed as he went out of the hall.

"What a little wizard he is! Half the serving folk are afraid of him already," he said, "but he is clever and well grown for his years, and I am proud of him. I wish, though, that you had told me that you had gotten Melisendra with child. It would have saved her, and me too, some angry words from my Lady; I did not know that Melisendra was being kept virgin for the Sight. And so we all suffered, for Jerana was wonderfully cross, to lose her *leronis* so young."

"I did not tell you because I did not know," Bard said, "and Melisendra's foresight could not have been so wonderful after all, if it did not keep her out of my chamber when I was alone and wanting a woman." After he said it he was a little ashamed, remembering that he had given her, after all, no choice in the matter. But, he told himself, if Melisendra had half as much *laran* as that red hair promised, she would never have fallen victim to that compulsion anyhow! He could not, for instance, have done it to Melora.

"Well, at least her son is handsome and clever, and I see you had him brought up in this house instead of fostering him out to some nobody!"

His father said, staring into the fire, "You were going into outlawry and exile. I feared he should be all I had left of you. And in any case," he added, defensively, as if he were ashamed of this weakness, "Jerana had not the heart to separate Melisendra from her baby."

Bard reflected that he had never suspected Lady Jerana of having any heart at all, so that was no surprise to him. He did not want to say that to his father, so he said, "I see that his mother has taught her son some of her craft too; already he bears a starstone, young as he is. And now enough of women and children, Father. I thought you would already have moved against that damned upstart of a Hastur who has tried to make himself master of this land."

"I cannot move against Geremy at once," said Dom Rafael, "for he still has Alaric in his keeping. I sent for you to try to devise some way to get your brother back, so that I can move freely against these Hasturs."

Bard said, enraged, "Geremy is a snake whose coils lie everywhere! I had him in my hand once, and forebore to kill him. Would I had been as foresighted as you say Melisendra was!"

"Oh, I bear the boy no ill will," Dom Rafael said. "In his boots I should have taken the same step, no doubt. He was hostage at Ardrin's court for the good will of King Carolin of Thendara! I have no doubt Geremy grew to manhood knowing that if ill will came between Ardrin and Carolin, his own head would be the first to fall, be he ever so much the foster-brother of Ardrin's son! And speaking of Ardrin's sons—you knew, did you not, that Beltran was dead?"

Bard set his teeth and nodded. Some day he would tell his father how Beltran had come to die; but not now. "Father," he asked what he had never thought to ask before. "Was I hostage at Ardrin's court for your good behavior?"

"I thought you had known that all your life," Dom Rafael said. "Ardrin never trusted me overmuch. Yet, no doubt, Ardrin valued you at your true worth, or he would never have promoted you to his own banner bearer, nor set you above his own son. You flung that away by your own folly, my boy, but you seem to have prospered in these years of exile, so we will say no more of that. But while you, and then Alaric, were at his court, Ardrin knew I would make no trouble, nor strive with him for the throne, though my claim to sit there was as good as his own, and better than that of his younger son. Now, however, with both Ardrin and Beltran dead, it would be catastrophe, in times like these, for a baby king to reign—rats make havoc in the kitchen when the cat's a kitten! If you are with me—"

"Can you doubt that, Father?" Bard asked, but before he could speak further, a woman came from the woman's fire, slender, with graying hair, clad in a richly embroidered and braided robe.

"So you are back again, foster son? Seven years outlawry seem to have done you no very great harm, after all. Indeed," she added, looking at his fur-trimmed garb, the jeweled dagger and sword hanging at his side, the warrior's braid banded with jewels, "you must have prospered in the foreign wars! This is no wolf's pelt!"

Bard bowed to the Lady Jerana. He thought, *still the same sour-faced, ill-spoken bitch, it would take three times seven years to make any improvement in her, and the best improvement would be a shroud*, but in seven years he had learned not to say everything that came into his head.

"Seven years indeed have made small change in you, foster mother," he said, and her smile was sour.

"Your manners, at least, are much improved."

"Why, *domna,* I have lived seven years by my wits and my sword; in such lands and circumstances, lady, one improves quickly or one dies, and as you see, I still walk among the living."

"But your father is remiss in hospitality," Lady Jerana said. "He has offered you no refreshment. How came you to ride so late in such times?" she added when she had signaled to her servants to bring food and wine.

"Is it so unsafe, *domna?* Old Gwynn said something of this, but I thought, at his age, his wits might well have gone roving."

"His wits are clear enough," Dom Rafael said. "It is I who have given orders for the gates to be barred every night at sunset, and that every beast and man and woman and child shall be within the walls. And I have set rangers to ride the borders, with beacon fires to warn us if more than three riders are sighted in a party—which is why we did not welcome you properly. It never occurred to us that you would ride alone, without bodyguard or paxman or even serving manor squire!"

"I am not called Wolf for nothing," Bard said. "*Lone wolf,* and *rogue,* are the kindest of the names they give me."

"Yet, despite all these precautions," Dom Rafael said, "raiders, bandits they said, but I think myself they may be Geremy's men, have broken into the villages and driven off some horses. We built stockades here in the castle, where they may keep their beasts if they will, but they have begun to keep them at home again. The raiders also took sacks of grains and nuts, and half the harvest of apples. There will be no great hunger, but the markets will go short, and people will have little coined money, and some of the village folk have armed themselves. There was even talk of hiring a *leronis,* to frighten away the raiders with sorcery, but nothing came of it, and I was not displeased; I like not that kind of warfare."

"Nor I," Bard said, "but little Erlend said something of being trained as *laranzu.*"

Lady Jerana nodded. "The boy has *donas,*" she said, "and his tutors think he has probably not the muscles for a swordsman." Servants had brought wine, and were handing around savory tidbits. Bard froze suddenly, looking down into the eyes of a small, round-bodied woman whose hair was like a living flame around her face, escaping in small fiery tendrils despite the modest braids coiled low on her neck.

"Melisendra?"

"My lord," she said, lowering her head in a bow. "Erlend said, when he came to me to be put back to bed, that he had seen you."

"He is a fine, likely-looking boy. Word came to me, just before I came here, of his existence; I had not thought of it before. Any man would be proud of such a son."

A faint smile touched her face. "And for such compliments, no doubt, a woman is rewarded for whatever price she paid. I think now, perhaps, he was a fair price for what I lost; but it took me many years to come to think so."

Bard studied the mother of his son in silence. Her face was still round, snub-chinned; she wore a sober gown of gray, over an under-tunic of blue, embroidered with a pattern of butterflies at neck and sleeves. She had a poise and dignity which reminded him, suddenly, of his young son's solemn way of speaking. He had not remembered her this way.

She said, "Lady Jerana has been kind to us both; and so has your father."

"I should hope so," said Bard. "I was brought up in my father's house, and there is no reason my son should not be treated as well."

Her eyes glinted with an ironic smile. "Why, yes, my lord, that was the last thing you said to me, that you were certain your father would not allow me and the babe to starve in the fields."

"A grandson is a grandson," Bard said. "Even if his birth was blessed with no ceremonious rubbish!"

Melisendra said quietly, "No birth is unblessed, Bard. Ceremonies are to comfort the heart of the ignorant; the wise know that it is the Goddess who gives a blessing. But how can anything which gives comfort be rubbish?"

"I take it, then, you are not among the ignorant who had need of such ceremonies?"

"When I had need of them, my lord, I was more ignorant than you can guess, being very young. Now I know that the Goddess alone can give more comfort than any ceremony devised by mankind or woman."

Bard chuckled. "Which goddess is she, among the dozens who comfort the ignorant in this countryside?"

"The Goddess is one, by whatever name she may call herself, or whichever name the ignorant may give her."

"Well, I suppose I must find some name by which to thank her," Bard said, "for giving me such a fine son. But I would rather think that I owe thanks to *you*, Melisendra."

She shook her head. "You owe me nothing, Bard," she said, and turned away. He would have followed her, but the minstrels began to play near the fire. Bard went and sat beside his father again. At the other end of the hall some of the women were dancing, but he noticed briefly that Melisendra was not among them.

He asked, "How is it that Geremy is trying to claim the throne? The very name *Asturias* means *land of Asturiens,* what has a Hastur to do with it?"

"He claims," said Dom Rafael, "that once all this land was held by the Hastur kin, and that Asturias was given to the di Asturiens only to hold at Hastur's will; that *Asturias* means, in the old tongue, *land of Hasturs.*"

"He is mad."

"If so, it is a self-serving madness, for he claims this land for King Carolin of Carcosa."

"What shadow of a claim—" Bard began, then amended himself. "Leaving aside the claim of Prince Valentine, and I would as soon leave *that,* for that land fares ill where the king's a child, what shadow of claim does he have, save the old myth of the sons of Hastur and Cassilda? I will not be ruled by a king whose claim comes from legend and myth!"

"Nor I," said Dom Rafael. "I would as soon believe that the Hasturs were once gods, as myth has it, and that the Hasturs were true sons of the Lord of Light! But even if the first Hastur were son to Aldones himself, I would not so peacefully give up my claim to the land the di Asturiens have held for all these years? I cannot move against him while he holds Alaric; but I think he knows that the people will cry out against a Hastur on the throne. Perhaps he holds Alaric to set him there as his puppet, but he must be shaking in his sandals, the wretch!"

"When he knows I have come back, he will have cause to tremble," Bard said. "But I thought, perhaps, he had chosen to marry the daughter of King Ardrin and hold the throne for his children."

"Carlina?" Dom Rafael inquired, and shook his head. "I know nothing of her, and certainly she is not married to Geremy; *that,* I would have heard."

Soon after that, the minstrels were dismissed, Lady Jerana sent her women away, and Dom Rafael bade his son an affectionate good night. Lady Jerana had sent a body servant to his old rooms, to take his boots and clothing, and see him to his bath; but when he came back to bed the servant omitted the customary courtesy of asking if he wanted a woman for his bed. Bard started to call him back, then shrugged; he had ridden far that day, and had seen no woman among Lady Jerana's maids who interested him. He put out the light and got into his bed.

And sat up in astonishment, for it was already occupied.

"Zandru's hells!"

"It is I, Bard." Melisendra sat up beside him. She was wearing a long thin bedgown in some pale color, her hair a luminous cloud. Bard laughed.

"So you have come back, though you whimpered and wailed when I had my will of you before!"

"Not my will, but Lady Jerana's will," Melisendra said. "Perhaps she does not wish to lose another of her virgin *leroni;* as for me, what I had to lose can be lost only once." She gave a cynical shrug. "She has allowed me to use these rooms, saying I had a right to them, and little Erlend and his nurse sleep yonder. You are no worse than any other; and the Goddess knows, I have had to protest often enough, to be left in peace here. Lady Jerana wishes to think of me as *barragana* to her foster son and I have borne you a child. But if you do not want me here I shall be more than happy to sleep elsewhere, even if I must share my child's cot."

Bard was infuriated by her quiet, indifferent acceptance, yet he realized he would have been equally angry if she had protested her distaste or dislike. He was ready to fling her out of his bed with a curse and a blow and bid her be gone from here. But he sensed that whatever he did she would accept with the same shrug of indifference, in order to infuriate him further. Damn the woman, one would think he had done her harm, instead of giving her a son of noble blood and a regular place as *barragana* in this great household!

And, since he could not have Carlina in his bed, one woman was very much like any other when the lamp was out.

"Come here, then," he said brutally, "and be quiet. I don't like women who make a lot of noise, and I don't want to hear any more of your impudent chatter."

She looked up at him, smiling, as he seized her. "Why, just as you like, my lord. All the gods forbid you must endure anything to displease you."

She said nothing more. If she had, Bard thought in dull rage, he would have hit her and tried to see whether that drove the damned smile from her face.

CHAPTER TWO

He wakened to a great clamor, and sat up, instantly awake. He had slept at too many battle posts not to know what that noise was. Melisendra sat up beside him.

"Are we under attack?"

"It sounds like it. How in hell's name should I know?" Bard was already out of bed, flinging on his clothes. She slid a long robe over her bedgown and said, "I must go to my lady and see the women and children safe. Let me help you with your boots," she added, and Bard wondered how she knew that he grudged the time to summon his body servant. "And here are your sword and cloak."

He hastened toward the stairs, flinging back over his shoulder, "See that the boy is safe!" He was vaguely surprised at himself; with a castle under attack it was no time to worry about women and children.

He found his father in the Great Hall, hastily dressed.

"Are we under attack?"

"No; a swift strike, they have come and gone in the villages, taking horses we could ill spare, and some sacks of grain. The noise was the villagers, riding in to tell us, and my guardsmen arming to chase them, perhaps to get the horses back. . . ."

"Geremy's men?"

"No, they would have struck at Great House, not villages. The men of Serrais, I think, swarming over our borders, taking advantage of anarchy to lead Dryland scum against us. . . . The land is overrun with them. I wish they would go and harry Geremy in Castle Asturias!"

Gwynn entered and Dom Rafael turned irritably toward the old *coridom*. "What now?"

"A king's messenger, my lord."

Dom Rafael scowled and demanded testily, "Where is there a king in this land to send a messenger?"

"Your pardon, my lord. I should have said a messenger from Dom Geremy Hastur. He arrived in the midst of all this confusion, while your men were saddling to ride after the bandits—"

"I should have ridden with them," Bard said, and his father shook his head.

"No doubt that is what they wished, that you waste your strength on bandits and random strikes!" He turned to Gwynn and said, "I will receive Geremy's man. Tell Lady Jerana to send a *leronis* to set truthspell in the hall. I will hear no Hastur lackey without that. Bard, will you attend me?"

By the time Geremy's envoy came into the Great Hall, bearing truce flag and the banner of the Hasturs of Carcosa, the silver fir tree on blue, differenced with the blazing candles, Bard had breakfasted hastily on a bowl of nut porridge from the kitchens, washed down with a cup of sour beer, washed the sleep from his eyes, and dressed himself in his father's colors, blue and silver for di Asturien. Dom Rafael was seated in a carven chair on the dais, two steps behind him, in the paxman's place, Bard stood with his hand just resting on the hilt of his sword. Melisendra, also in the di Asturien silver and blue— and how, Bard wondered, had the Hasturs and di Asturiens come to have the same household colors?—was seated on a low stool, bending over her starstone that spread the blue haze of truthspell over the chamber. The envoy paused in the doorway, displeased.

"My Lord, that is not necessary."

"In my hall," said Dom Rafael, "I judge what is necessary unless I greet my own overlord; and I do not recognize any son of Hastur as my overlord, or his messenger as the voice of my lawful king. State your business under truthspell, or forbear to speak it at all and take yourself out of my hall again."

The envoy was too well trained to his work to shrug, but somehow he gave the impression of having done so.

"Be it so, *vai dom*. Since I speak no falsehood, truthspell says more of the customs of your hall than the message of my master. Hear, then, the word of the high lord Geremy Hastur,

Warden of di Asturien and Regent of Asturias, holding this land for the rightful lord, King Carolin of Carcosa. . . ."

Dom Rafael interrupted, softly but audibly, "What is the *leronis* about? I thought truthspell was set in this room so that no falsehood could be spoken here, yet I hear a claim—"

Bard knew Dom Rafael had said this only to annoy; truthspell dealt with facts and intentions, not with disputed claims, and of course the messenger knew it too, and disregarded the interruption. His stance altered, and Bard knew he looked upon a Voice, or professional messenger-mimic, whose business was to speak a message in the very words and inflection exactly as it had been given. Any messenger could repeat his message verbatim; but the art of repeating them in the very voice of the speaker, and taking back any message in the very same tone, so that the recipient could judge for himself every subtlety, irony or innuendo, was a rare and special skill.

"To my kinsman and the old friend of my father, Dom Rafael of Asturias," the Voice began, and Bard shivered; it was uncanny. The Voice was a smallish fat man with gingery whiskers and nondescript livery, but through a trick of voice or glamour, it seemed that Geremy Hastur himself stood before them, a bent man, one shoulder higher than the other, one leg posed to take less weight, leaning on some kind of support. And Bard felt a cold grue running over him as he saw what the boyish quarrel had made of the embittered man before him. . . .

No. This was a trick, a trained Voice, a mimic, a special kind of servant; the real Geremy was far away.

"Kinsman, your claim and mine to the throne of Asturias may be disputed later; at the moment all of Asturias is under siege from the people of Serrais, who see the throne of Asturias under dispute and think this land a game bird flying free for any hawk to seize. Whatever the merits of your claim or mine, I ask truce, to drive these outsiders of Serrais from our borders; and after that, you and I may sit down as kinsmen and discuss who shall rule this land and how. I ask you to make common cause with me for the moment, as the greatest of the generals who served under my cousin Ardrin in the years past. I pledge the word of a Hastur that while the truce endures, your son Alaric, who dwells as a kinsman in my house, shall be safeguarded against the war; and when the invaders are driven forth, I pledge to meet with you myself, each of us unarmed and with no more than four paxmen, to discuss the fate of this land and the return of Alaric to his father's care."

And after a few seconds, the Voice added, now in his own voice, "And this is all of the message which the lord Geremy Hastur has sent to you at this time; except that he asks that you come as quickly as you can."

Dom Rafael sat scowling at the floor. It was Bard who asked, "How many of the invaders have crossed the borders of Asturias?"

"Sir, they are an army."

Dom Rafael said, "It seems we have no choice; otherwise these Serrais will fall upon us one by one, and pick us off at leisure. Say to my kinsman that I will join him, with all the able-bodied men I can raise, and as many *leroni* as I can bring, as soon as I have made certain of the defense of my own house and of my lady and my grandson; and you may tell him that I have said this under truthspell."

The Voice bowed and there were a few more formal speeches. Then the Voice withdrew, and Dom Rafael turned to Bard.

"Well, my son? I have heard of your renown in war, and look, here is one waiting for you as soon as you come home to Asturias!"

"I would rather fight against Geremy himself," Bard said, "but the throne of Asturias must be made secure before anyone can sit upon it! If Geremy thinks that our help will strengthen his claim to the throne, it will be for us to show him he is deluded when that time comes. When do we ride forth?"

All that day the beacon fires burned, summoning all men who owed service to Asturias, which meant every able-bodied man who could ride against invasion. As they rode out, more and more men joined them, noblemen in armor of metal-reinforced leather, bearing sword and shield and ahorse; bowmen afoot with arrows and fire arrows and long pikes, farmers and peasants riding donkeys and horned pack beasts, carrying ancient spears, maces studded with deadly spikes, even cudgels and pitchforks.

Bard rode with his father's paxmen, and near them rode a small group of men and women, unarmed, wearing long gray cloaks and hoods which hid their faces; the *leroni* who would fight alongside the warriors. Bard realized that all during his absence his father must have been recruiting and training these men, and suddenly he shivered a little. How long had his father been hatching this rebellion, like some monstrous egg sheltered in his mind? Had he wanted the crown for Alaric, so long ago?

Well, he, Bard, was better suited for war than governing; he would rather be the king's man than the king, and if the king was one day to be his well-loved brother, there was a good life before him. He began to whistle, and rode on, cheerful.

But an hour or so later he had a shock, for among the *leroni* he had recognized, even under the hood, the form and face of Melisendra.

"Father," he demanded, "why does the mother of my son ride with the armies? She is no camp follower!"

"No, she is the most skilled *leronis* in our service."

"Somehow, from what you said, I thought Lady Jerana blamed me for spoiling her for that service—"

"Oh, she is useless for the Sight," Dom Rafael said. "We have a maiden youth for that, not twelve years old. But for all else, Melisendra is highly skilled. I had thought of taking her for my own *barragana*, at one time, because Jerana is fond of her, and as you will know when you are wedded, it is useless to take a concubine who is detestable to your lawful wife. But—" he shrugged, "Jerana wished to keep her virgin for the Sight, and so I let her be; and you know what happened. I would rather have a grandson anyway. And since Melisendra has proved herself fertile to you, perhaps you should take her to wife."

Bard frowned with revulsion. He said, "I remind you, sir, that I have already a wife; I shall take no other woman while Carlina lives."

"You may certainly take Carlina for wife if you can find her," Dom Rafael said, "but she has not been at court since her father's death. She fled the court even before Queen Ariel took Valentine to her kinsfolk at Valeron."

Bard wondered if she had left court to avoid marriage to Geremy. He would certainly have seen this marriage as the best road to claim Ardrin's throne. Was she waiting for him, somewhere, to come and claim her?

"Where is Carlina, then?"

"I know no more than you, my son. For all I know, she is within a Tower somewhere, learning the ways of a *leronis,* or even—" Dom Rafael raised his eyes to the newest group of fighters who had joined their army on the road, "she may have cropped her hair and taken the vows of the Sisterhood of the Sword."

"Never!" said Bard, with a shudder of dismay, looking at the women in their scarlet cloaks. Women with their hair cropped shorter than a monk's, women without grace or beauty, women who wore the Renunciate's dagger, not in their boots as men did, but strapped across their breasts, in token that a man who laid a hand upon them would die, and that the woman herself would die before surrendering herself as a prize of war. Under their cloaks they wore the odd garb of their sworn sisterhood, breeches and long laced jerkins to their knees, low boots tied around their ankles; their ears were pierced like those of bandits, long hoops dangling from the left earlobe.

"I wonder, my Father, that you will have these—these bitches with us."

"But," said Dom Rafael, "they are fighters of great skill, pledged to die rather than fall to an enemy; not one has ever been taken prisoner, or betrayed her oath of service."

"And you mean to tell me that they live without men? I do not believe it," Bard jeered. "And what do the men think, riding with women who are not camp followers?"

"They treat them with the same respect as the *leroni*," said Dom Rafael.

"Respect? For women in breeches, with their ears holed? I would treat them as all such women deserve who give up the decencies of their sex!"

"I would not advise it," Dom Rafael said, "for I have heard that if one of them is raped, and does not kill herself or her ravisher, her sisters hunt her down and kill them both. As far as any man can say, they are as chaste as the priestesses of Avarra; but no one knows for certain what goes on among them. It may simply be that they are very adept at the art of secret whoring. And they are, as I say, skilled fighters."

Bard could not imagine Carlina among them. He rode on, silent and moody, until they called him, in midafternoon, to examine the weapons of a band of young farmers who had joined them. One bore an heirloom sword, but the others had axes, pikes which looked as if they had been handed down for generations, pitchforks and cudgels.

"Can you ride?" he asked the man with the sword. "If so you may join my horsemen."

The young peasant shook his head. "Nay, *vai dom,* not even a plowing beast," he confessed in his rude dialect. "The sword belonged to my great-grandsire, who bore it a hundred years gone at Firetop. I can fight wi' it, a wee bit, but e'en so, I better stay wi' my brethren."

Bard nodded in agreement. Weapons did not make a soldier.

"As you wish, man, and good fortune to you. You and your brothers may join those men there. They speak your tongue."

"Aye, they my neighbors, *vai dom,*" he said, then asked shyly, "Are ye no' the high lord's son, the one they call the Wolf, *dom?*"

Bard said, "I have been called so."

"What be ye doin' here, *dom?* I heard ye were outlawed, in foreign parts—"

Bard chuckled. "He who made me outlaw has gone to explain it in hell. Are you going to try to kill me for the head-prize, man?"

"Nay, no such thing," said the young peasant, his eyes round in dismay. "Not to the high lord's son. Only, with you to lead us, we canna' do other than win, *dom* Wolf."

Bard said, "May all the Serrais foxes and wild men think so, man," and watched as the peasants joined their own group. His eyes were thoughtful as he rode forward to join his father. Here and there he heard a snatch of conversation: *the Wolf, the Kilghard Wolf has come to lead us.* Well, perhaps it would serve them well.

When he joined his father, Dom Rafael gestured at the youngest of the *leroni,* a fresh-faced freckled boy, his hair blazing under the gray hood; he was only twelve or so. "Rory has seen something, Bard. Tell my son what you have seen, lad."

"Beyond the wood, Dom Wolf—Dom Bard," he amended quickly, "a party of men coming to ambush us."

Bard's eyes narrowed. "You saw this. With the Sight?"

The *laranzu* said, "I could not see so well, riding, as in the crystal, or in a pool of clear water. But they are there."

"How many? Where? How are they drawn up?" He fired questions at the boy. Rory got down from his pony, and taking up a twig, began to draw a pattern in the dust.

"Four, maybe five dozen men. About ten mounted, like

this—" He sketched a line at an angle to the rest. "Some of the rest have bows. . . ."

Melisendra bent over the boy and said, "Are there *leroni* with them?"

"I think not, *domna*. It is hard to see. . . ."

Bard looked quickly around at the great body of men straggling along behind them. Damn! He had not thought it necessary, yet, to form them up; but if they were taken on the flank this way, even a few men could do dreadful damage! Even before he thought seriously about the ambush, he snapped, "Rory, see this! Are there men following us?"

The boy squinted his eyes and said, "No Dom Wolf, the road is clear behind us all the way to Dom Rafael's stronghold and as far as the borders of Marenji."

That meant that the invading army from Serrais was somewhere between them and Castle Asturias. Would they have to fight their way through it, and find the castle under siege? Perhaps the invaders could wear out Geremy Hastur before they ever got there. No, that was no way to talk about an ally under truce. And meanwhile there was an ambush waiting for his army. A laughably small one, intended—he was sure—only to delay them awhile, so they would halt to tend their wounded, not arrive at the castle till after nightfall, or perhaps the next day. Which would mean an attack was planned for that night. An army of this size could not escape observation; if they had sentry birds or *leroni* with the Sight, the army of Serrais must surely know that they were on the way, and have some special interest in keeping them away for another day.

He said something of this to his father, and Dom Rafael nodded in agreement. "But what shall we do?"

"A pity we cannot get around them somewhere," Bard said, "and leave the men of this ambush to watch here like a cat at an empty mousehole. But we cannot take an army this size past this wood unseen. Rory says there is no *leronis* with them, but that does not mean there is no *leronis* in rapport with one of their leaders, seeing through his eyes. So we cannot attack them without also alerting the main army of Serrais." He considered for a time. "And if we do so, even though we annihilate them quickly—four dozen men cannot stand against all our army—it would give time for *leronis* or sentry bird to spy out our numbers and how we are positioned and weaponed. But what a *leronis* does not witness she cannot report. I think the main army must go past the wood where the ambushers will not see them. Father, give some man your cloak and let him ride your horse, and send him with me, with your banner, while you take the main army around the wood. Meanwhile, give me—" he paused to consider, "ten or twelve picked horsemen, and a dozen swordsmen with tall shields; and a couple of dozen bowmen. We will go the main path; and if we are fortunate, the watchers in rapport with the ambush will think that is all we have to lift the siege of Castle Asturias. Take all the *leroni* with you, and when you are past this wood, sit down with them and their sentry birds, and let them tell us what manner of army Serrais has sent against us this time."

This was quickly agreed to.

"Take the bowmen of the Guild," he was told, "and Lord Lanzell's horsemen—there are fifteen of them and they work well together and follow one man. Pick your foot soldiers yourself."

"Father, I do not know the men well enough, now, to find picked men so quickly."

"Jerrall does," Dom Rafael said, gesturing to his banner bearer. "He has been with me twenty years. Jerrall, go with my son and obey him as you would myself!"

Drawing up his picked men, watching the main army form up tightly to go the other way, Bard felt a queer tightening in his throat. He had been fighting since he was thirteen years old, but this was the first time he had fought under his father's banner; and the first time since he had been sent into outlawry that he fought for a land about whose welfare he cared a *sekal*.

They swept down on the ambush from behind, taking the mounted men unawares and killing half their horses before the foot soldiers could rally to them. Bard's men formed a shield wall and shot blazing arrows toward them. The battle lasted less than half an hour, after which Bard's men had the Serrais banner and the wounded remnant fled in all directions. Bard had lost two or three men, but they had captured or killed all of the enemy's horses. He gave orders to cut the throats of the most gravely wounded—they would not survive being moved, in any case, and this was more merciful than leaving them for *kyorebni* and wolves—to take up the gear and armor.

Rejoining the main army, they had their prisoners interrogated by a *laranzu* who could mind-probe. From this they learned that they would, indeed, have to fight their way through the whole

Serrais army before they came to Castle Asturias. The army, outside the walls of the castle, was preparing to attack, but was ready to hold it under siege if they could not capture it by surprise attack.

Bard nodded, grim-faced. "We must press on through the night. We cannot bring up all the supply wagons so quickly, but our best men must arrive in time to spoil the surprise those men of Serrais are planning!"

The nightly rain of this season was already beginning, but they went on at what haste they could, even after the rain had changed to light snow, and there was some grumbling in the ranks about this.

"Are you trying to tell us they'd attack Castle Asturias in *this?* They couldn't see the walls to shoot at them!"

It reminded Bard of the long-ago campaign, his first independent command. Melisendra, her bright hair covered by the gray hood of a *leronis*, reminded him, suddenly and with a stab of poignant regret, of Melora. Where was she now? Even Melisendra's voice was like hers, as she said softly, "The weather will clear before dawn, you may be sure of that. And you may be sure that their sorcerers are well aware of it, too. Inside the castle they may think themselves secure because of the storm. But when the skies clear, there will be moonlight."

The man looked at her with respectful awe, and said, "Do you know that with your wizardry, *domna?*"

"I know it because I know the cycles of the moons," Melisendra laughed. "Any farmer could tell you as much. There are four moons in the sky tonight, and Liriel and Kyrrdis are at the full. It will be bright enough to fly hawks! So we must be there in time for battle; but," she added thoughtfully, "there will be light enough for their sorcerers to work wizardry too, and we must be ready for *that.*"

Bard was glad of the intelligence; but he had no liking for wizardry in battle. He preferred honest swords and spears!

The storm grew to wild heights, so that the *leroni* were riding ahead, carrying lighted torches, and young Rory was spying out the trails with the Sight. Men and horses struggled along behind them, following the torches, fighting the snow and the drifts, cursing. Bard wondered if the enemy's *leroni* had brought the storm. It seemed too heavy to be natural. He had no way of knowing, and resolved, resentfully, that he would *not* ask Melisendra!

And then, suddenly, all was quiet; they moved out of the storm into clear night, the wind died, and overhead the great serene faces of the larger moons floated at full, pale Liriel, Kyrrdis glimmering bluish in the night. Bard heard the men's gasps of amazement. Atop a hill, they looked into the valley surrounding the castle.

It was eerie and quiet. He knew, from what the sorcerers had told him, that the whole army of Serrais lay there, encamped outside the castle, prepared to attack at dawn; but not a watch-fire glimmered, not a step rustled below them.

"Yet they are there," Melisendra said at his side, and through her mind he picked up the image of the valley below, not dark as he saw it, but lighted with strange flickers which, he knew, were men, and horses, and engines of war.

"How is it that you can see that, Melisendra?"

"I do not know. Perhaps my starstone feels the heat of their bodies, and translates it into a picture my mind can see . . . everyone sees it differently. Rory told me that he could *hear* them; perhaps he feels the movement of their breath, or feels the crying of the grass as their feet crush it."

Bard shivered, wishing he had not asked. He had possessed this woman, she had borne him a son, yet he knew nothing of her, and he was afraid of her. He had heard of a *laran* gift which could kill with a thought. Did she possess it? No, or she would surely have struck him down in defense of her chastity. . . .

"Do their *leroni* know we are coming?"

"I am sure they know we are somewhere about. The presence of all these men and beasts cannot be hidden from anyone with *laran*. But Rory and I have closed down our Gifts as much as we can, and hopefully, they think us much farther away than we are. We left old Master Ricot, and Dame Arbella, with the supply wagons, and instructed them to send out false pictures, as if the army were still there with them. . . . All we can do is wait and see."

They waited. Kyrrdis was lowering toward the horizon and the eastern sky was just beginning to flush red when Melisendra touched Bard's arm and said, "The word has been passed for attack, down there."

Bard said grimly, "Then we will attack them first." He beckoned to his page and gave the word. He was not weary, though he had slept but little for three nights. He gnawed at a hard bread roll with meat baked inside. It tasted like leather, but he knew from experience that if he went into battle with his stomach empty he would get dizzy or squeamish. Other men, he knew, were the other way round, Beltran always said that if he touched a bite of food he would spew it up like a breeding woman—why was he thinking of Beltran now? Why must that ghost come to sit on his shoulder?

So they would cut through the invading Serrais army to save Castle Asturias, and Geremy Hastur's worthless life. And then would they attack again? With Dom Rafael's army there, did Geremy really think he could make good his claim to the throne? Did Geremy think the truce would last any longer than Dom Rafael found it convenient? Yet he had asked Dom Rafael to bring his army here.

How many of the army would stand for Dom Rafael? Probably most of them were as unwilling to see a Hastur on the throne, as was their leader.

Below him a glimmer flashed, and he gave a quick command. "Lights!"

From everywhere, torches were brought from behind their shielding. A fire arrow blazed a long, screaming comet tail into the midst of the Serrais army.

"Attack!" Bard shouted.

Screaming the ancient battle cries of di Asturien, the army charged down the hill toward the army of Serrais, taking them from behind as they charged upon the walls of Asturias.

By the time the red sun came dripping up over the eastern hills, the Serrais army lay cut to pieces, the remnant fleeing in confusion; the heart had gone out of them with Bard's first charge, which had killed and wounded half of their rear-guard. They had never managed to bring up a single catapult or war engine, nor to get their clingfire alight; Bard had captured it all. Then some clingfire shells had been set to burn among them, fragile, exploding everywhere and bursting among their remaining horses, stampeding them in frenzy; and then it was all over but the slaughter, and the final surrender. The armed men inside the castle had covered them with bowmen from the walls, and at the end the *leroni* had massed to spread terror among the Serrais army, so that the rest of them fled shrieking as if all the demons in all of Zandru's nine hells were after them. Bard thought, having fought against *laran* terror himself, that the devils probably *were*—or at least the Serrais men *thought* they were, which amounted to the same thing.

Dom Eiric Ridenow of Serrais had been captured, and by the time Bard rode with his banner bearers into the castle, they were already debating whether to hold him as hostage for the good behavior of the other Serrais lords, ransom him and send him home after accepting an oath of neutrality or hang him from the castle walls as an example to others who might try to cross the borders of Asturias under arms.

"Do your worst," said the old man, setting his teeth so fiercely that his blond beard wagged. "Do you think my sons will not march on Asturias with all their might, now that they know what happened to their advance guard?"

"He is lying," said a young *laranzu*. "This army was no advance guard; it was made up of every man he could put into the field. His sons are not of an age to fight. They risked all on one throw of the dice."

"And they would have succeeded, had it not been for your efforts, kinsman," said Geremy Hastur to Dom Rafael. He was wearing a long robe, a scholar's robe of purple so deep that it was almost black. He was unweaponed save for a small dagger. The long robe hid the ungainly lameness, but could not conceal the uneven stance or his halting step, supported on a crutch like a man four times his age. His red hair was already graying at the temples, and he had begun, like an old man, to wear a fringe of beard at his jaws. Bard thought, with contempt, that his foster-brother looked less like a warrior than one of those Renunciates who had fought in his army!

Dom Rafael and Geremy embraced as kinsmen, but then they broke apart; Geremy's eyes fell on Bard where he stood two paces behind his father.

"You!"

"Are you surprised to see me, kinsman?"

"You were outlawed in this realm for seven years, Bard; and there is the blood of the royal house on your hands now. Your life is doubly forfeit here. Give me a single good reason I should not tell my men to take you out and hang you from the walls!"

Bard said hotly, "You know by what betrayal that blood came on my hands—" but Dom Rafael silenced him with a gesture.

"Is this gratitude, cousin Geremy? Bard led the assault

which saved Castle Asturias from falling into Serrais hands.
Had he not come, your head would now be hanging for a
popinjay, for Dom Eiric's men to use at target practice!"

Geremy's mouth tightened.

"I have never doubted that my cousin was brave," he said,
"and so, I suppose, I must grant him amnesty, life for life. Be
it so, Bard; come and go in this realm as your lawful duties
warrant. But not in my presence. When the army goes, go you
with them, and do not come into my court for your life's span,
for on the day I set eyes on you again, I will certainly have you
killed."

"As for that," Bard began, but Dom Rafael cut in.

"Enough. Before you go to passing sentences of death or
banishment, Hastur, you had better have a throne to speak
from. On what grounds do you claim to reign here?"

"As regent for Valentine, son of Ardrin, at Queen Ariel's request; and as warden for these lands, which have been, since
time out of mind, a part of the Hastur Domains, and shall be
again, when these years of anarchy are past. The Hasturs of
Carcosa are a peaceful folk, and will let the di Asturiens reign
here, as long as they swear allegiance to the Domain of Hastur, and Valentine has already done so."

"Oh, brave!" retorted Dom Rafael, "Great glory and gallant
deeds are yours, Geremy Hester, to extort an oath from a babe
not five years old! Did you promise the child a toy sword and
a new pony, or did you get it cheaply from him for a sugared
cake and a handful of candies?"

Geremy flinched at the sarcasm. "He listened to the persuasion of his mother, Queen Ariel," he said. "She knew well that
I would guard the boy's rights till he was grown; at which
time, he said to me, he would take oath as a man, to reign here
as warden for the Hasturs."

Dom Rafael said fiercely, "We want no Hasturs in this land
which the di Asturiens have held since they won it from the
cat-folk ages ago!"

"The men of this land will follow Valentine, their rightful
lord, in allegiance to the lawful Hastur King," Geremy said.

"Will they? If you believe it, you had better ask them, my
lord."

"I had believed," Geremy said, holding his temper with obvious effort, "that we were under truce, Dom Rafael."

"Truce while the Serrais armies held you here; but behold,

that army lies in ruins, and I doubt if Dom Eiric will muster
enough men to put an army in the field for ten years or more!
Even if we let him live! And as for that," he added, signaling
to one of his bodyguards, "take Dom Eiric away and keep him
secure."

"In a dungeon, my lord?"

Dom Rafael looked Eiric Ridenow up and down. "No," he
said. "That would be over hard on his old bones. If he will give
oath under truthspell not to attempt escape until we have determined his fate, we will house him in comfort befitting his
rank and his gray hairs."

"For every gray hair on my head," Dom Eiric said truthfully, "there are ten on yours, Rafael di Asturien!"

"Even so, I shall house you in comfort till your sons can
ransom you, for they will need you at home till they are grown.
Little boys are impetuous, and they might try something too
dangerous for them."

Dom Eiric glared, but at last he said, "Bring our *leronis*. I
will swear by the walls of Serrais that I will not leave this place
till you yourself dismiss me, dead or alive."

Bard laughed harshly. He said, "Take from him some oath
stronger than the walls of Serrais, Father, for I can go and
break those whenever I will."

Dom Eiric glowered, but he did not speak, for what Bard
said was true, and he knew it. Dom Rafael said to his guard,
"Take him to some comfortable chamber, and keep him there
secure until I can take his oath. Your life for it if he escapes before a *leronis* has his oath."

Geremy Hastur scowled as the old lord was led away.
"Don't presume too far on my gratitude, cousin. You are over
free, it seems to me, in disposing of my prisoners."

"Your prisoners? When will you face the truth, cousin?"
Dom Rafael asked. "Your rule here is ended, and I shall prove
it to you." He gestured to Bard, who stepped out on the balcony.

In the courtyard below, where the army was quartered, he
heard a wild outburst of cheering.

"The Wolf! The Kilghard Wolf!"

"Our general! He led us to victory!"

"Dom Rafael's son! Long live the house of di Asturien!"

Dom Rafael stepped out on the balcony, calling, "Listen to
me, men! You have won freedom from Serrais. Will you turn

Asturias over to the Hasturs? I claim that throne for the house of di Asturien; not for myself, but in ward for my son Alaric!"

Wild cheering drowned out his words. When there was quiet, he said, "Your turn, my lord Geremy. Ask if there are any men down there who wish to live for twelve years or so under the rule of Hastur while Ardrin's son Valentine grows to manhood."

Bard felt that he could taste Geremy's hate and wrath, it was so thick around them; but the young man did not speak, only stepped out on the balcony. There were one or two cries of "No Hasturs!" "Down with the Hastur tyrants!" but after a moment they quieted.

"Men of di Asturien," he called out. His voice was a strong, resonant bass which gave the lie to the frail body containing it. "In days past, Hastur, son of Light, won this realm and set the di Asturiens over it, in wardship! I stand here for King Valentine, son of Ardrin. Are you traitors, men, to rebel against your rightful king?"

"Where's that king, then?" shouted one man in the crowd. "If he's our rightful king, why isn't he here, being brought up among his lawful subjects?"

"No Hastur puppet kings here," another one shouted. "Get back to Hali where you belong, Hastur!"

"We'll have a real di Asturien on the throne, not a Hastur flunkey!"

"We'll kiss no Hastur arses in Asturias!"

Bard listened, with growing satisfaction, as the cries grew louder. Someone threw a stone. Geremy did not flinch; he flung up a hand and the stone exploded in a flare of blue light. There was a gasp and a yell of rage.

"No wizard kings in Asturias!"

"We'll have a soldier, not a damned *laranzu!*"

"Dom Rafael! Dom Rafael! Who stands for King Alaric?" they yelled, and there were even a few cries of "Bard! Bard di Asturien! We'll have the Kilghard Wolf!"

Someone threw another stone, which did not pass within a hand-span of Geremy. He did not bother to deflect this one. Then someone threw a handful of courtyard horse dung which splattered on the purple robe. Geremy's paxman caught him by the elbow and dragged him away from the balcony.

Dom Rafael said, "Do you still think you can claim the throne of Asturias, Dom Geremy? Perhaps I should send your head back to Queen Ariel and the folk at Carcosa, as warning to the lady to choose her servants more carefully."

Geremy's smile was as grim as the old man's. "I would not advise it. King Valentine loves his playmate Alaric; but I doubt not that Queen Ariel could persuade him to send you back gift for gift."

Bard stepped forward, fists clenched, but Dom Rafael shook his head. "No, my son. No bloodshed here. We mean no harm to the Hasturs while they rule their own lands and meddle not with ours. But you will remain my guest until my son Mario dwells again beneath this roof."

"Do you think Carolin of Carcosa will deal with an usurper?"

"Then," said Dom Rafael, "I shall be happy to entertain you as long as you desire, my lord. Should I not live long enough to see your return to Carcosa, I have a grandson who will reign as Warden of Asturias for my son Alaric." He said to Bard, "Conduct our royal guest to his chambers—he is royal in Carcosa, though he shall never be so in Asturias. And station servants to see that he lacks for nothing, and that he does not go exploring in the woods and perhaps fall and damage his lame leg. We must care for the son of King Carolin with great kindness."

"I shall see that he stays within his chamber in study and meditation, and takes no risk of injuring himself with exercise," Bard said, and laid a hand on Geremy's shoulder.

"Come, cousin."

Geremy shook off the touch as if it burned him. "You damned bastard, don't presume to put your hands on me!"

"I find no pleasure in the touch," Bard said. "I am no lover of men. You will not come at my courteous request? Why, then—" He signaled to two of the soldiers, "My lord Hastur is experiencing some difficulty in walking; he is lame, as you see. Kindly assist him to his chamber."

Geremy yelled and shouted as the husky men-at-arms picked him up bodily and carried him; then, recalling his dignity, subsided and allowed them to take him. But the look he gave Bard told him that if he ever again met Bard armed and ready, he could expect to fight him to the death.

I should have killed him when I had the chance, Bard thought bitterly. *But I had lamed him by mischance. I could not kill him unarmed.*

*I would rather have Geremy as foster brother and friend,
not enemy. What god hates me, that this has come to pass?*

The change of power in Castle Asturias was accomplished
within a few days, without much trouble. They had to hang a
few of Geremy's loyal men, who organized a palace rebellion,
but one of the *laranzu* smelled out the plot before it had gone
far. Soon all was quiet. Bard heard from Melisendra that one
of the exiled queen's ladies was bearing Geremy Hastur's
child, and had begged to join him in his imprisonment."

"I did not know Geremy had a sweetheart. Do you know
her name?"

"Ginevra," Melisendra said, and Bard raised his eyebrows.
He remembered Ginevra Harryl.

"You are a *leronis*," he said. "Can't you force her to miscarry, or something of that sort? It is bad enough to keep one
Hastur prisoner, without starting a dynasty."

Melisendra's eyes were pale with lambent wrath. "No *leronis* would so abuse her powers!"

"Do you think me a fool, woman? Don't tell me fairy tales
of virtue! Every camp follower who finds herself breeding
against her will knows a sorceress who will lighten her of that
inconvenient burden!"

At white heat, Meisendra retorted, "If the woman does not
wish to bear a child into squalor, or on campaign, or fatherless,
or when she knows she will have no milk for it—then, no
doubt, some *leronis* would take pity on her! But to kill a much-
longed-for babe, simply because some man finds it inconvenient to his throne?" Her eyes flamed at him. "Do you think I
wanted *your* child, Bard di Asturien? But it was done, and irrevocable, and whatever came of it, I had lost the Sight. . . . so
I kept from damaging an innocent life, even though I had not
desired it. And if I could keep from laying hands on *that,* do
you think I would harm Ginevra's child even in thought?
Ginevra loves her babe and its father! If you want your dirty
work done, send a man with a sword to cut her throat, and be
done with it!"

Bard found nothing to say. It was an unwelcome thought—
that Melisendra might have rid herself, so easily, of that child
who had become Erlend. Why had she held her hand?

And there was the problem of Ginevra. Damn women and
their idiotic scruples! Melisendra had killed in battle, he knew

that. Yet here was a potential enemy of the Asturiens, more dangerous than one who bore sword or pike, and that enemy was to live! He would not demean himself by arguing with her, but let her beware how she crossed him again! He told her so, and slammed out of the room.

Being forced to think of the woman he had and did not want reminded him, perforce, of the woman he wanted and could not have. And after a time he thought of a way to use Ginevra and her coming child.

When the countryside was quiet, and the armies had returned home, except for the standing army Bard was training for defense and perhaps conquest (for he knew perfectly well that the Hasturs would someday descend on them, hostages or no) Lady Jerana had lost no time in coming to court. Bard sought her out in the apartments that had been Queen Ariel's.

"The lady Ginevra Harryl, who is with child by Hastur—is she healthy and well? When will she be brought to bed?"

"Perhaps three moons," Lady Jerana said.

"Do me a kindness, foster mother? See to it that she is housed in comfort, with suitable ladies to care for her, and a good and trustworthy midwife in attendance."

The lady frowned. She said, "Why, so she is, she has three waiting-women known to have Hastur sympathies, and the midwife who delivered your own son waits on her; but I know you too well to think you do this out of any kindness to the Lady Ginevra."

"No?" Bard said. "Have you forgotten that Geremy is my own foster brother?"

Jerana looked skeptical, but Bard said no more. However, later that day, when he had verified for himself that all Dom Rafael's wife said was true, he went to Geremy's apartments.

Geremy was playing at a game called Castles with one of the pages who had been sent to wait on him. When Bard came in he put aside the dice and got awkwardly to his feet.

"You needn't stand on courtesy, Geremy. In fact, you need not stand at all."

"It is customary for a prisoner to stand in the presence of his jailer," Geremy said.

"Please yourself," Bard said. "I came to bring you news of the Lady Ginevra Harryl. I am sure you are too proud to ask news of her on your own, so I came to assure you that she is lodged in a suite next to that of my father's wife, and that her own women,

Camilla and Rafaella Delleray and Felizia MacAnndra have been sent to wait upon her; and that a midwife trained in our own household is in attendance upon her."

Geremy's fists clenched. "Knowing you," he said, "I am sure this is your way of telling me that you have taken revenge for some fancied insult by casting her and her women into some dirty dungeon with an accursed and filthy slut to mishandle her in childbirth."

"You misjudge me, cousin. She is housed in comfort considerably greater than your own, and I will say so under truth-spell, if you like."

"Why would you do that?" Geremy asked suspiciously.

"Because, knowing how a man is troubled for the thought of his womenfolk," Bard said, "I thought you might be as eager for news of your lady as I for mine. If you wish, it can be arranged for Ginevra to join you here. . . ."

Geremy dropped on his seat and covered his face with his hands. He said, "Do you take pleasure in tormenting me, Bard? You have no shadow of a quarrel with Ginevra, but if it gives you enjoyment to see me humiliated, I will crawl to you on my knees, if I must; do not harm Ginevra or her child."

Bard opened the door to admit a *leronis* of the household—not Melisendra. When the blue light of truthspell was in the chamber, he said, "Hear me now, Geremy. Lady Ginevra is housed in luxurious apartments, not a stone's throw from those of Queen Ariel when we were boys. She has ample food for a breeding woman, and such things as she best likes, by my orders. She has her own women with her, sleeping in her chamber so that no one will trouble her, and my own mother's midwife is within call."

Geremy watched the steady light of truthspell and it did not flicker. He was still suspicious, but he knew enough of *laran,* himself trained in that art, to know there had been no deceit in the setting of the spell. He demanded, "Why do you say all this to me?"

"Because," Bard said, "I too have a wife, whom I have not seen for seven long years of outlawry and exile. If you will tell me, under truthspell, where I can find Carlina, I am ready to allow Ginevra to join you here, or to move you, under guard, into her suite, until the birth of your child."

Geremy threw back his head and laughed, a long laugh of despair.

"Would that I could tell you!" he said. "I had forgotten how seriously you took that handfasting . . . we all took it seriously then, before your quarrel with Ardrin."

"Carlina is my wife," Bard said. "And since there is truth-spell here, tell me this truthfully, too: did not Ardrin repent of his promise and try to give her to you, Hastur-spawn?"

"He repented it early and late," Geremy said, "and with Beltran dead, and you fled into outlawry, he held the bond between you forfeit. And, indeed, he offered her to me. But don't clench your teeth and scowl like that, Wolf; Carlina would have nothing to do with me, and she told him so, though the old king threw a mighty tantrum about it, and swore he would not be so defied by any woman living!"

The light of the truthspell on his face did not waver; Bard knew he spoke the truth. He felt an upsurge of joy. Carlina remembered their bond, she had refused to set it aside even for Geremy!

"And where is she, Geremy? Speak, and Ginevra is free to join you here."

Geremy's laugh held the bitterness of despair. "Where is she now? Willingly, willingly I will tell you, cousin! She has sworn the vows of a priestess of Avarra, which even her father dared not gainsay," he said, "and she has fled the court and the kingdom, and made her way to the Isle of Silence, where she is sworn to live out the rest of her life in chastity and prayer. And if you want her, cousin, you will have to go there and take her."

CHAPTER THREE

After the conquest of Asturias, Bard's father had placed him in command of the armies. But Serrais had been subdued, for the moment, and he was not yet ready to take the field against the Hasturs, so he went to Dom Rafael and begged a few days' leave.

"To be sure, you have well earned it, my son. Where do you wish to go?"

"I induced Geremy to tell me where Carlina has gone," he said, "and I wish to take an honor guard and bring her back to me."

"But not if she has been married to any other man," his father said anxiously. "I know your feelings, but I cannot in good conscience give you leave to take the wife of any of my subjects! I rule this land under law!"

"What law is stronger than that which binds a man to the woman he has handfasted? But ease your mind, Father, Carlina is the wife of no man; she has taken refuge where she cannot be forced into marriage with any other."

"In that case," his father said, "take what men you will, and when you return with her, we will hold the marriage here in all splendor." He hesitated. "The lady Melisendra will be ill content to take her place as *barragana* when your wife is here. Shall I send her back to our estates? She can care for her son there and live honorably in retirement."

"No," he said savagely. "I will give her to Carlina for a handmaiden!"

Something in him rejoiced at the thought of Melisendra humbled, waiting on Carlina, combing her hair and fetching her shoes and ribbons.

"You must do as it seems good to you," Dom Rafael said, "but she is the mother of your eldest son, and in humiliating the mother, you belittle the son. Nor would Carlina, I suppose, find much pleasure in beholding, night and day, the face of her rival. I do not think you understand women very well."

"Perhaps not," said Bard, "and you may be sure that if Carlina wishes me to send Melisendra away, I will lose no time in doing so. As my lawful wife, it will be Carlina's duty to foster all my sons, and I will put Erlend in her care." That, he thought, would be better than letting Melisendra poison the child's mind against him. He liked little Erlend, and had no intention of being parted from him.

He chose an honor guard of a dozen men; that would be enough to show the women of the Island of Silence that he intended to have his wife, and that they should lose no time in handing her over to him. No very great force would be needed against a handful of unworldly female recluses!

In addition to the honor guard, he brought with him two sorcerers; the young *laranzu* Rory, and Melisendra herself. From childhood he had heard tales of the sorcery of the priestesses of Avarra, and he wished to have sorcery of his own to contend with them. And it would do Melisendra no harm to know that he did, indeed, have a lawful wife, and that she could expect nothing more from him!

The Island of Silence lay outside the kingdom of Asturias, in the independent shire of Marenji. Bard knew little of Marenji, except that their ruler was chosen every few years by acclamation from among the rabble; they had no standing army, and kept themselves free of any alliances with kings or rulers nearby. Once Bard's father had entertained the Sheriff of Marenji in his Great Hall, dealing with him for some casks of their fruit wine, and making an arrangement to guard his borders.

He rode across the peaceful countryside of Marenji, with its groves of apples and pears, plums and greenberries, its orchards of nut trees and featherpod bushes. In a hilly ravine he saw a stream dammed up to give power to a felting mill where featherpod fibers were made into batting for quilts. There was a village of weavers; he recalled that they made beautifully woven tartan cloth for skirts and shawls. There was no sign anywhere of defenses.

If this place were armed, Bard thought, and soldiers quartered in the villages, it would make a splendid buffer state to hold off the armies of Serrais when they came down again toward Asturias, and in return the men of Asturias could protect them. The Sheriff of Marenji could surely be made to see reason. And if he did not, well, there was no army to show resistence. He would advise his father as soon as he returned to lose no time in quartering armies in Marenji.

As they rode, the land grew darker. They rode in the shadow of the high mountains, past lakes and misty tarns. There were fewer and fewer farms, just an isolated steading here and there. Melisendra and the boy rode close together and looked ill at ease.

Bard reviewed in his mind everything that he knew of the priestesses of Avarra. They had dwelt, as long as any living man could remember, on the island at the center of the Lake of Silence; and always the law had been that any man who set foot on that island must die. It was said that the priestesses swore lifelong vows of chastity and prayer; but in addition to the priestesses, many women, wives or maidens or widows, went to the island in grief or piety or penitence to dwell for a time under the mantle of Avarra, the Dark Mother; and whoever they were, so that they worshipped Avarra and wore the garb of the sisterhood during their sojourn there and spoke to no man and observed chastity, they might dwell as long as they wished. No man really knew what went on among them, and the women who went there were pledged never to tell.

But women in grief and despair from the loss of a child or husband, women who were barren and longed for children, women worn from childbearing who wished to petition the Goddess for health or for barrenness, women suffering from any sorrow, these went there to the shrine of Avarra to pray for the help of the priestesses, or for that of the Mother.

Once an old woman who served Lady Jerana—Bard had been so young then that he was not even chased away when women talked among themselves—had said in his hearing, "Secret of the Island of Silence? The secret is that there is no secret! I spent a season there once. The women live in their houses, in silence, chaste and alone, and speaking only when necessary, or to pray, or for healing and charity. They pray at dawn and sunset, or when the moons rise. They are pledged to give help to any woman who asks it in the name of the Goddess, whatever her griefs or burdens. They know a great deal of healing herbs and simples, and while I dwelt with them they taught me. They are good and holy women."

Bard wondered how any women could be good, being pledged to murder any man who set foot on the island? Although, he conceded, (making a joke of it to himself, to allay his anxiety) they must at least be unlike other women if they were silent! That was always a virtue in women!

It seemed, though, wrong for women to dwell alone, unprotected; if he were Sheriff of Marenji he would send soldiers to protect the women.

They stood now on the lip of a valley, looking down at the wide waters of the Lake of Silence.

It was a quiet place and an eerie one. There was no sound, as they moved down toward the shores of the lake, except the sound of their horses' hooves; and the cry of a water bird, her nest disturbed, flying up with a sudden squawk into the air. Dark trees bent flexible branches over the dark waters, black against the low sunset light in the sky; and as they came nearer they heard the complaining of frogs. They picked their way through the soggy swamplands along the shore, and Bard heard sucking sounds as his horse's feet sloshed in the marsh.

Ugh, what a dismal place! Carlina should be grateful that he had come to take her away from it! Perhaps she had shown good sense in taking refuge here, so that no other marriage could be forced on her for political reasons, but surely seven years was long enough to spend in piety and prayer, apart from all men! Her life as the Princess Carlina, wife to the Commander of the King's Armies, would be very different!

And now there was fog, rising in swirls from the surface of the lake, thick wisps of it, swirling and streaming toward them until Bard could hardly see the path before him. The men were grumbling; the very air seemed thick and oppressive! Small Rory, on his pony at Bard's side, raised a pale, frightened face.

"Please, *vai dom,* we should go back. We will be lost in the fog. And they do not want us here, I can feel it!"

"Use the Sight," Bard commanded. "What do you see?"

The child took out the seeing-stone and obediently looked into it, but his face was contorted, as if he were trying not to cry.

"Nothing. I see nothing, only the fog. They are trying to hide from me, they say it is impious for a man to be here."

Bard jeered, "Do you call yourself a man?"

"No," said the child, "but *they* call me one and say I must not come here. Please, my Lord Wolf, let's go back! The Dark Mother has turned her face to me, but she is veiled, she is angry—oh, please, my lord, we are forbidden to come here, we must turn and go away again or something terrible will happen!"

Furious, frustrated, Bard wondered if those witches on the island thought they could frighten him by playing their witch tricks on a harmless little boy with a seeing-stone. "Hold your tongue and try to act like a man," he told the boy severely, and the child, sniffling, wiped his face and rode in silence, shaking.

The fog thickened and grew darker still. Was it an oncoming storm? Strange; for on the hill above the lake, the weather had been fine and bright. Probably it was the dampness from that unhealthy marsh.

What a superstitious lot his men were, grumbling that way about a little fog!

Suddenly the fog swirled and flowed and began to shape itself into a pattern; he felt his horse nervously step aside, as directly before him, it flowed, moved within itself and became the form of a woman. Not a fog ghost, but a woman, solid and real as he was himself. He could see every strand of the white hair, braided in two braids down the side of her face, covered, all but a few inches, by a thick, woven black veil. She wore a black skirt and the thickly knitted black shawl of a country woman, simple and unadorned over some form of chemise of coarse linen. Around her waist was a long belt, woven in colored patterns, from which hung a sickle-shaped knife with a black handle.

She held up her hand in a stern gesture.

"Go back," she said. "You know that no man may set foot here; this is holy ground, sacred to the Dark Mother. Turn your horses and go back the way you came. There is quicksand here, and other dangers about which you know nothing. Go back."

Bard opened his mouth and had a little trouble finding his voice. At last he said, "I mean no harm or disrespect, Mother, not to you or to any of the devout servants of Avarra. I am here to escort home my handfasted wife, Carlina di Asturien, daughter of the late King Ardrin."

"There are no handfasted brides here," said the old priestess. "Only the sworn sisters of Avarra, who live here in prayer and piety; and a few penitents and pilgrims who have come to dwell among us for a season for the healing of their hurts and burdens."

"You are evading me, old Mother. Is the Lady Carlina among them?"

"No one here bears the name Carlina," said the old priestess. "We do not inquire what name our sisters bore when they dwelt in the world; when a woman comes here to take vows among us, the name she bore is lost forever, known only to the Goddess. There is no woman here you may claim as your wife, whoever you are. I admonish you most sincerely: do not commit this blasphemy, or bring on yourself the wrath of the Dark Mother."

Bard leaned forward over his saddle. "Don't you threaten me, old lady! I know that my wife is here, and if you do not deliver her up to me, I will come and take her, and I will not be responsible for what my men may do."

"But," said the old woman, "you will certainly be held responsible, whether you take responsibility for it or not."

"Don't chop words with me! You would do better to go and tell her that her husband has come to take her away; and if you will do that, I will commit no blasphemy, but await her here outside your holy precincts."

"But I do not fear your threats," the ancient priestess said. "Nor does the Great Mother." And the fog swirled up around her face, and suddenly there was no one where she had been standing, only empty swirls of mist rising from the reeds at the water's edge.

Bard gasped. How had she vanished? Had she ever been there at all, or only an illusion? Perversely, he was more sure than ever that Carlina was there, and that they were hiding her from him. Why had the old lady not seen the sense of doing as he bade her, going to Carlina and telling her that he had come in peace, willing no harm or blasphemy, to take her home to his fireside and his bed? She was, after all, his lawful wife. Must he be forced, then, to commit a blasphemy?

He turned and drew up his horse beside Melisendra.

"Now is the time to use your sorcery," he said, "unless we are all to be caught in quicksand. Is there quicksand here?"

She drew out her starstone and gazed into it, her face taking on that same distant, abstracted look he had seen so often on Melora's face.

"There is quicksand near, though not dangerously near, I think. Bard, are you resolved on this folly? Truly, it is unwise to brave the wrath of Avarra. If Carlina wished to come to you, she would come; she is not held prisoner there."

"I have no way of knowing," Bard said. "These are mad-women, who try to live alone, putting chastity and prayer into the place of those things which are proper for women—"

"Do you think chastity and prayer improper for women?" she inquired, sarcastically.

"By no means; but surely a woman can pray as much as she wishes by her own fireside, and no wedded wife has the right to commit herself to chastity against the will of her lawful husband! What good are these priestesses to anyone if they flout the laws of nature and of man this way?"

He had meant the question rhetorically, but Melisendra took it literally. "I am told that they do many good works," she said. "They know much of herbs and medicines, and they can make the barren fertile; and prayer is always a good thing."

Bard ignored her. They had come through the fog and out on to a small sandy beach, free of the reeds that lined the lakeshore elsewhere; and there was a small hut there, and a tethered boat.

Bard got down from his horse and shouted.

"Hi! Ferryman!"

A small slouched figure, wrapped in shawls, came out of the hut. Bard was outraged to discover that it was no ferryman but a little old woman, crippled and gray and bent.

"Where is the ferryman?"

"I keep this ferry, *vai dom,* for the good ladies."

"Take me across this lake here to the island, quickly!"

"I can't do that, sir. It's forbidden. Now the lady there, if *she* wants to go over, I'll take her. But no man, it's not allowed, the Goddess forbids it."

"Rubbish," Bard said. "How dare you pretend to know what the immortals want, even assuming that there are any gods, or any goddesses either? And if the priestesses don't like it, well, there's nothing they can do about it."

"I won't be responsible for your death, *vai dom.*"

"Don't be foolish, old dame. Get into that boat and take me over, at once!"

"Don't call names like fool, sir; you don't know what you're talking about. That boat won't take you over to the other shore. Me, yes; the lady, yes; but it won't take you, not at all."

Bard decided the woman was a halfwit. Probably the priestesses had given her the task of ferrying, out of charity, but her main task was to scare people away. Well, he didn't scare. He drew his dagger.

"See this? Get into the boat! Now!"

"Can't do it," she wailed. "Indeed I can't! The water's not safe except when the priestesses want it to be! I never come over unless they call me from the other side!"

Frowning, Bard remembered the spelled ford near Moray's mill, where a quiet, shallow stream had suddenly become a torrent. But he gestured, menacing, with his dagger.

"The boat!"

She took a step and then another, shaking, then collapsed, sobbing, a sodden bundle of rags. "Can't," she wailed. "Can't!"

Bard felt like kicking her. Instead, his jaw set, he stepped over her cowering body and got into the boat, picking up the paddle and driving it, with a few long, strong strokes, out into the water.

The lake water was rough, with a savage undertow unlike anything Bard had ever felt before, tossing the little boat around like a cork; but Bard was very strong, and had learned to handle small boats on the troubled waters of Lake Mirion. He drove the boat through the water with firm strokes. . . .

. . . and discovered, to his dismay, that somehow he had gotten turned around, and instead of heading for the shore of the Island of Silence, the boat was heading right up on the sandy beach where the ferrywoman's hut was located.

Bard swore, impotently, as he felt the boat being rushed by the savage current, right back on the shore he had left. He thrust with the paddle, fending the boat out into the stream again. It took every scrap of his strength to keep the boat in the channel, but try as he might, he could make no headway toward the island. Slowly, inexorably, the boat turned in circles, drifting, no matter how he paddled it. The ferrywoman had hauled herself to her knees and was watching him, cackling with laughter. The boat moved on shore, no matter how hard he paddled, scooted up, scraping on the sand, and his last paddle stroke actually drove it hard aground.

The little ferrywoman cackled, "I told ye, sir. Not if you was to try all day and all night. That boat there won't go to the island unless the priestesses *call* it there."

Bard fancied he saw grins on the faces of some of his men.

He glared around with such rage that they quickly assumed total impassivity. He took a threatening step toward the old ferrywoman. He felt ready and willing to wring her neck. But she was only an old simpleton, after all.

He considered, standing over her. The ford at Moray's mill had been spelled. Evidently the boat, here, had been put under sorcery as well. In any case, if the priestesses really meant to keep Carlina from him, and it was fairly obvious that they did, one man alone would meet only more bewitchment and sorcery.

Perhaps a *leronis* could calm the waters, as Melora had done at Moray's mill; and his men could swim their horses across.

"Melisendra!"

She came quietly. He wondered if she had been laughing behind his back at his struggle with the boat.

"If the priestesses have put a spell on the water, you can calm it and reverse it!"

She looked straight at him and shook her head.

"No, my lord. I dare not risk the anger of Avarra."

"Is she the Goddess of whom you prate?" he demanded.

"She is the Goddess of all women, and I will not anger her."

"Melisendra, I warn you—" He raised his hand, ready to strike her.

She looked at him with deadly indifference. "You cannot do anything to me worse than you have done. After what has already befallen me, do you think that a few blows will make me obedient to your will?"

"If you dislike me as much as all that, I would think you would be glad to help me recover my wife! Then you will be free of me, if I am so hateful to you!"

"At the cost of betraying some other woman into your hands?"

"You are jealous," he accused, "and want no other woman in my arms!"

She kept her eyes on him, straight and level. She said, "If your wife were held captive on that island and wished to rejoin you, I would risk the anger of Avarra to help her to your arms. But she seems not very eager to leave her place of refuge and come over to you. And if you are wise, Bard, you will leave this place at once before something worse happens."

"Is that the Sight?" Frustration made his words sarcastic.

She bowed her head. She said, and he saw that she was

weeping silently, "No, my lord. That is—gone from me forever. But I know the Goddess cannot be defied with impunity. You had better come, Bard."

"Would you grieve if some dreadful fate befell me?" he asked, savagely, but she did not answer, only turned her horse about and rode slowly away from the lake.

Damn the woman! Damn all women, and their Goddess with them!

"Come on, men," he shouted. "Swim the horses; the spell is only on the boat!" He urged his horse right up to the water's edge, although it fought, shying nervously and backing from the water under its feet. He swiveled his horse and saw that they were not following him.

"Come on! What's the matter with you? After me, men! There are women on that island, and they have defied me, so I make you free of them all! Come on, men, plunder and women—not afraid of some old witch's jabberings, are you? Come on!"

About half of the men hung back, muttering fearfully.

"Nay, Dom Wolf, it's uncanny, it's forbidden!"

"The Goddess forbids it, lord! No, don't do this!"

"Blasphemy!"

But one or two of the others urged their horses forward, eagerly, hauling at the reins, forcing the unwilling beasts into the water.

The fog was rising again, thicker and thicker; and this time it had a strange, eerie greenish color. It seemed that there were faces within it, faces that grimaced and leered and menaced him, and slowly, slowly, the faces were drifting ashore. One of the men hanging back, unwilling to go near the water, suddenly howled like a madman, and cried, "No, no! Mother Avarra, have mercy! Pity us!" He jerked the reins savagely and Bard heard his horse's hoofs suck and splash as he turned about and galloped back the way they had come. One after another, although Bard rose in his stirrups and yelled and cursed them, his men turned and bolted their animals back up the trail, until Bard was alone at the water's edge. Damn them all! Frightened of a little fog! Cowards, he'd break them all and reduce them to the ranks, if he didn't hang them one and all for cowardice!

He sat defying the fog. "Come on," he said aloud, and clucked to the horse, but she did not move, quivering beneath him as if she stood in the chill of a blizzard. He wondered if she could see the horrid faces, drifting nearer and nearer the shore.

And suddenly a blind terror chilled Bard, too, to the bone. He *knew*, with every fiber in him, that if one of the faces touched him through the fog, all the courage and life in him would drain out, cold, and he would die, the fog would bite through to the bone and he would fall from his saddle, strengthless and screaming, and never rise again. He jerked at the reins of his horse and tried to gallop after Melisendra and his fleeing men, but he was frozen, and the mare sat trembling under him and did not stir. He had once heard that the Great Mother could take the form of a mare. . . . Had she bewitched his horse?

The faces drifted closer and closer, horrible and formless, the faces of dead men, ravished women, corpses with the flesh hanging from their bones, and somehow Bard knew they were all the men *he* had led into battle and death, all the men *he* had killed, all the women *he* had ravaged or raped or burned and driven from their houses, the screaming face of a woman in the pillage of Scaravel, when he had taken her child from her and flung it over the wall to be shattered on the stones below . . . a woman he had taken in the sack of Scathfell, her husband lying dead beside her . . . a child, bruised and bleeding from a dozen men who had used her . . . Lisarda, weeping in his arms . . . Beltran, all the flesh melted from his bones . . . the faces were so close now that they were formless, lapping at his feet, his knees, swirling higher and higher. They wrapped about his loins, sucking, biting, and under his clothing he felt his genitals shrink and wither, unmanning him, felt the cold rise in his belly; when they rose to bite at his throat his breath would fail and he would fall, choking, dying. . . .

Bard screamed, and somehow the sound gave him life enough to grab at the reins, to kick frantically at his horse's flanks. She bucked and bolted. He clung for his life, letting her run, letting her take him anywhere, anywhere away from that place. He lost the stirrups, he lost the reins as she bolted, but panic somehow gave him strength to cling to her back; at last he felt her slowing under him to a walk, and came to consciousness dazed, finding that he was riding at the rear of his men, next to Melisendra.

If she said a single word, he resolved, if she spoke a syllable indicating that she had warned him, or that he should have taken her advice, he would hit her! Somehow that damned woman always seemed to come off best in their encounters! He was sick to death of having her there to sneer at him! If she said one word about what a ludicrous figure he had cut, fleeing, clinging to his horse. . . .

"If you're so damned well suited by piety and chastity," he snarled at her, "and so glad of my defeat, why don't you go back to them yourself and stay there?"

But she was not jeering at him. She was not looking at him at all. She had her veil pulled over her face and she was weeping quietly behind its shelter.

"I would go," she said in a whisper. "I would go, so gladly! But they would not have me." And she lowered her head and would not look at him again.

Bard rode on, sick with rage. Once again, Carlina had escaped him! She had made a fool of him again, when he had been so sure of her! And he was tied still to Melisendra, whom he was beginning to hate! He turned as they rode up the steep path, and shook an angry fist at the lake which lay silent, pale in the falling dusk, behind them.

He would come back. The women there had defeated him once, but he would devise some way to come back, and this time he would not be driven away by their witchcraft! Let them beware!

And if Carlina was hiding there, let her beware too!

CHAPTER FOUR

Summer had come to the Kilghard Hills, bringing fire season, when the resin trees burst into flame and every available man was called out on fire-watch. On a day late in summer Bard di Asturien rode slowly southward, with a small group of picked men and bodyguards, and at last crossed the border from Marenji into Asturias.

No longer, he thought, *truly a border.* The Shire of Marenji, despite the protests of the sheriff, lay under arms, protected by soldiers quartered in every house and village in Marenji. A system of beacon fires and telepathic relays had been established to warn the people of Asturias of any attack from north or east, from bandits from over the Kadarin, or riders from Serrais.

The people of Marenji had protested. When had the people, he wondered, ever known what was good for them? Did they *want* to stand unarmed between Serrais and Asturias, being ridden over by armies every few years? If they did not want soldiers there from Astunias, they should have had their own armies to keep them out.

He spent one night in his old home, but no one was there except the old *coridom;* Erlend had been sent to join his mother at court. Soon, Bard thought, he would have to take thought about suitable fosterage for his son in some nobleman's house. Even if Erlend was destined to be a *laranzu,* he should know something of war and arms. Bard remembered that Geremy, who knew he would never carry arms in battle, had been nothing behind his foster brothers in swordplay. . . . he cut that thought off, clean, setting his jaw, refusing to think about it.

Erlend should be a *laranzu,* if his gifts lay that way; he was only a *nedestro* son. When he had found the right way to reclaim Carlina, she could give him lawful sons enough. But Erlend must be fostered as befitted his rank, and be supposed Melisendra would make some sort of scene over that. Damn the woman, all the disadvantages of having a wife, and none of the advantages! If she were not his father's most valued *leronis* he would send her away at once. Perhaps one of Dom Rafael's men would be willing to marry her, surely his father would give her some kind of dowry.

He rode in to Castle Asturias at dusk, finding the courtyard filled with strange horses, Hastur banners, embassies from all over the Hundred Kingdoms. What had happened? Had King Carolin sent at last to ransom Geremy?

That, he learned, was only a part of it. Forty days before, the Lady Ginevra Harryl had borne a son to Geremy Hastur; Geremy had chosen, first, to legitimatize the boy, and at the same time had chosen to marry the woman *di catenas.* As a way of proving that Geremy Hastur was no prisoner but an honored guest (the legal fiction, Bard thought wryly, about all hostages), Dom Rafael had chosen to perform the marriage himself, and to hold the wedding with great ceremony, with Hasturs coming from far and wide to attend the wedding. And while Dom Carolin would not venture, himself, into Asturias, he had sent one of his ministers, the *laranzu* Varzil of Neskaya, to solemnize the ceremony.

Bard cared little for this kind of merry-making, and the preparations reminded him, painfully, of the fact that he had hoped to hold this kind of wedding for himself some time this summer, before his defeat at the Lake of Silence. Nevertheless, the commander of the king's armies must be present; brooding, he got into his embroidered tunic and ceremonial cloak of blue, richly trimmed with copper threads and fine embroidery. Melisendra, too, looked noble and proud, her hair done high in looped braids, in a gown of green and a cape of marl-fur. Before they left the suite little Erlend came in, stopping wide-eyed to admire his parents.

"Oh, Mother, you are beautiful! And you too, Father, you are beautiful too!"

Bard chuckled and bent to lift up his son. Erlend said wistfully, "I wish I might go down and see the wedding and all the fine clothes and noblemen and ladies. . . ."

"There is no place for children—" Bard began, but Melisendra said, "Your nurse may take you into the gallery for a peep at them, Erlend, and if you are a good boy she will fetch you some cakes from the kitchen for your suppers." Bard put him down, and Melisendra knelt to kiss him.

Bard, jealous of the way the boy clung to his mother, said, "And you shall ride with me tomorrow." Erlend trotted away with his nurse, quite dazzled at the thought of the promised treats.

But Bard frowned as he went, at Melisendra's side, down the great stairway.

"Why in the name of all the gods did Father choose to hold Geremy's wedding in such state?"

"I think he has a plan, but I do not know what it is; I am sure it was not because of any good will he holds toward Geremy. Nor, I suppose, toward Ginevra; although Dom Regis Harryl is one of the oldest nobility of Asturias, and of the Hastur kin a few generations back."

Bard thought about this. Of course, Dom Rafael sought to hold the throne for Alaric, and must do it in part by keeping the goodwill of all the nobles who owed allegiance to the di Asturiens. A court wedding for the daughter of a valued supporter was a simple diplomatic move, well worth what it cost. Although personally Bard would have hesitated at showing such favor at one of his own allies marrying into the Hasturs when the Hasturs could, all too soon, be enemies.

"Do you really think we shall have to go to war with the Hasturs, Bard?"

Bard scowled, annoyed at Melisendra's habit of reading his mind, but said, "I see no way that it can be avoided."

Melisendra shivered a little. "Why, you are *pleased*. . . ."

"I am a soldier, Melisendra. War is my business, and the business of every loyal man of Asturias, so that we have to keep this realm by force of arms."

"I should think it would be easy to make peace with the Hasturs. They don't want war any more than we do."

Bard shrugged. "Well, let them surrender to us, then." He wished Melisendra would stop talking about things that did not really concern her.

"But it does concern me, Bard. I am a *leronis*, and no stranger to battle. And even if I were not, if I were such a woman as had nothing better to do than bide at home and keep my house, I should still have to deal with wounds and pillage and bearing of sons to ride into war . . . war is a concern of women, not only of men!"

Her face was flushed with indignation, but Bard only said, roughly, "Nonsense. And if you read my thoughts again, Melisendra, without leave, you will be sorry for it!"

She shrugged and said with composure, "I am sorry for *anything* I have to do with you, my lord. And if you wish me not to read your thoughts, you should refrain from sending them forth so that no one can help but hear them; I am seldom sure whether you have spoken aloud, or no."

Bard wondered about that. He had never thought he had any measurable *laran*. Why did Melisendra find him so easy to read?

The Great Hall was crowded with men and women. There was also the howling of two or three young infants; there had recently been a silly fad among noblewomen for suckling their babes themselves, instead of giving them properly to wet nurses, and Ginevra was recently a mother so that many other young matrons had seen fit to bring their unweaned babes into the hall. He hoped they would be carried out before the ceremonies began! He decided that when Carlina came to court he would insist that she should behave in a more dignified fashion; with all these squalling weanlings about, the place was like the pasture of mares in foal!

But Lady Jerana had evidently insisted that all the babies be taken away before the ceremony. The marriage bracelets were locked, with great solemnity, on the wrists of Geremy and Ginevra, as the Regent of Asturias said, "May you be forever one." Well, Geremy had a wife, and at least she was of proven fertility. He shrugged and went to congratulate his kinsman.

Ginevra and Melisendra were hugging one another and squealing inanities as young women always did at weddings. Bard bowed.

"I congratulate you, cousin," he said courteously. If Geremy were halfway intelligent, he thought, he would chalk their differences up to the fortunes of war, and have done with it. He bore Geremy no special ill will; he supposed that in Geremy's shoes he would have done much the same.

"I see your kinsmen have come far and wide to do honor to you, foster brother."

"Mostly, I think, to my lady," Geremy returned, and presented Ginevra to Bard. She was a small, swarthy woman, who looked almost as if she might have been born to the mountain forge-folk; even though Geremy did not stand straight, she came only up to his shoulder. She was flat-chested too, and had followed the stupid fashion of having her gown made with lacings so that she could nurse her infant in public; how undignified!

But he spoke politely, bowing.

"I hope your son is strong and hearty as a man-child should be."

She said a courteous word or two; and Geremy evidently shared Bard's feeling that it was prudent for them to be seen in civil chit-chat for a moment or two.

"Oh, yes, the women say he is a fine boy. I am no judge of such things. To me he looks like any other newborn babe, soggy at both ends, and howling early and late; but Ginevra thinks he is pretty, even after all the trouble he gave her."

"I was fortunate," Bard said, "for I made the acquaintance of my son only after he could walk and talk like a reasonable person, not an untrained puppy."

"I have seen young Erlend," Geremy said, "and he is handsome and clever. And his mother, I have heard, is a *leronis;* is the boy *laran*-gifted as well?"

"His mother tells me so."

"I should expect it, with the red hair of the Hastur kin," Geremy said. "Have you given thought to having the boy fostered at one of the Towers, Hali or Neskaya? I am sure they would be glad to have him. My kinsman Varzil of Neskaya is here, and he could arrange for it."

"I doubt it not. But it seems to me that Erlend is over young to be sent out of this realm in time of war, and I have no wish to see him held hostage."

Geremy looked shocked. "You misunderstand me, kinsman. The Towers are sworn to neutrality, which is how a Ridenow came to be Keeper at Hali. And after the burning of Neskaya, when the Tower was rebuilt, Varzil came there with a circle, and swore they would observe the Compact of the Hasturs, and fight no more wars with *laran* weapons."

"Except in the cause of the Hasturs, you mean," Bard said with a cynical grin. "Clever of Carolin, to insure their loyalty like that!"

"No, cousin, not even that. They are sworn not to fight even for the Hasturs, but to use their starstones only in the cause of peace."

"And Carolin lets their Tower stand unburned within his realm?"

"My father wishes it so," said Geremy. "This land is torn yearly with foolish and fratricidal wars, so that the peasants cannot even get in their crops. Clingfire is bad enough, but worse weapons are made now by sorcery. The Lady of Valeron used air-cars to spread bonewater dust north of Thendara, and I think perhaps no crops will ever grow there again, and any man who travels through that country dies, afterward, with blood turned to water and bones gone brittle . . . and worse things, such things as I would not speak of at a festival. And so we have all sworn that we will use no *laran* against any foe from these Towers, and all the lands near the Hastur realms have pledged themselves to observe the Compact."

"I know not of this Compact," Bard said. "What means it?"

"Why, where the Compact is in force no man may attack another with any weapon save one that brings the wielder within arm's reach of death. . . ."

"I had not heard of it," Bard said, "and I too would rather fight with honest sword and pike than with sorcery. I have no love for using *leroni* in battle, nor, I think, has any soldier. But I would not have *leroni* within my realm at all, unless they were sworn to fight with me, and protect my armies against the attack of wizardry. Tell me more."

"Why, I have not been within my father's realm since I was a boy, and I do not know much of it, except what my kinsman Varzil has told me."

"You own a Ridenow of Serrais as *kin?*"

"We are all Hastur kin," said Geremy, "and bear alike the blood of Hastur and Cassilda. Why should we be at strife?"

This sobered Bard and shocked him. If the Hastur and the Serrais were to make common cause, what would then become of the realm of Asturias? He wanted to rush off to his father with this new intelligence, but the minstrels had begun to play for dancing, and dancers were crowding onto the floor.

"Would you like to dance, Ginevra? You need not stay at my side because I am crippled; I am sure one of my kinsmen would lead you out."

She smiled, briefly pressing his hand. "At my wedding, I shall dance with no man, since my husband cannot join me. I will wait for a woman's ring dance and dance with my ladies."

"You have a loyal wife," Bard said, and Geremy shrugged.

"Oh, Ginevra has always known that I should never win acclaim in the field of war, nor on the dancing floor."

One of the Hastur kinsmen in his blue and silver came up to request a dance with the bride. Watching Ginevra's gracious refusal, Bard began to realize why his kinsman had chosen this scrawny, dark, plain little thing. She had the charm and graciousness of a queen; she would, in spite of her unremarkable features, grace any court.

"But you must not do that," protested the man. "Why, dancing with a bride is a powerful charm for any man who wishes to marry within the year! How can you have the heart to deprive us so, *domna?*"

Ginevra bantered gaily, "Why, I shall dance only with my unmarried ladies; that will help *them* to husbands, and since they must find some men to share the weddings, and so it will help the bachelors to find brides, too!" She signaled to the musicians, who began to play a ring dance. Taking Melisendra's hands, Ginevra drew her away on to the dancing floor, and many women and young girls, too young for dancing with strangers, or women whose husbands or brothers were committed elsewhere, came crowding out behind them. Bard watched Melisendra's green-clad form, weaving in and out of the patterns of the ring dance. Where, he wondered, was Melora now? Why did that memory haunt him so? The thought crossed his mind, and he knew it was insanity, that if he were tied to Melora like this, they would talk together, they could be friendly, close, in the way Geremy and Ginevra were. He remembered how Ginevra had pressed Geremy's hand against her cheek. No woman had ever behaved so with him, and yet he could imagine Melora doing such a thing.

Nonsense; he could not marry Melora, she was not well-born, and in any case she was committed to a Tower. That was not the way marriages were made. He had criticized Geremy in his mind for marrying Ginevra, who was, despite the old family and her gracious manners, considerably below him in rank. Only a fool would marry a woman who could not bring him some powerful alliance or rich dowry. He could not, for instance, resign himself to marrying Melisendra; she was the daughter of a humble *laranzu* . . . though what was it Geremy had said about Hastur kin and red hair? Melisendra could not be so low-born after all. . . .

"I had believed," said Geremy, "that we were soon to have

the honor of dancing at *your* wedding, Bard. Could you not persuade Carlina to leave the hospitality of the Sisterhood of Avarra?"

"I had no opportunity to speak with her. The shores of the Island of Silence are guarded with sorcery. It will take a regiment of *leroni* to break those spells! But mark my words, it shall be done!"

Geremy made a gesture which mimicked pious horror.

"And you do not fear the wrath of Avarra?"

"I do not fear any group of foolish women who pretend that their will is the will of some goddess or other!" Bard growled.

"But can it be that your bride prefers chastity and good works to the pleasures that await her when she is wedded to you? Why, how can she be so foolish!" Geremy's gray eyes flickered with malicious amusement, and Bard turned on his heel and walked away. He did not want to embarrass his father by quarreling at a great entertainment like this. Not even to himself did he admit that he had no wish to quarrel further with Geremy.

Later, while all the young people were dancing, he talked a little to his father about what he had done on the northern borders.

"It is not likely we shall be attacked from Serrais while we have Dom Eiric hostage," he said, "but seeing us beset by the Hasturs, they may come down on us too. I have heard of a truce between Aldaran and Scathfell; if they come at us together we would be hard put to it to hold them off, with so many of our armies holding off any threat from Serrais. And there are some who would be glad to ally with the Hasturs. If Varzil of Serrais has made an alliance with Hastur, I think we must try to win over the MacAran, at El Haleine, to guard our southern borders, as Marenji stands between us on the north."

"I do not think either the MacAran, or the people at Syrtis, would be willing to anger the Hasturs," Dom Rafael said. "They say of Lord Colryn of Syrtis that he can stand atop his keep and look out over all of his small country, and while the mouse in the walls may look from afar at a cat, he does well not to go squeaking about it; and Dom Colryn has no wish to be mouse to King Carolin's meowing! Carolin could gobble him up without blooding his whiskers!" He scowled. "And unless we return Dom Eiric to Serrais, all those who are allied with Serrais will come down on us before winter. Perhaps we must swear Dom Eiric to a truce and gain time. It is time we need!" He struck his knee with his open hand. "We may be forced to swear truce with the Hastur too!"

Bard said scornfully, "I will take the field against the Hasturs. I am not afraid of them! I held Scaravel with a handful of men, and I can do as much for Asturias!"

"But you are only one man," Dom Rafael said, "and can lead only one army. With Serrais to the east, and the Hasturs to the west, and perhaps all those across the Kadarin ready to come down on us from the north, Asturias cannot stand!"

"We have some protection in Marenji," Bard said, "for anyone who comes at us that way must fight, now, across their land; and I think perhaps we could raise mercenaries in the north, and in the Dry towns—they know my reputation and will fight under my command. And perhaps we can bind Dom Eiric to a truce; his sons are young and must keep from war for a time. If we bind him to truce for half a year—and a released hostage must expect that, at least—he cannot put an army against us in the field until spring thaw. And by spring perhaps we could have mercenaries, and even allies, enough that we could move against Serrais and reduce them to vassalage. Think of it, Father! To have all those lands to the east peaceful, without continual fighting! It seems we have been at war against Serrais since I was a babe in arms!"

"We have," Dom Rafael said, "and longer. But even if we conquer Serrais we will still have to face the Hasturs, for King Carolin claims that all these lands were once Hastur lands—"

"Geremy said something to that effect. I paid him little heed. But if Carolin is claiming that, we will simply have to teach him better."

"But I will have to take oaths and make truces," said Dom Rafael soberly. "It is still a matter of time; for time has run out for holding Geremy as hostage. Carolin has called our bluff and Varzil of Neskaya was sent to escort Geremy home. He brought your brother Alaric home to us."

"I shall not be sorry to see Geremy go forth from this court," said Bard, but he was aware that this represented a diplomatic loss for Dom Rafael. With a Hastur hostage, he had some leverage for diplomatic compromise with the Hasturs. Still, the return of Alaric was a gain to offset that loss.

"How is it with my brother?" Bard asked eagerly. "Is he

well and happy; has Carolin used him well? For when Queen Ariel fled there, I have no doubt he was in Carolin's hands and not hers."

"I have not seen him as yet," Dom Rafael said soberly. "He is still in the care of Varzil. The formal exchange will come later, for Varzil, I understand, is empowered with a message from Carolin, and has asked for formal audience in which to state his mission."

Bard raised his eyebrows. So the Keeper of Neskaya had sunk to the level of a Hastur flunkey? Perhaps it was worse than he thought, perhaps all the lands from the Kilghard Hills to Thendara lay under the Hasturs! Would the next few years see Asturias among them? *Over my dead body!*

And then he felt a small premonitory shudder. If it should indeed come about that way, well, it would certainly be over his dead body. But that was a soldier's fate in any case! And whatever happened, he was not likely to escape it.

If Alaric were returned, that would at least give Dom Rafael excuse to hold a coronation; for Rafael still insisted he was not king, but regent for Alaric. Bard wondered what was the difference between one child king and another. But in any case, Alaric was here, not, like Valentine, fled to the protection of another kingdom. Then Bard realized that he had been thinking of Alaric as he had been almost seven years ago; a child, pleased at the thought of his brother's outgrown toys. Now Alaric must be fourteen or fifteen, close to legal manhood. His own son Erlend was not so much younger than Alaric had been when they last parted!

Time. Time was the enemy of every man. He himself had lived longer than most men who earned their bread as mercenary soldiers. At least he should lose no time in marrying and getting himself some legitimate sons. He must make the kingdom secure for his brother, and then he must discover some way to attack the Island of Silence, even if it took a whole army of wizards, and regain Carlina.

While she lives, I shall marry no other woman! It occurred to him, for the first time, that perhaps he had made a great mistake. If Carlina truly did not want him, perhaps there were other women who would. Again he thought of Melora . . . but no. Carlina was King Ardrin's daughter, she was his handfasted wife, and if she did not want him, well, he would soon teach her where her duty lay. No woman ever wanted to refuse him a second time!

Rafael of Asturias released Dom Eiric of Serrais the next morning.

"But why *now*, Father?" Bard asked. "Certainly you could delay him a few tendays more!"

"A matter of protocol," Dom Rafael said grimly. "Varzil of Neskaya, who is a Ridenow, wishes to interview him, but he cannot in courtesy do so until he has transacted his main business here, the exchange of hostages; and he cannot speak with my prisoner without my leave. So I will take oath from Dom Eiric and set him on his way, *before* Varzil is free to speak with him. I want no more Ridenow lords making allies of Hastur!"

Bard nodded, absorbing this. Once Dom Eiric had taken his oath not to work against Rafael of Asturias for half a year, he could not lawfully ally with any enemy of Asturias, either. Bard had all manner of knowledge of military tactics and strategies, but diplomacy was still new to him. But with his father's knowledge of statecraft, and his own skill at war, perhaps they could hold all this countryside one day.

He found that he was curious to see this Varzil, who had allied with the Hasturs. Neskaya had been in Ridenow hands—though it lay far outside the Serrais lands proper—for more than two hundred years. In those days the Hasturs and the Ridenow had fought a prolonged war, and peace had been made in the reign of Allart of Thendara. Did the Hasturs still entertain dreams of reclaiming all the Serrais lands?

Bard was summoned to the council, as his father's high commander; and Melisendra, too, for the setting of truthspell. As Bard watched her come into the presence chamber, in her thin unadorned gray dress and cape, the mark of a *leronis* present upon official duties, he realized that Melisendra, as his father's chosen court sorceress, now had status and power in her own right, power that had nothing to do with her official position as the mother of the regent's grandson. The thought made him vaguely angry; there were *laranzu'in* enough, why did his father not, in decency, choose one of them? Was his father trying to put Melisendra in a position where she could flout her lawful lord and the father of her son?

He hoped Alaric had some skill at arms. As Ardrin's fosterling, he should have learned *something*. Bard himself was only one man; but if he had a knowledgeable military leader backing him up from the throne—and certainly a king should be able, like Ardrin, to lead his fighting men into battle—it augured well for Asturias in the years that would come.

Varzil of Neskaya was a small and slender man. In the gorgeous ceremonial dress he had worn at the wedding he had looked impressive, but now, in the green and gold of his House, he seemed small, narrow-shouldered; his features were lean, scholarly, and his hands, Bard noted with contempt, were as small and well-kept as a woman's, with no callouses from sword or dagger, and no hair worn away at his temples from the facepiece of the helmet. Not a man of war, then, but a sandal-wearer, a dandy. And this was Hastur's chosen embassy? Bard thought, with contempt, *I could break him with my two hands!*

Even Geremy, stooped though he was, dragging his lame leg, was taller than Varzil. Geremy wore his customary sober dress, unweaponed save for a small ornamental dagger, the hilt set with firestones. Bard watched, standing in the paxman's place, behind his father's throne, as the formalities and the setting of truthspell took place.

"Geremy Hastur," said Dom Rafael, "since my son is to be safely returned to me, I declare you free to return to your father's kingdom, or wherever you choose to go, with your wife, who is my subject, and your son, and your vassals, and all that is yours. Furthermore, as a mark of the esteem in which my lady wife holds your lady, if your wife's waiting-women wish to accompany the lady Ginevra to her new home, they are free to do so, if they have leave from their own fathers."

Geremy bowed and made a short and courteous speech thanking Dom Rafael and reassuring him of his gratitude for his kind hospitality. The irony was heavy-handed enough so that the truthspell light faltered on his face, but it was not worth taking issue. Courtesy, Bard thought wryly, was mostly lies anyhow.

"Geremy, you are free, if you will, to leave your son to be fostered in my house. His mother's father is my loyal man, and I give you my personal assurance that he will be brought up in all respects as my own son, and as a companion to my grandson."

Geremy thanked him courteously and declined that his son

was too young to be parted from his mother, being as yet un-weaned, and that Ginevra had a fancy to nurse him herself.

Varzil stepped forward. "And I have come," he said, "in the name of Carolin, High King at Thendara, guardian of Valentine di Asturien, rightful king of Asturias and overlord of all these lands, to return Alaric di Asturien, son of the Regent and Warden of Asturias, to his father. Alaric—?"

Bard drew in his breath, in audible shock. From behind Varzil, a slightly built boy limped forward; his uneven step and twisted shoulders were like a ghastly parody of Geremy's own; and Bard could not contain himself.

"Father!" he cried out, stepping forward, "Will you let them mock us thus in our own halls? Look what they have done to my brother, in revenge for Geremy's hurts! I will swear before truth-spell that Geremy was hurt by mischance, not by design, and Alaric has not deserved this of Carolin!" He drew his dagger. "Now, by all the gods, Hastur spawn, defend yourself, for *this* time your life is forefeit and it will be no accident! I'll make good what I should have done to you seven years ago—"

He grabbed Geremy's shoulder and spun him around.

"Draw your dagger, or I strike you down where you stand!"

"Cease! I command it!"

Varzil's voice was not loud, but it made Bard loosen his grip and fall back from Geremy, pale and sweating. He had not heard command voice for many years from the lips of a trained *laranzu*. Varzil's slender figure seemed to loom over him, menacing, as Bard's dagger fell from nerveless fingers.

"Bard di Asturien," Varzil said, "I do not war on children, nor does Carolin; your accusation is monstrous, and I stand here in the light of truthspell to give you the lie to your face. We told you nothing of Alaric's ills for fear you would come to exactly this conclusion. We had no hand in Alaric's laming. Five years ago he fell ill with the muscle fever which ravages so many children in the lake district, and although all of Ardrin's healers did their best for him, and sent him to Neskaya for healing as soon as he was able to travel—which is why he was not left here to rejoin you when Queen Ariel fled the country, since he was in my care at Neskaya—despite all our best efforts, his leg withered, and his back is weakened. He can walk now with only a leg brace to help him, and he has recovered his powers of speech; so you may ask Alaric himself if he has anything to complain of from our treatment."

Bard stared in dismay. So this poor cripple was the fine, strong, manly brother who would help him to lead his armies! He had the feeling that the gods were mocking him.

Dom Rafael held out his arms and Alaric limped forward, into his father's embrace.

"My dear son!" he said in dismay and consternation, and the boy looked from his father to Varzil in distress.

"Dear Father," he said. "Truly, what has happened is not the fault of my kinsman Ardrin, and certainly not of the Lord Varzil. When I fell ill, and for many years after, he, and his *leroni*, cared for me night and day. They have been so kind and good to me, neither you nor my mother could have done more."

"Gods above!" groaned Dom Rafael. "And Ardrin sent me no word? Nor Ariel, when she fled into exile?"

"I had been sent to Neskaya years before," Alaric retorted, "and since you never came to court, I did not think that you cared much what befell me! Certainly," he added, in a detached, ironical way which convinced Bard that, if his brother's body was crippled, there was certainly nothing wrong with his mind, "you were not so eager to have me back that you would contend very long with Carolin for me. I knew that you would hold your throne for me, at least until you saw me. After that, I was not sure whether you would care to ransom me at all."

Dom Rafael said loyally, "You are my own dear son, and I welcome you back to the throne I have claimed for you," but Bard heard the unspoken part of this, *if you can possibly hold it*, and was sure Alaric could hear it too.

Varzil's face was composed and compassionate; his eyes lingered on Alaric and Dom Rafael as if he had no thought except for the child and his stricken father. But Bard knew that Varzil, in spite of a very genuine concern for young Alaric, had nevertheless held him back to produce at the moment when it would cause the most confusion and consternation. He had intended to show them all, and as publicly as possible, that the young claimant to the throne of Asturias was no more than a pitiful little cripple!

Bard felt despair and rage—was *this* the strong young warrior who would ride to battle at his side? Yet his heart ached for the little brother he had loved. Whatever his father's disappointment and his own, Alaric must be feeling it more than either of them! It was inexcusable, to use the boy like this, to show forth the weakness of the Asturian throne! At this moment, had it not been for his knowledge of diplomatic immunity, he would willingly have strangled Varzil where he stood—yes, and Geremy too!

Yet—he thought, slowly coming to terms with this new knowledge—it could have been worse. Alaric was lamed, but otherwise he looked healthy and strong, and there was certainly nothing wrong with his mind! Geremy had a healthy son; there was no reason Alaric could not have a dozen. He would not, after all, be the first crippled king to hold a throne; and, after all, he had a loyal brother to command his armies.

I am not ambitious toward his throne, Bard thought. *I have no wit, nor yet skill, to govern; I would rather be the king's commander than the king!* He met Alaric's eyes and smiled.

Dom Rafael too had recovered his equilibrium. He rose from his presence seat and said, "In token that I reigned here only as regent, my son, I yield this place to you as rightful King of Asturias. My son and my lord, I beg you to take this place."

The boy's cheeks stained with color, but he had been well trained in protocol. When his father knelt at his feet, proffering his sword, he said, "I beg you to rise, Father, and take back your sword, as regent and warden of this realm, until I have reached years of manhood."

Dom Rafael rose, taking his place three steps behind the throne.

"My brother," Alaric said, looking at Bard, "I have been told that you are commander of the armies of Asturias."

Bard bent the knee before the boy and said, "I am here to serve you, my brother and my lord."

Alaric smiled, for the first time since he had stepped out from behind Varzil, and the smile was like a sun coming out and warming Bard's heart.

"I do not ask you for your sword, dear brother. I beg you to keep it in defense of this realm; may it be drawn only against my enemies. I name you first man in this realm after our father the Lord Regent, and I will think soon of some way to reward you."

Bard said briefly that his brother's favor was reward enough. He had hated this kind of ceremony, ever since he had been a boy in the king's house; he stepped back, grateful that at least he had not made a fool out of himself by tripping over something.

Alaric said, "And now, kinsman Varzil, I know you were entrusted with a diplomatic mission which, quite rightly, you did not confide to a child. Will you now reveal it to the throne of Asturias, and to my father and regent?"

Dom Rafael seconded the request. "I welcome Carolin's embassy," he said, "but would it be possible to hold it in a room more suited to this conference than this throne room where we must all stand about in ceremonial attitudes, waiting upon formalities?"

"I should be honored," Varzil said, "and I am willing to dispense with truthspell if you are; the matters to be discussed are not facts, but attitudes, claims, opinions and ethical considerations. Truthspell has no validity over honest differences of opinion where each side believes itself in the right."

Dom Rafael said ceremoniously, "This is true. By your leave, then, cousin, we will dismiss the *leronis* and her work, and meet again within the hour in my private drawing room, if that is not too informal for you, cousin. I offer more comfort, not any intended slight of the importance of your mission."

"I shall welcome informality and privacy," Varzil said. When the Hastur embassage had temporarily withdrawn, Dom Rafael and his sons delayed for a moment before leaving the presence chamber.

"Alaric, my son, you need not sit through the conference if it would weary you!"

"Father, by your leave, I will stay," Alaric said. "You are my regent and guardian, and I will defer to your judgment till I am declared a man, and after, too, no doubt, for many years. But I am old enough to understand these matters, and if I am to govern one day, I had better know what statecraft you intend."

Bard and Dom Rafael exchanged glances of approval.

"Stay by all means, your highness." Dom Rafael used the very formal phrase *va' Altezu*, used only to a superior and one very near the throne. Bard knew that his father was acknowledging the boy as an adult, though he had not—quite—arrived at the age for legal manhood. Alaric might look like a sick child, but there was little question in either mind that he had the maturity to take his place as a man.

In Dom Rafael's private study they gathered again, around

a table, and Dom Rafael sent for a servant to pour wine for them all. When the servant had withdrawn again Varzil said, "By your leave, Dom Rafael, and you, Highness," he added formally to Alaric, his tone quite in contrast to the affectionate informality he had shown Alaric before, "I am entrusted by Carolin of Thendara with a mission. I had intended to bring a Voice, that you might hear Carolin's very words. But, by your leave, I will dispense with this. I am Carolin's ally and his friend; I am Keeper of Neskaya Tower. And I have signed with him, for Neskaya, the Compact we now ask you to keep. As you know, Neskaya was destroyed by fire-bombing, a generation ago; and when Carolin Hastur had it rebuilt, we agreed upon the Compact. He did not require it of me as a sovereign lord, but requested it of me as a man of reason, and I was glad to do so."

"What is this Compact of which you speak?" asked Dom Rafael.

Varzil did not answer directly. Instead he said, "The Hundred Kingdoms are torn apart, every year, by foolish and fratricidal wars; your strife with Queen Ariel for the throne of Asturias is only one. Carolin of Thendara is willing to recognize the house of Rafael di Asturien as rightful warden of this realm, and Queen Ariel stands ready to withdraw, for herself and her son, any claim to this throne, if you sign the Compact."

"I grant the generosity of the concession," Dom Rafael said, "but I have no wish for Durraman's bargain, when he bought the donkey. I must know the precise nature of this Compact, cousin, before I agree to it."

"The Compact states that we will use no weapons of sorcery in war," Varzil said. "Perhaps war is inevitable among men; I confess that I do not know. Carolin and I are working for a day when all these lands will be united in peace. Meanwhile, we ask you to unite with us in a sacred pledge that fighting shall be done honorably by soldiers who go into battle and risk their own lives, not by coward's weapons to fling sorcery and chaos upon women and children, to burn forests and ravage towns and farmlands. We ask that you outlaw, within your realm, all weapons which go beyond the arm's reach of the man who wields them, so that fighting may be honorable and equal, and not endanger the innocent with evil weapons which strike from afar."

Dom Rafael said, "You cannot possibly be serious!" He

stared at Varzil in disbelief. "What insanity is this? Are we to march to war with swordsmen alone, while our enemies fall upon us with arrows and clingfire, bombs and sorcery? Dom Varzil, I am reluctant to think you a madman, but do you truly think war is a game of *castles,* played by women and children with dice for cakes or pennies? Do you truly think that any sane man would listen for a moment to such an idea?"

Varzil's calm, handsome face was wholly serious. "I give you my word, in all honesty. I mean what I say, and there are many small kingdoms that have already signed the Compact with King Carolin and the Hasturs. Coward's weapons, and *laran* warfare, are to be completely outlawed. We cannot prevent war, not in the present state of our world. But we can keep it within bounds, keep war from destroying croplands and forests, prevent such weapons as the evil that ravaged Hali nine years ago, where children swelled and sickened of the disease that turns their blood to water, because they had played in forests where the leaves had been destroyed with bonewater dust. . . . The lands there are still unlivable, Dom Rafael, and may be so in the times of young Alaric's grandchildren! War *is* a contest, Dom Rafael. It could, indeed, be settled by a throw of the dice, or a game of castles. The rules of warfare are not decreed by the gods, that we must go on to greater and greater weapons which will destroy all of us one day, victor and vanquished alike. Before that day comes, why not limit it to such weapons as can be used with honor for all?"

"As to that," said Dom Rafael, "my people would never agree. I am no tyrant, to take away their weapons, and leave them defenseless against those unscrupulous people who would always refuse to give up *their* weapons. Perhaps, when I am sure that all our enemies have already done this . . . but I do not think so."

"Bard di Asturien," Varzil said, surprisingly turning to him, "you are a soldier; most soldiers are men of reason. You are commander of your father's armies. Would you not willingly see these atrocious weapons outlawed? Have you not seen a village burned with clingfire, or little children dying of the bonewater sickness?"

Bard felt an inward wrench, remembering just such a village near Scaravel; the endless screaming and crying of children burned by clingfire. It seemed to go on for days, until one by one they had died, all of them, and then the silence seemed even more terrible, as if he could still hear their screams somewhere in his mind. . . . He would not, himself, use clingfire; but why was Varzil asking *him?* He was only a soldier, his father's loyal man who must follow orders.

He said, "Dom Varzil, I would gladly fight with swords and shields alone, if others could be brought to do likewise. But I am a soldier, and my business is to win battles. I cannot win battles when I lead men armed with swords against an army who bear clingfire, or set demons of sorcery and fear against my men, to raise wind and water and storms and earthquakes against me."

"It would not be asked of you," Varzil said. "But would you agree that if *laran* is not used against you, you will not be the first to use it, and especially not to use it against noncombatants?"

Bard began to say that it sounded reasonable, but Dom Rafael broke in angrily, "No! War is not a game!"

Varzil said in contempt, "If it is not a game, what is it? Surely it is for those who make war to set the rules as they wish!"

Dom Rafael said with a scornful twist of his mouth, "Why, then, why not carry your policy all the way? Suggest that in future all our wars shall be settled by a game of football—or even leapfrog? Send our old gaffers to settle the war by a game of king's-man on a squared board, or our little girls for a game of jump rope, to settle our disputes?"

Varzil said, "The subject of most wars is a matter which would be better settled by reasonable debate among reasonable men. When reason cannot bring about a settlement, it could be as well settled by a game of catch-ball among the children, as by these endless campaigns which prove only that the gods seem to love those who have the better trained soldiers!" He sounded immeasurably bitter.

"You speak like a coward," Dom Rafael said. "War may be disturbing to the squeamish, but you can't argue with facts, and since men aren't reasonable—and why should they settle for reason instead of what they want?—all arguments are, in the long run, going to be settled in favor of the one who can enforce settlement with the strongest hand. You cannot change the nature of mankind, and that's simply the knowledge we have from all the years of man. If a man isn't satisfied by the answer he gets, no matter how reasonable and right it may seem to others, he is going to go out and fight for what he wants. Otherwise we would all be born without hands or arms or the brains to use weapons. None but a coward would say otherwise; though I would expect it of a sandal-wearer, a *laranzu*."

Varzil said, "Hard words break no bones, sir. I am not so much afraid of being called coward that I would fight a war to avoid it, like schoolboys blacking each other's eyes over the cry of *whoreson* or *sixfathered!* Are you telling me that if soldiers come against you armed only with swords, you will burn them with clingfire?"

"Yes, of course, if I have the clingfire. I do not make the evil stuff, but if it is used against me, I must have it, and I must use it before it can be used against me. Do you really think anyone will keep this Compact, unless he is assured of victory already?"

"And you will fight this way, even when you know it means your own lands will be poisoned with bonewater dust, or the new poison which brings out black sores on every man, woman and child who breathes it, so that they now call it the masking sickness? I had thought you a merciful and reasonable man!"

"Why, so I am," Dom Rafael said, "but not so reasonable that I will lay down my arms and resign myself to surrendering my country, and my people, to live in slavery to some other country! In my mind, anything which gives a quick and decisive victory is a merciful and reasonable weapon. A war fought with swords, like a tournament, may drag on for years—we have been fighting the Serrais for most of my lifetime—while sensible men will think twice before carrying on a war against such weapons as I can bring against them. No, Dom Varzil, your words sound reasonable on the surface, but under them lurks insanity; men would enjoy your kind of war too much, and prolong it like a game, knowing they could play at warfare without being seriously hurt. You may go back to Carolin and tell him that I despise his Compact and I will never honor it. If he comes against me, he will find me prepared with every weapon my *leroni* can devise, and on his own head be it if he chooses to arm his men with swords and shields alone; for all I care he may arm them with tennis balls, and make my work easier; or tell them to surrender at once. Is this nonsense of Compact all you were sent to tell me, Dom Varzil?"

"No," said Varzil.

"What more is there? I do not want war with the Hasturs. I would prefer a truce."

"And so would I," Varzil said, "and so would King Carolin. I was sent and empowered to take your oath to abstain from war against us. You are a reasonable man, you say; why, then, should this land be torn apart with fighting?"

"I have no wish to fight," said Dom Rafael, "but I will not surrender to the Hasturs where di Asturiens have reigned since time out of mind."

"That is not true," said Varzil. "Written records in Nevarsin and Hali—which are perhaps more reliable than the patriotic legends and folk tales you use to rally your men—would reassure you that less than two hundred years ago this land was all ruled by Hasturs; but after an invasion of catmen, Lord Hastur gave the di Asturiens the task of guarding it, no more. And now all these lands have split up into little kingdoms, each one claiming an immemorial right to be independent and sovereign over its own people. This is chaos. Why not have peace again?"

"Peace? Tyranny, you mean," Dom Rafael said. "Why should the free people of Asturias bow their heads to the Hasturs?"

"Why, then, should they bow it to the di Asturiens, for that matter? Peace is bought at the cost of giving up some local autonomy. Suppose each of your farmsteaders insisted that he was a free man, and had a right to absolute individual self-rule, refusing any other man the right to cross his borders without paying tribute, and owing loyalty to nothing but his own whim?"

"That," said Dom Rafael, "would be foolish."

"Then why is it not foolish to say that El Haleine and Asturias and Marenji are all kingdoms, each with separate king and government and each cut off from others? Why not make peace under the sons of Hastur, and have freedom to move about, and trade, without armed men everywhere? You will be free in your own realm, you simply pledge not to meddle with any other free and independent realm, but to cooperate with your fellow lords as friends and equals—"

Rafael di Aa\sturien shook his head. "My ancestors won

this land. Ardrin's son Valentine forfeited his right to it when he fled to King Carolin with his traitor mother. But I shall keep it for my sons, and if Hasturs want it, they will have to come and take it if they can." He spoke bravely, but Bard knew that his father was remembering their conversation the night of Geremy's wedding.

Serrais to the east. Aldaran and Scathfell to the north. Hasturs to the west and all their allies, and no doubt, someday people from the Plains of Valeron to the south.

"Then," said Varzil, "you will not swear allegiance to Hastur, even though all he asks is a pledge that you will not take up arms against Hali or Carcosa or Castle Hastur or Neskaya which is under his protection?"

"The throne of Asturias," Rafael said, "is not subject to Hastur. And that's my last word on the subject. I have no intention of attacking Hasturs, but they cannot seek to rule here."

"Alaric," Varzil said, "you are lord of Asturias. You are not of an age to make compacts, but I ask you nevertheless, out of kindness to kin, to ask your father to see reason in this matter."

"My son is not your prisoner now, Dom Varzil," Rafael said, his chin jutting hard. "I do not know how much treason you may have taught him against his own people, but now—"

"Father, that is unjust," Alaric protested. "I ask you not to quarrel with my kinsman Varzil!"

"For your sake, my son, I hold my peace. Yet I beg of you, Dom Varzil, set aside this foolish talk of surrendering the throne of Asturias to the Hasturs!"

Varzil said, "Even now you are contemplating war against peaceful neighbors—not invaders! I know what you have done in Marenji. I am informed that in the spring you intend war against Serrais; and you intend to fortify the lands along the Kadarin—"

"And what is that to you?" Bard asked with cold hostility. "The lands along the Kadarin are not Hastur lands!"

"Neither are they the lands belonging to Asturias," said Varzil, "and Carolin is sworn to make them safe against attack from land-greedy little kingdoms! Do what you will within your own realm; but I warn you, unless you are prepared to fight against all of those who give allegiance to Hastur and to the Compact, do not move outside them!"

"Are you threatening me?"

"I am," Varzil said, "though I would rather not. I ask as

envoy of Hastur, that you and your two sons take oath not to move against the Compact lands who have sworn to one another as equals, or we will have an army in the field within forty days, and we will take the Kingdom of Asturias and put it into the wardenship of someone who will hold it in peace among the *com'ii* under Hastur."

Bard heard this with a dreadful sinking. They were not, in fact, prepared to make war against the Hasturs; not with the men rising past the Kadarin, not with Serrais on the east! And if the Hasturs came against them *now,* Asturias could not stand.

Dom Rafael clenched his fists with rage.

"What oath do you require of us?"

"I ask you to swear," Varzil said, "not to me, but to Geremy Hastur for his kinsman Carolin, an oath of kinsmen, not to be broken without warning of half a year on either side; which pledges you not to move against any land under Hastur protection; and in return you will be a part of this peace which reigns under the Alliance." He used the word *comyn* in a new way. "Will you swear?"

There was a long silence; but the di Asturiens were at the disadvantage and knew it. They had no choice but to swear. They were grateful when Alaric spoke, so that neither of them must lose face.

"Dom Varzil, I will swear the oath of kinsmen, although no oath to your Alliance. Will this suffice? I vow that I will not go to war against Carolin of Thendara unless half a year's warning is given. But," he added, and Bard saw the childish jaw clench, "this oath will endure only while my kinsman Carolin of Thendara leaves me in possession of the throne of Asturias; and on the day when he moves against the throne, on that same day I withdraw my oath and consider him my enemy!"

Geremy said, "I accept your oath, cousin. I swear to see it honored by Carolin. But how will you hold your father and your brother to this oath? For you are not yet of legal age, and they are the powers which hold your throne."

Alaric said, "By the gods and by the honor of my family; Bard, my brother, will you abide my oath?"

Bard said, "In the form the oath was given, my brother, I will." He gripped his sword. "Zandru seize this sword and this heart if I prove false to your honor."

"And I," said Dom Rafael, tight-lipped, closing his fingers

on his dagger, "by the honor of Asturien, which no man can gainsay."

No, Bard thought, as Geremy and Varzil, with endless formalities, took their leave, they had no choice, not with a crippled child on the throne, instead of the strong young warrior they had foreseen. They needed time, and this oath was only a way to give them time. His father maintained the façade of calm until the Hastur embassage had ridden away and Alaric, dreadfully pale from the strain of long ceremonial, was taken away to his rooms, then Dom Rafael broke down.

"My son! He is my son, I love him, I honor him, but in hell's name, Bard, is he fit to reign in times like these? Would to all the gods that *your* mother had been my lawful wife!"

"Father," Bard entreated, "it is only his legs that are crippled; his mind and wit are sound. I am a soldier, not a statesman; Alaric will make a better king than I!"

"But they look up to you, they call you Wolf and Commander, will they ever look up to my poor little lame lad that way?"

"If I stand behind his throne," Bard said, "they will."

"Alaric is blessed, then, in his brother! True is the old saying, *bare is back without brother. . . .* But you are only one man, and you are sworn to Hastur, which cripples you. If we had time, or if Alaric had been strong and fit—"

"If Queen Lorimel had worn trousers instead of skirts, she'd have been king and Thendara would never have fallen," said Bard, curtly. "There is no point in talking about *if,* and *would to all the gods,* and such rubbish. We must cut our coat as we find the cloth laid! The gods know I love my brother, and I could have bawled like Geremy's baby son to see him stand before us so bent and twisted, but what has come, has come; the world will go as it will. I am only one brother."

"It is the good fortune of the Hasturs that you were not born twins," said Dom Rafael with a despairing laugh, "for with two like you, dear son, I could conquer all the Hundred Kingdoms."

And then he stopped. His laugh broke off in mid-gasp, and he stared at Bard with such intensity that Bard wondered if the shock of Alaric's illness had turned the old man's brain.

"Two of you," he said, "with two such as you, Wolf, I could conquer all this land from Dalereuth to the Hellers. Bard, suppose that there were two of you," he said in a whisper, "that I had another son, just like you, with your skill at warfare and your genius for strategy and your fierce loyalty—two of you! And I know how to find another. Not another *just like you*—another *you!*"

CHAPTER FIVE

Bard stared at his father in dismay. *The gods grant,* he thought, *that Alaric is mature enough to rule, for our father has suddenly lost his wits!*

But Dom Rafael did not look mad, and his voice and manner were so matter-of-fact that another, more rational explanation occurred to Bard.

"You had not confided in me, sir; but do you mean that you have another bastard son, enough like to impersonate me when it should be necessary?"

Dom Rafael shook his head. "No. And I am aware that what I have just said sounds like a madman's raving, dear son, so you need not bother to humor me; I shall not begin to rave like a breeding woman in the Ghost Wind, nor chase butterflies in the snow. But what I must now suggest to you is very strange, and—" he glanced around the empty throne room—"in any case we cannot talk here."

In his father's private apartments, Bard waited while his father sent the servants away, poured them both some wine.

"Not too much," he said dryly. "I do not want you to think me drunk, as you thought I was mad. I said, Bard, that with two like you, two generals with your sense of war and strategy—and this must have been born with you, since those who fostered you show no sign of it, and it is certainly not due to my teaching—with two of you, Bard, I could conquer all this realm. If the Hundred Kingdoms are to be united into a single realm—and I admit it is a sound idea, for why should all these lands be torn with war spring and fall—why should the Hasturs be overlords? There were men bearing the di Asturien

name in these hills long before the Lord of Carthon gave his
daughter to the Hastur kin. There is *laran* in our line, too, but
it is the *laran* of humankind, of true men, not of the *chieri*-
folk; the Hasturs are *chieri,* or of *chieri*-kind, as you may see
if you care to count their fingers, and too many of them are still
born *emmasca*, neither man nor woman; Felix of Thendara was
born so, a few hundred years ago, and so *that* dynasty came to
an end."

"There are no people in these hills who have not some
chieri blood, father."

"But only the Hastur kin sought to preserve that blood in
their line with their breeding program," Dom Rafael said, "and
so many of the old families—Hastur, Aillard, Ardais, even the
Aldarans and the Serrais, bear in their blood and heritage so
many strange things that true men are wary of them! A child
may be born who can kill with a thought, or see into the future
as if time ran both ways, or cause fire to strike or the rivers to
rise. . . . There are two kinds of *laran;* the kind which all men
have and may use, aided with a starstone, and the evil kind
borne by the Hastur kin. Our line is not altogether free of it,
and when you got that redheaded son upon your mother's *leronis,* you brought the Hastur kin *laran* back into our folk. But
what's done is done, and Erlend may be useful to us one day.
Have you gotten the girl with child again yet? Why not?" But
he did not wait for Bard's answer.

"Still, I am sure you can see why I have no will to be ruled
by the Hasturs; they are riddled through and through with the
chieri blood, and their Gifts are not diluted by the normal humankind, but fixed into their line by that breeding program. I
feel that humankind should rule, not wizard-folk!"

"But," said Bard, "why tell me all this now? Or are you saying that when Erlend is grown he will be near enough to their
kin that he can claim their line?" He spoke sarcastically, and
his father did not bother to reply.

"What you do not know," he said, "is that I studied *laran*
craft when I was a young boy. I was not, as you know, reared
to king-craft, for Ardrin was the eldest, but I did not have the
stronghold of di Asturien either, for there were three brothers
between us, and I had leisure for study and learning. I was a
laranzu, and dwelt for a time in Dalereuth Tower, and learned
something of their craft."

Bard had known that his father bore a starstone, but that

was in no way uncommon, and not everyone who bore a starstone knew *laran* lore. He had not known that he had dwelt
within a Tower.

"Now there is a law in the use of the starstone," Dom Rafael
said. "I do not know who formulated it, or why it should be so,
but it is so; that everything which exists, except for a starstone,
exists in one, and only one, *exact* duplicate. Nothing is unique,
except for a starstone, which has no duplicate. However,
everything else—*everything,* every rabbithorn in the woods,
every tree and flower, every rock in the fields—has its precise
duplicate, and also every human being has *one* exact double
somewhere, more like him than his own twin. And that tells me
that somewhere, Bard, you have an exact double. He may
dwell in the Dry towns, or in the unknown lands beyond the
Wall Around the World, he may be the son of a peasant, or live
beyond the uncrossable gulf of the Sea of Dalereuth which
leads into the Unknown Sea. And he would be more like you
than your own twin, even though he dwelt far beyond the
Hundred Kingdoms. I hope it is not so, I hope he dwells in the
Kilghard Hills; otherwise it would be hard to teach him our
language and the manners of our people. But whatever he may
be, he will have *laran,* even if he has never been taught to use
it; and he will have your military genius, once again, though he
may not know yet how to use it; and he will look so much like
you that your own mother, if she were still alive, would not be
able to tell you apart by looks alone. Do you see now, dear son,
why this would be good to have?"

Bard frowned. "I am beginning to see—"

"And another thing. Your double would *not* be sworn to
Hastur, nor bound to him by any oath. Understand me?"

Bard saw. He saw indeed. "But where do we find this duplicate of myself?"

"I told you that I had studied *laran*-craft," Dom Rafael said,
"and I know the whereabouts of a screen, a set of relay starstones constructed to bring these duplicates together. When I
was a youth, we could, though it was difficult, bring men and
women, other *leroni,* from one set of starstones to another. If
we have one set of duplicates on the screen, we can bring your
duplicate from wherever he may be living."

"But," Bard asked, "when we have him, how do we know
he will be willing to help us?"

"He cannot help being what he is," said Dom Rafael. "If he

were already a great general, we would know about him. He may indeed be one of my own bastard sons, or of Ardrin's, living in poverty without knowledge of war. But once we give him the chance of power and greatness—not to mention a chance to exercise the military genius which, if he is your duplicate, he will possess, if only as potential—then he will be grateful to us and willing to serve as our ally. Because, Bard, if he is your double—then he will be ambitious too!"

Three days later, Alaric-Rafael, heir to Asturias, was solemnly crowned in the regency of his father. Bard repeated in public the oath he had sworn to his brother, and Alaric presented him with a beautifully worked heirloom sword—Bard knew it was one his father had kept for many years, hoping that his one legitimate son would bear it into battle one day. But it was abundantly clear that King Alaric, whatever kind of ruler he might be, would not be a great warrior; so Bard accepted the sword from his brother's hands, and with it the command of all the armies of Asturias and all her subject kingdoms.

At the moment, I am general of Asturias and Marenji, and no more. But that it only a beginning.

A day will come when I will be general of all the Hundred Kingdoms, and they will all know and fear the Wolf of Asturias!

And as general of Marenji, he thought, he was legally entitled to go into that country and deal with those damned women on the Island of Silence!

I could declare them a treasonable assembly, and give them notice to quit the island! He was sure the people of Marenji would consider this a blasphemy, at present. But he asked Alaric to issue a proclamation that the people of Marenji were believed to be hiding the handfasted wife of Bard di Asturien; and that any person concealing the whereabouts of Carlina di Asturien would be considered a traitor and subjected to the extreme penalties of the law.

Alaric issued the proclamation, but in private he expressed dismay to Bard.

"Why do you want a woman who doesn't want you? I think you ought to marry Melisendra. She's very nice, and she's the mother of your son, and Erlend ought to be legitimate, he's a fine boy, and *laran*-gifted. Marry her, and I'll give you a fine wedding."

Bard said firmly that his brother and his lord ought not to talk about things he would not understand until he was older.

"Well, if I were ten years older, I'd marry Melisendra myself, so there," Alaric said. "I like her. She's good to me, she never makes me feel like a cripple."

"She had better not," Bard growled. "If she dared to be rude to you, I'd break her neck, and she knows it!"

"Well, I *am* a cripple, and I must learn to live with it," said Alaric, "and Lady Hastur, the *leronis* who cared for me at Neskaya, who helped me to talk again, taught me that it does not matter if my body is lamed. And Geremy—he is crippled, and yet he is a fine man, strong and honorable—it will be very hard for me to learn to think of the Hasturs as enemies," he added with a sigh. "I find it hard to understand politics, Bard. I wish there could be peace among all people, and then we could be friends with the Lord Varzil, who has been like a foster father to me. But I am used to being treated like a cripple, because I *am*, and I must have help to dress myself, and walk—but someone like Melisendra, she helps me not to mind so much, because she helps me to feel, even when she is helping to tie me into my leg brace, that I am no worse off than anyone else."

"You are the king," Bard said, but Alaric sighed, a resigned sigh.

"You don't know what I mean *at all*, do you, Bard? You're so strong, and you've never been really sick, or frightened, so how could you know? Do you know what it's like to be really *scared*, Bard? When I first had the fever, and I couldn't even *breathe* . . . Geremy, and three of Ardrin's healer-women, sat up with me all night with their starstones, for seven nights, just helping me to breathe when I couldn't."

Bard thought against his will of the terror that had gripped him on the shores of the Lake of Silence when the eerie faces in the fog had drifted around him, turning his bowels to water . . . but even to his brother he would not confess that. "I was afraid when I rode first into battle," he said. That he did not mind saying.

Alaric sighed enviously. "You were no older than I am now, and you were made King Ardrin's banner bearer! But it's different, Bard; you had a sword, you could *do* something against your fear, and I could—could only lie there and wonder if I was going to die, and know I had no way to help it, one way or the other, I was wholly helpless. And after that you—you always know that it can happen again, that you can die, or be destroyed. No matter how brave I am, I know, now, that there will always be something I can't fight," Alaric said. "And with some people, I feel like that all the time, that poor, sick, paralyzed coward. And some, like Varzil, and Melisendra, remind me that I don't have to be that way, that life is really not so terrible—do you know what I mean, Bard? Even a little?"

Bard looked at the boy and sighed, knowing that his brother was pleading for understanding, and not knowing how to give it to him. He had seen soldiers like this, wounded almost to death, and when they lived, after all, something had happened within them that he did not understand. That had happened to Alaric, but it had happened to him before he was old enough to face it.

"I think you are alone too much," he said, "and it makes you fanciful. But I am glad Melisendra is kind to you."

Alaric sighed and held out his hand, small and white, to Bard, who engulfed it in his huge browned one. Bard, he thought, didn't understand him at all, but he loved him, and that was just as good.

"I hope you get your wife back, Bard. It's very wicked of people to keep her from you."

Bard said, "Alaric, Father and I must be away from court for a few days. Father and I and some of his *leroni*. Dom Jerral will be here to advise you, if you need him."

"Where are you going?"

"Father knows of someone who would be a great help in commanding the armies, and we are going to find him."

"Why not simply order him to come to court? The regent can command anyone to come."

"We do not know where he lives," Bard said. "We must find him by *laran*." That, he thought, was quite explanation enough.

"Well, if you must go, you must. But please, can Melisendra stay with me?" he asked, and Bard, though he knew Melisendra was one of the most skilled *leroni*, decided not to refuse his brother.

"If you want Melisendra," he said, "she shall certainly stay with you."

* * *

He had braced himself for an argument with his father, but to his surprise, Dom Rafael nodded.

"I had not intended to bring Melisendra in any case; she is the mother of your son."

Bard wondered what difference that made, but he did not bother to ask. It was enough for him that his brother wanted Melisendra's company.

They left the castle that night and rode toward Bard's old home. Three *leroni,* two woman and a man, had accompanied them, and Dom Rafael led them to a room Bard had never seen before, in an old tower room at the end of a broken staircase.

"I have not used any of these things in decades," be said, "but *laran*-craft, once learned, is not forgotten." He turned to the wizards and asked, "Do you know what this is?"

The man looked at the apparatus, and then at his two comrades, and Dom Rafael, in dismay. "I know, my lord. But I thought the use of such things was outlawed outside the safety of a Tower."

"In Asturias, there is no law but mine! Can you use it?"

The *laranzu* glanced again, uneasily, at the women. He said, "A duplicate under Cherillys' Law? I suppose so. But of what or whom?"

"Of my son here; the commander of King Alaric's armies."

One of the women looked at Bard and he caught the ironic flicker of her thought. *Another of the Kilghard Wolf? I should think one of him to be more than abundance!* He supposed she was a friend of Melisendra's. But they shrugged, quickly shielded again, and said, "Yes, my lord, if that is your wish."

He could sense their surprise, distaste, wonder; but they made no audible protest, making their preparations, setting seals on the room so that no alien presences could enter and no other *leroni* spy on them from elsewhere.

When all was prepared, Dom Rafael signaled to Bard to take his place before the screen, to remain silent and motionless. He obeyed, kneeling silently. He was so placed that he could not see his father, nor any of the three telepaths, but he sensed them near him. Bard did not think he had much *laran,* and what he did have had never been properly trained. He had always rather despised the art of sorcery, thinking it a skill or craft for women; he felt a little frightened as the almost tangible web of their thoughts tightened around him. He sensed that they were extending their thoughts *into* him, deep into brain and body, seeking out the very pattern of his being; he thought, fancifully, that they were seeking out his very soul, tying it up tight and imprisoning it in that glassy screen there.

He could not move a finger or a foot. He felt a moment of paralyzed panic . . . no. This was a perfectly ordinary piece of *laran* sorcery, with nothing to fear; his father would not let anything harm him.

He remained motionless, looking at his reflection in the glassy surface. Somehow he knew it was not only the reflected shadow on glass but *himself* there in that multilayered screen, reinforced at all levels with starstone crystals which resonated to the starstones of the *leroni* around him. He felt the combined web of their layered thoughts swing out over vast gulfs of empty space, extending, searching, searching to find something to fit that pattern, fit it *exactly* . . . something came near, close to touching . . . near to captive . . . no. It was not a duplicate, a resemblance, touching perhaps at ninety out of a hundred, but not the exact duplicate which alone could be captured within the screen. He felt the *other* slide away, vanish, as the search swung out again.

(Far away in the Kilghard hills, a man named Gwynn, an outlaw and fatherless—although his mother had told him he had been fathered in the sack of Scathfell by Ansel, son of Ardrin the first of Asturias, thirty years ago—woke from an evil dream in which faces had swung around him, circling, swooping like hawks on their prey, and one of the faces was like his own as twin to twin. . . .)

Again the web swung out, this time over greater gulfs, starless night, a tremendous void beyond space and time, with swirling, nightmarish vortexes of terrible nothingness. Again a shadow formed behind Bard on the screen, shimmered, wavered, twitched, struggled as a sleeper struggles to wake from nightmare; somewhere a spark flared in Bard's brain; myself, or the *other?* He did not know, could not guess. It struggled for freedom but they held it, imprisoned in their web, moving from point to point of the pattern encased in the screen . . . searching to see that every atom, every trifle was congruent, identical. . . .

Now!

Bard saw in his mind before his eyes saw the flare of lightnings in the room, a searing shock as the *other* was torn loose from the shadow in his mind, the pattern doubled and breaking, splitting apart . . . terror flamed in him; was it his own fear, or the terror of the *other*, unimaginably hurled across that great gulf of space. . . . He caught a glimpse of a great yellow sun, hurling worlds, stars flaming across the dark void, galaxies spinning and drifting in shock. . . . Lightning crashed through his brain and he lost consciousness.

He stirred, conscious now of savage headaches, pain, confusion. Dom Rafael was lifting him, feeling his pulse. Then he let him go and went past, and Bard, sick and stunned with the lightning, followed with his eyes; and the *leroni,* behind him, watching, looked dazed too. He caught a wisp of thought from one of them, *I don't believe it. I did it, I was part of it but still I don't believe it. . . .*

Lying on the floor at the opposite pole of the great screen lay the naked body of a man. And Bard, though he had been prepared intellectually for this, felt a surge of gut-wrenching terror.

For the man lying on the floor was himself.

Not someone very much like him. Not an accidental or close family resemblance. *Himself.*

Broad-shouldered, and halfway between them, the blackish blotch of a birthmark which he had seen only in a mirror. The muscles bunching in his sword arm, the same dark-reddish patch of hair at the loins, the same crooked toe on the left foot.

Then he began to see differences. The hair was cut a little shorter, though at the crown of his head there was the same unruly whorl. There was no scar across the knee; the double had not been at the battle of Raven's Glen and did not have the sword-slash he had taken there. The other did not have the thick callous at the inside of the elbow where the shield strap rested. And these little differences somehow made it worse. The man was not simply a magical duplicate created somehow by the *laran* of the screen; be was a real human being, from *somewhere else,* who was, none the less, precisely and exactly Bard di Asturien.

He didn't like it. Still less did he like the confusion and fear which the *other* was feeling. Bard, without much *laran,* could still somehow *feel* all that emotion.

He couldn't stop himself. He got up and went across the room to the naked man lying there. He knelt beside him and put an arm under his head.

"How are you feeling?"

Only after he had spoken did be stop to wonder if the alien *other* could understand his language. That would be luck entirely too good, though he supposed that perhaps his kin somewhere in the Kilghard Hills had probably fathered this duplicate. Could any man be so like without being kin somehow? The strange man's skin looked darker, as if it had been burned brown by a fiercer sun. . . . No, that was folly, the sun was the sun . . . but still, the picture was in his mind of spinning galaxies, a world with a single cold white moon, and the frightening thing was that somehow all those images seemed to *belong* in Bard's mind!

The strange man spoke. He was not speaking Bard's language; somehow Bard knew that no one else in the room could understand him. But Bard knew what he had said, as if they were linked in the strongest *laran* bond.

"I feel like hell. How do you expect me to feel? What happened, a tornado? Hell—you're *me!* And that's not possible! You're not the devil by any chance?"

Bard shook his head. "I'm not any of the devils, not even nearly," he said.

"Who are you? What is this? What happened?"

"You'll find out later," Bard said, then, feeling him stir urgently, held him unmoving. "No, don't try to move yet. What's your name?"

"Paul," the man said weakly, "Paul Harrell." And then he fell back, unconscious. Bard moved, spontaneously, to raise him, support him. He shouted for help. The *laranzu* came and examined the unconscious man.

"He's all right, but the energy expended in that journey was frightful," he said.

Dom Rafael said, "Get old Gwynn to help you carry him; I'd trust him with my life, and more." Bard helped the old *coridom* carry the stranger to his own old rooms, laid him in his bed, locked the door of the suite—not that it was necessary; the *laranzu* assured them that he would not wake for a day and a night, or perhaps more.

He returned, to find that Dom Rafael had ushered the *leroni* into an adjacent chamber, where the old *coridom* had laid ready a hot supper, with plenty of wine. Bard, desperately curious about the stranger, reached for contact with his father, but for some strange reason his father was wholly shielded against him.

Why should his father barricade his mind so strongly?

"Food and drink is prepared for you, my friends. I have been a *laranzu,* I know the terrible hunger and thirst of such work. Come, eat and drink and refresh yourselves. Then I have had rooms made ready for you to sleep, and rest as long as you will."

The three *leroni* went quickly to the table and began to raise the wine glasses. Bard was thirsty too; he began to pick up a glass, but his father seized his arm in an iron grip, preventing him. At that moment one of the women screamed, a dreadful raw-throated scream, and slithered down lifeless to the floor. The *laranzu* gulped, spluttered in shock, but it was already too late.

Poisoned, Bard thought with a thrill of fear, thinking how close he had come to drinking of that same wine. The other *leronis* raised her face in blind appeal, and Bard felt her terror, the dread of certain death; she had swallowed almost none of the wine, and he saw her look around, hunting against hope for a way of escape.

Bard hesitated, for the woman was young, and not without attractiveness. Sensing his confusion, she came and flung herself at his feet. "Oh no! Oh, my lord, don't kill me, I swear I'll never say a word—"

"Drink," said Dom Rafael, and his face was like stone. "Bard. Make her drink."

Bard's confusion was gone. His father was right; none of them could let the *leronis* live to tell of this night's work. Old Gwynn could be trusted with their lives; but a *leronis* whose mind could be read with another's starstone—no, not possible. Essential to their plan was the knowledge that he should not be known to have a double. The woman was still clutching his knees, babbling in terror. Reluctantly, he bent to his work, but before he could touch her the woman dodged away, springing to her feet, and ran. He sighed, foreseeing a really nasty chase and the need for cutting her down at the end of it; but she ran around the table, caught up the goblet and drank deeply. Even before the third swallow she gave a small strange cough and fell lifeless across the table, upsetting a tray of bread, which fell with a *clunk* to the floor.

So this was why his father had not brought Melisendra!

Dom Rafael poured out the rest of the poisoned wine on the stone floor.

"There is a wholesome bottle here," he said. "I knew we would need it. Eat, Bard, the food is untouched, and we have work to do. Even with Gwynn's help, it will be a night's work to bury them all three."

BOOK THREE

The Dark Twin

CHAPTER ONE

If he is me, then who in hell am I?

Paul Harrell was not sure whether the thought so strong in the forefront of his mind was his own thought, or that of the man who stood before him. It was immensely confusing. At the same time, two emotions warred in him: *this man would understand me,* and *I hate him; how dare he be so much what I am?* It was not his first experience with ambivalence, but it was his most disturbing awareness of it.

The man who had introduced himself as Wolf said his name again. "Paul Harrell. No, that is not one of our names, although the Harryls are among my father's most loyal men. It would have been too much to ask that you should have been one of them."

Paul felt his head again, finding, rather to his surprise, that it was all in one piece. Then he thought of the perfect way to test whether this was, after all, a bizarre nightmare of the stasis box.

"Where's the head?"

He knew that the other man had understood even the slang phrase—how the *hell* did he do that thought-reading trick?—when he pointed. "Across the corridor."

Paul got up, naked, and went through the indicated door. No locks. He wasn't a prisoner, whatever they wanted with him, so it had to be an improvement. The corridor was stone, filled with an icy draft, and his feet felt freezing. The room was a reasonably well-appointed bathroom. The fixtures were somewhat strange in appearance, and he couldn't even imagine what they were made of, though it certainly wasn't porcelain, but it was easy enough to figure out the plumbing; he supposed there were only a few designs among humans. There was hot water—in fact, there was a large sunken tub filled with steaming hot water that looked somewhat like a Japanese bath-house fixture, and from the faint medicinal smell he supposed it came right up from a volcanic spring somewhere. Relieving himself, Paul supposed this was the ultimate reality testing. He caught up a fur-lined rug or blanket from a bench and wrapped it around himself.

Returning to the room, the other looked at Paul in his improvised blanket, and said, "I ought to have thought of that. There's a bedgown on the chair."

It looked like an old-fashioned bathrobe, but bulkier, lined with some silky fabric that felt like fur, and fastened tightly up at the neck to keep out draughts. It was very warm; in his own world it would have been good for a topcoat intended for traveling in Siberia. He sat down on the bed, drawing up his bare feet under the warm robe.

"That'll do for a start. Now, where am I, and what is this place, and what am I doing here? And, incidentally, who are you?"

Bard repeated his name and Paul tried it over on his tongue. "Bard di Asturien." It was not so outlandish, after all. He was trying to assimilate what Bard had told him about the Hundred Kingdoms. He wondered what the name of the sun was—if they were a pre-space culture, they probably called it The Sun—and he didn't know of any world within the Confederacy which had a sun as large as this, or as red. The really big red suns usually didn't have habitable planets. "Are there really a Hundred Kingdoms?"

He was thinking of a kind of United Confederacy where the kings all met together, as in the four-yearly Congress of the Confederacy of Worlds. Only there weren't a hundred inhabited planets. A hundred kings together would be quite an assembly, especially if they got along no better than the embassies of the Confederacy usually did! And there were only forty-two of them!

Bard took his question quite seriously.

"I am better at strategy than at geography," be said, "and I have not consulted a map maker recently; there may have been some new alliances, and the Hasturs have recently taken over a vacant throne or two. I think perhaps there are seventy-five or eighty, no more. But the Hundred Kingdoms is a good round number and sounds well beyond their borders."

"And how did you manage to bring me here?" Paul asked. "The last I heard, even with hyper-drive, to go much farther than the Alpha colony took an enormous amount of time, and I notice that my hair and nails haven't grown all that much."

Bard scowled and said, "I haven't the least idea what you are talking about." *Does he have sorcery stronger than ours?* Paul heard the unspoken thought perfectly well.

"I take it, then, we're right outside the Confederacy of Worlds."

"Whatever they may be, we are," Bard said.

"And the Terran police have no jurisdiction here?"

"It, or they, certainly do not. The only law within this kingdom is that of my father, as regent for my brother Alaric. Why do you ask? Are you a fugitive from justice, or a criminal under sentence of death?"

"I spent enough time as a fugitive," Paul said. "I was remanded for rehabilitation twice before I was eighteen. At this time I am supposed to be in custody, and under sentence. . . ." It made no sense to speak of the stasis box. They evidently didn't have it here and there was no sense in giving them ideas.

"Your country imprisons, then, rather than giving death or exile?"

Paul nodded.

"And you were—imprisoned? Then, since I delivered you out of prison, you owe me service."

"That's a moot point," said Paul, "and we'll moot it later. How did you bring me here?"

But the explanation—*starstones, a circle of wizards*—made no more sense to him than, he suspected, the stasis box would have made to the Wolf. Come to think of it, it was as likely as anything else that could get him out of a stasis box. It had been tried, of course, but had never been managed before; or if it was, the government wasn't telling anybody.

"What about the people who brought me here?"

Bard's face was grim. "They're in no condition to go blabbing about it." Paul knew perfectly well what he meant. "In your own idiom, they are in earth, except for my father. He will meet you later; he is still sleeping. His night's work was—strenuous, for so old a man." Paul had a fragmentary picture: three graves, hastily dug by moonlight, and suddenly he turned cold. This was no place for frightened conformists. Well, that was the kind of place he had wanted all his life. The people in this place played by rules he could understand. He knew Bard was quite willing to frighten him, and he decided it was time to let this self-styled Wolf know that he didn't scare easy. *Who's afraid of the big bad wolf? Not me.*

Bringing him here this way must have been illegal; or else they wouldn't have killed off all the witnesses; so he had something already on Bard, and on his father.

"I don't suppose you brought me here out of pure-hearted love of knowledge," he said, "or you'd be shouting it from the housetops, instead of hiding me here and murdering anyone who knows about it."

Bard looked disconcerted. "Can you read my mind?"

"Some, yes." Not nearly as much as he wanted Bard to think he could. But he wanted to keep the Wolf a little off balance. He knew this was a man who played rough, played for keeps, and he needed every advantage he could get!

But Bard wouldn't have gone to all this trouble for nothing. He was probably safe until he knew what Bard wanted him for, and unless it was to impersonate the guest of honor at a public execution, it couldn't be worse than the stasis box.

"What do you want with me? I didn't get any good-conduct medals—any more than you did," he said, making a shrewd guess.

Bard grinned. "Right. I was outlawed at seventeen, and I've been a mercenary soldier ever since. This year I came back and helped my father claim the throne of Asturias for my brother."

"Not for yourself?"

"Hell, no. I've got better things to do with myself than sit in council with all the graybeards in the kingdom, making laws about keeping cattle in their pastures and mending roads and stocking travel shelters and whether the Sisterhoods of the Sword should share fire-watch with men!"

Put like that, Paul decided that the business of kingship sounded a bit dull after all. "You're a younger brother and your elder brother is the king?"

"No, the other way around. My younger brother is the legitimate son. I am *nedestro* . . . more than a bastard but not in line of succession."

"Born the wrong side of the blanket, huh?"

Bard looked briefly puzzled, then chuckled as he caught the

image. "You could put it that way. I've no complaint about the old man; he reared me in his own house and supported me in my quarrel with the old king. And now my brother's put me in charge of his armies."

"So what do you want me for?" Paul demanded, "and what's in it for me?"

"At the very least," Bard said, "freedom. If you're as much like me on the inside as you are on the outside, that means a lot to you. Beyond that? I don't know. Women, if you want them, and again, if you're anything like me, you want them and you'll get them, too. Riches, if you're not too greedy. Adventure. Maybe a chance at the regency of a kingdom. Anyway, a better life than you led in your prison. Isn't that a good start?"

It sounded like one. He'd have to keep an eye on Bard, but at least he hadn't been brought here for any prisoner-of-Zenda complications where he sat and rotted in prison so his double could get out and do things.

He caught pictures in Bard's mind that already excited him. This, damn it, might be a world worth living in, not a tame one that relied on keeping everybody mushed down to a level of bland conformity, and lopping off the head of everyone who stood up above the pack!

Plenty of important personages, generals, rulers, had doubles; but somehow he thought it was going to be more than that. They could probably have found someone who resembled Bard pretty well, a relative or kinsman, without going nearly so far, and minor differences would have been covered by the convenience of having someone who knew their language and customs. Somebody like Paul, who couldn't even dress himself in this society without being shown how, and who had to communicate by thought-reading so far—and only with one person, at that—that would be a grave inconvenience, so that there simply had to be a good reason, an *overpowering* reason to put up with him. They needed someone who was like Bard, but not just on the outside. They needed someone who was like him on the inside as well.

This might be a real world, then. Not just an existence within circumscribed limits, a real world where he could be a real man, among real men, not bloodless androids and clerics!

Bard stood up.

"Hungry? I'll have them bring you something to eat. From

what my father says, if it suits me, it ought to suit you. And I'll send you some clothes. You're about my size—" he remembered and broke into a mirthless laugh. "No, damn it, you *are* my size. We can't do anything until your hair grows out—I can't be seen without the warrior's braid. Which gives us some time to teach you the rudiments of civilized life here, I suppose you do know the rudiments of swordplay—no? Your world must be a stranger place than I can imagine! I'm no duelist, so you won't need to know the fancy stuff, but you have to know something of self-defense. And you have to learn the language. I won't always be around, and it's a nuisance to have to read each other's minds all the time. I'll see you later." He stood up unceremoniously and went out, leaving Paul to shake his hand and wonder, again, if this were only some bizarre dream inside the stasis box.

Well, if it was, he might as well enjoy it.

CHAPTER TWO

But it was only ten days later that they set out for Castle Asturias. Dom Rafael had been unwilling to leave the government longer in the inexperienced hands of Alaric. And so the plan to wait until Paul could completely impersonate Bard had had to be abandoned too. On the contrary, they decided, it would be well to have them seen together, and a slight resemblance between them noted; thus, later, when Paul was *actually* impersonating him, no one would believe that the kinsman who resembled him somewhat, but not much, could be enough like him to do it. He didn't want the idea to get around that there was actually someone carefully hidden away who was enough like him to impersonate him. People, Bard reminded his father, usually saw what they expected to see, and if he was seen often with a (supposed) kinsman who resembled him somewhat, but not too much, people who liked to gossip about things which were none of their business would be quick to point out that the resemblance was really not so great after all.

So, for the time being, Paul's short hair, sun-bleached from a brighter sun than Bard's, was darkened with streaks of a dye that made it gingery red, and he cultivated a small ragged moustache. Differences in manner and carriage, they felt, would do the rest. For the time being, it was to be given out that he was a *nedestro* grandson of one of the brothers of Ardrin and Dom Rafael who had died before Ardrin came to the throne, and therefore Bard's cousin, discovered by him during his years of exile.

It would be given out that he had been living far north of

the Kadarin, near to trailman country. This region was so remote that there was not the slightest chance of anyone who spoke that language, or observed those alien customs, coming to court; so that any mistakes Paul made would be put down to his rustic and uncouth fostering.

And it was good that Paul could be at court openly for a little while and learn for himself the manners and the political situation. Bard was relieved to see that Paul rode well, though not quite as well as he did himself. The thought-reading had helped. Paul already spoke *casta* somewhat, and his odd accent could be explained by his supposed rural upbringing in the Hellers. Their first task, Bard thought, must be to get rid of the last traces of that accent.

For the audacious plan was no less than this: to divide the armies they could raise, and send them on two separate campaigns, one against the Serrais to the west, the other to confront Carolin's armies in the east; with each army believing that Bard himself was leading them; and at last to unify all the realm, and in the end, all the Hundred Kingdoms, under the overlordship of Alaric of Asturias. Then, with the Hasturs subjugated, the domains could be united, and there would be peace, without the tyrannical rule of Varzil's infamous Compact! Peace, without the pressure of small fratricidal wars coming to the boil at every season from spring thaw to harvest, or a new kingdom springing up every time some little group of men didn't like their lord and resolved to set up a new kingdom without him!

And then, Bard thought, such a Golden Age might return as had not been known since the Lord of Carthon made compact with the forest folk!

Central to this plan, though, was the military genius of Bard di Asturien and the particular charisma of the Kilghard Wolf. Paul, riding slowly behind Bard and Dom Rafael—as his assumed character of a poor relation demanded—could pick up a little of his thought, even now. *So I am to be Dog to his Wolf? We'll see about that!*

Paul thought about the theory that had brought him here; that he and Bard were, in essence, the same man. He was inclined to believe it. He had always known himself to be larger than his fellows, not in body alone—though that helped—but cut out, in mind, for a bigger and more heroic age than the one into which he'd been born.

The way he put it to himself was that most men had brains but no guts, or maybe vice versa; and of the rare men who had brains *and* guts, most had no imagination whatever. Paul knew himself to have all three; but they were wasted in the world he lived in. One of his early psychiatrists, back when they were still trying to reclaim him for the establishment, had told him frankly that be belonged on a frontier, that in a primitive society he would have been outstanding. Which hadn't helped at all. The psychiatrist had owned up, just as frankly, that in Paul's own society, unless he could resign himself to conform, his assets would all be liabilities.

Now he was putting both brains and imagination to work on Bard's world. The four colored moons had already told him that this was none of the known colonies of the Confederated Worlds. Yet the inhabitants were perfectly human, so far, which would have strained credibility beyond endurance if they were not of Terran stock; and although he was no linguist, he knew that the *casta,* with its admixture of Spanish words, could not possibly have descended from anything but a Terran culture. He could only hypothesize, tentatively, that they had been descended from one of the Lost Ships—sent out, in the old days before hyper-drive, for colonization in a universe they had already found to be all but unpopulated. One of these ships had formed the Alpha colony, others the early ones, but most of them had vanished without trace and been assumed lost, with all aboard. Paul knew that the Confederated Worlds were prepared to find one or two survivor colonies, isolated, some day. He hoped they wouldn't find this one in his lifetime. It would be a tragedy to see it beaten down to the same mediocrity as Terra, or Alpha, or any other known world!

Riding down toward Castle Asturias, a little before midday, Paul realized that it was a form of fortified building which had not been built on Earth for a few thousand years. It did not look much like the pictures of historic castles he had seen. The building materials were different, the life-style which dictated the architecture was different. But in the past few days be had been introduced to the theory of fortifications and strategies, and he set his mind to the problem of wondering how he would take this castle. It wouldn't be easy, he thought.

But it could be done, and he was fairly sure that if it came to that, he could do it.

However, he reflected, it would be easiest with an accomplice inside. . . .

Dom Rafael went ceremoniously with his retainers to make his return known to Alaric and the councillors. Bard assigned Paul a couple of servants, a room or two in his own suite, and took himself off about unexplained business. Paul, left alone, went to explore the rooms he had been given.

He found a little stair which led down into a small enclosed courtyard, filled with late-summer flowers—though to Paul the climate still seemed cold for any kind of flowers. There were flagged walks everywhere, and the fragrance of herbs, and an old well. He sat down to enjoy the rare late-day sun, and think over the curious situation in which he found himself.

He heard a noise behind him and whirled—he had been a fugitive too long to ignore anyone or anything behind him—then relaxed, with a sense of foolish relief, to see that it was only a very small boy, bouncing a ball along the walks.

"Father!" the child cried. "They didn't tell me you were back—" Then he stopped his headlong rush toward Paul, blinked and said with a charming little dignity, "My apologies, sir. Now I see that you are not my father, though you are very like him. I ask pardon for disturbing you, sir—I suppose, I should say *kinsman.*"

"That's all right," he said, deciding—it didn't take much thought to figure it out—that this must be Bard's son. Funny—he hadn't thought Bard would be the kind to have a wife and kids, to tie himself down that way, any more than he was himself. Come to think of it, Bard had said something about arranged marriages, they'd probably married him off to somebody without asking, though he couldn't imagine Bard tamely going along with that, either. Well, he supposed he'd learn.

"I've been told that there *is* a resemblance, after all, to your father."

The child reproved solemnly, "You should say 'the Lord General' when you speak of my father, sir, even if he is a kinsman. Even I am supposed to say 'the Lord General' except among the family, for Nurse says I will be sent to be fostered soon, and I must learn to speak of him with the proper courtesy. So, she says, I should always call him so except when we are alone. But King Alaric says 'my father' when he speaks of my grandsire, Dom Rafael, and *he* does not call my father 'Lord General' even when they are in the throne room. I don't think that's fair, do you, sir?"

Paul, hiding a smile, said that royalty had privileges. Well, he had wanted a society where people were not worn down to a tiresome egalitarianism, and now he had it. At that, he had probably gotten a higher place in it than he deserved at the start!

"I suppose, kinsman, that you are from beyond the Hellers. I can tell by the way you speak," said the child. "What is your name?"

"Paolo," Paul said.

"Why, that is not so strange a name after all! Do you have names like ours in the far lands beyond the Hellers?"

"That is the *casta* for my name, or so your father tells me. My own name would sound strange enough to you, probably."

"Nurse says it is rude to ask a stranger's name without giving one's own. My name is Erlend Bardson, kinsman."

Well, Paul had guessed that already. "How old are you, Erlend?"

"I shall be seven at midwinter."

Paul raised his eyebrows. He would have thought the boy was nine or ten, at least. Well, perhaps their year was a different length.

"Erlend," called a woman's voice. "You must not bother your father's guests or his sworn men!"

"Am I bothering you, sir?" Erlend asked.

Paul, amused by the child's dignified manner, said, "No, indeed."

"It's all right, my lady," said Erlend, as a woman came along the curving path. "He *says* I am not bothering him."

The woman laughed. She had a sweet laugh, very low and mirthful. She was young, her face round and freckled, and she had two long braids that hung almost to her waist, as red as the boy's. She was not shabby, but she was dressed plainly, without richness or any jewelry except a small and shabby locket with a blue stone around her neck. She was probably the boy's nurse, he thought; some poor relation or hanger-on. From what he knew of Bard, the Wolf would have dressed his mistress or fancy-woman in something more elaborate, and his wife would have been dressed according to her rank.

But how had Bard managed to overlook her? For to Paul it seemed that the rounded, womanly body, the low laugh and graceful hands and quick, mirthful smile, were the very embodiment of woman—yes, and of sex. He wanted her, suddenly, with such violence that it was all he could do to keep his hands off her! If the child had not been there. . . .

But no. He wasn't going to risk his position here, not right away, anyhow, by woman trouble. That, he knew grimly, was what had wrecked the plot and the reason he'd wound up in the stasis box. He hadn't had the brains and judgment to keep his hands off the wrong woman. He had guessed, from random conversation among the bodyguards and paxmen, that the Kilghard Wolf was quite a man for the women—he'd have expected that, if Bard was his own duplicate—and he wasn't going to quarrel with him on trivial grounds like that. There were plenty of women.

But this one. . . . He watched her with fascination, her delicate hands, the movement of the ripe, womanly body in her plain, simple dress. Her cheek was dimpled, curving into a light laugh as she admonished the boy.

"But I have to know all their names, *domna*," said Erlend. "When 1 am old enough to be my father's paxman I will have to know all his men by name!"

She was wearing a rust-colored dress. Strange that he had never realized how that color set off red hair. The dress was the exact color of her freckles.

"But Erlend, you are not to be a soldier or paxman, but a *laranzu*," she said, "and in any case this is disobedience, for you were told to play quietly in the other court. I shall have to ask Nurse to watch you more carefully."

"I'm too big for a nurse," the boy grumbled, but went along obediently at the woman's side. Paul watched till she was out of sight. God, how he wanted that woman! It was all he could do to keep his hands off her. . . . He wondered if she were someone accessible to him. Well, a child's governess couldn't be very exalted in station, even if she was a relation—as he suspected from her faint resemblance to the boy. He wondered where Bard's wife was. Dead, perhaps. On primitive worlds, childbearing was a risky business and, he knew, the mortality rates were fairly high.

He thought, with a cynical grin, that he was reacting normally. Reprieved from death, recalled out of the stasis box, what better way to spend a few odd hours than with women? But just in case this was real, he wasn't going to make the same mistake that had got him into the box in the first place. If by some strange chance this was one of Bard's women, he'd adopt a strict hands-off policy! There were plenty of other women. . . .

But damn it, that was the one he wanted! Too bad the child had been there; he wasn't *quite* enough of a bastard to grab a woman with a youngster looking on. He had a feeling she wouldn't be coy. The ripeness of that bosom, the red mouth which looked well kissed, told him she was no innocent virgin! To do her justice, he couldn't say she'd given him any clear signals; she'd been modest enough, but he bet his life she wouldn't make any fuss once he got his hands on her!

Bard sent for him late that evening, and they sat before the fire over a stack of campaign maps which Bard had insisted Paul should understand thoroughly. It was not too early to start. They talked for a long time about tactics and campaigns, and although it was professional, strictly business, Paul had the sense that Bard welcomed this companionship, enjoyed teaching him this; that he seldom had anyone to share his interests.

He's like me, a man who doesn't often find anyone he can talk to as an equal. They call him Wolf, but I have a feeling that "Lone Wolf" would be more like it. He's been a loner all his life, I bet. Like me.

There just weren't that many people who could follow his mental processes. It wasn't at all an unmixed blessing—to be brighter than ninety percent of the people you met. It made men seem like fools, and women like worse fools, and most people never had the slightest idea what he was talking about or thinking about.

Even when Paul led the rebellion that had brought him to disaster, he had already known that it was hopeless. Not because the rebellion was impossible—it could have been successful, if he'd had a couple of intelligent allies who knew what the hell he was really trying to do—but because, basically, the men he led weren't half so committed as he was himself. He'd been the only one who really *cared,* deep down, what they were fighting about. The other men didn't have that rage at the center of themselves; he had suspected, sooner or later, that most of them would climb down—as, in fact, they had done—and crawl to the powers that be for another chance; even if that chance meant having their whole selves carved up until there was nothing left of them. Well, there'd been nothing much to them in the first place, small loss! But it meant he had always been alone.

I can make myself necessary to the Wolf.

Because I'm his equal, his duplicate, the nearest to an equal he'll ever have. He looked at Bard for a minute with something very akin to love, thinking, *He'd understand. If I'd had just one follower like him, we could have put some steel into the spines of the men who followed me. We could have done it, together. Two like us could have changed the world!*

Rebellions, Paul knew, usually failed, because the brains and guts and imagination to lead them came along only once in a century or so. But this time there were two of them.

I couldn't change my world alone. But the two of us can change his, together!

Bard looked up sharply, and Paul felt sudden disquiet. Was he doing that thought-reading trick again? But the Wolf only stretched and yawned and said it was late.

"I'm for my bed. By the way, I forgot to ask, shall I have the steward send you a woman? There are enough useless females, heaven knows, and most of them just as eager for a man in their bed as the men are for them. Have you, perhaps, seen one that's to your liking?"

"Only one," said Paul. "Your son's governess, I suppose; long braids, bright red, freckled—curvy, not very tall. *That* one—unless she's married, or something. I don't want trouble."

Bard flung his head back and laughed.

"Melisendra! I wouldn't advise—she has a tongue like a whip!"

"It was all I could do to keep my hands off her."

"I should have expected that," Bard said, still laughing. "If we're the same man! That was how I reacted when I was seventeen, and she wasn't, I suppose, fourteen yet! She made a great fuss, and my foster mother has never forgiven me for it, but damn it, it was worth it! Erlend's her son. And mine."

"Oh, well, if she's yours—"

Bard laughed again. "Hell, no! I'm sick to death of her, but my foster mother's shoved her off on me, and she's getting above herself! I'd enjoy teaching her a lesson, prove to her she's no better than any of the other women around here and that it's only by my good nature, not as a right, that she's allowed to be my woman and stay here to raise my son! Let me think—if I told her to go to you, she'd run whining to Lady Jerana, and I haven't the heart for a quarrel with my father's wife. But just the same—" He grinned with mischief. "Well, you are supposed to be my duplicate! I wonder if she would even know the difference? Her room is there, and she'll think it's me, and know better than to make a fuss!"

Something in Bard's tone bothered him, as Bard added with a sarcastic grin, "After all, you *are* me; she can't complain that I've given her to someone else!"

Who the hell did Bard think he was, to fling him at Melisendra this way? But the thought of the red-haired woman's lovely ripe body stopped any thought of resistance. No woman had ever aroused him so, like that, at first glance!

His heart was pounding, as, later, he went toward the darkened room Bard had pointed out to him. And behind the excitement, the thought of the woman, was a note of cynical caution.

Bard would find it hilarious, he sensed, to guide him, not into Melisendra's room, but into the room of some withered old hag, some ancient virgin who would rouse the house screaming.

But even if Bard tried that, he'd find her; somehow he'd hold Bard to his promise.

He's my size and he's been fighting all his life. And right now, after God knows how long in the stasis box, he's probably more fit than I am; but he's not any stronger. I bet I could take him. I doubt, for instance, if he knows much karate.

But he dropped the thought of their inevitable confrontation from his mind as he came into the room. Moonlight from an open window lay across the bed, and he could see the loosened waves of the copper hair, rich and thick, the freckled face he had seen before. Her eyes were closed and she slept. She was wearing a long nightgown, embroidered at neck and sleeves, but it could not conceal the round ripeness of her body. Carefully, he shut the door. In the darkness, how would she know he was not Bard? He wanted her, somehow, to *know,* to want him too! And yet, if this was the only way he could have her . . . what the hell was he delaying for? If she was the kind of woman who could be handed from man to man, would it matter? But she obviously was *not* that kind of woman, or Bard would simply have handed her over, without this ruse. . . .

Or perhaps not. He found that thinking of Bard's body, his own body, entangled with this woman, was curiously arousing. Somehow it gave him a charge to think of it. Did Bard have the same kink, that it would give him some kind of kick to think of *his* duplicate, making love to *his* woman?

He sat on the edge of the bed to take off his clothes. It was pitch dark, but he would not risk a light. She could have told the difference, perhaps, by the fact that he did not have the warrior's braid of hair. . . . He discovered, with an amused grimace, that he was actually shaking with anticipation, like a boy about to take his first woman.

What the hell?

And Bard had given Melisendra to him, not to please Paul but, he sensed, to humiliate Melisendra. Suddenly he was not sure he wanted to collaborate with Bard on humiliating this woman.

But she would probably never know the difference anyway; and if this was the only way he could have her, he wasn't going to give up that chance! He got into bed beside her, and lay a hand on her under the blankets.

She turned toward him with a little sigh, not of acceptance or welcome, but of resignation. Was Bard so inept a lover as all that, or did she simply dislike him? Surely there was no love lost between them now! Well, perhaps he could change her tune; no woman who gave him half a chance had ever failed to welcome him as a lover.

She lay passive under his caresses, net refusing his touch, not accepting, simply acting as if he were not there at all. Damn the woman, he didn't want her that way, he would rather she'd scream and fight him than accept him as a loathsome duty! But even as he formulated the thought, she sighed again, and put up her arms around his neck, and he pulled her to him. He could feel her growing excitement, and felt her trembling against him as his own arousal grew greater and greater.

He let himself fall, spent and gasping, across her. He lay there, his hands still caressing her, covering her with kisses, unwilling to let her go even for a moment. She said quietly into the darkness, "Who are you?"

He drew breath in astonishment. And then he realized he should have known. He and Bard were physically doubles, yes, doubles even in personality perhaps. But sex was, of all activities, the most subject to total cultural conditioning. He could not possibly expect to make love in the way a Darkovan would do. The mechanics of the act were the same, but the whole psychological milieu was entirely different; he might have deceived her with a familiar face and body while he kept still, but every caress, every movement, betrayed a whole world of conditioning too deep to be altered. He could no more have made love to her in Bard's way—even if his duplicate had, unimaginably, told him the customary method—than he could have performed the sexual act in the manner of a Cro-Magnon man!

He said quietly, "Please don't cry out, Melisendra. He sent me here; I could not resist, I wanted you so."

Her voice was low and agitated. "He has played a cruel trick on us both; it is not his first. No, I will not cry out. Do you mind if I strike a light?"

He lay back while she lit a small lamp and held it where she could see him.

"Yes," she said, "the resemblance is—is demoniacal. I noticed it when I saw you with Erlend. But it is more than just resemblance, is it not? Somehow I could sense a tie between you. Even though you are—are very different," she said, and her breath came, ragged.

He reached out and took the lamp away from her, setting it down on the bedside table. "Don't hate me, Melisendra," he pleaded. Her mouth trembled, and he discovered that he wanted to kiss away whatever troubled her. That was not at all the usual reaction he had toward women! Damn it, usually when he'd had what he wanted of them he couldn't get away fast enough! But this one did something very strange to him.

She looked at him, shaken.

"I thought—for a moment, I thought, perhaps, something had changed in him. I—I—I have always wanted him to be this way with me—" She swallowed, hard, choking, and he sensed that she was trying very hard not to cry. "But I have only deceived myself, for he is rotten, rotten to the core, and I despise him. But I despised myself more, for—for wishing that he were such a man as I could—could come to love. For, since I must belong to him, since I have been given to him, I cannot help but wish he were—were a man I could love—"

He pulled her down to him, kissing the shaking mouth, the streaming tears beneath the pale lashes.

"I can't regret anything," he said. "Not when it brought me to you, Melisendra. I'm sorry for your grief, I'm sorry you were frightened; I wouldn't have hurt you or frightened you willingly—but I'm glad to have had you, once, when you wouldn't protest—"

She looked at him soberly, her eyes still wet.

"I am not sorry either," she said. "Believe me. Even though I suppose he was trying to humiliate me. I always refused when Lady Jerana would have given me to another, even when she offered to marry me honorably to one of Dom Rafael's paxmen. I feared it would be even worse. Bard has done his worst to me, I have no more to fear from him, and I thought, better the cruelty that I knew than new cruelty from a stranger. . . . But you have taught me otherwise." She smiled at him suddenly in the lamplight, a very faint smile, but he knew he would never be wholly content until she smiled at him as today she had smiled at the child, a wholehearted, mirthful smile of love.

"I think I am grateful to you. And I do not even know your name."

With one hand he put out the light and with the other he drew her down to him.

"Then are you willing to show your gratitude?"

He heard her surprised, grateful sigh in the moment before she turned and kissed him, with a surprised delight which shook him to the roots.

"I have never hated Bard before," she said, trembling, holding herself tight to him. "Now, because of you, I have learned how to hate him, and I shall never cease to be grateful to you."

"But I want more than gratitude," be heard himself say, to his own surprise. "I want your love, Melisendra."

She said in the dark, with a frightening intensity, "I am not sure I know how to love. But I think if I could learn to love anyone, I would love you, Paul."

He said no more, drawing her fiercely against his mouth. But even in the midst of his wonder and delight, a troubling thought nagged at him.

Now I can't turn back, now I am committed to this world, now there is someone here who means more to me than anyone and anything in the world I came from. What will happen now that I can't treat it all as a crazy dream?

CHAPTER THREE

A tenday later, Paul Harrell rode to war for the first time beside Bard di Asturien.

"The men of Serrais have broken their oaths," Bard told him as they made their preparations. "We may not have to fight. But we do have to remind them of what they have sworn, and the best way to do that is with a show of force and a sight of our armies. You had better be ready to ride within the hour."

Paul's first thought was triumph, *so, there will be a chance to strike for power!* His second, displacing even that, was one of dismay; *Melisendra!* He did not want to be parted from her so swiftly. He had just begun to suspect, and for the first time in his life, that he did not want to be parted from her at all. Yet a moment's sober reflection told him that this parting was the best thing that could possibly have happened.

Sooner or later, he knew it soberly, he would quarrel with Bard over Melisendra. He wanted her, still, as he had never wanted any other woman. Ordinarily, a tenday's possession would have satiated him and he would be more than ready for anything that removed him from any woman's hold. But he still wanted Melisendra. He dreaded this parting, he wanted her—and he couldn't explain it—in a new way. He wanted her for all time, and with her own consent; he was dismayed to realize that her happiness had become more important to him than his own.

He had always thought that women were there for the taking, and that was that. Why, he wondered, should he feel differently about Melisendra?

I always swore I'd never let any woman lead me around by

*the balls. . . . I knew it in my heart that women wanted to be
mastered, to have a real man they couldn't dominate. . . . Why
is this one so different?*

He knew he still wanted Melisendra; and he wanted her,
undisputed, for the rest of their lives. But he also knew that
Bard, produced by a less sophisticated society, regarded
Melisendra as his property, his prize, his possession. He might
pass her on to Paul for a time, to humiliate her, but he was not
likely to give her up entirely. She was, after all, the mother of his
only son.

And at the moment there was nothing he could do about any
of it. A time would come when they would quarrel over
Melisendra, and when that happened, Paul knew he must be
prepared.

For when that time comes, he thought grimly, *either he will
kill me or I will have to kill him. And I don't intend to be killed.*

So he gathered his pack for riding, and told Bard, "I would
like to say farewell to Melisendra."

"Why, as to that, there is no need," said Bard, "for she rides
with the army."

Paul nodded, at first without much thought; he was accustomed to women soldiers, even to women generals. Then the
shock hit him. Yes, in warfare which was a matter of button-
pushing and guns, women would be as competent in combat as
men—but in this world, where war meant close-order fighting
with swords and knives?

"Oh, we have those too," said Bard, reading his mind. "The
women of the Order of Renunciates, the Sisterhood of the
Sword, ride into battle with men, and they fight like berserk-
ers. But Melisendra is a real woman, not one of those; she is a
leronis, a spell-caster who rides with the armies to fight off
sorcery."

Paul thought perhaps that might be more dangerous still,
but he did not say so. As they rode out an hour later, Bard said
that this was just as well.

"There are those who would recognize my style of fighting," he said, "and while we are on this campaign—since you
are supposed to be a *nedestro* kinsman of mine—it will not
strike anyone as significant if I have you given lessons from
my own arms-master."

Paul, riding unregarded with a small group of Bard's
aides, noted for himself how the armies greeted their general:

cries of "The Kilghard Wolf! The Wolf!" cheers and shouts of acclaim. His very presence seemed to encourage and inspire them with courage and enthusiasm for this war against the Serrais.

So Bard would someday trust him with that power—and believe that he would tamely render it back again when the time was past? Not likely. There was, Paul knew with a chill of certainty along the spine, only one explanation. Bard would use him on his climb to conquest—and then, rather than rewarding him and sending him away as he had pledged, it would be back to the stasis box, by the same sorcery that had brought him here. Or perhaps, more simply still, a knife in the ribs on some dark night, and a corpse to the *kyorebni* wheeling around the cliffs. Paul kept his face impassive, joining in with the men who cried out in Bard's acclaim. It would not be easy. For now, Bard had other things to think of than the duplicate being trained to be his double and his dupe; but at other times they could read one another's thoughts, and he had had no training in blocking them. Perhaps Melisendra could help him, if she was truly a sorceress; but Melisendra would not be all that eager, either, to kill the father of her son. She might say that she hated Bard, but Paul wasn't entirely sure of the depths of that hate.

Still, confronted with an accomplished fact, he could probably trust her to be silent about the substitution.

For now there was only one thing to do; and that was just what Bard wanted him to do—to ready himself, not only to impersonate, but to *become* Bard di Asturien, the Kilghard Wolf, general of all the armies of Asturias. And perhaps, one day, more.

To his own surprise—for he knew nothing of the Darkovan style of swordplay and war and had never held a sword—he took to it as if he had been born to it. A little thought told him why. He had been born with the identical reflexes and superb physical organization that made Bard an incomparable swordsman; and he had trained that physical mechanism to the utmost with martial arts and the skills of unarmed combat during the rebellion. Now it was just a case of adding another set of skills to the trained muscles and brain, as a trained dancer can learn variation of steps.

He found he enjoyed the campaign, riding lookout with the aides, making camp each night and sleeping beneath the four moons that waxed and waned again. He thought often that if he had been brought up to this life he would have been happier. Here there were few expectations of conformity, and those there were came naturally to him; there was plenty of outlet for aggression. In his first close-quarters battle he found that he had no fear and that he could kill, if he must, without fear and without malice, and, better, without squeamishness. A corpse hacked by spears and swords was neither more nor less dead than one riddled with bullets or blasted with fire.

Bard kept him close at hand and talked to him a good deal. Paul knew this was not out of good will; the Wolf simply had to know whether Paul had his gift for strategy as well. It seemed that he did; a talent for handling men, a sense for the strategy of battle or attack, as city after city fell, almost undefended, to the armies of Asturias, and the men of Serrais fled, or went down before them, to the very borders of the Serrais lands. In forty days they had conquered half as many towns, and the road lay open before them to the old lands of the Serrais people. And Paul discovered that he knew instinctively what was the best strategy to take each city, to strike down each fighting force spread against them.

"My father said once," Bard told him, "that with two like me we could conquer the Hundred Kingdoms. And damn it, he was right! I know now it's not only likeness skin deep; you and I are the same man, and when we can lead two armies at once, the whole of this land will lie open to us like a whore on the city wall!" He laughed and clapped Paul's shoulder. "We'll have to—one kingdom would never hold us both, but with a hundred, there ought to be room enough for us both!"

Paul wondered if Bard really thought he was as naïve as all that. Bard would certainly try to kill him. But not yet awhile, maybe not for years, because he would need him until all of the Hundred Kingdoms, or as many of them as he wanted, were in subjection.

And meanwhile, paradoxically, he enjoyed Bard's company. It was a new experience for Paul to have someone to talk to who could follow what he said and understand it intelligently. And he felt that Bard enjoyed his, too.

It would all have been quite perfect if he could have had Melisendra actually *with* him on this campaign; but Melisendra rode with the other *leroni*, men and women in gray robes sternly chaperoned by a gray-haired elderly man with a lame

leg, so severely lame that he rode with a special device attached to his saddle to prop it up before him, and another to
unfold and help him in dismounting. In all the first three tendays of the campaign he had no opportunity to exchange more
than half a dozen words with Melisendra, and those were such
as could be spoken in front of half the army.

The walls of Serrais were actually within sight when Paul,
riding with Bard's aides, saw that Bard had dropped back from
his usual leading place to ride with the *leroni*. After a moment,
seeing that Paul was watching them, he beckoned and Paul
rode back toward the cluster of gray-robed men and women.
Melisendra raised her eyes in greeting, with a secret smile beneath her gray hood, somehow as intimate as a kiss.

Paul asked, "Who is Master Gareth?"

"He is the chief among the *laranzu'in* of Asturias; also, he is
my father," Melisendra said. "I wish that I might tell him—"
she broke off, but Paul knew what she meant.

He said in a whisper, "I miss you," and she smiled again.

Bard beckoned imperatively to him and said, "Master
Gareth MacAran, captain Paolo Harryl."

The gray-haired sorcerer gave Paul a formal bow.

"Master Gareth was lamed in my first campaign," Bard
said, "but he seems to bear me no ill will, for all that."

The old wizard said genially, "You were not to blame, Master Bard—or must I call you Lord General now as the young
guardsmen do? No one could better have led such a campaign.
That I caught a poisoned dagger in the leg muscle was ill fortune, the fortunes of war, no more. Those of us who ride to war
must accept such things."

"It seems long since that campaign," said Bard, and Paul,
who was as always catching some spillage from his mind and
feelings, realized that the tone was the bitterness of regret.

And in truth Bard was feeling the sharp sting of regret, a longing for days long past, of which the presence of Master Gareth
was a sharp reminder, and the copper sheen of Melisendra's hair
beneath the gray sorcerer's cloak more poignant still. Beltran had
been at his side then, and still was his friend. And Melora. He
found he could not resist the temptation to ask, "And your elder
daughter, sir, how does she; where has she gone?"

"She is in Neskaya," Master Gareth said. "In the circle of
Varzil, Keeper there."

Bard frowned, displeased, and said, "She serves, then, the

enemies of Asturias?" And yet he felt it might be better to think of Melora as an enemy, since she had gone beyond his reach. She was the only woman alive who had ever come near to understanding him, yet he had never laid a hand upon her.

"Why, no," Master Gareth said. "The *leroni* at Neskaya have pledged to work with starstones and live only for the good of all mankind, and to give allegiance to no king or ruler whatsoever, but only to the gods, and to help or heal. So they are not the enemy, my lord Wolf."

"Do you really believe that?" Bard's voice was contemptuous.

"Sir, I know it; Melora does not lie, nor would she have reason to lie to me, nor can one *laranzu* lie to another. Dom Varzil is exactly what he says he is, sworn to the Compact, to use no weapons, make no weapons, allow no weapons by *laran*. He is an honorable man and I admire his courage. It cannot be an easy thing to renounce your weapons knowing that others still carry them, and that others may refuse to believe you disarmed."

"If you admire him so much, then," Bard said peevishly, "must I look for you too to desert my armies and rally to the standard of this wondrous great man Varzil? He is a Ridenow of Serrais."

"Born so, sooth," Gareth said, "but now he is Varzil of Neskaya, with no loyalties other than that. And your question, Master Bard, is needless. I have sworn to King Ardrin an oath lifelong and I will not forsake it for Varzil or for any other. I would have held to the standard of Ardrin's son, had Lady Ariel not fled the country with him. I follow your father's banner because I believe truly that this is best for Asturias. But I am not the keeper of Melora's conscience. And indeed she left Ardrin's court in that same night that you were exiled, sir, long before there was cause to choose between Valentine's cause and Alaric's—in fact, Valentine was yet unborn. And she left with the king's leave."

"Still," said Bard, "if she has chosen not to fight against the enemies of Asturias, should I not rank her among them?"

"That's as you see it, sir. But you might also say that she has chosen not to fight alongside the enemies of Asturias, either. She could have done that easily enough; all of Varzil's circle did not swear the Compact, but left him and went to the Hastur supporters among that army. She stayed in Neskaya at Varzil's side, and that meant she's chosen to stay neutral, sir. And my granddaughter Mirella went to Hali Tower, which has also sworn to stay neutral alongside Neskaya. I'm an old man, and I'm loyal to my king while he needs me, but I pray the young people may find some way to end these damnable wars year after year while our countryside is laid waste!"

Bard did not answer that. He said, "I would not like to think of Melora as my enemy. If she is not my friend, I think it well that she is neutral."

Paul, riding between Bard and Melisendra, wondered why Melora could bring to Bard's face that note of anger and grief and misery. Master Gareth said, "Indeed, she'd never be your enemy, sir. She always spoke well of you."

Bard, sensing that both Melisendra and Paul could read his emotions, made an angry effort to control them. What was that woman Melora to him anyhow? *That* part of his life was over. At the end of this campaign, he would put all his *leroni* to seeking out a way to attack the Island of Silence and bring Carlina home to him, and then he need never think of Melora again. Or—he thought, intercepting a look between Paul and Melisendra—of Melisendra. Paul could have her and welcome. It would, at least, keep Paul safely preoccupied for awhile.

For awhile. Until I am safely established, with Alaric king over all these lands. Then he will be too dangerous to me; an ambitious man, accustomed to wielding all that power. . . .

And then he felt an unexpected surge of pain. Was he never to have a friend, a brother, an equal, that he could trust? Was he to lose every friend and peer as he had lost Beltran and Geremy? Perhaps, after all, he could think of another way; perhaps Paul need not die.

I do not want to lose him as I lost Melora. . . . He stopped himself, furious. He would *not* think of Melora again!

Suddenly Melisendra jerked her horse to a violent stop; her face contorted, and at the same moment Master Gareth flung up his hands as if to ward off some invisible evil. One of the other *leroni* screamed; another choked aloud in terror, bending over his horse's saddle and clinging there by instinct, almost unable to sit. Bard looked at them in dismay and bewilderment. Paul moved swiftly to steady Melisendra, who sat swaying in her saddle, paler than the snow at the edges of the paths.

She paid no heed to him. "Oh—the death, the burning!" she cried, and her voice held terror beyond expressing. "Oh, the agony—death, death, falling from the sky—the fire—the screams—" Her voice died in her throat, and she sat with her eyeballs rolled up until only white showed, as if they stared at some inward horror.

Master Gareth choked, "Mirella! Dear gods, Mirella—she is there—"

This brought Melisendra back, but only for a moment. "We cannot be sure she has come there yet, dear Father, she—I have not heard her cry out, I am sure I should know if she were among them—but oh, the burning, the burning—" She screamed again, and Paul reached over from his own horse. She let her head fall against him, sobbing.

He whispered, "What is it, Melisendra, what is it—" but she was beyond answering him. She could only cling to him, weeping helplessly. Master Gareth, too, looked as if he were about to fall from his saddle. Bard put out a hand to steady the old *laranzu* and at the touch the images flooded into him.

Flaring light. Searing pain, intolerable agony as flames rose and struck inward, consuming, tearing . . . mounting fire, walls crumbling and falling . . . voices raised in shrieks of agony, terror, wild lamentation . . . air-cars booming and fire, death raining down from the sky. . . .

Paul had been immune, but as Bard's mind opened to the images, he saw and felt them too, and felt himself go pale in horror. "Fire-bombing," he whispered. He had believed this world civilized, too civilized for such warfare, and war almost a game, a manly test of courage, of domination and challenge. But *this. . . .*

A woman's body flaring like a torch, the smell of burning hair, burning flesh, agony searing. . . .

Bard steadied the old man, as he would have with his own father. He was sick with the horror of the images flaring through his mind. But Master Gareth managed somehow to pull himself free from the horrors within. *"Enough!"* he said harshly, aloud. "We cannot help them by sharing their death agonies! Barricade yourselves, all of you! At once!" He spoke in command voice, and suddenly the air around them was free of smoke and the smell of death and burning, the intolerable screams of agony gone. Paul looked around, dazed, at the peaceful trail and the soft silent clouds overhead, the small sounds of an army on the march. A horse whinnied some-where, supply wagons creaked and rumbled, a drover somewhere good-naturedly cursed his mules. Paul blinked with the suddenness of the falling quiet.

"What was it? What was *that,* Melisendra?" His arms were still around her; she straightened, a little abashed.

"Hali," she said, "the great Tower by the shores of the Lake; Lord Hastur had sworn that the Towers should be neutral, at least Hali and Neskaya—I do not know who struck them." Her face was still stunned with the horror she had shared. "Every *leronis* in the Hundred Kingdoms must have shared that death. . . . This is why the Lord Varzil has sworn neutrality. If this goes on, soon there will be no land to conquer. . . ."

They all looked sober; many of the *leroni* were weeping. Melisendra said, "Not one of us here but has a sister, a brother, a friend, a loved one at Hali. It is the largest of the Towers; there are thirty-six women and men there, three full Circles, with *leroni* from every one of the kingdoms and *laran*-bearing families. . . ." Her voice died again.

"So much for the Compact," said Master Gareth fiercely. "Shall they sit quietly in Elhalyn and limit their warfare to sword and crossbow when fire is sent against them from the sky? But who would have dared to strike them? It is not the forces of Asturias, surely?"

Bard shook his head, numbed.

"Serrais, now, has no such strength, and why should the Lord Hastur strafe his own Tower who were loyal to him and had sworn to hold themselves neutral? Can it be that the Aillard or the Aldaran have joined in this war, and that all the Hundred Kingdoms are aflame?"

Paul listened, shaken. On the surface this world was so simple, so beautiful, and yet *this,* this hideous telepathic warfare hidden. . . .

"It can be worse than fire-bombing," Melisendra said, picking up his thoughts as she so often did. "At least they were borne by aircraft and the defending Tower could have knocked them out of the sky. I once struck down an air-car bent on such attack. But I have known a circle of *leroni* to put a spell on the ground beneath a castle under siege—" she pointed to a ruin atop a distant hill—"and the ground opened, and shook—and the castle fell in ruins and everyone was killed."

"And is there no defense against such weaponry?"

"Oh, yes," Melisendra said indifferently, "If the Lord of the Castle had had his own circle of wizards and they were stronger than the attackers. For generations, all of our family—and all the great families of Darkover—had *laran* ever stronger bred into them; that was while all this land lay under the rule of the Hastur kin, the descendants of Hastur and Cassilda. But there is a limit to what can be done with breeding; sooner or later there is too much inbreeding, and lethal recessives take over. My father—" she gestured to Master Gareth, who still looked pale and exhausted—"was married to his half-sister, and of fourteen children, only the three survived, all daughters. There are no MacArans in these hills now, only a few away to the north who were never taken into the breeding program . . . and few Dellerays, and the old line of Serrais died out; the Ridenow took the name when they married into that line. And my sister Kyria died in bearing a daughter, so that Melora and I brought up her child. . . . Mirella is a *leronis* too, one of those kept virgin for the Sight, and I pray she may stay so, for I know she fears to die the same way."

Paul was not really in rapport with Melisendra now, but he could sense the waves of old, half-conquered fear; he remembered Melisendra had borne a child, and felt sudden sympathy for the terrors she must have known. Always before this he had had but little sympathy for the special problems of women; now it struck him with remorse. In his own world, a woman would have known enough to make certain she was not at risk of pregnancy, but he had not bothered, here, to inquire, and it occurred to him, troubled, that Melisendra had not stopped to weigh the cost of their lovemaking.

"It has begun to be lethal in our family," she went on, almost absently—Paul wondered if she was talking to him, or trying to ease her own tensions and fears. "Erlend is healthy, the Goddess be praised, but already he has *laran,* and he is young for it. . . . Bard is only distantly related to us, of course, and Kyria married a cousin, so that may be why. . . . Melora and I must be careful to whom we bear children; even if we survive, the children may be stillborn. . . . I do not think Mirella should have children at all. And there are certain *laran* gifts which could combine with mine so that I would not survive forty days of such a pregnancy. Fortunately those are rare now, but I do not think their virulence is wholly lost in the line, and since records are not now kept, and the old art of monitoring cell-deep is not known now, the last of those who knew all of it died before she could teach what she knew. . . . None of us can know, when we bear a child, what may come of it. And some of these new weapons. . . ." She shuddered and resolutely changed the subject again, but not much. "I was fortunate that Bard was not carrying any of that heredity. It was perhaps the only fortunate thing about that whole affair."

It took another day of marching before they came up with the armies of Serrais, and that meant another night encamped on the road. Under ordinary conditions, Paul did not even see Melisendra when they were with the army; but near the camp was a little grove of trees with a well, and when he strolled that way, as the nightly drizzle began to fall (Bard told him this was normal for the season, except in the high summer—what a climate!) Melisendra, wrapped in the gray cloak of a *leronis,* beckoned to him. They stood embracing for some minutes, but when he whispered to her, moving his head suggestively toward the concealing trees, she shook her head.

"It would not be seemly. Not like this, with the army. Don't you think I want to, my beloved? But our time will come."

He was about to protest—how did he know they would have any time at all, after this campaign?—but the look in her eyes stopped him. He could not treat Melisendra like a camp follower. Quite soon, she went back to the other *leroni*—her father, she said, would have been angry at even this surreptitious embrace, would have thought that she was behaving badly—not that he minded whom she loved, but to do it furtively, like this, on campaign, when all others must leave their loved ones behind, was shameful. When she had gone he stood watching her reflectively, thinking that this was the first time he had ever listened to a woman's refusal. If any other woman had done this, he would have considered her a cheap, manipulative slut, trying to lead him around by the balls. . . . What was happening to him? Why was Melisendra different?

And, an unwelcome thought, was it possible that his own attitude, in those days, had left something to be desired? Paul was not given to questioning the rightness of his own motives and actions, and this was a new idea to him, one he put aside at once. Melisendra was different, that was all, and love was the art of making exceptions.

But it seemed to be his night for unwelcome thoughts. He lay awake, unable to sleep, and wondered what would happen when Bard knew that it was not a casual affair with Melisendra but that he wanted her for all time. And if he and Bard were the same man, with the same sexual tastes and desires, why was it that he had not tired of Melisendra at once, as Bard had done?

I have no consciousness of guilt toward her, and so Melisendra does not make me uncomfortable . . . and Paul almost laughed; Bard, feel guilty about anything? Bard was as free of the neurotic pattern of guilt as any man Paul had ever known, as free of it as Paul was himself. Guilt was a thing created by women and priests to keep men from doing what they wanted to do and had the strength to do, a tool of the weak to get their own way. . . . Still it was a long time before Paul could get to sleep. He wondered dismally what was happening to him on this world.

At least it was better than the stasis box. And with this thought he finally managed to sleep.

The next day was gray and dismal, with rain landing down, and Paul was surprised that they tried to march; though a little thought told him that in this climate, if they let rain stop them, they'd never do anything. And indeed, he saw herdsmen, mounted on strange horned beasts, watching over flocks in the fields, flocks of what Bard told him were rabbithorns; and farmers, many of them women, shrouded in thick tartan cloaks and wrappings, digging in the fields. At least, he thought glumly, they didn't have to worry about watering their crops. He was glad he wasn't a farmer. From what little he knew of them, it was either too wet or too dry. They rode by a lake and saw small boats out in the rain, hauling in nets. He supposed fish-farming was a good trade to be carried on in the rain.

Around noon—the days were longer here, and Paul could never be sure of the time unless he could see the sun—they stopped to eat the cold trail rations served out by the quartermasters: bread, coarse, with raisins or some kind of dried fruit, and nuts baked into it, a kind of bland cheese, a handful of nuts in their shells and a pale, sourish wine which, nevertheless, had considerable body and was refreshing and warming. It was, he knew, the commonest home brew of the countryside, and he felt he could get to like it.

Halfway through the meal, Bard's aide came to summon Paul to him. As he rose to obey the summons, Paul was conscious of looks and comments; he should, perhaps, warn Bard that this supposed favoritism to one who was, after all, newcome to his armies, could get him into trouble. But when he mentioned it, Bard shrugged it off.

"I never do the expected thing; that's one of the reasons I got the name Wolf," he said. "It keeps them off balance." Then he told Paul that one of his runners had come in, bearing news that the Serrais army was not far away. As soon as the weather cleared, he would have to send out sentry birds to spot their exact position and formation. "But I have a young *laranzu* with the Sight," he said, "and it may be that we can take them by surprise in the rain. Ruyven," he said to another of his aides, "run and tell Rory Lanart, when he has finished his meal, to come to me at once."

When Rory came, Paul noted with dismay that the young *laranzu* was only about twelve years old. Did children fight battles of sorcery and wickedness in this world, too? It was bad enough to have women in the field, but children? Dismay struck more deeply as he thought of young Erlend, the starstone about his throat. Would Erlend grow up in a world like this? He watched the child looking into the starstone, relaying the information they wanted in a quiet, faraway voice, and wondered what Melisendra thought of having her son brought up to this.

Bard, after all, is no more than a barbarian chief in a barbarian world. He and I are not the same man. He is the man I might have been in this barbarian society. There but for the grace of God, and all that.

He raised his head to find Bard watching him; but his double did not give any sign or hint as to whether or not he had read Paul's mind this time. He only said, "Finished your meal? Bring along what you want to—I always put some nuts in my pocket to eat as I ride—and tell the aides to get the men started again. Rory, ride at the head of the army with me, I'm going to need you, and someone should lead your horse if you're going to be using the Sight."

They had not ridden for more than an hour, as Paul judged it, past the time of the nooning break when they came to the top of a hill; and Bard pointed, silently. Spread out in the valley below them, an army lay, formed up and waiting, and Paul identified, even at this distance, the green and gold banner of the Ridenow of Serrais. Between them and the Serrais army below was a little wood, a sparse grove of trees and undergrowth. A sudden flight of birds racketed upward, disturbed at their feeding in the bushes. Paul could hear Bard thinking: *that's done it, that's the end of any idea that we might possibly*

take them by surprise. But their leroni *would have better sense
than that. And surely they have* leroni *with them.*

Aides were riding along the ranks of the men, forming
them up in the battle plan Bard had discussed, briefly, with
Paul—one of the things which the other aides resented, he
knew, was that their leader spoke to Paul, outsider and new-
comer, as an equal. They had, of course, no idea quite how
much Paul was Bard's equal. But they sensed something and
it made them angry. Some day, Paul knew, when there was
time, he would have to deal with it. And he thought, with a
trace of amusement, that when he and Bard were leading separate armies, each believing that it was led by the Kilghard
Wolf himself, at least that source of friction would be gone;
there would be no intrusive outsider to come between the
Wolf and his loyal followers.

The signal was, as always, the drawing of Bard's sword.
Paul watched, his hand on the hilt of his own sword, waiting
for Bard to give the sign for the charge. The rain had drizzled
itself out, and only stray drops were falling. Now, suddenly,
through a great break in the clouds, the great red sun came out
and blazed, spreading light into the valley. Paul looked at the
sky, thinking offhand that it was better to fight without
the rain, but aware that the turf underfoot was still wet and the
horses would find it slippery in the charge. Master Gareth had
drawn his little army of sorcerers, gray-cloaked, off to one
side, to keep them out of the way of the charge. When Paul had
first ridden into battle, he had been anxious about Melisendra.
Now he knew that she was in no physical danger in a battle
such as this. Even under the concealing gray cloak, he could
tell Melisendra by her riding.

He saw Bard draw his sword—then heard him cry out, and
saw him raise the sword to slash at empty air. *What, in God's
name, does he see?* And all the men riding near him were behaving the same way—slashing at empty air, crying out, raising their arms to shield their eyes against some unseen
menace; even the horses were rearing and whinnying in
distress. Paul saw nothing, smelled nothing, even though one
of the men cried out, "Fire! Look there—" and fell crashing
from his horse, rolling away, screaming. And suddenly as he
caught Bard's eyes, in contact with his twin, he saw what
Bard saw: over their heads, wheeling and screeching, strange
birds flew, diving viciously at the eyes, causing the horses to

rear up as their foul breath pervaded everything; and the horror was that the birds had the faces of women, contorted with lewd grins. . . .

Paul saw this through Bard's eyes; and through his own eyes . . . the day lay quiet, sunlit below them, the armies of Serrais quickly moving to repel the charge. Paul rose in his stirrups, his own sword flashing out. He bellowed—in, he knew it, Bard's voice, "There's nothing there, men! It's illusion! What the hell are the *leroni* doing? Come on—*charge!*"

Bard's swift response to the words reassured him. He shouted, "Charge!" and led the charge, riding through the illusion—Paul saw through his eyes the evil harpy that dived at his eyes and felt Bard duck, even while he knew that it was illusion. He smelled the stench of the beast-woman, but the frozen horror had broken; Paul had snapped back to his own awareness and was thundering, sword in hand, toward the first rank of the oncoming Serrais army. A man cut upward at his horse and he slashed and saw the man fall. And then he was fighting hand to hand, without the least instant to spare for magic horrors, or for seeing them through Bard's eyes. At this moment he did not care what Bard might be seeing, whether or not it was there to be seen or was the product of sorcery or *laran* science.

They had still caught the Serrais army, who had relied on their sorcerers to delay the charge, at least partly by surprise. The battle was not brief; but not as long as Paul, helping Bard to assess the forces mastered against them, had believed. Bard came through miraculously unwounded. Miraculously, Paul thought, for throughout the battle, wherever he looked, Bard was in the thick of the fighting. Paul himself took a slash in the leg, which did more harm to his trousers than anything else. When the Serrais army, demoralized, fled, and Dom Eiric himself surrendered—Bard hanged him out of hand as an oath-breaker—the sun was setting, and Paul, his leg freezing under the flapping remnants of the leather breeches, rode to help the aides set up headquarters in one of the houses in the nearby village, commandeered. The men were set to plunder and rape, then burn the village, but Bard stopped them.

"These are my brother's subjects; rebellious, it is true, but still our subjects, and while they may have been terrified into doing the will of the Serrais army, they shall have a chance to prove their loyalty or otherwise when they can act freely without an army at their throats. It will go hard with any man in this army who touches one of our subjects, loyal or disloyal. Pay for what you take, and lay no hand on any unwilling women."

Paul, listening as Bard gave the order, reflected that he had not known Bard had this kind of sense, or that he could hold back men set on plunder. But when he spoke of this to Bard, Bard smiled. He said, "Don't be a fool. I'm not being generous, though what I said is true, of course, and even more that the royal house of Asturias, and I, will get the credit for being generous with our subjects. But it's more than that, much more. There's simply not enough, of either plunder or women, to satisfy this army. And when they'd taken all there was to take, they'd fall to quarreling over it and cut each other to pieces—and I can't have that in my army." He grinned wickedly and said, "Anyhow, the officers have a little leniency—and you'd get first choice since you led the charge. We may not be so like after all—you're braver than I, to lead the charge right through that nest of harpies! Or did you simply begin to suspect, earlier than I did, that they were illusion?"

Paul shook his head. "Neither," he said. "I simply didn't see anything."

Bard stared. "You didn't—not at all?"

"Nothing. I began, after a little, to see them through *your* mind—but then, I was only seeing what *you* saw, and I knew it."

Bard pursed his lips and whistled. "That's very interesting," he said. "You picked up the burning of the Tower of Hali—gods above and below, that was a ghastly business! Wars should be fought with swords and strength, not with sorcery and fire-bombing! That hellish stuff they use is made by sorcery in the Towers; no normal process can manufacture it!"

"I couldn't agree more," Paul said, "but I picked it up, again, through Melisendra's mind. I didn't see it myself."

"Yes. Sex creates a bond. And I've often suspected that Melisendra's a catalyst telepath. In a Tower she'd be used to awaken latent *laran* in someone who for some reason can't use it. I suspect, without meaning to, she's awakened what little of it I have. God knows, she'd never think she owed me any favors! And there are times I suspect that it's no favor at all, though most people would think it so; there are times I wish I was immune to *laran,* or at least to illusion. If you hadn't led the charge this morning, we'd have lost the last bit of our advantage. As for being immune to *laran*—unless you pick it up directly from my mind, or Melisendra's, or from someone very close to you—well, that might be an advantage. We'll talk about that afterward, maybe. I can think of a service you could do me." His eyes narrowed and he looked sharply at Paul. "I'll have to think about it. Meanwhile, I have this rebel village to deal with. Stand back there and listen to what's happening; you might have to deal like this sometime."

Paul, admonished, listened as he gave the commands about the men who had actively assisted the Serrais army. They were to pay double taxes this year; anyone who could not pay the taxes to do forty days of free labor on the roads—Paul had already learned that the forty-day cycle, corresponding to that of the larger moon, served the social purpose of a month, making up four tendays. Women, too, followed the forty-day menstrual cycle of the largest moon. At the end they cheered his leniency.

One of Bard's fellow officers said, "With respect, Lord General, you should have burned them right out," but Bard shook his head.

"We're going to need good subjects to pay taxes. Dead men support no armies, and we need the work of their hands; and if we hanged them we'd somehow have to support their wives and children. . . . Or are you suggesting we emulate the Drytowners and sell the women and children off into brothels to earn their keep? How would people like that feel about King Alaric, to say nothing of his armies?"

Master Gareth said quietly behind him, "I am surprised. When he was a boy, no one ever suspected that Bard di Asturien, brave as he might be, would have grown up to have any political sense at all."

A pretty, red-haired, round-bodied girl came up to them, bending in a low curtsy. "My father's house is your headquarters, Lord General. May I serve you wine from his cellars?"

"Now that," Bard said, "we'll gladly accept. Serve it to my staff as well, if you will. And all the more for your serving it, my dear." He smiled at her, and she returned the smile.

Paul, remembering that the women of the *leroni* had all been quartered at the far end of the village, in a house set apart, and that four guardsmen had been told to protect their privacy, remembered tales among the soldiers that Bard had a hell of a reputation with the women.

But before the girl could return with the wine there was a knock on the door, and one of the Sisters of the Sword, her scarlet tunic slashed and still battle-stained, burst into the room.

"My lord!" she exclaimed, and fell on her knees before Bard, "I appeal to the justice of the Kilghard Wolf!"

"If you are one of those who fought for us in the battle, *mestra*," Bard said, "you shall have it. What troubles you? If any man with my army has laid a hand upon you—I personally do not think women should be soldiers, but if you fight in my army, you are entitled to my protection. And the man who has touched you against your will shall be gelded and then hanged."

"No," said the woman in the red tunic, laying a hand upon the dagger at her throat. "Such a one should have perished already by my hand or that of my sworn sister. But there were mercenaries of the Sisterhood in the army of Serrais, my lord. Most of them fled when that army fled, but one or two were wounded and some of them stayed by their sisters; and now that the battle is over the men of your army are not treating them with the courtesy which is allowed by custom to captured prisoners of war. One of them has already been raped, and when I appealed to the sergeants to stop it, they said that if a woman took the field in war she should be sure not to lose her battle, or she should be treated not as a warrior but as a woman—" The woman soldier's mouth was trembling in outrage. Bard rose swiftly to his feet.

"I'll put a stop to that, certainly," he said, and gestured to Paul and one or two of his officers to follow him as he strode out of the tent.

They followed the woman in red through the village and through the hurly-burly outside that was the army making camp, but they had not far to go past the village when they knew what the woman had been talking about. They heard a screaming of women, and a group of men had gathered around one of the tents, making lewd noises of encouragement. At one side a fight was going on, where a group of women in red were fighting to get through. Into the noise and confusion came Bard's bellowing voice.

"What the hell is this all about? Stand back!"

"Lord General—" Murmurs, shocked noises of recognition. Bard thrust back the flap of the tent, and a minute later two men came staggering out under a savage kick. A woman was sobbing wildly inside. Bard paused to say something to the guard that Paul could not hear, then raised his voice again.

"Once and for all, I gave my orders: no civilian is to be touched, and no prisoner ill-used!" He jerked his head at the men he had kicked. They were sitting dazed on the ground, already drunk, their clothes undone, confused. "If these men have any friends here, take them back to their own quarters and sober them up."

There was muttering in the ranks, and one of the men called out, "We can take what the other army has, that's custom in war! Why do you refuse us what's customary, General Wolf?"

Bard turned toward the voice and said harshly, "You're allowed by custom to take their weapons, no more. Have any men in the opposing army been made your minions by force?"

There was a mutter of outrage at the notion.

"Then hands off these women, hear me? And while you're at it, let me repeat what I told the soldier here." He gestured toward the woman of the Sisterhood. "Any man who lays a hand on one of the Sisterhood who has fought beside us for the honor and strength of Asturias and the reign of King Alaric, shall be first gelded and then hanged, if I have to do it myself! Understand that, once and for all."

But the woman in red flung herself at Bard's feet.

"Won't you punish the men who have outraged my sisters?"

Bard shook his head. "I've put a stop to it; but my men acted in ignorance, and I won't punish them. No one else will touch a prisoner; but what's done is done and I won't give the women who fought against me the same kind of protection I give my own armies—or what's the good of being in my armies at all? If the mercenaries in your Sisterhood want to swear allegiance to Asturias and fight alongside my armies, I'll give them that protection; otherwise not. Although," he added loudly, glancing around at the assembled men, "if anyone touches a prisoner except as custom allows, I'll have him whipped and his pay stopped, is that clear?" The woman was about to say more, but he stopped her. "Enough," I said. No more fighting. Come on, men, break it up. Get about your business! Any more fighting and there'll be whippings and broken heads tomorrow!"

Back in the commandeered house, the staff had finished their wine and were going to make their own arrangements. The red-haired girl, who reminded Paul elusively of Melisendra, put a cup into his hand and smiled.

"Here, my lord, finish your wine before you go."

He raised his face to her and drank, sliding his arm about her waist. Her flirtatious smile made him understand; this was not an unwelcome advance, and he pulled her close. A hand fell on his shoulder, and Bard's voice boomed out, "Let her be, Paul. She's mine."

Mentally Paul cursed, knowing he should have expected this. Already, on campaign, he had discovered that he and Bard had the same taste in women. Naturally enough, if they were the same man, they'd want the same thing in women, and it wasn't the first time their eyes had fallen on the same camp follower or woman of pleasure in a fallen city. But it was the first time it had come to a direct confrontation. Paul thought, he owes me something for leading the charge, and his arm stayed stubbornly around the girl's waist. This time, damn it, he would *not* give in!

"Oh, hell," Bard said.

Paul realized that he was already drunk; also that the rest of the staff had gone, leaving them alone with the girl. He put a hand under the girl's chin and asked, "Which of us do you want, wench?"

Her smile turned from one to the other. She had been drinking too. He could smell the sweet fruitiness of wine on her breath, and either the drink had heightened her perceptions or she had a trace of *laran,* for she said, "How can I choose between you when you are so much alike? Are you twin brothers, then? What is a poor girl to do when if she chooses one she'll have to give up the other?"

"No need for that," Paul said, as he swallowed the wine, realizing it was much stronger than what he had had before, and was consolidating his drunkenness. "There's no need to prove one of us the better man this time, is there, brother?" He had never voiced this knowledge of their unconscious rivalry before this. And if Bard were somehow a hidden half of himself, was this not a way to come to terms with it?

The girl looked from one to the other of them, laughing, and turned to lead the way. "In here."

Paul was just drunk enough to retain a merciless clarity. Bard made some show of flipping a coin. Paul wasn't surprised—that kind of chance-choice was common in some very unlike cultures—but he stepped back, watching the clouded and elegant dance of bodies, Bard and the girl, *his* body and hers, as Bard sank down, pulling the girl atop him. Paul felt a momentary flicker of surprise—*he* would have pinned her down beneath his own body—but the thought was remote, dreamlike. He sank down beside them, his hands straying along her curving back, through the silken hair. She turned a little and her lips fastened on his even while she drew in a gasp of excitement as Bard entered her. She found a moment and a free hand to tease his manhood with her fingertips. Paul, embracing her, found that he had them both in his arms, but it didn't seem to matter; it was dreamlike, nothing now seemed forbidden, and he knew their three bodies, enlaced, became a shifting dance. The woman's softness seemed somehow only an excuse to savor *himself,* knowing Bard's excitement and sharing it. It was dreamily perverse; he knew that when he took her, Bard, in full rapport now, shared the pleasure even as he had shared his twin's. He never knew, never wanted to know, how long it lasted, or at what point, the girl forgotten, he found himself in Bard's hard clasp, all softness gone now, a struggle almost to the death, locked together in what he could not isolate as either passion or hatred; and in a final sardonic flicker of apartness he wondered if this could be called, if they were actually the same man, sex or the ultimate masturbation, and then it did not matter whether the violent explosion was orgasm or death.

He woke alone, his head thundering. The girl was gone, nor did he ever set eyes on her again. She had meant nothing, she had only been the excuse for that violent confrontation with his dark twin, his other half, his half-known unknown other. He sluiced his face with the icy water in the bucket, and was still gasping with the shock of it when Bard came in.

"My orderly brought me a pitcher of hot *jaco*. If your head's doing what mine is, you could use half of it," he said. The stuff smelled like bitter chocolate, but the effect was about the same as extra-strong black coffee, and Paul was glad to get it. Bard poured himself another mug.

"I want to talk to you, Paolo. You know you saved the day yesterday. That damned harpy illusion is a new one, and the *leroni* weren't prepared for it. It was so real! And you didn't see it at all?"

"Only through your mind, as I told you."

"So you're immune to that kind of illusion," Bard said. "I wish I dared confide in Master Gareth! He might be able to explain it. And among other things, it gives you an edge if you should have to lead the army some day. And the men will follow you; but you'll have to be careful about the *leroni,* they'll sense something strange about you." He barked short laughter. "One good thing about Varzil's God-forgotten Compact—we can fight without having those wretched corps of wizards along with us, if they ever decide to put the Compact into effect!"

"I thought you and Master Gareth were friends—that you depended on him!"

"True," Bard said. "He's known me since we were boys, my foster brothers and I. But I'd still be glad to dispense with his services and send him to spend a nice peaceful old age in a Tower! When this land is at peace again, perhaps Alaric will swear to the Compact after all. I don't like my future subjects being bombed out of their homes, and down where they spread bonewater dust last year I hear the midwives report children being born without arms or legs or eyes, cleft palates, backbone sticking through the skin at their butts, things you don't see twice in a year and there are *dozens* of them—got to be some connection! And men and women dying of thinned blood—and the worst of it is, it's *still* dangerous to ride there. I suspect the land will be blasted for years, maybe a generation or two! There's too much sorcery about!"

How, Paul wondered, had they managed, by mind-power, to make radioactive dust? For what Bard had described was certainly some kind of radiation product. Well, if *laran* could do the other things he knew it could do, it should be no very great trick to break down molecules into their component atoms, or to combine them into heavy radioactive elements.

He said wryly, "And to *that* kind of *laran* I should certainly not be immune!"

"No, I shouldn't think so. Your mind may be immune, but your body's no different from anyone else's. But there are kinds of *laran* to which you would be immune and I'm not; and so I have a task for you. Serrais' main strength is broken. I heard today that the Aillards, after the bombing of Hali, have sworn to the Compact, which means that all those lands down south on the plains of Valeron, twelve or thirteen kingdoms in all, will be ready for the taking. And so I have a task for you."

He frowned, staring at the floor. "I want you to go to the Lake of Silence and bring back Carlina. It is guarded by sorcery, but you won't mind that. You can get through their defenses and ignore their illusions, and kidnap her, and bring her here."

Paul asked, "Who is Carlina?" But he knew the answer before Bard spoke it.

"My wife."

CHAPTER FOUR

Dawn was breaking over the Lake of Silence, and on the Holy Isle a long procession of women, each robed in black, each with a dark mantle covering her head and the sickle-shaped knife of the priestess hanging from her girdle, wound slowly down along the shore, from the beehive-shaped temple toward the houses where they dwelt.

The priestess Liriel, who had, in the world, been known as Carlina, daughter of King Ardrin, walked silently among them, a part of her mind still hearing the morning prayer;

"Thy night, Mother Avarra, gives way unto dawn and brightness of day. But unto thy darkness, O Mother, all things must one day return. As we do thy works of mercy in the light let us never forget that all light must vanish and only thy darkness remain at last. . . ."

But as they turned into the large wattle-and-daub building which was the dining hall of the priestesses, Carlina's mind turned to other things; for it was her turn to help in the hall. She hung her heavy dark mantle on a hook in the hallway and went into the big dark kitchen, where she wrapped herself in a big white pinafore apron, covering her black skirt and tunic, tied up her head in a white towel and fell to dishing up the porridge which had simmered all night in a big kettle over the fire. When all the porridge had been ladled into wooden bowls, she sliced long loaves of bread and set them out on a wooden tray, filled the small crocks with butter and honey which were placed at intervals along the breakfast table, and as the benches filled with black-clad forms, passed among them, pouring from pitchers of cold milk or hot bark tea. At breakfast talking was permitted, though the other meals were taken in the silence of meditation. The tables were loud with chattering and cheerful laughter, a daily respite from the solemnity imposed at most times upon the priestesses. They giggled and gossiped as any group of women might do anywhere in the kingdoms. Carlina finally finished serving and took her appointed place.

"—But there is a new king in Marenji now," said one of the sisters at her left, speaking to a third, "—and it is not enough that they have to pay tribute to the king, but they have summoned every able-bodied man who can bear arms to fight against the Hasturs in the Lord General's army. King Alaric is only a boy, they say, but the commander of his armies was once a famous bandit they called the Kilghard Wolf, and now he's the Lord General. They say he's a terror; he's conquered Hammerfell and Sain Scarp, and the woman who came to bring leather for shoe soles, *she* told me that Serrais has fallen to him too. And now that he's marching on the plains of Valeron, he'll have all the Hundred Kingdoms raised against the Hasturs—"

"That seems to me impiety," said Mother Luciella, who was—they said—old enough to remember the reign of the old Hastur kings. "Who is this Lord General? Is he not of the Hastur kindred at all?"

"No. They say he's sworn to take the kingdom right out of Hastur hands," said the first speaker, "and all the Hundred Kingdoms. He's the king's half-brother, and he's the real ruler, whoever sits on the throne! Sister Liriel," appealed the priestess, "didn't you come from the court of Asturias? Do you know who this man could be, the one they call the Kilghard Wolf?"

Carlina was surprised into an unwary "yes," before she recalled herself and said severely, "You know better than that, Sister Anya. Whatever I was before this, now I am only Sister Liriel, priestess of the Dark Mother."

"Don't be that way," sulked Anya. "I thought you would be interested in news of your homeland, that perhaps you knew this general!"

It must be Bard, Carlina thought. *There is no one else it could be.* Aloud she said fiercely, "I have now no homeland but the Holy Isle," and dug her spoon fiercely into her porridge.

. . . No. She had now no interest in what went on in the

world beyond the Lake of Silence. She was no more, now, than priestess of Avarra, content to remain so for life.

"You may say so," said Sister Anya, "but when those armed men came against the island half a year ago, it was for you they asked, and by your old name. Do you think Mother Ellinen did not know that once you were called Carlina?"

The sound of the name rubbed raw on already lacerated nerves. Carlina, Sister Liriel, rose angrily. "You know well that it is forbidden to speak the worldly name of anyone who has sought refuge here and been accepted under the mantle of the Mother! You have broken a rule of the temple. Now, as your senior, I command you to do appropriate penance!"

Anya stared at her, round-eyed. Before Carlina's anger she dropped her head, then got out of her seat, kneeling on the cobblestone floor. "I humbly ask your pardon before us all, my sister. And I sentence myself to a half-day digging out the grass around the stones on the temple pathway, with no noon meal but bread and water. Will this suffice?"

Carlina knelt beside her. She said, "It is too harsh. Eat your proper food, little sister, and I will myself help you in digging the stones when I have done with my duties in the House of the Sick, for I was guilty, too, of losing my temper. But in the name of the Goddess, dear sister, I implore you, let the past be hidden under her mantle, and speak that name never again."

"Be it so," said Anya, rising, and she gathered up her porridge bowl and cup, carrying them to the kitchen.

Carlina, following with her own, tried self-consciously to smooth away the frown she could feel between her brows. The sound of the name she had laid aside—forever, she had hoped—had disturbed her more than she wanted to say, aroused emotions long since put aside. She had found peace here, companionship, useful work. Here she was happy. She had not, really, been troubled or frightened when Bard had come here with armed men; she had trusted in Avarra to protect her, and she was confident that the protection would hold true as it had done then. Her sisters would protect her; and the spells they had laid on the waters of the lake.

No, she had not been afraid. Let Bard seize all Asturias, all the Hundred Kingdoms, it was nothing to her, he was gone from her mind and from any meaning he might ever have had for her. She had been a young girl then; now she was a woman, a priestess of Avarra, and she was safe within the walls of her chosen place.

Sister Anya had gone to do the hard work on the stones of the path, which must be done but which could not be assigned to anyone and must wait until such time as someone saw fit to volunteer as penance for a broken rule or some real or fancied imperfection of conduct. Or, occasionally, as an outlet for superfluous energies. Carlina knew that she would welcome the hard physical work of pulling out the tightly knotted grass which was shifting the stones of the path, losing her anxieties in the strenuous and sweaty task of lifting and changing the stones and clearing the grass and thorns. But she was not yet free to seek that mind-soothing monotony; it was her day to tend the sick. She took off the pinafore and towel, laid her crockery for the young novices to wash, and went to her allotted work.

In the years since she had come to the Island of Silence, she had learned much of healing, and now was ranked as one of the most skillful healer-priestesses of the second rank. One day, she knew, she would be among the best, those entrusted with the training of others. It was only her youth which kept her, now, from that post. This was not vanity, it was merely a realistic awareness of the skills she had learned since she had come here, skills of which she had had no idea at home in Asturias, for no one at the court had ever troubled to coax them forth and teach their use.

First there was the minor routine of every day. A novice had burned her hand on the porridge kettle. Carlina dressed the burn with oil and gauze and gave her a little lecture about being mindful of what she was doing when she handled hot things. "Meditation is all very well," she said severely, "but when you are handling hot vessels over the fire, that is not the time for prayerful contemplation. Your body belongs to the Goddess; it is your business to care for it as her property. Do you understand, Lori?" She brewed tea for one of the Mothers who suffered from headache and a young novice who was suffering from cramps, went to pay a visit to one of the very old priestesses who was slipping away mindlessly into a calm, painless death—she could do little for her except to stroke her hand, for the old woman could no longer see or recognize her—and gave some liniment to a priestess who worked in the dairy and had been stepped on by the clumsy foot of a dairy animal.

"Rub it with this, sister, and in future remember, the beast is too foolish to keep from stepping on your foot, so you must be sensible enough to keep your feet out of her way. And do not go to the dairy again for a day or two. Mother Allida will probably die today; you may sit by her and hold her hand and speak to her if she seems restless. She may grow lucid if the end is near. If she should, send at once for Mother Ellinen."

Then she went to the Stranger's House, where, twice in a tenday, she had been given the task of first seeing the sick who came to ask help of the priestesses of Avarra, usually after the village healer-women had failed to help them.

Three women sat silently on a bench. She beckoned the first into a small inner room.

"In the name of the Mother Avarra, how may I help you, my sister?"

"In the name of Avarra," said the woman—she was a small, pretty, rather faded-looking woman—"I have been married for seven years and have never once conceived a child. My husband loves me, and he would have accepted this as the will of the gods, but his mother and father—we live on their land—have threatened to make him divorce me and take a fertile wife. I—I—" she broke down, stammering. "I have offered to foster and adopt any child he might father by another woman, but his family want him married to a woman who will give him many children. And I—I love him," she said, and was silent.

Carlina asked quietly, "Do you truly want children? Or do you look on them as your duty to your husband, a way to keep his love and attention?"

"Both," said the woman, furtively wiping her eyes on the edge of her veil. Carlina, her *laran* awareness tuned high enough to hear the overtones in the answer, could *feel* the woman's sincerity as she said, weeping, "I told him that I would foster his sons by any other woman he chose. We have his sister's baby to foster, and I have found that I love little children. . . . I see the other women with their children at their breasts and I want my own, oh, I want my own. You who are vowed to chastity, you can't know what it is like to see other women with their babies and know you will never have one of your own—I have my fosterling to love, but I want to bear one too, and I want to stay with Mikhail. . . ."

Carlina considered for a moment, then said, "I will see what I can do to help you." She made the woman lie on a long table. The woman looked at her apprehensively, and Carlina, still attuned to her, was aware that she had suffered the painful ministrations of midwives who had tried to help her.

"I will not hurt you," Carlina said, "nor even touch you; but you must be very quiet and calm or I can do nothing." Taking her starstone from about her neck, she let the awareness sink deep into the body, finding after a time the blockage which had prevented conception; and she let herself descend, in that consciousness, into nerves, tissues, almost cell by cell unblocking the damage.

Then she gestured to the woman to sit up.

"I can promise nothing," she said, "but there is now no reason you should *not* bear a child. You say your husband has fathered children for others? Then, within a year, you should have conceived yours." The woman began to pour out thanks, but Carlina stopped her.

"Give no thanks to me, but to the Mother Avarra," she said, "and when you are an old woman, never speak cruel words to a barren woman, or punish her for her barrenness. It may not be her fault."

She was glad, as she saw the woman go away, that she had actually found a physical blockage. When there was nothing to be found she must assume either that the woman did not really want a child and, with *laran* she was not aware she had, was blocking conception—or that the woman's husband was sterile. Few women—and fewer men—could believe that a virile man could be sterile. A few generations ago, when marriage had been a group affair and women as a matter of course bore children to different men, it had been simple; a matter of simply encouraging a shy or timid woman to lie with two or three other than her own husband, perhaps at Festival, so that the woman could sincerely believe that the child was fathered by the one she had chosen. But now, when inheritance of property rested so firmly on literal fatherhood, she had the unpalatable choice of counseling a woman to accept her barrenness, or take a lover and risk her husband's anger. The old way, she thought, had made more sense.

The second woman, also, was concerned with fertility—

which did not surprise Carlina, for it was to the Goddess that women usually came for this.

"We have three daughters, but all our sons died except the last," the woman said, "and my husband is angry with me, for I have had no children for five years, and he calls me worthless. . . ."

The old story, Carlina thought, and asked her, "Tell me, do you really want another child?"

"If my husband were content, I would be content too," said the woman, shakily, "for I have borne eight children, and four still live, and our son is healthy and well and already six years old. And our eldest daughter is already old enough to marry. But I cannot bear his anger. . . ."

Carlina said sternly, "You must say to him that it is the will of Avarra; and he must thank her mercy that a single son was spared to you. He must rejoice in the children he has, for it is not you who denies him children, but the Mother herself who has said to you that you have done your part in bearing so many children."

The woman could not conceal the relief in her eyes. "But he will be very angry and perhaps he will beat me—"

"If he does," said Carlina, and she could not conceal a smile, "I tell you in the name of Avarra to pick up a log of wood from the fire and hit him over the head with it; and while you are at it, hit him for me too." She added, more seriously, "And remind him, too, that the gods punish impiety. He must accept the blessings he has been given and not be greedy for more."

The woman thanked her, and Carlina thought, dazed, *Merciful Mother of All! Eight children, and she was willing to consider having more?*

The last woman was in her fifties, and when she was summoned into the little room told Carlina timidly that she had begun to bleed again when the time for such things was many years past. She was thin and sallow and had a bad color, and for the first time, Carlina, after asking many questions, examined her physically as well as with the starstone. Then she said, "I have not the skill to treat this myself; you must come again in a tenday to speak with one of the Mothers. Meanwhile, drink this tea—" she gave her a packet. "It will ease the pain and lessen the bleeding. Try to eat well and put on some flesh so you will have the strength to endure any treatment which she may feel is needed."

The woman went away, clutching her packet of herb tea, and Carlina sat sighing, thinking of what probably lay ahead. Neutering might save the woman; only the most skilled could decide whether it was worth it, or would only prolong suffering. If not, the Chief Priestess would give her another packet of tea, but this one would contain a slow poison which would give her death before the pain robbed her of humanity and dignity. She hated this sentence; but Avarra's mercy included easing the death of those for whom death was, in any case, inevitable. All the afternoon, while she labored at Anya's side with the tough grass and twisted thorns which had dislodged the stones of the pathway to the temple, she thought of them, the women she had sent away, content, the one she could not help. Shortly before the service at sunset, she was sent for again by the Mother Ellinen.

"Mother Amalie has had a seeing," she told Carlina, "that we shall need more protection. We will be invaded again. And I foresee it will be for your sake that they will come against us." She patted Carlina's hand. "I know it is not your fault, Sister Liriel. Evil dwells in the world, by the will of the gods, but the Mother will protect us."

I hope so, Carlina thought, trembling. *I hope so, indeed.*

But it seemed, in the far distance, that she could hear Bard speak her name, and hear the threat he had made.

Wherever you go, wherever you may try to hide from me, Carlina, I will have you, whether you will or no. . . .

"Carlina," Bard repeated, "my wife. And I cannot reach the Isle of Silence. But you can, you are immune to illusions, unless you pick them up from another mind you can read, and there are not many you can read. You can reach the Island of Silence and bring Carlina back to me. But make no mistake," he warned, "I know that we want the same women, and I have given you Melisendra. But I swear to you, if you lay so much as the tip of your finger upon Carlina, I will kill you. Carlina is mine, and wherever she may be hiding I will have her!"

And now Paul stood, surveying the quiet waters of the Lake of Silence. Hidden in the reeds, he had studied the ferry-boat on a rope by which it could be hauled over from either side, even though it took, laden, some rowing to steer it across. He could kill the old ferrywoman; but he had observed that two women rowed over, morning and night, to bring her food and a jug of wine. And they might notice her absence. After much thought, when she rowed the priestesses back to the isle, he sneaked into her hut and spiked the wine with a powerful, strong, colorless spirit. It would make her far too drunk to know what was going on, and if the priestesses found her drunk, she could say no more than that she had drunk her usual ration of wine and it had for some reason affected her. By the time they suspected she had been drugged it would be too late to do anything about it. Whereas if they should find her dead, or even unconscious, or bound and gagged, the first thing they would suspect was that there was an intruder on the island.

So he waited until she came back from returning the two priestesses, and sat down in front of her little dwelling to eat and drink. She ate heartily of the bread and fruit they had left, washing it down with thirsty draughts of the wine, and as he had foreseen, she quickly grew dizzy and staggered inside to lie down on her bed. Soon she was snoring in a heavy drunken stupor. Paul nodded, approving. Now, even if they sensed, psychically, that she was stupidly drunk, they could not be alarmed. She was, after all, an elderly woman who could not be expected to carry her wine like a young person.

He stepped into the boat and rowed quietly across the Lake, struck by the eerie silence of the water and the dark reeds. Bard had told him—briefly—of the spell put on the boat. He found the Lake depressing, and once or twice, briefly, he felt dizzy, with the curious feeling that he was rowing the wrong way, but he looked at the shore and the low line of the island against the water and rowed on. Paul had read in Bard's mind the terror he had known. Even for Carlina Bard had no wish to face it again, far less to set foot on the shores where, it was said, any man who set foot must die. He felt growing oppression, a mounting sense of doom, but he had been warned against that and it did not frighten him unduly. If he had been a man of this world, vulnerable to their spells and illusions, he supposed he would now have been gibbering in terror. Considering what he had read in Bard's mind and Melisendra's, Paul was glad for his own immunity.

The boat scraped on the island's shore where, so Paul had

been told, no man had set foot for more generations than could be counted. He had no sense of awe—what were their religious taboos to him? He himself had always considered religions something priests had invented to control others and support themselves in idleness. But accumulated custom could have its own force and Paul was not at all eager to face *that*.

A well-trodden path, lined with sparse shrubbery, led upward from the beach. Paul skirted it, keeping in the shadow of the trees, and hid behind the projecting curve of some building as a pair of women came down to the path. They wore dark dresses and had sharp, curved little knives hanging in their belts; and to Paul they looked formidable, hardly like women at all, with their gaunt, strong-chinned faces and big rough hands and shapeless garb that showed nothing of feminine curves. They scared him. He had no desire whatever to be seen by them, or to see any more of them than he had to. A scrap of memory flickered through his mind, that it had always been death to spy on women's mysteries and for that reason all sensible societies had always outlawed women's mysteries.

"I thought I heard the boat," one of them said.

"Oh, no, Sister Casilda. Look, the boat is on the shore over there," said the second, and Paul was glad that he had sent it back on the rope. The second woman was a hearty, double-chinned old matron and he wondered why she was here—he would have expected her to be somewhere terrifying her grown daughters and daughters-in-law and putting the fear of God into her grandchildren. He could imagine virgin priestesses as neurotic and beautiful young maidens, but solid, chunky, capable grandmother types? Somehow it caused his head to spin.

"But where is Gwennifer?" asked the scrawny Sister Casilda, and she reached up to the high pole anchoring the boat's rope. She struck the bell, hard, with the handle of her little knife. But there was neither sound nor movement on the opposite shore. "It is not like her to sleep at her post. I wonder if she is ill?"

"More likely," scoffed a third woman who had not spoken till now, "she has drunk all her two days' ration of wine at once and is lying there sodden drunk!"

"And if she is, it is not a capital crime," said the first

woman. "Still, I feel I should pull the boat back and go over. She may be lying there ill and untended, or she has fallen and broken a bone as old women can do all too easily. She might lie there for days until the next pilgrims come!"

"If that should happen, indeed I would never forgive myself," agreed the other, and they pulled down the rope and began to haul the boat ashore, got into it and began rowing across. Paul stole up the shore, glad that he had not injured the old ferrywoman. She would indeed be found lying there spectacularly drunk, but there was no evidence left that she had been harmed, or that anyone had come anywhere near her. In fact, he had *not* harmed the old lady—he had simply given her a pleasant drunk, and from the way the women talked, it was not the first time it had happened anyhow that she should get drunk and sleep at her post.

His spine prickled with dread—if he had followed his first impulse, to knock her down and tie her up before he got into the boat, an alarm would be out even now that an intruder was loose on the island.

He had assured himself that none of those women was the one he wanted. Bard had shown him a portrait of Carlina, first warning him that it was very much romanticized and had in any case been taken seven years ago; but he felt certain he would recognize Carlina when he saw her. And along with this he felt a certain grim dread. He and Bard had a bad habit of wanting the same women. But Bard had made it very clear: *this* one he could not have. He had read enough of Bard's thoughts to know that Carlina could, for a time at least, drive all thoughts of any other woman from him. It was something Paul had never sensed in Bard before: he was *obsessed* with Carlina, not so much the physical woman, but the *idea* of her.

God Almighty, Paul thought, *suppose when I set eyes on Carlina she has that effect on me and I can't resist her!*

Well, it would only mean that the inevitable confrontation with Bard would come a little sooner, that was all.

If he could deceive the girl into thinking that he *was* Bard— would that make it easier? Or did she hate and fear Bard as Melisendra had come to hate and fear him? The way Bard spoke, they had been childhood sweethearts, handfasted, separated by the old king's cruelty. But if she were as eager to join him as that indicated, what was she doing hiding here among the priestesses of Avarra?

He could pass himself off as Bard except to someone like Melisendra, who knew every nuance of Bard's behavior. But Carlina had no intimate experience of Bard. Paul knew from the mind of his double that the closest contact Bard had had with Carlina was a couple of chaste kisses—from which, in any case, the girl had shrunk away. If he could get Carlina to accept him as Bard, then the original of that name could be put quietly out of the way, and he would have freedom, and a kingdom. . . .

But he would not have the one thing that had made this world worthwhile to him. If he played Melisendra false, she would have no reason not to expose him. And in any case, he must be more like Bard than he had thought. The business of ruling a kingdom seemed dull to him. Unlike Bard, he had no taste for war for its own sake, though he seemed to share Bard's talent for it. War, to Paul, was simply the necessary prelude to an orderly state of affairs where things could be put in order, and he would be deadly bored with ruling over a kingdom once set in order. What did he want, then? Oddly enough, he'd never stopped to think about that, nor had Bard, sure that Paul, being his double, shared his goals, cared to ask him.

Well, he thought, *if I were free I'd like to take Melisendra and go off somewhere exploring. There's a lot to see here. Maybe, someday, settle down and have kids and raise them. And horses; I like horses. A place where things would make sense to me, and I wouldn't get into the kind of trouble that got me into the stasis box in the first place. A world where I wouldn't always be running up against impossible rules and regulations.*

It was a shame, really, that it couldn't end that way. Bard was welcome to the damned kingdom. All hundred of them, for that matter. Maybe he could convince Bard that he meant it—hell, why shouldn't he, they could read each other's minds; Bard would have to believe him! And if he had Carlina, he wouldn't want Melisendra. Erlend, maybe, but not Melisendra.

Only Bard would never believe that while Paul lived he could be safe. Perhaps he should make Carlina his ally at once; he'd never thought he'd stoop to making friends with a woman! Women were for one thing, and one thing *only*. But that wasn't how he felt about Melisendra. Somehow she had became his friend, too.

A crackle of bushes and steps on the path recalled him to his danger, and he slid into the shadow of the shrubbery again. Three women were coming along the path, and Paul, peering out, saw that one of them was Carlina.

She was pale and thin, and so small that she came barely up to his chest. Her hair was tied back into a long braid. She moved with the same calm, detached walk as the other priestesses, and her shapeless dress made her look clumsy. Paul stared from concealment, in shock. This—*this* was the Princess Carlina, the woman with whom Bard was so obsessed that he could think of nothing and no one else? And for this he would give up the beautiful ripeness of Melisendra, who was, moreover, the mother of his son? Melisendra was also beautiful, witty, intelligent, schooled in *laran,* and possessed of all the graces to adorn a court and become a queen, or at least a general's lady; and she had fought at Bard's side in battle. Paul had thought that he knew Bard well, but now he was shaken to the core by the knowledge that the differences lay deeper than he could have imagined.

But Bard did *not* want her, Paul thought as he watched Carlina moving away. He couldn't. He *knew* what Bard wanted. He had wanted Melisendra, till she had wounded his pride unendurably. He had wanted the round-bodied little wench they had shared after the battle. Want Carlina? Never.

He was *obsessed* with Carlina, and that was a different thing. As if Bard had told him so, he knew that what Bard wanted of Carlina was that she was King Ardrin's daughter, the reassurance that he was the king's lawful son-in-law, not an exiled outlaw desperately trying to reclaim some position, some identity.

All the more reason, Paul thought, *that I should make Carlina my ally at once . . . and yet, I could never give up Melisendra for this. Madness! Melisendra would even make a better queen.*

And yet, if Bard has Carlina, he will not contest with me for Melisendra. . . .

I must make sure, then, that Carlina is delivered into Bard's hands, and as quickly as possible. And about one thing, at least, I need not worry. It will be easy for me to keep my hands

*off her. I would not have her in my bed, not if she were thirty
times over a queen.*

A dynastic marriage with Carlina would give Bard—or
Paul in his place—a claim of his own to the throne, if the
sickly Alaric died childless—which seemed likely. Well, then,
the throne and Carlina for Bard. And for Paul—freedom and
Melisendra! Bard would never feel safe while he was alive—
but if he could manage to get away, preferably as soon as possible, then perhaps Bard would be too busy holding his throne
to send after them. But first, Bard must have Carlina.

The priestesses had gone along the path, and Paul stole after
them, keeping in the shadows. First one, then another went
into small houses at the side of the path. Carlina turned into
one, and after a moment, inside, he saw the tiny glow of a
lamp. Paul hid to consider. Not that he was really afraid of the
women. But there were a lot of them, and they had those
wicked little knives.

Carlina must be given no time to make an outcry. Not even
a mental one. There were sure to be other telepaths in this
place. Which meant—he considered it coldly—that he must
knock her down and render her completely unconscious with
one blow before she saw him or was alarmed at the idea of an
intruder. And he must have her well away from the island before she saw his face.

He slipped noiselessly through the door. Humming a tune to
herself, she stood trimming the tiny wick of the little lamp.
Then she took off her black mantle, hung it over a rod, and
reached up to unfasten her braids. He did not want to wait
while she undressed; in this cold he could not take her far without clothing, and he knew he could not put clothes back on her
limp body. He slid from his place of concealment and struck
one hard blow, watching her crumple soundlessly to the floor.
He was shocked, unaccustomed as yet to what little *laran* he
had, to the sudden *nothingness* where, a moment ago, there
had been a presence. Suddenly afraid, he bent to reassure himself that she was breathing. She was. He bundled her limp
body into the black cloak, wadding a couple of extra folds over
her nose and mouth. She could breathe, but the cloak would
stifle any outcry, though, if she woke and felt fear, the alarm
would be out and the hunt up within moments. He carried her
out, kicked the door shut behind him. Now came the one real
risk of the whole performance. If someone should see him

now, he would probably never get off the island alive. He carried her swiftly down the path to the boat and hauled it over. Half an hour later he was riding away from the Island of Silence, Carlina's limp body trussed across the back of his pack beast. He had made her as comfortable as he could, but he wanted to put as much distance as possible between himself and the island, as quickly as he could. With luck, they might not miss her till morning; and he had seen no riding horses on the island at all. But sooner or later she would recover consciousness and make some form of telepathic outcry. And he wanted to be far enough away, by then, so that it would make no difference.

She seemed still unconscious when he reached the place in the hills where he had left the escort. His men were ready saddled, with a horse-litter standing by.

He motioned to them. "Mount and get ready to ride. Have you got a fresh horse for me? Yes, and extra horses for the litter, so we won't have to stop anywhere for post horses." He dismounted, lifted the unconscious bundle that was Carlina into the litter, and closed the curtains.

"Let's go!"

The sun was rising when they stopped to breathe the horses. Paul dismounted, swallowed a bit of food—there was no time to stop and cook a meal—then went and thrust aside the curtains of the litter.

Carlina was conscious. She had gotten the gag out of her mouth. She was lying on her side, silently and desperately struggling to tear loose the knots around her hands.

"Do they hurt you, my lady? I will loosen them if you like," Paul said.

At the sound of his voice she shrank away.

"Bard," she said. "I should have known it was you. Who else would be impious enough to brave the wrath of Avarra!"

"I do not fear any Goddess," he said truthfully.

"That I can well believe, Bard mac Fianna. But you will not dare her with impunity."

"As for that," Paul said, "I do not intend to debate the matter. Your Goddess, if she exists, did not intervene to protect you from being taken from the island. And I do not think she will protect you now. If the thought that she will punish me comforts you, I do not begrudge you that comfort. I came only to say that if you are weary of those bonds, I will loosen them; you need only give me your word of honor not to escape."

She glared at him with implacable defiance. "I will certainly escape if I can."

Damn the woman, Paul thought with exasperation, *doesn't she know when she's beaten?* With an unfamiliar feeling he did not recognize as guilt, he realized that he did not want to hurt her, or even to tie her up more tightly. With a curse, he thrust the curtains together and strode away.

CHAPTER FIVE

Bard had had another unwelcome piece of news as he rode back toward Castle Asturias: his second-in-command had come to him and told him that three days after the battle all the mercenaries of the Sisterhood of the Sword had come to the officer, demanded what pay was owing to them, and left the camp.

Bard stared. "I paid them generously, and what is more, I put them under my personal protection," he said in outrage. "Did they give any reason?"

"Yes. They said that your men had raped the women prisoners of war, and you had not punished them," the officer said. "To tell you the truth, Lord General, I think we're well rid of them. There is something about them that makes me uneasy. They're—" he hesitated, thought it over a minute, and said, "obsessed, that's what it is. Tell you what, my lord, you remember when we rode against the Island of Silence, and that old witch there who cursed us? Those damned Sword Sisters make me think of *her,* them and their Goddess!"

Bard scowled. Mention of the Island of Silence made him realize that Paul should have returned by now. Unless the curse of the island, and of Avarra had caught Paul too. His officer misread the scowl and thought he was angry at having that defeat mentioned; he stared uneasily at the floor. "I never thought a batch of women would drive us off that way, Lord General. They're all mad there, them and their Goddess alike, see? It's unlucky to have anything to do with them, and if you'll take my advice, sir, you won't have anything to do with the Sisterhood either. Did you know? They ransomed the prisoners of

war, the women of the Sisterhood, that is, and took them along
with them. They said they ought to have known they were both
fighting on the same side, they ought never to have taken up
arms against their sisters—some rubbish like that. Crazy, they
are, sir. Glad to see them gone."

"They didn't kill the prisoners themselves? I heard that if a
woman of the Sisterhood is raped her sisters hunt her down
and kill her if she doesn't kill herself."

"Kill them? No, sir, the guards heard them all crying together in the tents. And they gave them back their weapons and
put decent clothes on 'em—the soldiers tore their own clothes
off, you remember—and gave them horses, and they all rode
off together. I tell you, you can't trust women like that, no
sense of loyalty, see?"

When he arrived at Castle Asturias, he sent word to his father and to his brother, King Alaric, that he had arrived, and as
he gave his horse to the grooms, he noticed the horse Paul had
ridden to the Lake of Silence standing in the yard. He went in,
hurrying to the presence chamber. His father met and embraced him, and Alaric hobbled toward him, holding him in a
kinsman's embrace.

"Bard, your lady is here. The Princess Carlina."

He had known this, but he was surprised to hear that Alaric
and his father knew.

"She is?" he asked numbly.

"She came in a horse-litter a little while ago; your paxman
Paolo Harryl escorted her here," Alaric said. "But I still think
you should marry Melisendra, Bard. Erlend's too good a son to
you to be a *nedestro*. When I am crowned king, I shall give
him a patent of legitimacy. Then he will be your son whether
you marry Melisendra or not!"

"She is in her old rooms?"

"What else," Alaric said, staring. "I gave orders she should
be taken to them and should have women to wait on her and
bathe her and so forth. She had been riding all day in a horse-
litter, she must have been tired and dirty."

Was it possible, Bard wondered, that Carlina had come
willingly?

Alaric went on, "Paolo said she was too tired and too travel-
worn to see anyone, but that I should send waiting-women to
look after her. She is King Ardrin's daughter, and your wife.
When you have the *catenas* ceremony, I will perform it, if you

wish, it is supposed to be an honor if the king performs the wedding."

Bard thanked his brother and asked leave to withdraw. Alaric's smile was childish.

"You don't have to ask me, Bard. I keep forgetting I'm the king and have to give people permission to go and come, even Father, isn't it foolish?"

He had been assigned rooms near Carlina's old rooms. When he came into them, Paul was waiting for him.

"I gather," Bard said dryly, "that you had success on your mission. Did she come willingly?"

Paul shook his head ruefully, indicating a long scratch on his cheek. "The first night I was unwise enough to let her go— to loosen her bonds for a few minutes so that she could relieve herself. That was the only time I made *that* mistake. Fortunately, none of the men were from Asturias, or knew who the lady was. They were all mercenaries from Hammerfell and Aldaran, and most of them couldn't speak her language. But when she saw where I had brought her—to her own home— she gave me her word of honor not to try to escape tonight. I thought it would be too humiliating for the lady to come into her own home tied hand and foot like a sack of washing, so I accepted it. And the king sent ladies to wait on her. I imagine you'll find her pretty tame—I didn't touch her, except when I had to knock her out—I didn't put a hand on her until she scratched me. Even then, I just bundled her up like a sack of beans and dumped her back into the litter. No more force than absolutely necessary, I promise you that."

"Oh, I believe you," Bard said. "So where is she now?"

"In her own rooms; and by tomorrow, I suppose, you can talk her out of wanting to go, or put a guard on her yourself," Paul said. He wondered if it was the right time to talk about Melisendra to Bard, and decided it probably wasn't.

Bard went and called his body servant, had himself shaved and dressed. He'd give Carlina a little time to rest from the long arduous journey, and make herself pretty. He was hoping against hope that Carlina would welcome him, resigned to their marriage. Of course she had struggled when she was abducted, but when she found herself in her own home, she had been willing to give her parole. Surely, that meant she knew she had nothing to fear. Certainly, Carlie knew he wouldn't hurt a hair of her head. After all, she was his wife, by all the laws of the gods and of the Hundred Kingdoms!

A guard before her door came to attention as Bard approached, and Bard, returning the man's salute, wondered if Paul had doubted the validity of Carlina's parole. But why? Probably Carlina, being carried off so suddenly without a word, had feared that she was being kidnapped; held for ransom, or forced into a marriage of state with someone. Surely her parole meant she was glad to find herself safe at home?

He found Carlina in one of the inner rooms, lying across a bed, sleeping. She was pale and looked like a schoolgirl, wearing some sort of dark plain robe; she had pulled a thick, graceless black mantle around herself like a blanket. Her eyes were red, against the ivory paleness of her face. He had never been able to endure Carlina's tears. After a moment her eyes opened and she looked up at him, her face contracting in fear. She sat bolt upright, and clutched the black mantle around her body.

"Bard," she said, blinking. "Yes. It is really you this time, isn't it? Who was the other man—one of your bastard kin from the Hellers? You will not hurt me, will you, Bard? After all, we were children together, playmates."

He heard her long sigh, like an explosion of relief. He said, fastening on an irrelevancy, "How did you know?"

"Oh, you are certainly very much alike," she said. "Even your voices; but I scratched his face to the bone, thinking it was you. If he was only your witless tool, perhaps I owe *him* an apology."

He went back to what she had said before. "Certainly I would never hurt you, Carlie. After all, you are my wife, and even now, the King of Asturias waits to join us with the *catenas*. Would tonight suit you, or would you rather wait until some of your kinsmen and kinswomen can be summoned?"

"Neither tonight nor any other time," Carlina said, and her hands were white as skeleton joints against the black mantle. "I have sworn an oath to the priestesses of Avarra, and to the Mother, that I will devote my life to prayer, in chastity. I belong to Avarra, not to you."

Bard's face hardened. He said, "Who is false to a first oath will be false also to the second. Before ever you gave oath to Avarra you and I were handfasted before all men."

"But not married," Carlina retorted, "and a handfasting can

be broken, being unconsummated! You have no more right to me than—than—than that guard out there in the hall!"

"That's a matter of opinion. Your father gave you to me—"

"And took me back at your exile!"

"I do not accept his right to do so."

"And I did not accept his right to give me to you without my consent in the first place, so we are even," Carlina flung back at him, her eyes blazing.

Bard thought that she looked more beautiful than he had ever seen her, color high in her cheeks, her eyes bright with wrath. Women had defied or refused him before this, but he had never waited nearly so long for any one of them. Now the time of waiting was over. She would not leave this suite until she was his wife in fact, as she had really been all these years. He was excited by her nearness, and by the element of challenge in her voice and her eyes. Even Melisendra had not resisted him this way. No woman had ever been able to resist him, except Melora, and she—angrily, he banished the thought of Melora. She meant nothing to him. She was gone.

"Bard, I cannot believe you could harm me. We were children together. I bear you no ill will; let me go back to the island, and to the Mother, and I will intercede with them so that there shall be no punishment and no curse."

He snapped his fingers. "I do not care *that* much for any curses, whether of Avarra or any other spook!"

Carlina made a horrified, pious gesture. "I beg you not to speak such blasphemies! Bard, send me back to the island."

He shook his head. "No. Whatever happens, that is over. You belong here, with me. I call upon you to carry out your duty to me, and become my wife tonight."

"No. Never." Her eyes filled with tears. "Oh, Bard, I don't hate you. You were my foster brother, with Geremy and poor Beltran! We were all children together, and you were always kind to me. Be kind to me now, and don't insist on this. There are so many women you could have, ladies of high degree, *leroni,* beautiful women—there is Melisendra, who is the mother of your son, and a fine little boy he is—why do you want *me,* Bard?"

He looked straight into her eyes and told her the literal truth.

"I don't know. But there is never any woman I have wanted as I want you. You are my wife and I will have you."

"Bard—" her face paled. "No. Please."

He said, "You managed to break the handfasting by a trick, because it had not been consummated, and you will not trick me that way again. You will do your duty to me, willing or unwilling, Carlina."

"Are you saying that you are intending to rape me?"

He sat on the bed beside her, reaching for her hand. "I would rather have you willing than unwilling. But one way or another, I will have you, Carlie, so you must resign yourself to it."

She snatched her hand out of his reach and flung herself down, as far away from him as she could, pulling the heavy mantle around her, and he could hear her sobbing in its shelter. He pulled the heavy mantle off her, though she clung to it, and flung it angrily to the floor. He could not bear to see Carlina cry. He had never been able to endure her tears, even when she cried because a kitten had scratched her. It seemed that he could see her now, nine years old, thin as a stick, with her hair in thin plaits like black ropes, sucking her scratched thumb and weeping.

"Damn it, stop crying, Carlie! I can't stand to see you cry! Do you think I could ever hurt you? I don't *want* to hurt you, but I have to make sure you can't get away from me on that pretense again. You won't be angry with me afterward, that I promise you. No woman has ever minded, *afterward*."

"Do you really believe that, Bard?"

He didn't bother to answer that. He didn't believe it, he *knew* it. Women had all kinds of excuses to keep them from doing what they wanted to do anyway. He remembered Lisarda, wretched little slut, she hadn't minded afterward, either, she'd loved it! But women weren't brought up to be honest about these things. Instead of answering, he bent over her and pulled her into his arms; but she struggled away, fighting, and her nails ripped down his cheek.

"Damn you, Bard, now you have one to match your pax-man, and you're no better than he is!"

His helpless frustration turned to anger; he grabbed her hands roughly, holding them both in one of his own.

"Stop it, Carlie! I don't want to hurt you, you are *forcing* me to hurt you!"

"You always justify yourself, don't you?" she flared at him, raging. "Why should I make this easy for you?"

"Carlie, there's no way you can talk me, or trick me, or persuade me out of this. I am going to have you and that is all there is to it, and while I don't want to hurt you, I'll do whatever I have to to keep you quiet. I let you escape me before and all my troubles came from that. If Geremy hadn't come interfering, that Festival, you'd be my wife and we'd have lived happy all these years; Beltran would still be alive—"

"Do you dare to blame me for that?"

"I blame you for everything that has happened to me since I let you refuse me," he said, angry now, "but I am willing still to take you as my wife, and this is your chance to make amends!"

"Amends? You must be quite mad, Bard!"

"You owe me this, at least! Now if you will be sensible and not struggle so foolishly, it could be as pleasant for you as for me, and that's the way I'd rather have it. But whether or no, I'm stronger than you are, and if you're sensible you'll know there's no use whatever in fighting me. Here—" He pulled at her shawl. "Let's have these clothes off."

"No!" Her voice was frantic; she backed away in terror. Bard set his teeth. If the little cat was set on fighting, he'd stop her now. He pulled off the shawl and flung it away, grabbed the top of her tunic and tore it down all the way, pulling off the torn fabric and hurling it to the floor. The under-tunic followed, the thin cloth tearing down quickly. Her nails left scratches on his hands, and she beat and battered at his face, but he ignored her. He lifted her, still struggling, and dumped her into the center of the bed, lowered himself beside her. She kicked him, and he struck her, brutally, with his open hand. She cowered away, in her thin chemise, and began to cry.

"Carlie, my sweetheart, my love, I don't want to hurt you, there's no sense in fighting me." He tried to take her close in his arms, but she turned her head away and wept, twisting her head from his searching mouth. Infuriated by her crying, when he intended so much tenderness, he slapped her again, hard, and she stopped fighting, and lay quiet, tears pouring down her face. Damn her! It could have been so good for both of them! Why had she forced him to do this?

Enraged—and simultaneously aroused—by the way in which she was spoiling the moment he had dreamed of for years, he flung himself on her and pulled up her chemise, roughly parting her legs with his hand. She arched her body and tried to throw him off, but he pressed her roughly down. She gasped and lay still, shrinking away, sobbing. She did not struggle again, though he *knew* he was hurting her; he saw her teeth clamp hard in her lower lip and saw flecks of blood there. He tried to bend and kiss it away, but she jerked her head roughly aside, rigid as a corpse in his arms, except for the tears still flooding down her face as if only they were alive.

"Lord General—" a voice interrupted Paul as he strode along the hall. For a moment he thought Bard had suddenly turned up in the hallway nearby, then realized that he was being addressed. So he had come to look *that* much like Bard! He was about to reveal his identity, then realized that no one was supposed to know that Paolo Harryl and Bard were so much alike. He scrabbled swiftly in his mind for memory of the man's name.

"Lerrys."

The man's eyes rose to the scratch on Paul's face. "You look like you've been fighting with one of those bitches in red," he said, chuckling. "1 hope you tore her earrings right out of their holes, sir." In *casta* the phrase assumed a slight double entendre, and Paul, though the joke was a little less sophisticated than he'd have found funny in his own world, laughed companionably and didn't answer, except with a knowing grin.

"I heard they'd all deserted, sir. Going to punish them, or outlaw them, or anything? Might give the troops some fun, and it would teach women to stay in their proper place."

Paul shook his head. "Falcons don't fly after cagebirds. Let them go, and good riddance to them," he said, and went on to his own rooms, thoughtfully. As he had foreseen, Melisendra was waiting for him.

She put up her arms and kissed him, and he realized that all the way back from the Island of Silence, he had been looking forward to this moment. What had happened to him that a woman could get under his skin that way?

"How is Erlend?"

"Well enough, though I wish we could send him to safety in the country," she said, "or better, in the Tower. Although—" she paled, "after what befell Hali, I am not sure there is any safety in the Tower, or anywhere else in this land."

"Send him to the country, if you will," Paul said. "I am sure

Bard will not object; but why do you think he would not be safe here, Melisendra?"

"I have Aldaran blood," she said, hesitating, "and there is the *laran* of precognition in that line. It is not reliable—I cannot always control it. But sometimes. . . . It may be only my fear, but I have seen fire, fire in this place, and once when I looked at King Alaric I saw his face surrounded in flame. . . ."

"Oh, dearest!" Paul held her close, realizing suddenly that if anything should happen to her, nothing would be left in this world or any other that could contain light of happiness for him. What had happened to *him?*

She raised her soft hand to touch the scratch on his face, "How did you get this? It looks too small for a battle wound."

"And it is not," Paul said, "for I got it from a woman."

She smiled and said, "I never inquire what a man chooses to do when he is on campaign. I imagine you have had enough women, but can't you find willing ones? I shouldn't think, my handsome one, that anyone would refuse you."

Paul felt himself blushing, remembering the beautiful redheaded wench he and Bard had shared. God knows she had been willing enough. But she had been, at first, only comfort for the knowledge that Melisendra was not there, and later, an excuse for confrontation with Bard. "Such women as I take are willing, my love," he said, wondering why he bothered to explain this—what in the world had come over him in the last few months? "This was a captive, a woman Bard ordered me to bring to him."

That was it. I resented getting a woman for him. I'm not his damned pimp! Angrily, he identified the cause of his anger, and Melisendra, dropping into rapport with him, said, "I'm surprised at that. There are few enough women to refuse Bard. Although the Princess Carlina, I am told, fled the court, there had been some talk of marrying them when they were boy and girl." And as again she followed his thought, her small hands flew to her mouth and she stared at him.

"Carlina, in the name of the Goddess! He sent *you*—to incur the wrath of Avarra, to shift the curse to you."

"I don't think that was all his reason," Paul said, and explained that he was immune to the spells laid on the Island of Silence.

She listened, troubled, shaking her head in despair. "Any man who sets foot on the Holy Isle must die. . . ."

"First of all," Paul said, "I'm not afraid of your Goddess. I told Carlina that. And she's his wife—"

Melisendra shook her head. "No, the Goddess has claimed her. Perhaps it is through her that Avarra's vengeance will strike. Nevertheless he cannot escape it." She shuddered, her face white with horror. "I thought even Bard had had his warning, when he was driven from the island before," she whispered. "I don't hate Bard; he is the father of my son, and yet—and yet—"

She paced the floor, distracted, distressed. "And the penalty for him who rapes a priestess of Avarra . . . it is terrible! First he has incurred the enmity of the Sisterhood, who are under the protection of the Goddess, and now this."

Paul watched her, troubled. All his life he had believed that women really wished to be mastered, that in their deepest womanhood they wished to be taken, and if they did not know it, then a man was doing them no harm by showing them what they really wanted. Watching Melisendra, he had no doubt that she was capable of knowing what she wanted, and it was a new and rather disturbing idea to him. Yet Bard had taken her against her will . . . he found he did not want to follow that thought through, or he would find himself ready to kill Bard.

I don't want to kill Bard, he has somehow become a part of myself. . . .

"But what about the Sisterhood, Melisendra? They go among men; have they any right to display their womanhood and say, yes, I am here, but you can't touch? I agree that women who stay at home, protected by their men, should never be touched, but these women have forfeited this protection—"

"Do you think all women are alike? I do not know the Sisters of the Sword, although I have spoken now and again with one of them. I know very little of their ways, but if they choose to take up their swords, I do not see why they should not do so in peace—" Realizing what she had said, she giggled. "No, of course I don't mean that. But they should do so undisturbed; why should an accident of birth deprive them of the right to make war, if they prefer it to sewing cloaks and embroidering cushions and making cheese?"

"Next," Paul said, smiling at her vehemence, "you will be saying that men should have the right to spend their lives embroidering tablecloths and washing babies' breechclouts!"

"Do you doubt that some men are more fitted for it than for

war?" she demanded. "Even if they wish to put skirts about their knees, and keep at home boiling porridge for dinner! A woman, at least can marry, or be a *leronis,* or pledge to the Sisterhood and pierce her ears and take up the sword, but God help the man who wishes to be other than a soldier or a plowman or a *laranzu!* Why should a woman who takes up the sword have to fear rape, if she is defeated? I am a woman—would you see me used so?"

"No," said Paul, "I would kill any man who tried, and I would not let him die easy; but you are a woman, and they—"

"And they are women too," she interrupted him angrily. "Men do not think women are unwomanly, or subject them to rape and disasters if they must follow the plow to scratch a living for their orphaned children or herd animals in the wild. The man who rapes a solitary herdwoman or fisherwoman is everywhere scorned as a man who cannot get a woman willing! Why should only swordswomen be subject to this? When you capture a foeman, you take his weapons and force him to ransom them, in the evil old days you could keep him as your servant for a year's space, but you did not force him to lie down for you!"

"That's what Bard said," said Paul. "He said that his men should use them honorably as prisoners of war, and would have them whipped otherwise."

She said, "Truly? That is the best thing you have ever told me about Bard di Asturien. He may, as he grows older, be changing, becoming more of a man, and less of a wild wolf—"

Paul looked at her sharply. "You don't really hate him, do you, Melisendra? Even though he raped *you*—"

"Oh, my dear," she said, "that was not rape; I was willing enough, though it was true he threw a glamour over me. But I have come to know that many women lie with a man under a glamour, and sometimes they do not even know it. I hope the Goddess Avarra may forgive Bard as readily as I have forgiven him." She put her arms around him and said, "But why are we talking of him? We are together, and it is not likely that he will disturb us this night."

"No," Paul said, "I think Bard will have a great deal else to think of. Between the Lady Carlina and the wrath of Avarra, I do not think he will spare much thought for us."

*　　*　　*

Carlina had been crying for a long time; now her sobs had subsided at last, and she lay with tears just slipping down her cheeks, running out from under the swollen eyelids and soaking into the damp pillow.

"Carlina," Bard said at last, "I beg you, don't cry any more. The thing is done. I am sorry I had to hurt you, but now it will be better, and I give you my word I will never lay a rough hand on you again. For the rest of our lives, Carlie, we can live happily together, now that you can no longer refuse me."

She turned over and stared at him. Her eyes were so swollen with crying that she could hardly see him. She said, in a hoarse little voice, "Do you still believe that?"

"Of course, my beloved, my wife," he said, and reached out to take her slender hand in his, but she pulled it away.

"Avarra's mercy," he exploded, "why are women so unreasonable?"

She looked up, and a strange small smile played around the corner of her mouth. She said, "*You,* to call upon the mercy of Avarra? A day will come, Bard, when I think you will not take that oath so lightly. You have forfeited, I think, all claim to her mercy, when you had me taken from the island; and again, last night."

"Last night—" Bard shrugged. "Avarra is Lady of Birth and Death—and of the hearth fire; surely she could not be angered at a man taking his wife, who had been pledged to him before ever you swore your traitor's oath to the Goddess. And if she is a Goddess who will come between husband and wife, then I will swear to put down her worship everywhere within this kingdom."

"The Goddess is the protectress of all women, Bard, and she will punish rape."

"Do you still claim that you were raped?"

"Yes," she said implacably.

"I didn't think you minded too much. Your Goddess knows, you didn't try to fight me—"

"No," she said in a low voice, but he heard the unspoken part of that, *I was afraid.* . . . He had taken her, a second time, and she had not struggled, nor tried to fight him away, but lay quiet and passive, letting him do what he would as if she were a rag doll.

He looked at her with contempt. "No woman has ever complained of me—afterward. You will come to it too, Carlina, with time. Why can you not be honest about your feelings? All women are the same; in your hearts you desire a man who will take you, and master you, and you will one day stop fighting and acknowledge that you wanted me as much as I wanted you. But I had to make you admit it to yourself. You were too proud, Carlie. I had to break through that pride of yours before you could admit that you wanted me."

She sat up in the bed, reaching for the black cloak of Avarra.

He wrenched it away from her and threw it angrily into a corner. "Never let me see you wearing that damned thing again!"

She shrugged, standing in her torn chemise as straight and proud as if she were wearing court dress. The tears were still flooding down her face with their own life, but she brushed them impatiently away. Her voice was still and cold, even through the hoarseness of many tears. "Do you really believe that, Bard? Or is it your way to protect yourself from knowing what a cruel thing you have done, what a wretched, miserable excuse for a man you really are?"

"I am no different from any other man," he defended himself, "and you, my dear lady, no different from any other woman, except for your pride. I have even known women to kill themselves before they can admit to the man that their desires are no different from men's—but I had thought you were more honest than that, that you could admit to yourself, now that I have made it inevitable, that you had wanted me. . . ."

"That," she said, very low, "is a lie, Bard. A lie. And if you believe it, it is only because you do not dare to know what you are or what you have done."

He shrugged. "At least I know women. I have known enough of them since my fourteenth year."

She shook her head.

"You have never known anything about any woman, Bard. You have known only what you yourself wished to believe about them, and that is a very long way from the truth."

"And what in the truth?" His voice held scathing contempt.

"You ask me," she said, "but you do not dare to know, do you? Have you ever even thought of trying to find out the truth—the real truth, Bard, not the soothing lies men tell themselves so that they can live with what they are and the things they do?"

"Do you suggest I ask a woman, and listen to the lies they tell *themselves?* I tell you, all of them—yes, and you too, lady—they want to be mastered, to have their pride overcome, so that they can admit to their real desires. . . ."

She smiled, just a little. She said, "If you believe that, then, Bard, you will have no hesitation in knowing the real truth, mind to mind, so that neither can lie to the other."

"I did not know you were a *leronis,*" Bard said, "but I am sure enough of myself, lady, that if you have courage to show me your inner mind I do not fear what I will see."

Carlina touched her throat, where the starstone hung within its small leather pouch on a braided leather thong. She said, "Be it so, Bard. And Avarra have mercy on you; for I shall have no more pity than you had on me last night. Know, then, what I am—and what you are."

She unwrapped the stone, and Bard felt a faint sickness at the blueness, the little ribbons of light that curled inside.

"See," she said in a low voice. "See from inside, if you will."

For a moment nothing except distance, strangeness, and then Bard knew he was seeing himself, in memory, as Carlina had seen him when he first came to court as their foster brother; big, loutish, a clumsy boy who could not dance, over-grown, stumbling over his own feet . . . *Did she pity me, then? No more than pity?* No, he saw himself in her eyes, handsome, frightening, even a little glamorous, the big boy who fetched down her kitten from the tree—and suddenly, when she was most grateful, threatened to wring its neck, so that her gratitude was swallowed up in sudden fear, *if he would do that to a kitten, what would he do to me?* To Carlina, Bard knew, he had seemed huge, terrifying, big as the world, and when they were to be handfasted, and she had first thought of Bard as a possible husband, he felt, with her, the terrifying revulsion, big arms that would crush her, rough hands touching her, the kiss he had given her there before all, shamed and shrinking; and her anger at him when she had held Lisarda weeping in her arms, the girl not even knowing what Bard had done or why, only that she had been used, shamed, humiliated, and that she could not resist him, even through her hate and sickness at what had been done to her body and how he had made her compliant in her own rape. . . .

And then the Festival, where he had led her into the gallery

and she knew that he meant to have from her, willing or unwilling, what he had had from Lisarda; only it was worse for
her, because she *knew* what he wanted and why. . . .

*Bard does not want me, only, in his pride, he wants to lie
with the king's daughter so that he will be the king's son-in-
law; he has no identity or pride of his own, so he must have the
king's daughter for wife, to give him legitimacy. And he wants
my body . . . as he wants every woman's body he sees. . . .* Bard
felt with Carlina her physical sickness at his touch, the revulsion of his tongue thrusting into her mouth, his hands on her,
the dizzying relief when Geremy had interrupted. Through her
eyes he watched himself draw that accursed dagger on Geremy,
and heard Geremy's screams and the convulsion of agony—

"No more—" he begged aloud, but the matrix held him,
pitiless, dragging him into Carlina's shame that at one time she
had admired him, that at one time she had felt the first stirrings
of desire for him. . . . It was as if he had crushed them out with
his own hands, so that she felt nothing when she stood and
watched him, outlawed, going forth into exile; and it was as if
his hands on her had crushed out any desire ever to marry.
When Geremy's hand was offered, she had fled to the safety of
the Island of Silence, and there the peace had wiped out the
memory . . . or almost wiped it out. Bard felt he would swoon
in terror as he felt with Carlina the mortal dread of being alone,
bound and gagged . . . *helpless, wholly helpless* . . . in a horse-
litter, going in the hands of she knew not whom, toward she
knew not where. Every emotion of Carlina's thrust itself agonizingly into him, the fear of strange hands, the dread when
she had seen Bard's face—as she thought—peering hatefully
into her litter—and knew that she could expect no mercy from
his pride and ambition. He lived through the gasping struggle
when, freed for a moment to relieve herself, she had run like a
horned *chervine,* only to be caught and snatched up, fighting
and scratching, (in the midst of terror the momentary satisfaction as she felt her nails draw blood from Paul's cheek) and
dumped back in the litter. The humiliation of lying there hour
after hour, bound and gagged, the shame of lying in a dress
soaked with her own urine. The knowledge, when she had
been brought and carried to her own apartments, that she was
beaten, that there was no escape; hearing herself, shamed, but
too exhausted to do otherwise, give her parole just for the ease
of the bonds knifing her flesh, for food and care and a bath and

clean garments. *After that, I will never again be able to think myself brave. . . .*

When Bard came to her she was already half beaten. Bard felt with Carlina the staccato terror of her frantic prayers, *Mother Avarra, help me now, save me, protect me who is sworn to you, don't let this happen . . . why, why must this happen, why do you abandon me, I have done all that I vowed, I have served you faithfully as your priestess . . .* and the awful sense of abandonment as she realized that the Goddess would not help her, that no one would help her, that she was alone with Bard and he was stronger than she. . . .

Mortal terror, and awful humiliation, as she lay with her clothes torn off, impaled, tearing pain, but worse than the pain, the horror of knowing herself only a thing to be used. The battering of his body inside her deepest and most secret parts, and a sense of worthlessness, a shamed self-disgust that she could let herself be used like this, self-hatred and horror that she had not forced him to kill her first, that she had not fought to the death; certainly nothing, nothing he could have done would have been worse than this . . . and as his seed spurted into her the fear and knowledge of her own vulnerability, that she would be no more than a womb for his child, *his . . .* a horrid, hateful parasite that could grow in her and take over her clean body . . . but she had let him do this, she could have fought harder, she deserved no better. . . .

Bard did not know that he was on the floor, writhing, that he screamed aloud, in the depth of this violation, as Carlina had not screamed, feeling his teeth bite into his lip, a beaten, battered, outraged thing. The world was darkness and his own sobs as he felt with Carlina the horror of being taken again, used again, that *he* had dared to find pleasure in this horror . . . stillness and self-contempt that she deserved only this and no more. . . .

But that was not all. Somehow, the flood of *laran* had wakened, and he felt other memories, other awarenesses flood through him. He saw himself from Lisarda's eyes, naked, monstrous, bewildering, dealing pain and violation . . . saw himself through Melisendra's eyes, hateful compulsion and a pleasure that created self-contempt, the dread of being humiliated and despoiled for the Sight, her terror of punishment and the scornful tongue of Lady Jerana, and worse, Melora's pity. . . .

He stood again on the shore of the Lake of Silence, and a

priestess in a dark robe cursed him, and then the faces of all those he had killed and despoiled drifted in and gnawed at his soul, and he writhed and howled in the grip of self-knowledge so deep that there was nothing left; he saw himself a small sick shameful thing . . . *what a miserable excuse for a man you really are* . . . and knew it to be true. He had looked deep into his own soul, and found it wanting; and with all his heart he longed for death as it went on . . . and on . . . and on. . . .

At last it was over, and he lay curled into withdrawal, exhausted, on the floor of the chamber. Somewhere, a million miles away, farther than the moons, the avenging Avarra thrust a matrix out of sight and the world went into merciful darkness.

Hours later, the world began to clear. Bard stirred, hearing a single voice through the torment of hatred and accusation and self-contempt which was all he could hear.

Bard, I think you are two men . . . and that other, I shall never cease to love. . . .

Melora, who had loved him and valued him. Melora, the only woman in whose eyes he had never destroyed himself.

Even my brother, even Alaric, if he knew what I have done, would hate me. But Melora knows the worst of me and she does not hate me. Melora, Melora. . . .

Like a man in a daze, he dressed himself, looking across where Carlina lay, flung in deep exhaustion across the bed. She had been too weary even to pull her black mantle across her body; she still wore the torn, blood-stained chemise, and her eyes were raw with crying, sunk deep into her face. He looked at her with a terrible fear and dread, and thought, *Carlie, Carlie, I never wanted to hurt you, what have I done?* Tiptoeing for fear she should wake and look at him again with those terrible eyes, he went out into the hallway. *Melora!* Only one thought was in his mind, to get to Melora, Melora who alone could heal his hurts. . . . Yet before all else Bard was a soldier, and even as he longed to hurl himself down the stairs and to his home, he forced himself to take the alternate path, along the hail to his own suite of rooms.

Paul looked up in dismay as Bard came in. He started to say, good God, man, I thought you spent the night with your wife, and you look as if you'd been chasing demons in one of the hells . . . but he held his peace at the look in Bard's eyes. What had *happened* to him? He saw Bard look at Melisendra, wearing a green chamber-robe, her hair tied loosely up, fresh from her bath, and then look away, in torment.

"Bard," she said, in her sweet, musical voice, "what has come to you, my dear? Are you ill?"

He shook his head. "I have no right—no right to ask—" and Paul was amazed and shocked at the hoarseness of his voice. "Yet—in the name of Avarra—you are a woman. I beg you to go to Carlina; I would not—not let her be humbled further by—by her own serving-maids seeing her in this condition. I—" his voice broke. "I have destroyed her. And she has destroyed me." He raised his hand, refusing her ready questions, and Melisendra knew that the man was at the very end of his endurance.

He turned to Paul, summoning a final remnant of his old manner.

"Until I return—until I return, you are Lord General of the Army of Asturias," he said. "It has come sooner than we thought, that is all."

Paul opened his mouth in protest, but before he could speak, Bard had plunged out of the room.

As the sound of his booted feet died away, Paul turned to Melisendra, in astonishment and dismay.

"What in hell has happened to *him?* He looks like the wrath of God!"

"No," said Melisendra gently, "of the Goddess. I think that he has come face to face with the wrath of Avarra; and that she has not been gentle with him." She put Paul's hand aside. "I must go to the Lady Carlina; he asked it of me in the name of the Goddess, and that request no woman, and no priestess, may ever refuse."

CHAPTER SIX

All the long road to Neskaya, Bard, clinging to his galloping horse, riding alone, could barely sit in his saddle. He was sick and exhausted, pain and despair pounding in him with the hoofbeats on the road; the agonizing awareness of humiliation, he was not sure whether it was his own or Carlina's, the ache of a violated body and a shame that went searingly deep into his very soul. He felt her pain, her self-contempt, and marveled at it. . . . Why should she hate herself for what *I* did to her? Yet he knew that she blamed herself for not letting him kill her first. Searing more deeply yet was the memory of Melisendra's gentle voice as she said, *Bard, what has come to you, my dear? Are you ill?* How could she be so forgiving when he had done to her no less than to Carlina? And yet it was genuine, she felt real care and concern for him; was it only that he had fathered her son? Or did she have some source of comfort unknown to him? *When I had need of the comfort of the Goddess, I was younger and more ignorant than you could possibly imagine,* she had said once to him. She had outlived her pain, or at least survived it, but in Carlina it was all fresh and raw, the memory of the moment when she had cried out to the Goddess and realized that her Goddess could not, or would not intervene to save her. *Yet the Goddess struck through Carlina and avenged her—her and all the other women I have ill-used. But why did Carlina have to suffer so that the Goddess should strike me?*

Am I going mad?

He rode all day, and when the night came, since already he could see the Tower of Neskaya over the hills, he rode on by moonlight. He had not stopped for food or rest, or for anything except to give his horse a few minutes of rest. Now remembering that he had neither eaten nor drunk all day, and had had little sleep, he dismounted for a few moments and gave his horse some grain. His heavy cloak kept out the evening drizzle well enough, but as he watched the sky cleared and the green face of Idriel peered palely through ragged flaps of cloud.

She is watching me. It is the face of the Goddess watching me.

Yes. Surely, surely, she is going mad. No, it is I who am going mad. But a sane little voice beneath his despair remarked that he was not going mad, that there was no such merciful escape from the pain of self-knowledge.

You dare not go mad. You must somehow pull yourself together so that you can make amends . . . though nothing, nothing can wipe out what I have done. . . .

How did I have enough laran *to see all that?*

Melisendra. She is a catalyst telepath.

Why did Melisendra never show me what Carlina showed me? She had the power. Was it pity for me that stayed her hand? And why should she pity me after what I did to her?

Melora, Melora. If he had had any sense at all, he would have known—a thousand little things should have told him— that Carlina did not want him as a husband, and that he did not want her for a wife. He had wanted to marry the king's daughter in order that he would be secure in his place as the king's son-in-law. But why had he felt so little self-confidence and pride? *I always thought that, if anything, I was too proud; yet all I did, I did because I felt I was never good enough.*

But he was the king's *nedestro* nephew; King Ardrin was his father's brother and bastardy never counted for all that much against his skills at war and strategy. He could have had a good career and achieved honor and position as the king's champion and banner bearer . . . but he hadn't believed in himself enough to be sure of it, he had had to force himself on Carlina.

And if King Ardrin had indeed had his heart set on it, he and Carlina could have enjoyed a formal marriage no worse than that of many other couples at the court. But after that successful campaign with the clingfire he should have had enough confidence to know that the king would value him even without that marriage. He should have freed Carlina, and asked leave of Master Gareth to pay his addresses to Melora. *If she*

*would have had me; I think I knew then that I was not good
enough for her!*

Melora was the only person who had ever loved him. His
mother had given him up for fostering by his father, as far as
he knew, without a moment's hesitation. Had his father ever
loved him, or had he seen Bard only as a tool to his own ambition? His little brother Alaric had loved him . . . *but Alaric
never knew me, and if he had known what I really was he
would not love me . . . he would have hated me, held me in
contempt.* He had never had a woman to love him. *I put compulsion on them to come to my bed because I felt none of them
would want me, of her own free will. . . .*

His foster brothers had loved him—and he had lamed one
for life, and made an enemy of the other, then killed him. . . .

*And why did Beltran become my enemy? Because I mocked
him . . . and I mocked him because he exposed to me my fears
about my own manhood. Because he was not ashamed to admit
his weakness or his wish to reassure himself with the old
pledge we had made when we were boys . . . but I was afraid
he would find me less manly than himself!*

*And when I reach Neskaya, no doubt Melora will reveal to
me what a fool I was to think that she could care for me . . . but
perhaps she will take pity on me. She is a* leronis, *and perhaps
she will know what I must do to put my life right again. Not
that what I have done can be wiped out, but I must try. Perhaps
I can appease the Goddess. . . .*

Is it too late?

His horse was now very tired and went slowly, but Bard
was weary too, weary beyond telling, and pulled his cloak
around him in a way that reminded him intolerably, with that
new raw awareness, of the way Carlina had bundled herself
into her black mantle. And he had stripped from her even that
rag of weak protection. . . . Bard felt he could not live with this
awareness, that he would die if it went on much longer, and yet
he knew, on a deep level, that it would never really cease. No
matter what amends he made, he would live the rest of his life
this way, agonizingly aware of what torment he wrought to
others. He would live forever knowing what he had done to
those he loved.

Loved. For in his own bewildered way, he had loved Carlina. His love was selfish and gross, but it had been real love
too, love for the shy little girl who had been his playmate. And

he had loved Geremy, and Beltran too, and they had forever gone between his reach, and all the punishment for their loss was to know that he had himself driven them away, Geremy to alienation, Beltran to death. And he loved Erlend, and he knew he would never deserve his son's affection or regard. If he had it nevertheless, somehow (for children loved without reason) he would always know that he had it because of Erlend's goodness and not his own, that if Erlend knew his depths Erlend would hate him too, as Alaric would hate him, as his father would hate him . . . as Melora, who was so good and honest, would certainly hate him when she knew. And he must tell her.

And then he knew of the pain it would give her when he told, and wondered how he could possibly lay this burden upon Melora, how he could possibly seek to ease his own heart at the cost of weighing hers with his pain. He wondered if he ought to kill himself at once, so that he could never again hurt another person. And then he knew that that, too, would hurt others. It might burden Carlina's guilt, already overweighed with shame and humiliation, beyond recovery. It would hurt Erlend, who loved him and needed him, and it would hurt Alaric, in whose fragile hands the kingdom rested—but only with Bard's strong help. And beyond all these it would hurt Melora; and so he knew he could not do it. He rode into the courtyard of Neskaya and asked the sleepy guard there if he might manage to speak to the *leronis* Melora MacAran.

The man lifted his eyes a little, but apparently at the Tower of Neskaya the arrival of a solitary night rider was not all that strange an event. He sent someone to tell Melora she was wanted, and meanwhile, seeing Bard's exhaustion, brought him inside the lower floor and offered him some biscuits and wine. Bard ate the biscuits greedily, but did not touch the wine, knowing that if he drank half a cupful in his starved and exhausted state he would be drunk at once. Much as he might have welcomed the oblivion of that drunkenness, he knew there was now no such easy escape for him.

He heard Melora's voice before he saw her. "But I haven't the faintest idea who could come here wanting me at this God-forgotten hour, Lorill." And then Melora stood in the door. At first glance he could only see that she was heavier of body and rounder of face than ever, standing in the light of a lamp in her hand; but he could see the sheen of her red hair through the modest veil she had thrown over it. She had evidently been disturbed as she was about to retire, and was wearing a loose pale chamber robe through which, dimly silhouetted, he could see the outline of her body.

"Bard?" she said, looking at him in question and surprise, and then, with that new and terrible awareness of other people's emotions, he *felt* her shock as she took in his haggard face, the lines of exhaustion there. "Bard, my dear, what is it? No, Lorill, it's all right, I'll take him to my sitting room. Can you walk at all, Bard? Come, then—come in out of the cold!"

He followed her, will-less, unable to do anything but obey like a child, remembering that Melisendra, too, had said "my dear" when she saw his face. How could they? She turned in at the door of a room whose firelit warmth made him realize that he was half frozen.

"Sit here, Bard, by the fire. Lorill, just throw a few more logs there on the fire and then you can go back to your post— don't be foolish, man, I'm no maiden *leronis* to be sheltered and chaperoned, and I've known Bard since he rode his first campaign! He'll offer me no harm!"

So there was still one person alive who trusted in him. It wasn't much, but it was a start, a seed of creeping warmth which lighted the frozen waste inside him, as the fire warmed his chilled and exhausted body. Lorill had gone away. Melora lifted a small, fragile table and set it between them.

"I was having a late supper before going up into the relays. Share it with me, Bard, there's always more than enough for two."

There was a basket of fragrant nut bread, still warm, sliced into slightly crumbly chunks, some rolls of soft cheese flavored with herbs, rich and pungent, and a crock of hot soup. Melora poured half of it into a mug which she shoved in his direction, picking up the crock and drinking her share from it. He sipped, feeling the hot soup, and her calm trustfulness, spread life back into him. She finished her soup and set the crock down, spreading the cheese on the bread, which crumbled so that she had to hold it together with her fingers; even so, it dropped crumbs in her lap, which she gathered up and flung into the fire.

"More soup? I can send for more, there's always some in the kitchen over the fire—you're sure? Have that last piece of bread, if you want it. I'm stuffed, and you've ridden a long way in the cold. You're beginning to look a little less like banshee bait! Well, Bard, what's happened? Tell me about it, why don't you?"

"Melora!" He crossed the room in a rush to kneel at her feet. She sighed, looked down at him. He knew she was waiting, and suddenly all the enormity of what he was doing struck him, how could he ease the enormous agony of his new burden of knowledge by laying it on Melora's shoulders? He said, and heard his voice, harsh and uncertain like the new baritone of a boy whose voice is just changing, "I should never have come here, Melora. I'm sorry. I—I'll go now. I can't—"

"Can't *what?* Don't be foolish, Bard," she said, and reached out, with those fat but curiously graceful hands, to lift his face up to hers. And at the touch of his temples, suddenly he knew that she could read it all, that she *knew* it all, in one enormous rush of awareness. The rawness of his new pain communicated itself to her, without words, and she knew what he had done, and how it now seemed to him, and what had happened.

"Merciful Avarra!" she whispered in horror; then, softly, "No—she was not so merciful to you, was she, my poor fellow? But you have not deserved her mercy yet, have you? Oh, Bard!" And her arms went out to fold him close against her breast. He knelt there as if she was, for that one moment, the mother he had never known, and he knew he was near to tears. He had not wept since Beltran died, but he knew that he would weep in another moment, and so he struggled upright, holding himself taut against further breakdown.

"Oh, my dear," Melora said in a whisper, "how did it ever come to this? I blame myself, Bard—I should have seen how very much you needed love and reassurance, I should have found some way to come to you. But I was so proud of myself for keeping to the rules, as if they were not meant to be set aside for human needs, and in my pride I set all this in motion! We all live with the mistakes we make—that's the dreadful part. We can look back and see the very moment where it all went wrong, and that's all the punishment we ever need, I think; to live with what we do, and know how we did it. I should have found a way."

Sudden memory of Mirella, that night in the camp when Melora had sent him away, reminding him proudly of the proper thing, came back to him; Mirella, at the door of the tent, whispering "She cried herself to sleep. . . ." Melora had wanted him as much as he wanted her. If he had even known *that!* If he had even been sure of that, he could have been gentler with Beltran . . . but how could Melora blame herself for *his* sins and mistakes? She did, and he could never ease her of *that,* and so in a terrible way he had wronged *her*, too.

"Is there no help for it? Is there no help for any of it? I can't live like this, with this—this burden of knowledge, I can't—"

Still gently touching his face, she said, with infinite gentleness, "But you must, my dear, as I must, as Carlina must, as we all must. The only difference is that some of us never know why we suffer as we do. Tell me, Bard, would you rather this had not happened? Do you truly wish it?"

"Wish I had not done what I did? Are you crazy? Of course—that's the hell of it, that I can never undo any of it—"

"No, Bard, I mean, do you really wish that Carlina had never shown you this, that you were still the man you were a few days ago?"

He started to cry out: yes, yes, I cannot bear knowing, this way, I want to go back to ignorance. Carlina had laid this burden upon him with *laran,* perhaps with *laran* a way could be found to take this monstrous knowledge from him again. And then he realized, head bent, with a new kind of pain, that it was not true. For him, to go back to ignorance would be to risk repeating what he had done, becoming, once again, the kind of man who could commit such atrocities; who could wound a brother, lame a foster brother for life unheeding, rape and torment women who cared for him . . . he said, his head still bowed, "No." For even if he did not know about it, all the pain of Carlina, all Melisendra's suffering and the beauty of her forgiveness, would still be there, but he would be unaware of any of it. He could no longer imagine what it would be like, not to know; he would be like a blind man in a garden of blossoming flowers, treading down beauty without caring.

"I'd rather know. It hurts, but—oh, I'd rather know!"

"Good," Melora said, in a whisper. "That's the first step— to know, and not to block it away."

"I want—I want, some way, to—to try to make amends— for what I can—"

She nodded. "You will. You can't help it. But there will be so many things you *can't* make amends for, and even when it tortures you, you have to learn to—to go on, somehow, carrying the weight of it. Knowing you can't undo anything you've done." She looked at him sharply. "For instance, should you have left Carlina alone with this?"

He said, still unable to look at her, "I should think I would be the one person she would not want to see."

"Don't be too sure of that; you have shared something, after all, and some day you will have to face her again."

"I—I know. But after—after that I couldn't be there—reminding her—and I couldn't bear it. I—I sent Melisendra to her. She's—she's kind. I don't know how she *can* be, after all she's been through, all I did to her, but she *is*."

Melora said, "Because she sees into people. The same way you do, now. She knows what they are and what's tormenting *them*."

"You do, too," he said after a moment. "What is it? Is it just—having *laran?*"

"Not entirely. But it's the first step in our training. Which is why Carlina returned you, really, good for evil. She gave you the gift of *laran,* which was the first thing she herself had been given."

"Some gift!" Bard said bitterly.

"The gift to see *ourselves.* It is a gift, and you'll know it in time. Bard, it's late and I must go into the relays—no, I won't leave you like this. Let me send word to Varzil—he is our *tenerézu,* our Keeper—and he can send someone else to take my place there; your need is greater right now." Bard remembered that he had seen Varzil of Neskaya—was it at Geremy's wedding? He could not remember; time was telescoping into a blurred and continuous past. He did not know when or how or why he had done anything, only the enormous conviction of a guilt past endurance and a horror of himself, so great that he felt he could never again hold up his head. Anything he did, anything, was going to create endless catastrophe. How could he live this way? Yet dying would create catastrophe too, so he could not settle anything by taking himself away from the opportunity to do more harm. . . .

Melora touched his hand.

"Enough!" she said sharply. "Now you are beginning to indulge yourself in self-pity, and that will only make it worse. What you feel now is only the aftermath of exhaustion. No more! I tell you—" and her voice was softened—"when you are rested, and can absorb what has happened to you, you will be able to go on. Not to forget, but to put it behind you, and live with what you can't mend. What you need now is rest and sleep. I'll stay near you." She rose and picked up the little table, replacing it, tugged a heavy footstool, thickly upholstered, in front of the chair.

"I should have moved that for you—"

"Why? I'm not exhausted or crippled. Here, put your feet up—yes, like that. Let me get those boots off. And take off your sword-belt, you don't need it. Not here." She pulled aside a curtain to an alcove at the far end of the room. He realized that it was where she slept. She brought him a pillow from her own bed. "The chair's comfortable enough, I've slept here plenty of nights when someone was sick, and I knew I'd be called at any moment. If you need to go out in the night," she added forthrightly, "the place you're looking for is just past the end of this corridor down the stairs, and it has a door painted red. It's for the guards; it *would* be a scandal if I let you use the bath in my suite, since you're not one of us here." She tucked a knitted shawl around him. "Sleep well, Bard."

She went past him, extinguishing the lamp. He heard the creak of her bed as she climbed into it. Strange, how light-footed she was for such a big woman; he could not hear her steps at all. Bard touched the fuzzy texture of the shawl under his chin. It made him feel, somehow, as if he were very small and young; he had a curious flash of his foster mother tucking him up in a shawl like this after some childish illness. Strange. He had always thought of Lady Jerana hating him and treating him cruelly; why had he forgotten the times when she had been kind to him? Had he *wanted* to believe she hated him and wanted ill for him? It could not be easy for a childless woman to foster her husband's strong, healthy, well-loved child by some other woman.

As he dropped off to sleep he could hear Melora breathing; the sound was oddly reassuring, that she would let him—a man who had never treated a woman with anything but cruelty—sleep in her very room. Not that he had any designs on her—he wondered, suddenly, if he would ever be able to feel desire for a woman again without this terrible awareness of all the harm he could do. *Carlina has had her revenge*, he thought, and then in a wry flash of insight he wondered if, since his own mother gave him up, he had never believed he was loved because he'd felt, without knowing it, that even she did not find him worthy of love. He didn't know; he was beginning to think he knew nothing about love. But he knew that Melora's trust was, somehow, the first step in his healing. Clasping the pillow that smelled sweetly of some fresh scent about Melora, he slept.

When he woke, it was a day of soft-falling snow, one of the first snowfalls of the year in the Kilghard Hills, and silent flakes, melting as they fell, were drifting across the windows. Melora sent him to borrow a razor and a fresh shirt from one of the guards, and to join their mess at breakfast "That way," she said, smiling at him merrily, "they will know that I am not entertaining a lover from outside the Tower, which is not proper during my term of service here. I'm not overly concerned for my reputation, but it's not done—to bring scandal on the Towers that way. Varzil has enough to contend with, without that."

As he went to eat hot, fresh nutbread and salt fish fried into cakes, with the guards of Neskaya, Bard felt a little shamefaced pride; the Lord General of Asturias, to join a common guardsmen's mess? But this was not his own country, he would probably not be recognized, and if he was, well, it was none of anyone's business; surely even a general could come to consult a *leronis* on urgent private business? Shaved, cleanly clothed, he felt better. After breakfast, a youngster, red-headed, in blue and silver, with the indefinable stamp of the Hastur kin on his face, brought a message that the Lord Varzil of Neskaya wished to see him.

Varzil of Neskaya. An enemy, a Ridenow of Serrais; but Alaric had loved him, and he himself had been favorably impressed by the man when he had come to exchange Alaric for Geremy. Even when he believed Varzil an ally of King Carolin of Thendara, he had been somewhat impressed.

It cannot be easy, to swear to neutrality in a world torn by war! When all the lands lie in flames about you, surely it is easier to join with one side or another!

Bard had remembered Varzil as young, but the man who faced him in the small stone-floored study, wearing a simple robe and sandals rather than the ceremonial robe of office, seemed old; there were heavy lines in the care-worn face, young as it was, and the bright red hair was already graying. Varzil, after all, could not be so young; he had rebuilt Neskaya after its fire-bombing, and that had been before Bard was born, although, he had heard, Varzil had been very young then.

"Welcome, Bard mac Fianna. I will speak with you presently—but I have a few matters to arrange first. Sit there," he said, and continued speaking with the young man, wearing Hastur colors, who was facing him. At first this made Bard's skin prickle—so much for the vaunted neutrality of Varzil and the Tower—but after he had heard a few words he relaxed.

"Yes, tell the people of Hali that we will send healers and *leroni* to care for the worst-burnt cases, but they must realize that the physical wounds that can be seen are not all that has happened. The pregnant women must be monitored; most of them will miscarry, and they are the lucky ones, for of those who bear children from the time of this disaster, at least half will be born marred or deformed; they must be monitored, too, from birth. Women of childbearing age must be taken out of the area as soon as possible, or they will run the same risk, if they conceive children before the land has healed, and that may not be for years."

"The people will not want to leave their estates or their farms," the Hastur man said, "and what shall we tell them?"

"The truth," Varzil said with a sigh, "that the land is poisoned past redemption and will be so for years; no one can live there, conquered nor conquerors either. Only one good thing has come of all this."

"A good thing? And what is that, *vai laranzu?*"

"The Dalereuth Tower has joined us in neutrality," Varzil said. "They have sworn to make no more *laran* weapons, whatever the inducement; and their overlord, Marzán of Valeron, has pledged to the Compact, and Queen Darna of Isoldir. And Valeron and Isoldir have taken the oath of fealty under the Hasturs."

Bard's teeth were set on edge by this. Would all this land lie under Hastur command someday? And yet . . . if the Hasturs were sworn to fight no more wars except under the Compact, there would be no more such atrocities as at Hali. He had been a soldier all his life, and he felt no special guilt for the men he had struck down face-to-face with the sword; they had had an equal chance to strike *him* down. But for the men slain by spells and sorcery, for the women and children killed in fire-bombings, he felt nothing could atone, not ever. He felt, too, that his armies could face, and conquer, the Hastur armies with any weapons they chose; why should they need sorcerers too?

When Varzil had finished with the Hastur envoy, he said, "Say to *Domna* Mirella that I would like to speak with her."

Bard heard the name without surprise—it was not so uncommon as that—but when the young woman came in, he recognized her at once. She was still slight and pretty, wearing the white robe of a monitor.

"Are you working in the relays, child? I thought you were simply resting, after your ordeal at Hali," Varzil said. Mirella was about to answer, but stopped when she saw Bard.

"*Vai dom,* I heard from Melora that you were Lord General of Asturias now—forgive me, Lord Varzil, may I ask news of my family? Is my grandsire well, sir, and Melisendra?"

Bard found, from somewhere, the strength to face her. It was too much to hope Mirella did not know of his depravity; for all he knew, everyone in the Hundred Kingdoms knew, and
➤ was ready to spit on the name of Bard mac Fianna, called di Asturien. "Master Gareth is very well, though of course he grows old," he told her. "He rode with us on the campaign against the Ridenow before they surrendered." He glanced hesitantly at Varzil. Not a tenday ago, he had hanged this man's overlord, Dom Eiric of Serrais, after the battle, as an oathbreaker. But although Varzil looked sad, there seemed to be, in him, no hatred for Bard or his armies.

"And Melisendra?"

Melisendra is mother's-sister to this girl. What has she said of me? "Melisendra is well," he said, then, on an impulse. "I think she is happy; I—I think she wishes to marry one of my paxmen, and if that is her wish, I will not prevent her. And King Alaric has promised Erlend a patent of legitimacy, so his status need not trouble her."

Melora said I would find a way to make what amends could be made. This is only a beginning, and so little, but it was a place to begin. Paul's almost as bad as I am, but for some reason she cares for him.

Mirella smiled at him, sweetly, and said, "I thank you for your good news, *vai dom.* And now, Dom Varzil, I am at your command."

"We are happy to have you here while you recover from the shock of what happened at Hali," Varzil said. "How came you not to be within the Tower?"

"I had had leave to ride in the hills, hunting, with two of my *bredin-y,*" Mirella said. "And we were just about to turn homeward when the rain came, and we sheltered in a herdsman's hut—and then, oh merciful Goddess, we—we felt the burn-

ing—the cries—" her face turned pale, and Varzil reached out
his hand and gripped the young woman's in his own strong
clasp.

"You must try to forget, dear child. It will be with you always—indeed, none of us in any of the Towers will ever be
able to forget," Varzil said. "My youngest sister, Dyannis, was
a *leronis* at Hali, and I felt her die . . ." his voice trailed off and
for a moment he looked inward at horror. Then, recovering
himself, he said firmly, "What we must remember, Rella, is
that their heroism has taken another step toward the time when
all this land will lie under Compact. For you know, they deliberately broadcast what happened—while they were dying they
kept their minds open so that we should all see, and hear, and
feel what they suffered, instead of quickly taking their way out
of life . . . which they could have done, so easily—"

Mirella shuddered and said, "I could not have done it! At
the first touch of fire I think I should have stopped my heart
and died a merciful death—"

"Perhaps," Varzil said gently. "We are not all equally heroic.
And yet you might, surrounded by the others, have found your
own courage."

Bard saw in his mind the picture of a woman's body, blazing like a torch . . . but Varzil shut it away, and said, "You
must go to another Tower, Rella; do you wish to go to Arilinn
or Tramontana?"

"Tramontana is the post of danger," she said, "for Aldaran
has not yet sworn the Compact, and may strike at Tramontana.
I owe a death to all of you; I will go to Tramontana."

"That is not necessary," Varzil said gently. "There will be
plenty of work for *leroni* here, healing the wounds of children
burned and damaged at Hali, or in the Venza hills where they
sowed bonewater dust and children are dying."

"That task," said Mirella, "I will leave to the healer-women
and to the priestesses of Avarra, if they can bring themselves
to leave their isolation on the Island of Silence. My task lies at
Tramontana; it is laid on me, Varzil."

Varzil bowed his head. "Be it so," he said. "I am not the
keeper of your conscience. And I foresee no peace at Aldaran,
nor any safety at Tramontana for my lifetime, or many life-
times to come. But if it is laid on you to go to Tramontana,
Mirella, then all the gods go with you, little one." He rose, and

took Mirella in his arms, pressing her close. "Take my blessing, sister. And be certain to speak to Melora before you go."

When he released her, she turned to Bard.

"Carry my greetings to my grandfather and to Melisenda,
via dom. And say to them that if we do not meet again, it is the
fortunes of war. You, who were the commander when I first
rode to war as a *leronis,* will understand that." She looked
more sharply at him, and something she saw in his face caused
her eyes to soften. She said, "Now that you are one of us, I
shall pray for your peace and enlightenment, sir. May the gods
protect you."

When she had gone away, Bard turned to Varzil in puzzle-
ment.

"What the hell did she mean—one of us?"

"Why, she saw that you were *laran*-gifted, newly so,"
Varzil said. "Do you think one *leronis* cannot tell another with
donas?"

"Does it—by the wolf of Alar—does it *show?*" His consternation was so apparent—did he bear a visible mark of what
he had become?—that Varzil almost laughed.

"Not physically. But she sees it, as any of us would—we
don't look at one another much with our physical eyes, you
know; we see it in—in the *outside* of your mind. None of us
would read your thoughts uninvited, not even I. But, in general, we can tell one another." He smiled. "After all, do you
think that the Keeper of Neskaya gives audience to anyone
who comes here—even the Lord General of Asturias and
Marenji and Hammerfell and God knows how many other little countries up in rebel territory? I don't care *that* for the Lord
General," he said, with a smile which made the words somehow inoffensive, "but Bard mac Fianna, the friend of Melora,
whom I love, and newly made aware of his *laran*—Bard mac
Fianna is another matter. As *laranzu* I have a duty toward you.
You are—how shall I say this—you are a pivot."

"I don't know what you mean."

"Neither do I," said Varzil, "nor how I know it; I only know
that when first I set eyes on you I knew it was on you that
many great events of our time would turn. I am also one of
those pivots, people who can change history, and who have a
duty to do so if they can, whatever happens. This, I think, is
why you became Lord General of Asturias."

"That sounds a bit too mystical for me, *vai dom,*" Bard said, scowling. He had won back from exile, by his own efforts, and he didn't like the metaphysical notion that he might just be a pawn of fate.

Varzil shrugged. "Maybe so. I've been a *laranzu* all my life, and one of my gifts is to see time lines—not many, not very clearly, not in a way that would let me choose clearly between the many paths I might take. I heard there was a gift like that, once, but it died out. But sometimes I can recognize a pivot when I see it, and choose what has to be done to keep from wasting an opportunity."

Bard's mouth twisted. He said, "And suppose you can't get anyone else to go along with your idea of what should happen? Do you just tell them they have to do so-and-so or the world will collapse?"

"Ah, no, alas, that would be too easy, and I don't suppose the gods will that we should have perfection," Varzil said. "No, everyone else does his best as *he* sees it, and it isn't always what I see. Otherwise I'd be a god, not just Keeper of Neskaya. I do what I can, that's all, and I'm always terribly conscious of the mistakes I make, and have made, and even the ones I *will* make. I just have to do the best I can, and—" suddenly his voice hardened—"in view of your experience, Bard mac Fianna, I think that's something you're going to have to learn, *fast*—to do the best you can, where you can, and live with what mistakes you can't help making. Otherwise you'll be like the donkey who died of hunger between two bales of hay, trying to decide which one to eat first."

Was this, Bard wondered, why Melora had sent him to Varzil?

"Partly," said Varzil, picking up his thought, "but you are in command of the Army of Asturias, and one of your tasks is to unify all this land. So you must go back."

It was the last thing Bard had expected him to say.

"I will send Melora with you," Varzil said. "I think she may be needed in her homeland. Asturias is where the important things of our world are happening. But before you go, I will ask you once again what I asked of you when we met before, in Asturias: will you pledge yourself to Compact?"

Bard's first impulse was to say yes, I will. Then he bowed his head.

"I would do so willingly, *tenerézu*. But I am a soldier, and under orders. I have no right to do so without the command of my king and his regent. For good or ill, I am sworn to obey them, and I cannot do so without their leave; and if I did it would be dishonorable. He who is false to his first oath will be false to his second." With crawling shame, he remembered how he had taunted Carlina with that same proverb, but that did not lighten his duty at this moment.

I have broken and trampled all else. But my honor as a soldier, and my loyalty to my father and my brother—these are still untarnished. I must try to keep them so.

Varzil looked at him steadily. After a moment he held out his hand to Bard, touched him very lightly on the wrist. He said, "If your honor demands it, so be it; I am not the keeper of your conscience either. Then I must come with you to Asturias, Bard. Wait until I speak to my deputies and be certain who can be left in charge here."

CHAPTER SEVEN

Carlina woke from an uneasy sleep, aching in every nerve and muscle of her body, to see a woman standing in the doorway of her room. She shrank away, pulling the black cloak over her; then, shaking, remembered that she had no right to it. Not now. She would have let it fall away, but remembered that she was still half naked, wearing the torn, bloody chemise which was the only garment Bard had left her. She felt numb and battered, and now she recognized the woman, who was tall and rounded, wearing a handsome green gown trimmed with fur; it was Bard's concubine, Lady Jerana's household *leronis,* who had borne him a son years ago. All she knew of her was that her name was Melisendra, and she had seen something hazy about her in Bard's mind and memory. . . . She could not remember the details, but felt sure they were sickening. She hid under the black mantle, thinking she could not endure to let this calm, self-possessed woman see her shame.

"Vai domna," said Melisendra, coming into the room, "you do not want your servants to see you like this; I beg of you, let me help you." She sat down on the bed beside Carlina, gently touching the darkening bruise on Carlina's cheek. "Believe me, I know what you are feeling. I was a *leronis,* kept virgin for the Sight, and I could not even guard myself against a glamour—in a sense I was more shamed than you, for I was not beaten into submission, but laid down my maidenhood without a struggle. And I can see that you defended yourself with all your strength, as I had not the will to do; I saw the marks of your nails in his face."

Carlina began to cry again, helplessly. Melisendra pulled the other woman against her breast and held her close.

"There now, there now, cry if you will . . ." she murmured, rocking her. "Poor little lady, I know, I know, believe me. I woke like this, too, and there was none to comfort me, my sister was far away in the Tower, and I had to face my lady's anger. There now, there. . . ."

When Carlina had cried herself into quiet, Melisendra went into the bath and put Carlina into a hot tub, stripping away the torn chemise. "I shall have this burned," she said. "I am sure you will not want to wear it again." With it she put the torn clothing Bard had ripped away from Carlina. She washed her as if she had been a small child, and dressed her bruises with soothing creams. Then she dressed her like a doll, and sent for one of the waiting-women in the suite.

"Bring my lady some food," she said, and when it came, she sat and encouraged Carlina to eat, spoonful by spoonful, some soup and some custard. Carlina found it hard to eat with her bruised jaw, but Melisendra reassured her that it was not broken.

When the waiting-women had taken away the trays, Carlina looked at her tremulously, saying, "I feel it must look strange to them—that they all know how I am shamed—and you here—"

Melisendra smiled at her. She said, "Surely not; it is nothing new that a *barragana* should wait on the lawful wife. And, my lady, if the truth be told, I am certain that in this land where so many marriages are made with unwilling women you are not the only noblewoman to go to her bridal as if it were rape."

Carlina said, with a bitter smile, "Why, so they do. I had almost forgotten—I suppose this has made me Bard's lawful wife, and I need only wait, now for the *catenas* to be locked on my wrists, as if I were a Dry-town whore! Where is Bard?"

"He rode away earlier today . . . I do not know where; but he looked as if he had met the avenging Avarra," Melisendra said quietly. "I do not know what will come of this; I do not know if the political situation will force him to keep you as wife. I don't know anything about such things. But I am sure, very sure, that he will never misuse you again. I am a *leronis,* and I knew something had happened within him. I do not think he will ever mishandle any woman again."

"How can you be such a friend to me," Carlina asked, "considering that, if I must remain here as his wife, you will be only *barragana?*"

"I was never more than that, my lady. Bard's father would willingly have seen us married, but Bard cares nothing for me. I was only a diversion when he was angry and bitter at all the world. If I had not borne his son, I would have been cast out. . . ."

"Why, then," Carlina whispered, "you are a victim too. . . ." Reaching out, she kissed the older woman, on impulse. She said, shyly, "Under the vow of the priestesses of Avarra, I am," she quoted, "mother and sister and daughter to every other woman. . . ."

". . . and under her mantle you are my sister," said Melisendra softly. Carlina looked up at her in numb amazement.

"Are you one of us?"

"I would willingly have been so," said Melisendra, and her eyes filled with tears. "But you know Her law. No woman may renounce the world for the Holy Island while she has a child too young for fostering, or aged parents who need her care. They would not have me while I had these responsibilities; my other sister is a *leronis* at Neskaya, and I am the only remaining support for my old father, and Erlend is only six years old. So they would not accept my vow. And—further—a *laranzu* told me, once, that I had work to do in the world, though he would not say how or when. But the Mother Ellinen allowed me to pledge myself, privately, to the obligations of a priestess, though I am not bound to chastity; she said I might one day wish to marry."

"And you still—wished for the love of a man—" Carlina asked her shakily. "I feel—I will die—I cannot bear the thought that any man will ever again touch me in lust—or even in love—"

Melisendra stroked her hand gently. "That will pass, sister. That will pass, if the Goddess wills. Or it may be her will that somehow, you shall serve her again in chastity, on the island or elsewhere. We are all under her mantle." She lifted up the black cloak and said, "Shall I have this cleaned and readied for you?"

Carlina whispered, "I am not fit to wear it—"

"Hush!" said Melisendra sternly. "You know better than

that! Do you think she does not know how well you defended yourself?"

Carlina'a eyes filled with tears again. She said, "That is what I am afraid of. I could have fought harder—I could have let him kill me—I wish that I had—"

"*Vai domna*—sister," Mellsendra said gently, "I think it blasphemous to believe the Goddess could be less understanding than a weak woman like myself. And if I can understand and condone your weakness, why, then, the Dark Mother can certainly do no less."

"Perhaps I have been on the Holy Island too long," said Carlina, and her voice was shaking. "I have forgotten the real things of the world. You are at war here."

"Did you even know when Hali was fire-bombed and they—died?"

"We knew. But Mother Ellinen bade us shut it out, saying we could do no good by sharing their death agony—"

"My father said the same. But we were on the march with the armies," said Melisendra.

"But the Mothers said that we must not entangle ourselves in the making of war, that our business was with eternal things, birth and death, and that war was a man's business—that it was nothing to do with us, patriotism and men's pride and royalty and succession, that women had nothing to do with it—"

Melisendra said a rude word. "Forgive me, lady. But I have fought alongside men in the field, unarmed except for a starstone and a dagger to make sure I did not fall into the enemy's hands. And the Sisterhood of the Sword fight with such weapons as they have, even though they know that, for them, the penalties of defeat are even more cruel. Some of the prisoners suffered that fate only a few days ago, after the last defeat of Serrais."

Carlina said faintly, "The priestesses of Avarra are always being asked to leave their island and do healing in the world. Perhaps we should ask the Sisterhood to protect us. At least we could not harm them in that way. . . ." Her voice trailed off. "Perhaps the Mother Ellinen is wrong when she says we should take no part in the struggles around us. . . ."

"I am not the keeper of anyone's conscience," Melisendra ventured. "Perhaps there are different callings for different women. . . ."

Carlina asked bitterly, "But where will you find a man to grant us that?" and the women were silent.

Neither of them had warning of what happened next. There was a small, faint, droning sound—all the survivors agreed upon that. A moment later, there was a great crash, a booming noise, the ground rocked under their feet, and they involuntarily caught at one another. The first explosion was followed by another and another.

"Erlend!" screamed Melisendra, and ran wildly down the corridor, stumbling as the walls rocked with a fourth explosion. "Erlend! Paolo!"

Paul shouted Melisendra's name and caught her at the entrance to their rooms, grabbing her by force and dragging her under one of the doorways, where he stood, bracing himself against a further explosion. Melisendra clutched at him and stood, swaying, reaching out for the mind of her son. He was safe! Praise to all the gods, he was safe in the stables where he had gone to visit a litter of puppies! Paul felt her relief as his own, her mind open to him as she stood, swaying, holding to him with both hands. Again and again the floors rocked with repeated explosions, the rumble and crash of collapsing stone.

"Come on," Paul said tersely. "We've got to get out!"

"The Lady Carlina—"

Paul followed Melisendra as she fled back. He found Carlina cowering under overturned furniture, and snatched her up in his arms, hurrying with her toward the small private stairway into the small garden where he had first seen Melisendra with her son. Melisendra hurried at his heels. Safely outside, he set Carlina on her feet. In the confusion of terror, she had not seen him; now, staring at him, she shrank away in renewed fear.

"You—but no, you are not Bard, are you?"

"No, my lady. But it was I who took you from the Island of Silence."

"You are very like him," she said. "It is very strange."

Stranger than you can know, Paul thought, but he could not tell her and knew that she would probably not believe him if he did. What could she possibly know of his world and the stasis box? That was behind him, anyway, that had been another life and the man he had been on that world was dead beyond recall. What good would it do to tell her?

Somehow, some way, he must make Bard believe that he, Paul, was no threat. Perhaps now, with Bard fled on some mysterious errand, and the castle in confusion, under attack like this—by sorcery?—was the time to take Melisendra and flee into the Kilghard Hills and farther, past the Hellers. Back in that wild and undiscovered country, perhaps, they could make another life somehow. But would Melisendra agree to leave her son?

"Look! Oh, merciful gods, *look!*" cried Melisendra, looking back at the building they had escaped. One whole wing of the castle bad fallen in, and she clutched at Paul in horror. Through her mind he saw. . . .

A young face, drawn with terror; a crippled body too slow and cumbersome on the stairs, an old man hastening to safety, turning back to give an arm to the lame child . . . a flight of stairs collapsing, sliding away under their feet, the roof opening to admit the sky . . . and the world wiped out in a fall of masonry that buried them, instantly, together. . . .

"Dom Rafael! Alaric!" Melisendra whispered, in horror. She began to weep. "The old man was always so kind to me. And the boy—his life had been so hard, poor little lad, and to die like this. . . ."

Carlina's face was set and implacable. She said, "I am sorry for your grief, Melisendra. But the usurper of the throne of Asturias is dead. And I cannot find it in me to grieve."

Now, all through the gardens and grounds of Castle Asturias, men and women, courtiers and servants, nobles and kitchen girls and grooms, were emerging, yelling and shouting in confusion, crowding together to look in horror at the fallen wing. But even while one of the majordomos was calling out, telling everyone not to go near the still-quaking building, there was a terrific final explosion, the remainder of the stonework of that wing collapsed and crashed down, with a rising of stone dust and muffled cries, and silence descended.

In that stillness Paul heard Master Gareth shouting, "Are there any of the king's *leroni* yet alive? To me! Quickly! We must find out who is attacking us!"

"I must go," said Melisendra, and hurried away before Paul could catch at her hand, urge her to escape during the confusion. He stood beside Carlina, watching the sorcerers, not now in their gray robes, but wearing everything from nightcaps and chamber robes to one, the young boy Rory, wrapped in a towel and evidently fresh from his bath, assembling beneath the flowering trees in the orchard. Master Gareth, hobbling on his bad leg gathered the *leroni* around him; two or three were missing, for some of them had been in the other wing in attendance on Dom Rafael and the king, but there were four women and two men besides the boy, and Master Gareth spoke to them in hushed tones. Paul, at this distance, could not hear what he said. The soldiers were rallying, trying to keep people away from the fallen walls. Paul went toward them—what had Bard said?

You are Lord General till I return. It has come a little sooner than we thought, that is all.

One of the men ran up to him and saluted. "Sir, you'll be worrying about your son. He's safe, one of the sergeants has him in charge, since his mother will be with the old wizard and all the other *leroni*. Come, sir, show yourself to him and let the little fellow know he's still got a father and a mother."

Yes, that was only fair. He saw Erlend, looking pale and shaken, clinging to a puppy with both hands.

"Your mother is safe, Erlend, she's there with your grandda," said the soldier, "and look, *chiyu*, here's the Lord General come to take you to mammy."

Erlend raised his head. He said, "That's not—" and for a panicky moment Paul *knew* the game was over already, before it began, that Erlend was about to say, *That's not my father,* but he met Paul's eyes for a split second, and said instead, "That's not the way to talk to me, Corus, I'm not a baby." He thrust the puppy into the soldier's hands and said, "Take *him* to his mammy, he's the one howling for milk! I should be with the *leroni,* some of us are dead; they will need every starstone."

"He's a one, he is, Lord General," said the soldier. "Like wolf, like cub! Good lad!"

Paul said to Erlend, carefully and with dignity, "I do not think they will need you, Erlend, but you may go and inquire if they have need of you."

"Thank you, sir." Erlend walked at his side, steadily, but Paul could feel that the boy was shaking, and after a moment he held out his hand. The boy gripped it in his small sweaty one. When they were out of earshot he said fiercely to Paul, "Where is my father!"

"He—he rode away this morning." After a moment he said, "I feared they would think he had deserted them in trouble, so

I answered to his name when they thought I was your father."
He wondered why he bothered to explain to a child of six.

"Yes. He should be here," Erlend said, and there was a
shade of condemnation in his voice. It made Paul wonder, for
the first time, if or when Bard would return!

"He said before he left, *Until I return you are the Lord General,*" and Erlend looked up at him, strangely. He said, "I saw
him ride away. I did not know, then, what it meant," and was
silent. At last he said, "You must do as he told you."

As the boy walked away toward the little group of *leroni*
under the trees, Paul watched, disturbed. Carlina was still
standing where he had left her. She said, "Is that Bard's son?"

"Yes, lady."

"He does not look at all like Bard. I suppose he is like
Melisendra—certainly he has her hair and eyes."

"I should go and see what the soldiers are doing," Paul said,
resuming what he had been intending before finding Erlend.
Melisendra would be reassured by the sight of her son; but the
army was like an anthill somebody had kicked over, without
any kind of leader, milling restlessly. He bawled, "Form up,
men! Sergeants, take muster, find out who was buried in the
wreckage! Then we can find out if we're under attack! Form
up!"

There were shouts of, "It's the Wolf! The Lord General's
here!"

Leadership reestablished, the men went about the business
of forming up, taking muster, listening for the silences when a
called name was not answered. Some of the men considered
dead in that first random muster would later be found alive, absent for some reason or other from their post, off-duty and in
the village for a drink, or a woman, one or two soundly asleep
in barracks, to turn up later wondering what all the shouting
was about. But at least they had some faint idea of who was
there and who was not, the form of the army had been reestablished if not its totality.

And still it continued to be silent. There was no sign of any
further explosion, no sign of any enemy or attack, no attacking
force. Paul wondered who was the enemy. Serrais had surrendered, Hammerfell had not the strength, the Hasturs had sworn
to the Compact, and while their armies were still on the road,
they had sworn not to use *laran* weapons. Had the Altons or
the Aldaran joined the war, and the news somehow failed to

reach Paul while he was on his errand to the Island of Silence? Was it the little kingdom of Syrtis, long known for powerful *laran?* There *had* been, so far, no word from the *leroni* who were searching out the direction of the attack. Paul wondered if they had accepted Erlend's offer to work with them. Later that afternoon, with two of the army engineers, he was going into the undamaged part of the building to see what was safe and what was not, and make sure that any fires caused by collapsing braziers or untended lamps had been put out. He saw Erlend trotting busily off, and the boy saluted him gravely and said that the *leroni* had put him to work running errands for them, having food brought to them, and wine, because they had no isolated place to work, and the presence of a nontelepath waiting on them would be disturbing. Paul wondered what tactful *leronis* had thought of this, and whether it was just a way to use the boy's energy and keep him out of trouble. It might even be true—it sounded reasonable.

Inside, the castle was chaos. One wing, and the main part, were almost totally undamaged, and most of the main Keep had not suffered. Whatever the strike, it must have hit a little off center. Paul, searching the wreckage, found no debris that would indicate actual, physical bombs smuggled in, which had been his first thought. He was inclined to agree with the appraisal of the army engineer, that it had been a strike with *laran.*

"We won't know that until we get Master Gareth, or Mistress Melisendra, or Mistress Lori, up here to make sure," the man said. "They can sniff out whether it's *laran* or not; but for now they're busy elsewhere, and rightly so, I suppose, trying to find who hit us, and how to hit back! They may end up by putting a shield over the castle—don't be surprised I know something of that, sir, my sister was a *leronis* in Hali Tower; she died when the Tower was fire-bombed. And my father died thirty years ago when Neskaya was burned. Some day, sir, they've got to get rid of the *laran* weapons. Nothing against your lady, Mistress Melisendra's a good woman, but with respect, sir, the army's no place for women, not even in a corps of wizards, and I'd like to see wars fought honestly with steel instead of witchcraft!"

Paul surprised himself by saying heartily, "So would I! Believe me, man, so would I!"

"But as long as they're sending *laran* weapons against us, I reckon that we'll have to shield ourselves. Nothing evil about putting up a *laran*-proof shield, sir, that no sorcery can get through."

"I'll speak to them about it," said Paul wryly, and the man said, "You do that, Lord General. And if the new king, whoever he is, wants to sign the Compact, sir, tell him the army's all for it!"

Carlina, in her black mantle, was moving around among the few that had been dragged out of the rubble still alive, healing and supervising the healers. Paul saw that her very presence somehow inspired and comforted the sufferers. "Look, a priestess of Avarra, a woman from the Holy Isle has come to tend us!" The other healers did what they could, but reverent silences seemed to follow Carlina as she moved among the sufferers. No one knew or cared that she was, or had been, Ardrin's daughter, the princess Carlina; it was the priestess of Avarra they cared about, and the few who recognized her did not speak of it—or if they did, there was no one to hear.

By nightfall, some semblance of order had been restored. The injured had been moved into the Great Hall, and were being cared for there. Carlina, looking around in a daze, realized that eight years ago she had been handfasted to Bard in this hall, and half a year later had heard him outlawed. It seemed like something in another life. It *had* been something in another life.

The body of King Alaric, crushed and pitiful, had been recovered from the ruin of the great stair in the far wing, and that of Dom Rafael, who had tried, apparently, to cover the boy with his own body as they fell. They were lying in state in the ancient chapel, watched over by old servants, among them old Gwynn. Paul took care not to go inside. He knew that his absence would be remarked—or rather, Bard's absence would be remarked—but he did not trust old Gwynn's sharp eyes.

But outside the chapel, Paul was accosted by two of the chief advisers.

"Lord General—we must speak with you."

"Is this the time, with—" Paul drew a breath and said deliberately, "with my father and brother not yet laid to rest?" He had never seen Alaric; and of Dom Rafael he knew only that the man had brought him here by wizardry. He felt no grief and did not dare try to simulate it.

"There is no more time," said Dom Kendral of High Ridge,

who Paul knew to be the chief Councillor of the Kingdom of
Asturias, "Alaric of Asturias is dead, and his regent with him.
That is the objective situation. Valentine, Ardrin's son, is a
child, and we'll have no Hastur puppets here. The army's with
you, sir, and that's the important thing. We stand ready to support your claim as king, Bard di Asturien."

Paul could only stand and stammer, "Good Lord!"

It was sufficiently bizarre that the chief Councillors of the
kingdom should stand ready to offer the crown to Bard mac Fianna, *nedestro* outlaw, the Kilghard Wolf.

It was unthinkable that they should offer it to Paul Harrell,
exile, rebel, condemned criminal and murderer! Fugitive from
the stasis box!

"Time's the thing, sir. We're at war, and you know what to
do with the army; the army would never accept a child for
king, not now. And you're the Lord General."

Where the hell, Paul wondered savagely, *was Bard anyhow?* What was he doing away at this juncture?

"We have to have a king, sir. If the Hasturs march in on us,
there's nothing we can do about it! We saw how you calmed
down the soldiers this morning. You're the only king I think
the people would accept."

Grimly, Paul knew he had no chance to refuse. Bard had
gone, no one knew where, and everyone here believed he was
Bard. Bard had said, often enough, that he did not want to be
king; but Paul thought that if Bard had been here, in a ruined
castle, with a leaderless army and a kingless country, he too
would have succumbed to the logic of the situation.

"I suppose I have no choice."

"That you don't, sir. There's really nobody else, you see."
Lord Kendral hesitated. "One thing more, sir. You were handfasted once to Ardrin's younger daughter, but Ardrin's line
isn't popular right now. Not since Queen Ariel ran off that way.
You'll have to designate an heir, sir, and since you haven't any
brothers, none living, you'll have to legitimize your son.
Everybody knows who his mother is; it might be a good thing
if you married Mistress MacAran—the Lady Melisendra, of
course, I mean, *vai dom.* The army would like that."

And so, by lamplight in the old presence chamber in the undamaged wing of the castle, Paul Harrell, rebel and condemned criminal from the stasis box, was crowned king,
and married *di catenas* to Melisendra MacAran, *leronis.* Two

thoughts were uppermost in his mind as Master Gareth linked their hands together above the ritual bracelets and said, "May you be forever one."

One was gratitude for Erlend had been put to bed.

The other was a raging curiosity; just where in the hell was Bard di Asturien, and how would he feel when he found out that his double had usurped the throne . . . and presented him with a queen!

CHAPTER EIGHT

Varzil had had to delay most of the day to find someone who could carry on at Neskaya, and it was not till the next morning that they set out for Asturias. Melora, having her donkey saddled, warned Bard with a laugh that she was no better at riding than she had been years ago, on that faraway campaign. Watching her ride, Bard thought that she still sat her donkey like a sack of meal dumped into a saddle. Strange, Melisendra rode gracefully and well. Why was it that he had never had any interest in Melisendra, beyond her beautiful body, and this one meant so much to him?

Perhaps there was a time when I could have cared for Melisendra. But whenever I looked at her, afterward, I was ashamed, and I did not want to know what I had done to her; and so I could not bear to look at her. And was more cruel to her than ever. . . .

I have destroyed everyone I loved. And I have destroyed my own life. And I cannot even die because there are things I must do. Bard rode through the fresh early-autumn beauty of the Kilghard Hills, but his eyes looked inward to a bleak and barren land, and the taste of ashes was cold in his mouth.

Somehow he must set Asturias in order. There was a war to be won, or at least a peace to be made. Since the burning of Hali, there had not, Bard thought, been much taste for the war remaining among the Hasturs, or anywhere else. He had touched Mirella's mind for a moment, and Varzil's, and Melora's, when they spoke of the burning of Hali, and there was a sickness in him now, when he thought of that kind of strike, with clingfire, or the bonewater dust spread around the Venza mountains, and children dying with their blood thinned and pale . . . this was not war! This was nightmare. Bard resolved that at the very least he would dismiss his sorcerers and *leroni*; and if his father refused to swear the Compact, then he could find some other to command his armies. He, Bard, had earned his porridge as a mercenary soldier, in exile, before this. He could do it again.

He thought, grimly, that if his father was resolved on a great general who would lay all these lands waste, and bring all of the Hundred Kingdoms under the lordship of Asturias, he could get Paul to do it for him.

Paul . . . Paul is as ruthless as I was. As I was until . . . gods above, was it only the night before last? I have lost count of the time. It seems that man lived centuries ago. . . .

Paul cannot even see the horrors of laran *warfare, he is immune to the horrors that get inside a man's brain and mind and soul. . . .*

He knew suddenly that he was prepared to kill Paul. Not as he had been, while they rode together on campaign, because eventually his dark twin would pose a threat to his own power and position; but because Paul was the man he himself had been until a day or two ago, and now he was prepared to kill Paul to save his people from the overlordship of the cruel and ruthless man he had been then. He knew it would hurt Melisendra, and he was prepared to try everything short of murder to persuade Paul to give up that ambition. But Paul had not had the experience he had had, and there was nothing in Paul to halt that pitiless ambition. Paul was still capable, as Bard had once been, of riding roughshod over anyone and anything—even Melisendra—to achieve power and pride.

I do not know that for sure. Maybe I have misjudged Paul as I misjudged everything and everyone else. Perhaps he can be brought to see reason. But if he cannot—I do not want to inflict any more pain on Melisendra—but I will not allow him to inflict any more harm. They must know, at the very least, that he is an imposter. I should not have left the command of the army in his hands; he could do infinite harm.

And then he realized that he had meddled—or rather, his father had meddled—in Paul's life without reason, and anything Paul did to him in return was just retribution. It all came back to the old knowledge which, he now knew, had lain dormant within him since first he looked upon the face of his dark twin:

A day will come when I will have to kill him, or he will kill me first.

They followed the road west from Neskaya; but when the road turned north to Asturias, Varzil said, grimly, that they must leave the road for a time and continue west.

"Melora is still of child-bearing years, and so, Bard, are you. That land is blighted; any child born to either of you in after years could be damaged, cell-deep. Even coming this close—I am not even sure Neskaya is safe. We do not know everything, yet, about what that stuff does to the cells. The danger of Neskaya we must all bear, but I will not willingly expose either of you to more danger. At my age it does not matter so much. But you two will probably have children some day. Either of you could have, I mean," he added, and then laughed, spreading his hands as if to say, *That wasn't what I meant* . . . but Bard, looking at Melora in the bright morning, saw a smile as intimate as a kiss of welcome, a smile that warmed him all through the death inside him. In all his life it had never occurred to him that a woman could look at him and smile at him that way.

. . . and that man, Bard, I shall never cease to love. . . .

So she loved him still. It would not be easy. He had made Carlina his wife by force; the law stated that a handfasting, once consummated, was lawful marriage. No doubt Carlina would be glad enough to be rid of him, and he could not make a *leronis* of Neskaya into his *barragana;* so he had little enough to offer Melora. But perhaps they could find some honorable solution.

Strange. All these years he had dreamed of possessing Carlina, and now that he had her he was trying to work out a way to get rid of her. There was a saying in the hills: *Take care how you beseech the gods, they may answer you.*

The worst irony of all, he thought, the worst catastrophe he could envision, would be if Carlina should actually have come to love him, as he had always felt she must do if he once possessed her. He could not restore what he had taken from her, no more than he could make real amends to Melisendra, give her back her virginity and the Sight. But what he could do, he must. If Melisendra wanted Paul, she should have him, even though she might find, in the end, that Paul was no better than himself.

Or was he? He knew no more about Paul than . . . really . . .

he knew about himself. Paul and he were the same man at root. Paul was the man he might have been, no more. Perhaps the differences went deeper than he could guess.

The long detour around the blasted lands took time, and the sun was angling downward past noon when Melora cried out in shock and dismay. Varzil pulled his horse to a stop, his face drawn, and seemed to listen for something out of the range of normal hearing. He reached from his seat in the saddle and took Bard's hand, with an instinctive gesture, as if to offer comfort.

"Alaric!" Bard whispered in shock, and somewhere, distant, in his mind, felt and saw his brother's last sight of the roof buckling to admit the sky, his last frantic clutching at his father for support, the instant and merciful darkness.

Oh, my brother! Merciful gods! My brother, my only brother!

He did not cry the words aloud in agony; he only thought that he did. Varzil held out his arms and Bard let his head fall on the older man's shoulder, in voiceless grief, shaking with an anguish too deep for tears.

"I am sorry," Varzil said in his gentle, muted voice. "He was like a fosterling to me, who have no son, and I cared for him long when he was so very ill."

And Bard knew that Varzil's grief was like his own. He said, shaking, "He loved you, *vai dom,* he told me so . . . it is why I could . . . could trust you."

Varzil's eyes were filled with tears; Melora was weeping. Varzil said, "Do not call me *vai dom,* Bard, I am your kinsman as I was his . . ." and Bard, tears stinging his own eyes, realized that he had never known what it was to have a kinsman, a peer, an equal, since Beltran died . . . he tightened his throat. He could not cry, not now, or he would weep all the tears he had not shed since he saw Beltran lying dead on his own sword, and said farewell to Geremy whom he had maimed for life, and nevertheless had embraced him and wept. . . .

Aldones! Lord of Light! Geremy loved me, too, and I never could believe it, accept it, I drove him away from me, too . . .

He straightened in his saddle, looking across at the older man, his face tightening into control.

He said, "I must ride on and see what is happening at my home—cousin," he said, a little hesitantly. "Please—you must not feel obligated to keep to the pace I set; I must get home as quickly as I can, I will be needed. You may follow at a speed that is comfortable to you. Melora is not a good rider, and you—you are not young."

Varzil's face was set, too. "We will keep pace with you. We may well be needed, too. I think it is safe to turn directly toward Asturias, now, and to take the high road." He wheeled his horse. "If we cut across the fields here, we will be back on the high road within the hour—"

Melora said, "My donkey will not keep up with your horses. We will stop at the first inn where they have staging horses, and I shall leave the donkey there and get a horse that can carry me. I can keep up with you if I must."

Vaszil started to protest, looked at the taut mouth and didn't. Bard wondered what knowledge Melora and Varzil shared from which he was excluded. Varzil only said, "It is your choice, Melora. Do what you feel you must do." They began to ride across the fields.

Within the hour they had exchanged Melora's donkey, leaving him in the care of the staging inn, and found her a gentle saddle horse and a lady's saddle. After that, they made better time, and as they rode toward Asturias, Bard found grim pictures in his mind, whether cast up by his own developing *laran* or adrift on the rapport with Varzil and Melora he did not know and did not care, of ruin and chaos at Castle Asturias. *And all over this land, all over the Hundred Kingdoms. . . .*

This laran *warfare must somehow be ended, or there will be no land to conquer and nothing left for the conquerors. Only in the Compact is there hope for all these lands.* Bard felt that this came from Varzil, and not from his own mind, then he was not so sure.

He is right. He is right. I could not see it, before, but he is altogether right.

He said once, into the grim silence, "I would that you were king instead of the Hastur lord, sir," and Varzil shook his head.

"I want nothing to do with kingship. It is too much temptation for me—to feel that I can set all things right with a word. Carolin of Thendara is not a proud man, or an ambitious one, and he does not mind being ruled by his advisers; he was trained to kingcraft, which is just this—to know that you are not king in yourself, but steward for your people. A good king cannot be a good soldier, or a really good statesman—he must be content to know that he can search out the best soldiers and the best statesmen and be advised by them, and be content to be no more than a visible sign of his reign. I would meddle too much in my own reign, if I were a king," he said with a smile. "As Keeper of Neskaya, I have, perhaps, more power than is good for me. In these times it is useful, perhaps, but maybe it is just as well that I am an old man; times may be coming when a Keeper has not so much power. This, I think, is why I hoped to send Mirella to Arilinn."

"A woman?" Melora asked, startled. "Has a woman the strength to be Keeper?"

"Certainly, as much so as any *emmasca,* and after all, we do not need physical strength, or swordcraft, but strength of will and of mind . . . and women are less inclined to meddle in politics; they know what is real, and what a Tower needs, perhaps, is not a strong man to rule, but a mother, to guide. . . ." Varzil was silent, frowning, and Melora and Bard forbore to disturb his thoughts.

As they rode on, and the day wore toward nightfall, thick clouds began to obscure the horizon. When they paused, near sunset (but the sun was hidden) to eat a little bread and dried meat, they drew their cloaks about them, anticipating rain or even snow, but gradually the weather cleared. Three moons, near full, floated in the dark-purple sky; the green face of Idriel, the blue-green face of Kyrrdis and the pearl disk of Mormallor; Liriel, a shy crescent, lingered near the horizon. In the bright moonlight they could see the road ahead, and, when they came up to the hill overlooking the valley of Asturias, they could see below them the dark mass that was the castle.

Ruin. Chaos. Deaths. . . .

"It is not so bad as that," Melora said quietly.

Varzil said, "I see lights, cousin. Lights, moving, and the shapes of buildings undisturbed. It may not be so bad—forgive me, cousin, I know you have suffered a dreadful loss, but you may not find your home in such ruin as you think. And certainly all is not lost."

But my father. And Alaric. It is not only that I have lost my kinsmen. But certainly the kingdom lies in ruins, with king and regent dead. And what of my men, the army, and I not there to see to them!

I said it to Paul: until I return, you are the Lord General. But what does he know of commanding my men? I taught him how to wield the power. But what does he know of the responsibility, the care for men who look to their leader for direction, for their hope, their comforts and even the necessities of life? Will he know how to make sure that they are well quartered, safe, cared for? Bard realized that in a life where there had been few to love, few to love him, he had loved his men and been loved by them, and he had left them in another man's hands, at a moment which had turned out to be more crucial than he knew!

His father had raised the army for conquest, and for his own ambition, but now his father was dead, and what would become of the army, how could he settle his men? As they rode downward to the castle, not knowing how much ruin they would find, Bard wondered what was to be done with the army. He would return to his father's estate—his father had left no legitimate sons, after all, and there was no other to inherit—and Erlend must, of course, be legitimated, at once, in case he should die before he had any other children. But what of his men? Who would reign over Asturias, and what would that ruler do with the chaos he had inherited, the wreck in the wake of one man's ambition?

He could do nothing until he knew what was left.

It was not so bad as he had feared. One wing of the castle, stark in the moonlight, lay in fallen rubble; lights were still moving in the ruins where workmen sought to dig out any remaining bodies. The main building, and the keep, and the west wing stood intact, enduring and straight against the flooding moonlight. And as they rode to the gates, Bard saw with relief that all was not utter chaos, for the voice of one of his soldiers rang out strong and clear.

"Who rides there? Stand, and declare yourself friend or foe!"

Bard started to call out his name—surely the man would know his voice—but the Keeper of Neskaya was not given to deference to any man alive. His voice was strong and sure.

"Varzil of Neskaya, and a *leronis* of his Tower, Melora MacAran."

"And," Bard added firmly, "Bard mac Fianna, Lord General of Asturias!"

The man's voice was deferential. "*Dom* Varzil! Come away in sir, you'll be welcome, and the *leronis,* her father is here. But by your leave, sir, that man with you isn't the Lord General, you've been gulled by an imposter."

"Nonsense," said Varzil impatiently. "Do you think the Keeper of Neskaya does not know to whom he speaks?"

"I don't know who he is, Lord Varzil, but he's not the Lord General and that's sure. The Lord General is *here*."

Bard said sharply, "Hold that lantern here! Come on, Murakh, don't you know me? The man who's here is my paxman Harryl!"

The man held up the lantern, beginning to be uncertain. He said, uneasily, "Sir, whoever you are, you sure *look* like the Lord General, and you sound like him, too . . . but you can't be the Lord General. I—he's not the Lord General now, he's the king. I was on guard tonight, and I saw him crowned. And married!"

Bard swallowed, unable to do more than stare at the man.

Varzil said quietly, "I assure you, man, this man here beside me is Bard mac Fianna of Asturias, son to Dom Rafael and brother to the late king."

The soldier looked troubled, staring up from Varzil to Bard, shifting the lantern in a shaking hand.

"I've got my duty, sir. It's my business to make sure people are who they say they are. Even if you were the king, begging your pardon, my lord."

Bard said to Varzil, "I'll never fault a soldier for doing his duty. We can settle who I am tomorrow. Don't argue. There are people here who know me beyond doubt. If I'm supposedly married to Lady Carlina—"

The Guardsman shook his head. "I don't know anything about any Lady Carlina, sir, I thought she'd left the court years ago and was in a Tower or a house of priestesses or something like that. But the queen's father, Master Gareth MacAran, he's in the Great Hall tending the hurt folk they dug out of the ruins, and if you're a *leronis,* my lady, they'll welcome you there. . . ."

Bard smiled with grim humor. So he had arrived at Castle Asturias to find that he was king, and married, and now he was to be shut out of the gates as an imposter. Well, he had told Paul to fill his place till he returned, and it seemed that the other man had done so.

Varzil said in his deep voice, "I'll vouch for this man; his identity's something we can settle tomorrow. But I might be needed inside, too."

"Oh, I'll admit him as a member of your suite, Lord Varzil," said Murakh deferentially, and they rode through the gates, giving up their homes in the undamaged stables.

The Great Hall was crowded with wounded men and, divided off by blankets, women; a hospital ward of those who had been injured in the collapse of the east wing, or in the search for bodies. Master Gareth welcomed Varzil, with deference which held no hint of too much humility, as a fellow craftman.

"It's good of you to offer your help, sir. We're short on it and there's so many men here hurt and dying. . . ."

"What happened here?" Varzil demanded.

"As near as we can tell, it's the men of Aldaran, taking this time to get into the war. Tomorrow the Lord General—the king, sir—will have to decide what's to be done, perhaps we can stop 'em at the Kadarin, but right now we've put a *laran*-shield over the castle . . . they won't strike at us again with *that*, but of course we can't maintain it all that long; it's taking four men and a boy. They must have known the army was here and wanted to put us about, so we wouldn't know what they were doing . . . but right now I have to see to the wounded. And you, Melora, there's need enough for someone among the women. As usual in any commotion, two or three women, one of the court ladies and one of the kitchen girls, and yes, one of the army's washerwomen, took just *this* time to go a-birthing, so there's more work than one midwife can handle. Avarra be praised, a priestess of Avarra was here, only the Goddess knows why, and she's caring for them, but there were women hurt on the rockfalls, too, so if you'd go and help the healer-women, Melora—"

"Certainly I will go," Melora said, turning her steps toward the other part of the hall, and after a moment's thought, Bard followed. Carlina, here—and as a priestess of Avarra! When, if he had been crowned king of this land, she should be queen. . . .

He found her bending over a woman with a bandaged arm and leg, her eye and skull bandaged. She saw Melora first and said curtly, "Are you a healer, and do you know anything of midwifery? One of the women has borne children before, I can safely leave her to the maids, but this woman is going to die, and there is a woman in labor who is past thirty, and bearing her first child, and another young girl with her first. . . ."

"I am not a midwife, but I am a woman and I have been taught something of healing," Melora said, and Carlina looked her full in the face by the shaded lamp.

"Melisendra—" she said, and then stopped and blinked. "No, you are not even much like her, are you? You must be her sister, the *leronis*—there is no time to ask now how you came here, but in the name of Avarra I bless you! Will you come, then, and help me with the wounded?"

"Gladly," Melora said. "Where are the women in labor?"

"We carried them into that room there, it was the old king's study once . . . I will be with you in a moment," Carlina said. She bent again to the dying woman, put a hand to her forehead, shook her head.

"She will not wake again," she said, and went toward the room where she had sent Melora; but Bard laid a light hand on her sleeve.

"Carlie," he said.

She started away in shock; then, perhaps sensing in his voice that he was no threat to her, she let her breath go and said, "Bard. I did not expect to see you here—"

He saw the darkening bruise on her cheekbone. *Merciful Avarra, I did that to her . . .* but he had no time even for shame or self-pity. Even abasing himself to Carlina could wait. His land was under attack by Aldaran, and in the hands of an usurper.

"What's this nonsense about my being crowned tonight, and married to someone else?"

"Crowned, married? I don't know, Bard, I have been here all day since the other wing of the castle collapsed, tending the sick and hurt. I've had no time for anything else—I have had time for nothing, only to swallow a little bread and cheese. . . ."

"Is there no one else to do this, Carlie? You look so weary—"

"Oh, I am used to it, this is the work of a priestess—" she said with a faint smile. "And, although you may not believe it, Bard, that is what I am. Although perhaps I have been sheltered too long, perhaps we need the priestesses more in the world than on the Holy Isle."

"Melisendra—is she—"

"She was with me at the time of the attack; she was unhurt. And your son, he is well, I heard. He was with Master Gareth all day," she said. "But Bard, I have no time for you now, these women are dying. And the men, too . . . do you know there were over a hundred men hurt, and twelve of them have already died, so tomorrow we will have to have a whole regiment of soldiers to dig graves somewhere, and someone to send word to their families. . . . Bard, can you send someone to the Holy Isle, to beg priestesses to come and help me with the hurt and dying? If you send express riders, they can be there by daylight—"

"Certainly I can do that," said Bard, sobered, "but will they listen to any man, will they come?"

"Not for the King of Asturias, perhaps. But perhaps for me, if they know it is I who ask it, Sister Liriel—"

"But there is no man can win through even to the shores of the Lake of Silence, Carlie, without incurring their evil sorceries—" he stopped. No, the sorceries were not evil; they were only protecting themselves. He said humbly, "No man can win through the protections they have laid about themselves without dying of terror."

"But a woman may do so," said Carlina. "Bard, with your army, have you any of the sworn Sisterhood of the Sword? They too ride under the protection of Avarra."

"I think they have all left me, Carlina. But I will go and ask my sergeants; some of them will surely know."

"Then send one of the Sisterhood, Bard. Beg her to ride there and bear the message from me, that they will come—"

Bard started to say that he did not *beg* anyone in his army to do what he—or she—was bidden to do by a lawful commander, then stopped himself. If Carlina could beg, he could too. He said, "I will send express riders at once, lady," and went away, leaving Carlina staring after him, knowing that something very strange had happened, not only in the kingdom of Asturias, but within Bard too.

Bard went away toward the stables, thinking, with relief, that at least Carlina had not taken that moment to rail and upbraid him. She had a right to make a scene if she wanted to. He had done her wrong enough. But the greater tragedy had wiped out any personal consideration, as it had in himself.

One of his sergeants told him that when the prisoners and the mercenaries in his army had ridden away together, one of the women had been too sick to ride, and another of the sworn Sisters had remained to nurse her and care for her. The two

were living together in a little tent near where the army's camp
followers and washer women were housed, beyond the regular
army barracks. Bard started to say, tell her to ride express at
once and send someone to look after her friend, then he realized
that he was asking an extraordinary service of someone whom
he had denied proper protection. He had better go himself.

He lost himself in the army encampment two or three times,
before he finally found the quarters of the army camp followers.

Even in the wake of the disaster, here where the army was
quartered things were reasonably normal. Men not badly hurt
were being nursed by their comrades, and some of the women
had been pressed to help. A few of the women who followed
the army looked at Bard with a sidelong smile, and he knew he
had not been recognized. It reminded him of his days as a mercenary soldier, and that in turn made him think of Lilla, and
her son, who was probably his son as well. He had not harmed
Lilla as he had harmed so many women; that was probably because she had neither expected nor needed anything from him,
except what little money he could spare from a soldier's pay to
care for her son. She had given him no power to hurt her, and
so he could not harm her in any way.

*Yes, I harmed many women. But perhaps the women were
not all blameless either. They lived in such a way that they
could be destroyed by men . . .* in a sense he was no more to
blame than any man in his world. Every man in his world. Was
the whole world to blame, then?

"Well, Captain," said one of the camp followers, "are you
looking for some fun?"

He shook his head. Evidently she had not recognized his
rank and thought him a common soldier, *captain* was flattery,
no more. "Not tonight, my girl, I have more important things
on my mind. Can you tell me where the sworn Sisters, the Renunciates, are lodged?"

"You won't get any pleasure from that pair, sir, they've got
daggers for kisses, and the general said he'd have something
worse for anyone who meddles with them," the pleasure woman
said.

Bard grinned companionably and said, "Believe it or not,
pretty one, a man does have other things on his mind now and
then, hard as it is to imagine it." There was no harm in the girl.
"I've a message for one of them from the—" he hesitated, "the

leronis working in the field hospital. And if you can get your mind to it, there's work there for anyone."

She said, staring at the pebbles under her feet, "What would the likes of me do, helping a *leronis,* sir?"

"Well, you could carry water and roll bandages and feed the folks who can't sit up to feed themselves," Bard said. "Why not go and try it?"

"You're right, captain, this is no time to be lying about with people hurt," said the woman. "I suppose plenty of us could be used in the nursing. I'll go and see. And if you're wanting the Sisterhood, sir, there's two of 'em in that tent there, but—" she glared at him, "don't be getting any dirty ideas. One of them's so badly hurt she can't sit up, and her friend's just nursing her. The men got at her before the general gave his orders, and it's not with them like it is with—with women like me, sir, she wasn't accustomed—and they hurt her pretty bad." Her scowl was fierce. "Men like that ought to be treated worse than whipping, sir."

Avarra's mercy! All the old scalding shame and guilt washed heavily over Bard again. He said, to the woman's surprise, "You're absolutely right," and went toward the indicated tent. He did not dare to approach it. The women there would probably, after all they had been through, strike first at any man who came near, and ask questions afterward. He called softly from outside *"Mestra—"*

A woman appeared in the door of the tent, crawled out and rose to her feet. She wore the red tunic of the Sisterhood, red leather, knee-length and split in front for riding, and her hair, clipped short, was tousled all over her head. She said fiercely, "Keep your voice down! My sister is very bad!" She was tall and thin, and wore a knife in her belt. A golden circlet gleamed in her ear.

"I'm sorry for her hurts," Bard said, "but I have a message from the *leronis* at the hospital. I need someone to ride express at once for Marenji and the Island of Silence." He explained, and the woman looked at him, troubled. Bard moved into the circle of light from a lantern hung on a pole over the camp street, and she recognized him.

"Lord General! Well, sir, I'd go and welcome, but—but my sister needs me badly, sir. You heard what happened—"

"Yes, I know," Bard said, "but can't you take her to the field hospital? If she's as badly off as that, she needs more care than you can give her, and surely the priestess of Avarra will help her."

The Renunciate scowled at him, but there were tears in her eyes. She said, "The priestesses—they're holy virgins, sir, and they wouldn't want to be involved with the Sisterhood. They think, no doubt, that we're not proper women. And what would they know of a woman who's been raped again and again, and—and she's *infected,* sir—"

"I think you'll find she's more sympathetic than you know," Bard said. "The priestesses of Avarra are sworn to help *all* women." That much he had seen from Carlina's mind. "But you must ride at once. I'll arrange for a stretcher to have her carried up to the hospital." He strode back toward the barracks, shouting for a stretcher. In a few minutes the hurt woman was being lifted out, carefully, and her sister/friend bending over her.

"Tresa, *breda,* these people will take you to a *leronis* who can help you better than I can—"

She turned to Bard and said, her voice shaking, "I hate to leave her with strangers—"

He said "I'll see her into the hands of the *leronis* myself, *mestra*, but yours is a task only a woman can do; no man may approach the Island of Silence." Carlina would care for her and if for some reason or another Carlina could not, he was sure Melora would know what to do for her.

Carllna was still distractedly going between the injured women in one room, and the midwifery in the other, when he had the woman carried in. Melora was wrapping up a newborn child.

"I have another for you to help," Bard said, and explained what had happened.

"Yes, certainly, I'll look after her," Carlina promised, and he fancied that the look she gave him was puzzled, *since when do you trouble yourself about such things?*

He said, angry, defensive, "She is a soldier and a prisoner; and it was my men who hurt her, damn it! Are you too virtuous to tend her?"

"Of course not, Bard," she said. "I told you we would look after her. You women—" she gestured to the women who had insisted on carrying the litter, taking over from the soldiers, "I can use every pair of hands! Even those of you who don't know the first thing of nursing, you can feed people and carry trays and boil water and make porridge!"

Bard glanced at the sky, lightening outside the castle. It was near dawn. "I'll send the army cooks to make the porridge," he promised. Any soldier on duty could be dispatched with that message, and it took him only a moment to have it handled, and to put a sergeant at the immediate disposal of Master Gareth and Varzil. The sergeant was a veteran who had known Bard on many campaigns and never thought to question Bard's identity. As he saluted and said, "As the Lord General wishes," Bard reflected that his father had brought Paul to this world so that, in effect, Bard could be in two places at once. Well, that was happening; the Lord General, newly crowned king, was in his royal suite with his newly made queen, and the Lord General was down here giving orders in the field hospital.

My father cared for me only as a tool for his ambition!

He had believed that all his life. But now he knew it was not true. For long before Dom Rafael di Asturien could have known whether his son would be a soldier, or a statesman, or a *laranzu* or a feeble-minded ne'er do well, his father had had him taken from his mother, had him reared in his own house, schooled and taught in all the manly arts, fostered by his lady, given horses and hounds and hawks, reared as a nobleman's son, deprived himself, even, of what company his son could have given him in order to have him fostered at court with princes and noblemen for foster brothers. Yes, his father had loved him unselfishly, not only for his own good. And even the mother who had given him up—Bard knew, staring at the red dawn and the great red sun rising over the jagged teeth of the Kilghard Hills, that his mother must have loved him, too; loved him enough to give up her child so that he might be reared as a nobleman's son and not scratch his living on a bare hill farm. He wondered, literally for the first time in his life, if that unknown mother was still living. He could never, now, ask his father. But Lady Jerana might know, and she had been kind to him, in her own way; would have been kinder, if he had allowed it. He would, if he must, humble himself to Lady Jerana and beg from her the name of his mother, and where in the hills she dwelled, so that he could kneel before her and do her honor for loving him enough to give him up to his father's love.

His eyes blurred with tears.

I have been loved, all my life, and I never knew.

What's happening to me? I want to weep all the time! Is it only laran, *or have I become a milksop, a mollycoddle, the kind of man I always despised.* . . .

He would grow accustomed to what had happened; he knew it. But he also knew, deep and hard within himself, that he had become a different man. He was surprised, but not ashamed, of the man he had become. His shame was reserved for the man he had been, and that man was *dead*. He need waste neither guilt nor shame on that former Bard.

He must find time to speak with Carlina again. They had not finished what lay between them. But her business was with the living, too, and the dead Bard could not be much more interesting to her than he was to himself. And so, as the first streaks of real daylight lightened the sky, he went in search of Paul Harrell and of Melisendra.

CHAPTER NINE

By dawn Varzil had done all that he could do in the field hospital, had sent Master Gareth, protesting, to rest. "A few hours will make no difference."

Master Gareth said, "You've worked all night too, and ridden all the day before. And you're not young either, Dom Varzil!"

"No, but younger than you are, and I'll deal with what needs to be dealt with. Go and rest!" he said, suddenly drawing himself up to his full height—he was not very tall—and speaking in command voice, and Master Gareth sighed.

"It's a long time since any man commanded me, sir, but I'll obey you."

When the old *laranzu* had gone, Varzil detailed orderlies to feed those who were able to eat and to look after those who were not, and went into the women's part of the Great Hall. He found Melora there, her dress pinned up and a sheet tucked around her.

"Well, child, how is it with you?"

She grinned. "Asturias has three new subjects," she said, "whoever the king may be. A soldier's son and a kitchen maid, and to judge by the red hair, a *leronis* for his council. I did not know that I had talent to be a midwife, but then, I did not know till yesterday that I could ride a horse, either."

"Well, moving around is the best way to keep from getting saddle sores after all that riding," he told her, "but now, *breda*, you must go and rest. And you too, good mother," he said, looking at Carlina in her black mantle.

"Yes," she said, tiredly drawing her hand across her eyes, "I think I have done all I can here. These women can care for them while I rest a little."

"But you *vai tenerézu?*" Melora asked.

He said, "The army has been put at my disposal; I will consult Bard, whether he is Lord General or king, but before that—" he looked at the lightening sky, "I will go and have sentry birds flown, to see if we are under attack from Aldaran. If they are sending an army against Asturias, Bard must somehow manage to stop them at the Kadarin. And if not—well, we will think of that later."

He went away, and Carlina stood watching, suddenly aware that she had neither eaten nor drunk since Melisendra had fed her soup and custard yesterday. She said, "Varzil spoke to me as if I were a priestess of Avarra."

Neither of the women thought it strange that Melora should know precisely what had happened to Carlina or why. She said, "You belong to the Goddess still, do you not?"

"Always. But even if I could return to the Island of Silence, I am not sure I should do so. I think we have been too isolated, on our safe little island, protected by powerful spells, and not caring what goes on in the world outside. And yet—how can women live together, unwed, in safety?"

"The Sisterhood of the Sword do so," Melora said.

"But they have means of protection we do not have," Carlina said, and thought, *I could never wield a sword; I am a healer, I am a woman . . . and it seems to me no part of a woman's life to make war, but to care for others. . . .*

"Perhaps," said Melora hesitantly, "the Goddess needs both of your sisterhoods, one to be strong, and the other to help and heal. . . ."

Carlina's smile was shaky. She said, "I do not think they have much more respect for our way of life than we—" the smile was rueful now, "than we have for theirs."

"Then," said Melora, and her clear voice was not command voice but it might just as well have been, "you must learn respect for one another's ways. You are Renunciates too. And people can change, you know."

Yes, Carlina thought, *if Bard can change so much, there should be hope that anyone on the face of this restless world can change! I must speak to Varzil about this; as Keeper of Neskaya, perhaps he has some answers for us.*

Melora said, "Forgive me, Mother—" using the title of respect given to a priestess, "but you are the Princess Carlina, are you not?"

"I was. I renounced that name many years ago." With a pang Carlina realized that, as the laws stood, she was lawfully married to Bard. And if Bard should have made her pregnant! *What would I do with a child? His child!*

"I thought so; I last saw you at midsummer Festival, but I do not think you saw me, I was only Master Gareth's daughter—"

"I saw you. Dancing with Bard," Carlina said, and then, because she too had *laran,* she said, "You love him. Don't you?"

"Yes, I do not think he knows it yet." Melora giggled, suddenly, nervously. "I am told that the Lord General was crowned, and married, yesterday. And as the laws stand also, you are his wife, handfasted. So, at the moment, he has at least one lawful wife too many. I am sure he will want to be free of at least one of them . . . and, if I know him at all, of both. Perhaps, Carlina—Mother Liriel—this misunderstanding will all turn out for the best, since the whole matter of his marriage must be cleared up by the laws."

"Let us hope so," Carlina said, and impulsively took Melora's hand.

"Come and rest, *vai leronis*. I can find a place for you among the ladies-in-waiting; I will send them down to do what they can for the wounded and the sick, and you must sleep."

Meanwhile, Bard di Asturien walked along the halls of the castle toward the rooms he had occupied since Alaric was crowned and had appointed him Lord General. There was a guardsman before the door, telling him that the Lord General—supposedly—was within.

Bard thought for a moment. He could, of course, walk up to the door and demand, as Lord General, to be admitted. Most of the men in the army knew the Kilghard Wolf by sight. But he was not quite ready for that confrontation yet. So after a moment's thought he went around through a hallway to a back entrance whose very existence was known only to his most trusted men.

He walked through the rooms as if he had never seen them before. He hadn't; the man who had slept here only a few nights ago was a different man. In the great bedchamber they lay sleeping; Paul, on his back, and Bard looked on his own face with strange, dispassionate interest. Melisendra lay curled against him, her head on his shoulder, and even in sleep Bard could see the protective way his arm curled around the woman. Her red curls were scattered, covering Paul's face.

Bard reflected, distantly, that had he found them like this, in his own rooms, *before,* he would have lost no time in whipping out his dagger and cutting their throats. Even now he reflected on it for a moment, Paul had tried to unsurp his throne; had been crowned in his name, and by marrying Melisendra in the sight of half the kingdom, had provided the Throne of Asturias with a queen who would, somehow, have to be publicly repudiated. Even if Paul were willing to yield up the identity of Lord General, that still left Bard married to Melisendra. What a tangle! And by what he had done, he had made Carlina lawfully his wife, and he could not publicly repudiate her, either! How in the name of all the gods was he to solve this? For a moment, Bard contemplated slipping out of the room as quietly as he had entered it, taking his horse, and riding away into the hills again. He did not want the Kingdom of Asturias. He had been sure they would find someone else, even when he had the shocking knowledge of his father's death and Alaric's. Beyond the Kadarin there were dozens of little kingdoms, and he had earned his way as a mercenary before. . . .

But what of his men, if he did that? Paul had not the knowledge or the interest to care for them. What of Carlina, of the pledge he had made to the Sisterhood of the Sword, of Melisendra, of Melora? No, he still had responsibilities here. And after all, he had left Paul, knowingly, to fill the place of the Lord General. Perhaps Paul had simply been protecting his good name and reputation—how would it look, after all, if it had been known that at the time of the sneak attack on Castle Asturias, the Lord General had run to weep on a woman's shoulder for his crimes? Paul must have his chance to explain; he would not kill him sleeping.

He leaned across Melisendra, looking down with a tenderness that surprised him, at her sandy eyelashes resting on her cheek, at the fullness of her breast where the thin nightgown, so thin that the skin showed pink through it, was gathered in flimsy folds. She had given him Erlend, and for that, at least, he must always show her love and gratitude.

Then he shook Paul's shoulder lightly.

"Wake up," he said.

Paul sat up in bed, with a start. Instantly alert, he saw Bard's drawn face, and knew at once that he was in immediate danger of death. His first thought was to protect Melisendra. He leaped upright, putting himself between Bard and the woman.

"None of this is her fault!"

Bard's smile surprised him. He looked, simply, amused. "I know that," he said. "Whatever happens, I'm not going to hurt Melisendra."

Paul relaxed a little, but he was still wary. "What are you doing here, like this?"

"I had intended to ask *you* that," Bard said. "It's my room, after all. I hear they crowned you last night. And—married you. To Melisendra. Can you blame me for wondering if you've got it into your head to claim the throne to Asturias? They almost didn't let me into the castle last night because they had a firm notion I was some kind of imposter."

For some reason, Bard noted, they were both speaking in whispers. But even so, their voices woke Melisendra, and she sat up in bed, her hair spilling down over the breast of her gown. She stared, wide-eyed, at Bard. Then, in a rush, she said, "Bard! No! Don't hurt him! He didn't intend—"

"Let him answer for himself as to what he intended!" Bard snarled, and his voice was like steel.

Paul set his teeth. He said, "What did you expect me to do? They came to me, they said I was the king, they demanded that I marry Melisendra! Did you expect me to say, Oh no, I'm not the Lord General, the Lord General was last seen heading for Neskaya? They didn't ask me what to do; they *told* me! If you'd come back in time—but no, you were off on some business of your own and left me to see to things—you haven't even asked about your son! You're about as fit to command this kingdom as—as *he* is, and that's not much of a compliment, because I imagine anything in pants could handle it better than you will! If you could get your mind off your women for ten minutes, and pay attention to what you're supposed to be doing—"

Bard whipped his dagger out of his sheath. Melisendra screamed, and three guardsmen burst into the room. Seeing Bard in a common soldier's dress, and Paul in his nightshirt, they leaped at once to the obvious conclusion, and went for Bard with drawn swords.

"Draw steel in the presence of the king, will you?" one of them yelled, and moments later, Bard stood disarmed, held between two of the guardsmen.

"What shall we do with him, Lord General—beg pardon—your Majesty?"

Paul stood staring from the guardsmen to Bard, realizing that he had jumped from the frying pan full tilt into the fire. He did not want to have the father of Melisendra's son killed before his eyes. He realized, painfully and just a second too late, that he was not angry with Bard at all.

Hell, in the long run, I got the stasis box because I couldn't keep my hands off the wrong women. Who am I to be slanging at him? And yet, if I admit that he is the king, and the Lord General, then I am in bed with the queen, and from all I know about this country that's going to be a fairly serious crime too—not to mention Bard's pride! If I have him killed, Melisendra will probably tell them the truth. If I don't, I'd be a hell of a lot better off in the stasis box! Because I have no doubt they have the death penalty here—and probably some clever ways of enforcing it!

The senior guardsman looked at Paul and demanded, "My lord—"

Bard said, "There's some mistake here, I should think—"

"Somebody's making one all right," said one of the guardsmen grimly. "This man tried to get into the palace last night claiming that he was the Lord General; he'd even managed to fool the lord Varzil of Neskaya! I think he's a Hastur spy. Shall we take him out and hang him, sire?"

Melisendra jumped out of bed, in her thin nightgown, careless of the stare of the guardsmen. She opened her mouth to speak. And at that moment there was an outcry in the halls, and a messenger entered.

"My lord King! An envoy from the Hasturs, under truce flag! Varzil of Neskaya sends word that you should see them at once in the throne room!"

The guardsmen whipped round. Bard said, "Impossible. The throne room's full of the sick and wounded; we'll have to see the envoys on the lawn. Ruyvil—" he said to the youngest of the guardsmen, "you know me, don't you? Remember the campaign to Hammerfell, when I argued with King Ardrin and got you to ride with us, and how Beltran's banner got tangled around your pike?"

"Wolf!" the guardsmen said, then turned, menacing, to Paul.

"Who is *this* man?"

Bard said quickly, "My paxman, and my proxy. I had to go on urgent business to Neskaya, and left him here; and he was crowned by proxy—"

The oldest of the guardsmen—who had demanded to take Bard and hang him—said suspiciously, "And married by proxy too?"

Young Ruyvil said, "Don't talk that way to the king, nithead, or you'll find your own head's loose on your shoulders! Do you think I don't know the Kilghard Wolf? I could have been booted right out of the army for that! Do you think an imposter would know about it?"

Paul said smoothly, picking up the loophole Bard had left for both of them, "I am not daring enough to meddle in my king's marriage. He had promised me Melisendra; and I married *her*. His Majesty—" he looked at Bard swiftly, and the message was clear, *get yourself out of this one any way you want to, now,* "could not have married the Lady Melisendra even if he wished; he is lawfully married to someone else."

Bard gave Paul an undeniably grateful look. He said, "Go and tell the envoy that I will meet with them as soon as I have shaved and dressed. And send word to Lord Varzil of Neskaya, as well." When the guardsmen and the messenger had gone, he turned to Melisendra and said, "Believe it or not, I had intended to marry you to Paul; but you have forstalled me. I'll have to have Erlend; he is all the heir I have."

Her chin quivered, but she said, "I won't stand in his way." And Bard thought of the unknown mother who had given him to Dom Rafael to be reared as a nobleman. Were all women this selfless? He said gruffly, "I'll see that he remembers he's *your* son, as well. Now, damn it, no bawling before breakfast! Send my body servant to me, with some proper clothes for an audience! And Paulo, cut your hair—we want to play *down* the resemblance—you're not out of the woods yet!"

As Paul went into the inner room, Melisendra laid on a hand on his arm.

"I am glad—" she said, and smiled. He put his arm around her.

"What else could I have done?" he demanded. "If I'd done anything else. I'd have been stuck with the kingdom!"

And he realized, with complete astonishment, that he had spoken the truth. He did not envy Bard. Not even a little. And perhaps—just perhaps—things had been settled so that he need not kill Bard in order to keep from being killed by him. With the Bard he had known before—that would never have been possible. But something had happened to Bard, in the short space since he brought Carlina from the Island of Silence. He did not know what it was; but somehow, subtly, this was a different man. Melisendra, he thought, knew what the change was, and perhaps, some day, she would tell him.

Or maybe Bard would. Nothing would surprise him, now.

Shaved, dressed, his blond braid bound with the red cord of a warrior, Bard glanced at himself in the mirror. He looked the same man, but he was still a stranger in his own skin, not knowing what he would do next. Paul had done the right thing, unwittingly—though he had not expected it; he had been afraid Paul would try to bluff it through, and he'd have had no choice except to have him killed.

No. I wouldn't have had him killed. I have destroyed too many people already. I might have struck him down myself, in anger, but I could not have stood there in cold blood and ordered him killed. He is too much a part of myself now. And it has turned out well, for I am free of Melisendra.

But he was still bound by law to Carlina, and if she needed the protection of this marriage—if, for instance, all merciful gods forbid, he had made her pregnant—he could not, now, honorably deny her the position of his queen. His whole heart cried out for Melora; but although he knew he would love her as long as he lived, he could not come to her by trampling Carlina into the dust or ignoring her claim on him.

Take care how you beseech the gods for a gift; for they will give it to you. And he remembered Melora, on that fated and faraway Festival night, saying that she would not step on the hem of Carlina's robe.

If I had only had sense enough to go to Carlina, then, and offer her freedom from a marriage neither of us wanted . . . but not even a god can bring back the leaves that have fallen. He had woven this tangle with Carlina, and unless it could be honorably untied, he would live in its coils.

It seemed to him, though he stood as straight as he could, that the man in the mirror bent under a heavy burden. Yes, this land of Asturias, where he had no will to reign, lay now on his shoulders, *Oh, my brother! I would so willingly have been your general, not worn your crown!* But the wine had been poured and must be drunk. He turned away from the mirror, setting his teeth and squaring his shoulders. His armies had chosen the Kilghard Wolf to rule over them, and rule he must.

A canopy and a chair in lieu of throne had been set up for him on the lawn. He looked, with grim incredulity, at the lines of bowing courtiers, the soldiers and guards coming to swift attention as he passed. He had never seen this formality when it surrounded his father, or King Ardrin. He had simply taken it for granted. He thought briefly that it was just as well that for this first ascent to his throne it was a canopy and a chair. He remembered stumbling at the foot of Ardrin's throne when he had been granted the red cord.

"Sir, the envoy from the Hasturs."

It was Varzil who had spoken, and Bard remembered, with what little he knew of protocol, that the Keeper of a major Tower ranked with any king. He beckoned Varzil to approach the chair where he sat.

"Cousin, must this be a formal assembly?"

"Only if you wish."

"Then send away all these people and let me speak to the envoys in peace," Bard said, and as Varzil dismissed the courtiers and all but the skeleton of a personal guard, Bard looked at the envoy. As he had known it would be, there was the truce flag of King Carolin, and in blue and silver of the Hasturs, Geremy Hastur.

He stepped toward Geremy to take him into a formal kinsman's embrace, and at the touch, all the old affection flooded back. Could he some day rediscover Geremy, too?

Geremy has *laran,* too, he thought, he knows. And as he raised his eyes to Geremy's face, he saw in that look, though Geremy looked drawn and careworn, the same acceptance, the same understanding he had seen in Melora's.

He said, and knew that his voice was shaking with the emotion he could no longer pretend not to feel, "Welcome to Asturias, cousin. It is a sad welcome indeed, and based on a bereavement—my father and brother are not yet at rest, but lie unburied until there is some order in this kingdom. We are under attack from Aldaran, and I find myself, undesired, on a throne I do not know how to fill. But although it is a poor welcome, I am glad to have you here—" and his voice broke. He stopped, knowing he would break down and weep in the sight of them all if he did not. He felt Geremy's hand, hard, over his.

"Would that I could bring you some comfort—foster brother," Geremy said, and Bard swallowed hard. "I grieve deeply for your bereavement. I did not know Dom Rafael well, but I knew Alaric and loved him, and he was overyoung to be torn so swiftly out of life. But even in this hour of sorrow we must care for the living. Varzil has told me news which I believe you have not yet heard. Varzil, kinsman, tell Bard what your sentry birds have seen."

"Aldaran has joined this war," Varzil said. "We knew from Master Gareth, last night, and his *leroni,* that they had sent the sorcery which broke the castle walls. Now there is an army on the march from the Darriell forest, and he is allied with Scath-fell and other little kingdoms to the north. They are still many days north of the Kadarin, but I believe they think they will take you in chaos and bereavement. But I have later news still. Tramontana has sworn neutrality; they will make no more *laran* weapons. And they are the last of the Towers to swear, for Arilinn has so sworn to the Hasturs."

"So," Geremy said, "the martyrs at Hali died to some purpose, then. For now there is no single Tower in this land which will manufacture clingfire, or bonewater dust, or the blight which has attacked the Venza hills. I came to ask Dom Rafael, not knowing of his death—I came to ask him, for a second time, to swear Compact, and join with me and my *leroni,* if only to disable the stocks of *laran* weapons which remain. We have sworn not to use them, but we can defend ourselves against them."

Bard considered this, silently, staring at the fallen wing of the castle. Aldaran had come against him with *laran,* and how did they know what he had left in his arsenal? At last he said, "I would gladly do so, Geremy. When there is peace again in this land, I will swear to Compact, and woe to any man who breaks it, and the *leroni* may go back to telling fortunes for lovesick maidens and telling breeding women whether they will bear sons or daughters, or to healing the sick and sending relay messages faster than an express rider. But while the land is at war, I dare not. I must put my army on the road within three days if I am to stop Aldaran and hold him on his own side of the Kadarin!"

"For that, I offer you an alliance," Geremy said. "I am empowered by Carolin to send his men beside you against Aldaran. He is welcome to reign across the Kadarin, but we do not want him in the Hundred Kingdoms."

"I will accept Carolin's help gratefully," Bard said. "But I cannot swear to Compact until I have put my kingdom in order. And I will swear an alliance with the Hasturs." He knew, as he spoke, that he was tearing down, in a few words, all that his father had fought to do. But it had been his father's ambition, not his own. He would rule, but he had no further desire to conquer. Let those who owned and ruled over the land possess it in peace. He had enough trouble with a kingdom; he shuddered at the thought of ruling over an empire. He was only one man; he had set his dark twin free.

Geremy sighed. "I had hoped you were ready for Compact, Bard, now you have seen what the lack of it has done to this land. And it is worse in Hastur country. Have you seen the children being born in the Venza hills and near Carcosa?"

Bard shook his head. "I said, Geremy, we will talk of it again when Aldaran is resigned to staying on his own side of the Kadarin. And now, if you please, I have to set my army ready for the march." Who would rule while he was with the army? Could he trust Carlina to reign as his regent? Could he induce Varzil to stay at his court and see all things done well? How could he decide? He smiled grimly, thinking that once again he needed to be in two places at once, on his throne here, and with his army on the march! Would the army follow Paul? Should he put it into his hands of one of his father's experienced veteran commanders?

He summoned four or five of his father's men, veteran commanders, and talked with them for a considerable time about the deployment of the army. He stepped briefly into the Great Hall to move for a few minutes among the wounded men there. The army had organized plenty of orderlies, and the women were being tended by every woman in the castle who was not busy elsewhere. He recognized Lady Jerana's own personal maid, and realized even she must be dressing herself this morning.

He had had no glimpse of Melora; where had she gone? He hungered to have a sight of her, although till this tangle with Carlina should be settled, he knew he could not say a word to her about what was in his heart. Master Gareth came toward him, and he asked, "What is doing, my old friend? Are there enough *leroni* to maintain the shield of the castle?"

"We're trying, sir," Master Gareth said, "although I don't know how long we can keep it up, and I'd take it kindly if you'd ask Lord Geremy Hastur to lend you his sorcerers too."

"I'll do that, or you may ask him yourself."

"Ah, but the request would mean more from you, sir."

"And what of Mistress Melora? The Lord Varzil lent her to you last night to care for the sick—"

"She's leaving that to the Mother Liriel, the priestess, you know, this morning," said Master Gareth. Bard, in a split-second flash of insight, realized that Carlina, Mother Liriel as she was now calling herself, had no more wish to recognize that lapsed marriage contract and handfasting than he did. Was he truly free? He and Carlina must talk together, have it clear and understood, but his spirits lifted, even as Master Gareth said, "I sent Melora to fly her sentry birds; she's the best at handling them that I ever knew. She sent me to tell you there's a great column of priestesses on the road from the Island of Silence, and they're being escorted by riders in red."

"So the Sisterhood of the Sword has done as they said—" Bard began, but at that very moment Melora appeared at the back of the lawn, waving her arms and calling frantically, distraught.

Bard ran toward her, Master Gareth puffing behind on his elderly legs.

"What is it, Melora?"

"Send for Varzil! Oh, in the name of all the gods, send for Dom Varzil," she cried out. "Rory, who has the Sight, has seen for us! The *laran* shield had remained in place, but there are air-cars heading this way, and we have now no defenses against them! Get the army to it—we must get the wounded into the open air before the roof falls in on them!"

Master Gareth's face paled, but his voice was severe.

"Nothing can be gained by panic, Melora—you can reach Varzil easier than I!"

Melora's face went still and remote. Bard, falling into swift rapport with her, heard her soundless cry to Varzil, and within seconds he saw not Varzil alone but Geremy, on unsteady feet, hurrying toward them.

"Bard," Geremy snapped, "you haven't enough *laran* to be any good at this, not yet—you attend to getting the wounded out of the hall, in case we can't stop them!"

It did not occur to Bard that Geremy, who was not even in his own kingdom, was giving orders to the reigning king. What Geremy said seemed so completely rational that he hurried to obey. As he ran he beckoned to a guardsman.

"Find me Paolo Harryl and the Lady Melisendra!" And then, with his new *laran,* he wondered if he could use his closeness to either of them. He had always been in contact with Paul's mind. And this was a time when he needed to be in two places at once!

Paul! Get enough men up here to carry the wounded out safely!

From a corner of his eye he saw Melora and Geremy, Master Gareth and Varzil of Neskaya, hands linked, incongruously looking as if they were about to join in a ring and dance one of the children's dances! But even Bard, newly opened to *laran,* could see the psychic force, an almost tangible barrier building around them. Then he hurried inside the hall and started giving orders to the soldiers.

"Everybody who can walk, get outside, and as far away from the buildings as you can! Orderlies, help the people who can walk with a little help! We've had warning, we may be fire-bombed! Get everybody outside!" he commanded. "We'll have all the stretchers we need, pretty soon—don't panic, anybody, we'll get you out!" He could feel the fear like a visible miasma, and he raised his voice. "Walk, I said, don't run! I'll court-martial anyone who falls over another hurt man! Take it easy, we've had plenty of warning!" He stepped into the other room. "Carlie—Mother Liriel, have the ones who can walk help the ones who can't, we'll get stretchers up here soon!"

Carlina spoke softly to the women, and Bard saw, within minutes, orderly rescue being made. Paul had arrived, leading a whole squadron of stretcher-bearers. He stopped beside the stretcher of one of the women who lay with her newborn child in her arms.

"Ah, this is one of my new subjects? Well, mother, don't worry, she's a fine child, and she's going to be safe, believe me," he said, and passed on, hearing the murmur behind him.

"That's the *king!*"

"Don't be silly," said another woman on the next stretcher, "The king wouldn't come down here, that's the paxman of his, the one who looks so much like him."

"Well, whether it was or not," said the first one, "he spoke to me kindly, and I'm going to call the girl Fianna, after him. And the king's paxman is as good as the king, anyhow!"

Bard was supervising the last of the stretcher cases, stopping here and there to speak to a veteran he recognized, a courtier friend of his father's, a servant he had known for many years. Not all of them remembered to call him Sire, or Your Majesty, and he was just as glad. There would be time enough for formality in the years to come, and he was proud of being the Kilghard Wolf. And if it eased the terror of an ancient servant to call him Master Bard, it couldn't diminish him any, he supposed.

"Are they all out?"

"All but the old woman in the corner there. I'm afraid if we move her, she'll die," Carlina said, hesitating, "and I don't want to send four men with a stretcher—" She was white with fear, and he remembered that Carlina too had *laran,* and perhaps a touch of foresight. At that moment there was a strange droning sound, and a cry from the circle of *leroni* standing hands joined in the garden. Bard ran into the corner of the Great Hall and bent over the old woman. She stared up at him, her face gray with fear and pain.

"You get out, son, I'm done for."

"Nonsense, granny," Bard said, bending over her, and scooped her up in his arms. "Can you put your arm around my neck? There you are—come on, let's get out of here!" As he ran he suddenly remembered that Carlina had feared to move the old woman even on a stretcher, for fear she might die if she was moved. Well, she would certainly die if he left her there and the roof fell in on her! He ran, stumbling, into the air, and as he came out on the lawn there was a tremendous concussion, a blast of air struck him and he stumbled and fell heavily atop the old woman, feeling that his ears would burst with the noise.

When he knew what was happening, Paul and one of his guardsmen were picking him up, and the old woman, still miraculously breathing, was taken gently from his arms and lain on a stretcher.

One of the remaining wings of the castle sprouted a tall, graceful plume of dust and collapsed with a roar. Bard, who had himself given the order to have all fires extinguished, even cooking fire, saw with relief that there was no flame rising. There was another explosion and another, and a stable collapsed, but the army under Paul had been working; the horses were all outside by now. There was another explosion, and screams followed; it had landed in the very center of a little cluster of soldiers around the wounded men, and Bard, looking, sickened, saw arms and legs flying, and writhing, shrieking bodies.

Overhead the droning noise grew louder. Then a blue light shot up from the clustered *leroni* under the trees, and suddenly, with a roar as of a thunderclap, an air-car fell out of the sky, dropping like a stone. It fell into the orchard, landing in an apple tree from which flames suddenly sprouted sky-tall.

"Buckets!" bellowed one of Bard's commanders. "Get that fire there!"

A dozen men went running in the direction of the fire.

Another blue light; and another air-car went down in flames, this one striking harmlessly on a rocky peak and tumbling over and over until it came to rest in shattered fragments. Another soared over the main turret of the castle, dropping small, harmless-looking eggs as it came, which split asunder as they dropped.

"Zandru's hells!" Bard yelled. "Clingfire!" And indeed, as they struck, fire was shooting up from the very rock walls of the castle. The hellish stuff, Bard remembered, would burn *anything,* even rock, and go on burning and burning. . . .

So Alaric, and his father, would have a funeral pyre.

The last of the air-cars exploded in a rattling roar and fell out of the sky, but Bard saw Melora break away and run directly toward the castle. Was she mad? He had tried so hard to get everyone *out* of there—what was she doing?

Paul, working with the guardsmen to clear away burning debris from the stables, suddenly heard Melisendra cry out, as if with his physical ears. Gods above, had contact with Bard made him able to reach out that way too? He could see her, clearly, hurrying up those back stairs from the garden where he had first seen her, and heard her thoughts, panicking. *Erlend! Erlend! He was up late last night, running errands for the leroni, he still sleeps in his room! Oh, Merciful Avarra, Erlend!*

She was away and up the stairs, but Paul was directly on her heels. Halfway up the stairs he was met by a stifling cloud of smoke; but Melisendra had disappeared into the smoke, and he ripped away his shirt, tied it over his face, and dropping below the smoke level, began to crawl up the stairs on his hands and knees.

And in some strange doubling, as if he and Bard were truly linked in mind, he saw Bard try to dash into the building after Melora, and saw and felt the guardsmen who caught him, holding him fast.

"No! No, my lord, it's too dangerous!"

"But Melora—"

"We'll send someone in to get the *leronis* out, my lord, but you must not risk yourself. You are the king. . . ."

Bard struggled with them, fighting, seeing Melora running up the stairs, forcing her way over fallen debris, and through and above all this, the picture of Erlend, lying peacefully in his bed, the starstone at his throat clutched in his hand, and the curls of smoke overpowering him, turning his sleep to stupor as the walls above him began to burn.

"Let me go! Damn you. I'll have all your heads for that! It's my son—he's in there, burning!"

He fought against them, tears running down his face. "Damn you! Damn you all, let me go!"

But the guardsmen held him, and for the first time in his life, Bard's giant strength availed nothing. "They'll get him out, sir, but the whole reign's depending on you. Ruyvil, Jeran—help us hold his Lordship!"

And even while Bard struggled in their hands, some part of him was with Paul, climbing those stairs, he *was* Paul, so that in the guardsmen's hands he choked, his own eyes streaming tears as Paul struggled upward. . . .

Paul, feeling the smoke blind him, dropped on hands and knees to the floor. Behind him, Bard was suddenly lax in the hands of his captors as the essential part of him that fought upward was Paul; trying with every atom of his strength to lend his own strength to Paul, to *breathe* for him, if he must. It seemed, to both of them, that they crept *together* up those stairs, and at the top, inched their way along the corridor . . . found the door by touch, for the smoke was so thick Paul could not see. And just inside the door, Melisendra, lying overcome by smoke, her face dark and congested. For a terrifying moment Paul could not feel her breathing. The whole room was heavy with the acrid stuff, aching in Paul's lungs, and without Bard's strength he knew he could not have gone on but must have dropped to the floor there beside her, unconscious.

But somewhere a child whimpered, as if crying in his sleep, and Bard's awareness, in Paul, made him struggle, cursing, to his feet. The walls were beginning to blaze, and the edge of Erlend's mattress smoldered, sending now coils of thick smoke upward into the thick haze in the room. Paul—or Bard, he never knew which—hauled the child upright, hearing him shriek in pain and terror as he saw the flames blazing up. He smashed a carafe of water beside the bed, grabbed some garment off the floor and soaked it, tied it around his face; then, Erlend clinging weakly to his breast, knelt again beside Melisendra, slapping at her face with the wet cloth. He must rouse her! Perhaps, Bard's strength in him, he would have left Melisendra to rescue his son . . . but no, Melisendra was the child's mother, he could not leave her here to burn!

He smelled singing hair, the acrid smell of burning cloth, and Melora, her face blackened by smoke, was standing over him.

"Here! Give Erlend to me—" she said, coughing, choking, trying to force the words out. "You can carry Sendra, I can't—"

Paul wondered, in a fragment of separate consciousness, if she thought he was Bard, but the part of him that was Bard had already stretched out his arms, handing over the unconscious child into Melora's arms. He knew that tears of relief and thankfulness were flooding down his face, even while all of his doubled attention turned to Melisendra. He saw Melora stumble on a half-burned board at the edge of the door, fall heavily with the child in her arms, haul herself upright, clutching at a blazing beam and somehow, miraculously, stagger into the burning corridor, Erlend's face hidden on her bulky breasts. She was crying, he could hear her sobbing in pain and terror, but she stumbled on with the little boy in her arms.

Paul hoisted Melisendra to his shoulder, and a fragment of memory from another world and another life came irrelevantly into his mind, that this lift was called the fireman's carry and he had never known why. The walls were blazing now, an inferno, a hell of heat and smoke, but he hurried back the way he had come, bumped into Melora, who was at the top of the stairs, staring down in horror at the blazing stairs. How could they get down there?

Melora's breathing was loud and harsh, rasping in and out of her lungs, and her voice so hoarse that she could not speak above a shaky whisper. He saw her draw something from around her neck.

"Go on! Go down! I . . . *leronis* . . . the flames. . . ."

He hesitated, and the thick voice was frantic.

"Go! Go on! Only . . . hold fire . . . an instant . . . star-stone. . . ."

Before him the flames wavered, drew back, and Paul stood frozen gasping in amazement . . . but Bard, within him, accepted the sorcery of this world, the way in which a trained *leronis* could handle flame, took a firmer hold on Melisendra and hurried down the stairs. Melisendra was limp in his arms, unconscious, but Erlend was screaming in terror in Melora's arms. The flames retreated, wavered before them as they stumbled down the stairs, Melora's step heavy and blundering because all of her conscious will was focused on the starstone, on the flames that died, sprang up, drew back and hung there in terrible menace. He plunged through the burning door and into the blessed air, and again with the frightening split consciousness, saw Bard, with a last, berserker strength, fight away from the guardsmen and come to take Melisendra from his arms as he fell, half conscious, his tormented lungs sobbing air in and out with a whistling sound. A dozen women rushed to take Melisendra and lay her on the grass, and Bard, frenzied, plunged through the last flames, blazing up as Melora fell, unconscious. Bard grabbed Erlend from her arms, passed him quickly to a Varzil's waiting arms. Geremy, stumbling after him, held Bard upright as he caught at Melora in relief and dread.

She fell against him, so heavily that even Bard's giant strength stumbled and for a moment he thought they would roll to the ground, all three of them, but the arms of guardsmen steadied them all. Melora's face was covered with soot and smoke and she screamed in pain as Bard's arms went around her, but as he loosened his grip, fearfully—had she paid with her own life for rescuing his son?—she clutched at him again, weeping.

"Oh, it hurts—I'm burned, Bard, but not badly—for the love of the Goddess, get me a drink, something—" She choked, coughing, sobbing, tears running black with soot down her face. Someone thrust a tankard of water into her hand and she gulped at it, choked, spat, coughed again and again. Bard held her, bellowing for someone to come and attend to her, but she drew herself upright as Master Gareth came to them.

"No, Father, it's all right, really, just a little burn," she said. Her voice was still thick and hoarse. Geremy, kneeling on the grass beside Erlend now, raised his face to Bard, in deep thankfulness.

"He breathes, thank the gods," he said, and as if to underline that, Erlend began to wail loudly. But he stopped when he caught sight of Bard.

"You came to get me, Father, you came and got me, you didn't let me burn up, I knew my father wouldn't leave me to burn . . ."

Bard started to speak, to disclaim it, to say it had been Paul who physically climbed those stairs while he, the child's father, had been held helpless by his own guards, king or no; but Paul said loudly from where he bent over Melisendra, "That's right, my Prince, your father came to fetch you out of the fire!" He said fiercely in an undertone, "Don't you ever tell him anything else! You *were* there! I couldn't have made it without your strength! And he's got to *live* with you!"

His eyes met Bard's, and suddenly Bard knew they were free of one another forever. He had given Paul life, from the death of the stasis box; and now Paul had given him back a life more precious than his own, the life of his only son. No longer bound with a deadly tie, dark twins, but brothers, lord and respected paxman, friends.

He bent over Erlend and kissed his son. This *nedestro* heir should never feel himself unloved, or suffer the torments he had known. Melora might never bear him a child—she was older than he, she had worked long as a *leronis* and healer in the blighted zone—but she had given him Erlend's life. And as he watched Carlina, in her dark robes, bending over Melisendra's limp body—now tortured with the racking coughs as they forced the smoke from her lungs—he knew that he was free of them both. Melisendra would find her own happiness with Paul; and Carlina's life was given to the Goddess. He would deny it no further. In his lifetime, he would see the priestesses of Avarra leave their Lake of Silence and come into the world as healers under Varzil's protection. The priestesses and the Sisterhood of the Sword would form a new Order of Renunciates, and Carlina would be one of their founders and saints; but that was all in the future.

With a tremendous roar, the roof of the main wing of the castle fell in and the flames engulfed it. Bard, sitting beside

Melora as the healers dressed the burn on her arm and breast, shook his head and sighed.

"I am a king without a castle, my beloved. And if the Hasturs have their way, a king without a kingdom; lord of no more than my father's estate—I should think they'd give me that. Will you be a queen without a country, Melora, my own love?"

She smiled up at him, and it seemed that the morning sun was no brighter than her eyes. Bard beckoned to Varzil, smiling up at him, and said, "After the wounded are cared for, there is a Compact to be sworn. And an alliance to be made."

And, turning back to Melora, he kissed her full on the lips. "And a queen to be crowned," he said.

DARKOVER

Marion Zimmer Bradley's Classic Series

Now Collected in New Omnibus Editions!

Heritage and Exile   0-7564-0065-1
The Heritage of Hastur & Sharra's Exile

The Ages of Chaos   0-7564-0072-4
Stormqueen! & Hawkmistress!

The Saga of the Renunciates   0-7564-0092-9
The Shattered Chain, Thendara House
& City of Sorcery

The Forbidden Circle   0-7564-0094-5
The Spell Sword & The Forbidden Tower

A World Divided   0-7564-0167-4
The Bloody Sun, The Winds of Darkover
& Star of Danger

Darkover: First Contact   0-7564-0224-7
Darkover Landfall & Two to Conquer

To Save a World   0-7564-0250-6
The World Wreckers & The Planet Savers

To Order Call: 1-800-788-6262

www.dawbooks.com

Sherwood Smith

Inda

"A powerful beginning to a very promising series by a writer who is making her bid to be a major fantasist. By the time I finished, I was so captured by this book that it lingered for days afterward. I had lived inside these characters, inside this world, and I was unwilling to let go of it. That, I think, is the mark of a major work of fiction…you owe it to yourself to read *Inda*." -Orson Scott Card

INDA
978-0-7564-0422-2

THE FOX
978-0-7564-0483-3

KING'S SHIELD
978-0-7564-0500-7

And now available in hardcover:

TREASON'S SHORE
978-0-7564-0573-1

To Order Call: 1-800-788-6262
www.dawbooks.com

DAW 110

Patrick Rothfuss
THE NAME OF THE WIND
The Kingkiller Chronicle: Day One

"It is a rare and great pleasure to come on some-body writing not only with the kind of accuracy of language that seems to me absolutely essential to fantasy-making, but with real music in the words as well.... Oh, joy!"   —Ursula K. Le Guin

"Amazon.com's Best of the Year...So Far Pick for 2007: Full of music, magic, love, and loss, Patrick Rothfuss's vivid and engaging debut fantasy knocked our socks off."   —Amazon.com

"One of the best stories told in any medium in a decade. Shelve it beside *The Lord of the Rings* ...and look forward to the day when it's mentioned in the same breath, perhaps as first among equals."   —*The Onion*

"[Rothfuss is] the great new fantasy writer we've been waiting for, and this is an astonishing book."   —Orson Scott Card

0-7564-0474-1

To Order Call: 1-800-788-6262
www.dawbooks.com

DAW 111

Kristen Britain

The **GREEN RIDER** series

"Wonderfully captivating...a truly
enjoyable read." —Terry Goodkind

"A fresh, well-organized fantasy debut,
with a spirited heroine and a reliable
supporting cast." —*Kirkus*

"The author's skill at world building and her
feel for dramatic storytelling make this first-rate
fantasy a good choice." —*Library Journal*

"Britain keeps the excitement high from beginning to end, balancing epic magical battles with
the humor and camaraderie of Karigan and her
fellow Riders." —*Publishers Weekly*

GREEN RIDER
0-88677-858-1 (mass)   978-0-7564-0548-9 (trade)
FIRST RIDER'S CALL
0-7564-0209-3 (mass)   978-0-7564-0572-4 (trade)
THE HIGH KING'S TOMB
978-0-7564-0588-5 (mass)   978-0-7564-0489-5 (trade)

To Order Call: 1-800-788-6262
www.dawbooks.com